COMBAT

COMBAT

EDITED AND WITH AN INTRODUCTION BY

STEPHEN COONTS

A TOM DOHERTY ASSOCIATES BOOK
NEW YORK

COMBAT

This book is printed on acid-free paper.

A Forge Book
Published by Tom Doherty Associates, LLC
175 Fifth Avenue
New York, NY 10010

www.tor.com

Library of Congress Cataloging-in-Publication Data

Combat / edited and with an introduction by Stephen Coonts.—1st ed.
p. cm.
"A Tom Doherty Associates book."
Contents: Leadership material / Dale Brown—Lash-up / Larry Bond—Cav / James Cobb—Cyberknights / Harold W. Coyle—Flight of Endeavour / R.J. Pineiro—Breaking point / David Hagberg—Inside job / Dean Ing—Skyhawks forever / Barrett Tillman—There is no war in Melnicca / Ralph Peters—al'Jihad / Stephen Coonts.
ISBN 0-312-87190-2 (regular edition)
ISBN 0-765-30028-1 (limited edition)
1. War stories, American. 2. Science fiction, American. 3. Imaginary wars and battles—Fiction. I. Coonts, Stephen

PS648.W34 C65 2001
813'.609358—dc21

00-048451

First Edition: January 2001

Printed in the United States of America

0 9 8 7 6 5 4 3 2 1

To the memory of the seventeen sailors who lost their lives on the USS *Cole*

Contents

INTRODUCTION

The milieu of armed conflict has been a fertile setting for storytellers since the dawn of the written word, and probably before. The *Iliad* by Homer was a thousand years old before someone finally wrote down that oral epic of the Trojan War, freezing its form forever.

Since then war stories have been one of the main themes of fiction in Western cultures: *War and Peace* by Leo Tolstoi was set during the Napoleonic Wars, Stephen Crane's *The Red Badge of Courage* was set during the American Civil War, *All Quiet on the Western Front* by Erich Maria Remarque was perhaps the great classic of World War I. Arguably the premier war novel of the twentieth century, Ernest Hemingway's *For Whom the Bell Tolls*, was set in the Spanish Civil War.

World War II caused an explosion of great war novels. Some of my favorites are *The Naked and the Dead, The Thin Red Line, War and Remembrance, From Here to Eternity, The War Lover,* and *Das Boot.*

The Korean conflict also produced a bunch, including my favorite, *The Bridges at Toko-Ri* by James Michener, but Vietnam changed the literary landscape. According to conventional wisdom in the publishing industry, after that war the reading public lost interest in war stories. Without a doubt the publishers did.

In 1984 the world changed. The U.S. Naval Institute Press, the Naval Academy's academic publisher, broke with its ninety-plus years of tradition and published a novel, *The Hunt for Red October*, by Tom Clancy.

This book by an independent insurance agent who had never served in the armed forces sold slowly at first, then became a huge best-seller when the reading public found it and began selling it to each other by word of mouth. It didn't hurt that President Ronald Reagan was photographed with a copy.

As it happened, in 1985 I was looking for a publisher for a Vietnam flying story I had written. After the novel was rejected by every publisher in New York, I saw *Hunt* in a bookstore, so I sent my novel to the Naval Institute Press. To my delight the house accepted it and published it in 1986 as *Flight of the Intruder*. Like *Hunt*, it too became a big best-seller.

Success ruined the Naval Institute. Wracked by internal politics, the staff refused to publish Clancy's and my subsequent novels. (We had no trouble selling these books in New York, thank you!) The house did not publish another novel for years, and when they did, best-seller sales eluded them.

Literary critics had an explanation for the interest of the post-Vietnam public in war stories. These novels, they said, were something new. I don't know who coined the term "techno-thriller" (back then newspapers always used quotes and hyphenated it) but the term stuck.

Trying to define the new term, the critics concluded that these war stories used modern technology in ways that no one ever had. How wrong they were.

Clancy's inspiration for *The Hunt for Red October* was an attempted defection of a crew of a Soviet surface warship in the Baltic. The crew mutinied and attempted to sail their ship to Finland. The attempt went awry and the ringleaders were summarily executed by the communists, who always took offense when anyone tried to leave the workers' paradises.

What if, Clancy asked himself, the crew of a nuclear-powered submarine tried to defect? The game would be more interesting then. Clancy's model for the type of story he wanted to write was Edward L. Beach's *Run Silent, Run Deep*, a World War II submarine story salted with authentic technical detail that was critical to the development of the characters and plot of the story.

With that scenario in mind, Clancy set out to write a submarine adventure that would be accurate in every detail. Never mind that he had never set foot on a nuclear submarine or spent a day in uniform—his inquiring mind and thirst for knowledge made him an extraordinary researcher. His fascination with war games and active, fertile imagination made him a first-class storyteller.

Unlike Clancy, I did no research whatsoever when writing *Flight of the Intruder*. I had flown A-6 Intruder bombers in Vietnam from the deck of the USS *Enterprise* and wrote from memory. I had been trying to write a flying novel since 1973 and had worn out two typewriters in the process. By 1984 I had figured out a plot for my flying tale, so after a divorce I got serious about writing and completed a first draft of the novel in five months.

My inspiration for the type of story I wanted to write was two books by Ernest K. Gann. *Fate Is the Hunter* was a true collection of flying stories from the late 1930s and 1940s, and was, I thought, extraordinary in its inclusion of a wealth of detail about the craft of flying an airplane. Gann also used this device for his novels, the best of which is probably *The High and the Mighty*, a story about a piston-engined airliner that has an emergency while flying between Hawaii and San Francisco.

Gann used technical details to create the setting and as plot devices that moved the stories along. By educating the reader about what it is a pilot does, he gave his stories an emotional impact that conventional storytellers could not achieve. In essence, he put you in the cockpit and took you flying. That, I thought, was an extraordinary achievement and one I wanted to emulate.

Fortunately, the technology that Clancy and I were writing about was state-of-the-art—nuclear-powered submarines and precision all-weather attack jets—and this played to the reading public's long-standing love affair with scientific discoveries and new technology. In the nineteenth century Jules Verne, Edgar Allan Poe, Wilkie Collins, and H. G. Wells gave birth to science fiction. The technology at the heart of their stories played on the public's fascination with the man-made wonders of that age—the submarine, the flying machines that were the object of intense research and experimentation, though they had yet to get off the ground, and the myriad of uses that inventors were finding for electricity, to name just a few.

Today's public is still enchanted by the promise of scientific research and technology. Computers, rockets, missiles, precision munitions, lasers, fiber optics, wireless networks, reconnaissance satellites, winged airplanes that take off and land vertically, network-centric warfare—advances in every technical field are constantly re-creating the world in which we live.

The marriage of high tech and war stories is a natural.

The line between the modern military action-adventure and science fiction is blurry, indistinct, and becoming more so with every passing day. Storytellers often set technothrillers in the near future and dress up the technology accordingly, toss in little inventions of their own here and there, and in general, try subtly to wow their readers by use of a little of that science fiction "what might be" magic. When it's properly done, only a technically expert reader will be able to tell when the writer has crossed the line from the real to the unreal; and that's the fun of it. On the other hand, stories set in space or on other planets or thousands of years in the future are clearly science fiction, even though armed conflict is involved.

In this collection you will find ten never-before-published techno-thriller novellas by accomplished writers, a category in which I immodestly include myself. I hope you like them.

STEPHEN COONTS

AL-JIHAD

BY STEPHEN COONTS

One

Julie Giraud was crazy as hell. I knew that for an absolute fact, so I was contemplating what a real damned fool I was to get mixed up in her crazy scheme when I drove the Humvee and trailer into the belly of the V-22 Osprey and tied them down.

I quickly checked the stuff in the Humvee's trailer, made sure it was secure, then walked out of the Osprey and across the dark concrete ramp. Lights shining down from the peak of the hangar reflected in puddles of rainwater. The rain had stopped just at dusk, an hour or so ago.

I was the only human in sight amid the tiltrotor Ospreys parked on that vast mat. They looked like medium-sized transports except that they had an engine on each wingtip, and the engines were pointed straight up. Atop each engine was a thirty-eight-foot, three-bladed rotor. The engines were mounted on swivels that allowed them to be tilted from the vertical to the horizontal, giving the Ospreys the ability to take off and land like helicopters and then fly along in winged flight like the turboprop transports they really were.

I stopped by the door into the hangar and looked around again, just to make sure, then I opened the door and went inside.

The corridor was lit, but empty. My footsteps made a dull noise on the tile floor. I took the second right, into a ready room.

The duty officer was standing by the desk strapping a belt and holster to her waist. She was wearing a flight suit and black flying boots. Her dark hair was pulled back into a bun. She glanced at me. "Ready?"

"Where are all the security guards?"

"Watching a training film. They thought it was unusual to send everyone, but I insisted."

"I sure as hell hope they don't get suspicious."

She picked up her flight bag, took a last look around, and glanced at her watch. Then she grinned at me. "Let's go get 'em."

That was Julie Giraud, and as I have said, she was crazy as hell.

Me, I was just greedy. Three million dollars was a lot of kale, enough to keep me in beer and pretzels for the next hundred and ninety years. I followed this ding-a-ling bloodthirsty female along the hallway and through the puddles on the ramp to the waiting Osprey. Julie didn't run—she strode purposefully. If she was nervous or having second thoughts about committing the four dozen felonies we had planned for the next ten minutes, she sure didn't show it.

The worst thing I had ever done up to that point in my years on this planet was cheat a little on my income tax—no more than average, though—and here I was about to become a co-conspirator in enough crimes to keep a grand jury busy for a year. I felt like a condemned man on his way to the gallows, but the thought of all those smackers kept me marching along behind ol' crazy Julie.

We boarded the plane through the cargo door, and I closed it behind us.

Julie took three or four minutes to check our cargo, leaving nothing to chance. I watched her with grudging respect—crazy or not, she looked like a pro to me, and at my age I damn well didn't want to go tilting at windmills with an amateur.

When she finished her inspection, she led the way forward to the cockpit. She got into the left seat, her hands flew over the buttons and levers, arranging everything to her satisfaction. As I strapped myself into the right seat, she cranked the left engine. The RPMs came up nicely. The right engine was next.

As the radios warmed up, she quickly ran through the checklist, scanned gauges, and set up computer displays. I wasn't a pilot; everything I knew about the V-22 tiltrotor Osprey came from Julie, who wasn't given to long-winded explanations. If was almost as if every word she said cost her money.

While she did her pilot thing, I sat there looking out the windows, nervous as a cat on crack, trying to spot the platoon of FBI agents who were probably closing in to arrest us right that very minute. I didn't see anyone, of course: The parking mat of the air force base was as deserted as a nudist colony in January.

About that time Julie snapped on the aircraft's exterior lights, which made weird reflections on the other aircraft parked nearby, and the landing lights, powerful spotlights that shone on the concrete in front of us.

She called Ground Control on the radio. They gave her a clearance to a base in southern Germany, which she copied and read back flawlessly.

We weren't going to southern Germany, I knew, even if the air traffic controllers didn't. Julie released the brakes, and almost as if by magic, the Osprey began moving, taxiing along the concrete. She turned to pick up a taxiway, moving slowly, sedately, while she set up the computer displays on the instrument panel in front of her. There were two multifunction displays in front of me too, and she leaned across to punch up the displays she wanted. I just watched. All this time we were rolling slowly along the endless taxiways lined with blue lights, across at least one runway, taxiing, taxiing . . . A rabbit ran across in front of us, through the beam of the taxi light.

Finally Julie stopped and spoke to the tower, which cleared us for takeoff.

"Are you ready?" she asked me curtly.

"For prison, hell or what?"

She ignored that comment, which just slipped out. I was sitting there wondering how well I was going to adjust to institutional life.

She taxied onto the runway, lined up the plane, then advanced the power lever with her left hand. I could hear the engines winding up, feel the power of the giant rotors tearing at the air, trying to lift this twenty-eight-ton beast from the earth's grasp.

The Osprey rolled forward on the runway, slowly at first, and when it was going a little faster than a man could run, lifted majestically into the air.

The crime was consummated.

We had just stolen a forty-million-dollar V-22 Osprey, snatched it right out of Uncle Sugar's rather loose grasp, not to mention a half-million dollars' worth of other miscellaneous military equipment that was carefully stowed in the back of the plane.

Now for the getaway.

In seconds Julie began tilting the engines down to transition to forward flight. The concrete runway slid under us, faster and faster as the Osprey accelerated. She snapped up the wheels, used the stick to raise the nose of the plane. The airspeed indicator read over 140 knots as the end of the runway disappeared into the darkness below and the night swallowed us.

Two weeks before that evening, Julie Giraud drove into my filling station in Van Nuys. I didn't know her then, of course. I was sitting in the office reading the morning paper. I glanced out, saw her pull up to the pump in a new white sedan. She got out of the car and used a credit card at the pump, so I went back to the paper.

I had only owned that gasoline station for about a week, but I had already figured out why the previous owner sold it so cheap: The mechanic was a doper and the guy running the register was a thief. I was contemplating various ways of solving those two problems when the woman with the white sedan finished pumping her gas and came walking toward the office.

She was a bit over medium height, maybe thirty years old, a hardbody wearing a nice outfit that must have set her back a few bills. She looked vaguely familiar, but this close to Hollywood, you often see people you think you ought to know.

She came straight over to where I had the little chair tilted back against the wall and asked, "Charlie Dean?"

"Yeah."

"I'm Julie Giraud. Do you remember me?"

It took me a few seconds. I put the paper down and got up from the chair.

"It's been a lot of years," I said.

"Fifteen, I think. I was just a teenager."

"Colonel Giraud's eldest daughter. I remember. Do you have a sister a year or two younger?"

"Rachael. She's a dental tech, married with two kids."

"I sorta lost track of your father, I guess. How is he?"

"Dead."

"Well, I'm sorry."

I couldn't think of anything else to say. Her dad had been my commanding officer at the antiterrorism school, but that was years ago. I went on to other assignments, and finally retired five years ago with thirty years in. I hadn't seen or thought of the Girauds in years.

"I remember Dad remarking several times that you were the best Marine in the corps."

That comment got the attention of the guy behind the register. His name was Candy. He had a few tattoos on his arms and a half dozen rings dangling from various portions of his facial anatomy. He looked at me now with renewed interest.

I tried to concentrate on Julie Giraud. She was actually a good-looking woman, with her father's square chin and good cheekbones. She wasn't wearing makeup: She didn't need any.

"I remember him telling us that you were a sniper in Vietnam, and the best Marine in the corps."

Candy's eyebrows went up toward his hairline when he heard that.

"I'm flattered that you remember me, Ms. Giraud, but I'm a small-business owner now. I left the Marines five years ago." I gestured widely. "This grand establishment belongs to me and the hundreds of thousands of stockholders in BankAmerica. All of us thank you for stopping by today and giving us your business."

She nodded, turned toward the door, then hesitated. "I wonder if we might have lunch together, Mr. Dean."

Why not? "Okay. Across the street at the Burger King, in about an hour?" That was agreeable with her. She got in her car and drove away.

Amazing how people from the past pop back into your life when you least expect it.

I tilted the chair back, lifted my paper and sat there wondering what in hell Julie Giraud could possibly want to talk about with me. Candy went back to his copy of *Rolling Stone*. In a few minutes two people came in and paid cash for their gas. With the paper hiding my face, I could look into a mirror I had mounted on the ceiling and watch Candy handle the money. I put the mirror up there three days ago but if he noticed, he had forgotten it by now.

As the second customer left, Candy pocketed something. I didn't know if he shortchanged the customer or just helped himself to a bill from the till. The tally and the tape hadn't been jibing and Candy had a what-are-you-gonna-do-about-it-old-man attitude.

He closed the till and glanced at me with a look that could only be amusement.

I folded the paper, put it down, got out of the chair and went over to the counter.

"So you was in the Marines, huh?"

"Yeah."

He grinned confidently. "Wouldn't have figured that."

I reached, grabbed a ring dangling from his eyebrow and ripped it out.

Candy screamed. Blood flowed from the eyebrow. He recoiled against the register with a look of horror on his face.

"The money, kid. Put it on the counter."

He glanced at the blood on his hand, then pressed his hand against his eyebrow trying to staunch the flow. "You bastard! I don't know what you—"

Reaching across the counter, I got a handful of hair with my left hand and the ring in his nose with my right. "You want to lose all these, one by one?"

He dug in his pocket, pulled out a wadded bill and threw it on the counter.

"You're fired, kid. Get off the property and never come back."

He came around the counter, trying to stay away from me, one hand on his bleeding eyebrow. He stopped in the door. "I'll get you for this, you son of a bitch."

"You think that through, kid. Better men than you have died trying. If you just gotta do it, though, you know where to find me."

He scurried over to his twenty-five-year-old junker Pontiac. He ground and ground with the starter. Just when I thought he would have to give up, the motor belched a cloud of blue smoke.

I got on the phone to a friend of mine, also a retired Marine. His name was Bill Wiley, and he worked full time as a police dispatcher. He agreed to come over that evening to help me out for a few hours at the station.

It seemed to me that I might as well solve all my problems in one day, so I went into the garage to see the mechanic, a long-haired Mexican named Juan.

"I think you've got an expensive habit, Juan. To pay for it you've been charging customers for work you didn't do, new parts you didn't install, then splitting the money with Candy. He hit the road. You can work honest from now on or leave, your choice."

"You can't prove shit."

He was that kind of guy, stupid as dirt. "I don't have to prove anything," I told him. "You're fired."

He didn't argue; he just went. I finished fixing the flat he had been working on, waited on customers until noon, then locked the place up and walked across the street to the Burger King.

Of course I was curious. It seemed doubtful that Julie Giraud wanted to spend an hour of her life reminiscing about the good old days at Quantico with a retired enlisted man who once served under her father, certainly not one twenty-five years older than she was.

So what did she want?

"You are not an easy man to find, Mr. Dean."

I shrugged. I'm not trying to lose myself in the madding crowd, but I'm not advertising either.

"My parents died twelve years ago," she said, her eyes on my face.

"Both of them?" I hadn't heard. "Sorry to hear that," I said.

"They were on an Air France flight to Paris that blew up over Niger. A bomb."

"Twelve years ago."

"Dad had been retired for just a year. He and Mom were traveling, seeing the world, falling in love with each other all over again. They were on their way to Paris from South America when the plane blew up, killing everyone aboard."

I lost my appetite for hamburger. I put it down and sipped some coffee.

She continued, telling me her life story. She spent a few more years in high school, went to the Air Force Academy, was stationed in Europe flying V-22 Ospreys, was back in the States just now on leave.

When she wound down, I asked, as gently as I could, why she looked me up.

She opened her purse, took out a newspaper clipping, offered it to me. "Last year a French court tried the men who killed my parents. They are Libyans. Moammar Gadhafi refused to extradite them from Libya, so the French tried them in absentia, convicted them, sentenced them to life in prison."

I remembered reading about the trial. The clipping merely refreshed my memory. One hundred forty people died when that Air France flight exploded; the debris was scattered over fifty square miles of desert.

"Six men, and they are still in Libya." Julie gestured at the newspaper clipping, which was lying beside my food tray. "One of the men is Gadhafi's brother-in-law, another is a key figure in Libyan intelligence, two are in the Libyan diplomatic service." She gripped the little table between us and leaned forward. "They blew up that airliner on Gadhafi's order to express the dictator's displeasure with French foreign policy at the time. It was raw political terrorism, Mr. Dean, by a nation without the guts or wit to wage war. They just murder civilians."

I folded the clipping, then handed it back.

"Ms. Giraud, I'm sorry that your parents are dead. I'm sorry about all those people who died on that airliner. I'm sorry the men who murdered them are beyond the reach of the law. I'm sorry the French government hasn't got the guts or wit to clean out the vermin in Tripoli. But what has this got to do with me?"

"I want you to help me kill those men," she whispered, her voice as hard as a bayonet blade.

Two

I grew up in a little town in southwestern Missouri. Dad was a welder and Mom waited tables in a diner, and both of them had trouble with the bottle. The afternoon of the day I graduated from high school I joined the Marines to get the hell out.

Sure, I killed my share of gomers in Vietnam. By then I thought life was a fairly good idea and wanted more of it. If I had to zap gomers to keep getting older, that was all right by me. It helped that I had a natural talent with a rifle. I was a medium-smart, whang-leather kid who never complained and did what I was told, so I eventually ended up in Recon. It took me a while to fit in; once I did, I was in no hurry to leave. Recon was the place where the Marine Corps kept its really tough men. The way I figured it, those guys were my life insurance.

That's the way it worked out. The guys in Recon kept each other alive. And we killed gomers.

All that was long ago and far away from Julie Giraud. She was the daughter of a Marine colonel, sure, a grad of the Air Force Academy, and she looked like she ran five miles or so every day, but none of that made her tough. Sitting across the table looking at her, I couldn't figure out if she was a fighter or a get-even, courthouse-stairs back-shooter. A lot of people like the abstract idea of revenge, of getting even, but they aren't willing to suffer much for the privilege. Sitting in Burger King watching Julie Giraud, listening to her tell me how she wanted to kill the men who had killed her parents, I tried to decide just how much steel was in her backbone.

Her dad had been a career officer with his share of Vietnam chest cabbage. When they were young a lot of the gung ho officers thought they were bulletproof and let it all hang out. When they eventually realized they were as mortal as everyone else and started sending sergeants to lead the patrols, they already had enough medals to decorate a Panamanian dictator. Whether Julie Giraud's dad was like that, I never knew.

A really tough man knows he is mortal, knows the dangers involved to the tenth decimal place, and goes ahead anyway. He is careful, committed, and absolutely ruthless.

After she dropped the bomb at lunch, I thought about these things for a while. Up to that point I had no idea why she had gone to the trouble of looking me up; the thought that she might want my help getting even with somebody never once zipped across the synapses. I took my time thinking things over before I said, "What's the rest of it?"

"It's a little complicated."

"Maybe you'd better lay it out."

"Outside, in my car."

"No. Outside on the sidewalk."

We threw the remnants of our lunch in the trash and went outside.

Julie Giraud looked me in the eye and explained, "These men are instruments of the Libyan government—"

"I got that point earlier."

"—seventeen days from now, on the twenty-third of this month, they are going to meet with members of three Middle East terrorist organizations and a representative of Saddam Hussein's government. They hope to develop a joint plan that Saddam will finance to attack targets throughout western Europe and the Middle East."

"Did you get a press release on this or what?"

"I have a friend, a fellow Air Force Academy graduate, who is now with the CIA."

"He just casually tells you this stuff?"

"She. She told me about the conference. And there is nothing casual about it. She knows what these people have cost me."

"Say you win the lottery and off a few of these guys, what's she gonna tell the internal investigators when they come around?"

Julie Giraud shook her head. "We're covered, believe me."

"I don't, but you're the one trying to make a sale, not me."

She nodded, then continued: "Seventeen days from now the delegates to this little conference will fly to an airstrip near an old fortress in the Sahara. The fortress is near an oasis on an old caravan route in the middle of nowhere. Originally built by the ancient Egyptians, the fortress was used by Carthaginians and Romans to guard that caravan route. The Foreign Legion did extensive restoration and kept a small garrison there for years. During World War II the Germans and British even had a little firefight there."

I grunted. She was intense, committed. Fanatics scare me, and she was giving me those vibes now.

"The fortress is on top of a rock ridge," she explained. "The Arabs call it the Camel."

"Never heard of it," I retorted. Of course there was no reason that I should have heard of the place—I was grasping at straws. I didn't like anything about this tale.

She was holding her purse loosely by the strap, so I grabbed it out of her hand. Her eyes narrowed; she thought about slapping me—actually shifted her weight to do it—then decided against it.

There was a small, round, poured-concrete picnic table there beside the Burger King for mothers to sit at while watching their kids play on the gym equipment, so I sat down and dug her wallet out of the purse. It contained a couple hundred in bills, a Colorado driver's license—she was twenty-eight years old—a military ID, three bank credit cards, an expired AAA membership, car insurance from USAA, a Sears credit card, and an ATM card in a paper envelope with her secret PIN number written on the envelope in ink.

Also in the wallet was a small, bound address book containing handwritten names, addresses, telephone numbers, and e-mail addresses. I flipped through the book, studying the names, then returned it to the wallet.

Her purse contained the usual feminine hygiene and cosmetic items. At the bottom were four old dry cleaning receipts from the laundry on the German base where she was stationed and a small collection of loose keys. One safety pin, two buttons, a tiny rusty screwdriver, a pair of sunglasses with a cracked lens, five German coins and two U.S. quarters. One of the receipts was eight months old.

I put all this stuff back in her purse and passed it across the table.

"Okay," I said. "For the sake of argument, let's assume you're telling the truth—that there really is a terrorists' conference scheduled at an old pile of Foreign Legion masonry in the middle of the goddamn Sahara seventeen days from now. What do you propose to do about it?"

"I propose to steal a V-22 Osprey," Julie Giraud said evenly, "fly there, plant enough C-4 to blow that old fort to kingdom come, then wait for the terrorists to arrive. When they are all sitting in there plotting who they are going to murder next, I'm going to push the button and send the whole lot of them straight to hell. Just like they did to my parents and everyone else on that French DC-10."

"You and who else?"

The breeze was playing with her hair. "You and me," she said. "The two of us."

I tried to keep a straight face. Across the street at my filling station people were standing beside their cars, waiting impatiently for me to get back and open up. That was paying business and I was sitting here listening to this shit. The thought that the CIA or FBI might be recording this conversation also crossed my mind.

"You're a nice kid, Julie. Thanks for dropping by. I'm sorry about your folks, but there is nothing on earth anyone can do for them. It's time to lay them to rest. Fly high, meet a nice guy, fall in love, have some kids, give them the best that you have in you: Your parents would have wanted that for you. The fact is they're gone and you can't bring them back."

She brushed the hair back from her eyes. "If you'll help me, Mr. Dean, I'll pay you three million dollars."

I didn't know what to say. Three million dollars rated serious consideration, but I couldn't tell if she had what it takes to make it work.

"I'll think about it," I said, and got up. "Tomorrow, we'll have lunch again right here."

She showed some class then. "Okay," she said, and nodded once. She didn't argue or try to make the sale right then, and I appreciated that.

My buddy, Gunnery Sergeant Bill Wiley, left the filling station at ten that night; I had to stay until closing time at 2 A.M. About midnight an older four-door Chrysler cruised slowly past on the street, for the second or third time, and I realized the people inside were casing the joint.

Ten minutes later, when the pumps were vacant and I was the only person in the store, the Chrysler drove in fast and stopped in front of the door. My ex–cash register man, Candy, boiled out of the passenger seat with a gun in his hand, a 9-mm automatic. He and the guy from the backseat came charging through the door waving their guns at me.

"Hands up, Charlie Dean, you silly son of a bitch. We want all the money, and if you ain't real goddamn careful I'm gonna blow your fucking brains out."

The guy from the backseat posted himself by the door and kept glancing up and down the street to see who was driving by. The driver of the car stayed outside.

Candy strutted over to me and stuck his gun in my face. He had a butterfly bandage on his eyebrow. He was about to say something really nasty, I think, when I grabbed his gun with my left hand and hit him with all I had square in the mouth with my right. He went down like he had been sledgehammered. I leaped toward the other one and hit him in the head with the gun butt, and he went down too. Squatting, I grabbed his gun while I checked the driver outside.

The driver was standing frozen beside the car, staring through the plate-glass window at me like I was Godzilla. I already had the safety off on Candy's automatic, so I swung it into the middle of this dude's chest and pulled the trigger.

Click.

Oh boy!

As I got the other pistol up, the third man dived behind the wheel and slammed the Chrysler into gear. That pistol also clicked uselessly. The Chrysler left in a squall of rubber and exhaust smoke.

I checked the pistols one at a time. Both empty.

Candy's eyes were trying to focus, so I bent down and asked him, "How come you desperate characters came in here with empty pistols?"

He spit blood and a couple teeth as he thought about it. His lips were swelling. He was going to look like holy hell for a few days. Finally one eye focused. "Didn't want to shoot you," he mumbled, barely understandable. "Just scare you."

"Umm."

"The guns belong to my dad. He didn't have any bullets around."

"Did the driver of the car know the guns were empty?"

Candy nodded, spit some more blood.

I'll admit, I felt kind of sorry for Candy. He screwed up the courage to go after a pint or two of revenge, but the best he could do for backup help was a coward who ran from empty pistols.

I put the guns in the trash can under the register and got each of them a bottled water from the cooler. They were slowly coming around when a police cruiser with lights flashing pulled up between the pumps and the office and the officer jumped out. He came striding in with his hand on the butt of his pistol.

"Someone called in on their cell phone, reported a robbery in progress here."

I kept my hands in plain sight where he could see them. "No robbery, officer. My name's Dean; I own this filling station."

"What happened to these two?" Spittle and blood were smeared on one front of Candy's shirt, and his friend had a dilly of a shiner.

"They had a little argument," I explained, "slugged each other. This fellow here, Candy, works for me."

Candy and his friend looked at me kind of funny, but they went along with it. After writing down everyone's names and addresses from their driver's licenses while I expanded on my fairy tale, the officer left.

Candy and his friend were on their feet by then. "I'm sorry, Mr. Dean," Candy said.

"Tell you what, kid. You want to play it straight, no stealing and no shortchanging people, you come back to work in the morning."

"You mean that?"

"Yeah." I dug his father's guns from the trash and handed them to him. "You better take these home and put them back where they belong."

His face was red and he was having trouble talking. "I'll be here," he managed.

He pocketed the pistols, nodded, then he and his friend went across the street to Burger King to call someone to come get them.

I was shaking so bad I had to sit down. Talk about luck! If the pistols had been loaded I would have killed that fool kid driving the car, and I didn't even know if he had a gun. That could have cost me life in the pen. Over what?

I sat there in the office thinking about life and death and Julie Giraud.

At lunch the next day Julie Giraud was intense, yet cool as she talked of killing people, slaughtering them like steers. I'd seen my share of people with that look. She was just flat crazy.

The fact that she was a nut seemed to explain a lot, somehow. If she had been sane I would have turned her down flat. It's been my experience through the years that sane people who go traipsing off to kill other people usually get killed themselves. The people who do best at combat don't have a death grip on life, if you know what I mean. They are crazy enough to take the biggest risk of all and not freak out when the shooting starts. Julie Giraud looked like she had her share of that kind of insanity.

"Do I have my information correct? Were you a sniper in Vietnam, Mr. Dean?"

"That was a war," I said, trying to find the words to explain, taking my time. "I was in Recon. We did ambushes and assassinations. I had a talent with a rifle. Other men had other talents. What you're suggesting isn't war, Ms. Giraud."

"Do you still have what it takes?"

She was goading me and we both knew it. I shrugged.

She wouldn't let it alone. "Could you still kill a man at five hundred yards with a rifle? Shoot him down in cold blood?"

"You want me to shoot somebody today so you can see if I'm qualified for the job?"

"I'm willing to pay three million dollars, Mr. Dean, to the man with the balls to help me kill the men who murdered my parents. I'm offering you the job. I'll pay half up front into a Swiss bank account, half after we kill the men who killed my parents."

"What if you don't make it? What if they kill you?"

"I'll leave a wire transfer order with my banker."

I snorted. At times I got the impression she thought this was some kind of extreme sports expedition, like jumping from a helicopter to ski down a mountain. And yet . . . she had that fire in her eyes.

"Where in hell did a captain in the air farce get three million dollars?"

"I inherited half my parents' estate and invested it in software and internet stocks; and the stocks went up like a rocket shot to Mars, as everyone north of Antarctica well knows. Now I'm going to spend the money on something I want very badly. That's the American way, isn't it?"

"Like ribbed condoms and apple pie," I agreed, then leaned forward to look into her eyes. "If we kill these men," I explained, "the world will never be the same for you. When you look in the mirror the face that stares back won't be the same one you've been looking at all these years—it'll be uglier. Your parents will still be dead and you'll be older in ways that years can't measure. That's the god's truth, kid. Your parents are going to be dead regardless. Keep your money, find a good guy, and have a nice life."

She sneered. "You're a philosopher?"

"I've been there, lady. I'm trying to figure out if I want to go back."

"Three million dollars, Mr. Dean. How long will it take for your gasoline station to make three million dollars profit?"

I owned three gas stations, all mortgaged to the hilt, but I wasn't going to tell her that. I sat in the corner of Burger King working on a Diet Coke while I thought about the kid I had damn near killed the night before.

"What about afterward?" I asked. "Tell me how you and I are going to continue to reside on this planet with the CIA and FBI and Middle Eastern terrorists all looking to carve on our ass."

She knew a man, she said, who could provide passports.

"Fake passports? Bullshit! Get real."

"Genuine passports. He's a U.S. consular official in Munich."

"What are you paying him?"

"He wants to help."

"Dying to go to prison, is he?"

"I've slept with him for the past eighteen months."

"You got a nice ass, but . . . Unless this guy is a real toad, he can get laid any night of the week. Women today think if they don't use it, they'll wear it out pissing through it."

"You have difficulty expressing yourself in polite company, don't you, Charlie Dean? Okay, cards on the table: I'm fucking him and paying him a million dollars."

I sat there thinking it over.

"If you have the money you can buy anything," she said.

"I hope you aren't foolish enough to believe that."

"Someone always wants money. All you have to do is find that someone. You're a case in point."

"How much would it cost to kill an ex-Marine who became a liability and nuisance?"

"A lot less than I'm paying you," she shot back. She didn't smile.

After a bit she started talking again, telling me how we were going to kill the bad guys. I didn't think much of her plan—blow up a stone fortress?—but I sat there listening while I mulled things over. Three million was not small change.

Finally I decided that Julie's conscience was her problem and the three million would look pretty good in my bank account. The Libyans—well, I really didn't give a damn about them one way or the other. They would squash me like a bug if they thought I was any threat at all, so what the hell. They had blown up airliners, they could take their chances with the devil.

Three

We were inside a rain cloud. Water ran off the windscreen in continuous streams: The dim glow of the red cockpit lights made the streams look like pale red rivers. Beyond the wet windscreen, however, the night was coal black.

I had never seen such absolute darkness.

Julie Giraud had the Osprey on autopilot; she was bent over fiddling with the terrain-avoidance radar while auto flew the plane.

I sure as hell wasn't going to be much help. I sat there watching her, wondering if I had made a sucker's deal. Three million was a lot of money if you lived to spend it. If you died earning it, it was nowhere near enough.

After a bit she turned off the radios and some other electronic gear, then used the autopilot to drop the nose into a descent. The multifunction displays in front of us—there were four plus a radar screen—displayed engine data, our flight plan, a moving map, and one that appeared to be a tactical display of the locations of the radars that were looking at us. I certainly didn't understand much of it, and Julie Giraud was as loquacious as a store dummy.

"We'll drop off their radar screens now," she muttered finally in way of explanation. As if to emphasize our departure into the outlaw world, she snapped off the plane's exterior lights.

As the altimeter unwound I must have looked a little nervous, and I guess I was. I rode two helicopters into the ground in Vietnam and one in Afghanistan, all shot down, so in the years since I had tried to avoid anything with rotors. Jets didn't bother me much, but rotor whop made my skin crawl.

Down we went until we were flying through the valleys of the Bavarian Alps below the hilltops. Julie sat there twiddling the autopilot as we flew along, keeping us between the hills with the radar.

She looked cool as a tall beer in July. "How come you aren't a little nervous?" I asked.

"This is the easy part," she replied.

That shut me up.

We were doing about 270 knots, so it took a little while to thread our way across Switzerland and northern Italy to the ocean. Somewhere over Italy we flew out of the rain. I breathed a sigh of relief when we left the valleys behind and dropped to a hundred feet over the ocean. Julie turned the plane for Africa.

"How do you know fighters aren't looking for us in this goop?" I asked.

She pointed toward one of the multifunction displays. "That's a threat indicator. We'll see anyone who uses a radar."

After a while I got bored, even at a hundred feet, so I got unstrapped and went aft to check the Humvee, trailer and cargo.

All secure.

I opened my duffel bag, got out a pistol belt. The gun, an old 1911 Colt .45 automatic, was loaded, but I checked it anyway, reholstered it, got the belt arranged around my middle so it rode comfortable with the pistol on my right side and my Ka-Bar knife on the left. I also had another knife in one boot and a hideout pistol in the other, just in case.

I put a magazine in the M-16 but didn't chamber a round. I had disassembled the weapon the night before, cleaned it thoroughly, and oiled it lightly.

The last weapon in the bag was a Model 70 in .308. It was my personal rifle, one I had built up myself years ago. With a synthetic stock, a Canjar adjustable trigger, and a heavy barrel custom-made for me by a Colorado gunsmith, it would put five shots into a half-inch circle at a hundred yards with factory match-grade ammunition. I had the 3×9 adjustable scope zeroed for two hundred. Trigger pull was exactly eighteen ounces.

I repacked the rifles, then sat in the driver's seat of the Humvee and poured myself a cup of coffee from the thermos.

We flew to Europe on different airlines and arrived in Zurich just hours apart. The following day I opened a bank account at a gleaming pile of marble in the heart of the financial district. As I watched, Julie called her banker in Virginia and had $1.5 million in cold hard cash transferred into the account. Three hours after she made the transfer I went to my bank and checked: The money was really there and it was all mine.

Amazing.

We met for dinner at a little hole-in-the-wall restaurant a few blocks off the main drag that I remembered from years before, when I was sight-seeing while on leave during a tour in Germany.

"The money's there," I told her when we were seated. "I confess, I didn't think it would be."

She got a little huffy. "I'd lie to you?"

"It's been known to happen. Though for the life of me, I couldn't see why you would."

She opened her purse, handed me an unsealed envelope. Inside was a passport. I got up and went to the men's room, where I inspected it. It certainly looked like a genuine U.S. passport, on the right paper and printed with dots and displaying my shaved, honest phiz. The name on the thing was Robert Arnold. I put it in my jacket pocket and rejoined her at the table.

She handed me a letter and an addressed envelope. The letter was to her banker, typed, instructing him to transfer another $1.5 million to my account a week after we were scheduled to hit the Camel. The envelope was addressed to him and even had a Swiss stamp on it. I checked the numbers on my account at the Swiss bank. Everything jibed.

She had a pen in her hand by that time. After she had signed the letter, I sealed it in the envelope, then folded the envelope and tucked it in my pocket beside the passport.

"Okay, lady. I'm bought and paid for."

We made our plans over dinner. She drank one glass of wine, and I had a beer, then we both switched to mineral water. I told her I wanted my own pistol and rifles, a request she didn't blink at. She agreed to fly into Dover Air Force Base on one of the regularly scheduled cargo runs, then take my duffel bag containing the weapons back to Germany with her.

"What if someone wants to run the bag through a metal detector, or German customs wants to inspect it?"

"My risk."

"I guess there are a few advantages to being a well-scrubbed, clean-cut American girl."

"You can get away with a lot if you shave your legs."

"I'll keep that in mind."

That was ten days ago. Now we were on our way. Tomorrow we were going to case the old fort and come up with a plan for doing in the assembled bad guys.

Sitting in the driver's seat of the Humvee sipping coffee and listening to the drone of the turboprops carrying us across the Mediterranean, I got the old combat feeling again.

Yeah, this was really it.

Only this time I was going to get paid for it.

I finished the coffee, went back to the cockpit, and offered Julie a cup. She was intent on the computer screens.

"Problems?" I asked.

"I'm picking up early warning radar, but I think I'm too low for the Libyans to see me. There's a fighter aloft too. I doubt if he can pick us out of ground return."

All that was outside my field of expertise. On this portion of the trip, I was merely a passenger.

I saw the land appear on the radar presentation, watched it march down the scope toward us, as if we were stationary and the world was turning under us. It was a nice illusion. As we crossed the beach, I checked my watch. We were only a minute off our planned arrival time, which seemed to me to be a tribute to Julie's piloting skills.

The ride got bumpy over the desert. Even at night the thermals kept the air boiling. Julie Giraud took the plane off autopilot, hand-flew it. Trusting the autopilot in rough air so close to the ground was foolhardy.

I got out the chart, used a little red spotlight mounted on the ceiling of the cockpit to study the lines and notes as we bounced along in turbulence.

We had an hour and twenty minutes to go. Fuel to get out of the desert would have been a problem, so we had brought five hundred gallons in a portable tank in the cargo compartment. Tomorrow night we would use a hand pump to transfer that fuel into the plane's tanks, enough to get us out of Africa when the time came.

I sat back and watched her fly, trying not to think about the tasks and dangers ahead. At some point it doesn't pay to worry about hazards you can't do anything about. When you've taken all the precautions you can, then it's time to think about something else.

The landing site we had picked was seven miles from the Camel, at the base of what appeared on the chart to be a cliff. The elevation lines seemed to indicate a cliff of sixty or seventy feet in height.

"How do you know that is a cliff?" I had asked Julie when she first showed the chart to me. In reply she pulled out two satellite photos. They had obviously been taken at different times of day, perhaps in different seasons or years, but they were obviously of the same piece of terrain. I compared them to the chart.

There was a cliff all right, and apparently room to tuck the Osprey in against it, pretty much out of sight.

"You want me to try to guess where you got these satellite photos?"

"My friend in the CIA."

"And nobody is going to ask her any questions?"

"Nope. She's cool and she's clean."

"I don't buy it."

"She doesn't have access to this stuff. She's stealing it. They'll only talk to people with access."

"Must be a bunch of stupes in the IG's office there, huh."

She wouldn't say any more.

We destroyed the photos, of course, before we left the apartment she had rented for me. Still, the thought of Julie's classmate in the CIA who could sell us down the river to save her own hide gave me a sick feeling in the pit of my stomach as we motored through the darkness over the desert.

Julie had our destination dialed into the navigation computer, so the magic box was depicting our track and time to go. I sat there watching the miles and minutes tick down.

With five miles to go, Julie began slowing the Osprey. And she flipped on the landing lights. Beams of light seared the darkness and revealed the yellow rock and sand and dirt of the deep desert.

She began tilting the engines toward the vertical, which slowed us further and allowed the giant rotors to begin carrying a portion of our weight.

When the last mile ticked off the computer and we crossed the cliff line, the Osprey was down to fifty knots. Julie brought the V-22 into a hover and used the landing lights to explore our hiding place. Some small boulders, not too many, and the terrain under the cliff was relatively flat.

After a careful circuit and inspection, Julie set the Osprey down, shut down the engines.

The silence was startling as we took off our helmets.

Now she shut down the aircraft battery and all the cockpit lights went off.

"We're here," she said with a sigh of relief.

"You really intend to go through with this, don't you?"

"Don't tell me you still have doubts, Charlie Dean."

"Okay. I won't."

She snapped on a flashlight and led the way back through the cargo bay. She opened the rear door and we stepped out onto the godforsaken soil of the Sahara. We used a flashlight to inspect our position.

"I could get it a little closer to the cliff, but I doubt if it's worth the effort."

"Let's get to work," I said. I was tired of sitting.

First she went back to the cockpit and tilted the engines down to the cruise position. The plane would be easier to camouflage with the engines down. We would rotate the engines back to the vertical position when the time came to leave.

Next we unloaded the Humvee and trailer, then the cargo we had tied down in piles on the floor of the plane. I carried the water jugs out myself, taking care to place them where they wouldn't fall over.

The last thing we removed from the plane was the camouflage netting. We unrolled it, then began draping it over the airplane. We both had to get up on top of the plane to get the net over the tail and engine nacelles. Obviously we couldn't cover the blade of each rotor that stuck straight up, so we cut holes in the net for them.

It took us almost two hours of intense effort to get the net completely rigged. We treated ourselves to a drink of water.

"We sure can't get out of here in a hurry," I remarked.

"I swore on the altar of God I would kill the men who killed my parents. We aren't going anywhere until we do it."

"Yeah."

I finished my drink, then unhooked the trailer from the Humvee and dug out my night-vision goggles. I uncased my Model 70 and chambered a round, put on the safety, then got into the driver's seat and laid it across my lap.

"We can't plant explosives until tomorrow night," she said.

"I know that. But I want a look at that place now. You coming?"

She got her night-vision goggles and climbed into the passenger seat. I took the time to fire up the GPS and key in our destination, then started the Humvee and plugged in my night-vision goggles. It was like someone turned on the light. I could see the cliff and the plane and the stones as if the sun were shining on an overcast day.

I put the Humvee in gear and rolled.

Four

The Camel sat on a granite ridge that humped up out of the desert floor. On the eastern side of the ridge, in the low place scooped out by the wind, there was an oasis, a small pond of muddy water, a few palm trees, and a cluster of mud huts. According to Julie's CIA sister, a few dozen nomads lived here seasonally. Standing on the hood of the Humvee, which was parked on a gentle rise a mile east of the oasis, I could just see the tops of the palms and a few of the huts. No heat source flared up when I switched to infrared.

The old fort was a shattered hulk upon the skyline, brooding and massive. The structure itself wasn't large, but perched there on that granite promontory it was a presence.

I slowly did a 360-degree turn, sweeping the desert.

Nothing moved. I saw only rock and hard-packed earth, here and there a scraggly desert plant. The wind had long ago swept away the sand.

Finally I got down off the hood of the Humvee. Julie was standing there with her arms crossed looking cold, although the temperature was at least sixty.

"I want you to drive this thing back into that draw, and just sit and wait. I'm going to walk over there and eyeball it up."

"When are you coming back?"

"Couple hours after dawn, probably. I want to make sure there are no people there, and I want to see it in the daylight."

"Can't we just wait until tonight to check it out?"

"I'm not going to spend a day not knowing what in hell is over the hill. I didn't get to be this old by taking foolish risks. Drive down there and wait for me."

She got in the Humvee and did as I asked.

I adjusted my night-vision goggles, tucked the Model 70 under my arm and started hiking.

I had decided on South Africa. After this was over, I was going to try South Africa. I figured it would be middling difficult for the Arabs to root me out there. I had never been to South Africa, but from everything I had seen and heard the country sounded like it might have a future now that they had made a start at solving the racial problem. South Africa. My image of the place had a bit of a Wild West flavor that appealed to my sporting instincts.

Not that I really have any sporting instincts. Those all got squeezed out of me in Vietnam. I'd rather shoot the bastards in the back than in the front: It's safer.

The CIA and FBI? They could find me anywhere, if they wanted to. The theft of a V-22 wasn't likely to escape their notice, but I didn't think the violent death of some terrorists would inspire those folks to put in a lot of overtime. I figured a fellow who stayed out of sight would soon be out of mind too.

With three million dollars in my jeans, staying out of sight would be a pleasure.

That's the way I had it figured, anyhow. As I walked across the desert hardpan toward the huts by the mudhole, I confess, I was thinking again about South Africa, which made me angry.

Concentrate, I told myself. Stay focused. Stay alive.

I was glad the desert here was free of sand. I was leaving no tracks in the hard-packed earth and stone of the desert floor that I could see or feel with my fingers, which relieved me somewhat.

I took my time approaching the huts from downwind. No dogs that I could see, no vehicles, no sign of people. The place looked deserted.

And was. Not a soul around. I checked all five of the huts, looked in the sheds. Not even a goat or puppy.

There were marks of livestock by the water hole. Only six inches of water, I estimated, at the deepest part. At the widest place the pond was perhaps thirty feet across, about the size of an Iowa farm pond but with less water.

The cliff loomed above the back of the water hole. Sure enough, I found a trail. I started climbing.

The top of the ridge was about three hundred feet above the surrounding terrain. I huffed and puffed a bit getting up there. On top there was a bit of a breeze blowing, a warm, dry desert breeze that felt delicious at that hour of the night.

I found a vantage point and examined the fort through the night-vision goggles, looked all around in every direction. To the west I could see the paved strip of the airport reflecting the starlight, so it appeared faintly luminescent. It too was empty. No people, no planes, no vehicles, no movement, just stone and great empty places.

I took off the goggles and turned them off to save the battery, then waited for my eyes to adjust to the darkness. The stars were so close in that clear dry air it seemed as if I could reach up and touch them. To the east the sky was lightening up.

As the dawn slowly chased away the night, I worked my way toward the fort, which was about a third of a mile from where the trail topped the ridge. Fortunately there were head-high clumps of desert brush tucked into the nooks and crannies of the granite, so I tried to stay under cover as much as possible. By the time the sun poked its head over the earth's rim I was standing under the wall of the fort.

I listened.

All I could hear was the whisper of the wind.

I found a road and a gate, which wasn't locked. After all, how many people are running around out here in this wasteland?

Taking my time, I sneaked in. I had the rifle off my shoulder and leveled, with my thumb on the safety and my finger on the trigger.

A Land Rover was parked in the courtyard. It had a couple five-gallon cans strapped to the back of it and was caked with dirt and dust. The tires were relatively new, sporting plenty of tread.

When I was satisfied no one was in the courtyard, I stepped over to the Land Rover. The keys were in the ignition.

I slipped into a doorway and stood there listening.

Back when I was young, I was small and wiry and stupid enough to crawl through Viet Cong tunnels looking for bad guys. I had nightmares about that experience for years.

Somewhere in this pile of rock was at least one person, perhaps more. But where?

The old fort was quiet as a tomb. Just when I thought there was nothing to hear, I heard something . . . a scratching . . .

I examined the courtyard again. There, on a second-story window ledge, a bird.

It flew.

I hung the rifle over my shoulder on its sling and got out my knife. With the knife in my right hand, cutting edge up, I began exploring.

The old fort had some modern sleeping quarters, cooking facilities, and meeting rooms. There were electric lights plugged into wall sockets. In one of the lower rooms I found a gasoline-powered generator. Forty gallons of gasoline in plastic five-gallon cans sat in the next room.

In a tower on the top floor, in a room with a magnificent view through glass windows, sat a first-class, state-of-the-art shortwave radio. I had seen the antenna as I walked toward the fort: It was on the roof above this room. I was examining the radio, wondering if I should try to disable it, when I heard a nearby door slam.

Scurrying to the door of the room, I stood frozen, listening with my ear close to the wall.

The other person in the fort was making no attempt to be quiet, which made me feel better. He obviously thought he was very much alone. And it was just one person, close, right down the hallway.

Try as I might, I could only hear the one person, a man, opening and closing drawers, scooting something—a chair probably—across a stone floor, now slamming another door shut.

Even as I watched he came out of one of the doors and walked away from me to the stairs I had used coming up. Good thing I didn't open the door to look into his room!

I got a glimpse of him crossing the courtyard, going toward the gasoline generator.

Unwilling to move, I stood there until I heard the generator start. The hum of the gasoline engine settled into a steady drone. A lightbulb above the table upon which the radio sat illuminated.

I trotted down the hallway to the room the man had come out of. I eased the door open and glanced in. Empty.

The next room was also a bedroom, also empty, so I went in and closed the door.

I was standing back from the window, watching, fifteen minutes later when the man walked out of a doorway to the courtyard almost directly opposite the room I was in, got into the Land Rover, and started it.

He drove out through the open gate trailing a wispy plume of dust. I went to another window, an outside one, and waited. In a moment I got a glimpse of the Land Rover on the road to the airport.

In the courtyard against one wall stood a water tank on legs, with plastic lines leading away to the kitchen area. I opened the fill cap and looked in. I estimated the tank contained fifty gallons of water. Apparently people using this facility brought water with them, poured it into this tank, then used it sparingly.

I stood in the courtyard looking at the water tank, cursing under my breath. The best way to kill these people would be to poison their water with some kind of delayed-action poison that would take twenty-four hours to work, so everyone would have an opportunity to ingest some. Julie Giraud could have fucked a chemist and got us some poison. I should have thought of the water tank.

Too late now.

Damn!

Before I had a chance to cuss very much, I heard a jet. The engine noise was rapidly getting louder. I dived for cover.

Seconds later a jet airplane went right over the fort, less than a hundred feet above the radio antenna.

Staying low, I scurried up the staircase to the top of the ramparts and took a look. A small passenger jet was circling to land at the airport.

I double-timed down the staircase and hotfooted it out the gate and along the trail leading to the path down to the oasis, keeping my eye on the sky in case another jet should appear.

It took me about half an hour to get back to the oasis, and another fifteen minutes to reach the place where Julie was waiting in the Humvee. Of course I didn't just charge right up to the Humvee. Still well out of sight of the vehicle, I stopped, lay down, and caught my breath.

When I quit blowing, I circled the area where the Humvee should have been, came at it from the east. At first I didn't see her. I could see the vehicle, but she wasn't in sight.

I settled down to wait.

Another jet went over, apparently slowing to land on the other side of the ridge.

A half hour passed, then another. The temperature was rising quickly, the sun climbing the sky.

Finally, Julie moved.

She was lying at the base of a bush a hundred feet from the vehicle and she had an M-16 in her hands.

Okay.

Julie Giraud was a competent pilot and acted like she had all her shit in one sock when we were planning this mission, but I wanted to see how she handled herself on the ground. If we made a mistake in Europe, we might wind up in prison. A mistake here would cost us our lives.

I crawled forward on my stomach, taking my time, just sifting along.

It took me fifteen minutes to crawl up behind her. Finally I reached out with the barrel of the Model 70, touched her foot. She spun around as if she had been stung.

I grinned at her.

"You bastard," Julie Giraud said.

"Don't you forget it, lady."

Five

Blowing up the fort was an impractical idea and always had been. When Julie Giraud first mentioned destroying the fort with the bad guys inside, back in Van Nuys, I had let her talk. I didn't think she had any idea how much explosives would be necessary to demolish a large stone structure, and she didn't. When I finally asked her how much C-4 she thought it would take, she looked at me blankly.

We had brought a hundred pounds of the stuff, all we could transport efficiently.

I used the binoculars to follow the third plane through the sky until it disappeared behind the ridge. It was some kind of small, twin-engined bizjet.

"How come these folks are early?" I asked her.

"I don't know."

"Your CIA friend didn't tip you off about the time switch?"

"No."

The fact these people were arriving a day early bothered me and I considered it from every angle.

Life is full of glitches and unexpected twists—who ever has a day that goes as planned? To succeed at anything you must be adaptable and flexible, and smart enough to know when backing off is the right thing to do.

I wondered just how smart I was. Should we back off?

I drove the Humvee toward the cliff where we had the Osprey

parked. The land rolled, with here and there gulleys cut by the runoff from rare desert storms. These gulleys had steep sides, loose sand bottoms, and were choked with desert plants. Low places had brush and cacti, but mainly the terrain was dirt with occasional rock outcroppings. One got the impression that at some time in the geologic past the dirt had blown in, covering a stark, highly eroded landscape. I tried to keep off the exposed places as much as possible and drove very slowly to keep from raising dust.

Every so often I stopped the vehicle, got out and listened for airplanes. Two more jets went over that I heard. That meant there were at least five jets at that desert strip, maybe more.

Julie sat silently, saying nothing as we drove along. When I killed the engine and got out to listen, she stayed in her seat.

I stopped the Humvee in a brushy draw about a mile from the Osprey, reached for the Model 70, then snagged a canteen and hung it over my shoulder.

"May I come with you?" she asked.

"Sure."

We stopped when we got to a low rise where we could see the V-22 and the area around it. I looked everything over with binoculars, then settled down at the base of a green bush that resembled greasewood, trying to get what shade there was. The temperature must have been ninety by that time.

"Aren't we going down to the plane?"

"It's safer here."

Julie picked another bush and crawled under.

I was silently complimenting her on her ability to accept direction without question or explanation when she said, "You don't take many chances, do you?"

"I try not to."

"So you're just going to kill these people, then get on with the rest of your life?"

I took a good look at her face. "If you're going to chicken out," I said, "do it now, so I don't have to lie here sweating the program for the whole damned day."

"I'm not going to chicken out. I just wondered if you were."

"You said these people were terrorists, had blown up airliners. That still true?"

"Absolutely."

"Then I won't lose any sleep over them." I shifted around, got comfortable, kept the rifle just under my hands.

She met my eyes, and apparently decided this point needed a little more exploring. "I'm killing them because they killed my parents. You're killing them for money."

I sighed, tossed her the binoculars.

"Every few minutes, glass the area around the plane, then up on the ridge," I told her. "Take your time, look at everything in your field of view, look for movement. Any kind of movement. And don't let the sun glint off the binoculars."

"How are we going to do it?" she asked as she stared through the glasses.

"Blowing the fort was a pipe dream, as you well know."

She didn't reply, just scanned with the binoculars.

"The best way to do it is to blow up the planes with the people on them."

A grin crossed her face, then disappeared.

I rolled over, arranged the rifle just so, and settled down for a nap. I was so tired.

The sun had moved a good bit by the time I awakened. The air was stifling, with no detectable breeze. Julie was stretched out asleep, the binoculars in front of her. I used the barrel of the rifle to hook the strap and lift them, bring them over to me without making noise.

The land was empty, dead. Not a single creature stirred, not even a bird. The magnified images I could see through the binoculars shimmered in the heat.

Finally I put the thing down, sipped at the water in my canteen.

South Africa. Soon. Maybe I'd become a diamond prospector. There was a whole lot of interesting real estate in South Africa, or so I'd heard, and I intended to see it. Get a jeep and some camping gear and head out.

Julie's crack about killing for money rankled, of course. The fact was that these people were terrorists, predators who preyed on the weak and defenseless. They had blown up an airliner. Take money for killing them? Yep. And glad to get it, too.

Julie had awakened and moved off into the brush out of sight to relieve herself when I spotted a man on top of the cliff, a few hundred yards to the right of the Osprey. I picked him up as I swept the top of the cliff with the binoculars.

I turned the focus wheel, tried to sharpen the dancing image. Too much heat.

It was a man, all right. Standing there with a rifle on a sling over his shoulder, surveying the desert with binoculars. Instinctively I backed up a trifle, ensured the binoculars were in shade so there would be no sun reflections off the glass or frame. And I glanced at the airplane.

It should be out of sight of the man due to the way the cliff outcropped between his position and the plane. I hoped. In any event he wasn't looking at it.

I gritted my teeth, studied his image, tried by sheer strength of will to make it steadier in the glass. The distance between us was about six hundred yards, I estimated.

I put down the binoculars and slowly brought up the Model 70. I had a variable power scope on it which I habitually kept cranked to maximum magnification. The figure of the man leaped at me through the glass.

I put the crosshairs on his chest, studied him. Even through the shimmering air I could see the cloth he wore on his head and the headband that held it in place. He was wearing light-colored trousers and a shirt. And he was holding binoculars pointed precisely at me.

I heard a rustle behind me.

"Freeze, Julie," I said, loud enough that she would plainly hear me.

She stopped.

I kept the scope on him, flicked off the safety. I had automatically assumed a shooting position when I raised the rifle. Now I wiggled my left elbow into the hard earth, settled the rifle in tighter against my shoulder.

He just stood there, looking right at us.

I only saw him because he was silhouetted on the skyline. In the shade under this brush we should be invisible to him. Should be.

Now he was scanning the horizon again. Since I had been watching he had not once looked down at the foot of the cliff upon which he was standing.

He was probably a city soldier, I decided. Hadn't been trained to look close first, before he scanned terrain farther away.

After another long moment he turned away, began walking slowly along the top of the cliff to my right, away from the Osprey. I kept the crosshairs of the scope on him until he was completely out of sight. Only then did I put the safety back on and lower the rifle.

"You can come in now," I said.

She crawled back under her bush.

"Did you see him?" I asked.

"Yes. Did he see the airplane?"

"I'm certain he didn't."

"How did he miss it?"

"It was just a little out of sight, I think. Even if he could have seen it, he never really looked in the right direction."

"We were lucky," she said.

I grunted. It was too hot to discuss philosophy. I lay there under my bush wondering just how crazy ol' Julie Giraud really was.

"If he had seen the plane, Charlie Dean, would you have shot him?"

What a question!

"You're damned right," I muttered, more than a little disgusted. "If he had seen the plane, I would have shot him and piled you into the cockpit and made you get us the hell out of here before all the Indians in the world showed up to help with the pleasant chore of lifting our hair. These guys are playing for keeps, lady. You and me had better be on the same sheet of music or we will be well and truly fucked."

Every muscle in her face tensed. "We're not leaving," she snarled, "until those sons of bitches are dead. All of them. Every last one."

She was over the edge.

A wave of cold fear swept over me. It was bad enough being on the edge of a shooting situation; now my backup was around the bend. If she went down or freaked out, how in the hell was I going to get off this rock pile?

"I've been trying to decide," she continued, "if you really have the balls for this, Charlie Dean, or if you're going to turn tail on me when crunch time comes and run like a rabbit. You're old: You look old, you sound old. Maybe you had the balls years ago, maybe you don't anymore."

From the leg pocket of her flight suit she pulled a small automatic, a .380 from the looks of it. She held it where I could see it, pointed it more or less in my direction. "Grow yourself another set of balls, Charlie Dean. Nobody is running out."

I tossed her the binoculars. "Call me if they come back," I said. I put the rifle beside me and lay down.

Sure, I thought about what a dumb ass I was. Three million bucks!—I was going to have to earn every damned dollar.

Hoo boy.

Okay, I'll admit it: I knew she was crazy that first day in Van Nuys.

I made a conscious effort to relax. The earth was warm, the air was hot, and I was exhausted. I was asleep in nothing flat.

The sun was about to set when I awoke. My binoculars were on the sand beside me and Julie Giraud was nowhere in sight. I used the scope on the rifle to examine the Osprey and the cliff behind it.

I spotted her in seconds, moving around under the plane. No one else visible.

While we had a little light, I went back for the Humvee. I crawled up on it, taking my time, ensuring that no one was there waiting for me.

When we left it that morning we had piled some dead brush on the hood and top of the vehicle, so I pulled that off before I climbed in.

Taking it slow so I wouldn't raise dust, I drove the mile or so to the Osprey. I got there just as the last rays of the sun vanished.

I backed up to the trailer and we attached it to the Humvee.

"Want to tell me your plan, Charlie Dean?" she asked. "Or do you have one?"

As I repacked the contents of the trailer I told her how I wanted to do it. Amazingly, she agreed readily.

She was certainly hard to figure. One minute I thought she was a real person, complete with a conscience and the intellectual realization that even the enemy were human beings, then the next second she was a female Rambo, ready to gut them all, one by one.

She helped me make up C-4 bombs, rig the detonators and radio controls. I did the first one, she watched intently, then she did one on her own. I checked it, and she got everything right.

"Don't take any unnecessary chances tonight," I said. "I want you alive and well when this is over so you can fly me out of here."

She merely nodded. It was impossible to guess what she might have been thinking.

I wasn't about to tell her that I had flown helicopters in Vietnam. I was never a rated pilot, but I was young and curious, so the pilots often let me practice under their supervision. I had watched her with the Osprey and thought that I could probably fly it if absolutely necessary. The key would be to use the checklist and take plenty of time. If I could get it started, I thought I could fly it out. There were parachutes in the thing, so I would not need to land it.

I didn't say any of this to her, of course.

We had a packet of radio receivers and detonators—I counted them—enough for six bombs. If I set them all on the same frequency I could blow up six planes with one push of the button. If I could get the bombs aboard six planes without being discovered.

What if there were more than six planes? Well, I had some pyrotechnic fuses, which seemed impractical to use on an airplane, and some chemical fuses. In the cargo bay of the Osprey I examined the chemical fuses by flashlight. Eight hours seemed to be the maximum setting. The problem was that I didn't know when the bad guys planned to leave.

As I was meditating on fuses and bombs, I went outside and walked around the Osprey. There was a turreted three-barreled fifty-caliber machine gun in the nose of the thing. Air Force Ospreys didn't carry stingers like this, but this one belonged to the Marine Corps, or did until twenty-four hours ago.

I opened the service bay. Gleaming brass in the feed trays reflected the dim evening light.

Julie was standing right behind me. "I stole this one because it had the gun," she remarked. "Less range than the Air Force birds, but the gun sold me."

"Maximum firepower is always a good choice."

"What are you thinking?" she asked.

We discussed contingencies as we wired up the transfer pump in the bladder fuel tank we had chained down in the cargo bay. We used the aircraft's battery to power the pump, so all we had to do was watch as three thousand pounds of jet fuel was transferred into the aircraft's tanks.

My plan had bombs, bullets, and a small river of blood—we hoped—just the kind of tale that appealed to Julie Giraud. She even allowed herself a tight smile.

Me? I had a cold knot in the pit of my stomach and I was sweating.

Six

We finished loading the Humvee and the trailer attached to it before sunset and ate MREs in the twilight. As soon as it was dark, we donned our night-vision goggles and drove toward the oasis. I stopped often to get up on the vehicle's hood, the best vantage point around, and take a squint in all directions.

I parked the vehicle at the foot of the trail. "If I'm not back in an hour and a half, they've caught me," I told Julie Giraud. I smeared my face with grease to cut the white shine, checked my reflection in the rearview mirror, then did my neck and the back of my hands.

"If they catch you," she said, "I won't pay you the rest of the money."

"Women are too maudlin to be good soldiers," I told her. "You've got to stop this cloying sentimentality. Save the tears for the twenty-five-year reunion."

When I was as invisible as I was going to get, I hoisted a rucksack that I had packed that evening, put the M-16 over my shoulder, and started up the trail.

Every now and then I switched the goggles from ambient light to infrared and looked for telltale heat sources. I spotted some small mammal, too small to be human. I continued up the ridge, wondering how any critters managed to make a living in this godforsaken desert.

The temperature had dropped significantly from the high during the afternoon. I estimated the air was still at eighty degrees, but it would soon go below seventy. Even the earth was cooling, although not as quickly as the air.

I topped the ridge slowly, on the alert for security patrols. Before we committed ourselves to a course of action, we had to know how many security people were prowling around.

No one in sight now.

I got off to one side of the trail, just in case, and walked toward the old fortress, the Camel. Tonight light shone from several of the structure's windows, light visible for many miles in that clean desert air.

I was still at least five hundred yards from the walls when I first heard the hum of the generator, barely audible at that distance. The noise gradually increased as I approached the structure. When I was about fifty yards from the wall, I circled the fort to a vantage point where I could see the main gate, the gate where I entered on my last visit. It was standing open. A guard with an assault rifle sat on a stool near the gate; he was quite clear in the goggles. He was sitting under an overhang of the wall at a place where he could watch the road that led off the ridge, the road to the oasis and the airfield. He was not wearing any night-vision aid, just sitting in the darkness under the wall.

The drone of the gasoline generator meant that he could hear nothing. Of course, it handicapped me as well.

I continued around the structure, crossing the road at a spot out of sight of the man at the gate. Taking my time, slipping through the sparse brush as carefully as possible, I inspected every foot of the wall. The main gate was the only entrance I noticed on my first visit, yet I wanted to be sure.

A man strolled on top of the wall on the side opposite the main gate; the instant I saw him I dropped motionless to the ground. Seconds passed as he continued to walk, then finally he reversed his course. When he disappeared from view I scurried over to a rock outcrop and crouched under it, with my body out of sight from the wall.

If he had an infrared scope or any kind of ambient light collector, he could have seen me lying on the open ground.

I crouched there waiting for something to happen. If they came streaming out of the main gate, they could trap me on the point of this ridge, hunt me down at their leisure.

As I waited I discovered that the M-16 was already in my hands. I had removed it from my shoulder automatically, without thinking.

Several minutes passed as I waited, listening to the hypnotic drone of the generator, waiting for something to happen. Anything.

Finally a head became visible on top of the wall. The sentry again, still strolling aimlessly. He leaned against the wall for a while, then disappeared.

Now I hurried along, completed my circumnavigation of the fort.

I saw only the two men, one on the gate and the man who had been walking the walls. Although I had seen the man on the wall twice, I was convinced it was the same person. And I was certain there was only one entrance to the fort, the main gate.

I had to go through that gate so I was going to have to take out the guard. I was going to have to do it soon, then hope I could get in and out before his absence from his post was noticed or someone came to relieve him. Taking chances like that wasn't the best way to live to spend that three million dollars, that's for sure, but we didn't have the time or resources to minimize the risk. I was going to have to have some luck here or we had no chance to pull off this thing.

This whole goddamn expedition was half-baked, I reflected, and certainly no credit to me. Man, why didn't I think of poisoning their water supply when we were brainstorming in Germany?

In my favor was the fact that these people didn't seem very worried about their safety or anything else. A generator snoring away, only two guards? An open gate?

I worked my way to the wall, then turned and crept toward the guard. The generator hid the sounds I made as I crept along. He was facing the road.

I got about ten feet from him and froze. He was facing away from me at a slight angle, but if I tried to get closer, he was going to pick me up in his peripheral vision. I sensed it, so I froze.

He changed his position on the stool, played with the rifle on his knees, looked at the myriad of stars that hung just over our heads. Finally he stood and stretched. For an instant he turned away from me. I covered the distance in two bounds, wrapped my arm around his mouth, and jammed my knife into his back up to the hilt.

The knife went between his ribs right into his heart. Two convulsive tremors, then he was dead.

I carried him and his rifle off into the darkness. He weighed maybe one-eighty, as near as I could tell.

One of the outcroppings that formed the edge of the top of the ridge would keep him hidden from anyone but a determined searcher. After I stashed the body, I hurried back to the gate. I took off my night-vision goggles, waited for my eyes to adjust. I took off my rifle, leaned it against the wall out of sight.

As I waited I saw the man on the ramparts walking his rounds. He was in no hurry, obviously bored. I got a radio-controlled bomb from the rucksack, checked the frequency, and turned on the receiver.

The Land Rover was in the courtyard. When the man on the wall was out of sight, I slipped over to it and lay down. I pulled out the snap wire and snapped it around one of the suspension arms. The antenna of the bomb I let dangle.

This little job took less than thirty seconds. Then I scurried across the courtyard into the shelter of the staircase.

The conferees were probably in the living area; I sure as hell hoped they were. My edge was that the people here were not on alert. And why should they be? This fort was buried in the most desolate spot on the planet, hundreds of miles from anyplace.

Still, my life was on the line, so I moved as cautiously as I could, trying very hard to make no noise at all, pausing to listen carefully before I rounded any corner. My progress was glacial. It took me almost five minutes to climb the stairs and inch down the corridor to the radio room.

The hum of the generator was muted the farther away from it I moved, but it was the faint background noise that covered any minor noise I was making. And any minor noise anyone else was making. That reality had me sweating.

The door to the radio room was ajar, the room dark.

Knocking out the generator figured to be the easiest way to disable the radio, unless they had a battery to use as backup. I was betting they did.

After listening for almost a minute outside the door, I eased it open gently, my fighting knife in my hand.

The only light came through the interior window from the floods in the courtyard. The room was empty of people!

I went in fast, laid my knife on the table, got a bomb out of the rucksack. This one was rigged with a chemical fuse, so I broke the chemicals, shook the thing to start the reaction, then put the package—explosive, detonator, fuse and all—directly behind the radio. As I turned I was struck in the face by a runaway Freightliner.

Only partially conscious, I found myself falling. A rough hand gripped me fiercely, then another truck slammed into my face. If I hadn't turned my head to protect myself, that blow would have put me completely out.

As it was, I couldn't stay upright. My legs turned to jelly and I went to the floor, which was cold and hard.

"What a pleasant surprise," my assailant said in highly accented English, then kicked me in the side. His boot almost broke my left arm, which was fortunate, because if he had managed to get a clean shot at my ribs he would have caved in a lung.

I wasn't feeling very lucky just then. My arm felt like it was in four pieces and my side was on fire. I fought for air.

I couldn't take much more of this. If I didn't do something pretty damned quick he was going to kick me to death.

Curling into a fetal position, I used my right hand to draw my hideout knife from my left boot. I had barely got it out when he kicked me in the kidney.

At first I thought the guy had rammed a knife into my back—the pain was that intense. I was fast running out of time.

I rolled over toward him, just in time to meet his foot coming in again. I slashed with the knife, which had a razor-sharp two-sided blade about three inches long. I felt it bite into something.

He stepped back then, bent down to feel his calf. I got my feet under me and rose into a crouch.

"A knife, is it? You think you can save yourself with that?"

While he was talking he lashed out again with a leg. It was a kick designed to distract me, tempt me to go for his leg again with the knife.

I didn't, so when he spun around and sent another of those iron-fisted artillery shots toward my head, I was ready. I went under the incoming punch and slashed his stomach with the knife.

I cut him bad.

Now he grunted in pain, sagged toward the radio table.

I gathered myself, got out of his way, got into a crouch so I could defend myself.

He was holding his stomach with both hands. In the dim light I could see blood. I had really gotten him.

"Shouldn't have played with you," he said, and reached for the pistol in the holster on his belt.

Too late. I was too close. With one mighty swing of my arm I slashed his throat. Blood spewed out, a look of surprise registered on his face, then he collapsed.

Blood continued to pump from his neck.

I had to wipe the sweat from my eyes.

Jesus! My hands were shaking, trembling.

Never again, God! I promise. Never again!

I stowed the little knife back in my boot, retrieved the rucksack and my fighting knife from the table.

Outside in the corridor I carefully pulled the door to the radio room shut, made sure it latched.

Down the stairs, across the courtyard, through the gate. Safe in the darkness outside, I retrieved my M-16 and puked up my MREs.

Yeah, I'm a real tough guy. Shit!

Then I trotted for the trail to the oasis. It wasn't much of a trot. My side, back, and arm were on fire, and my face was still numb. The best I could manage was a hell-bent staggering gait.

As I ran the numbness in my side and back wore off. I wheezed like an old horse and savored the pain, which was proof positive I was still alive.

Julie Giraud was standing beside the Humvee chewing her fingernails. I took my time looking over the area, made sure she was really alone, then walked the last hundred feet.

"Hey," I said.

My voice made her jump. She glanced at my face, then stared. "What happened?"

I eased myself into the driver's seat.

"A guy was waiting for me."

"What?"

"He spoke to me in English."

"Well . . ."

"Didn't even try a phrase in Arabic. Just spoke to me in English."

"You're bleeding under your right eye, I think. With all that grease it's hard to tell."

"Pay attention to what I'm telling you. He spoke to me in English. He knew I understood it. Doesn't that worry you?"

"What about the radio?"

"He knew I was coming. Someone told him. He was waiting for me."

"You're just guessing."

"He almost killed me."

"He didn't."

"If they knew we were coming, we're dead."

Before I could draw another breath, she had a pistol pointed at me. She placed the muzzle against the side of my head.

"I'll tell you one more time, Charlie Dean, one more time. These people are baby-killers, murderers of women and kids and old people. They have been tried in a court of law and found guilty. We are going to kill them so they can never kill again."

Crazy! She was crazy as hell!

Her voice was low, every word distinctly pronounced: "I don't care what they know or who told them what. *We are going to kill these men. You will help me do it or I will kill you.* Have I made it plain enough? Do you understand?"

"Did the court sentence these people to die?" I asked.

"*I* sentenced them! *Me!* Julie Giraud. And I am going to carry it out. *Death*. For every one of them."

Seven

The satellite photos showed a wash just off the east end of the runway. We worked our way along it, then crawled to a spot that allowed us to look the length of it.

The runway was narrow, no more than fifty feet wide. The planes were parked on a mat about halfway down. The wind was out of the west, as it usually was at night. To take off, the planes would have to taxi individually to the east end of the runway, this end, turn around, then take off to the west.

"If they don't discover that the guards are missing, search the place, find the bombs and disable them, we've got a chance," I said. "Just a chance."

"You're a pessimist."

"You got that right."

"How many guards do you think are around the planes?"

"I don't know. All of the pilots could be there; there could easily be a dozen people down there."

"So we just sneak over, see what's what?"

"That's about the size of it."

"For three million dollars I thought I was getting someone who knew how to pull this off."

"And I thought the person hiring me was sane. We both made a bad deal. You want to fly the Osprey back to Germany and tell them you're sorry you borrowed it?"

"They didn't kill your parents."

"I guarantee you, before this is over you're going to be elbow-deep in blood, lady. And your parents will still be dead."

"You said that before."

"It's still true."

I was tempted to give the bitch a rifle and send her down the runway to do her damnedest, but I didn't.

I took the goddamn M-16, adjusted the night-vision goggles, and went myself. My left side hurt like hell, from my shoulder to my hip. I flexed my arm repeatedly, trying to work the pain out.

The planes were readily visible with the goggles. I kept to the waist-high brush on the side of the runway toward the planes, which were parked in a row. It wasn't until I got about halfway there that I could count them. Six planes.

The idea was to get the terrorists into the planes, then destroy the planes in the air. The last thing we wanted was the terrorists and the guards out here in this desert running around looking for us. With dozens of them and only two of us, there was only one way for that tale to end.

No, we needed to get them into the planes. I didn't have enough radio-controlled detonators to put on all the planes, so I thought if I could disable some of the planes and put bombs on the rest, we would have a chance. But first we had to eliminate the guards.

If the flight crews were bivouacked near the planes, this was going to get really dicey.

I took my time, went slowly from bush to bush, looking at everything. When I used infrared, I could see a heat source to the south of the planes that had to be an open fire. No people, though.

I was crouched near the main wheel of the plane on the end of the mat when I saw my first guard. He was relieving himself against the nearest airplane's nosewheel.

When he finished he zipped up and resumed his stroll along the mat.

I went behind the plane and made my way toward the fire.

They had built the thing in a fifty-five-gallon drum. Two people stood with their backs to the fire, warming up. I could have used a stretch by that fire myself: The temperature was below sixty degrees by that time and going lower.

No tents. No one in sleeping bags that I could see.

Three of them.

I settled down to wait. Before we made a move, I had to be certain of the number of people that were here and where they were. If I missed one I wouldn't live to spend a dollar of Julie Giraud's blood money.

Lying there in the darkness, I tried to figure it all out. Didn't get anywhere. Why that guy addressed me in English I had no idea. He was certainly no Englishman; nor was he a native of any English-speaking country.

Julie Giraud wanted these sons of the desert dead and in hell—of that I was absolutely convinced. She wasn't a good enough actress to fake it. The money she had paid me was real enough, the V-22 Osprey was real, the guns were real, the bombs were real, we were so deep in the desert we could never drive or hike out. Never.

She was my ticket out. If she went down, I was going to have to try to fly the Osprey myself. If the plane was damaged, we were going to die here.

Simple as that.

Right then I wished to hell I was back in Van Nuys in the filling station watching Candy make change. I was too damned old for this shit and I knew it.

I had been lying in the dirt for about an hour when the guy walking the line came to the fire and one of the loafers there went into the darkness to replace him. The two at the fire then crawled into sleeping bags.

I waited another half hour, using the goggles to keep track of the sentry.

The sentry was first. I was crouched in the bushes when he came over less than six feet from me, dropped his trousers and squatted.

I left him there with his pants around his ankles and went over to the sleeping bags. Both the sleeping men died without making a sound.

Killing them wasn't heroic or glorious or anything like that. I felt dirty, coated with the kind of slime that would never wash off. The fact that they would have killed me just as quickly if they had had the chance didn't make it any easier. They killed for political reasons, I killed for money: We were the same kind of animal.

I walked back down the runway to where Julie Giraud waited.

I got into the Humvee without saying anything and started the motor.

"How many were there?" she asked.

"Three," I said.

We placed radio-controlled bombs in three of the airplanes. We taped a bomb securely in the nosewheel well of each of them, then dangled the antennas outside, so they would hang out the door even if the wheel were retracted.

When we were finished with that we stood for a moment in the darkness discussing things. The fort was over a mile away and I prayed the generator was still running, making fine background music. Julie crawled under the first plane and looked it over. First she fired shots into the nose tires, which began hissing. Then she fired a bullet into the bottom of each wing tank. Fuel ran out and soaked into the dirt.

There was little danger in this, as Julie well knew. The tanks would not explode unless something very hot went into a mixture of fuel vapor and oxygen: She was putting a bullet into liquid. The biggest danger was that the low-powered pistol bullets would fail to penetrate the metal skin of the wing and the fuel tank. In fact, she fired six shots into the tanks of the second plane before she was satisfied with the amount of fuel running out on the ground.

When she had flattened the nose tires of all of the unbooby-trapped planes and punched bullet holes in the tanks, she walked over to the Humvee, reeking of jet fuel.

"Let's go," she said grimly.

As we drove away I glanced at her. She was smiling.

For the first time, I began to seriously worry that she would intentionally leave me in the desert.

I comforted myself with the fact that she didn't really care about the money she was going to owe me. She could justify the deaths of these men, but if she killed me, she was no better than they.

I hoped she saw it that way too.

She let me out of the Humvee on the road about a quarter of a mile below the fort. From where I stood the road rose steadily and curved through three switchbacks until it reached the main gate.

With my Model 70 in hand, I left the road and began climbing the hill straight toward the main gate. The night was about over. Even as I climbed I thought I could see the sky beginning to lighten up in the east.

The generator was off. No light or sound came from the massive old fort, which was now a dark presence that blotted out the stars above me.

Were they in bed?

The gate was still open, with no one in sight on top of the wall or in the courtyard. That was a minor miracle or an invitation to a fool—me. If they had discovered King Kong's body they were going to be waiting.

I stood there in the darkness listening to the silence, trying to convince myself these guys were all in their beds sound asleep, that the miracle was real.

No guts, no glory, I told myself, sucked it up, and slipped through the gate. I sifted my way past the Land Rover and began climbing the stairs.

I didn't go up those stairs slow as sap in a maple tree this time. I zipped up the steps, knife in one hand and pistol in the other. Maybe I just didn't care. If they killed me, maybe that would be a blessing.

The corridor on top was empty, and the door to the radio shack was still closed. I eased it open and peeked in. King Kong was still lying in a pool of his own blood on the floor, just the way I had left him.

I pulled the door shut, then tiptoed along the corridor toward an alcove overlooking the courtyard.

I heard a noise and crouched in the darkness.

Someone snoring.

The sound was coming from an open door on my left. At least two men.

I eased past the door, moving as quietly as I could, until I reached the alcove.

Nothing stirred in the quiet moment before dawn.

From the rucksack hanging from my shoulder I removed three hand grenades, placed them on the floor near my feet.

And I waited.

Eight

Dawn took its own sweet time arriving. I was sore, stiff, hungry, and I loathed myself. I was also so exhausted that I was having trouble thinking clearly. What was there about Julie that scared me?

It wasn't that she might kill me or leave me stranded in the desert surrounded by corpses. She didn't strike me as the kind to double-cross anyone: If I was wrong about that I was dead and that was that. There was something else, something that didn't fit, but tired as I was, I couldn't put my finger on it.

She stole the V-22, hired me to help her . . .

Well, we would make it or we wouldn't.

I sat with my rifle on my lap, finger on the trigger, leaned back against the wall, closed my eyes just for a moment. I was so tired . . .

I awakened with a jerk. Somewhere in the fort a door closed with a minor bang.

The day was here, the sun was shining straight in through the openings in the wall.

Someone was moving around. Another door slammed.

I looked at my watch. The bombs should have gone off twenty minutes ago. I had been asleep over an hour.

I slowly rose from the floor on which I had been sitting, so stiff and sore I could hardly move. I picked up the grenades and pocketed them. Moving as carefully and quietly as I could, I got up on the railing, put my leg up to climb onto the roof.

The rifle slipped off my shoulder. I grabbed for the strap and was so sore I damn near dropped it.

The courtyard was thirty feet below. I teetered on the railing, the rifle hanging by a strap from my right forearm, the rucksack dangling, every muscle I owned screaming in protest.

Then I was safely up, pulling all that damn gear along with me.

Taking my time, I spread out the gear, got out the grenades, and placed them where I could easily reach them.

I took a long drink from my canteen, then screwed the lid back on and put it away.

The radio that controlled the bombs was not large. I set the frequency very carefully, turned the thing on, and let the capacitor charge. When the green light came on, I gingerly set the radio aside.

Three minutes later, a muffled bang from the bomb behind the shortwave radio slapped the air.

I lay down on the roof and gripped the rifle.

Running feet.

Shouts. Shouts in Arabic.

It didn't take them long to zero in on the radio room. I heard running feet, several men, pounding along the corridor.

They didn't spend much time in there looking at the remains of King Kong or the shortwave. More shouts rang through the building.

Julie Giraud and I had argued about what would happen next. I predicted that these guys would panic, would soon decide that the logical, best course of action was a fast plane ride back to civilization. I suspected they were bureaucrats at heart, string-pullers. Julie thought they might be warriors, that their first instinct would be to fight. We would soon see who was right.

I could hear the voices bubbling out of the courtyard, then what sounded like orders given in a clean, calm voice. That would never do. I pulled the pin from a grenade, then threw it at the wall on the other side of the courtyard.

The grenade struck the wall, made a noise that attracted the attention of the people below, then exploded just before it hit the ground.

A scream. Moans.

I tossed a second grenade, enjoyed the explosion, then hustled along the rooftop. I lay down beside a chimney in a place that allowed me to watch the rest of the roof and the area just beyond the main gate.

From here I could also see the planes parked on the airfield, gleaming brightly in the morning sun.

Someone stuck his head over the edge of the roof. He was gone too quick for me to get around, but I figured he would pop up again with a weapon of some kind, so I got the Model 70 pointed and flicked off the safety. Sure enough, fifteen seconds later the head popped back up and I squeezed off a shot. His body hit the pavement thirty feet below with a heavy plop.

The Land Rover could not carry them all, of course. Still, I thought this crowd would go for it as if it were a lifeboat on the *Titanic*. I was not surprised to hear the engine start even though I had tossed two grenades into the courtyard where the vehicle was parked: The Rover was essentially impervious to shrapnel damage, and should run for a bit, at least, as long as the radiator remained intact.

Angry shouts reached me. Apparently the Rover driver refused to wait for a full load.

I kept my head down, waited until I heard the Rover clear the gate and start down the road. Then I pushed the button on the radio control.

The explosion was quite satisfying. In about half a minute a column of smoke from the wreckage could be seen from where I lay.

I stayed put. I was in a good defensive position, what happened next was up to the crowd below.

The sun climbed higher in the sky and on the roof of that old fort, the temperature soared. I was sweating pretty good by then, was exhausted and hungry . . . Finally I had had enough. I crawled over to one of the cooking chimneys and stood up.

They were going down the road in knots of threes and fours. With the binoculars I counted them. Twenty-eight.

There was no way to know if that was all of them.

Crouching, I made my way to the courtyard side, where I could look down in, and listen.

No sound but the wind, which was out of the west at about fifteen knots, a typical desert day this time of year.

After a couple minutes of this, I inched my head over the edge for a look. Three bodies lay sprawled in the courtyard.

I had a fifty-foot rope in the rucksack. I tied one end around a chimney and tossed it over the wall on the side away from the main gate. Then I clambered over.

Safely on the ground, I kept close to the wall, out of sight of the openings above me. On the north side the edge of the ridge was close, about forty yards. I got opposite that point, gripped my rifle with both hands, and ran for it.

No shots.

Safely under the ledge, I sat down, caught my breath, and had a drink of water.

If there was anyone still in the fort waiting to ambush me, he could wait until doomsday for all I cared.

I moved downslope and around the ridge about a hundred yards to a place where I could see the runway and the airplanes and the road.

The figures were still distinct in my binoculars, walking briskly.

What would they do when they got to the airplanes? They would find the bodies of three men who died violently and three sabotaged airplanes. Three of the airplanes would appear to be intact.

The possibility that the intact airplanes were sabotaged would of course occur to them. I argued that they would not get in those planes, but would hunker down and wait until some of their friends came looking for them. Of course, the only food and water they had would be in the planes or what they had carried from the fort, but they could comfortably sit tight for a couple of days.

We couldn't. If the Libyan military found us, the Osprey would be MiG-meat and we would be doomed.

A thorough, careful preflight of the bizjets would turn up the bombs, of course. We needed to panic these people, not give them the time to search the jets or find holes to crawl into.

Panic was Julie's job.

She had grinned when I told her how she would have to do it.

I used the binoculars to check the progress of the walking men. They were about a mile away now, approaching the mat where the airplanes were parked. The laggards were hurrying to catch up with the leaders. Apparently no one wanted to take the chance that he might be left behind.

Great outfit, that.

The head of the column had just reached the jets when I heard the Osprey. It was behind me, coming down the ridge.

In seconds it shot over the fort, which was to my left, and dived toward the runway.

Julie was a fine pilot, and the Osprey was an extraordinary machine. She kept the engines horizontal and made a high-speed pass over the bizjets, clearing the tail of the middle one by about fifty feet. I watched the whole show through my binoculars.

She gave the terrorists a good look at the U.S. Marine Corps markings on the plane.

The Osprey went out about a mile and began the transition to rotorborne flight. I watched it slow, watched the engines tilt up, then watched it drop to just a few feet above the desert.

Julie kept the plane moving forward just fast enough to stay out of the tremendous dust cloud that the rotors kicked up, a speed of about twenty knots, I estimated.

She came slowly down the runway. Through the binoculars I saw the muzzle flashes as she squeezed off a burst from the flex Fifty. I knew she planned to shoot at one of the disabled jets, see if she could set it afire. The fuel tanks would still contain fuel vapor and oxygen, so a high-powered bullet in the right place should find something to ignite.

Swinging the binoculars to the planes, I was pleasantly surprised to see one erupt in flame.

Yep.

The Osprey accelerated. Julie rotated the engines down and climbed away.

The terrorists didn't know how many enemies they faced. Nor how many Ospreys were about. They were lightly armed and not equipped for a desert firefight, so they had limited options. Apparently that was the way they figured it too, because in less than a minute the first jet taxied out. Another came right behind it. The third was a few seconds late, but it taxied onto the runway before the first reached the end and turned around.

The first plane had to wait for the other two. There was just room on the narrow strip for each of them to turn, but there was no pullout, no way for one plane to get out of the way of the other two. The first two had to wait until the last plane to leave the mat turned around in front of them.

Finally all three had turned and were sitting one behind the other, pointing west into the wind. The first plane rolled. Ten seconds later the second followed. The third waited maybe fifteen seconds, then it began rolling.

The first plane broke ground as Julie Giraud came screaming in from the east at a hundred feet above the ground. The Osprey looked to be flying almost flat out, which Julie said was about 270 knots.

She overtook the jets just as the third one broke ground.

She had moved a bit in front of it, still ripping along, when the second and third plane exploded. Looking through the binoculars, it looked as if the nose came off each plane. The damaged fuselages tilted down and smashed into the ground, making surprisingly little dust when they hit.

The first plane, a Lear I think, seemed undamaged.

The bomb must have failed to explode.

The pilot of the bizjet had his wheels retracted now, was accelerating with the nose down. But not fast enough. Julie Giraud was overtaking nicely.

Through the binoculars I saw the telltale wisp of smoke from the nose of the Osprey. She was using the gun.

The Lear continued to accelerate, now began to widen the distance between it and the trailing Osprey.

"It's going to get away," I whispered. The words were just out of my mouth when the thing caught fire.

Trailing black smoke, the Lear did a slow roll over onto its back. The nose came down. The roll continued, but before the pilot could level the wings the plane smeared itself across the earth in a gout of fire and smoke.

Nine

Julie Giraud landed the Osprey on the runway near the sabotaged planes. When I walked up she was sitting in the shade under the left wing with an M-16 across her lap.

She had undoubtedly searched the area before I arrived, made sure no one had missed the plane rides to hell. Fire had spread to the other sabotaged airplanes, and now all three were burning. Black smoke tailed away on the desert wind.

"So how does it feel?" I asked as I settled onto the ground beside her.

"Damn good, thank you very much."

The heat was building, a fierce dry heat that sucked the moisture right out of you. I got out my canteen and drained the thing.

"How do you feel?" she asked after a bit, just to be polite.

"Exhausted and dirty."

"I could use a bath too."

"The dirty I feel ain't gonna wash off."

"That's too bad."

"I'm breaking your heart." I got to my feet. "Let's get this thing back to the cliff and covered with camouflage netting. Then we can sleep."

She nodded, got up, led the way into the machine.

We were spreading the net over the top of the plane when we heard a jet.

"Getting company," I said.

Julie was standing on top of the Osprey. Now she shaded her eyes, looked north, tried to spot the plane that we heard.

She saw it first, another bizjet. That was a relief to me—a fighter might have spotted the Osprey and strafed it.

"Help me get the net off it," she demanded, and began tossing armloads of net onto the ground.

"Are you tired of living?"

"Anyone coming to visit that crowd of baby-killers is a terrorist himself."

"So you're going to kill them?"

"If I can. Now drag that net out of my way!"

I gathered a double armful and picked it up. Julie climbed down, almost dived through the door into the machine. It took me a couple minutes to drag the net clear, and took Julie about that long to get the engines started and the plane ready to fly.

The instant I gave a thumb-up, she applied power and lifted off.

I hid my face so I wouldn't get dirt in my eyes.

Away she went in a cloud of dirt.

She shot the plane down. The pilot landed, then tried to take off when he saw the Osprey and the burned-out jets. Julie Giraud used the flex Fifty on him and turned the jet into a fireball a hundred yards off the end of the runway.

When she landed I got busy with the net, spreading it out.

"You are the craziest goddamn broad I ever met," I told her. "You are no better than these terrorists. You're just like them."

"Bullshit," she said contemptuously.

"You don't know who the hell you just killed. For all you know you may have killed a planeload of oil-company geologists."

"Whoever it was was in the wrong place at the wrong time."

"Just like your parents."

"Somebody has to take on the predators," she shouted at me. "They feed on us. If we don't fight back, they'll eat us all."

I let her have the last word. I was sick of her and sick of me and wished to Christ I had never left Van Nuys.

I got a little sleep that afternoon in the shade under a wing, but I had too much on my mind to do more than doze. Darkness finally came and we took the net off the plane for the last time. We left the net, the Humvee, the trailer, everything. I put all the stuff we didn't need over and around the trailer as tightly as I could, then put a chemical fuse in the last of the C-4 in the trailer and set it to blow in six hours.

When we lifted off, I didn't even bother to look at the Camel, the old fortress. I never wanted to see any of this again.

She flew west on autopilot, a few hundred feet above the desert floor. There were mountain ranges ahead of us. She used the night-vision goggles to spot them and climbed when the terrain forced her to. I dozed beside her in the copilot's seat.

Hours later she shook me awake. Out the window ahead I could see the lights of Tangier.

She had the plane on autopilot, flying toward the city. We went aft, put on coveralls, helped each other don backpacks and parachutes, then she waddled forward to check how the plane was flying.

The idea was to fly over the city from east to west, jump over the western edge of the city and let the plane fly on, out to sea. When the fuel in the plane was exhausted it would go into the ocean, probably break up and sink.

Meanwhile we would be on our way via commercial airliner. I had my American passports in my backpack—my real one and Robert Arnold's—and a plane ticket to South Africa. I hadn't asked Julie where she was going when we hit the ground because I didn't want to know. By that point I hoped to God I never set eyes on her again.

She lowered the tailgate, and I walked out on it. She was looking out one of the windows. She held up a hand, signaling me to get ready. I could just glimpse lights.

Now she came over to stand beside me. "Fifteen seconds," she shouted and looked at her watch. I looked at mine too.

I must have relaxed for just a second, because the next thing I knew she pushed me and I was going out, reaching for her. She was inches beyond my grasp.

Then I was out of the plane and falling through the darkness.

Needless to say, I never saw Julie Giraud again. I landed on a rocky slope, a sheep pasture I think, on the edge of town and gathered up the parachute. She was nowhere in sight.

I took off my helmet, listened for airplane noise . . . nothing.

Just a distant jet, maybe an airliner leaving the commercial airport.

I buried the chute and helmet and coveralls in a hole I dug with a folding shovel. I tossed the shovel into the hole and filled it with my hands, tromped it down with my new civilian shoes, then set off downhill with a flashlight. Didn't see a soul.

The next morning I walked into town and got a room at a decent hotel. I had a hot bath and went to bed and slept the clock around, almost twenty-four hours. When I awoke I went to the airport and caught a flight to Capetown.

Capetown is a pretty city in a spectacular setting, on the ocean with Table Mountain behind it. I had plenty of cash and I established an account with a local bank, then had money wired in from Switzerland. There was three million in the Swiss account before my first transfer, so Julie Giraud made good on her promise. As I instinctively knew she would.

I lived in a hotel the first week, then found a little place that a widow rented to me.

I watched the paper pretty close, expecting to see a story about the massacre in the Libyan desert. The Libyans were bound to find the wreckage of those jets sooner or later, and the bodies, and the news would leak out.

But it didn't.

The newspapers never mentioned it.

Finally I got to walking down to the city library and reading the papers from Europe and the United States.

Nothing. *Nada.*

Like it never happened.

A month went by, a peaceful, quiet month. No one paid any attention to me, I had a mountain of money in the local bank and in Switzerland, and neither radio, television, nor newspapers ever mentioned all those dead people in the desert.

Finally I called my retired Marine pal Bill Wiley in Van Nuys, the police dispatcher. "Hey, Bill, this is Charlie Dean."

"Hey Charlie. When you coming home, guy?"

"I don't know. How's Candy doing with the stations?"

"They're making more money than they ever did with you running them. He's got rid of the facial iron and works twelve hours a day."

"No shit!"

"So where are you?"

"Let's skip that for a bit. I want you to do me a favor. Tomorrow at work how about running me on the crime computer, see if I'm wanted for anything."

He whistled. "What the hell you been up to, Charlie?"

"Will you do that? I'll call you tomorrow night."

"Give me your birth date and social security number."

I gave it to him, then said good-bye.

I was on pins and needles for the next twenty-four hours. When I called again, Bill said, "You ain't in the big computer, Charlie. What the hell you been up to?"

"I'll tell you all about it sometime."

"So when you coming home?"

"One of these days. I'm still vacationing as hard as I can."

"Kiss her once for me," Bill Wiley said.

At the Capetown library I got into old copies of the *International Herald Tribune*, published in Paris. I finally found what I was looking for on microfiche: a complete list of the passengers who died twelve years ago on the Air France flight that blew up over Niger. Colonel Giraud and his wife were not on the list.

Well, the light finally began to dawn.

I got one of the librarians to help me get on the Internet. What I was interested in were lists of U.S. Air Force Academy graduates, say from five to ten years ago.

I read the names until I thought my eyeballs were going to fall out. No Julie Giraud.

I'd been had. Julie was either a CIA or French agent. French, I suspected, and the Americans agreed to let her steal a plane.

As I sat and thought about it, I realized that I didn't ever meet old Colonel Giraud's kids. Not to the best of my recollection. Maybe he had a couple of daughters, maybe he didn't, but damned if I could remember.

What had she said? That the colonel said I was the best Marine in the corps?

Stupid ol' Charlie Dean. I ate that shit with a spoon. The best Marine in the corps! So I helped her "steal" a plane and kill a bunch of convicted terrorists that Libya would never extradite.

If we were caught I would have sworn under torture, until my very last breath, that no government was involved, that the people planning this escapade were a U.S. Air Force deserter and an ex-Marine she hired.

I loafed around Capetown for a few more days, paid my bills, thanked the widow lady, gave her a cock-and-bull story about my sick kids in America, and took a plane to New York. At JFK I got on another plane to Los Angeles.

When the taxi dropped me at my apartment, I stopped by the super's office and paid the rent. The battery in my car had enough juice to start the motor on the very first crank.

I almost didn't recognize Candy. He had even gotten a haircut and wore clean jeans. "Hey, Mr. Dean," Candy said after we had been chatting a while. "Thanks for giving me another chance. You've taught me a lot."

"We all make mistakes," I told him. If only he knew how true that was.

STEPHEN COONTS is the author of eight *New York Times* best-selling novels, the first of which was the classic flying tale *Flight of the Intruder*, which spent over six months on the *New York Times* best-seller list. He graduated from West Virginia University with a degree in political science, and immediately was commissioned as an ensign in the Navy, where he began flight training in Pensacola, Florida, training on the A-6 Intruder aircraft. After two combat cruises in Vietnam aboard the aircraft carrier USS *Enterprise* and one tour as assistant catapult and arresting gear officer aboard USS *Nimitz*, he left active duty in 1977 to pursue a law degree, which he received from the University of Colorado. His novels have been published around the world and have been translated into more than a dozen different languages. He was honored by the U.S. Navy Institute with its Author of the Year award in 1986. His latest novel is *Hong Kong*. He and his wife, Deborah, reside in Clarksville, Maryland.

LEADERSHIP MATERIAL

BY DALE BROWN

ACKNOWLEDGMENTS

Thanks to Don Aldridge, Lt. General, USAF (ret.), former vice commander of the Strategic Air Command, for his help and insights on the inner workings of an Air Force promotion board, and to author and former B-52 radar nav Jim Clonts for his help on living and working on Diego Garcia.

Special thanks to my friends Larry and Maryanne Ingemanson for their generosity.

March 1991

The alarm goes off at 6 A.M., the clock radio set to a soothing easy-listening music station. Air Force Colonel Norman Weir dresses in a new Nike warm-up suit and runs a couple of miles through the base, returns to his room, then listens to the news on the radio while he shaves, showers, and dresses in a fresh uniform. He walks to the Officers' Club four blocks away and has breakfast—eggs, sausage, wheat toast, orange juice, and coffee—while he reads the morning paper. Ever since his divorce three years earlier, Norman starts every workday exactly the same way.

Air Force Major Patrick S. McLanahan's wake-up call was the clatter of the SATCOM satellite communications transceiver's printer chugging to life as it spit out a long stream of messages onto a strip of thermal printer paper, like a grocery-store checkout receipt gone haywire. He was sitting at the navigator-bombardier's station with his head down on the console, taking a catnap. After ten years flying long-range bombers, Patrick had developed the ability to ignore the demands of his body for the sake of the mission: to stay awake for very long periods of time; sit for long hours without relief; and fall asleep quickly and deeply enough to feel rested, even if the nap only lasted a few minutes. It was part of the survival techniques most combat aircrew members developed in the face of operational necessity.

As the printer spewed instructions, Patrick had his breakfast—a cup of protein milk shake from a stainless-steel Thermos bottle and a couple pieces of leathery beef jerky. All his meals on this long overwater flight were high-protein and low residue—no sandwiches, no veggies, and no fruit. The reason was simple: no matter how high-tech his bomber was, the toilet was still the toilet. Using it meant unfastening all his survival gear, dropping his flight suit, and sitting downstairs nearly naked in a dark, cold, noisy, smelly, drafty compartment. He would rather eat bland food and risk constipation than suffer through the indignity. He felt thankful that he served in a weapon system that *allowed* its crew members to use a toilet—all of his fighter brethren had to use "piddle packs," wear adult diapers—or just hold it. *That* was the ultimate indignity.

When the printer finally stopped, he tore off the message strip and read it over. It was a status report request—the second one in the last hour. Patrick composed, encoded, and transmitted a new reply message, then decided he'd better talk to the aircraft commander about all these requests. He safetied his ejection seat, unstrapped, and got to his feet for the first time in what felt like days.

His partner, defensive systems officer Wendy Tork, Ph.D. was sound asleep in the right seat. She had her arms tucked inside her shoulder straps so she wouldn't accidentally trigger her ejection handles—there had been many cases of sleeping crew members dreaming about a crash and punching themselves out of a perfectly good aircraft—her flying gloves on, her dark helmet visor down, and her oxygen mask on in case they had an emergency and she had to eject with short notice. She had her summerweight flight jacket on over her flight suit, with the flotation-device harness on over that, the bulges of the inflatable pouches under her armpits making her arms rise and fall with each deep sleepy breath.

Patrick scanned Wendy's defensive-systems console before moving forward—but he had to force himself to admit that he paused there to look at Wendy, not the instruments. There was something about her that intrigued him—and then he stopped himself again. *Face it, Muck*, Patrick told himself: *You're not intrigued—you're hot for her. Underneath that baggy flight suit and survival gear is a nice, tight, luscious body, and it feels weird, naughty, almost* wrong *to be thinking about stuff like this while slicing along forty-one thousand feet across the Gulf of Oman in a high-tech warbird. Weird, but exciting.*

At that moment, Wendy raised the helmet's dark visor, dropped her oxygen mask, and smiled at him. Damn, Patrick thought as he quickly turned his attention to the defensive-systems console, those eyes could melt titanium.

"Hi," she said. Even though she had to raise her voice to talk cross-cockpit, it was still a friendly, pleasant, disarming sound. Wendy Tork, Ph.D., was one of the world's most renowned experts in electromagnetic engineering and systems development, a pioneer in the use of computers to analyze energy waves and execute a particular response. They had been working together for nearly two years at their home base, the High Technology Aerospace Weapons Center (HAWC) at Groom Lake Air Station, Nevada, known as Dreamland.

"Hi," he said back. "I was just . . . checking your systems. We're going over the Bandar Abbass horizon in a few minutes, and I wanted to see if you were picking up anything."

"The system would've alerted me if it detected any signals within fifteen percent of detection threshold," Wendy pointed out. She spoke in her usual hypertechnical voice, female but not feminine, the way she usually did. It allowed Patrick to relax and stop thinking thoughts that were so out of place to be thinking in a warplane. Then, she leaned forward in her seat, closer to him, and asked, "You were looking at me, weren't you?"

The sudden change in her voice made his heart skip a beat and his mouth grow dry as arctic air. "You're nutty," he heard himself blurt out. Boy, did *that* sound nutty!

"I saw you though the visor, Major Hot Shot," she said. "I could see you looking at me." She sat back, still looking at him. "Why were you looking at me?"

"Wendy, I wasn't . . ."

"Are you sure you weren't?"

"I . . . I wasn't . . ." *What is going on?* Patrick thought. *Why am I so damned tongue-tied? I feel like a school kid who just got caught drawing pictures of the girl he had a crush on in his notebook.*

Well, he did have a crush on her. They'd first met about three years ago when they were both recruited for the team that was developing the Megafortress flying battleship. They had a brief, intense sexual encounter, but events, circumstances, duties, and responsibilities always prevented anything more from happening. This was the *last* place and time he would've guessed their relationship might take a new, exciting step forward.

"It's all right, Major," Wendy said. She wouldn't take her eyes off him, and he felt as if he wanted to duck back behind the weapons bay bulkhead and stay there until they landed. "You're allowed."

Patrick found himself able to breathe again. He relaxed, trying to look cool and casual even though he could feel sweat oozing from every pore. He held up the SATCOM printer tape. "I've got . . . we've got a message . . . orders . . . instructions," he stammered, and she smiled both to chide him and to enjoy him at the same time. "From Eighth Air Force. I was going to talk to the general, then everybody else. On interphone. Before we go over the horizon. The Iranian horizon."

"You do that, Major," Wendy said, a laugh in her eyes. Patrick nodded, glad that was over with, and started to head for the cockpit. She stopped him with, "Oh, Major?"

Patrick turned back to her. "Yes, Doctor?"

"You never told me."

"Told you what?"

"Do all my systems look OK to you?"

Thank God she smiled after that, Patrick thought—maybe she doesn't think I'm some sort of pervert. Regaining a bit of his lost composure, but still afraid to let his eyes roam over her "systems," he replied, "They look great to me, Doc."

"Good," she said. "Thank you." She smiled a bit more warmly, let her eyes look him up and down, and added, "I'll be sure to keep an eye on your systems too."

Patrick never felt more relieved, and yet more naked, as he bent to crawl through that connecting tunnel and make his way to the cockpit. But just before he announced he was moving forward and unplugged his intercom cord, he heard the slow-paced electronic "DEEDLE . . . DEEDLE . . . DEEDLE . . ." warning tone of the ship's threat-detection system. They had just been highlighted by enemy radar.

Patrick virtually flew back into his ejection seat, strapped in, and unsafed his ejection seat. He was in the aft crew compartment of an EB-52C Megafortress bomber, the next generation of "flying battleships" Patrick's classified research unit was hoping to produce for the Air Force. It was once a "stock" B-52H Stratofortress bomber, the workhorse of America's long-range heavy-bombardment fleet, built for long range and heavy nuclear and nonnuclear payloads. The original B-52 was designed in the 1950s; the last rolled off the assembly line twenty years ago. But this plane was different. The original airframe had been rebuilt from the ground up with state-of-the-art technology not just to modernize it, but to make it the most advanced warplane . . . that no one had ever heard of.

"Wendy?" he radioed on interphone. "What do we got?"

"This is weird," Wendy responded. "I've got a variable PRF X-band target out there. Switching between antiship and antiaircraft search profiles. Estimated range . . . damn, range thirty-five miles, twelve o'clock. He's right on top of us. Well within radar-guided missile range."

"Any idea what it is?"

"Could be an AWACS plane," Wendy replied. "He looks like he's scanning both surface and air targets. No fast PRFs—just scanning. Faster than an APY scan, like on an E-2 Hawkeye or E-3 Sentry, but same profile."

"An Iranian AWACS?" Patrick asked. The EB-52 Megafortress was flying in international airspace over the Gulf of Oman, just west of the Iranian coastline and just south of the Strait of Hormuz, outside the Persian Gulf. The director of the High Technology Aerospace Weapons Center, Lieutenant General Brad Elliott, had ordered three of his experimental Megafortress bombers to start patrolling the skies near the Persian Gulf to provide a secret, stealthy punch in case one of the supposedly neutral countries in the region decided to jump into the conflict raging between the Coalition forces and the Republic of Iraq.

"Could be a 'Mainstay' or 'Candid,' " Patrick offered. "One of the aircraft Iraq supposedly surrendered to Iran was an Ilyushin-76MD airborne early-warning aircraft. Maybe the Iranians are trying out their new toy. Can he see us?"

"I think he can," Wendy said. "He's not locking on to us, just scanning around—but he's close, and we're approaching detection threshold." The B-52 Stratofortress was not designed or ever considered a "stealth" aircraft, but the EB-52 Megafortress was much different. It retained most of the new antiradar technology it had been fitted with as an experimental test-bed aircraft—nonmetallic "fibersteel" skin, stronger and lighter than steel but nonradar-reflective; swept-back control surfaces instead of straight edges; no external antennas; radar-absorbent material used in the engine inlets and windows; and a unique radar-absorbing energy system that retransmitted radar energy along the airframe and discharged it back along the wing trailing edges, reducing the amount of radar energy reflected back to the enemy. It also carried a wide variety of weapons and could provide as much firepower as a flight of Air Force or Navy tactical fighters.

"Looks like he's 'guarding' the Strait of Hormuz, looking for inbound aircraft," Patrick offered. "Heading two-three-zero to go around him. If he spots us, it might get the Iranians excited."

But he had spoken too late: "He can see us," Wendy cut in. "He's at thirty-five miles, one o'clock, high, making a beeline for us. Speed increasing to five hundred knots."

"That's not an AWACS plane," Patrick said. "Looks like we picked up some kind of fast-moving patrol plane."

"Crap," the aircraft commander, Lieutenant General Brad Elliott, swore on intercom. Elliott was the commander of the High Technology Aerospace Weapons Center, also known as Dreamland, and the developer of the EB-52 Megafortress flying battleship. "Shut his radar down, Wendy, and let's hope he thinks he has a bent radar and decides to call it a night."

"Let's get out of here, Brad," Patrick chimed in. "No sense in risking a dogfight up here."

"We're in international airspace," Elliott retorted indignantly. "We have as much right to be up here as this turkey."

"Sir, this is a combat area," Patrick emphasized. "Crew, let's get ready to get the hell out of here."

With one touch, Wendy ordered the Megafortress's powerful jammers to shut down the Iranian fighter's search radar. "Trackbreakers active," Wendy announced. "Give me ninety left." Brad Elliott put the Megafortress in a tight right turn and rolled out perpendicular to the fighter's flight path. The plane's pulse-Doppler radar might not detect a target with a zero relative closure rate. "Bandit at three o'clock, thirty-five miles and steady, high. Moving to four o'clock. I think he lost us."

"Not so fast," the crew mission commander and copilot, Colonel John Ormack, interjected. Ormack was HAWC's deputy commander and chief engineering wizard, a commander pilot with several thousand hours in various tactical aircraft. But his first love was computers, avionics, and gadgets. Brad Elliott had the ideas, but he relied on Ormack to turn those ideas into reality. If they gave badges or wings for techno-geeks, John Ormack would wear them proudly. "He might be going passive. We've got to put some distance between us and him. He might not need a radar to intercept us."

"I copy that," Wendy said. "But I think his IRSTS is out of range. He . . ."

At that moment, they all heard a loud, faster-paced "DEEDLE DEEDLE DEEDLE!" warning on the intercom. "Airborne interceptor locked on, range thirty miles and closing fast! His radar is huge—he's burning right through my jammers. Solid radar lock, closure rate . . . closure rate moving to *six hundred knots*!"

"Well," John Ormack said, "at least that water down there is warm even this time of year."

Making jokes was the only thing any of them could think about right then—because being highlighted by a supersonic interceptor alone over the Gulf of Oman was just about the most fatal thing a bomber crew could ever face.

This morning was a little different for Norman Weir. Today and for the next two weeks Weir and several dozen of his fellow Air Force full colonels were at Randolph Air Force Base near San Antonio, Texas, for a lieutenant colonel's promotion board. Their task: pick the best, the brightest, and the most highly qualified from a field of about three thousand Air Force majors to be promoted to lieutenant colonel.

Colonel Norman Weir knew a lot about making choices using complex objective criteria—a promotion board was right up his alley. Norman was commander of the Air Force Budget Analysis Agency at the Pentagon. His job was to do exactly what he was now being asked to do: sift through mountains of information on weapon and information systems and decide the future life-cycle costs and benefits of each. In effect, he and his staff of sixty-five military and civilian analysts, accountants, and technical experts decided the future of the United States Air Force every day. Every aircraft, missile, satellite, computer, "black box," and bomb, along with every man and woman in the Air Force, came under his scrutiny. Every item on every unit's budget had to pass his team's rigorous examination. If it didn't, by the end of the fiscal year it would cease to exist with a single memo to someone in the Secretary of the Air Force's office. He had power and responsibility over billions of dollars every week, and he wielded that power with skill and enthusiasm.

Thanks to his father, Norman decided on a military career in high school. Norman's father was drafted in the mid-sixties but thought it might be safer serving offshore in the Navy, so he enlisted and served as a jet power-plant technician on board various aircraft carriers. He returned from long Pacific and Indian Ocean cruises with incredible stories of aviation heroism and triumph, and Norman was hooked. Norman's father also came home minus half his left arm, the result of a deck munition explosion on the aircraft carrier USS *Enterprise*, and a Purple Heart. That became Norman's ticket to an appointment to the United States Naval Academy at Annapolis.

But Academy life was hard. To say Norman was merely introverted was putting it mildly. Norman lived inside his own head, existing in a sterile, protected world of knowledge and reflection. Solving problems was an academic exercise, not a physical or even a leadership one. The more they made him run and do push-ups and march and drill, the more he hated it. He failed a physical-conditioning test, was dismissed with prejudice, and returned to Iowa.

His father's almost constant niggling about wasting his appointment and dropping out of the Naval Academy—as if his father had chosen to sacrifice his arm so his son could go to Annapolis—weighed heavily on his mind. His father practically disowned his son, announcing there was no money for college and urging his son to get out and find a job. Desperate to make his father happy, Norman applied and was accepted to Air Force Reserve Officer Training Corps, receiving a degree in finance and an Air Force commission, becoming an accounting and finance specialist and earning his CPA certification a few months later.

Norman loved the Air Force. It was the best of all worlds: He got respect from the folks who respected and admired accountants, and he could demand respect from most of the others because he outranked and outsmarted them. He pinned on a major's gold oak leaves right on time, and took command of his own base accounting service center shortly thereafter.

Even his wife seemed to enjoy the life, after her initial uncertainty. Most women adopted their husband's rank, and Norman's wife spit-shined and paraded that invisible but tangible rank every chance she got. She was "volunteered" by the higher-ranking officers' wives for committeeships, which at first she resented. But she soon learned that she had the power to "volunteer" lower-ranking officers' wives to serve on her committee, so only the wives of lower-ranking officers and noncommissioned officers had to do the heavy work. It was a very neat and uncomplicated system.

For Norman, the work was rewarding but not challenging. Except for manning a few mobility lines during unit deployments and a few late nights preparing for no-notice and annual base inspections, he had a forty-hour workweek and very little stress. He accepted a few unusual assignments: conducting an audit at a radar outpost on Greenland; serving on advisory staffs for some congressional staffers doing research for a bill. High-visibility, low-risk, busywork assignments. Norman loved them.

But that's when the conflicts began closer to home. Both he and his wife were born and raised in Iowa, but Iowa had no Air Force bases, so it was guaranteed they weren't going home except to visit. Norman's one unaccompanied overseas PCS assignment to Korea gave her time to go home, but that was small comfort without her husband. The frequent uprooting hurt the couple unequally. Norman promised his wife they'd start a family when the cycle of assignment changes slowed down, but after fifteen years it was apparent that Norman had no real intention of starting a family.

The last straw was Norman's latest assignment to the Pentagon to become the first director of a brand new Air Force budget oversight agency. They said it was a guaranteed four-year assignment—no more moving around. He could even retire from that assignment if he chose. His wife's biological clock, which had been ringing loudly for the past five years, was deafening by then. But Norman said wait. It was a new shop. Lots of late nights, lots of weekends. What kind of life would that be for a family? Besides, he hinted one morning after yet another discussion about kids, wasn't she getting a little old to be trying to raise a newborn?

She was gone by the time he returned home the next evening. That was over three years ago, and Norman hadn't seen or spoken to her since. Her signature on the divorce papers was the last thing he ever saw that belonged to her.

Well, he told himself often, he was better off without her. He could accept better, more exotic assignments; travel the world without having to worry about always going either to Iowa in the summer or to Florida in the winter, where the in-laws stayed; and he didn't have to listen to his ex-wife harping about how two intelligent persons should be having a better, more fulfilling—meaning "civilian"—life. Besides, as the old saying went: "If the Air Force wanted you to have a wife, they'd have issued you one." Norman began to believe that was true.

The first day at the promotion board at the Selection Board Secretariat at the Air Force Military Personnel Center at Randolph was filled with organizational minutiae and several briefings on how the board worked, the criteria to use during the selection process, how to use the checklists and grading sheets, and an overview of the standard candidate's personnel file. The briefings were given by Colonel Ted Fellows, chief of the Air Force Selection Board Secretariat. Fellows gave a briefing on the profile of the candidates—average length of service, geographical distribution, specialty distribution, and other tidbits of information designed to explain how these candidates were selected.

Then, the promotion board president, Major General Larry Dean Ingemanson, the commander of Tenth Air Division, stepped up before the board members and distributed the panel assignments for each board member, along with the Secretary of the Air Force's Memorandum of Instruction, or MOI. The MOI was the set of orders handed down by the Secretary of the Air Force to the board members, informing them of who was going to receive promotions and the quotas for each, along with general guidelines on how to choose the candidates eligible for promotion.

There were three general categories of officers eligible for promotion: in-, above-, and below-the-primary zone candidates. Within each category were the specialties being considered: line officers, including flying, or rated, officers, nonrated operations officers such as security police and maintenance officers, and mission-support officers such as finance, administration, and base services; along with critical mission-support subspecialties such as Chaplain Corps, Medical Service Corps, Nurse Corps, Biomedical Sciences Corps, Dental Corps, and Judge Advocate General Corps. General Ingemanson also announced that panels could be convened for any other personnel matters that might be required by the Secretary of the Air Force.

The board members were randomly divided up into eight panels of seven members each, adjusted by the president so each panel was not overly weighted by one specialty or command. Every Air Force major command, direct reporting unit, field operating agency, and specialty seemed to be represented here: logistics, maintenance, personnel, finance, information technology, chaplains, security police, and dozens of others, including the flying specialties. Norman noticed right away that the flying or "rated" specialties were especially well represented here. At least half of all the board members were rated officers, mostly unit commanders or staff officers assigned to high-level posts at the Pentagon or major command headquarters.

That was the biggest problem Norman saw in the Air Force, the one factor that dominated the service to the exclusion of all else, the one specialty that screwed it up for everyone else—the flyers.

Sure, this was the U.S. *Air* Force, not the U.S. Accountant Force—

the service existed to conduct battles in the national defense by taking control of the sky and near space, and flyers were obviously going to play a big part. But they had the biggest egos and the biggest mouths too. The service bent over backward for their aviators, far more than they supported any other specialty no matter how vital. Flyers got all the breaks. They were treated like firstborns by unit commanders—in fact, most unit commanders were flyers, even if the unit had no direct flying commitment.

Norman didn't entirely know where his dislike for those who wore wings came from. Most likely, it was from his father. Naval aircraft mechanics were treated like indentured servants by flyers, even if the mechanic was a seasoned veteran while the flyer was a know-nothing newbie on his first cruise. Norman's dad complained loud and long about officers in general and aviators in particular. He always wanted his son to be an officer, but he was determined to teach him how to be an officer that enlisted and noncommissioned officers would admire and respect—and that meant putting flyers in their place at every opportunity.

Of course, it was an officer, a flyer, who ignored safety precautions and his plane captain's suggestions and fired a Zuni rocket into a line of jets waited to be fueled and created one of the biggest noncombat disasters at sea the Navy had ever experienced, which resulted in over two hundred deaths and several hundred injuries, including Norman's father. A cocky, arrogant, know-it-all flyer had disregarded the rules. That officer was quickly, quietly dismissed from service. Norman's unit commanders had several times thrown the book at nonrated officers and enlisted personnel for the tiniest infractions, but flyers were usually given two, three, or even four chances before finally being offered the opportunity to resign rather than face a court-martial. They always got all the breaks.

Well, this was going to be different. *If I get a flyer's promotion jacket,* Norman thought, *he's going to have to prove to me that he's worthy of promotion.* And he vowed that wasn't going to be easy.

"Let's hit the deck," Patrick said.

"Damn fine idea," Brad said. He yanked the Megafortress's throttles to idle, rolled the plane up onto its left wing, and nosed the big bomber over into a relatively gentle six-thousand-foot-per-minute dive. "Wendy, jam the piss out of them. Full spectrum. No radio transmissions. We don't want the whole Iranian air force after us."

"Copy," Wendy said weakly. She scrambled to catch flying pencils and checklists as the negative Gs sent anything unsecure floating around the cabin. Switching her oxygen regulator to "100%" helped when her stomach and most of its contents threatened to start floating around the cabin too. "I'm jamming. He's . . ." Suddenly, they all heard a fast-pitched "DEEDLEDEEDLEDEEDLE!" warning, and red alert lights flashed in every compartment. "*Radar missile launch, seven o'clock, twenty-five miles!*" Wendy shouted. "*Break right!*"

Elliott slammed the Megafortress bomber into a hard right turn and pulled the throttles to idle, keeping the nose down to complicate the missile's intercept and to screen the bomber's engine exhaust from the attacker as much as possible. As the bomber slowed it turned faster. Patrick felt as if he were upside down and backwards—the sudden deceleration, steep dive, and steep turn only served to tumble his and everyone's senses.

"*Chaff! Chaff!*" Wendy shouted as she ejected chaff from the left ejectors. The chaff, packets of tinsel-like strips of metal, formed large blobs of radar-reflective clouds that made inviting spoof targets for enemy missiles.

"Missiles still inbound!" Wendy shouted. "Arming Stingers!" As the enemy missiles closed in, Wendy fired small radar- and heat-seeking rockets out of a steerable cannon on the Megafortress's tail. The Stinger airmine rockets flew head to head with the incoming missiles, then exploded several dozen feet in the missile's path, shredding its fuselage and guidance system. It worked. The last enemy missile exploded less than five thousand feet away.

It took them only four minutes to get down to just two hundred feet above the Gulf of Oman, guided by the navigation computer's terrain database, by the satellite navigation system, and by a pencil-thin beam of energy that measured the distance between the bomber's belly and the water. They headed southwest at full military power, as far away from the Iranian coastline as possible. Brad Elliott knew what fighter pilots feared—low-altitude flight, darkness, and heading out over water away from friendly shores. Every engine cough was amplified, every dip of the fuel gauge needles seemed critical—even the slightest crackle in the headset or a shudder in the flight controls seemed to signal disaster. Having a potential enemy out there, one that was jamming radar and radio transmissions, made the tension even worse. Few fighter pilots had the stomach for night overwater chases.

But as Wendy studied her threat displays, it soon became obvious that the MiG or whatever it was out there wasn't going to go away so easily. "No luck, guys—we didn't lose him. He's closed inside twenty miles and he's right on our tail, staying high but still got a pretty good radar lock on us."

"Relaying messages to headquarters too, I'll bet," Elliott said.

"Six o'clock, high, fifteen miles. Coming within heater range." With the enemy attacker's radar jammed, he couldn't use a radar-guided missile—but with IRSTS, he could easily close in and make a heat-seeking missile shot.

"Wendy, get ready to launch Scorpions," Brad said.

"Roger." Wendy already had her fingers on the keyboard, and she typed in instructions to warm up the Megafortress's surprise weapon—the AIM-120 Scorpion AMRAAM, or Advanced Medium-Range Air-to-Air Missile. The EB-52 carried six Scorpion missiles on each wing pylon. The Scorpions were radar-guided missiles that were command-guided by the Megafortress's attack radar or by an onboard radar in the missile's nose—the missiles could even attack targets in the bomber's rear quadrant by guidance from a tail-mounted radar, allowing for an "over-the-shoulder" launch on a pursuing enemy. Only a few aircraft in the entire world carried AMRAAMs—but the EB-52 Megafortress had been carrying one for three years, including one combat mission. The enemy aircraft was well within the Scorpion's maximum twenty-mile range.

"Twelve miles."

"When he breaks eight miles, lock him up and hit 'em," Brad said. "We gotta be the one who shoots first."

"Brad, we need to knock this off," Patrick said urgently.

Wendy looked at him in complete surprise, but it was Brad Elliott who exclaimed, "What was that, Patrick?"

"I said, we should stop this," Patrick repeated. "Listen, we're in international airspace. We just dropped down to low altitude, we're jamming his radar. He knows we're a bad guy. Forcing a fight won't solve anything."

"He jumped us first, Patrick."

"Listen, we're acting like hostiles, and he's doing his job—kicking us out of his zone and away from his airspace," Patrick argued. "We tried to sneak in, and we got caught. No one wants a fight here."

"Well, what the hell do you suggest, nav?" Brad asked acidly.

Patrick hesitated, then leaned over to Wendy, and said, "Cut jamming on UHF GUARD."

Wendy looked at him with concern. "Are you sure, Patrick?"

"Yes. Do it." Wendy reluctantly entered instructions into her ECM computer, stopping the jamming signals from interfering with the 243.0 megahertz frequency, the universal UHF emergency channel. Patrick flipped his intercom panel wafer switch to COM 2, which he knew was set to the universal UHF emergency channel. "Attention, Iranian aircraft at our six o'clock position, one hundred and seventy-six kilometers southeast of Bandar Abbas. This is the American aircraft you are pursuing. Can you hear me?"

"Patrick, what in *hell* are you doing?" Elliott shouted on interphone. "Defense, did you stop jamming UHF? What in hell's going on back there?"

"That's not a good idea, Patrick," John offered, sternly but not as forcefully as Elliott. "You just told him we're Americans. He's going to want to take a look now."

"He'd be crazy to answer," Brad said. "Now stay off the radio and . . ."

But just then, they heard on the radio, "*Shto etah? Nemalvali pazhaloosta.*"

"What the hell was that?" Wendy asked.

"Sounded like Russian to me," Patrick said.

Just then, in broken English, they heard, "American aircraft at my twelve of the clock position from my nose, this is Khaneh One-Four-One of the Islamic Republic of Iran Air Force. I read you. You are in violation of Iranian sovereign airspace. I command you now to climb to three thousand meters of altitude and prepare for intercept. Reduce speed now and lower your landing-gear wheels. Do you understand?"

"One-Four-One, this is the American aircraft. We have locked defensive weapons on to your aircraft. Do not fly closer than twelve kilometers from us or you will be attacked. Do you understand?"

"Range ten miles."

"You are at sixteen kilometers," Patrick radioed. "Do not come any closer."

"Patrick, this is *nuts*," Brad said. "You're going to try to convince him to turn around? He'll never go for it."

"Nine miles. Closure speed five hundred knots."

"One-Four-One, you are at fourteen-point-five kilometers, closing at thirteen kilometers per minute. Do not, I repeat, do not fly closer than twelve kilometers to us, or you will be attacked. We are not in Iranian airspace, and we are withdrawing from the area. This is my final warning. Do you understand?"

"Eight miles . . ."

"One-Four-One, we have you at twelve kilometers! Break off now!"

"Stand by to shoot, Wendy! Damn you, McLanahan . . . !"

"Here he comes!" Wendy shouted. "Closure rate . . . wait, his closure rate dropped," Wendy announced. "He's holding at eight miles . . . no, he's slowing. He's climbing. He's up to five thousand feet, range ten miles, decelerating."

"Cease jamming, Wendy," Patrick said.

"What?"

"Stop jamming them," Patrick said. "They broke off their attack. Now we need to do the same."

"Brad?"

"You're taking a big damned chance, Muck," Brad Elliott said. He paused, but only for a moment; then: "Cease jamming. Fire 'em up again if they come within eight miles."

"Trackbreakers and comm jammers to standby," Wendy said, punching instructions into the computer. "Range nine miles. He's climbing faster, passing ten thousand feet."

"You Americans, do not try to approach our Iran, or we will show you our anger," the Iranian MiG pilot said in halting English. "Your threats mean nothing to us. Stay away or be damned."

"He's turning north," Wendy said. "He's . . . oh no! He's diving on us! Range ten miles, closure rate seven hundred knots!"

"Jammers!" Brad shouted. "*Lock on and shoot!*"

"No! Withhold!" Patrick shouted. He keyed the UHF radio mike button again: "One-Four-One, don't come any closer!"

"I said *shoot* . . . !"

"Wait! He's turning and climbing!" Wendy reported with relief. "He's climbing and turning, heading northeast."

"Prick," John Ormack said with a loud sigh of relief. "Just a macho stunt."

"Scope's clear," Wendy said. "Bandit at twenty miles and extending. No other signals."

"Pilot's clearing off," Brad said. He didn't wait for John's acknowledgment, but safetied his ejection seat, whipped off his straps, and stormed out of his seat and back to the systems officer's compartment.

"He doesn't look happy, guys," John warned Patrick and Wendy on interphone.

The instrument console was right behind the hatch leading to the lower deck, so Brad couldn't go all the way back. He plugged into a free interphone cord, so everyone on board could hear his tirade, stood over the console with eyes blazing, pointed a gloved finger at Patrick, and thundered, "Don't you *ever* countermand my orders again, Major! He could've blown us away—twice! You're not the aircraft commander, I am!" He turned to Wendy Tork and shouted, "If I say 'shoot,' Tork, you obey my orders instantly or I will kick your ass, then kick your ass into prison for twenty years! And don't you dare cease jamming an enemy aircraft unless I give the order to stop! You copy me?"

"I hear you, General," Wendy shot back, "but you can go straight to hell." Elliott's eyes bulged in rage. Wendy hurried on: "Who gave us the order to shoot? Who even gave us permission to jam a foreign power's radar and radios?" Elliott remained silent.

"Brad?" John Ormack asked. "This mission is supposed to be a contingency mission, in case Iran opens a second front against the Coalition. We're not supposed to be flying so close to disputed territory—I don't think we were supposed to engage anyone."

"In fact, I don't ever recall being given an order to fly *at all*, sir," Patrick said. "I read the warning order, and it says we were supposed to stand by for possible action against Iran or any other nation that declares neutrality that might be a threat to the U.S. I never saw the execution order or the rules of engagement. We never received any satellite photos or tactical printouts. Nothing to help us in mission planning."

"What about that, General?" Wendy asked. "I never saw the execution order for our mission either. I never got the order of battle or any intelligence reports. Is this an authorized mission or not?"

"Of course it is," Brad said indignantly. His angry grimace was melting away fast, and Patrick knew that Wendy had guessed right. "We were ordered to stand by for action. We're . . . standing by. This is tactically the best place to be standing by anyway."

"So if we fired on an Iranian fighter, it would be unauthorized."

"We're authorized to defend ourselves . . ."

"If we were on an authorized mission, we'd be authorized to defend ourselves—but this isn't authorized, is it?" Patrick asked. When Brad did not answer right away, Patrick added, "You mean, *none* of the Megafortresses we have in-theater is specifically authorized to be up here? We've got three experimental stealth warplanes loaded with weapons flying ten thousand miles from home and just a few miles from a war zone, and no one knows we're up here? Jesus, General . . ."

"That will be all, Major," Elliott interjected. "The sorties were authorized—by me. Our orders were to stand by and prepare for combat operations in support of Desert Storm. That is what we're doing."

Patrick unstrapped, unplugged his interphone cord, got to his feet, leaned close to Brad Elliott, and said cross-cockpit, so no one else could hear, "Sir, we can't be doing this. You're risking our lives . . . for what? If we got intercepted by Iranians or Iraqis or whoever, we'd have to fight our way out—but we'd be doing it without sanction, without orders. If we got shot down, no one would even know we were missing. *Why?* What the hell is all this for?"

Brad and Patrick looked into each other's eyes for a very long moment. Brad's eyes were still blazing with indignation and anger, but now they were shadowed by a touch of . . . what? Patrick hoped it would be understanding or maybe contrition, but that's not what he saw. Instead, he saw disappointment. Patrick had called his mentor and commanding officer on a glaring moral and leadership error, and all he could communicate in return was that he was disappointed that his protégé didn't back him up.

"Is it because you didn't participate in Desert Storm?" Patrick asked. The Persian Gulf War—some called it "World War III"—had just ended, and the majority of troops had already gone home. They were enjoying celebrations and congratulations from a proud and appreciative nation, something unseen in the United States since World War II. "Is it because you know you had something that could help the war effort, but you weren't allowed to use it?"

"Go to hell, McLanahan," Elliott said bitterly. "Don't try any of that amateur psychoanalyst crap with me. I'm given discretion on how to employ my forces, and I'm doing it as I see fit."

Patrick looked at his commanding officer, the man he thought of as a friend and even as a surrogate father. His father had died before Patrick went off to college, and he and his younger brother had been raised in a household with a strong-willed, domineering mother and two older sisters. Brad was the first real father figure in Patrick's life in many years, and he did all he could to be a strong, supportive friend to Elliott, who was without a doubt a lone-wolf character, both in his personal and professional life.

Although Bradley James Elliott was a three-star general and was once the number four man in charge of Strategic Air Command, the major command in charge of America's long-range bombers and land-based ballistic nuclear missiles, he was far too outspoken and too "gung ho" for politically sensitive headquarters duty. To Brad, bombers were the key to American military power projection, and he felt it was his job, his duty, to push for increased funding, research, and development of new long-range attack technologies. That didn't sit well with the Pentagon. The services had been howling mad for years about the apparent favoritism toward the Air Force. The Pentagon was pushing "joint operations," but Brad Elliott wasn't buying it. When he continued to squawk about reduced funding and priority for new Air Force bomber programs, Brad lost his fourth star. When he still wouldn't shut up, he was banished to the high Nevada desert either to retire or simply disappear into obscurity.

Brad did neither. Even though he was an aging three-star general occupying a billet designated for a colonel or one-star general, he used his remaining stars and HAWC's shroud of ultrasecrecy and security to develop an experimental twenty-first-century long-range attack force, comprised of highly modified B-52 and B-1 bombers, "superbrilliant" stealth cruise missiles, unmanned attack vehicles, and precision-guided weapons. He procured funding that most commanders could only wish for, money borrowed—many said "stolen"—from other weapons programs or buried under multiple layers of security classification.

While the rest of the Air Force thought Brad Elliott was merely sitting around waiting to retire, he was building a secret attack force—and he was using it. He had launched his first mission in a modified B-52 bomber three years earlier, dodging almost the entire Soviet Far East Air Army and attacking a Soviet ground-based laser installation that was being used to blind American reconnaissance satellites. That mission had cost the lives of three men, and had cost Brad his right leg. But it proved that the "flying battleship" concept worked and that a properly modified B-52 bomber could be used against highly defended targets in a nonnuclear attack mission. Brad Elliott and his team of scientists, engineers, test pilots, and technogeeks became America's newest secret strike force.

"It's not your job or place to second-guess or criticize me," Elliott went on, "and it sure as hell isn't your place to countermand my orders or give orders contrary to mine. You do it again, and I'll see to it that you're military career is terminated. Understand?"

Patrick thought he had noted just a touch of sadness in Brad's eyes, but that was long gone now. He straightened his back and caged his eyes, not daring to look his friend in the eye. "Yes, sir," he replied tonelessly.

"General?" John Ormack radioed back on interphone. "Patrick? What's going on?"

Brad scowled one last time at Patrick. Patrick just sat down without meeting Brad's eyes and strapped into his ejection seat again. Elliott said, "Patrick's going to contact Diego Garcia and get our bombers some secure hangar space. We're going to put down until we get clarification on our mission. Plot a course back to the refueling track, get in contact with our tankers and our wingmen, and let's head back to the barn."

When Brad turned and headed back to the cockpit, Wendy reached across the cabin and touched Patrick's arm in a quiet show of gratitude. But Patrick didn't feel much like accepting any congratulations.

"I want to go over the highlights of the Secretary's MOI with you before we get started," Major General Larry Ingemanson, the president of the promotion board, said. He was addressing the entire group of board members just before they started their first day of deliberations. "The

MOI defines the quotas set for each promotion category, but you as voting members aren't required to meet those quotas. We're looking for quality, not quantity. Keep that in mind. The only quotas we must fill for this board are for joint-service assignments, which are set by law, and the Secretariat will take care of that. The law also states that extra consideration be given to women and minorities. Bear in mind that your scores are not adjusted by the Secretariat if the candidate happens to be female or a member of a minority—no one can adjust your score but you. You are simply asked to be aware that these two groups have been unfairly treated in the past.

"You are also asked to keep in mind that since the start of hostilities in the southwest Asian theater, some candidates may not have had the opportunity to complete advanced degrees or professional military education courses. Eventually I believe this will become more and more of a concern as deployment tempos pick up, but so far the law has not been changed. You're just asked to keep this fact in mind: If a candidate hasn't completed PME or advanced degrees, check to see if he or she is serving in some specialty that requires frequent or short-notice deployments, and take that into consideration."

General Ingemanson paused for a moment, closed his notes, and went on: "Now, this isn't in the MOI—it's from your nonvoting board president. This is my first time presiding over a board but my fourth time here in the box, and I have some thoughts about what you are about to undertake:

"As you slug through all the three thousand-plus files over the next several days, you may get a little cross-eyed and slack-jawed. I will endeavor to remind you of this as the days go on, but I'll remind you now, of the extreme importance of what you're doing here: If you have ever thought about what it would be like to shape the future, this, my friends, is it.

"We find ourselves in a very special and unique position of responsibility," Ingemanson went on solemnly. "We are serving on the Air Force's first field grade officers' promotion board just days after the end of Operation Desert Storm, which many are calling the reawakening of America and the reunification of American society with its armed forces. We are seeing the beginning of a new era for the American military, especially for the U.S. Air Force. We are tasked with the awesome responsibility of choosing the men and women who will lead that new military into the future."

Norman Weir rolled his eyes and snorted to himself. What drivel. It was a promotion board, for Christ's sake. Why did he have to try to attach some special, almost mystical significance to it? Maybe it was just the standard "pep talk," but it was proceeding beyond the sublime toward the ridiculous.

"I'm sure we've all heard the jokes about lieutenant colonels—the 'throwaway' officer, the ultimate wanna-bes," Ingemanson went on. "The ones that stand on the cusp of greatness or on the verge of obscurity. Well, let me tell you from the bottom of my soul: I believe they are the bedrock of the Air Force officer corps.

"I've commanded four squadrons, two wings, and one air division, and the O-5s were always the heart and soul of all of my units. They did the grunt work of a line crewdog but had as much responsibility as a wing commander. They pulled lines of alert, led missions and deployments, and then had to push paper to make the bosses happy. They had the most practical hands-on experience in the unit—they usually were the evaluators, chief instructors, and most certainly the mentors. They had to be the best of the best. Us headquarters weenies could get away with letting the staff handle details—the 0-5s pushing squadrons never got that break. They had to study and train just as hard as the newest nugget, but then they had to dress nice and look sharp and do the political face time. The ones that do all that are worth their weight in gold."

Norman didn't understand everything Ingemanson was talking about, and so he assumed he was talking flyer-speak. Naturally, Ingemanson himself was a command pilot and also wore paratrooper's wings, meaning he probably graduated from the Air Force Academy. It was going to be a challenge, Norman thought, to break the aviator's stranglehold on this promotion board.

"But most importantly, the men and women you'll choose in the next two weeks will be the future leaders of our Air Force, our armed forces, and perhaps our country," Ingemanson went on. "Most of the candidates have completed one or more command and staff education programs; they might have a master's degree, and many even work on doctorates. They've maxed out on flying time, traveled to perhaps five or six different PCS assignments plus a few specialty and service schools. They're probably serving in the Sandbox now, and perhaps even served in other conflicts or actions. They are beginning the transition from senior line troop, instructor, or shop chief to fledgling unit commander. Find the best ones, and let's set them on track to their destinies.

"One more thing to remember: Not only can you pick the candidates best eligible for promotion, but you are also charged with the task of recommending that candidates be *removed* from extended active duty. What's the criterion for removal? That, my friends, is up to you. Be prepared to fully justify your reasons to me, but don't be afraid to give them either. Again, it's part of the awesome responsibility you have here.

"One last reminder: it is still *our* Air Force. We built it. I'd guess that most of the candidates you'll look at didn't serve in Vietnam, so they don't have the same perspective as we do. Many of our buddies died in Vietnam, but we survived and stayed and fought on. We served when it was socially and politically unpopular to wear a uniform in our own hometowns. We played Russian roulette with nuclear weapons, the most deadly weapons ever devised, just so we could prove to the world that we were crazy enough to blow the entire planet into atoms to protect our freedom. We see the tides turning in our favor—but it is up to us to see that our gains are not erased. We do that by picking the next generation of leaders.

"It is our Air Force. Our country. Our world. Now it's our opportunity to pick those who we want to take our place. In my mind, it is equally important a task as the one we did in creating this world we live in. That's our task. Let's get to it. Please stand, raise your right hand, and prepare to take the oath of office to convene this promotion board." General Ingemanson then administered the service oath to the board members, and the job was under way.

Norman and the other board members departed the small theater and headed toward the individual panel meeting rooms. There was a circular table with comfortable-looking chairs arrayed around it, a dry-marker board with an overhead slide projector screen, a bank of telephones, and the ever-present coffeepot and rack of ceramic mugs.

Norman's seven-member panel had five rated officers—four pilots and one navigator, including one officer who looked as if he had every possible specialty badge one person could have: He wore command pilot and senior paratrooper wings, plus a senior missile-launch officer badge on his pocket. The flyers all seemed to know each other—two were even from the same Air Force Academy class. To them, it was a small, chummy Air Force. None of the flyers wore any ribbons on their uniform blouses, only their specialty badges on one side, name tags on the other, and rank on their collar; Norman almost felt self-conscious wearing all of his three rows of ribbons before deciding that the flyers were probably out of uniform.

Introductions were quick, informal, and impersonal—unless you were wearing wings. Along with the flyers and Norman, there was a logistics planning staff officer from the Pentagon. Norman thought he recognized the fellow Pentagon officer, but with almost five thousand Air Force personnel working at the "five-sided puzzle palace," it was pretty unlikely anyone knew anyone else outside their corridor. None of the panel members were women—there were only a couple women on the entire board, a fact that Norman found upsetting. The Air Force was supposed to be the most progressive and socially conscious branch of the American armed services, but it was as if they were right back in the Middle Ages with how the Air Force treated women sometimes.

Of course, the five flyers sat together, across the table from the nonflyers. The flyers were relaxed, loud, and animated. One of them, the supercolonel with all the badges, pulled out a cigar, and Norman resolved to tell him not to light up if he tried, but he never made any move to do so. He simply chewed on it and used it to punctuate his stories and jokes, shared mostly with the other flyers. He sat at the head of the semicircle of flyers at the table as if presiding over the panel. He looked as if he was very accustomed to taking charge of such groups, although each panel didn't have and didn't need a leader.

The supercolonel must've noticed the angry anticipation in Norman's eyes over his cigar, because he looked at him for several long moments during one of the few moments he wasn't telling a story or a crude joke. Finally, a glimmer of recognition brightened his blue eyes. "Norman Weir," he said, jabbing his cigar. "You were the AFO chief at Eglin four years ago. Am I right?"

"Yes; I was."

"Thought so. I'm Harry Ponce. I was the commander of 'Combat Hammer,' the Eighty-sixth Fighter Squadron. Call me 'Slammer.' You took pretty good care of my guys."

"Thank you."

"So. Where are you now?"

"The Pentagon. Chief of the Budget Analysis Agency."

A few of the other flyers looked in his direction when he mentioned the Budget Analysis Agency. One of them curled his lip in a sneer. "The BAA, huh? You guys killed an ejection-seat modification program my staff was trying to get approved. That seat would've saved two guys deploying to the Sandbox."

"I can't discuss it, Colonel," Norman said awkwardly.

"The first ejection seat mod for the B-52 in twenty years, and you guys kill it. I'll never figure that one out."

"It's a complicated screening process," Norman offered disinterestedly. "We analyze cost versus life cycle versus benefit. We get all the numbers on what the Pentagon wants to do with the fleet, then try to justify the cost of a modification with its corresponding . . ."

"It was a simple replacement—a few feet of old worn-out pyrotechnic actuators, replacing thirty-year-old components that were predicted to fail in tropical conditions. A few thousand bucks per seat. Instead, the budget weenies cut the upgrade program. Lo and behold, the first time a couple of our guys try to punch out near Diego Garcia—actuator failure, two seats. Two dead crewdogs."

"Like I said, Colonel, I can't discuss particulars of any file or investigation," Norman insisted. "In any case, every weapon system from the oldest to the newest has a cost-reward break-even point. We use purely objective criteria in making our decision . . ."

"Tell that to the widows of the guys that died," the colonel said. He shook his head disgustedly and turned away from Norman.

What an idiot, Norman thought. *Trying to blame me or my office for the deaths of two flyers because of a cost-analysis report.* There were thousands, maybe tens of thousands of factors involved in every accident—it couldn't all be attributed to budget cuts. He was considering telling the guy off, but he saw the staff wheeling carts of personnel folders down the hallway, and he kept silent as they took seats and got ready to work.

In a nutshell, Norman observed, careers were made or destroyed by a simple numbers game. The Selection Board Secretariat's staff members wheeled in a locked lateral file cabinet on wheels with almost four hundred Officer Selection Reports, or OSRs, in them. Although there was supposedly no time limit on how long each panel member considered each OSR, the board members were asked to finish up the first round of scoring in the first week. That meant they had no more than about five minutes to score each candidate.

Five minutes to decide a career, Norman thought as he opened the first file. Five minutes to decide whether this person deserved to be promoted, or should stay where he was, or even if he or she should even be in the Air Force to begin with.

Well, maybe it won't be that hard, Norman thought as he scanned the OSR. The first thing he saw on the right side of the folder was the candidate's photo, and this guy was a mess. Hair too long, touching the ears. A definite five o'clock shadow. Cockeyed uniform devices. Norman had a chart available that showed the proper order ribbons should be displayed on the uniform, but he didn't need to refer to it to know that the Air Force Training Ribbon was not placed over the Air Force Achievement Medal.

Each board member had a checklist of things to look for in a personnel jacket, along with a sheet for notes or questions and a scoring summary block. Each jacket was given a score between 6.0 and 10.0 in half-point increments. The average score was 7.5. Norman decided he would start at the maximum score and deduct half points for every glitch. So this guy was starting out with a 9.5, and he hadn't even gotten to the job performance and effectiveness reports and ratings yet. Below the photo was a list of the officer's decorations and awards and an officer selection brief, outlining the candidate's duty history. This guy was not wearing a ribbon he had been awarded, so Norman deducted another half point. How inept could one officer be?

And yes, Norm noted that he was a flyer.

On the left side of the OSR were the candidate's OERs, or Officer Effectiveness Reports, starting with the most recent. Norman scanned through the files, paying close attention to the three rater's blocks on the back page. Each OER was endorsed by the officer's three sequential superior officers in his chain of command. He received either a "Below Average," "Average," "Above Average," or "Outstanding" rating, plus a block below for personal comments. An OER with all "Outstanding" ratings was called a "firewalled" OER, and all officers seeking promotion aspired to it.

After filling out hundreds of OERs in his career, Norman knew that anything short of an "Outstanding" rating was cause for concern, and he dinged a candidate for any "Above Average" or lower ratings. But since some commanders always "firewalled" OERs, Norman had to take a quick glance at the rater's comments, even on "firewalled" OERs. He looked for examples of deficiencies or nuances in the wording to suggest what the rater really thought of the candidate. Most all raters used the word "Promote" in his comments, so if the word was missing, that was a big ding—the rater obviously did not think the candidate was worthy of promotion, so why should Norman? If the candidate was really good, the rater might put "Promote ASAP" or "Promote without fail;" if the candidate was exceptionally good, he might say "Promote immediately" or "Promote ahead of contemporaries." Some were more creative: They sometimes wrote "Promote when possible," which was not a strong endorsement and earned a ding, or "Promote below the zone immediately without fail" for a really outstanding candidate. Sometimes they just said "Promote," which Norman considered a big ding too.

By the first lunch break, Norman was slipping right into the groove, and he realized this was not going to be a really difficult exercise. Patterns began to emerge right away, and it soon becomes clear who the really great officers were and who were not. Out of thirty or so OSRs, Norman had only marked a few above 8.0. Most of his scores drifted below the 7.5 average. No one was ranked over 8.5—not one. Norman had to adjust his own scoring system several times because he started to read better and better OERs and realized that what he thought were good comments were actually average comments. Occasionally, he had to ask the flyers what this school or that course was. Norman disliked acronyms on OERs and dinged a candidate for them if he couldn't understand what it meant—especially if he or she was a flyer.

So far, Norman was not too impressed. Some of the candidates they were reviewing were above-the-primary-zone candidates, meaning they had not been promoted when they should have been, and they seemed worse than the others. It was as if they had already given up on the Air Force, and it showed—missing or outdated records, snotty or whining letters to the board attached to the record, old photos, and evidence of stagnated careers. Most were in-the-primary-zone candidates, meeting the board at the proper time commensurate with their date of rank, and most of them had a polished, professional, well-managed look.

Most all of the flyers' OERs were "firewalled," and Norman scrutinized those even more closely for telltale signs of deficiency. The non-flying line officer OERs always seemed more honest, forthright evaluations. The flying community was indeed a closed fraternity, and Norman took this opportunity to take some chips out of their great steel wall every chance he could. If a flyer's OER wasn't firewalled, Norman mentally tossed it aside, taking big dings out of the score.

The chips he was breaking off flyers' OERs quickly became chunks, but Norman didn't care. If a flyer was really great, he would get a good rating. But just being a flyer wasn't a plus in Norman's book. Everyone had to earn their score, but the flyers would have to really shine to pass Norman's muster.

The British Indian Ocean Territories, or BIOT, was a chain of fifty-six islands covering twenty-two thousand square miles of the Indian Ocean south of India. The total land area of the BIOT was only thirty-six square miles, about half the size of the District of Columbia. Located only four hundred miles south of the equator, the weather was hot and humid year-round. The islands were far enough south of the Indian subcontinent, and the waters were colder and deeper, so typhoons and hard tropical storms were rare, and the islands only received about one hundred inches of rain per year. If there had been any appreciable landmass or infrastructure in the BIOT, it might be considered an idyllic tropical paradise. The tiny bits of dry land and coconut groves on the islands had saved many hungry, storm-tossed sailors over the centuries since the islands were discovered by Western explorers in the late seventeenth century, although the reefs had also claimed their share of wayward sailors as well.

The largest and southernmost island in the BIOT was Diego Garcia, a V-shaped stretch of sand, reefs, and atolls about thirty-four miles long, with a thirteen-mile-long, six-mile-wide lagoon inside the V. The British

Navy claimed Diego Garcia and other islands of the Chagos Archipelago in the late eighteenth century and established copra, coconut, and lumber plantations there. The island was an isolated and seldom-used stopover and resupply point for the British Navy until after the independence of India, when it began to languish. Native fishermen from the African nation of Mauritius claimed Diego Garcia, citing historical and cultural precedents, and it appeared as if the British might hand over the island to them.

The United States stepped into the fray in December of 1966. Eager for a listening post to monitor Soviet Navy activity in the Indian Ocean during the height of the Cold War, the United States signed a bilateral agreement to improve and jointly administer the BIOT for defensive purposes. The native Iliots on the islands were relocated back to Mauritius with a promise that if the islands were no longer needed for defense, they would be returned to them. The U.S. Navy immediately landed a Seabee battalion on Diego Garcia and began work.

Seven years later, the U.S. Navy commissioned a "naval communications facility"—an electronic and undersea surveillance post—on Diego Garcia, along with limited naval-vessel support facilities and an airstrip. Five years later, the facility was expanded, making it a full-fledged—albeit still remote—Navy Support Facility. The few dozen sailors assigned there—donkeys, left over from copra and coconut-harvesting operations, far outnumbered humans—lived in primitive hootches and lived only for the next supply ship to take them off the beautiful but lonely desert island.

But the facility took on a more important role when the Soviet Navy began a rapid buildup of forces in the region in the late 1970s, during the oil crisis, and during the Iranian Revolution of the early 1980s. With Western influence in the Middle East waning, Diego Garcia suddenly became the only safe, secure, and reliable port and air facility in southwest Asia. Diego Garcia became a major forward predeployment and prepositioning base for the U.S. Central Command's operations in the Middle East. The facilities were greatly expanded in the early 1980s to make it "the tip of the spear" for American rapid-deployment forces in the region. The U.S. Navy began flying P-3 Orion antisubmarine patrols from Diego Garcia, and several cargo ships loaded with fuel, spare parts, weapons, and ammunition were permanently prepositioned in the little harbor to support future conflicts in the southwest Asia theater.

There was only one highway on the island, the nine-mile-long main paved road leading from the Naval Supply Facility base on Garcia Point to the airfield. Until just a few years ago, both the road and the runway were little more than crushed coral and compacted sand. But as the importance of the little island grew, so did the airfield. What was once just a lonely pink runway and a few rickety shacks, euphemistically called Chagos International Airport, was now one of the finest airfields in the entire Indian Ocean region.

With the advent of Operation Desert Shield, the rapid buildup of forces in the Middle East to counter the threat of an Iraqi invasion of the Arabian Peninsula, Diego Garcia's strategic importance increased a hundredfold. Although the tiny island was almost three thousand miles away from Iraq, it was the perfect place to deploy long-range B-52 Stratofortress bombers, which have an unrefueled range in excess of eight thousand miles. As many as twenty B-52G and-H model bombers and support aircraft deployed there. When the shooting started, the "BUFFs"—Big Ugly Fat Fuckers—began 'round-the-clock bombing missions against Iraqi forces, first using conventionally armed cruise missiles and then, once the Coalition forces had firm control of the skies over the region, pressing the attack with conventional gravity bombs. One-half of all the ordnance used in Operation Desert Storm was dropped by B-52 bombers, and many of them launched from Diego Garcia.

The lone runway on Diego Garcia was eleven thousand feet long and one hundred and fifty feet wide, only four feet above sea level, on the western side of the island. At the height of the air war against Iraq, the aircraft parking ramps were choked with bombers, tankers, transports, and patrol planes; now, only days after the Coalition cease-fire, only a token force of six B-52G and -H bombers, one KC-10 Extender aerial-refueling tanker/cargo plane, and three KC-135 Stratotanker aerial-refueling tankers remained, along with the usual and variable number of cargo planes at the Military Airlift Command ramp and the four P-3 Orion patrol planes on the Navy ramp. Things had definitely quieted down on Diego Garcia, and the little atoll's peaceful, gentle life was beginning to return to normal after months of frenetic activity.

Before the war there was only one aircraft hangar on the island for maintenance on the Navy's P-3 Orion subchasers—the weather was perfect, never lower than seventy-two degrees, never warmer than ninety degrees, with an average of only two inches of rain per week, so why work indoors?—but as the conflict kicked off the U.S. Air Force hastily built one large hangar at the southernmost part of the airfield complex, as far away from curious observers in the harbor as possible. Many folks speculated on what was in the hangar: Was it the still-unnamed B-1B supersonic intercontinental heavy bomber, getting ready to make its combat debut? Or was it the rumored supersecrect stealth bomber, a larger version of the F-117 Goblin stealth fighter? Some even speculated it was the mysterious Aurora spy/attack plane, the hypersonic aircraft capable of flying from the United States to Japan in just a couple of hours.

In reality, the hangar had mostly been used as a temporary overflow barracks during the Persian Gulf War, or used to store VIP aircraft out of the hot sun to keep it cool until just before departure. Since the cease-fire, it had been used to store dozens of pallets of personal gear for returning troops before loading on transport planes. Now, it held two aircraft—two very special aircraft, tightly squeezed in nose to tail.

The two EB-52 Megafortress bombers had arrived separately—Brad Elliott's plane was returning from its patrol near Iran, while the second bomber had been en route to replace the first when it had been diverted to Diego Garcia—but they had arrived within minutes of one another. The airfield had been closed down and blacked out, and all transient ships in the harbor had been moved north toward the mouth of the harbor, until both aircraft touched down and were parked inside the Air Force hangar. A third Megafortress bomber involved in the 'round-the-clock aerial patrols near Iran remained back at its home base in Nevada, with crews standing by ready to rotate out to Diego Garcia if a conflict developed. Roving guards were stationed inside and outside the hangar, but the lure of the island's secluded, serene tropical beauty and every warrior's desire to escape the stress and strains of warfighting combined to keep all curious onlookers away. No one much cared what was inside that hangar, as long as it didn't mean they had to go back to twenty-four-hour shifts to surge combat aircraft for bombing raids.

Patrick McLanahan had spent all night buttoning up the Megafortress, downloading electronic data from the ship's computers, and preparing a detailed intelligence brief for the Air Force on the strange aircraft they had encountered near the Strait of Hormuz. Now it was time to summarize their findings and prepare a report to send to the Pentagon.

"We need to come up with a best guess at what we encountered last night," Brad Elliott said. "Wendy? Start us off."

"Weird," Wendy said. "He had a big, powerful multimode X-band surface-search radar, which meant it was a big plane, maybe bomber-class, like a Bear, Badger, Backfire, Nimrod, or Buccaneer attack plane. But it also had an S-band air-search radar, like a Soviet Peel Cone system or like an AWACS. He was fast, faster than six hundred knots, which definitely eliminates the Bear and AWACS and probably eliminates a Badger, Nimrod, or Buccaneer attack plane. That leaves a Backfire bomber."

"Or a Blackjack bomber," Patrick offered, "or some other class of aircraft we haven't seen yet." The Backfire and Blackjack bombers were

Russia's most advanced warplanes. Both were large intercontinental supersonic bombers, still in production. The Backfire bomber, similar to the American B-1 bomber, was known to have been exported to Iran as a naval attack plane, carrying long-range supersonic cruise missiles. Little was known about the Blackjack bomber except it was larger, faster, more high-tech, and carried many more weapons than any other aircraft in the Communist world—and probably in the *entire* world.

"But with air-to-air missiles?" John Ormack remarked. "Could we have missed other planes with him, maybe a fighter escort?"

"Possible," Wendy said. "But normally we'd spot fighter intercept radars at much longer distances, as far as a hundred miles. We didn't see him until he was right on top of us—less than forty miles away. In fact, we probably wouldn't have detected him at all except he turned on his own radar first and we detected it. He was well within our own air-search radar range, but we never saw him."

"A *stealth bomber*?" Patrick surmised. "A stealthy Backfire or Blackjack bomber?"

"There's nothing stealthy about a Backfire," Wendy said, "but a Blackjack bomber—interesting notion. Armed with air-to-air missiles?"

"It's the equivalent of a Megafortress flying battleship, except built on a supersonic airframe," Patrick said. "Three years after we first flew the EB-52 Megafortress, someone—probably the Russians—builds their own copy and sells it to the Iranians. Remember we thought we heard a Russian voice on the radio before we heard the Iranian pilot respond in English? *The Russians built a Megafortress flying battleship and sold it to the Iranians.*"

"Hol-ee shit," Brad Elliott murmured. "It would sure keep the Russians in the Iranians' good graces to sell them a hot jet like a Megafortress. That would be worth a billion dollars in hard currency, something I'm sure the Russians need badly. It would be the ultimate weapon in the Middle East."

"We know how capable our system is—we *know* we can sneak up on any ship in the U.S. Navy and launch missiles and drop bombs before they know we're there," John Ormack said. "If the Iranians have a similar capability . . ."

"The entire fleet in the Persian Gulf could be in danger," Brad Elliott said ominously. "With Iraq all but neutralized and the Coalition forces going home, this could be Iran's best chance to take over the Persian Gulf. I want an abbreviated after-action and intelligence summary ready to transmit in thirty minutes, and then I want a detailed report prepared and ready to send out to Washington on the next liaison flight. Let's get busy."

The crew had the report done in twenty minutes, and they were hard at work on the after-action report when a communications officer brought in a message from the command post. Brad read it, his face darkened, and he crumpled it up into a ball and stormed out of the room, muttering curses.

John picked up the message form and read it. "We've been ordered to stand down," he said. "Apparently the Iranians filed a protest with the State Department, claiming an American warplane tried to violate Iranian airspace and attack a patrol. Almost every Gulf country is demanding an explanation, and the President doesn't have one . . ."

"Because he didn't know what we were doing," Patrick said. "The President must be ready to bust a gut."

"We've been ordered to bring the Megafortresses back to Groom Lake immediately." He gulped, then read, "And Brad's been relieved of duty." Patrick shook his head and made an exasperated sigh, then closed his classified notebook, collected his papers, and secured them in a catalog case to turn back in to the command post. "Where are you going, Patrick?"

"Out. Away from here. I'm on a beautiful tropical island—I want to enjoy a little of it before I get tossed into prison."

"Brad wanted us to stay in the hangar . . ."

"Brad's no longer in charge," Patrick said. He looked at John Ormack with a mixture of anger and weariness. "Are you going to order me to stay, John?" Ormack said nothing, so Patrick stormed out of the room without another word.

After turning in his classified materials, Patrick went to his locker in the hangar, stripped off his smelly survival gear and flying boots, found a beach mat and a bottle of water, took a portable walkie-talkie and his ID card, grabbed a ride from the shuttle bus to one of the beautiful white-sand beaches just a few yards from the Visiting Officers' Quarters, found an inviting coconut tree, stripped off his flight suit and undergarments to the waist, and stretched out on the sand. He heard the walkie-talkie squawk once—someone asking him to return to answer a few more questions—so Patrick finally turned the radio off. But he immediately felt bad for doing that, so he set his "internal alarm clock" for one hour and closed his eyes.

He was exhausted, bone-tired, but the weariness would not leave his body—in fact, he was energized, ready to go again. There was so much excitement and potential in their group—and it seemed it was wasted because Brad Elliott couldn't control himself. He was too eager simply to charge off and do whatever he felt was right or necessary. Patrick didn't always disagree with him, but he wished he could channel his energy, drive, determination, and patriotism in a more productive direction.

It seemed as if only a few minutes passed, but when Patrick awoke a quick glance at his watch told him fifty minutes had gone by. The sun was high in the sky, seemingly overhead—they were close enough to the equator for that to happen—but there was enough of a breeze blowing in off the Indian Ocean to keep him cool and comfortable. There were a few sailors or airmen on the beach a few dozen yards away to the east, throwing a Frisbee or relaxing under an umbrella.

"Helluva way to fight a war, isn't it?"

Patrick looked behind him and saw Wendy Tork sitting cross-legged beside him. She had a contented, pleased, relaxed look on her face. Patrick felt that same thrill of excitement and anticipation he had felt on the Megafortress. "I'll say," Patrick commented. "How long have you been sitting there?"

"A few minutes." Wendy was wearing nothing but her athletic bra and a pair of dark blue cotton panties; her flying boots and flight suit were in a pile beside her. Patrick gulped in surprise when he saw her so scantily clad, which made her smile. She motioned toward the Visiting Officers' Quarters down the beach. "Brad decided to let us get rooms in the Qs rather than sleep in the hangar."

Patrick snorted. "How magnanimous of him."

"What were *you* going to do—sleep on the beach?"

"Damn right I was," Patrick said. He shook his head disgustedly. "We were cooped up in that plane for over seventeen hours."

"And it was all unauthorized," Wendy said bitterly. "I can't believe he'd do that—and then have the *nerve* to chew you out for what you did."

"You mean, you can't believe he'd do that *again*," Patrick said. "That's Brad Elliott's MO, Wendy—do whatever it takes to get the job done."

"Flying the Kavaznya sortie—yes, I agree," she said. The first flight of the experimental EB-52 Megafortress bomber three years earlier, against a Soviet long-range killer laser system in Siberia, was also unauthorized—but it had probably saved the world from a nuclear exchange. "But with half the planet involved in a shooting war in the Middle East, why he would commit three Megafortresses to the theater without proper authorization and risk getting us all killed like that? Hell, it boggles my mind."

"No one said Brad was the clearheaded all-knowing expert in everything military," Patrick pointed out. "If he was, he'd probably build Megafortresses for just one person. He has a crew behind him." He turned toward her. "Rank disappears when we step into that bird,

Wendy. It's our job, our responsibility, to point out problems or discrepancies or errors."

"Aren't you obligated to follow his orders?"

"Yes, unless I feel his orders are illogical or illegal or violate a directive," Patrick replied. "Brad wanting to engage that unidentified aircraft—that was wrong, even if we were on an authorized mission. We can't just go around shooting down aircraft over international airspace. We did what we were supposed to do—disengage, identify ourselves, turn, run, and get out. We prevented a dogfight and came home safely." He paused, then smiled.

"Why are you smiling?"

"You know, I was a little miffed at Brad ordering us up on this mission at first," Patrick admitted. "But you know, I probably . . . no, I *definitely* wanted to go. I *knew* we had no tasking or execution order. If I wanted, I could have asked the question, demanded he get authorization, and stopped this sortie from ever leaving the ground. The fact is, I wanted to do it." His expression grew a bit more somber as he added, "In fact, I probably betrayed you, maybe even betrayed myself for *not* saying anything. I had a responsibility to speak up, and I didn't. And if things went completely to shit and some of us were killed or captured or hurt, I know that Brad would be the one responsible. I accused Brad of being irresponsible, of wanting to get into the fighting before it was over—and at the same time, I was thinking and doing the exact same thing. What a hypocrite."

"You are not a hypocrite," Wendy said, putting a hand on his shoulder as his eyes wandered out across the beach toward the open ocean. "Listen, Patrick, there's a war on. There might be a cease-fire now, but the entire region is still ready to explode. You know this, Brad knows this, I know this—and soon some smart desk jockeys in Washington will know this. They really did want our team warmed up and ready to go in case we were needed. Brad just advanced the timetable a little . . ."

"No, a *lot*," Patrick said.

"You played along because you recognized the need and our unit's capabilities. You did the right thing." She paused and took a deep breath, letting her fingers slide along his broad, naked shoulders. Patrick suppressed a pleased, satified moan, and Wendy responded by beginning to massage his shoulders. "I just wish Brad was a little more . . . user-friendly," she went on absently. "Commanders need to make decisions, but Brad seems a little too eager to pull the trigger and fight his way in or out of a scrape." She paused for a few long moments, then added, "Why can't *you* be our commander?"

"Me?" He hoped his surprised reaction sounded a lot less phony than it sounded to himself. In fact, ever since joining the High Technology Aerospace Weapons Center, Patrick thought about being its commander—now, for the first time, someone else had verbalized it. "I don't think I'm leadership material, Wendy," Patrick said after a short chuckle.

His little laugh barely succeeded in hiding the rising volts of pleasure he felt as her fingers aimlessly caressed his shoulder. "Sure you are," she said. "I think you'd be a great commanding officer."

"I don't think so," Patrick said. "They made me a major after the Kavaznya mission only because we survived it, not because I'm better than all the other captains in the Air Force . . ."

"They made you a major because you deserve to get promoted."

Patrick ignored her remark. "I think I might be meeting a lieutenant-colonel promotion board sometime this month—a two-year below-the-primary-zone board—but I have no desire to become a commander," he went on. "All I want to do is fly and be the best at whatever mission or weapon system they give me. But they don't promote flyboys to O-5 if they want to just stay flyboys."

"They don't?"

"Why should they? If a captain or a major can do the job, why do they need a lieutenant colonel doing it? L-Cs are supposed to be leaders, commanding squadrons. I don't want a squadron." Wendy looked at the sand for a long moment, then drummed her fingers on his shoulder. He glanced at her and smiled when she looked up at him with a mischievous smile. "What?"

"I think that's bull, Major-soon-to-be-Lieutenant-Colonel McLanahan." Wendy laughed. "I think you'd make an ideal commanding officer. You're the best at what you do, Patrick—it's perfectly understandable that you wouldn't want to spoil things by moving on to something else. But I see the qualities in you that other high-ranking guys lack. John Ormack is a great guy and a fine engineer, but he doesn't have what it takes to lead. Brad Elliott is a determined, gutsy leader, but he doesn't have the long-range vision and the interpersonal skills that a good commander needs.

"So stop selling yourself short. Those of us who know you can see it's total bull. The Strategic Air Command has got you so brainwashed into believing the mission comes first and the person comes last that you're starting to believe it yourself." She lay on the warm sand, facing him. "Let's talk about something else—like why you were watching me last night."

Her frankness and playfulness, combined with the warm sand, idyllic tropical scenery, fresh ocean breezes—not to mention her semiundressed attire—finally combined to make Patrick relax, even smile. He lay down on the sand, facing her, intentionally shifting himself closer to her. "I was fantasizing about you," he said finally. "I was thinking about the night at the Bomb Comp symposium at Barksdale that we spent together, how you looked, how you felt."

"Mmm. Very nice. I knew you were thinking that. I thought it was cute, you trying to stammer your way out of it. I've been thinking about you too."

"Oh yeah?"

Her eyes grew cloudy, tumultuous. "I had been thinking for the longest time if we'd ever get back together again," Wendy said. "After the Kavaznya mission, we were so compartmentalized, isolated—I thought I'd never touch you ever again. Then you joined Brad in the Border Security Force assignment, and that went bust, and it seemed like they drove you even deeper underground. And then the Philippines conflict . . . we lost so many planes out there, I was sure you weren't coming back. I knew you'd be leading the force, and I thought you'd be the first to die, even in the B-2 stealth bomber."

Wendy rolled over on her back and stared up into the sky. The clouds were thickening—it looked like a storm coming in, more than just the usual daily late-afternoon five-minute downpour. "But then Brad brought us back to refit the new planes to the Megafortress standard, and you were back at work like nothing ever happened. We started working together, side by side, sometimes on the same workstation or jammed into the same dinky compartment, sometimes so close I could feel the heat from your temples. But it seemed as if we had never been together—it was as if we had always been working together, but that night in Barksdale never happened. You were working away like crazy and I was just another one of your subcontractors."

"I didn't mean to hurt you, Wendy . . ."

"But it did hurt," she interjected. "The way you looked at me at Barksdale, the way you treated me at Dreamland, the way you touched me on the Megafortress just before we landed in Anadyr . . . I felt something between us, much more than just a one-night stand in Shreveport. That felt like an eternity ago. I felt as if I waited for you, and you were never coming back. Then I caught you looking at me, and all I could think of to do was come up with subtle ways to hurt you. Now, I don't know what I feel. I don't know whether I should punch your damned lights out or . . ."

He moved pretty quick for a big guy. His lips were on hers before she knew it, but she welcomed his kiss like a pearl diver welcomes that first deep, sweet breath of air after a long time underwater.

The beach was beautiful, soothing and relaxing, but they did not spend much time there. They knew that the world was going to come crashing down on them very, very soon, and they didn't have much time to get reacquainted. The Visiting Officers' Quarters were only a short walk away. . . .

"Damn shit-hot group we got, that's what I think," Colonel Harry Ponce exclaimed. He was "holding court" in the Randolph Officers Club after breakfast, sitting at the head of a long table filled with fellow promotion board members and a few senior officers from the base. Ponce jabbed at the sky with his unlit cigar. "It's going to be damn hard to choose."

Heads nodded in agreement—all but Norman Weir's. Ponce jabbed the cigar in his direction. "What's the matter, Norm? Got a burr up your butt about somethin'?"

Norman shrugged. "No, Colonel, not necessarily," he said. Most of the others turned to Norman with surprised expressions, as if they were amazed that someone would dare contradict the supercolonel. "Overall, they're fine candidates. I wish I'd seen a few more sharper guys, especially the in-the-primary-zone guys. The above-the-primary-zone candidates looked to me like they'd already thrown in the towel."

"Hell, Norman, ease up a little," Ponce said. "You look at a guy that's the ops officer of his squadron, he's got umpteen million additional duties, he flies six sorties a week or volunteers for deployment or TDYs—who the hell cares if he's got a loose thread on his blues? I want to know if the guy's been busting his hump for his unit."

"Well, Colonel, if he can't put his Class A's together according to the regs or he can't be bothered getting a proper haircut, I wonder what else he can't do properly? And if he can't do the routine stuff, how is he supposed to motivate young officers and enlisted troops to do the same?"

"Norm, I'm talkin' about the *real* Air Force," Ponce said. "It's all fine and dandy that the headquarters staff and support agencies cross all the damned t's and dot the i's. But what I'm looking for is the Joe that cranks out one hundred and twenty percent each and every damned day. He's not puttin' on a show for the promotion board—he's helping his unit be the best. Who the hell cares what he looks like, as long as he flies and fights like a bitch bulldog in heat?"

That kind of language was typical in the supercolonel's verbal repertoire, and he used it to great effect to shock and humor anyone he confronted. It just made Norman more defensive. Anyone who resorted to using vulgarity as a normal part of polite conversation needed an education in how to think and speak, and Ponce was long overdue for a lesson. "Colonel, a guy that does *both*—does a good job in *every* aspect of the job, presenting a proper, professional, by-the-book appearance as well as performing his primary job—is a better choice for promotion than just the guy who flies well but has no desire or understanding of all the other aspects of being a professional airman. A guy that presents a poor appearance may be a good person and a good operator, but obviously isn't a complete, well-balanced, professional officer."

"Norm, buddy, have you been lost in your spreadsheets for the past nine months? Look around you—we're at war here!" Ponce responded, practically shouting. Norman had to clench his jaw to keep from admonishing Ponce to stop calling him by the disgusting nickname "Norm." "The force is at war, a real war, for the first time since Vietnam—I'm not talkin' about Libya or Grenada, those were just finger-wrestling matches compared to the Sandbox—and we're kicking *ass*! I see my guys taxiing out ready to launch, and I see them practically jumpin' out of their cockpits, they're so anxious to beat the crap outta Saddam. Their crew chiefs are so excited they're pissin' their pants. I see those guys as heroes, and now I have a chance to promote them, and by God I'm gonna do it!

"The best part is, none of our officers are over there in the 'Sandbox' ordering someone to paint the rocks or having six-course meals while their men are dying all around them. We're going over there, kicking ass and taking names, and we're coming home alive and victorious. Our troops are being treated like professionals, not conscripts or snot-nosed kids or druggies or pretty-boy marionettes. Our officers are applying what they've learned over the years and are taking the fight to Saddam and shovin' Mavericks right down his damned throat. I want guys leading the Air force that want to train hard, fight hard, and come home."

"But what about . . . ?"

"Yeah, yeah, I hear all the noise about the 'whole person' and the 'total package' crapola," Ponce interjected, waving the cigar dismissively. "But what I want are *warriors*. If you're a pilot, I want to see you fly your ass off, every chance you can get and then some, and then I want to see you pitch in to get the paperwork and nitpicky ground bullshit cleaned up so everyone can go fly some more. If you're an environmental weenie or—what are you in, Norm, accounting and finance? Okay. If you're a damned accountant, I want to see you working overtime if necessary to make your section hum. If your squadron needs you, you slap on your flying boots, fuck the wife good-bye, and report in on the double. Guys who do that are aces in my book."

Norman realized there was no point in arguing with Ponce—he was just getting more and more flagrant and bigoted by the second. Soon he would be bad-mouthing and trash-talking lawyers, or doctors, or the President himself—everyone except those wearing wings. It was getting very tiresome. Norman fell silent and made an almost imperceptible nod, and Ponce nodded triumphantly and turned to lecture someone else, acting as if he had just won the great evolution vs. creation debate. Norman made certain he was not the next one to leave, so it wouldn't appear as if he was retreating or running away, but as soon as the first guy at the table got up, Norman muttered something about having to make a call and got away from Ponce and his sycophants.

Well, Norman thought as he walked toward the Military Personnel Center, attitudes like Ponce's just cemented his thoughts and feelings about flyers—they were opinionated, headstrong, bigoted, loud-mouthed Neanderthals. Ponce wasn't out to promote good officers—he was out to promote meat-eating jet-jockeys like himself.

It was guys like Ponce, Norman thought as he entered the building and took the stairs to the Selection and Promotion Branch floor, who were screwing up the Air Force for the rest of us.

"Excuse me, Colonel Weir?" Norman was striding down the hallway, heading back to his panel deliberation room. He stopped and turned. Major General Ingemanson was standing in the doorway to his office, smiling his ever-present friendly, disarming smile. "Got a minute?"

"Of course, sir," Norman said.

"Good. Grab a cup of coffee and c'mon in." Norman bypassed the coffee stand in the outer office and walked into Ingemanson's simple, unadorned office. He stood at attention in front of Ingemanson's desk, eyes straight ahead. "Relax and sit down, Colonel. Sure you don't want some coffee?"

"I'm fine, sir, thank you."

"Congratulations on finishing up the first week and doing such a good job."

"Thank you, sir."

"You can call me 'Swede'—everybody does," Ingemanson said. Norman didn't say anything in reply, but Ingemanson could immediately tell Weir wasn't comfortable calling him anything but "General" or "sir"—and of course Ingemanson noticed that Weir didn't invite him to call him by his first name, either. "You're a rare species on this board, Colonel—the first to come to a promotion board from the Budget Analysis Agency. Brand-new agency and all. Enjoying it there?"

"Yes, sir. Very much."

"Like the Pentagon? Wish you were back in a wing, running a shop?"

"I enjoy my current position very much, sir."

"I had one Pentagon tour a couple years ago—hated it. Air Division is okay, but boy, I miss the flying, the flight line, the cockpit, the pilots' lounge after a good sortie," Ingemanson said wistfully. "I try to keep current in the F-16 but it's hard when you're pulling a staff. I haven't released a real-live weapon in years."

"Yes, sir. Sorry, sir." He was sorry he didn't get to drop bombs and get shot at anymore? Norman definitely didn't understand flyers.

"Anyway, all the panel members have been instructed to call on you to explain any technical terminology or references in the personnel files relating to the accounting and finance field," Ingemanson went on. "A few line officer candidates had AFO-type schools, and some of the rated types on the panels might not know what they are. Hope you don't mind, but you might be called out to speak before another panel anytime. Those requests have to come through me. We'll try to keep that to a minimum."

"Not at all. I understand, sir," Norman said. "But in fact, no one has yet come to me to ask about the accounting or finance field. That could be a serious oversight."

"Oh?"

"If the flyers didn't know what a particular AFO school was, how could they properly evaluate a candidate's file? I see many flyers' files, and I have to ask about a particular school or course all the time."

"Well, hopefully the panel members either already know what the school or course is, or had the sense to ask a knowledgeable person," Ingemanson offered. "I'll put out a memo reminding them."

"I don't suppose too many AFOs will rate very highly with this board," Norman said. "With the war such a success and the aircrews acquitting themselves so well, I imagine they'll get the lion's share of the attention here."

"Well, I've only seen MPC's printout on the general profile of the candidates," Ingemanson responded, "but I think they did a pretty good job spreading the opportunities out between all the specialties. Of course, there'll be a lot of flyers meeting any Air Force promotion board, but I think you'll find it's pretty evenly distributed between the rated and nonrated specialties."

"If you listen to the news, you'd think there was a pilot being awarded the Medal of Honor every day."

"Don't believe everything you hear in the press, Colonel—our side practices good propaganda techniques too, sometimes better than the Iraqis," Ingemanson said with a smile. "The brass didn't want to give kill counts to the press, but the press eats that up. Helps keep morale up. The talking heads then start speculating on which fictional hero will get what medal. Stupid stuff. Not related to the real world at all." He noticed Weir's hooded, reserved expression, then added, "Remember, Colonel—there was Operation Desert Shield before there was Operation Desert Storm, and that's where the support troops shone, not just the aircrew members. None of the heroics being accomplished right now would be even remotely possible without the Herculean efforts of the support folks. Even the AFOs." Weir politely smiled at the gentle jab.

"I haven't seen any of the personnel jackets, but I expect to see plenty of glowing reports on extraordinary jobs done by combat support and nonrated specialties," Ingemanson went on. "I'm not telling you how I want you to mark your ballots, Colonel, but keep that in mind. Every man or woman, whether they're in the Sandbox or staying back in the States, needs to do their job to perfection, and then some, before we can completely claim victory."

"I understand, sir. Thank you for the reminder."

"Don't mention it. And call me 'Swede.' Everyone does. We're going to be working closely together for another week—let's ease up on some of the formalities." Norman again didn't say a word, only nodded uncomfortably. Ingemanson gave Weir a half-humorous, half-exasperated glare. "The reason I called you in here, Colonel," Ingemanson went on, "is I've received the printout on the scoring so far. I'm a little concerned."

"Why?"

"Because you seem to be rating the candidates lower than any other rater," the general said. "The board's average rating so far is 7.92. Your average line officer rating is 7.39—and your average rating of pilots, navigators, and missile-launch officers is 7.21, far below the board average."

Norman felt a brief flush of panic rise up to his temples, but indignation shoved it away. "Is there a problem, sir?"

"I don't know, Colonel. I asked you here to ask that very same question of you."

Norman shrugged. "I suppose someone has to be the lowest rater."

"Can't argue with that," Ingemanson said noncommittally. "But I just want to make sure that there are no . . . hidden agendas involved with your ratings decisions."

"Hidden agendas?"

"As in, you have something against rated personnel, and you want your scores to reflect your bias against them."

"That's nonsense, sir. I have nothing against flyers. I don't know many, and I have little interaction with them, so how can I have a bias against them?"

"My job as board president is to make sure there is no adverse bias or favoritism being exercised by the panel members," Ingemanson reminded him. "I look at the rater's individual average scores. Generally, everyone comes within ten or fifteen percent of the average. If it doesn't, I ask the rater to come in for a chat. I just wanted to make sure everything is okay."

"Everything is fine, sir. I assure you, I'm not biasing my scores in any way. I'm calling them like I see them."

"A flyer didn't run over your cat or run off with your wife . . . er, pardon me, Colonel. I forgot—you're divorced. My apologies."

"No offense taken, sir."

"I'm once divorced too, and I joke about it constantly—way too much, I'm afraid."

"I understand, sir," Norman said, without really understanding. "I'm just doing my job the way I see it needs to be done."

Ingemanson's eyes narrowed slightly at that last remark, but instead of pursuing it further, he smiled, rubbed his hands energetically, and said, "That's good enough for me, then. Thanks for your time."

"You aren't going to ask me to change any of my scores? You're not going to ask me how I score a candidate?"

"I'm not allowed to ask, and even if I was, I don't really care," the two-star general said, smiling. "Your responsibility as a member of this board is to apply the secretary's MOI to the best of your professional knowledge, beliefs, and abilities. I certify to the Secretary of the Air Force that all board members understand and are complying with the Memorandum of Instruction, and I have to certify this again when I turn in the board's results. My job when I find any possible discrepancies is to interview the board member. If I find any evidence of noncompliance with the MOI, I'll take some action to restore fairness and accuracy. If it's a blatant disregard of the MOI, I might ask you to rescore some of the candidates, but the system is supposed to accommodate wild swings in scoring.

"I'm satisfied that you understand your responsibilities and are carrying them out. I cannot change any ratings, try to instruct you in how to rate the candidates, or try to influence you in any way about how to carry out your responsibilities, as long as you're following the MOI. End of discussion. Have a nice day, Colonel."

Norman got to his feet, and he shook hands with General Ingemanson when he offered it. But before he left, Norman turned. "I have a question, sir."

"Fire away."

"Did you have this same discussion with anyone else . . . say, Colonel Ponce?"

General Ingemanson smiled knowingly. Well well, he thought, maybe he's not as stuck in the world between his ears as he thought. "As a matter of fact, Colonel, I did. We spoke last Saturday evening at the O Club over a few drinks."

"You spoke with Colonel Ponce about the board, at the Officers' Club?"

Ingemanson chuckled, but more out of exasperation than humor. "Colonel, this is not a sequestered criminal jury," he said. "We're allowed to speak to one another outside the Selection Board Secretariat. We're even allowed to discuss promotion boards and the promotion process in general—just not any specifics on any one candidate or anything about specific scores, or attempt to influence any other board members. You probably haven't noticed, but Slammer spends just about every waking minute that he's not sitting the panel at the Club. That seemed to me the best place to corral him."

" 'Slammer'?"

"Colonel Ponce. That's his call sign. I thought you two knew each other?"

"We were assigned to the same wing, once."

"I see." Ingemanson filed that tidbit of information away, then said with a grin, "If I'd run into you at the Club, Norman, I would've spoken to you there too. You seem to spend most of your time in your VOQ or out jogging. Neither is conducive to a heart-to-heart chat."

"Yes, sir."

"Harry and I have crossed paths many times—I guess if you've been around as long as we have in the go-fast community, that's bound to happen. I've got seven years on the guy, but he'll probably pin on his first star soon. He might have been one of the Provisional Wing commanders out in Saudi Arabia or Turkey if he wasn't such a hot-shit test pilot. He designed two weapons that were developed in record time and used in the war. Pretty amazing work." Norman could tell Ingemanson was mentally reliving some of the times they'd had together, and it irritated Norman to think that he could just completely drift off like that—take a stroll down Memory Lane while talking to another officer standing right in front of him.

"Anyway," Ingemanson went on, shaking himself out of his reverie with a satisfied smile, "we spoke about his scores. They're a little skewed, like yours."

"All in favor of the flyers, I suppose."

"Actually, he's too *hard* on flyers," Ingemanson admitted. "I guess it's hard to measure up with what that man's done over his career, but that's no excuse. I told him he's got to measure the candidates against each other, not against his own image of what the perfect lieutenant colonel-selectee is."

"Which is himself," Norman added.

"Probably so," Ingemanson said, with a touch of humor in his eyes. He looked at Norman, and the humor disappeared. "The difference is, Slammer is measuring the candidates against a rigid yardstick—himself, or at least his own image of himself. On the other hand, you—in my humble nonvoting opinion—are not measuring the candidates at all. You're chipping away at them, finding and removing every flaw in every candidate until you come up with a chopped-up thing at the end. You're not creating anything here, Colonel—you're destroying."

Norman was a little stunned by Ingemanson's words. He was right on, of course—that was exactly Norman's plan of attack on this board: Start with a perfect candidate, a perfect "10," then whittle away at their perfection until reaching the bottom-line man or woman. When Ingemanson put it the way he did, it did sound somewhat defeatist, destructive—but so what? There were no guidelines. What right did he have to say all this?

"Pardon me, sir," Norman said, "but I'm not quite clear on this. You don't approve of the way I'm rating the candidates?"

"That's not what I'm saying at all, Colonel," Ingemanson said. "And I didn't try to correct Slammer either—not that I could even if I tried. I'm making an unofficial, off-the-record but learned opinion, on a little of the psychology behind the scoring if you will. I have no authority for any of this except for my experience on promotion boards and the fact that I'm a two-star general and you have to sit and listen to me." He smiled, trying to punctuate his attempt at humor, but Weir wasn't biting. "I'm just pointing out to you what I see."

"You think I'm destroying these candidates?"

"I'm saying that perhaps your attitude toward most of the candidates, and toward the flyers in particular, shows that maybe you're gunning them down instead of measuring them," Ingemanson said. "But as you said, there's no specific procedure for scoring the candidates. Do it any way as you see fit."

"Permission to speak openly, sir?"

"For Pete's sake, Colonel . . . yes, yes, *please* speak openly."

"This is a little odd, General," Norman said woodenly. "One moment you criticize my approach to scoring the candidates, and the next moment you're telling me to go ahead and do it any way I want."

"As I said in my opening remarks, Colonel Weir—this is *your* Air Force, and it's your turn to shape its future," Ingemanson said sincerely. "We chose you for the board: you, with your background and history and experience and attitudes and all that other emotional and personal baggage. The Secretary of the Air Force gave you mostly nonspecific guidelines for how to proceed. The rest is up to you. We get characters like you and we get characters like Slammer Ponce working side by side, deciding the future."

"One tight-ass, one hard-ass—is that what you're saying?"

"Two completely different perspectives," Ingemanson said, not daring to get dragged into that most elegant, truthful observation. "My job is to make sure you are being fair, equitable, and open-minded. As long as you are, you're in charge—I'm only the referee, the old man what's in charge. I give you the shape of one man's opinion, like Eric Sevareid used to say. End of discussion." Ingemanson glanced at his watch, a silent way of telling Norman to get the hell out of his office before the headache brewing between his eyes grew any worse. "Have a nice day, Colonel."

Norman got to his feet, stood at attention until Ingemanson—with an exasperated roll of his eyes—formally dismissed him, and walked out. He thought he had just been chewed out, but Ingemanson did it so gently, so smoothly, so affably, that Norman was simply left wondering, replaying the general's words over and over in his head until he reached the panel deliberation room.

The other panel members were already seated, with Ponce at his usual place, his unlit cigar clenched in his teeth. "Gawd, Norm, you're late, and you look a little tight," Ponce observed loudly. "Had a wild weekend, Norm?"

"I finished my taxes and ran a ten-K run in less than forty minutes. How was your weekend?"

"I creamed the general's ass in three rounds of golf, won a hundred bucks, met a cute señorita, and spent most of yesterday learning how to cook Mexican food buck naked," Ponce replied. The rest of the room exploded in laughter and applause. "But shit, I don't have my taxes done. What kind of loser am I?" They got to work amidst a lot of chatter and broad smiles—everyone but Norman.

The day was spent on what was called "resolving the gray area." In the course of deliberations, many candidates had a score that permitted them to be promoted, but there weren't enough slots to promote them all. So every candidate with a potentially promotable score had to be rescored until there were no more tie scores remaining. Naturally, when the candidates were rescored, there were candidates with tie scores again. Those had to be rescored, then the promotable candidates lumped together again and rescored yet again until enough candidates were chosen to fill the slots available.

In deliberating the final phase of rescoring the "gray area," panel members were allowed to discuss the rationale behind their scores with each other. It was the phase that Norman most dreaded, and at the same time most anticipated—a possible head-to-head, peer-to-peer confrontation with Harry Ponce.

It was time, Norman thought, for the Slammer to get slammed.

"Norm, what in blue blazes are you thinking?" Ponce exploded as the final short stack of personnel jackets were passed around the table. "You torpedoed Waller again. Your rating pushes him out of the box. Mind tellin' me why?"

"Every other candidate in that stack has Air Command and Staff College done in residence or by correspondence, except him," Norman replied. He didn't have to scan the jacket—he knew exactly which candidate it was, knew that Ponce would want to go to war over him. "His PME printout says he ordered the course a second time after failing to finish it within a year. Now why do you think he deserves to get a promotion when all the others completed that course?"

"Because Waller has been assigned to a fighter wing in Europe for the past three years."

"So?"

"Jesus, Norm, open your eyes," Ponce retorted. "The Soviet Union is doin' a free fall. The Berlin Wall came down and Russia's number one ally, East Germany, virtually disappears off the map overnight. A Soviet premier kicks the bucket every goddamned year, the Baltic states want to become nonaligned nations, and the Soviet economy is in meltdown. Everyone expects the Russkies to either implode or break out and fight any day now."

"I still don't get it."

"Fighter pilots stationed in Europe are practically sleeping in their cockpits because they have so many alert scrambles and restricted alert postures," Ponce explained, "and Waller leads the league in sorties. He volunteers for every mission, every deployment, every training mission, every shadow tasking. He's his wing's go-to guy. He's practically taken over his squadron already. His last OER went all the way up to USAFE headquarters. He flew one-fifth of all his squadron's sorties in the Sandbox, and still served as ops officer and as acting squadron commander when his boss got grounded after an accident. He deserves to get a promotion."

"But if he gets a promotion, he'll be unavailable for a command position because he hasn't completed ACSC—hasn't even officially started it, in fact," Norman pointed out. "And he's been in his present assignment for almost four years—that means he's ready for reassignment. If he gets reassigned he'll have to wait at least a year, maybe two years, for an ACSC residence slot. He'll get passed up by officers junior to him even if he maintains a spotless record. A promotion now will only hurt him."

"What the hell kind of screwed-up logic is that, Weir?" Ponce shouted. But Norman felt good, because he could see that the little lightbulb over Ponce's head came on. He was getting through to the supercolonel.

"You know why, Colonel," Norman said confidently. "If he doesn't get promoted, he'll have a better chance of staying in his present assignment—in fact, I'd put money on it, if he's the acting squadron commander. He's a kick-ass major now—no one can touch him. He's certainly top of the list in his wing for ACSC. As soon as he gets back from Saudi Arabia, he'll go. When he graduates from ACSC in residence, he'll have all the squares filled and then some. He'll be a shoo-in for promotion next year."

"But he'll miss his primary zone," Ponce said dejectedly. He knew Norman was right, but he still wanted to do everything he could to reward this outstanding candidate. "His next board will be an above-the-primary-zone board, and he'll be lumped in with the has-beens. Here's a guy who works his butt off for his unit. Who deserves it more than him?"

"The officers who took a little extra time in professional career development and got their education requirements filled," Norman replied. "I'm not saying Waller's not a top guy. But he obviously knew what he had to do to be competitive—after all, he's taken the course twice, and he still didn't do it: That's not a well-rounded candidate in my book. The other candidates have pulled for their units too, but they also took time to get the theoretical and educational training in. Four other guys in that stack finished ACSC, and two of *them* have been selected to go in residence already. They're the ones that deserve a promotion."

"Well of course they had time to do ACSC—they're ground-pounders," Ponce shot back.

The remark hit a nerve in Norman's head that sent a thrill of anger through his body. "*Excuse* me?"

"They're ground-pounders—support personnel," Ponce said, completely ignorant of Norman's shocked, quickly darkening expression. "They go home every night at seventeen hundred hours and they don't come to work until oh-seven-thirty. If they work on weekends, it's because there's a deployment or they want face time. They don't have to pull 'round-the-clock strip alert or fly four scrambles a day or emergency dispersals."

"Hey, Colonel, I've done plenty of all those things," Norman retorted angrily. "I've manned mobility lines seventy-two hours straight, processing the airmen at the end of the line who've been up working all night because all the flyers insisted on going first. I've worked lots of weekends in-processing new wing commanders who don't want to be bothered with paperwork or who want to get their TDY money as soon as they hit the base or their precious teak furniture from Thailand got a scratch on it during the move and they want to sue the movers. Just because you're a flyer doesn't mean you got the corner on dedication to duty."

Ponce glared at Norman, muttered something under his breath, and chomped on his cigar. Norman steeled himself for round two, but it didn't happen. "Fine, fine," Ponce said finally, turning away from Norman. "Vote the way you damned want."

Resolving the "gray area" candidates took an entire workday and a little bit of the evening, but they finished. The next morning seemed to come much too quickly. But it started a little differently—because General Ingemanson himself rolled a small file cabinet into the room. He carried a platter of breakfast burritos and other hot sandwiches from the dining hall atop the file cabinet.

"Good morning, good morning, folks," he said gaily. "I know you all worked real hard yesterday, and I didn't see most of you in the Club this morning, so I figured you probably skipped breakfast, so I brought it for you. Take a couple, grab some coffee, and get ready for the next evolution." Hungry full birds fairly leaped for the food.

When everyone was seated a few moments later, General Ingemanson stepped up to the head of the room, and said, "Okay, gang, let's begin. Since you worked hard yesterday to finish up your gray area candidates, you're a little ahead of the game, so I have a treat for you today.

"As you may or may not know, once a promotion board is seated, the Military Personnel Center and the Pentagon can pretty much use and abuse you any way they choose, which means they can use you for any other personnel or promotion tasks they wish. One such task is below-the-zone promotions. We're going to take two hundred majors who are two years below their primary promotion zone, score them, then combine them with the other selected candidates, resolve the gray areas, and pass their names along for promotion along with the others. This panel gets one hundred jackets."

"Shit-hot," Harry Ponce exclaimed. "We get our hands on the best of the best of the best."

"I don't fully understand, sir," Norman said, raising a hand almost as if he were in grade school. "What's the purpose of such a drastic promotion? Why do those officers get chosen so far ahead of their peers? It doesn't make sense to me. What did they do to deserve such attention?"

"As in all promotion boards, Colonel," Ingemanson replied, "the needs of the Air Force determine how and why officers get promoted. In this case, the powers that be determined that there should be a handful of individuals that represent the absolute best and most dedicated of the breed."

"But I still don't . . ."

"Generally, below-the-zone promotions are incentives for motivated officers to do even better," Ingemanson interrupted. "If you know that the Air Force will pick a handful above the rest, for those who care about things like that, it's their chance to work a little harder to make their jacket stand out. It's been my experience that generally the BTZ guys become the leaders in every organization."

"That's to be expected, I suppose," Norman said. "You give one person a gold star when everyone else gets silver stars, and the one with the gold star will start behaving like a standout, whether he really is or not. Classic group psychology. Is this what we want to do? Is this the message we want to send young officers in the Air Force?"

Ponce and some of the others rolled their eyes at that comment. Ingemanson smiled patiently and responded, "It sounds like a never-ending 'chicken-or-the-egg' argument, Colonel, which we won't get into here. I prefer to think of this as an opportunity to reward an officer whose qualities, leadership, and professionalism rise above the others. That's your task.

"Now, I must inform you that some of these jackets are marked 'classified,' " General Ingemanson went on. "There is nothing in these files more classified than 'NOFORN' and 'CONFIDENTIAL,' but be aware that these files do carry a security classification over and above a normal everyday personnel file. The files may contain pointers to other, more sensitive documents.

"Bottom line is, that factoid is none of your concern. You evaluate each candidate by the physical content of the file that you hold in your hands. You won't be given access to any other documents or records. You should not try to speculate on anything in the file that is not on a standard promotion board evaluation checklist. In other words, just because a candidate has annotations and pointers regarding classified records doesn't mean his file should be weighed any heavier than someone else, or because a candidate doesn't have any such annotations shouldn't count against him. Base your decisions on the content of the files alone. Got it?" Everyone nodded, even Norman, although he appeared as perplexed as before.

"Now, to save time, we do below-the-primary-zone selections a little differently," Ingemanson went on. "Everyone goes through the pile and gives a yes or no opinion of the candidate. The candidate needs four of seven 'yes' votes to go on to round two. This helps thin out the lineup so you can concentrate on the best possible candidates in a shorter period of time. Round two is precisely like a normal scoring routine—minimum six, maximum ten points, in half-point increments. Once we go through and score everyone, we'll resolve the gray areas, then put those candidates in with the other candidates, then rescore and resolve until we have our selectees. We should be finished by tomorrow. We present the entire list to the board on Thursday, get final approval, and sign the list Friday morning and send it off to the Pentagon. We're on the home stretch, boys. Any questions?"

"So what you're saying, sir," Norman observed, "is that these below-the-zone selectees could displace selectees that we've already chosen? That doesn't seem fair."

"That's a statement, not a question, Colonel," Ingemanson said. There was a slight ripple of laughter, but most of the panel members just wanted Norman to shut up. "You're right, of course, Colonel. The BTZ selectees will be so identified, and when their OSRs are compared with the other selectees, you panel members will be instructed that a BTZ selectee must really have an outstanding record in order to bump an in-the-primary-zone or above-the-primary-zone selectee. As you may or may not know, BTZ selectees usually represent less than three percent of all selectees, and it is not unusual for a board to select *no* BTZ candidates for promotion. But again, that's up to you. No more questions? Comments? Jokes?" Ingemanson did not give anyone a chance to reply. "Good. Have fun, get to work."

The Officer Selection Reports began their circulation around the table, each member receiving a stack of about fifteen. Norman was irked by having to do this chore, but he was intrigued as well. These guys must be really good, he thought, to be chosen for promotion so far ahead of their peers.

But upon opening his first folder, he was disappointed again. The photograph he saw was of a chunky guy with narrow, tense-looking blue eyes, a crooked nose, irregular cheeks and forehead, thin blond hair cut too short, uneven helmet-battered ears, a thick neck underneath a shirt that appeared too small for him, and a square but meaty jaw. He wore senior navigator's wings atop two and a half rows of ribbons—one of the smallest numbers of ribbons Norman had seen in six days of scrutinizing personnel files. The uniform devices appeared to be on straight, but the Class A uniform blouse looked as if it had a little white hanger rash on the shoulders, as if it had hung in the closet too long and had just been taken out for the photograph.

He was ready to vote "no" on this guy right away, but he didn't want to pass the folder too early, so he glanced at the Officer Effectiveness Reports. What in hell were they thinking—this guy wasn't anywhere ready to be promoted *two years* ahead of his peers! He had only been to *two* assignments in eight years, not including training schools. Up until recently, he was a line navigator—an instructor, yes, but still basically a line officer, virtually the same as a second lieutenant fresh out of tech school. Sure, he had won a bunch of trophies at the Strategic Air Command Giant Voice Bombing and Navigation Competition, and several raters had called him "the best bombardier in the nation, maybe the world."

But one rater, a year before he left his first PCS assignment, had only rated him "Above Average," not "Outstanding." He didn't have a "firewalled" OER. One of his last raters at his first assignment had said "A few improvements will result in one of the Air Force's finest aviators." Translation: He had problems that he apparently wasn't even trying to fix. He wasn't officer material, let alone a candidate for early promotion! He wasn't even promotable, let alone leadership material! How in the world did he even get promoted to major?

What else? A master's degree, yes, but only Squadron Officer School done, by correspondence—no advanced leadership schools. What in hell was he doing with his time? One temporary assignment with the U.S. Border Security Force—which went bust before the end of its third year, disgraced and discredited. His OERs at his second PCS assignment in Las Vegas were very good. His last OER had one three-star and two four-star raters—the four-star raters were the chief of staff of the Air Force and the chairman of the Joint Chiefs of Staff, a very impressive achievement. But there were very few details of exactly what he did there to deserve such high-powered raters. He had some of the shortest rater's comments Norman had ever seen—lots of "Outstanding officer," "Promote immediately," and "A real asset to the Air Force and the nation" type comments, but no specifics at all. His flying time seemed almost frozen—obviously he wasn't doing much flying. No flying, but no professional military schools? One temporary assignment, totally unrelated to his primary field? This guy was a joke.

And he didn't have a runner's chin. Norman could tell immediately if a guy took care of himself, if he cared about his personal health and appearance, by looking at the chin. Most runners had firm, sleek chins. Nonexercisers, especially nonrunners, had slack chins. Slack chins, slack attitudes, slack officers.

Norman marked Patrick S. McLanahan's BTZ score sheet with a big fat "No," and he couldn't imagine any other panel member, even Harry Ponce, voting to consider this guy for a BTZ promotion. Then, he had a better idea.

For the first time as a promotion board member, Norman withdrew an Air Force Form 772—"Recommendation for Dismissal Based on Substandard OSR," and he filled it out. A rated officer who didn't fly, who was obviously contently hiding out at some obscure research position in Las Vegas twiddling his thumbs, was not working in the best interest of the Air Force. This guy had almost nine years in service, but it was obvious that it would take him many, many years to be prepared to compete for promotion to lieutenant colonel. The Air Force had an "up or out" policy, meaning that you could be passed over for promotion to lieutenant colonel twice. After that, you had to be dismissed. The Air Force shouldn't wait for this guy to shape up. He was a waste of space.

A little dedication to yourself and dedication to the Air Force might help, Norman silently told the guy as he signed the AFF772, recommending that McLanahan be stripped of his regular commission and either sent back to the Reserves or, better, dismissed from service altogether. Try getting off your ass and do some running, for a start. Try to act like you give a damn . . .

Mother Nature picked that night to decide to dump an entire week's worth of rain on Diego Garcia—it was one of the worst tropical downpours anyone had seen on the little island in a long time. The British civilian contracted shuttle bus wasn't authorized to go on the southeast side of the runway, and Patrick wasn't going to wait for someone to pick him up, so he ran down the service road toward the Air Force hangar. He had already called ahead to the security police and control tower, telling them what he was going to do, but in the torrential storm, it was unlikely anyone in the tower could see him. Patrick made it to the outer perimeter fence to the Air Force hangar just as one of the security units was coming out in a Humvee to pick him up.

Patrick dashed through security in record time, then ran to the hangar to his locker for a dry flight suit. Inside he saw maintenance techs preparing both Megafortress flying battleships for fueling and weapons preloading. Patrick decided to grab his thermal underwear and socks too—it looked as if he might be going flying very soon.

"What happened?" Patrick asked as he trotted into the mission planning room.

"An American guided-missile cruiser, the USS *Percheron*, was transiting the Strait of Hormuz on its way into the Persian Gulf when it was attacked by several large missiles," Colonel John Ormack said. "Two of them missed, two were shot down, two were near misses, but two hit. The ship is still under way, but it's heavily damaged. Over a hundred casualties."

"Do they know who launched the missiles?"

"No idea," Ormack replied. "Debris suggests they were Iraqi. The missiles were fired from the south, across the Musandam Peninsula over Oman. The warhead size was huge—well over five hundred pounds each. AS-9 or AS-14 class."

"The *Percheron* couldn't tag the missiles?"

"They didn't see them until it was too late," Ormack reported. "They were diving right on top of the cruiser from straight overhead. They were already supersonic when they hit. No time to respond. The *Percheron* is a *California*-class cruiser, an older class of guided-missile cruiser—even though it was fitted with some of the latest radars, it wasn't exactly a spring chicken."

"I thought every ship going into the Gulf had to be updated with the best self-defense gear?"

"That's the Navy for you—they thought they had cleaned up the Gulf and could just waltz in with any old piece of shit they chose," Lieutenant General Brad Elliott interjected as he strode into the room. He glared at Patrick's wet hair and heavy breathing, and added, "You don't look very rested to me, Major. Where's Tork?"

"On her way, sir," Patrick replied. "I didn't wait for the SPs to come get me."

"I guess it's not a very good night for a romantic stroll on the beach anyway," Elliott muttered sarcastically. "I could've used both of you an hour ago."

"Sorry, sir." He wasn't really that sorry, but he tried to understand what kind of hell Brad had to be going through—stripped of the command that meant so much to him—and he felt sorry for Brad, not sorry that he wasn't there to help out.

"The Navy's officially started an investigation and is not speculating on what caused the explosions," Elliott went on. "Defense has leaked some speculation to the media that some older Standard SM-2 air-to-air missiles might have accidentally exploded in their magazines. Hard to come up with an excuse for an above-deck explosion in two different sections of the ship. No one is yet claiming responsibility for the attack.

"Unofficially, the Navy is befuddled. They had no warning of the attack until seconds before the missiles hit. No missile-launch detection from shore, no unidentified aircraft within a hundred miles of the cruiser, and no evidence of sub activity in the area. They were well outside the range of all known or suspected coast defense sites capable of launching a missile of that size. Guesses, anyone?"

"How about a stealth bomber, like the one we ran into?" Patrick replied.

"My thoughts exactly," Brad said. "The Defense Intelligence Agency has no information at all about Iran buying Blackjack bombers from Russia, or anything about Russia developing a bomber capable of launching air-to-air missiles. They got our report, but I think they'll disregard it."

"I wonder how much DIA knows about us and *our* capabilities?" Wendy asked.

"I think we've got to assume that Iran is flying that thing, and it's got to be neutralized before it does any more damage," Patrick said. "One more attack—especially on an aircraft carrier or other major warship—could spark a massive Middle East shooting war, bigger and meaner than the war with Iraq." He turned to Brad Elliott and said, "You've got to get us back in the fight, Brad. We're the only ones that can secretly take on that Blackjack battleship."

Elliott looked at Patrick with a mixture of surprise, humor, and anger. "Major, are you suggesting that we—dare I even say it?—launch *without* proper authorization?" he asked.

"I'm suggesting that perhaps we should follow orders and return the Megafortresses to Dreamland," Patrick said. "But I don't recall any specific instructions about a specific route of flight we should take."

"You think it makes any sense for us to fly from Diego Garcia all the way to the Strait of Hormuz and tell the Pentagon we were on the way back to Nevada?" Brad asked, a twinkle of humor in his eyes.

"We always file a 'due regard' point in our flight plans, which means we disappear from official view until we're ready to reenter American airspace," Patrick said. Classified military flights, such as spy plane or nuclear-weapon ferry flights, never filed a detailed point-by-point route flight plan—they always had a "due regard" point, a place where the flight plan was suspended, the rest of the flight secret. In effect, the flight "disappears" from official or public purview. The flight simply checks in with authorities at a specific place and time to reactivate the flight plan, with no official query about where it was or what it did. "Even the Pentagon doesn't know where we go. And our tankers belong to us, so we don't have to coordinate with any outside agencies for refueling support. If we, for example, fly off to Nevada and, say, develop an in-flight emergency six hours in the mission and decide to head on back to Diego Garcia, I don't think the Air Force or the Pentagon can blame us for that, can they?"

"I don't see how they can," John Ormack said, smiling mischievously. "And we very well can't fly a Megafortress into Honolulu, can we?"

"And in five hours, we can be back on patrol over the Strait of Hormuz," Wendy Tork said. "We know what that Blackjack looks like on our sensors. We keep an eye on him and jump him if he tries to make another move." Everyone on the crew was getting into it now.

"In the meantime, we get full authorization to conduct a search-and-destroy mission over the Strait of Hormuz for the mysterious Soviet-Iranian attack plane," Patrick said. "If we don't get it, we land back here at Diego, get 'fixed,' and return to Dreamland. We've done all we can do."

"Sounds like a plan to me," Brad Elliott said, beaming proudly and clasping Patrick on the shoulder. "Let's work up a weapons list, get our guys busy loading gas and missiles, and let's get this show on the road!" As they all got busy, Brad stepped over to Patrick, and said in a low voice, "Nice to be working together with you again, Muck."

"Same here, Brad," Patrick said. Finally, thankfully, the old connection between them was back. It was more than reestablishing crew connectivity—they were back to trusting and believing in one another again.

"Any idea how we're going to find this mystery Iranian Megafortress?" Brad asked. "We've only got one chance, and we have no idea where this guy's based, what his next target is, or even if he really exists."

"He exists, all right," Patrick said. He studied the intelligence reports Elliott had brought into the mission-planning room for a moment. "We must have a couple dozen ships down there protecting the *Percheron*."

"I think the Navy's going to move a carrier battle group to escort the cruiser back to Bahrain."

"A carrier, huh?" Patrick remarked. "A cruiser is a good target, but a carrier would be a great target. Iraq made no secret of the fact they wanted to tag a carrier in the Gulf. Maybe Iran would like to claim that trophy."

"Maybe—especially if they could pin the blame on Iraq," Brad said. "But that still doesn't solve our problem: How do we find this mystery attack plane? The chances of him and us being in the same sky at the same time is next to impossible."

"I see only one way to flush him out," Patrick said. "It'll still be a one-in-a-thousand chance, but if he's up flying, I think we can make him come to us."

At over three hundred tons gross weight and with a wingspan longer than the Wright Brothers' first flight, the Tupolev-160 long-range supersonic bomber, code-named "Blackjack" by the West, was the largest attack plane in the world. It carried more than its own empty weight in fuel and almost its own weight in weapons, and it was capable of delivering any weapon in the Soviet arsenal, from dumb bombs to multimegaton gravity weapons and cruise missiles, with pinpoint precision. It could fly faster than the speed of sound up to sixty thousand feet, or at treetop level over any terrain, in any weather, day or night. Although only forty Blackjack bombers had been built, they represented the number one air-breathing military threat to the West.

But as deadly as the Tu-160 Blackjack was, there was one plane even deadlier: the Tupolev-160E. The stock Blackjack's large steel and titanium vertical stabilizer had been replaced by a low, slender V-tail made of composite materials, stronger but more lightweight and radar-absorbing than steel. Much of the skin not exposed to high levels of heat in supersonic flight was composed of radar-absorbent material, and the huge engine air inlets for the four Kuznetsov NK-32 afterburning engines had been redesigned so the engines' compressor blades wouldn't reflect radar energy. Even the jet's steeply raked cockpit windscreens had been specially shaped and coated to misdirect and absorb radar energy. All this helped to reduce the radar cross section of this giant bird to one-fourth of the stock aircraft's size.

The only thing that spoiled the Blackjack-E's sleek, stealthy needle-like appearance was a triangular fairing mounted under the forward bomb bay and a smaller fairing atop the fuselage that carried the aircraft's phase-array air and surface search radars. The multimode radar electronically scanned both the sky and the sea for aircraft and ships, and passed the information both to allied ground, surface, and airborne units, as well as automatically programming its attack and defensive weapons.

The Blackjack-E and its weaponry were the latest in Soviet military technology—but that meant little to a starving, nearly bankrupt nation on the verge of total collapse. The weapon system was far more useful to the Soviet Union as a commodity—and they found a willing buyer in the Islamic Republic of Iran. Still oil-rich—and, with the rise in oil prices because of the war, growing richer by the day—but with a badly shaved-back military following the devastating nine-year Iran-Iraq War, Iran needed to rebuild its arsenal quickly and effectively. Money was no object. The faster they could build an arsenal that could project power throughout the entire Middle East, the faster they could claim the title of the most powerful military force in the region, a force that had to be reckoned with in any dealings involving trade, commerce, land, religion, or legal rights in the Persian Gulf.

The Blackjack-E was the answer. The bomber was capable against air, ground, and surface targets; it was fast, it had the range to strike targets as far away as England without aerial refueling, and it carried a huge attack payload. After watching the Americans destroy nearly half of the vaunted Iraqi army with precision-guided weapons, the Iranians were positive they had spent their money wisely—any warplane they invested in had to be stealthy, had to be fast, had to have all-weather capability, and had to have precision-guided attack capability, or it was virtually useless over today's high-tech battlefield. The Russians were selling—not just the planes, but the weapons, the support equipment, and Russian instructors and technicians—and the Iranians were eagerly buying.

The USS *Percheron* was the first operational test of the new attack platform. A large American warship, transiting the shallow, congested, narrow waters of the Strait of Hormuz alone, was an inviting target. The *Percheron* was a good test case because its long-range sensors and defensive armament were highly capable, some of the best in the world against all kinds of air, surface, and subsurface threats. If the Blackjack-E could penetrate the *Percheron*'s defenses, it was indeed a formidable weapon.

The test was a rousing success. The Blackjack-E's crew—an Iranian pilot as aircraft commander, a Russian instructor pilot in the copilot's seat, two Iranian officers as bombardier and defensive-systems officer, and one Russian systems instructor in a jump seat between the Iranian systems officers—launched their entire warload of six Kh-29 external missiles—painted and modified with Iraqi Air Force markings—from maximum range and medium altitude. The missiles dived to sea-skimming altitude, then popped up to five hundred meters when only five kilometers from their targets and then dived straight down at their target. Two of the missiles missed the cruiser by less than a half a kilometer; two made direct hits. The explosions could be seen and heard by observers twenty kilometers away. Although the *Percheron* was still able to get under way, it was certainly out of action.

This time, however, the Blackjack-E would have a full weapons load. This would be the ultimate test. On this flight, the Blackjack-E was loaded for a multirole hunter-killer mission. In the aft bomb bay, it carried a rotary launcher with twelve Kh-15 solid-rocket attack missiles. Each missile had a top speed of Mach 5—five times the speed of sound—a range of almost ninety miles when launched from high altitude, and a three-hundred-and-fifty-pound high-explosive warhead. The missiles, covered with a rubbery skin that burned off while in flight, were targeted by the Blackjack's navigator by radar, or they would automatically attack large ships using its onboard radar, or home in on preprogrammed enemy radar emissions. Designed to destroy target defenses and attack targets well beyond surface-to-air missile range, the Kh-15s were unjammable, almost invisible to radar, and almost impossible to intercept or shoot down.

Externally, the Blackjack-E carried eight R-40 long-range air-to-air missiles, four under the attach point of each swiveling wing; two of the missiles on each wing were radar-guided missiles and two were heat-seeking missiles. It was the first Soviet heavy bomber to carry air-to-air missiles. Also under each wing were two Kh-29 multirole attack missiles, which had a range of sixteen miles, a top speed of just over Mach 2, and a massive six-hundred-pound high-explosive warhead. The Kh-29 was steered to its target by a TV datalink, giving it a precision-guided capability day or night or in poor weather, or it would home in on enemy radar emissions. Once locked on to its target, the Kh-29 would automatically fly an evasive sea-skimming or ballistic trajectory, depending on the target, followed by a steep dive into its target. The Kh-29 was designed to deliver a killing blow to almost any size target, even a large surface vessel, underground command post, bridges, and large industrial buildings and factories.

As predicted, the Americans erected an air umbrella around the stricken USS *Percheron* to protect it against sneak attacks. Because it was the closest, they moved CV-41, the venerable USS *Midway*, and its eight-ship escort group south to cover the *Percheron*'s crippled retreat. The *Midway*, the oldest carrier in active service in the U.S. fleet and the only carrier homeported on foreign soil, was overdue for decommissioning and reserve duty when Operation Desert Shield began. It was sent to the Persian Gulf and played mostly a short-range land-attack role with its three squadrons of F/A-18 Hornet fighter-bombers and one squadron of A-6 Intruder bombers.

If there was more time, or the need to get the crippled ship out of harm's way not so pressing, the Navy would have chosen another ship to protect the *Percheron*. The *Midway* was the lightest armed ship for self-defense, with only two Sea Sparrow surface-to-air missile launchers, two Phalanx close-in Gatling gun systems, and no F-14 Tomcat fighters for long-range defense—it relied heavily on its escorts for protection. It had little up-to-date radars and electronic-countermeasure equipment, since it was on its way to reserve status before the start of the war. The second carrier battle group stationed in the Persian Gulf, the USS *America*, maintained its patrol in the northern half of the Gulf, about two hundred and fifty miles away—too far from *Midway* to be of any help in case some disaster took place.

The Blackjack-E, call sign Lechtvar ("Teacher"), launched from its secret base near Mashhad, about six hundred kilometers east of Tehran, using an Iran Air, the official Iranian government airline, flight number. It followed the commercial air-traffic route, overflying the Persian Gulf and central Saudi Arabia on its way to Jiddah, Saudi Arabia. In late February, with air superiority established over the entire region and no threat from Iraq's air force, the Coalition forces agreed to reopen commercial air routes from Iran and other Islamic countries to the east into Jiddah to accommodate pilgrims visiting the Muslim holy cities of Mecca and Medina. As long as a flight plan was on file and the flight followed a strict navigation corridor, overflying Saudi Arabia was permitted during the conflict.

The flight was handed off from Riyadh Air Traffic Control Center to Jiddah Approach, just before coming within range of American naval radar systems operating in the Red Sea. As it descended over the Hijaz Mountains south of Jiddah, the Blackjack-E bomber crew activated their terrain-following radar system, deactivated its transponder radar tracking system, and descended below radar coverage in less than two minutes. The crew allowed a few seconds of a "7700" transponder signal—the international code for Emergency—before shutting off all radios and external lights completely and descending into the mountains. Within moments, the flight had completely disappeared from radar screens.

Saudi and Coalition rescue teams, both civilian and military, immediately started fanning out from Jiddah south to the suspected crash site. But by the time the rescuers launched, the Blackjack-E was already far to the east, speeding across the deserts of the central Arabian Peninsula.

As the Blackjack-E sped across the sands and desolate high plains of eastern Saudi Arabia, air-defense radar sites began popping up all across their intended route of flight. It seemed as if there was a surface-to-air missile site stationed every forty of fifty miles apart along the Persian Gulf from Al-Khasab on the tip of Cape Shuraytah in Oman all the way to Kuwait City, with more sprinkles of air-defense radars on warships on or over the Persian Gulf itself. But the sites that were the most dangerous threat to the Blackjack-E—the various Coalition Patriot, Rapier, and Hawk antiaircraft batteries—were all fixed sites, and their precise locations had been known for weeks—they would make easy targets. In addition, although all of them were capable of attacking targets in any direction, they were set up and oriented to attack targets flying in from the Persian Gulf or Strait of Hormuz, not from the Arabian Peninsula. There were a few scattered mobile antiaircraft artillery emplacements, and the shipborne Aegis, Standard, and Sea Wolf antiaircraft missile systems represented a significant threat, but those would not be able to engage a fast-moving low-flying stealthy target in time.

Just before starting its attack, the Blackjack-E accelerated to just under supersonic speed—it was now traveling more than a mile every ten seconds. From fifty miles away, the Blackjack-E crew launched inertially guided Kh-15 missiles against the known antiaircraft emplacements in the United Arab Emirates. As the plane sped closer, it polished off any remaining antiaircraft radar sites with radar-homing Kh-15 missiles. As the bomber neared the United Arab Emirates coastline heading east, many radar sites saw the big bomber coming, but before they could direct their missile units to fire, the Kh-15 missiles were blowing the radars and communications nets off the air. Coalition air-defense fighters based all up and down the Persian Gulf, from half a dozen bases, launched in hot pursuit. The aircraft carrier *Midway* had ten F/A-18 Hornet fighter-bombers in air-defense configuration airborne in combat air patrols all around the carrier group, and it quickly launched another pair and prepared more launches, even though no one had a definite fix on the unknown aircraft.

The biggest threat to the Blackjack-E crew, however, was the French-made Mirage 5 and Mirage 2000 air-defense fighters based in Dubai. One Mirage 2000 acquired the Blackjack shortly after liftoff along with his wingman, but it was blown out of the sky by a radar-guided R-40 missile before the Mirage could even complete its first vector to the bandit. The second Mirage disengaged when he saw his leader explode in a ball of fire, and by the time he was ready to pursue and engage again, the Blackjack-E was almost out of radar range and on its missile attack run against the USS *Midway*.

The gauntlet was squeezing tighter and tighter on the Blackjack-E, but it was still heading for its target. The crew accelerated to supersonic speed, staying less than one hundred feet above the dark, shallow waters of the Persian Gulf as the bomber closed in on its quarry. The Blackjack climbed higher only to launch Kh-15 radar-homing missiles on the greatest threats in front of them, the *Perry*-class guided-missile frigate guarding the *Midway*'s western flank. It took five Kh-15 missiles fired at the frigate to finally shut its missile-search-and-guidance radars down. The *Midway*'s Hornets' APG-65 attack radar was not a true look-down, shoot-down-capable system; although F/A-18 Hornets had the Navy's first two aerial kills of the Gulf War, the fighter was designed primarily as a medium bomber and attack plane, not as a low-altitude interceptor. Three Hornets took beyond-visual-range shots at the Blackjack with AIM-7 radar-guided Sparrow missiles, and all missed.

Strange, the Blackjack crew remarked to themselves—the Americans were all around them, taking long-range shots but not pressing the attack. It was a stiff defense, but not nearly as severe as they expected. Why . . . ?

But it didn't matter—now there was nothing to stop the Blackjack-E. At three minutes to launch point, the Blackjack's attack radar had locked on to the *Midway* and fed inertial guidance information to the four Kh-29 attack missiles. The final launch countdown was under way . . .

The UHF GUARD radio channel had been alive for several minutes with warnings from American and Gulf Cooperative Council air-defense networks in English, French, Arabic, and Farsi, demanding that the unidentified aircraft leave the area. The Blackjack crew ignored it . . .

. . . until new warning messages in English on both UHF and VHF emergency radio channels began: "Unidentified intruder, unidentified intruder, this is the Islamic Republic of Iran Army Air Defense Network command center, you are in violation of sovereign Iranian airspace. You are directed to leave the area immediately or you will be attacked without warning. Repeat, reverse course and leave the area immediately!"

The Iranian pilot in command of the Blackjack-E bomber looked at the Russian copilot in surprise. "What is happening?" he asked in English, their common language.

"Ignore it!" the Russian shouted. "We are on the attack run, and we still have many American warships to contend with. Stay . . ."

"Attention, attention, all air-defense units, this is Abbass Control," they heard in Farsi, "implement full air-defense configuration protocols, repeat, full air-defense protocols, all stations acknowledge." The message was repeated; then, in Farsi, Arabic, and English, they heard, "Warning, warning, warning, to all aircraft on this frequency, this is the

Islamic Republic of Iran Army Air Defense Network, full air-defense emergency restrictions are in effect for the Tehran and Bandar Abbass Flight Information Regions, repeat, full air-defense emergency restrictions are now in effect. All aircraft, establish positive radio contact and identification with your controller immediately. All unidentified aircraft in the Tehran and Bandar Abbass Flight Information Regions may be fired upon without warning!"

"What should we do?" the Iranian bombardier asked. "Should we ask . . . ?"

"We maintain radio silence!" the Russian shouted. "The Americans can home in on the briefest radio transmission! Stay on the attack run!"

"Our Mode Two—should we transmit?" the defensive-systems officer asked. The Mode Two was an encrypted identification signal. Although it could only be decoded by Iranian air-defense sites, transmitting any radio signals was dangerous over enemy territory, so they had it deactivated.

"*No!*" the Russian responded. "Pay attention to the attack run! Ignore what is happening . . ."

Just then, they saw a bright flash of light far off on the horizon. The weather was ideal, cloudy and cool, with no thunderstorms predicted. That wasn't lightning.

"Did you get the transfer-alignment maneuver yet, bombardier?" the Russian systems officer instructor asked.

"I . . . no, I have not," the Iranian bombardier replied, still distracted by what was happening over his own country. The transfer-alignment maneuver was a required gyroscopic routine that removed the last bit of inertial drift from their missiles' guidance system.

"Then get busy! Program it in and inform the crew. You had better hurry before . . ."

"Birjand Four-Oh-Four flight, cancel takeoff clearance!" the Blackjack crew heard on the emergency channel in Farsi. "Maliz Three, hold your position, emergency vehicles en route, passing on your right side. Attention all aircraft, emergency evacuation procedure in effect, report to your shelter assignments immediately."

"Shelter assignments?" the defensive systems officer shouted. "It sounds like one of our bases is under air attack!"

"I don't understand what you're saying!" the Russian copilot shouted. "But ignore any radio messages you are hearing. They could be fake messages. Stay on the attack run!"

But the defensive-systems officer couldn't ignore it. He switched his radio over to the tactical command frequency: "Abbass Control, Abbass

Control, this is Lechtvar, we copy your emergency reports, requesting vectors to last-known position of enemy aircraft. We are able to respond. Over." No response, just more emergency messages. "Abbass Control, this is Lechtvar, we are en route to your location, sixty miles southwest, request you pass vectors to enemy aircraft, we can respond! Over! Respond!"

"Damn your eyes, I said stay off the radios!" the Russian pilot shouted. "Don't you understand, the Americans can track your transmissions! Now get back on the attack run! That's an order!"

But just then they heard in English on their own tactical command frequency: "Attention, Iranian Blackjack bomber, this is your old friend from the Strait from last week. Do you recognize my voice?"

The Iranian pilot of the Blackjack-E was stunned. It was the same voice that had contacted them, the unidentified American military flight!

"Calling Abbass Control," they heard an Iranian voice say in English, "this is an official military frequency. Do not use this frequency. It is a violation of international law. Vacate this frequency immediately."

"Abbass Control, this is Lechtvar," the Iranian Blackjack pilot called. "We copied your emergency evacuation messages. Give us vectors to the enemy aircraft and we will respond immediately."

"Lechtvar, this is Abbass Control, negative!" the confused controller replied after a few moments. "We detected some unidentified aircraft, and then a flare was set off over the Strait. But there are no Iranian installations under attack and no one has implemented any evacuation procedures. Clear this channel immediately!"

The Blackjack crew finally realized they had been tricked. The crew was stunned into embarrassed silence. The Russian crew members cursed loud enough in Russian to be heard without the interphones—they realized that their chances of surviving this mission suddenly went from very good to very poor. The bombardier directed the transfer-alignment maneuver, a forty-five-degree left turn followed by two more turns back to course—all missiles were fully functional and . . .

"Hey, Blackjack. We know you're up here listening to us. We'll have you on our radar any second now. You'll never finish your attack. Why not forget about the carrier and come get us? We're waiting for you."

It was impossible! The mystery plane was back—and they knew all about their mission! How was that possible? How could they . . . ?

Suddenly, the radar-warning indicators blared a warning—an enemy airborne radar had swept across them. Seconds later, with sixty seconds to launch, the radar-warning receiver indicated a radar lock. They had been found! The Blackjack's radar jammers were functioning perfectly, but they were unable to keep the enemy tracking radar from completely breaking lock—it changed frequencies too fast and changed in such a broad range that the Blackjack's trackbreakers could not quite keep up.

"Got ya, Blackjack," the American said. "You're not as stealthy tonight as last time. You must be carrying some heavy iron tonight. Got some more air-to-air missiles loaded up tonight? Maybe a few big antiship missiles? Why don't you just jettison all that deadweight and come on up here and let's you and me finish this thing, once and for all?"

"We must break off the attack," the Iranian defensive-systems officer shouted. "If they have us on radar, they can vector in the other fighters. We'll be surrounded in seconds."

"Process the launch!" the Russian mission commander shouted. "Ignore this American bastard! He did not attack us before—perhaps he cannot stop us."

As if they could hear their interphone conversation, the American said, "Hey, Blackjack, you better bug out now. I just relayed your position to my little buddies, the F/A-18 Hornets from the *Midway*. They're not very happy that you've come to try to blow up their ship. In about two minutes you'll have an entire squadron of Hornets on your ass."

The Iranian pilot could no longer contain his anger. He opened the channel to the GUARD frequency and mashed his mike button: "You cowardly pig-bastard! If you want us, come and get us!"

"Hey, there you are, Blackjack," the American said happily. "Nice to talk to you again."

"You know who I am—who are you?"

"I'm the pig-bastard at your two o'clock position and closing fast," the American replied. "I'll bet my interceptor missiles are faster and have longer range than your attack missiles—I'll reach my firing point in about ten seconds. You don't want to die flying straight and level, do you? C'mon up here and let's get it on."

"You will never stop us!" the Iranian shouted.

"Oops—I think I overestimated our firing point. Here they come." And just then, the radar-warning receiver blared a shrill MISSILE LAUNCH warning—the Americans had fired radar-guided missiles!

The Russian pilot reacted instinctively. He immediately started a shallow climb and a steep right bank into the oncoming missiles. "Chaff! Chaff!" he shouted; then: "Launch the Kh-29s! *Now!*"

"We are not in range!" the bombardier shouted.

"Launch anyway!" the Russian ordered. "We will not get another chance! Launch!" The bombardier immediately commanded the Kh-29 missiles to launch. The missiles all had solid lock-ons, and with the slightly greater altitude, the Kh-29s had a little greater range . . . it might be enough to score a hit.

"They launched missiles!" Patrick shouted. The Megafortress's attack radar, a derivative of the APG-71 radar from the F-15E Eagle, immediately detected the big Kh-29 missiles speeding toward the *Midway*. "I got four big missiles, very low altitude, going supersonic. Wendy . . . ?"

"I got 'em," Wendy Tork reported. The APG-71 weapon system had immediately passed targeting information to Wendy's defensive system, and all Wendy had to do was launch-commit her AIM-120 Scorpion missiles. "We're at extreme range—I'm going to have to ripple off all our Scorpions. Give me forty right and full military power."

As Brad Elliott followed Wendy's orders, the fire-control computers went to work. Within twenty seconds, eight Scorpions fired off into space. At first they used the Megafortress's attack radar for guidance, but soon they activated their own active radars and tracked the Russian missiles with ease. All four Kh-29 missiles were shot down long before they reached the *Midway*.

"Splash four missiles," Wendy reported. "But we're in trouble now—we used up all our defensive missiles." And, as if the Blackjack crew heard them, Wendy saw that the Iranian attack plane was turning very, very quickly—heading right for them. "We got a big, big bandit at fifteen miles, low. He . . ." Just then, the EB-52C's threat-warning receiver issued a RADAR WARNING, a MISSILE WARNING, and a MISSILE LAUNCH warning in rapid succession. *"Break right!"* Wendy shouted. "Stingers coming on-line! Chaff!"

The Soviet-made R-40 missiles were well within their maximum range, and the Blackjack's big fire-control radar had a solid lock-on. The Megafortress's rear-defense fire-control radar locked on to the incoming missiles and started firing Stinger airmine rockets, but this time they couldn't score a hit. One R-40 missile was decoyed enough for a near miss, but a second R-40 scored a hit, blowing off the left V-tail stabilator on the Megafortress and shelling out two engines on the left side.

The force of the explosion and the sudden loss of the two left engines threw the Megafortress into a jaw-snapping left swerve so violent that the big bomber almost succeeded in swapping nose for tail. Only Brad Elliott's and John Ormack's superior airmanship and familiarity with the EB-52C Megafortress saved the crew. They knew enough not to automatically jam on full power on all the operating engines, which would have certainly sent them into a violent, unrecoverable flat Frisbee-like spin—instead, they had to *pull* power on the right side back to match the left, trade precious altitude so they could gain some even more precious flying airspeed, recover control, and only then start feeding in power slowly and carefully. The automatic fire-suppression systems on the Megafortress shut down the engines and cut off fuel, preventing a fatal fire and explosion. They lost two hundred knots and five thousand feet of altitude before the bomber was actually flying in some semblance of coordinated flight and was not on the verge of spiraling into the Persian Gulf.

But the Megafortress was a sitting duck for the speedy Blackjack bomber. "His airspeed has dropped off to less than five hundred kilometers per hour," the defensive-systems officer reported as he studied his fire-control radar display. "He has dropped to one thousand meters, twelve o'clock, ten miles. He is straight and level—not maneuvering. I think he's hit!"

"Then finish him off," the Iranian pilot shouted happily. "Finish him, and let's get out of here!"

"Stand by for missile launch!" the defensive-systems officer said. "Two missiles locked on . . . ready . . . ready . . . *launch*! Missiles . . ."

He never got to finish that sentence. A fraction of a second before the two R-40 missiles left their rails, three pairs of AIM-9 Sidewinder heat-seeking missiles from three pursuing F/A-18 Hornet fighters from the USS *Midway* plowed into the Blackjack-E bomber, fired from less than five miles away. They had used guidance information from the as-yet-unknown but friendly aircraft, so were able to conduct the intercept and lock on to the enemy attack plane without having to use their telltale airborne radars. The Sidewinders turned the Blackjack's four huge turbofan engines into four massive clouds of fire that completely engulfed, then devoured the big jet. The pieces of Blackjack bomber not incinerated in the blast were scattered across over thirty square miles of the Persian Gulf and disappeared from sight forever.

"Hey, buddy, this is Dragon Four-Zero-Zero," the lead F/A-18 Hornet pilot radioed on the UHF GUARD channel. "You still up?"

"Roger," Brad Elliott replied. "We saw that bandit coming in to finish us off. I take it we're still alive because you nailed his ass."

"That's affirmative," the Hornet pilot replied happily. "We saw the hit you took. You need an escort back to King Khalid Military City?"

"Negative," Brad replied. "That's not our destination. We've got a tanker en route that'll take us home."

"You sure, buddy? If you're not going to KKMC, it's a long and dangerous drive to anywhere else."

"Thanks, but we'll limp on outta here by ourselves," Brad replied. "Thank for clearing our six."

"Thank you for protecting our home plate, buddy," the Hornet pilot responded. "We owe you big-time, whoever you are. Dragon flight, out."

Brad Elliott scanned his instruments for the umpteenth time that minute. Everything had stabilized. They were in a slow climb, less than three hundred feet a minute, nursing every bit of power from the remaining engines. "Well, folks," he announced on interphone, "we're still flying, our refueling system is operable, and we've still got most essential systems. I want everyone in exposure suits. If we have to ditch, it's going to be a very, very long time before anyone picks us up. Might as well get up and stretch a bit—at this airspeed, it's going to be a real long flight back to Diego Garcia."

"The good news is," John Ormack interjected, "the weather report looks pretty good. I can't think of a nicer place to be stuck at fixing our bird."

"Amen," Brad Elliott agreed. He waited a few moments; then, not hearing any other comments, added, "You agree, Muck, Wendy? Can you use a few weeks on Diego while our guys fix us up? Patrick? Wendy? You copy?"

Patrick let his lips slowly part from Wendy's. He returned once more for another quick kiss, then drank in Wendy's dancing eyes and heavenly smile as he moved his oxygen mask to his face, and replied, "That sounds great to me, sir. Absolutely great."

"Ladies and gentlemen, thank you for your time, energy, dedication, and professionalism," Major General Larry Dean Ingemanson said. He stood before the last assembly of the entire promotion board in the Selection Board Secretariat's main auditorium. "The final selection list has been checked and verified by the Selection Board Secretariat staff—it just awaits my final signature before I transmit the list to the Secretary of the Air Force. But I know some of you have planes to catch and golf games to catch up on, so I wanted to say 'thank you' once again. I hope we meet again. The board is hereby adjourned." There was a relieved round of applause from the board members, but most were up and out of their seats in a flash, anxious to get out of that building and away from OSRs and official photographs and sitting in judgment of men and women they did not know, deciding their futures.

Norman Weir felt proud of himself and his performance as a member of the board. He was afraid he'd be intimidated by the personalities he'd encountered, afraid he wouldn't match up to their experience and knowledge and backgrounds. Instead, he discovered that he was just as knowledgeable and authoritative as any other "war hero" in the place, even guys like Harry Ponce. When it came to rational, objective decision-making, Norman felt he had an edge over all of them, and that made him feel pretty damned special.

As he walked toward the exits, he heard someone call his name. It was General Ingemanson. They had not spoken to one another since Ingemanson accepted the Form 772 on McLanahan, recommending he be dismissed from the active-duty Air Force. Ingemanson had requested additional information, a few more details on Norman's observations. Norman had plenty of reasons, more than enough to justify his decision. General Ingemanson accepted his additional remarks with a serious expression and promised he'd upchannel the information immediately.

He did warn Norman that a Form 772 would probably push the candidate completely out of the running for promotion, not just for this board but for any other promotion board he might meet. Norman stuck to his guns, and Ingemanson had no choice but to continue the process. McLanahan's jacket disappeared from the panel's deliberation, and Norman did not see his name on the final list.

Mission accomplished. Not only strike back at the pompous prima donnas that wore wings, but rid the Air Force of a true example of a lazy, selfish, good-for-nothing officer.

"Hey, Colonel, just wanted to say good-bye and thank you again for your service," General Ingemanson said, shaking Norman's hand warmly. "I had a great time working with you."

"It was my pleasure, sir. I enjoyed working with you too."

"Thank you," Ingemanson said. "And call me 'Swede'—everybody does." Norman said nothing. "Do you have a minute? I'm about ready to countersign your Form 772 to include in the transmission to the Secretary of the Air Force, and I wanted to give you an opportunity to look over my report that goes along with your 772."

"Is that necessary, sir?" Norman asked. "I've already put everything on the 772. McLanahan is a disgrace to the uniform and should be discharged. The Reserves don't even deserve an officer like that. I think I've made it clear."

"You have," Ingemanson said. "But I do want you to look at my evaluation. You can append any rebuttal comments to it if you wish. It'll only take a minute." With a confused and slightly irritated sigh, Norman nodded and followed the general to his office.

If Norman saw the man in a plain dark suit sitting in the outer office behind the door talking into his jacket sleeve, he didn't pay any attention to him. General Ingemanson led the way into his office, motioned Norman inside, and then closed the door behind him. This time, Norman did notice the second plain-clothed man with the tiny silver badge on his lapel and the earpiece stuck in his right ear, standing beside Ingemanson's desk.

"What's going on, General?" Norman asked. "Who is this?"

"This is Special Agent Norris, United States Secret Service, Presidential Protection Detail," General Ingemanson replied. "He and his colleagues are here because that man sitting in my chair is the President of the United States." Norman nearly fell over backwards in surprise as he saw the President of the United States himself swivel around and rise up from the general's chair.

"Smooth introduction, Swede," the President said. "Very smooth."

"I try my best, Mr. President."

The President stepped from behind Ingemanson's desk, walked up to the still-dumbfounded Norman Weir, and extended a hand. "Colonel Weir, nice to meet you." Norman didn't quite remember shaking hands. "I was on my way to Travis Air Force Base in California to meet with some of the returning Desert Storm troops, and I thought it was a good idea to make a quick, unofficial stopover here at Randolph to talk with you."

Norman's eyes grew as wide as saucers. "Talk to . . . *me*?"

"Sit down, Colonel," the President said. He leaned against Ingemanson's desk as Norman somehow found a chair. "I was told that you wish to file a recommendation that a Major Patrick McLanahan should be discharged from the Air Force on the basis of a grossly substandard and unacceptable Officer Selection Record. Is that right?"

This was the grilling he'd expected from Harry Ponce or General Ingemanson—Norman never believed he'd get it from *the President of the United States*! "Yes . . . yes, sir," Norman replied.

"Still feel pretty strongly about that? A little time to think about it hasn't changed your opinion at all?"

Even though Norman was still shocked by the encounter, now a bunch of his resolve and backbone started to return. "I still feel very strongly that the Air Force should discharge Major McLanahan. His background and experience suggests an officer that just wants to coast through his career, without one slight suggestion that he has or wants to do anything worth contributing to the Air Force or his country."

"I see," the President said. He paused for a moment, looked Norman right in the eye, and said, "Colonel, I want you to tear up that form."

"*Excuse* me?"

"I want you to drop your indictment."

"If you drop your affidavit, Colonel," Ingemanson interjected, "McLanahan will be promoted to lieutenant colonel two years below the primary zone."

"What?" Norman retorted. "You can't . . . I mean, you shouldn't do that! McLanahan has the worst effectiveness report I've seen! He shouldn't even be a major, let alone a lieutenant colonel!"

"Colonel, I can't reveal too much about this," the President said, "but I can tell you that Patrick McLanahan has a record that goes way beyond his official record. I can tell you that not only does he deserve to be a lieutenant colonel, he probably deserves to be a four-star general with a ticker-tape parade down the Canyon of Heroes. Unfortunately, he'll never get that opportunity, because the things he's involved in . . . well, we prefer no one find out about them. We can't even decorate him, because the citations that accompany the awards would reveal too much. The best we can do for him in an official manner is to promote him at every possible opportunity. That's what I'm asking you to do, as a favor to me."

"A . . . favor?" Norman stammered. "Why do you need me to agree to anything? You're the commander in chief—why don't you just use your authority and give him a promotion?"

"Because I'd prefer not to disrupt the normal officer selection board process as much as possible," the President replied.

"The President knows that only a board member can change his rating of a candidate," Ingemanson added. "Not even the President has the legal authority to change a score. McLanahan received a high enough score to earn a below-the-zone promotion—only the 772 stands in his way. The President is asking you to remove that last obstacle."

"But how? How can McLanahan possibly earn a high enough rating?"

"Because the other board members recognized something that exists in Patrick McLanahan that you apparently didn't, Colonel," the President replied. "Great officers exhibit leadership potential in many other ways than just attending service schools, dress, and appearance, and how many different assignments they've had. I look for officers who perform. True, Patrick hasn't filled the squares that other candidates have, but if you read the personnel file a little closer, a little differently, you'll see an officer that exhibits his leadership potential by doing his job and leading the way for others."

The President took the Form 772 from Ingemanson and extended it to Norman. "Trust me, Colonel," he said. "He's a keeper. Someday I'll explain some of the things this young man has done for our nation.

But his future is in your hands—I won't exercise whatever authority I have over you. It's your decision."

Norman thought about it for a few long moments, then reached out, took the Form 772, and ripped it in two.

The President shook his hand warmly. "Thank you, Colonel," he said. "That meant a lot to me. I promise you, you won't regret your decision."

"I hope not, sir."

The President shook hands and thanked General Ingemanson, then stepped toward the door. Just before the Secret Service agent opened it for him, he turned back toward Norman, and said, "You know, Colonel, I'm impressed."

"Sir?"

"Impressed with you," the President said. "You could've asked for just about any favor you could think of—a choice assignment, a promotion of your own, even an appointment to a high-level post. You probably knew that I would've agreed to just about anything you would have asked for. But you didn't ask. You agreed to my request without asking for a thing in return. That tells me a lot, and I'm pleased and proud to learn that about you. That's the kind of thing you'll never read in a personnel file—but it tells me more about the man than any folder full of papers."

The President nodded in thanks and left the office, leaving a still-stunned, confused—and very proud—Norman Weir to wonder what in hell just happened.

GLOSSARY

ACSC—Air Command and Staff College, an Air Force military school for junior field grade officers that prepares them for more leadership and command positions.

AFO—Accounting and Finance Officer—handles pay and leave matters

ASAP—"as soon as possible"

AWACS—Airborne Warning and Control System, an aircraft with a large radar on board that can detect and track aircraft for many miles in all directions

Backfire—a supersonic Russian long-range bomber

Badger—a subsonic Russian long-range bomber

Bear—a subsonic turboprop Russian long-range bomber and reconnaissance plane

BIOT—British Indian Ocean Trust, a chain of small islands in the Indian Ocean administer by the United Kingdom

Blackjack—an advanced supersonic Russian long-range bomber

Buccaneer—a British long-range bomber

Candid—a Russian cargo plane

Chagos—the Iliot native name for the islands administered by the British Indian Ocean Trust

Class A's—the business-suit-like uniform of the U.S. Air Force

DIA—Defense Intelligence Agency, the U.S. military's intelligence-gathering service

Diego Garcia—the largest island of the Chagos Archipelago in the Indian Ocean, part of the British Indian Ocean Trust

Dreamland—the unclassified nickname for a secret military research facility in south central Nevada

Extender—a combination aerial-refueling tanker and cargo plane operated by the U.S. Air Force

firewalled—on an Officer Effectiveness Report, when all raters rate the officer with the highest possible marks

Goblin—nickname for the U.S. Air Force F-117 stealth fighter

GUARD—the universal radio emergency frequency, 121.5 KHz or 243.0 MHz

HAWC (fictional)—the High Technology Aerospace Weapons Center, one of the top-secret Air Force research units at Dreamland

Iliots—the natives of Diego Garcia in the British Indian OceanTrust

IRSTS—Infrared Search and Track System, a Russian heat-seeking aircraft attack system where the pilot can detect and feed targeting information to his attack systems without being detected

Mainstay—a Russian airborne radar aircraft

Megafortress (fictional)—an experimental, highly modified B-52H bomber used for secret military weapons and technology tests

MiG—Mikoyan-Gureyvich, a Soviet military aircraft design bureau

MOI—Memorandum of Instruction, the directives issued by the Secretary of the Air Force to a promotion board on how to conduct candidate evaluations and scoring

MPC—Military Personnel Center, the U.S. Air Force's manpower and personnel agency

Nimrod—a British reconnaissance and attack plane

NOFORN—"No Foreign Nationals," a security subclassification that directs that no foreign nationals can view the material

O-5—in the U.S Air Force, a lieutenant-colonel

OER—Officer Effectiveness Report, an officer's annual report on his job performance and his or her commander's remarks on his suitability for promotion

Orion—a U.S. Navy antisubmarine warfare aircraft

OSR—Officer Selection Report, the file members of a promotion board receive to evaluate and score a candidate for promotion

PCS—Permanent Change of Station, a long-term job change

Peel Cone—a nickname for a type of Soviet airborne radar

PME—Professional Military Education, a series of military schools that teach theory and practice to help develop knowledge and skills in preparation for higher levels of command

PRF—Pulse Repetition Frequency, the speed at which a radar is swept across a target: a higher PRF is used for more precise tracking and aiming; when detected, it is usually a warning of an impending missile launch

SATCOM—Satellite Communications, a way aircraft can communicate with headquarters or other aircraft quickly over very long distances by sending messages to orbiting satellites

Scorpions (fictional)—the AIM-120, a radar-guided medium-range U.S. Air Force antiaircraft missile

SP—Security Police

Strait of Hormuz—the narrow, shallow, winding waterway connecting the Persian Gulf with the Gulf of Oman, considered a strategic chokepoint for oil flowing out of the Gulf nations

Stratotanker—the U.S. Air Force's KC-135 aerial-refueling tanker aircraft

USAFE—U.S. Air Forces in Europe, the major Air Force command that governs all air operations in Europe

warning order—a document notifying a combat unit to prepare for possible combat operations

DALE BROWN is a former U.S. Air Force captain and the superstar author of eleven consecutive *New York Times* best-selling military-action-aviation adventure novels, including *Flight of the Old Dog, Silver Tower, Day of the Cheetah, Hammerheads, Sky Masters, Night of the Hawk, Chains of Command, Storming Heaven, Shadows of Steel, Fatal Terrain,* and *The Tin Man*. He graduated from Penn State University with a degree in Western European history and received his Air Force commission in 1978, serving as a navigator-bombardier on the B-52G Stratofortress heavy bomber and the FB-111A supersonic medium bomber. During his military career he received several awards, including the Air Force Commendation Medal with oak leaf cluster and the Combat Crew Award. He is a member of the Writers' Guild and a Life Member of the Air Force Association and the U.S. Naval Institute. A multiengine and instrument-rated private pilot, he can be found in the skies all across the United States, piloting his own plane. He also enjoys tennis, skiing, scuba diving, and hockey. He lives with his wife, Diane, and son, Hunter, near the shores of Lake Tahoe, Nevada.

LASH-UP

BY LARRY BOND

One

Unexpected Losses

San Diego, California
September 16, 2010

Ray McConnell was watching the front door for new arrivals, but he would have noticed her anyway. Long straight black hair, in her late twenties, casually dressed but making jeans and a knit top look very good. He didn't know her, and was putting a question together when he saw Jim Naguchi follow her in. Oh, that's how she knew.

Ray stood up, still keeping one eye on the screens, and greeted the couple. The woman was staring at the wall behind Ray, and he caught the tail end of her comment. ". . . why you're never at home when I call."

Jim Naguchi answered her, "Third time this week," then took Ray's offered hand. "Hi, Ray, this is Jennifer Oh. We met at that communications conference two weeks ago—the one in San Francisco."

As Ray took Jennifer's hand, she said, "Just Jenny, please," smiling warmly.

"Jenny's in the Navy, Ray. She's a computer specialist . . ."

"Which means almost anything these days," McConnell completed. "Later we'll try to trick you into telling us what you really do."

Jenny looked a little uncomfortable, even as she continued to stare. Changing his tone a little, Ray announced, "Welcome to the McConnell Media Center, the largest concentration of guy stuff in captivity."

"I believe it," she answered. "Those are Sony Image Walls, aren't they? I've got a twenty-four-incher at home."

McConnell half turned to face the Wall. "These are the same, still just an inch thick. But larger," he said modestly.

"And four of them?" she said.

Every new guest had to stop and stare. The living room of Ray's ranch house was filled with electronic equipment, but the focus of the room was the four four-by-eight flat-screen video panels. He'd removed the frames and placed them edge to edge, covering one entire wall of his living room with an eight-foot-by-sixteen-foot video screen—"the Wall."

Just then it was alive with flickering color images. Ray pointed to different areas on the huge surface. "We've set up the center with a map of the China-Vietnam border. We've got subwindows," Ray said, pointing them out, "for five of the major TV networks. That larger text subwindow has the orders of battle for the Vietnamese and Chinese and U.S. forces in the region."

He pointed to a horseshoe-shaped couch in the center of the room, filled with people. "The controls are at that end of the couch, and I've got two dedicated processors controlling the displays."

"So is this how the media keeps track of an international crisis?" Jennifer asked.

"Maybe." Ray shrugged, and looked at Jim Naguchi, who also shrugged. "I dunno. We're engineers, not reporters."

"With a strong interest in foreign affairs," she responded.

"True," he added, "like everyone else here." He swept his arm wide to include the other guests. Half a dozen other people watched the screens, talked, or argued.

"There's people from the military, like you, and professionals from a lot of fields. We get together at times like this to share information and viewpoints."

"And watch the game," she added. Her tone was friendly, but a little critical as well.

"That window's got the pool on the kickoff times," Ray answered, smiling and indicating another area filled with text and numbers. "Most of the money is on local dawn, in"— he glanced at his watch—"an hour or so."

"And I brought munchies," Naguchi added, holding up a grocery bag.

"On the counter, Jim, like always," Ray responded. One side of the living room was a waist-high counter, covered with a litter of drinks and snacks.

"It's my way of feeling like I have some control over my life, Jenny. If we know what's going on, we don't feel so helpless." He shrugged at his inadequate explanation. "Knowledge is Power. Come on, I'll introduce you around. This is a great place to network."

Raising his voice just a little, he announced, "People, this is Jenny Oh. Navy. She's here with Jim." Everyone waved or nodded to her, but most kept their attention on the Wall.

McConnell pointed to a fortyish man in a suit. "That's Jim Garber. He's with McDonnell Douglas. The guy next to him is Marty Duvall, a C coder at a software house. Bob Reeves is a Marine." Ray smiled. "He's also the founding member of the 'Why isn't it Taiwan?' Foundation."

"I'm still looking for new members," the Marine answered. Lean, and tall even sitting down, with close-cropped black hair, he explained, "I keep thinking this is some sort of elaborate deception, and while we're looking at China's southern border, she's going to suddenly zig east, leap across the straits, and grab Taiwan."

"But there's no sign of any naval activity west of Hong Kong," Jenny countered, pointing to the map. "The action's all been inland, close to the border. I'm not in intelligence," she warned, "but everything I've heard say it's all pointed at Vietnam . . ."

"Over ten divisions and a hundred aircraft," Garber added. "That's INN's count this morning, using their own imaging satellites."

"But why Vietnam at all?" countered Reeves. "They're certainly not a military threat."

"But they are an economic one," replied Jenny. "They're another country that's trading communism for capitalism, and succeeding. The increased U.S. financial investment makes Beijing even more nervous."

Ray McConnell smiled, pleased as any host. The new arrival was fitting in nicely, and she certainly improved the scenery. He walked behind to the counter into the kitchen and started neatening up, trashing empty bags of chips and soda bottles. Naguchi was still laying his snacks on the counter.

"She's a real find, Jim," McConnell offered. "Not the same one as last week, though?"

"Well, things didn't work out." Naguchi admitted. "Laura wanted me to have more space. Like Mars." He grinned.

"Where's she stationed?"

"All she'll tell me is NAVAIR," Naguchi replied. "She knows the technology, and she's interested in defense and the military."

"Well, of course, she's in the business," McConnell replied. "She's certainly involved in the discussion." Ray pointed to Jenny, now using the controls to expand part of the map.

"That's how we met," Naguchi explained. "The Vietnam crisis was starting to heat up, and everyone at the conference was talking about it between sessions, of course. She was always in the thick of it, and somewhere in there I mentioned your sessions here."

"So *this* is your first date?" Ray grinned.

"I hope so," Naguchi answered hopefully. "I'm trying to use color and motion to attract the female."

"Ray! You've got a call." A tall African-American man was waving to Ray. McConnell hurried into the living room, picked up the handset from its cradle, and hit the VIEW button. Part of the Wall suddenly became an image of an older man, overweight and balding, in front of a mass of books. Glasses perched on his nose, seemingly defying gravity. "Good . . . evening, Ray."

"Dave Douglas. Good to see you, sir. You're up early in the morning." The United Kingdom was eight hours ahead of California. It was five in the morning in Portsmouth.

"Up very late, you mean. I see you've one of your gatherings. I thought you'd like to know we've lost the signals for two of your GPS satellites."

Naguchi, who'd moved next to Jennifer, explained. "Mr. Douglas is head of the Space Observer Group. They're hobbyists, mostly in Britain, who track satellites visually and electronically. Think high-tech birdwatchers."

"I've heard of them," she answered, nodding, "and of Douglas. Your friend knows *him*?" She sounded impressed.

Naguchi replied, "Ray's got contacts all over."

Jennifer nodded again, trying to pick up the conversation at the same time.

". . . verified Horace's report about an hour ago. It was number seventeen, a relatively new bird, but anything mechanical can fail. I normally wouldn't think it worth more than a note, but then Horace called back and said another one's gone down as well, and quite soon after the first one."

"Why was Horace looking at the GPS satellite signals?" McConnell asked.

"Horace collects electronic signals. He's writing a piece on the GPS signal structure for the next issue of our magazine."

Ray looked uncertain, even a little worried. "Two failures is a little unusual, isn't it?" It was a rhetorical question.

Douglas sniffed. “GPS satellites don’t fail, Raymond. You’ve only had two go down since the system was established twenty-five years ago. By the way, both satellites are due over southern China in less than an hour.”

Ray could only manage a “What?” but Douglas seemed to understand his query. “I’m sending you a file with the orbital data for the constellation in it. I’ve marked numbers seventeen and twenty-two. They’re the one’s who’ve failed.” He paused for a moment, typing. “There . . . you have it now.”

“Thank you, Dave. I’ll get back to you if we can add anything to what you’ve found.” Ray broke the connection, then grabbed his data tablet.

While McConnell worked with the system, speculation filled the conversation. “. . . so we turned off two of the birds ourselves. Deny them to the Chinese,” Reeves suggested.

“If so, why only two?” countered Jenny.

“And the most accurate signal’s encrypted anyway,” added Garber. “The Chinese can only use civilian GPS.”

“Which still gives them an asset they wouldn’t otherwise have,” reminded Reeves.

“Unless the Chinese have broken the encryption,” countered Duvall.

“But we need GPS even more,” said Garber. “It’s not just navigation, it’s weapons guidance and command and control.”

Jennifer added, “All of our aircraft mission planning uses GPS now. If we had to go back, it would be a lot harder to run a coordinated attack. We could never get the split-second timing we can now.”

“Here’s the orbital data,” McConnell announced.

The smaller windows on the Wall all vanished, leaving the map showing southern China and Vietnam. A small bundle of curved lines appeared in the center, then expanded out to fill the map, covering the area with orbital tracks. As Ray moved the cursor on his data pad, the cursor moved on the map. When it rested on a track, a tag appeared, naming the satellite and providing orbital and other data. Two of the tracks were red, not white, and were marked with small boxes with a time in them.

“Where are the satellites right now?” someone asked.

Ray tapped the tablet and small diamonds appeared on all the tracks, showing their current positions.

“Can you move them to where they’d be at local dawn for Hanoi?” suggested Garber.

“And what’s the horizon for those satellites at Mengzi?” Jennifer prompted, pointing to a town just north of the Chinese-Vietnamese border. "That's one of the places the Chinese are supposed to be massing."

"Stand by," answered Ray. "That's not built in. I'll have to do the math and draw it." He worked quickly, and in absolute silence. After about two minutes, an oval drawn in red appeared on the map, centered on the location. Everyone counted, but Ray spoke first. "I count three."

". . . and you need four for a fix," finished Naguchi.

National Military Command Center, The Pentagon
September 17

". . . and without the GPS, General Hyde had to issue a recall." The assistant J-3 looked uncomfortable, as only a colonel can look when giving bad news to a room full of four-star generals.

The meeting had originally been scheduled to review results of the first day's strikes in Operation CERTAIN FORCE. A total of eighty-three targets in China had been programmed to be hit by 150 combat aircraft and almost two hundred cruise missiles. It hadn't happened.

"The gap in coverage was only twenty minutes," Admiral Kramer complained. "Are we so inflexible that we couldn't delay the operation until we had full coverage?"

"It would have meant issuing orders to hundreds of units through two levels of command," answered General Michael Warner. Chief of Staff of the Air Force, it was one of his men, General Tim Hyde, who was Joint Task Force Commander for CERTAIN FORCE. Warner, a slim, handsome man whose hair was still jet-black at sixty, looked more than a little defensive.

"Sounds like 'set-piece-itis' to me," muttered the Army Chief of Staff.

The Chairman, also an Army general, shot his subordinate a "this isn't helping" look and turned back to Warner. The Air Force, through the Fiftieth Space Operations Wing, operated the GPS satellites.

"Mike, have your people found out anything else since this morning?"

"Only that both birds were functioning within norms. Number seventeen was the older bird. They'd recently fired up the third of her four clocks, but she was in good shape. Number twenty-two was still on her first atomic clock. All attempts to restart them, or even communicate with them, have failed. Imaging from our telescopes shows that they're still there, but they're in a slow tumble, which they shouldn't be doing . . ."

"And the chance of both of them suffering catastrophic failure is nil," concluded the Chairman.

"Yes sir. The final straw is that we started warm-up procedures on the two reserve birds twenty-eight and twenty-nine. Or rather, we tried to warm them up. They don't answer either."

General Sam Kastner, Chairman of the Joint Chiefs, was a thinker, more a listener than a speaker, but he knew he had to take firm charge of the meeting. He sighed, knowing the answer before he started, "What about Intelligence?"

The J-2, or Joint Intelligence officer, was a boyish-looking rear admiral. His normal staff was two or three assistants, but this time he had a small mob of officers and civilians behind him. The admiral moved to the podium.

"Sir, the short answer is that we don't know who did this or how. If we knew who, we could start to guess how they did it. Similarly, knowing how would immediately narrow the list of suspects.

"We know that the DSP infrared satellites detected no launches, and we believe that they also would have detected a laser powerful enough to knock out a GPS bird—although that's not a certainty," he added quickly, nodding to an Army officer with a stern expression on his face.

"The Chinese are the most likely actors, of course, but others can't be ruled out. CIA believes the attack was made by agents on the ground or in cyberspace, but we've detected no signs of this at any of the monitoring stations. The Navy believes they've adapted their space-launch vehicles for the purpose. Although it's a logical proposition, we've seen no sign of the launch, or the considerable effort it would require. And we track their space program quite closely."

The frustration in his voice underlined every word. "It's possible that the Russians or someone else is doing it to assist the Chinese, but there aren't that many candidates, and we've simply seen no sign of activity by any nation, friendly or hostile." He almost threw up his hands.

"Thank you, Admiral," replied Kastner. "Set up a Joint Intelligence Task Force immediately. Until we can at least find out what's being done, we can do nothing, and that includes reliably carry out military operations. Spread your net wide."

He didn't have to say that the media were also spreading their net. Television and the Internet were already full of rumors—the attack had been scheduled but called off for political reasons, that the entire exercise was just a bluff, that the U.S. had backed down because of the risk of excessive casualties, and others more fanciful. U.S. "resolve" had been shattered.

Gongga Shan Mountain Launch Complex, Xichuan Province, Southern China
September 23

General Shen Xuesen stood quietly, calmly, watching the bank of monitors, but wishing to be on the surface. He had a better view of the operation from here, but it did not seem as real.

It was their fifth time, and he could see the staff settling down, nowhere as nervous as the first launch, but China was committed now, and her future hung on their success.

Everyone saw the short, solidly built general standing quietly in the gallery. In his early fifties, he'd spent a lot of time in the weather, and it showed. An engineer, he looked capable of reshaping a mountain, and he had Gongga Shan as proof. It was a commander's role to appear calm, even when he knew exactly how many things could go wrong, and how much was at stake, both for him and for China.

Shen had already given his permission to fire. The staff was counting down, waiting until they were in the exact center of the intercept window. The 'Dragon's egg' sat in the breech, inert but vital, waiting for just a few more seconds.

The moment came as the master clock stepped down to zero. The launch controller turned a key, and for a moment, the only sign of activity was on the computer displays. Shen's eyes glanced to the breech seals, but the indicators all showed green. He watched the video screen that showed the muzzle, a black oval three meters across.

Even with a muzzle velocity of four thousand meters per second, it took time for the egg to build up to full speed. Almost a full second elapsed between ignition and . . .

A puff of smoke and flame appeared on the display, followed by a black streak, briefly visible. Only its size, almost three meters in diameter, allowed it to be seen at all. Shen relaxed, his inward calm now matching his outward demeanor. His gun had worked again.

"Hatching," reported the launch controller. Everyone had so loved the egg metaphor that they used the term to report when the sabots separated from the meter-sized projectile. Designed to hold the small vehicle inside the larger bore, they split and fell away almost instantly. Effectively, the projectile got the boost of three-meter barrel but the drag of a one-meter body.

Speed, always more speed, mused Shen as he watched the monitors.

The crews were already boarding buses for their ride up the mountain to inspect the gun. Other screens showed helicopters lifting off to search for the sabots. Although they could not be used again, they were marvels of engineering in their own right and would reveal much about the gun's design.

The goal was eight kilometers a second, orbital velocity. First, take a barrel a kilometer long and three meters across. To make it laser-straight, gouge out the slope of a mountain and anchor it on the bedrock. Cover it up, armor and camouflage it, too. Put the muzzle near the top, seventy-nine hundred meters above sea level. That reduces air resistance and buys you some speed. Then use sabots to get more speed. You're halfway there. Then . . .

"Ignition," announced one of the controllers. Put a solid rocket booster on the projectile to give it the final push it needed. "She's flying! Guidance is on-line, sir. It's in the center of the basket. Intercept in twenty minutes."

General Shen had seen the concept described in a summary the Iraqis had provided of Supergun technology after the American Persian Gulf War. American technological superiority had been more than a shock to the People's Liberation Army. It had triggered an upheaval.

The Chinese military had always chosen numbers over quality, because numbers were cheap, and the Politburo was trying to feed one and a half billion people. They'd always believed that numbers could overwhelm a smaller high-tech force, making them reluctant even to try. Everyone knew how sensitive the Americans were to casualties, and to risk.

But if the difference in quality is big enough, numbers don't matter anymore. Imagine using machine guns in the Civil War, or a nuclear sub in WW II. Shen and his colleagues had watched the Americans run rings around the Iraqis, suffering trivial casualties while they hammered the opposition.

So the Chinese army had started the long, expensive process of becoming a modern military. They'd bought high-tech weapons from the Russians, fortunately willing to sell at bargain-basement prices. They'd stolen what they couldn't buy from Western nations. They'd gotten all kinds of exotic technologies: rocket-driven torpedoes for their subs, exotic aircraft designs.

It wasn't enough. Running and working as hard as they could, they'd cut the technology lag from twenty to fifteen years. They were following the same path as the West, and it would just take time to catch up.

General Shen had seen the answer. He'd seen a vulnerability, then planned, convinced, plotted, and argued until the Politburo had listened and backed his plan. If your opponent strikes at you from above, take away his perch. Take away that technological edge.

Build a prison camp deep in the mountains, in a remote spot in southern China. Send the hard cases and malcontents there. The State has useful work for them. Watch the prisoners dig away the side of a mountain. You need a rail line to the nearest city, Kangding, 250 kilometers southwest. That had been a job in itself. Then add army barracks, the launch-control center, and SAM and AAA defenses. It had taken years before it looked like anything more than a mistake.

Meanwhile, design the "T'ien Lung," or Celestial Dragon, to fly in space. And design a gun, the biggest gun in the history of the world, the Dragon's Mother, to fire it. Such designs were well within the grasp of the West, but they were barely possible for China's limited means. Her civilian space program had provided a lot of the talent, as well as a convenient excuse for foreign study and purchases.

"Control has been passed to Xichuan," the senior controller announced. "Intercept in ten minutes." A look of relief passed over his face. If a screwup occurred after this, it was their fault, not his.

Shen longed to be in two places at once, but the gun was his, and Dong Zhi, the scientist who had actually designed the Dragons, was at the space complex. Xichuan handled China's civilian space program, and they had the antennas to watch the intercept.

Everyone in the room watched the central display, even though it was only a computer representation. Two small dots sat on curved lines, slowly moving to an intersection point. Then the screen changed, becoming completely black, with the characters for "Terminal Phase," displayed in one corner.

General Shen Xuesen smiled. He had insisted on the television camera for terminal-phase guidance. Not only was it hard to jam, it made the result understandable. Seeing the target grow from a speck to a shape to a recognizable satellite had made it real, not only for the leadership who had watched the tests, but for the people who had to do the work, who fought the war from so far away.

The image was a little grainy, because of the lens size, but it also had the clarity of space. He could see the boxy, cluttered body of the American GPS satellite, and the outspread solar panels, each divided into four sections.

The controller started counting down as the image slowly expanded. "Five seconds, four, three, two, one, now." He uttered the last word softly, but triumphantly, as the image suddenly vanished. A few people clapped, but they'd all seen this before, and most didn't feel the need now.

All that work, all that money, to put a ten-pound warhead in orbit.

More like a shotgun shell, the explosive fired a cone of fragments at the unarmored satellite. Filled with atomic clocks and delicate electronics, it didn't have a hope of surviving the explosion. The carcass would remain in its orbit, intact, but pocked with dozens of small holes.

In fact, the kill was almost an anticlimax. After all the work of getting the vehicle up there, it was over far too quickly.

Skyhook One Seven, Over the South China Sea
September 23

"We just lost GPS," reported the navigator. "Switching to inertial tracker." The navigator, an Air Force major, sounded concerned but not alarmed.

"Is it the receiver?" asked the mission commander. A full colonel, it was his job to manage the information gathered by the ELINT, or Electronic Intelligence, aircraft. Running racetracks off the China coast, it listened for radar and radio signals, analyzing their contents and fixing their location. The digested information was datalinked directly back to Joint Task Force Headquarters.

"Self-test is good, sir, and the receiver is still picking up satellites, but we just lost one of the signals, and now we're outside our error budget." Each satellite over the minimum required narrowed the area of uncertainty around a transmitter's location. GPS was accurate enough to target some missiles directly, or give pilots a good idea of where to search for their objective.

"So we've lost another one," muttered the colonel.

USS *Nebraska* (SSBN—739), On Patrol
September 24

The sub's Operations Officer knocked on the captain's open door. "Sir, they've lost another one." He handed the priority message to the skipper. It detailed the loss and showed how coverage was affected for their patrol area.

The captain looked over the printout. "Have you compared this with our navigation plan?"

"Yes, sir. We have to change one of our planned fix times. It falls in one of the new 'dark windows.' We can move it ahead two hours or back six."

The captain scowled, more than one might think appropriate for a minor inconvenience. But ballistic missile subs had to come up to periscope depth periodically to check their navigation systems' accuracy. A few meters of error at the launch point could be hundreds of times that at the target.

When the full GPS constellation had been operational, the captain could take a fix anytime he chose. Now there were times he couldn't. That made him less flexible, more predictable, and thus easier to find. He really didn't like that.

"Move it up," ordered the captain. "Let's take a fix before they lose any more birds. And draw up a new schedule reducing the interval between fixes."

INN News
September 24

"With the loss of another satellite, emotions at the Fiftieth Space Operations Wing have changed from grim or angry to fatalistic." Mark Markin, INN's defense correspondent, stood in front of the gate to Cheyenne Mountain. The Fiftieth's operations center was actually located at Schriver Air Force Base nearby, but the drama of the mountain's tunnel entrance was preferable to Schriver's nondescript government buildings.

Markin wore a weather-beaten parka, zipped up against the chill Colorado wind. His carefully shaped hair was beginning to show the effects of the wind as well, and he seemed to rush through his report in an effort to get out of the weather.

"Although it is widely acknowledged that loss of the GPS satellites is no fault of the people here at the Fiftieth, they are still suffering a deep sense of helplessness.

"Since the GPS network became active in 1989, it has become almost a public utility. The men and women here took pride in providing a service that not only gave the U.S. armed forces a tremendous military advantage, but benefited the civilian community in countless ways.

"Now, someone, possibly the Chinese, but certainly an enemy of the United States, has destroyed at least three and possibly as many as five satellites. Yesterday's loss shows that last week's attack was not an isolated act.

"And the United States can do nothing to stop it."

San Diego, California
September 24

Jim Avrell had gone to only a few of Ray's gatherings. His "discussion groups" were famous throughout SPAWAR, and were always worthwhile. Although Arvell would have liked to go, two preschoolers and another on the way limited his free time.

Tonight, though, he'd made the time. In fact, his wife Carol had urged him to go. After he'd described Ray's sudden leave of absence and the rumors from the other coworkers, she'd urged him to go and get the straight story.

Avrell was an antenna design specialist in Ray's working group. He knew and liked the outgoing engineer, even if McConnell could be a little fierce in technical "discussions." He was worried about their project, which was suffering in Ray's absence, and about Ray himself. With the brass so upset about GPS, it was no time for Ray to play "missing person."

The car's nav console prompted, "Turn left here," and he signaled for the turn onto Panorama Drive. It had been over a year since he had visited Ray's place, that time with Carol at a reception for a visiting astronaut. That had been an occasion.

But nothing like this. As he made the turn, Avrell saw the street almost completely lined with cars. This was definitely not typical for a quiet residential community. Avrell ended up parking a block away.

As he hurried up the path, he heard the expected hubbub, but Ray didn't meet him at the door, and everyone wasn't in the living room. A group of four men huddled around a coffee table there, and he could see another clustered in the kitchen. McConnell appeared out of the one of the bedroom doors, hurrying. He looked tired.

"Jim Avrell! It's great to see you." Genuine pleasure lit up Ray's face, but there was a distracted air to it. And surprise.

Avrell saw no point in dissembling. "Ray, what's going on over here? You haven't been at work . . ."

"I've got bigger fish to fry, Jim. Promise you won't tell anyone what's going on here? Unless I OK it?"

"Well, of course."

Ray looked at him intently. "No, Jim, I mean it. You can't tell anyone. Treat this as classified."

Avrell studied McConnell carefully, then agreed. "I promise not to tell anyone what I see here." He fought the urge to raise his right hand.

McConnell seemed to relax a little, and smiled again. "You'll understand in a minute, Jim." He called over to the group at the coffee table. "I'll be right there."

One of them, whom Avrell recognized as Avrim Takir, a mathematician from the work group, answered. "Fine, Ray. We need another ten minutes, anyway." Takir spotted Avrell and waved, but quickly returned his attention to the laptop in front of him.

McConnell led his coworker down the hall into his home office.

Ray's desk was piled high with books and disk cases and printouts. The center display, another Image Wall mounted above the desk, showed an isometric design for an aircraft—no, a spacecraft, Avrell realized.

Used to polished CAD-CAM designs where they worked, he was surprised. This one was crude. Some of it was fully rendered in 3-D space, but parts of it were just wireframes. At least one section was a two-dimensional image altered to appear three-dimensional.

"*Defender* isn't pretty, but we're a little pressed for time," McConnell declared. He had the air of a proud parent.

Avrell, surprised and puzzled, studied the diagram, which filled the four-by-eight display. Data tables hovered in parts of the screen not covered by the vehicle. He started tracing out systems: propulsion; communications; weapons? He shot a questioning look at McConnell.

Ray met his look with one of his own. "Question, Jim. What's the best way to protect a satellite? If someone's shooting them down, how can you stop them?"

"They haven't even confirmed it's the Chinese . . ."

"Doesn't matter who's doing it!" McConnell countered. "Someone is." He paused and rephrased the question. "Can you effectively protect a satellite from the ground?"

Avrell answered quickly. "Of course not. You're on the wrong end of the gravity well, even if you're near the launcher site, and you might be on the wrong side of the planet."

"Which we probably are," McConnell agreed. "Here on the surface, even with perfect information, we can't defend a satellite until something is launched to attack it, so we're always in a tail chase. If we're above the launcher, with the satellite we're trying to defend, Isaac Newton joins our team."

"And this is going to do the job?" Avrell asked, motioning toward the diagram. He tried to sound objective, but skepticism crept into his voice in spite of his efforts.

McConnell seemed used to it. "It can, Jim. There's nothing startling in here. The technology is all there: an orbital vehicle, sensors, and weapons."

"And you've been tasked by . . ."

"It's my own hook, Jim. This is all on my own," Ray admitted. Then he saw his friend's question and answered it without waiting.

"Because I can't wait for the government to think of it, that's why. The answer is obvious, but by the time they hold all the meetings and write all the Requirements we won't have any satellites left."

McConnell sat down heavily, fatigue and strain showing on his face.

"This isn't about just GPS or the Chinese, Jim. Someone's developed the capability to attack satellites in space. That means they could attack manned spacecraft. They can probably launch orbital nuclear weapons at us, or anyone else they don't like. And we certainly know they don't like us."

Avrell leaned back against the edge of a table and looked carefully at Ray. "So you're going to design the answer to our problems." He phrased it as a statement, but it was still a question.

"Me and all the other people here," Ray corrected. "Why not, Jim? I've got a good idea, and I'm running with it. I might not be in the right bureau in the right branch, but I believe in this. Ideas are too precious to waste."

Inside, Avrell agreed with his friend, but practicality pushed that aside. "You can't build it," he stated quietly.

"Well, that's the rub," McConnell said, actually rubbing the back of his neck in emphasis. "I've made a lot of friends over the years. I'm going to shotgun it out—only within the system," he hurriedly added, referring to the procedures for handling classified material. "I won't go public with this. It's a serious design proposal."

"Which needs a Requirement, a contractor, and research and development . . ."

"And congressional hearings and hundreds of man-hours deciding what color to paint it," continued McConnell. "A small group can always move faster and think faster than a large one. I want to present the defense community with a finished design, something so complete they'll be able to leapfrog the first dozen steps of the acquisition process." He grinned. "We can skip one step already. The other side's writing the Requirement for us."

Ray stood and turned to face Avrell directly. "I know I'm breaking rules, but they're not rules of physics, just the way DoD does business. I'm willing to push this because it needs to be done, and nobody else is doing it."

Avrell sighed. "So who's working on your comm system?"

McConnell grinned. "The guys in the kitchen, but they've got almost all the electronics. There's lots to do. Come on, I'll introduce you . . ."

"Wait a minute, Ray." Avrell held up his hand. "Let me make a call first."

"Carol?"

"No. Sue Langston. She's in graphics."

Ray laughed and pointed to the phone. Heading out of the office and down the hall, his intention was to check with the propulsion group in the living room, but then he heard the doorbell again. Fighting impatience, he hoped for another volunteer, or the Chinese takeout he'd ordered.

Jennifer Oh stood on the doorstep, and Ray blinked twice in surprise. Another unexpected caller.

"Can I come in?" she finally asked.

"Oh, certainly, please come in, Jenny," trying to sound as hospitable as he could. His distraction increased. She'd obviously come straight from work, and her naval uniform, with lieutenant commander's stripes, jarred after the casual outfit he'd seen her in last week. Her long black hair was tied up in an ornate bun.

She didn't wait for him to speak. "Jim Naguchi told me a little about what you're doing here. I think it's an incredible idea." She held up three square flat boxes. "And I brought pizza."

"Thank you on both counts, Jenny. Jim's not here tonight, though."

"I came to help you, Ray. I can see what you're doing. I've got a lot of experience in command and control systems," she offered.

Ray suddenly felt that *Defender* was going to work.

Two

Suggestions

National Military Command Center, The Pentagon
September 25

The Joint Chiefs of Staff didn't normally meet at two in the morning, but Rear Admiral Overton's call was worth getting out of bed for.

Most of the Chiefs had been in the Pentagon anyway, trying to manage the crisis, the troops, and the media. Although only three active GPS satellites had been lost out of a constellation of twenty-four, it had still created periods when there was no coverage in some parts of the world at some times, and there was no indication that they'd be able to fill the gaps soon. Everyone was assuming it would get much worse before it got better.

There was also the continuing problem of the Vietnam Crisis. U.S. forces could not execute a coordinated, precision attack without complete GPS coverage, but they could not maintain such high readiness levels forever. And what if China had started attacking American satellites? Had a war already started?

As they hurried into the Command Center, the J-2, Frank Overton, compared the generals' normal polished appearance with the tired, overworked men in front of him. He was glad he had good news.

The Chief of Staff of the Air Force and the Chief of Naval Operations were both last, coming in together and breaking off some sort of disagreement as they walked through the door. Overton didn't even wait for them to sit down.

"We have proof it's the Chinese. We figured out where, and that led to how," he announced.

Overton's data pad and the screen at the head of the table showed a black-and-white satellite photo. A date in the corner read "Jun 2006."

"This is the Gongga Shan prison camp in southern China—at least, we had identified it as a prison camp. We named it after the mountain." Using his pointer, he showed areas marked as "Prisoners' Barracks, Guard Barracks," and so on. "As far as we know, it was built about five years ago, and can accommodate several thousand prisoners."

He pressed the remote again, and the first image slid to one side, and a second, of the same area, appeared alongside it. "This was taken about six hours ago. This construction work"—he indicated a long scar on the side of the mountain in the first photo—"has been finished or just stopped. We think finished, because if they'd just abandoned it, the excavation would still be there. In fact, if you look in the second photo, the mountain's been restored to its original state. The original analysis four years ago speculated that the prisoners might be mining, or building an observatory, or an antenna. The site goes right up to the top of the mountain, and it's one of the tallest around."

Admiral Overton paused, looking at the group. A hint of embarrassment appeared on his face. "That analysis was never followed up." He shrugged.

General Kastner spoke for the group. "And the real answer is?"

Overton pressed the remote again. A gray-green infrared image appeared, superimposed over the second photo. "We wanted to see what they'd been working on. This is a satellite infrared picture taken about an hour ago. We were lucky," he explained. "There was one already tasked to cover the region because of the crisis."

Most of the shapes in the image duplicated the buildings and other structures, but one shape was unique: a long, thick, straight line, laid east–west along the spine of the mountain.

"It's one kilometer long, and based on careful measurements, we know it's angled along the western face of the mountain at about forty degrees elevation. At the base you'll see a series of buried structures, including what we think are several bunkers for the launch crew. The buildings at the base are warm, and the entire structure is slightly warmer than the surrounding rock. We think it's made of metal."

"A buried rocket launcher?" wondered the Army Chief of Staff.

"No, sir. A buried gun barrel. See these shapes?" He used the cursor to indicate two round structures. "We believe these are tanks for the liquid-propellant fuel. Here where the barrel widens is the breech and combustion chamber."

"The barrel looks to be about ten feet in diameter. We're still working on the numbers, but I believe it's capable of launching a boosted projectile into earth orbit."

Even while the generals and their staffs took in the news, Kastner replied, "Great job, Frank. We're pressed for time, but I've got to know how you found this."

"We're putting together a complete report right now, sirs; you'll all have it in a few hours." He paused for a moment, then said, "Elimination and luck. Two of our satellites were killed in the same area just east of Okinawa. We assumed a west-to-east trajectory, back-calculated the origin, and tried to find a launching site in the region. We got lucky because we figured they'd start with an established installation, and the Gongga Shan Prison Camp was on the list. It probably never was anything but a construction site for the gun. That still took us over a week." He didn't sound proud.

Kastner was complimentary but grim. "Well, Frank, your work is just beginning. We need to know a lot more about this weapon. First, is this the only one? It probably is, but I've got to know absolutely. How many more satellites can they kill with it? And what would it take to stop it?"

Overton nodded silently, as grim as the general. He and his staff quickly left.

Kastner turned to the others. "Immediate impressions, gentlemen? After we finish here, I'll wake the President."

INN News,
September 25

Mark Markin stood in front of a map of China and Vietnam, a familiar image after weeks of confrontation. He read carefully from a data pad.

"Xinhua, the official Chinese News Service, today released a statement claiming a victory over 'an American plan to seize control of Southeast Asia.' "

Markin's image was replaced by Chinese Premier Li Zhang, speaking to a crowd of cheering citizens. Thin, almost scrawny, the elderly leader spoke with energy in Chinese. English subtitles appeared at the bottom of the image.

"In response to preparations for a massive attack on Chinese territory, the forces of the People's Liberation Army have hamstrung the Imperialist aggressor by shooting down his military satellites.

"Deprived of his superiority and given pause by our new technological strength, the Americans have canceled their attack plan. This shows that America is not all-powerful, that any bully can be stopped if one faces him directly and exposes his inner weakness.

"We call on all the nations of the world, oppressed and suffering under American world hegemony, to topple the corrupt giant."

Markin reappeared, looking concerned. "U.S. defense officials have refused to comment officially, but it has been a working assumption that the Chinese were responsible for the missing spacecraft. They also were unable to say how or when U.S. military forces would react to this news.

"Sources at the State Department were slightly more forthcoming, but only about the reasons for the Chinese announcement. They believe that the Chinese are openly challenging the U.S. in a field the Americans consider theirs exclusively: their technical edge. They hope to leverage their victory into an alliance of nations opposed to American policy.

"There was no comment from the White House, except that the President and his advisors are considering all options to protect American interests in this widening crisis."

China Lake Naval Weapons Center, California
September 26

Tom Wilcox worked in the Test and Evaluation shop at China Lake. The entire base's mission was to evaluate new weapons systems for the Navy, but his shop was the one that did the dirty work. He spent a lot of time in the desert and would be out there at dawn, half an hour from now.

Wilcox looked like someone who's spent a lot of time on the desert. Lean, tanned, his face showed a lot of wear, although he would joke that was just from dealing with the budget. He'd been in his current job for twenty-five years, and claimed he was good for that many more.

This morning, he had to inspect the foundations for a new test stand. Before too long they'd be mounting rocket motors on it, and he didn't want a motor, with stand still attached, careening across the landscape.

First, though, he always checked his e-mail. Working on his danish, and placing his coffee carefully out of the way, he said, "New messages."

The computer displayed them on his wall screen, a mix of personal and professional subjects listed out according to his own priority system. The higher the rank of the sender, the less urgent the message had to be. Anything from an admiral went straight to the bottom of the pile.

He noted one unusual item. Ray McConnell had sent a message, with a medium-sized attachment. He'd known Ray for quite a while as a colleague, but he hadn't seen him since Wilcox had been to SPAWAR for that conference last spring, about six months ago. They'd exchanged some notes since then.

Wilcox noted that it had a long list of other addressees, and it had been sent out at four this morning. He recognized a few of the addressees. They were all at official DoD installations.

The cover letter was brief: "I think you'll know what to do with this. It's completely unclassified, but please only show it to people inside the security system. Thanks."

Well, that was mysterious enough to be worth a few minutes. He downloaded the attached file, waited for the virus and security check sums to finish, then had a look.

It was a hundred-page document. The cover page had a gorgeous 3-D-rendered image of a wedge-shaped airfoil. It had to be a spacecraft, and the title above it read, *"Defender."*

Wilcox's first reaction was one of surprise and disappointment. He almost groaned. Engineers in the defense community receive a constant stream of crackpot designs from wanna-be inventors. The unofficial ones were ignored or returned with a polite letter. The official ones, that came though a congressman or some other patron, could be a real pain in the ass. Why was Ray passing this on to him?

Then he saw the name on the front. It was Ray's own design! *What is this? It's not an official Navy project. McConnell must have put some real time into this, and he's no flake,* thought Wilcox. *Or at least, not until now.*

He opened the cover and glanced at the introduction. "The Chinese attack on our satellites is the beginning of a new stage of warfare, one that we are completely unprepared for. Even if the source of the attacks is found and destroyed, the technology now has been demonstrated. Others, hostile to U.S. interests, will follow the Chinese example.

"*Defender* is a vehicle designed to protect spacecraft in orbit from attack. It uses proven technology. Please consider this concept as an option to protect our vital space assets."

Below that was a long list of names, presumably people who either endorsed the idea or who had helped him with the design. Wilcox scanned the list. They were helpers. He didn't recognize any of the names, and there were none with a rank attached.

He skimmed the document, watching the clock but increasingly absorbed in the design. Ray had done his homework, although his haste was obvious. At least the art was good. Diagrams were important for the higher-ups. They had problems with numbers and large words.

The phone rang, and Wilcox picked it up. "We need you in five," his assistant reminded him.

"I'll be there," Wilcox replied, and hung up.

He sat for another ten seconds, thinking and staring at the screen. *All right, Ray's got a hot idea, and he wants to share it. In fact,* Wilcox realized, *he wants me to share it, to send it up the line. He's trying to jump-start the design process.*

Wilcox knew, and so did anyone else who worked for the DoD, that it took million of dollars and years of effort to produce a design like this, and that only happened after an elaborately crafted Requirement for such a design was issued by the Pentagon. The U.S. didn't have time for that kind of deliberate care.

Wilcox knew it was a good idea. The U.S. had no way of protecting their satellites.

Taking the few minutes it needed, he had the computer call up his address book and flagged ten names. Most were senior engineers, like him, but a few were military officers of senior rank. He wanted to see if they were still capable of recognizing an original idea when they saw it.

That morning, Ray had sent his document out to over thirty friends and colleagues. All had clearances, and all worked in some area of defense. By lunchtime, eight hours after its transmission, over 150 copies existed. By close of business, it was over five hundred and growing.

Crystal Square 3, Arlington, Virginia
September 27

Captain "Biff" Barnes was more than ready to leave for the day. His skills as a pilot were supposed to be essential for this project, but he spent most of the day wrestling with the Pentagon bureaucracy.

"Biff's" name was Clarence, but he'd acquired the nickname, any nickname, as quickly as he could. He hated "Clarence." Barnes was a little short, only five-eight, but average for a pilot. He kept in very good shape, counting the months and weeks until his desk tour was finished. His thin, almost angular face showed how little fat he carried. His hair was cut as short as regulations would allow. The Air Force didn't like bald pilots, but he'd have shaved his head if he could.

He'd flown F-15s before being assigned to the Airborne Laser project. He understood the work was important, but doing anything other than flying was a comedown. He'd been promised a billet in an F-22 squadron once this tour was complete.

His job was interesting, when he actually got to do it. He had to determine, as accurately as possible, how vulnerable aircraft were to laser attack. He'd gotten to look at a lot of foreign hardware up close, and his degree in aeronautical engineering was proving quite useful.

But most of the time he futzed with the system. Some congressman wanted to be briefed on the status of the project. That was easy. Some other agency didn't want to provide information he needed. That took some doing. The General Accounting Office wanted to review their phone records. Or some reporter on a fishing expedition filed a Freedom of Information Act request. That had to be dealt with immediately.

Because the project was classified, and only a limited number of people could be cleared into the program, everyone involved had to do double or triple duty. The junior troops, like Barnes, drew most of the nasty ones.

He couldn't have dodged the latest flap, anyway. A government office concerned with equal opportunity needed to know if Barnes, who was African American, felt his "capabilities were being fully utilized," and had included a five-page form to fill out. He'd used all of the comments section to share his feelings about "utilization."

He sat at his desk, closing up files and locking his safe, but still reluctant to go without something productive to show for his day. He checked his mail, at that point even willing to read Internet humor.

The page opened, and the first thing he noticed was another two copies of the *Defender* document, from separate friends at Maxwell and Wright-Pat. He'd gotten the first one yesterday morning from a pilot buddy at March Air Force Base in California, and another copy later in the day. He'd tabled it then, busy with paperwork, but his mind was ready for distraction now.

He opened the file and almost laughed when he saw the cover. Someone had taken the new VentureStar, a single-stage-to-orbit space vehicle, and tried to arm it, using "his" laser. The introduction had touted it as a way of defending the GPS satellites.

A worthy goal, although Barnes had no expectation that this lash-up was anything more than a time-wasting fantasy. Still he was motivated by curiosity to see what this McConnell had said about the Airborne Laser.

Carried by a modified Boeing 747, the Airborne Laser could engage ballistic or cruise missiles, or even aircraft, at long range. Just what range was one of the problems Barnes was trying to solve. The prototype aircraft, which had been flying for several years, was still in test, proving not just the laser but the basic concept of engaging aircraft with a beam of light. How much did weather affect it? What if some country developed a cheap antilaser paint?

McConnell had taken the laser out of the 747 and mounted it in the cargo bay of the spacecraft. Barnes flipped to the section labeled "Laser Weapon," and started to read. Whoever this McConnell was, thought Barnes, he didn't write science fiction. He hadn't made any obvious mistakes, but he didn't have detailed information, which of course was classified. There certainly wasn't any weather in space. The laser would be much more effective in a vacuum.

But what about targeting? He started working through the document, answering questions and become increasingly impressed with McConnell's idea.

He knew about spacecraft, not only because of his degree but because he'd actually been selected for the Astronaut Corps after his first squadron tour. He'd flown one mission, but then left the program. He hated the constant training, the public relations. And what he really hated was the lack of flight time.

Barnes's stomach growled, and he looked up from the screen to see it was seven-forty-five. He'd missed the rush hour, anyway. Biff said, "Print file," and pages started to fill the hopper. He wanted to show this to his buddies.

Barnes pulled himself up short. His friends would be interested, but they didn't have security clearances, and the cover message had explicitly asked that it not be shown to anyone who wasn't cleared. Respect for the design made him want to respect the author's wishes, and treat it seriously.

The Vietnam Crisis, another Desert Storm/Balkans exercise in U.S. diplomacy, had suddenly transformed itself into a much wider challenge. McConnell proposed this *Defender* as an answer—maybe the only answer, since he hadn't heard of any others.

He looked at the proposal. Did he buy into it? He did, Biff realized. McConnell had gotten the laser right. He knew what he was doing.

Biff sat back down at the keyboard. He had some friends in high places.

U.S. Navy Space Warfare Command, San Diego, California
September 27

Ray McConnell came back to his office and shut the door quickly. He was shaken, almost physically trembling, after his meeting with Admiral Carson.

Rear Admiral Eugene Carson was not just the head of Communications, which was Ray's division, but of the entire Space and Naval Warfare Systems Command. It had taken Ray two days to work his way up the chain, first with Rudy White, his own division head, then Dr.

Krauss, the technical director, and Admiral Gaston. With increasing force, he'd made his case for *Defender*. His unsolicited, unrequired, unwanted proposal had been shown dozens of times.

Rudy White had been concerned with the lost time from Ray's assigned projects. "Why haven't you put some of that creative energy into the new communications system?" he'd demanded.

"Because someone's shooting down GPS satellites right now," Ray had responded. He'd worked with White for years, and knew he could press his point. "I thought of this, but I can't build it, and it needs to be built, and soon."

White had agreed to let McConnell see the technical director, with the strict understanding that the *Defender* proposal was Ray's own idea. White was relaxed enough about his career to take the risk.

Dr. Krauss had been even less helpful, wondering aloud if *Defender* was SPAWAR property, since a SPAWAR employee had created it. Ray had been nonplussed, unsure whether Krauss was greedy or simply trying to cover his bureaucratic ass.

He'd decided to play the doctor's game. Krauss had been shocked when he heard about the several hundred copies of the proposal already circulating through the defense community.

"I'd be delighted to have official SPAWAR endorsement of *Defender*. I'm sure that would be all the help she needed." Ray fought hard to keep a straight face when he saw the look of horror. Krauss hadn't been able to get him out of his office quickly enough.

The vice commander had been the final hurdle, Ray thought. He'd been more than aware of *Defender*'s popularity. "You realize that you have no credibility as a spacecraft design engineer," Gaston explained coolly. He'd been polite, but a little condescending.

"I didn't think I had to be qualified to have a good idea, sir."

Gaston shook his head. "I disagree. Without credentials, why should anyone waste their time looking at this design? As far as the Navy is concerned, you're no different that anyone off the street, bringing it some design it didn't ask for. And to the wrong agency," he added.

"I know that this isn't SPAWAR's area, sir, but I'm SPAWAR's employee. I didn't want to go outside our own chain of command."

Gaston nodded, smiling approvingly. "Quite right. Your actions have been correct, although"—he glanced at his data pad—"your supervisor's concerned with the amount of leave you've taken lately."

"All of this work had been on my own time, sir. I didn't want to do it on Navy time."

Gaston scowled. "We're on Navy time now." He sat silently for a moment, pretending to consider the issue, while Ray fretted.

To be truthful, Gaston had made up his mind before McConnell ever walked in the room. He'd just wanted to interview the engineer himself before letting him go on to Carson.

Defender was too widely known, at least at the lower levels. It was a miracle the media hadn't picked it up already. It was popular, the kind of grassroots concept reporters loved. No matter that it would never be built. If he said no, then he'd be blamed as one of the people who kept it from happening. Better to let McConnell hang himself. Gaston didn't have to support it, just pass it on.

"All right, I'll forward it 'without endorsement.' "

Ray had begun to hope.

The meeting with Admiral Carson had begun poorly. The admiral had granted him fifteen minutes between other appointments, and appeared distracted. Ray had started his pitch, but Carson had cut him off after only a few words, chopping with one hand as if to cut off the stream.

"I'm familiar with the design, Mr. McConnell," Carson had said with irritation. "I've received three copies in the past two days, besides this one. I'm also familiar with the problem. I've spent most of the last week in Washington, answering questions about our own vulnerability and what SPAWAR could do to counter it.

"I've also been fully briefed about Chinese antisatellite threat," he said finally. "The current estimation is that the Chinese can't possibly have many more of the kill vehicles."

He walked over to where McConnell sat, almost leaning over him. "I've also looked over your personnel file. I was looking for your academic credentials. They're bad enough: No doctorate, a master's in electrical engineering and an undergraduate degree in physics. What made you think we'd take a spacecraft designed by you seriously?"

Carson picked up a data pad and checked something on the display. "And then I found this: After your master's degree, you applied for the astronaut program. Correct?"

Ray nodded. "Yes."

"And were turned down. And then you joined the Air Force. You served six years as a junior officer, and during that time applied three more times to become an astronaut. Also correct?" His tone was more than hostile.

"Yes sir. Each time I missed by just a few percentage points. I hoped . . ."

"You hoped to get into space with this half-baked fantasy!" shouted

Carson, pointing to *Defender*. "Did you plan on scoring the theme music for your little adventure, too?"

"Admiral, I've always been interested in space, but that doesn't have anything to do with this. I just want to get this idea to where it will do the most good."

Carson had sat, glowering, listening while Ray protested.

"Your idea is worthless, Mr. McConnell. At best, it's a distraction at a very difficult time. At worst, it's a personal attempt at empire building, but a very crude one.

"Although you've broken no rules I'm aware of, I am directing the Inspector General's office to review your activities and your work logs to see if any of your fantasizing has been done on government time. If that is the case, docking your pay will be the weakest punishment you will suffer. Now get back to work and hope I never hear about *Defender* again!"

Sitting in his office, Ray struggled with his feelings. He'd created *Defender* because he'd seen the need for it. Why didn't the chain see that need as well? Was he wrong? Maybe he didn't know enough to do it. But he'd had lots of help in designing *Defender*. And he'd gotten lots of mail back, some critical, but more supportive, some even offering help.

Was it time to sit down and shut up? He liked his job and the people he worked with. He didn't want to lose it over *Defender*.

He hadn't expected the command to be hostile. Indifferent, yes, but once he'd shown them the logic of the design, he'd hoped for some support.

He picked up the phone then, remembering, put it down, and pulled out his personal cell phone. No personal calls on a Navy line. He looked up a number and punched it in.

"Jennifer Oh."

"Hi, Jenny. It's Ray McConnell." He tried to sound cheerful, but even he could tell it didn't work.

"Ray, you don't sound too good. What's wrong? Problems with *Defender*?"

"Only if I want to keep my job." He sighed. "Let's just say that the Space and Naval Warfare Systems Command won't be giving me its endorsement. Admiral Carson almost had me thrown in the brig."

She laughed, half at his joke and also to cheer him up. "You're joking." He could hear the smile in her voice.

"He's siccing the IG on me, to see if I've wasted any Navy time on this quote half-baked fantasy unquote."

"That's not good." She paused, then asked, "So, you've gone all the way up your chain of command with no success?"

"I'd call that an understatement," he replied.

"Well, then it's time to try another chain," she said forcefully. "Let me make some calls."

"What?" McConnell was horrified. "Jenny! I'm poison. Please, just ditch anything you have with my name on it. *Defender*'s all over the Web. We'll just have to hope someone picks it up and uses it."

"No, Ray. We're not going to just sit. *Defender*'s a good idea, and I'm going to do everything I can for it." She paused again, and her tone softened, almost calming. "Let me call some of my friends on the NAVAIR staff. Admiral Schultz is a pilot and an 'operator,' not some bureaucrat. I've met him, and I think he'll give you a chance."

Ray didn't know what to say except, "Thanks, Jenny. I hope this doesn't backfire on you."

"Anything worthwhile is worth a risk, Ray. I'll call you this evening and tell you what I find out."

Office of the Chief of Naval Operations, The Pentagon, September 28

"I am not going to go into the Joint Chiefs of Staff and propose that we adopt some crackpot design that came off the Internet!" Admiral John Kramer was so agitated he was pacing, quickly marching back and forth as he protested.

Admiral William Schultz, Commander in Chief, Naval Aviation, sat quietly in his chair. He'd expected this reaction, and waited for Kramer to calm down a little. Schultz was calm, sure of himself and his mission.

"I've checked out this design, John, and the engineer. Both are OK. There are some technical questions, but nothing he's done here is science fiction. The man who designed it, Ray McConnell, had a lot of help. It may be unofficial"—Schultz leaned forward for emphasis—"but it's good work."

He sat back, straightening his spine. "It's also the only decent idea I've heard in almost two weeks."

Kramer and Schultz were both pilots, and had served together several times in their Navy careers, but where Kramer was tall, and almost recruiting-poster handsome, Schultz was only of middle height, and stockier. And his looks would never get him any movie deals. His thinning sandy hair was mussed whenever he put his navy cap on, while he was sure Kramer kept his in place with mousse. Kramer was a good pilot, but he'd also been the staff type, the "people person." Or so he thought.

Used to the convoluted, time-consuming methods of the Pentagon, the CNO continued to object. "Even if we did propose it, and even if it was accepted, where would we get the money?"

"Somewhere, John, just like we've done before. The money's there. We just have to decide what's the most important thing to spend it on."

Schultz continued, mentally assigning himself three Our Fathers and three Hail Marys. "Look, I've heard the Air Force is buying into *Defender* in a big way. They think it can work, and as far as they're concerned, if it's got wings, it belongs to them."

Kramer looked grim. The Air Force was shameless when they talked about "aerospace power." He nodded agreement.

"Let them get their hands on any armed spacecraft, and the next thing you know, we'll lose SPAWAR. Remember the time they tried to convince Congress that we should scrap our carriers and buy bombers with our money?" Kramer frowned, listening.

Schultz pressed his point. "Do we have any viable alternative for stopping the Chinese, sir?"

Kramer shook his head. "The launch site is out of Tomahawk range, and the President has already said that he won't authorize the use of a ballistic missile, even with a conventional warhead. And you'd need lots of missiles. The way that site is hardened, I'm not certain a nuke would do it."

"Air Force B-2s could reach it," Schultz said quietly.

"But they can't be sure they'd get out alive. The defenses are incredibly thick, and they're expecting us to use bombers. And it would take several aircraft to destroy the gun. We might have to commit as many as ten and expect to lose half."

"This is better, John. Look, McConnell's flying in here tomorrow. You can meet him yourself. I've listened to him, and I'm convinced."

"Then that's what we'll try to sell," Kramer decided.

Three

Indecision

Office of the Chief of Staff of the Air Force
September 30

General Michael Warner was an unusual Chief of Staff. He flew bombers, not fighters. In an Air Force that gave fighter pilots most of the stars, it was a sign of his ability, not only as an officer, but as a politician. Looking more like a banker than a bomber pilot, he had an almost legendary memory, which he used for details: of budgets, people, and events.

Pilots lived and died because of details. They won and lost battles because of them. And the general kept looking for some small detail that his deputy, General Clifton Ames, had missed. The three-star general had put the target analysis together personally.

Ames had nothing but bad news. An overhead image of the Gongga Shan launch site filled the wall screen. "I've confirmed there's no way the Navy can stretch the range of their Tomahawk missiles. They've got smaller warheads than our air-launched cruise missiles anyway. And even if we could adapt a ballistic missile with a conventional warhead, they aren't accurate enough for this target."

His data pad linked to the screen, Ames indicated various features of the site as he talked. "The Chinese built this installation expecting it to be attacked by cruise missiles. It has heavy SAM and AAA defenses. They've mounted radar on elevated towers to give them additional warning time of an attack. They've even constructed tall open framework barriers across the approach routes a cruise missile might use." He pointed to the large girder structures, easily visible in the photograph.

"The barrel and all vital facilities are hardened, and there's the matter of the gun itself. Given its three-meter bore, intelligence says the barrel thickness is at least a foot. Damaging that will require precision at a distance—precisely the capability we're now lacking."

"To get an eighty percent chance of success would take twelve B-2s, each carrying eight weapons." Ames knew he was talking to a bomber pilot, and watched for Warner's reaction. The chief just nodded glumly, and Ames continued.

"And the worst part is that the Chinese would have the gun back in operation again within a few months, possibly a few weeks. We're certain the barrel is constructed in sections, like the Iraqi gun. If a section is damaged, you remove it and replace it with a spare section. We've even identified in the imagery where they probably keep the spares.

"We estimate follow-up strikes would be needed every two weeks—indefinitely."

Even as he said it, Ames knew that wasn't an option. Airpower provided shock and speed, but it had to be followed up by something besides more air strikes.

"What about losses?" Warner asked.

"Using the standard loss rates," Ames replied, "there's a good chance we'll lose several bombers in the first few raids. And part of the flight path is over Chinese territory." The implications for search and rescue were not good.

"All right, Cliff. Send this on to the Chairman's office with my respects. And my apologies," Warner muttered.

"Sir, I've been looking at *Defender*," Ames offered. "One of my friends in the ABL Program Office passed it to me with his analysis. I think we should consider it."

Warner had heard about *Defender*, of course, but hadn't had time to do more than dismiss it as a distraction. "Are we that desperate?" the chief asked.

Gongga Shan Mountain, Xichuan Province, China
September 30

General Shen Xuesen stood nervously in the launch center. It was hard to maintain the unruffled demeanor his troops needed to see. He needed all of his experience to look calm and relaxed.

Visitors at such a time would make anyone nervous, and worse, distract the launch team. A television crew was unthinkable, but there they were. It was a State-run crew, of course, and they were being carefully supervised, but they brought lights and confusion and, worst of all, exposure.

Now they were filming an actual launch. Beijing had even asked if they could film the intercept, but Shen had refused absolutely, on security grounds. He understood the propaganda value of the Dragon launch, and offered to supply tapes of previous shots. They all looked alike. Who would know?

But the piece needed shots of activity in the launch center, and the reporter would add his narration. At least the general had been able to avoid an interview, again citing security reasons.

INN News
September 30

The oval opening erupted in flame, and a dark blur shot upward. Mark Markin's voice accompanied the video. "Released less than two hours ago, this dramatic footage from Gongga Shan Mountain in China shows the launch of a *T'ien Lung*, or Celestial Dragon." Markin's voice continued as the scene shifted to a more distant shot. The mountaintop, a rugged texture of browns, was capped by a small white cloud of smoke that lingered in the still morning air.

"That is their name for the spacecraft, or 'ASAT vehicle,' as U.S. officials describe the weapon. They also confirmed the destruction of another GPS satellite just a short time ago, the time of loss consistent with the launch shown here.

"This footage was released through Xinhua, the Chinese official news agency. The narrator claimed that China had now demonstrated military superiority over the United States, and that their superiority had halted American aggression in the region."

The mountaintop and its fading smoke were replaced by a computer-drawn representation of the gun, angled upward inside a transparent mountain.

"Intelligence officials here believe that the gun is based on the work of Dr. Gerald Bull, who designed a smaller weapon for Iraq. That weapon had a barrel of almost a hundred feet and a bore of nearly a meter. It was capable of launching a projectile several hundred kilometers, and although it was fired successfully in tests, it was never put into service. The Chinese would have no problem obtaining this technical knowledge from the Iraqis, probably in exchange for weapons."

Computer animation showed the process of loading the projectile, the launch, and sabots falling away from the projectile before a rocket booster fired.

"Before he was killed, possibly by foreign agents, Bull wrote of using such guns to launch spacecraft. Sources have hinted that a smaller gun, believed capable of firing across the straits of Taiwan, was built and tested. They now speculate that gun may never have been made fully operational, and have just served as a test bed for this much larger weapon."

The animation disappeared, replaced with Markin, with an image of a GPS satellite behind him. "This brings to four the number of GPS satellites known to have been destroyed by China. While American officials have wondered publicly about how many *T'ien Lung* vehicles the Chinese can build, China threatened during the broadcast to destroy the entire GPS constellation unless 'America abandoned its plans for Pacific hegemony.' "

United Flight 1191, En Route to Washington, D.C. September 30

Ray McConnell turned off the screen and put his head back against the seat. He hated being right, and he knew those "American officials" were indulging in wishful thinking. China's space program had a good base of design experience. The kill vehicle, the *T'ien Lung*, was not trivial, but it was well within their capabilities. The GPS satellites were unarmored and had only the most limited ability to maneuver. Technically, it wasn't a problem.

And logically, if they'd committed themselves to this premeditated confrontation, would they only have four or five bullets for their gun? *I'd have two dozen stockpiled, and a factory making more*, Ray mused.

It was bad news, although it helped strengthen his case.

He said it again. His case. Schultz had called him from Washington last night, telling him to come out ASAP, on Navy orders.

Sitting in his apartment, still depressed about his meeting with Carson, Schultz's call had struck like lightning. McConnell hadn't known what to think or hope.

He'd called Jenny to thank her, then frantically packed. He'd spent most of the night trying to organize the jumble of material that had supported the *Defender* design effort. McConnell hadn't even phoned work, just sending an e-mail asking for leave.

Ray glanced at his watch, still on California time. By rights, Rudy only got the e-mail at seven, about the same time the plane had taken off. Ray would be on the ground in another few hours, and hopefully by the time the brass heard anything, he'd know one way or the other.

McConnell decided he did feel hopeful, but he couldn't tell whether it was for *Defender* or his own personal success. Ray hadn't even realized that he personally had anything at stake until his meeting with Carson yesterday. He'd thought of *Defender* as just an engineering project. His personal stake in it was greater than he'd realized, but that was all right. Other people, like Jenny, were committed to it as well, and that spurred him on.

He hooked his data pad up to the screen built into the chair back and started opening files. *Defender* still needed a lot of work. He'd seen enough Pentagon briefings to know what was expected. He couldn't make her perfect, but he could at least hit the high points.

"Ladies and gentlemen, this is the pilot. We've just received word that Air Traffic Control has rescheduled our arrival into Dulles to four-fifteen instead of three-ten this afternoon. There's no problem with the weather, but because of the recent problems with the GPS system, they've just announced they'll be spacing aircraft farther apart near the airports, as a precaution.

"United apologizes for the delay. Passengers with connecting flights . . ."

McConnell smiled. For once, he was glad for the extra time in the air.

Office of the Chief of Staff of the Air Force, The Pentagon September 30

Captain "Biff" Barnes tapped his data pad and the file collapsed down into a small spaceship icon. His presentation had condensed McConnell's hundred-page design document down to fifteen minutes. It had been a long fifteen minutes, with Warner, his deputy, General Ames, and a flock of colonels watching intently. They'd all asked a lot of questions. Barnes had been able to answer many of them, especially about the laser installation, but not all. *Defender* was definitely a work in progress.

General Warner opened the discussion. "Captain, you've told General Ames that you think *Defender* will fly."

Well, thought Barnes, *actually I passed the file to Ed Reynolds in the ABL Program Office and Eddie gave it to the general. Also, I only told Eddie that* Defender *was better than anything else I'd heard of. The next thing I know, I've got two hours to prep a brief for the Chief of Staff of the Air Force.*

But Barnes didn't feel like correcting either general. "It's the best shot we have, sir," trying to sound positive, "unless there's something in the 'black' world." The armed forces ran a lot of "black" programs, secret projects with advanced technology. The F-117 had been one of the most famous. Was there one to deal with this threat?

"Nothing that will help us, I'm afraid." The general shook his head, half-musing to himself. "The X-40's operational, but she was never supposed to be more than a test bed. She doesn't have the payload for this in any case."

Looking at Barnes directly, Warner continued, "Yes, Captain, there is technology in the classified world that would help us—in anywhere from five to twenty years. The Chinese have jumped the gun on us." He sounded angry.

"We should own this crisis, and we just don't have the tools to deal with it! And now some SPAWAR employee and his buddies in their free time have come up with this, and we're all taking it seriously?"

Barnes waited for the general to continue. When it appeared he'd run down, the captain said, "Well, sir, at least he's former Air Force."

Warner laughed, a little grimly, then looked at the wall clock. "All right, then, Captain. Let's go see if the Joint Chiefs have a sense of humor."

National Military Command Center, The Pentagon
September 30

Ray McConnell looked around the fabled War Room. Every available chair was filled, usually by someone in uniform, and often by a uniform with stars on it.

The Joint Chiefs themselves sat on both sides of a long table, with the Chairman at the head on the left. A briefer's podium stood empty at the head, and behind the podium, the entire wall was an active video display. Ray almost felt at home.

He also felt rushed and a little unorganized. His plane had landed just a short time before. The Metro had taken him straight from Dulles to the Pentagon, and Admiral Schultz himself had met Ray. The outgoing admiral had quickly filled him in and shared some of his enthusiasm with the hurried engineer. They'd dropped his bags in the CNO's office, of all places, and made the meeting with only minutes to spare.

Several rows of chairs to one side of the main table were filled with a gaggle of aides, experts, and assorted hangers-on, including Ray. Nervously, he typed on his data pad, working on the design that was never finished.

The Vice Chairman, a Navy admiral, stepped up to the podium, and the buzz in the room quickly died. "Gentlemen, the Chairman."

Everyone rose, and Ray saw General Kastner, the Chairman of the Joint Chiefs of Staff, enter and take his seat. McConnell wasn't normally awed by rank, but he realized that this collection of stars could really make things happen. They literally were responsible for defending the country, and that's what they'd met to do.

The Vice Chairman, Admiral Blair, tapped the data pad built into the podium. A bullet chart appeared on the screen. It was titled "Protection of Space Assets."

"Gentlemen, our task today is find a course of action that will protect our satellites from Chinese attack. Any solution we consider"—and he started to tick off items on the list—"must include the cost, the technological risk, the time it would take to implement, and the political repercussions." He glanced over at Kastner, who nodded approvingly.

Blair continued. "Above all," he said, scanning the entire room, "it must work, and work soon. The material costs alone have been severe, and the potential effects on American security and the economy are incalculable.

"For purposes of this discussion, while cost should be considered, it is not a limitation. Also, the President considers these attacks by China an attack on American vital interests, although he has not made that decision public."

Nor will he, Ray thought, *until we can do something about them*. So cost wasn't a problem, just shut down the Chinese, and do it quickly.

Blair put a new page up on the display, listing some conventional methods of attack. "You've all sent analyses indicating that these are not viable options. Our purpose is to see what other means you've developed since those initial reports."

Kastner stood up, taking Blair's place at the podium. Blair sat down at his left. The Chairman looked around the room. "To save time, let me ask a few questions. The President has asked me if we can arm a shuttle and use it to defend the satellites." His tone was formal, as if he already knew the answer.

Kastner looked at General Warner, who glanced around the table before replying. "The Air Force would recommend against that. Not only would it take too long to prepare, it's too vulnerable during launch. Certainly if they can shoot down a GPS satellite, they can shoot down a shuttle."

The Chairman nodded, then looked at the Chief of Naval Operations. "Can we use a missile to shoot down the kill vehicle?"

Admiral Kramer answered quickly. "We'd hoped that would work, sir, but we're sure now that we can't. We had two Aegis ships in a position to track the last ASAT shot seven days ago. We've been analyzing the data since."

"The *T'ien Lung*," Kramer pronounced the Chinese name carefully, "is too fast. Our Standard Block IVs can shoot down a ballistic missile, but as hard as a ballistic intercept is, it's easier than this. At least a ballistic missile is a closing target, but the ASAT is outbound. It's a tail chase from the start. Even if we launched at the same moment, the intercept basket is nonexistent."

"Does the Army concur?" Kastner looked at the Army's Chief of Staff. The Army also had an active antiballistic-missile system.

"Yes, sir. It has to be from above." General Forest didn't look pleased.

Ray realized the general had just told the Chairman that the Army didn't have a role in solving the crisis. Of course, the Commandant of the Marine Corps looked even unhappier. This was one beach his men couldn't hope to storm.

General Kastner announced, "I'm also allowed to tell you that there are no special assets that might be able to destroy the launch site using unconventional methods."

In other words, Ray thought, *they can't get an agent into the area.* McConnell didn't even want to think about how he'd destroy the launcher. Talk about the Guns of Navarone . . .

Which meant they were getting desperate. McConnell saw what Kastner was doing, eliminating options one by one. He knew about *Defender*. He had to know. Ray didn't know what to feel. Was this actually going to happen? Fear started to replace hope.

General Warner finally broke the silence. "Sir, the Air Force thinks we can make the *Defender* concept work."

Admiral Kramer shot a look at Schultz, sitting next to Ray. Then both looked at McConnell, who shrugged helplessly. Warner's aide was loading a file into the display, and Ray saw *Defender*'s image appear on the wall. This was becoming a little surreal.

"Captain Barnes from our ABL Program Office has put together a presentation on the design." Ray saw a black Air Force captain with astronaut's wings step up to the podium. As he started to describe the spacecraft, McConnell felt irritation, an almost proprietary protectiveness about the ship. His ship. Ray wanted to speak up, to protest that he could describe it better than anyone, but Kramer wasn't saying anything, and Ray could only remain silent.

It seemed to take forever for Barnes to work his way through the different sections: space frame, weapons, sensors, flight control. The final slide was a list of unsolved design issues.

Ray spoke softly to Schultz beside him. "He's got an old copy of the file. I've solved two of those questions and added a new one."

Schultz nodded, then pulled out his data pad and typed quickly. Kramer, watching the presentation, looked down at his pad, and tapped something, then turned to look at Schultz, nodding.

General Forrest had started to ask about one of the issues when Admiral Kramer spoke up. "Excuse me, General, but that list may be a little old. Mr. McConnell, the engineer who designed *Defender*, is here, and has solved some of those problems."

Schultz nudged Ray, and the engineer stood up and moved toward the podium. As he passed Admiral Kramer, the naval officer muttered, "Go get 'em, Ray." The engineer never felt less like getting anyone in his life.

As he approached the podium, Captain Barnes shot him a hard look, seemingly reluctant to leave. Ray said, "Hello," conscious of the captain's sudden obsolescence, and tried to smile pleasantly. Barnes nodded politely, if silently, picked up his notes and data pad, and returned to his chair.

Ray was acutely aware of the many eyes on him. He linked his pad into the screen and transferred the most recent version of the file to the display. He used the moment's fiddling to gather his wits. He'd given dozens of briefs. This was just a little more impromptu than most. And much more important.

"I'm Ray McConnell, and I designed *Defender* to protect assets in space from ground-based attacks. It uses the Lockheed VentureStar prototype with equipment currently available to detect launches, maneuver to an intercept position, and kill the attacking vehicle. It also has the capability to destroy the launch site from orbit."

Barnes had said that much, Ray knew, but he'd felt a need to also make that declaration, to say to these men himself what *Defender* was and what it could do.

He opened the file, and rapidly flipped through the large document. McConnell realized that the pilot had done a pretty good job of summarizing *Defender*, so he concentrated instead on the work that had gone into selecting and integrating the different systems. That was his specialty, anyway, and it improved the credibility of his high-tech offspring.

A message appeared on his data pad from Admiral Schultz as he talked. "Are there any Army or Marine systems in the design?" Ray understood immediately what Schultz was driving at, and spent a little time on the kinetic weapons, adapted from Army antitank rounds. There wasn't a piece of Marine gear anywhere on the ship, and McConnell mentally kicked himself for not understanding the importance of Pentagon diplomacy.

Ray made it to the last slide as quickly as he could, and felt positive as he assured the assembled generals that all the questions listed there could be answered.

"Thank you, Mr. McConnell." Kastner rose again and Ray quickly returned to his seat, barely remembering to grab his data pad. "I'm much more confident about *Defender*'s ability, and probability, than I was at the start of this meeting. It is my intention to recommend to the President that *Defender* be built, and soon."

McConnell felt a little numb. Schultz gave him a small nudge and smiled.

"We haven't really discussed the political implications of arming spacecraft." General Forest's tone was carefully neutral, but his expression was hard, almost hostile. Would he fight *Defender*?

Kastner was nodding, though. "A good point, Ted, and part of our task." He looked around the table. "Admiral Kramer?"

"I believe the Chinese have solved that issue for us, sir. They've fired the first shot, and said so proudly and publicly." He smiled. "I think *Defender*'s name was well chosen."

General Warner added quickly, "I concur. GPS is dual-use. The gaps are already starting to affect civilian applications, and that will only get worse. And those civilian applications are worldwide, not just here in the U.S."

"All of our public statements will emphasize that we are taking these steps only as a result of Chinese attacks," Kastner stated.

Admiral Kramer quickly asked, "Should *Defender* even be made public? With enough warning, the Chinese might be able to take some sort of countermeasure."

Kastner considered only a moment before answering. "All right, my recommendation will be that *Defender* remain secret until after its first use."

General Warner announced, "I'll have my people look for a suitable development site immediately. With all the Air Force bases we've closed . . ."

"Your people aren't the only ones with runways, General. This is a Navy program. Mr. McConnell is a Navy employee."

"And that's why he put his design on the Internet, because of the tremendous Navy support he was receiving." Warner fixed his gaze on Kramer, almost challenging him to interrupt. "It was my understanding that he offered this design to the DoD as a private citizen. Certainly the

Air Force is the best service to manage an aerospace-warfare design. We'll welcome Navy participation, of course."

"The Navy has just as much technological expertise as the Air Force. And more in some of the most critical areas . . ."

Ray understood what was going on even as it horrified him. *Defender* would mean a new mission, and if it worked, a lot of publicity. That mattered in these lean times, for money, for recruiting, maybe for the future in ways they couldn't guess. But now they were arguing over the prize like children.

"The Army's experience with ballistic-missile defense means we should be able to contribute as well." General Forest's tone wasn't pleading, but his argument almost was.

Kastner spoke forcefully. "We will meet again at 0800 hours tomorrow morning. Every service will prepare a summary of the assets it can contribute, and any justification it might feel for wanting to manage the project."

Oh, boy, thought McConnell. *It's going to be a long night.*

INN Early News, London
October 1

Trevor West stood outside Whitehall while morning traffic crept past him. His overcoat and umbrella protected him against a rainy London day, but the wind fought his words. He spoke up, and held the microphone close.

"After an emergency meeting of Parliament this morning, in which the Prime Minister spoke on the Chinese antisatellite attacks, the British government has officially condemned the Chinese and demanded that they stop. The Official Note, which was given to the Chinese ambassador here approximately half an hour ago, protests not only the attacks themselves but the 'militarization of space.'

"The Chinese ambassador received the Note without comment.

"The American ambassador, provided with a copy of the Note, welcomed the British support and stated that the United States was doing everything in its power to defend its property.

"Ministry of Defense sources are unsure what the Americans plan to do about the Chinese attacks. They believe a direct attack on the launcher in southern China would be difficult, and the GPS satellites themselves are defenseless.

"One source speculated that the Americans may try to threaten Chinese interests elsewhere in Asia, pressuring them into stopping their attacks. They say they've even seen some signs that this may already be occurring. Of course, military pressure risks a wider conflict—a general war between the United States and China.

"MoD officials refused to speculate what Britain's position would be in such a case."

Office of the Chief of Staff of the Air Force, The Pentagon, October 1

Biff Barnes sat in a conference room with half a dozen other officers. Printouts and data pads covered the table, mixed with a litter of coffee cups, Chinese food from last night, and doughnut boxes from this morning.

The past twenty-four hours had been a blur to the captain. First the flurry of preparing to brief the Chief of Staff, then the JCS meeting. Barnes considered himself a good pilot, but a minor cog in a much greater machine. Suddenly he'd been asked to do new and challenging things, all at breakneck speed. And those things might change the Air Force. A corner of his mind also asked if this was going to help or hurt his chances for major.

As they had left the meeting yesterday, General Ames had said, "You did a good job on your presentation, Clarence."

Barnes, already in a foul mood, interrupted. "Please, sir, just 'Biff.' " Why was the general getting on a first-name basis?

Ames smiled. "Fine, Biff. Who knew they would back *Defender* as well? You did fine."

"Thank you, sir." Biff was unsure where this was going, but the back of his neck was starting to tingle.

"I need someone to put that presentation together, Biff. I'll give you as many of the staff as you need, and you can set up in my conference room. We've got until 0800 to come up with the arguments that will sell General Kastner on the Air Force owning *Defender*."

"Maybe you should get a lawyer," Biff suggested. He was half-serious.

"No, I want a pilot, and you're the only one in sight who's been an astronaut."

By now they'd reached Ames's office, but Biff didn't respond immediately. Finally, the general asked him flatly, "Do you want it?"

Biff knew he could say no if he wanted to. He believed Ames was a fair enough officer not to hold it against him. But Barnes was still mad at the Navy, and McConnell in particular. "Yes, sir. It's in the bag." He grinned, a fighter-pilot grin.

Now, the summary was almost ready, deceptively small for all the effort that had gone into it. Barnes was staring at the file's icon, wondering what he'd missed, when General Ames hurried into the room. He'd checked on their progress several times during the night, and Biff started to report when Ames cut him off.

"Turn on the news," Ames ordered a lieutenant at the far end of the room. The officer looked for the remote and grabbed it, then fumbled for the power control. ". . . no response to the Chinese demands yet. The spokesman only repeated demands by U.S. government that the Chinese stop their attacks."

The INN defense reporter, Mark Markin, stood in front of a sign that read, U.S. DEPARTMENT OF STATE.

"To repeat, the Chinese have now stated what their price is for stopping their attacks on the NAVSTAR GPS satellites. The U.S. must reduce its forces in the region below precrisis levels, especially in Korea and Japan. According to the statement this is 'to permanently remove the threat of U.S. aggression against China.' If the U.S. does so, the Chinese promise to cease their attacks. The ambassador also hinted that they might restart the stalled talks on human rights, piracy, and other long-standing disputes."

Ames said, "That's enough," and the lieutenant turned it off.

The general looked at Barnes. "The answer's 'Hell, no,' of course, but you've gotta love the way they're taking it to the media. And some of the reporters aren't helping the situation. 'Think about all those poor commuters without their GPS.' " Ames sounded disgusted.

Biff announced, "We're ready. Let's clean up and go get us a program."

National Military Command Center, The Pentagon
October 1

Ray McConnell had gotten about three hours of jet-lagged sleep last night, and that only because his eyes wouldn't focus on the screen any longer. He'd worked like a fiend, trying to finish *Defender* in one night while the CNO and his staff tried to figure out a way to keep her a Navy project.

He realized he should be on cloud nine right now. Not only was *Defender* going to be built, but the services were fighting over who would run it! Maybe it was fatigue, or the idea of the Air Force taking it away from him, but he wasn't even feeling optimistic.

Schultz had gotten no sleep, and looked it, but they'd all been energized in the morning by the Chinese ultimatum. Anger could substitute for sleep, for a little while anyway.

A group only slightly smaller than yesterday's waited for the Chairman's arrival. He arrived within seconds of eight o'clock, but followed by the Secretary of Defense. Both were hurrying, and the Secretary reached the podium before everyone had even finished standing.

Secretary of Defense Everett Peck was a political appointee, with little experience in the government. The balding, professorial lawyer had served as campaign manager for the President's election two years ago. He'd stayed out of trouble by letting the DoD alone while he dealt with Congress.

He motioned everyone back down, saying, "Seats, please, everyone," and then waited for half a moment while General Kastner took his chair.

The Secretary spoke, sounding rushed. "The Chairman and I have just come from a meeting with the President. This follows another meeting last night when General Kastner briefed us on *Defender*."

He paused, and tried to look sympathetic. "I understand the purpose of this meeting was to choose a service to run the *Defender* program, but that decision has been taken out of the Chairman's hands."

What? McConnell looked at the admirals, who looked as puzzled as he felt. In fact, everyone was exchanging glances. Secretary Peck was carefully reading from his data pad.

"The President has decided to create a new service to manage this new military resource. It will be structured similarly to the Special Operations Force, with assets and personnel seconded to it from the other services on an as-needed basis."

Peck didn't wait for that to sink in, but continued reading. "This service will be known as the Space Force and will be headed by Admiral Schultz." McConnell looked at Admiral Schultz, who looked thunderstruck.

The Secretary looked at Admiral Schultz, who was slowly recovering from the surprise announcement. "Your title would be 'Head of U.S. Space Forces.' You would retain your current rank. Do you accept?"

Just like that. Sitting next to Schultz, Ray heard the admiral mutter, "Ho boy," then stand. "I accept, sir."

"Good. Admiral, you will notify your deputy at NAVAIR to take over your duties immediately. You will no longer report to the CNO, but to the Chairman on administrative matters. You will report to me regarding operational matters. You can establish your headquarters wherever you wish, but I assume you will want to be colocated with the construction effort, wherever that is based."

Kramer, suddenly Schultz's former boss, still looked confused, as did most of the officers in the room. Kastner was smiling, and didn't seem like someone who'd had a decision taken out of his hands.

"I won't congratulate you, Admiral. You'll come to regret it, I'm sure, but I'm also sure you'll give it your best effort. And we are desperately in need of that. You have Presidential authority to call on any resources of the Department of Defense to get *Defender* built and stop the Chinese."

Peck glanced at his pad again, but didn't read verbatim. "Now for the bad news. Most of you know that the two spare satellites in orbit are also nonfunctional and presumed destroyed."

Ray's heart sank. He hadn't known that, and had assumed the spares were being kept in reserve.

"I will also tell you that although contracts have been let for replacement satellites, the President has decided that none be launched until the threat is contained."

Reasonable, Ray thought. *No sense giving the Chinese another three-hundred million-dollar target to shoot down. It'll take a long time for those replacements to be built, though.*

Peck continued. "The Chinese appear to be able to launch one vehicle a week. Given the number of satellites destroyed, at that rate the system will be fifty percent destroyed in seventy days. That is how much time we have to build *Defender*."

Suddenly, that three hours of sleep seemed like a lot.

Four

Skunk Works

Andrews Air Force Base, Washington, D.C.
October 1

One of Admiral Schultz's first requisitions had been an Air Force C-20F transport plane. The militarized Gulfstream executive jet was equipped for "special missions," which meant transporting high-ranking officers and government officials. It was loaded with communications equipment.

As the plane taxied for takeoff, Ray McConnell listened to Admiral Schultz as he argued with the Office of Personnel Management. Technically, as a civil servant, Ray worked for them.

"Of course I understand that you'd want to verify such an unusual order," he said calmly, almost pleasantly. "It's now been verified. And I need you to process it immediately. I know you've spoken to your director." His voice hardened a little. "I'm sure I won't have to speak to the director as well."

Schultz smiled, listening. "Certainly. There will be other personnel requests coming though this same channel, possibly quite a few. I'm certain you'll be able to deal with them all as swiftly as this one."

He turned off the handset and turned to Ray. "Congratulations. Say good-bye to Ray McConnell, SPAWAR engineer, and hello to Ray McConnell, Technical Director, U.S. Space Force."

Automatically, Ray protested. "I'm not senior enough . . ."

The admiral cut him off. "You're as senior as you need to be. You're now an SES Step 3, according to OPM." Schultz saw Ray's stunned look and smiled. "It's not about the money. You're going to be doing the work of a technical director, and you'll need the horsepower. If there was ever a test of the Peter Principle, this will be it."

Schultz leaned forward, and spoke softly and intently. "Listen, Ray, you're going to have to grow quickly. I gave you this job not because *Defender* was your idea, but because you had an original idea and put the pieces together to make it happen. Now you're going to have to do a lot more original thinking. You're going to build *Defender*, and set speed records doing it. Don't worry about bureaucratic limitations. Those are man-made. Our only barrier is the laws of physics, and I want you to bend those if you need to."

Schultz leaned even closer. "I'm also going to give you this to think about. This isn't just an engineering problem. You're going to deal with people—a lot of them, and you can't expect them all to automatically commit to *Defender* the way you have. There's a transition everyone in charge goes through as they increase in rank, from foot soldier to leader. Foot soldiers only have to know their craft, but leaders have to know their people as well."

He straightened up in his chair. "End of lecture. We're due to land in San Diego in five hours. By then, I've got to find us a headquarters and a place to build *Defender*. Your first job is to set up your construction team. Use names if you can, or describe the skills you need and let the database find them. After that—" He paused. "Well, I'll let you figure out what to do next."

Ray thought of plenty of things to do next. During the flight, Ray found himself searching thousands of personnel records, balancing the time it took to review the information with the need to fill dozens of billets. Taking a page from Admiral Schultz, he was careful to take people from all the military services, and to look for key phrases like "team player" as well as professional qualifications. He also included people from NASA, the National Weather Service, and even the FCC.

Then he went outside the government, requesting people from private industry. The government couldn't order them to participate, but if he had to, he'd hire them out from under their employers.

Remembering the JCS meeting and Captain Barnes, he called up the officer's service record. Eyes widening slightly, he'd added the pilot to his list. He could find a use for a man with his qualifications.

He added Jenny as well, without looking at her record. Somehow it seemed improper. He knew he needed comm specialists, and that he'd never have to wonder about her commitment to the project.

He also took five minutes to call Jim Naguchi at home. Ray had decided not to include Jim on the list. Although he was a good friend, he was very much involved with his own work, designing a new naval communications system. Naguchi had never shown up for any of the design sessions, either, although he knew all about *Defender*. Ray had been a little disappointed, but not everyone was as crazy as he was.

It was just before seven in California, and McConnell knew the engineer was still getting ready for work. "Naguchi here."

"Jim, I need you to clean out my office for me, and keep the stuff for a day or two. I'll send someone around to collect it."

"What?" Naguchi sounded surprised and worried at the same time. "I knew Carson was pissed. Did he bar you from the building?"

"No, it's nothing like that, Jim." Ray almost laughed. "I can't tell you everything, but I'm going to be very busy for a while. Remember *Defender*?"

"Sure."

"Has Jenny been keeping you briefed?" Ray asked.

"No, I haven't seen her for a while," he replied. "We only saw each other a few times. I was too laid-back for her. She's really competitive, Ray. We weren't good together."

"She's been over at the house a few times, with the design group," Ray remarked.

"Good for you, Ray. Brains and looks. But watch out. She's a hard charger."

Ray grinned. "I will. But get all my stuff from my office, would you please?"

"Sure, if someone doesn't think I'm ripping you off."

"No, I sent an e-mail to Rudy. He'll know. And don't tell anyone about this."

"Okay, and later you can explain where you are."

"I promise." McConnell hung up and sat, holding the phone. He had a hundred things to think about, but Jenny kept on moving to the top of the pile. Deal with it, Ray.

He used the phone to send her some flowers, with the message, "You've saved *Defender*."

Miramar Marine Corps Air Station, Near San Diego
October 2

Miramar was a big base, over twenty-three thousand acres of desert west of San Diego. During the Cold War it had been a Naval Air Station, home to the famous "Top Gun" fighter school. During the defense build-downs of the 1990s the Navy had moved out and the Marine Corps had moved in. They hadn't needed the whole base, though, and that made it attractive to the new U.S. Space Force.

Miramar had several airstrips, and the newly formed Defense Systems Integration Facility took over the most remote, along with a complex of unused buildings nearby. Authorization for the transfer had come in within an hour of Schultz's request, and they'd diverted the Gulfstream from their intended destination, North Island Naval Air Station, to land at Miramar.

They'd spent yesterday afternoon, after their arrival, speeding around the base with the commandant, a Marine general, in tow. General Norman had made it clear he'd been told to ask no questions, believe anything Schultz told him, and give them all the help he could.

By the time they'd finished the tour, transport aircraft had already started arriving. Schultz, as part of the security program, had ordered that as much of the supplies and as many people as possible be brought in by air.

General Norman had been more than true to his orders. Squads of Marines had appeared to unload transports. Armed patrols suddenly beefed up the perimeter. Teams of engineers had helped Public Works open and ready the buildings for use. A Marine Corps air-control unit had been flown in to handle the extra traffic, and a field kitchen had turned out their first dinner in their new home.

Besides the Marines, a gaggle of Navy officers had met the plane. During the flight to Miramar, Ray had heard the admiral dickering with his newly promoted replacement over how many of his staff could come with him and who had to stay. NAVAIR was located in nearby Coronado, so they'd all been able to get to Miramar in time to meet the plane. They would form the nucleus of the Space Forces administrative staff.

Ray had gone to sleep in a bare barracks room feeling almost optimistic.

October 3

The next morning, their first full day at Space HQ, had taught Ray more about engineering, and people, than he'd thought there was to learn.

Breakfast at 0530 had been a good start, but quickly interrupted. He and Schultz had been planning out the day when a civilian in an expensive suit and tie had hurried into the conference room being used as a mess hall. Escorted by an armed Marine, the middle-aged man had spotted the admiral and almost rushed to the table. Schultz saw him coming and stood.

The civilian had been looking for him. "Admiral Schultz? I'm Hugh Dawson, head of VentureStar Development." Dawson was tall, in his mid-fifties, and well built. Ray wondered if he'd played football in college.

Schultz smiled broadly and extended his hand. "Mr. Dawson. Please sit down and join us. We'll be working closely . . ."

Dawson did not sit down. "I don't know what we'll be working on," he replied, a little impatiently. "Yesterday afternoon my security director suddenly calls me in and briefs me into a new secret program. Then I get orders from the head of Lockheed Martin, Mr. Peter Markwith himself, to prepare VentureStar for immediate shipment here. Trash the rest of the test program, never mind the next set of modifications, just trundle her on up here for God knows what."

Schultz looked concerned, and asked, "Didn't you get the file on *Defender*?"

The executive was still standing. "I spent most of last night reading it. That has to be the worst cover story I've ever seen. Arming VentureStar? In two months? I came up here this morning to find out what's really going on."

Schultz said calmly, "That's not a cover story."

Dawson sat down.

The admiral motioned to one of the mess cooks. "Bring Mr. Dawson some coffee." He sat down facing the civilian. "I'd like you to meet Mr. Ray McConnell, Technical Director for the project, and for the U.S. Space Forces. He designed *Defender*."

Dawson automatically took McConnell's hand, but was still reacting to Schultz's words. "There's a U.S. Space Force?"

Schultz smiled proudly. "As of yesterday morning there was, and you and VentureStar are going to be a big part of it. Did you start the preparations to move her?"

Dawson nodded, replying automatically. "Yes, we've started. You don't argue with Peter Markwith. They're finishing up some work on the flight-control systems, but that will be done by the time the carrier plane arrives. Figure two days to make her safe and preflight the carrier, and a day to mate the two." He paused, suddenly.

"Markwith said you paid four billion for the VentureStar program. The whole thing. All of a sudden, we're a DoD program."

Ray looked over at Schultz, waiting for him to respond, but the admiral said nothing. In fact, he was looking sideways at McConnell. All right, then.

"Mr. Dawson, the design is sound," Ray ventured. "The Joint Chiefs, even the President have signed off on this. I know it can work."

Dawson sat, impassive. He wasn't convinced.

Damn it. McConnell realized he knew nothing about this man. *What does he care about? There has to be one thing.*

He tried again. "The Chinese are shooting down our GPS satellites, Mr. Dawson. VentureStar can stop that. She's the only platform with the space and payload to carry all the equipment we need. In seventy days we'll have her flying, doing things nobody ever imagined her able to do, and you'll be the one making the changes. She'll still be your project."

Dawson responded, "But the time! We can't possibly do it."

"We can if we decide we can, Hugh." McConnell was getting motivated himself. "No papers, no bureaucracy, no congressional briefings. Just results."

"Some of that paper is necessary," Dawson reminded him. "They laid out the P-51 on the floor of a barn, but that doesn't work anymore."

"We'll keep some, of course, but how much of that paper is needed to do the work? A lot just fills the government in on how you're doing, or tells the boss what he needs to know. A lot of it takes the place of good supervision. I'm not here to document a failure."

Ray pressed his point. "The rules will be different here. We're going to keep this group small. And I'm the government, as far as *Defender* goes. You won't have to write a memo to me because I'll be there on the floor with you."

Dawson sat, considering for a moment. "Marilyn's going to think I've taken up with another woman," he observed, smiling. "What about security?" Dawson asked. "Our PR people will want to know . . ."

Ray smiled. One down.

By late afternoon, enough people had arrived and been settled in so that they could start preparations to receive the vehicle. Or rather, preparing to prepare.

One of the hangars was big enough, but only with extensive modifications. A launchpad would have to be built next to it. A new computer hub, independent from the net, needed to be established, and some of the buildings were so old they weren't even wired for a network. They had to decide where to put launch control. Housing needed to be expanded. And the galley arrangements. And what about recreation?

Ray's to do list made him wish for a larger data pad. He had one idea and ran it past Schultz. "I love it," the admiral said. "I'll have one of my staff get right on it."

At Ray's suggestion, the evening meal was held outside. Even in the fall, San Diego's weather was excellent, and the Marine Corps cooks fixed an impromptu barbecue.

It was an important occasion. Almost everyone was a stranger to each other, and combined with the uncertainty of the times and the mission, he'd felt the stress level ramp up all day. McConnell realized he needed to get these people together, make them one team, with one mission. Schultz had approved of this idea as well.

Ray waited just long enough for everyone to be served. It was nothing special, just burgers and fried potatoes and greens and soft drinks. Ray was too nervous to eat himself. He'd tried to eat something, at Schultz's urging, but the first two bites started circling each other in his stomach, like angry roosters squaring off.

The time had finally come, though, and Ray had climbed up on an improvised stage. The portable amplifier gave its customary squeal as he adjusted the volume, and suddenly everyone's eyes were on him.

"Welcome to Space Force HQ." He paused for a moment, and heard a few snickers, mostly from the civilians. He smiled broadly, so he could be seen in the back, "I like the sound of it. The good news is, you are all founding members of America's newest and most modern military service."

He made the smile go away. "The bad news is, we're at war. The Chinese are killing our satellites, denying us the use of space, for both military and civilian use. *Defender* is going to regain control of space for us, for our use.

"You all understand the danger we face. They aren't on our shores, or bombing our cities, but they are overhead. And we know about the high ground.

"I'm expecting each of you, once you're settled, to take your job and run with it. More than that, though, if you see something that needs doing, don't wait for someone else to notice.

"There are going to be a lot more people coming in over the next few weeks. By the time the last of them arrives, you'll be the old hands, and I want you to tell them what I'm telling you now.

"You'll also wish we were twice as many. It's not for lack of resources. We've got a blank check from the President himself for anything or anyone we need. You're here because you're some of the best. I could have asked for more, but I didn't. A small organization thinks fast and can change fast.

"Some of you may think that this is an impossible task, or that even if it's possible, we don't have enough time to do it. It's just a matter of adjusting your thinking. The question to ask is not, 'Can this be done in time?' but 'What needs to be done to finish it in time?' "

Ray got down quickly, to gratifying applause. Schultz nodded approvingly, and Ray noticed someone standing next to him, still holding an overnight bag. Suddenly recognizing him as Barnes, Ray hurried over.

The captain took his hand, and was complimentary, although he didn't smile. "Good speech." He motioned to the crowd of perhaps fifty, eating and talking. "Did they buy it?"

Ray pointed out a small group of men and women. They sat around a circular table, talking as they ate. Their attention was on a sheet of paper in the center. One would point, or draw, and then someone else would take a turn.

"They'll never stop working on it," McConnell replied. "We should probably have a curfew so that we'll know they're getting enough sleep."

"So what do you have for me?" Barnes asked.

"We need someone to survey all the "black" DoD programs to see if there's any technology that we can use." Ray said it simply, like he wanted a list of names out of the phone book.

Barnes felt like telling him he was crazy, but only for a second. The Department of Defense ran dozens, possibly scores of "black" programs, not only classified, but also "compartmented." In other words, you didn't even know they existed unless you needed to know they existed. Each had its own security program, and it normally took a week or longer to get "briefed" into a program. Biff didn't think he had that much time.

McConnell was watching him closely. Was this some sort of test? He didn't think they had time to waste on such things. How to do it quickly?

"We'll have to go through the head of DoD security," Barnes suggested. "He's the only one who can grant me blanket access, and tell everyone to honor it."

"I'll call him tomorrow morning," said Schultz. "You'll have that clearance by lunchtime, along with Ray and me."

"We'll need a secure facility," Barnes added. High-security information was supposed to be kept in special rooms, electronically shielded, with carefully controlled access.

"We'll get you a shielded laptop tomorrow as well. That will be our secure facility until Public Works gets a real one set up."

Coronado Hotel, San Diego, California
October 4

The outside line rang, and Geoffrey picked up the phone. "Good morning, Coronado Hotel Concierge Desk. Geoffrey Lewis speaking."

"Mr. Lewis? This is Captain Munson, U.S. Navy. I'm sorry to call you at work, but we couldn't reach you before you left your home."

"The Navy?" Geoffrey was a little confused. He'd served in the Navy ten years ago, as a storekeeper. That was before he'd gotten his hotel management degree, before he started work here.

"I'll be brief, Mr. Lewis. I need someone to take care of a large group of people. They're very busy. You and a small staff will see to their needs while they work on other matters."

"Captain Munson, I'm not sure I understand. I'm quite happy . . ."

Munson named a figure over twice what Geoffrey made as a junior concierge. Lewis wasn't sure the senior concierge made that much.

"The job will last at least three months. You'll work hard for that money, and you'll have to live on site."

"And where is that site, exactly?" Geoffrey asked. The mystery of it was intriguing.

"Not too far," answered Munson carefully. "Your quarters will be quite comfortable. What's your decision?"

"Just like that?"

"Just like that," replied Munson. "We're a little pressed for time."

"The money's good," Lewis admitted. "But you don't know enough about me."

"We know quite a bit about you, Mr. Lewis. Please, if you don't want the job, I have other calls to make."

Geoffrey looked at the first thing on his list. Theater tickets for a couple from Kansas. Whoopie.

Space Forces Headquarters
October 5

Ray woke up thinking about housing. He'd gone to bed worrying about it, and was still thinking about it this morning. He was supposed to be building *Defender*, and instead he had to find places for people to live. But the first contingent of the Lockheed Skunk Works people would arrive from Palmdale this afternoon.

He hurried from the barracks past the office complex to the mess hall. None of the buildings he passed had originally served that purpose, but those were their present functions. The compound was already bustling, with people hurrying about on different errands. He could hear the sound of power tools from inside one empty building.

Coffee and a bagel were all he usually had for breakfast, and he could have had that at his desk, but people were already expecting him to put in an appearance in the morning, to be available. It was a tradition he'd decided to encourage.

He was taking his first bite when Biff Barnes walked in the door. Ray still felt uneasy about Barnes, guilty about embarrassing him at the JCS meeting. Was that why he'd picked him to work on *Defender*? But his qualifications made him a natural.

Barnes walked over to the table, and Ray motioned for the officer to join him. Ray's eyes were automatically drawn to Biff's astronaut wings.

"When were you in the astronaut program?" Ray asked. He tried not to sound like some autograph seeker.

"From '05 to '08," Barnes replied casually. "I flew one mission, then missed another because of mission change. I'd only missed one tour with the regular Air Force, so I decided to get back to real flying." His voice hardened a little. "And now this. I was supposed to get major and an Ops Officer billet after my tour in the program office. God knows what's happened to that."

Ray hadn't expected to hear that Barnes had voluntarily left the astronaut program. McConnell had worked as hard as he could for as long as he could remember to become an astronaut. And Barnes had walked away from it?

Almost without thinking, McConnell asked, "It wasn't medical?" His tone was incredulous.

"No," replied Barnes with a little irritation. "People do leave the program voluntarily. Proficiency time on T-38s is not the same as helping run a squadron or flying a fighter."

It was clear Barnes didn't think of his time as an astronaut fondly. And he was not happy with his assignment here. He liked to fly.

Ray offered, "I'm sorry I disrupted your tour, but I need pilots to help build *Defender*. In addition to all your other skills, you're a reality check on what's going on around here."

Barnes smiled, the first time Ray had seen the pilot pleased. "I think you'll need a bigger dose of reality than I can provide."

McConnell automatically smiled back. "Look, I'm sorry I upstaged you at that meeting. We had no idea the Air Force was going to back *Defender*."

"Yeah. I was the guy who suggested it to the brass." Biff looked like he was regretting the idea.

"And thanks for that support. I'm sorry I can't promise to make it up to you."

"Stop apologizing," Biff ordered. "I'm here, and I'll help you build her."

Ray nodded silently. It wasn't a ringing commitment, but he felt the air was clear.

Biff looked around, making sure there were no eavesdroppers, then turned on his data pad and passed it to McConnell. "Here's the review of those classified programs you asked for. It took me most of the night, but it was so interesting I didn't want to stop."

McConnell took the pad, handling it carefully. As he studied the long list, his eyes widened. "I had no idea . . ."

"Neither did I. After this is all over, we'll both have to burn our brains. The point is, there are some programs here that we might be able to use. I need a secure facility to work in, to store stuff."

Ray grimaced. "The engineers are working on beefing up the handling crane. Without that, we can't lift the VentureStar off her carrier. And after that they have to start work on the pad."

"Can we get more engineers?"

McConnell shook his head. "Not quickly. We're already using all the ones available on the West Coast. We'll have more in a week." He paused, considering. "Where are the programs you're interested in located?"

Biff saw where he was going. "They're spread all over the map, but they all have offices in D.C." He paused. "I leave right away, right?"

"You can take the C-20," Ray told him. "Hell, you can *fly* the C-20. We'll have something with metal walls set up by the time you get back."

Barnes face suddenly brightened. "Ray, the C-20 has metal walls."

McConnell smiled, nodding. "We'll need to post a guard, but Marines like guarding things. It lets them carry guns. Go get it set up."

Biff nodded and left quickly, almost running. Someone else was waiting.

Space Forces Headquarters
October 5
0430

They'd scheduled the arrival carefully. You couldn't count on overcast, especially in the California desert, so they'd chosen a satellite-free window after dark.

They all got up early to see it. Ray, standing by the end of the runway with a cup of coffee, saw them start to stream out of the buildings, walking slowly over to the tarmac. The handling crews were ready, and General Norman had arranged for a "nighttime base security exercise" that filled the area with patrols. The base fire department had also sent their equipment. Ray approved, but the thought made a small knot in his stomach.

Ray waited, impatient. They'd heard nothing, so everything should be fine. But nothing would be fine, not until it was all over.

Admiral Schultz walked up with a civilian in tow. "Ray, meet Mr. Geoffrey Lewis, our new morale officer." Seeing McConnell's distracted look, he reminded Ray, "Your idea? The concierge?"

Suddenly remembering, Ray shook the man's outstretched hand. "Welcome to the Space Force, Mr. Lewis." Lewis was a sandy-haired man, in his mid-thirties. Large glasses on his round face made his head seem large for the rest of his spare frame. While most of the civilians wore jeans and polo shirts, Lewis was dressed in khakis and a sport coat.

"Thank you, Mr. McConnell. The admiral's explained what you want done. I'm to take care of the people here. Run their errands, reduce their distractions. I've never had to sign a security form to be a concierge before."

McConnell grinned. "And you've never had Army quartermasters as your staff. But these people have all had their lives and jobs interrupted to work here. Do as much as you can to take care of their personal needs."

Lewis smiled. "I've already got a few ideas."

"Here she comes," said Schultz softly.

Ray turned as Schultz spoke, his attention drawn by the plane's landing lights as they came alive. The 747's white underside reflected the lights, but everything above the wing was in shadow.

Instinctively, Ray stepped back, awed by the size of the four-engined monster. It looked a lot bigger from the ground than it did from an airport jetway. The noise of the jet engines also grew until it was almost unbearable.

Ray began to fear that some terrible mistake had been made, that the jet had come in alone, but as it descended, the light finally caught the broad white wedge on top of the 747's fuselage.

The VentureStar was just half the length of the jumbo jet, and as wide as it was long. A smooth, blended shape, two short wings jutted out from the back, angling up and back. He knew it was huge, but it looked so fragile perched on top of the big jet.

He was suddenly afraid, and his insides tightened as he watched the plane come down and touch the runway. The engines crescendoed and the noise washed over him as the pilot cut in the thrust reversers. He could smell jet exhaust and burnt rubber as the plane's wake shook his clothing. He didn't relax until the plane came to a stop, then turned to taxi over to the hangar.

VentureStar was the prototype for a fleet of commercial single-stage-to-orbit space vehicles. In development since the early 1990s, an experimental small-scale version, the X-33, had successfully completed testing just after the turn of the century.

Like the space shuttle, VentureStar carried its payload in a big cargo bay, fifteen feet wide by fifty feet long. It used the same fuel, as well, liquid hydrogen and liquid oxygen. But the shuttle took months to prepare for a launch, and used expendable boosters that had to be reconditioned after each launch. VentureStar launched using her own aerospike engines, and landed conventionally like the shuttle. She could take fifty tons to low-earth orbit after two weeks' preparation.

The engineers were already preparing to lift VentureStar off the carrier aircraft. They had barely enough time before the satellite window closed. Teams also stood by to unload the 747, which carried instruments and spare parts. Some of them had strange looks on their faces, and Ray made a note on his pad to check with the security director. There was . . .

"Thanks for the flowers, Ray." A voice startled him, breaking his concentration. He turned to see Jenny smiling at him. She explained, "I came out to watch the landing and saw you over here."

"You're welcome," he replied automatically. Gathering his wits, he asked, "Are you okay with your job?"

"Setting up communications for an entire space program?" She laughed. "I could have waited ten years for that big a job, if I ever got it at all." She knew what he wanted to ask, and told him before he could. "I can do it. I've had to expand my consciousness a little, but I'll get it done."

She looked up at the huge spacecraft, perched on the even larger carrier plane. "This makes it real, doesn't it?" Her tone was half pride, half pleasure.

Ray caught himself about to say something stupid, about to brag about it all being his idea. But it only took one man to have an idea. It had taken a lot more to get it going, and would take that many more to bring it to life.

"It's starting to be real, Jenny." He wanted to stay, and talk, and he could see she would if he wanted to, but that wasn't why they were there.

Wishing each other good luck, they went to work.

Space Force Headquarters
October 7

His phone rang while Ray was inspecting the hangar. He'd been waiting all day. It was Schultz's voice, sounding resigned. "They've done it again. Check your pad."

McConnell activated his data pad. ". . . have confirmed the latest Chinese claim, made less than fifteen minutes ago. Another 'American targeting satellite' has been destroyed, and the Chinese renewed their promise to do the same to every American satellite unless they 'acknowledge Asian territorial rights.' "

The correspondent's face was replaced by a press conference, while his voice added, "In response to growing pressure to act, U.S. defense officials today announced a new program."

Ray's heart sank to the floor. Has some fool decided to take them public? Automatically, he started walking, while still watching the pad.

The official at the podium spoke. "To deal with this new threat to American commerce and security, an Aerospace Defense Organization has been established under the direct command of General David Warner, Chief of Staff of the Air Force. The other services will also take part. Its mission will be to defend American space assets against any aggression. Here is General Warner, who will take a few questions."

By now Ray was walking quickly, still watching the pad. He made it to Schultz's office just as the general was assuring the press that he had no intention of taking over NASA.

Ray's data pad was echoed by Schultz's wall screen. The admiral saw Ray and waved him in, with one eye on the screen. The rest of the admiral's attention was on the phone. "I appreciate the need for security, Mr. Secretary, but the effects on staff morale should have been considered. A little warning would have let us brief them. And I must have your assurance this will not affect our resources. Thank you. I'll call tonight, as always, sir. Good day."

Schultz hung up, almost breaking the little handset as he slammed it into its cradle. "Peck assures me this new organization is a blind, designed to distract attention away from us."

"And get rid of some of the heat DoD's been taking," Ray added.

"For about one week, I'll bet," Schultz agreed. "As soon as the Chinese shoot down another satellite, they'll be all over the general, asking him why he hasn't done something."

"And what about resources?" Ray asked, concerned.

"Well, he's going to need people, and money, and I have a hunch

Warner's going to take his charge seriously. I'd have to agree with him, too. I'm a belt-and-suspenders kind of a guy. So he might get people or gear we need."

Ray suggested, "Well, can we draw on his program? Use it as a resource?"

Schultz sharply disagreed. "No way. We don't want any links with them. Any contacts might get traced back. And if we start poaching, we'll make enemies. We have the highest possible priority, but we can't throw our weight around. There are people in every branch of the government who would love to see us fail, if they knew we existed."

Ray sighed. "I'll put a notice on the local net, and I'll speak personally to every department head, especially Security."

Schultz's attention was drawn to the wall display. A new piece, labeled REACTION, was on. A congressman was speaking on the Capitol steps to a cluster of reporters. Schultz turned up the volume. ". . . done the math, this new Aerospace Defense Organization will have to act quickly or we'll have nothing left to defend."

Space Force Headquarters
October 13

Barnes knocked on McConnell's open door, then stepped in almost without pausing. Everything was done quickly, Barnes thought, with the formalities honored, but only barely.

McConnell, in the middle of a phone call, waved him into a folding chair, the only other seat in the office, then said into the phone, "I'll call you back." He hung up and turned to face Barnes.

Expecting to be questioned about the technology survey, Barnes started to offer his data pad to McConnell, but Ray waved it back.

"You're close to done, aren't you?"

"Yes," agreed Biff. "We've already started to receive some material. But there's a lot of follow-up to be done."

"That's old business, Biff. I need you to turn it over to someone else as soon as you can." McConnell paused, but kept looking at him. "We need you to be mission commander for the flight."

Biff didn't say anything. He absorbed the information slowly. Although he'd wondered in his few spare moments who would get to fly the mission, he'd assumed NASA would supply rated astronauts.

Did he want the job? Well, hell yes. Biff suddenly realized how much he wanted to fly in space again, and on what would be a combat mission. He knew he could do it. He was a fighter pilot, after all.

McConnell pressed a key on his data pad. "Here's a list of the prospective flight-crew candidates." Biff heard his pad chirp and saw the file appear. He opened it and scanned the list as Ray explained.

"Most are already here, a few are not, but all met the criteria Admiral Schultz and I came up with. You'll need six: A mission commander, a pilot, a copilot and navigator, a weapons officer, a sensor officer, and an engineer. We listed all our requirements. If you disagree with any . . ."

"Your name isn't here," Biff interrupted.

"What? Of course not. It's not the whole team, just the . . ."

"No," Barnes insisted. "You're flight crew. You should be the engineer. You're putting her together. You know her best."

McConnell was as surprised as Barnes had been. "What?"

"Articulate answer, Ray." Barnes grinned. "Look at it this way. It's the ultimate vote of confidence. You build it, you fly it."

McConnell couldn't say no. "This only fulfills one of my lifelong ambitions," he answered, a little light-headed.

"One of mine, too. I get to boss you around."

Five

Exposure

INN News
October 26

Mark Markin's backdrop for his scoop was an artist's animation of the Chinese ASAT weapon, the Dragon Gun as it had been dubbed in the Western press. The artist had added a hundred-foot-long tongue of flame emerging from the barrel as a projectile left the muzzle. Markin didn't know if it was accurate, but it looked dramatic.

"With the crisis now into its second month, and seven GPS satellites destroyed, continued inaction by the United States has been taken as proof of their helplessness. Their refusal to act to protect these vital assets has been puzzling.

"But the situation may not be as it seems. Presuming that the administration would not stand idle, I was able to find hints that they may be acting after all. Residents surrounding the Miramar air base east of San Diego have reported heavy traffic at the front gate and cargo aircraft arriving at all hours."

The image shifted to a picture of Miramar's front gate. "On a visit to the base yesterday, we noticed increased security, and we were not allowed to take photographs on the base. There are also portions of the base we were not allowed to visit at all. All these provisions were blamed on an increased terrorist threat, but the Marine spokesman could not tell me the source of that threat.

"There have also been stories of hurried requests at defense contractors for personnel and equipment, but these could not be verified.

"All this could be attributed to activities of the Air Force's new Aerospace Defense Organization, but why at a U.S. Marine base? And why did this activity start weeks before the ADO was announced?"

Gongga Shan Mountain
October 28

The smoke was still swirling out of the muzzle when they left the command bunker. The group was small, just the general, Secretary Pan, and their aides.

Pan Yunfeng was First Party Secretary, and General Shen continually reminded himself of that as he answered the same questions he'd answered dozens of times now.

It was impossible to speed up the firing rate. The ablative lining inside the barrel had to be replaced after each launch. In tests, two-thirds of the projectiles had been damaged when the lining was reused, and there had been one near burn-though. Better lining would be more durable, but required exotic materials that were unavailable in sufficient quantity.

No, more men would not get the tubes relined more quickly. Although a kilometer long, it was just three meters in diameter, so only a limited number of men could work inside. All the old lining had to be removed, then each section of new lining had to be anchored and tested before the next section could be added.

Unlike many of China's leaders, Pan was relatively young, in his late fifties. His hair was black, and there was an energy about him that was missing from some of the other men Shen had dealt with. His impatience personified the feeling of the entire Chinese leadership. Why was it taking so long?

Now Pan stood on the side of the mountain, nudging one of the used liners with the toe. The ten-meter section was one quarter of a circle, and several inches thick. The outside was smooth, marked with attachment points and dimples, which Shen explained allowed for some flexing as the projectile passed.

The inside curve of the liner told the real story. The concave metal surface showed hints of the former mirror polish, but the heat and gun gases had pitted the lining, some of the pits deep enough to fit a fingertip. The different layers that made up the lining were visible, a mix of metal and ceramic and advanced fibers.

"Dr. Bull came up with this solution," Shen had explained. "The best steel in the world can't withstand the forces inside that barrel when it fires. Instead we just replace the liner after each launch."

"Which takes a week," the Secretary remarked with a sour face.

"It's not wasted, First Secretary. We use the time to upgrade the control system, test the breech, even improve the antiaircraft defenses." He pointed to a nearby hilltop, a new excavation on the side holding a massive billboard radar antenna.

"That radar is part of a new bistatic system designed to detect stealthy aircraft. We've also increased the depth of the antiaircraft belt and added more standing fighter patrols."

Later, in the general's office, Pan had questioned Shen even more, looking for ways of shaving a few days, even a few hours, off the interval between launches.

"We're concerned about the time it's taking, General. In any campaign of several months, we have to assume the enemy will take some action to counter our plans."

Shen listened respectfully. "I've seen the intelligence reports. I'm expecting, of course, that the Americans will do something eventually, but by then we will have won the first battle. And in a few months, we will have our advanced version of the T'ien Lung ready. And when you approve the construction of the second launcher, we will be even less vulnerable."

"But what measures have you taken in the meantime?"

"You know about the Long March booster modifications. You know our intelligence services are blanketing America and her allies."

Shen tried to reassure the official. "All we have to do is deny them the use of space. It's easier to shoot spacecraft down than it is to put them up. Have the Americans tried to replace any of the lost satellites? Have they launched any satellites at all since we started our campaign?"

The Secretary didn't answer, but Shen knew they both saw the same data.

Shen wanted to make his point, but was careful to keep his tone neutral. It didn't pay to argue Party officials into a corner. "The Americans have no choice. They'll either lose their valuable satellites, or publicly acknowledge our rights in the Pacific region. I think they'll wait until the last minute, refusing to accept the inevitable for as long as possible. When they do see they're backed into a corner, they'll give in. Either way, America is weaker, and we are the new champion of the countries opposing imperialism."

Space Force Headquarters, Miramar
November 5

They all looked at the wall display in Schultz's office. It showed a spiderweb of lines linking boxes. One box at the left was labeled "Begin Construction," and a dozen lines angled out of it. All the lines eventually led to a single box at the end that said "Launch." A dotted line with that day's date ran vertically across the diagram. Colors indicated the status of a task, ranging from deep red to grass green. Over half the chart was red, and a lot of the red was on the wrong side of the line.

Ray McConnell had called the meeting, officially to "brief" Schultz, unofficially to ask him to make a decision Ray couldn't.

"We've made tremendous progress." Ray hated the words as soon as he'd said them. *Trite, Ray. Be specific.* Using his data pad, he started to highlight boxes on the chart.

"The kinetic weapon rack will be installed this week, and the mounts for the laser are being installed right now. Sensor integration is time-consuming, but we've got good people on it."

He came to one box, labeled FABRICATE LASER PROPELLANT TANKS. "It's the one thing we couldn't plan for. Palmdale only had two fabrication units, and one has gone down. The parts to fix it will take two weeks to obtain and install."

McConnell nodded in the direction of Hugh Dawson, who had become a de facto department head at Space Forces HQ. "Lockheed Martin has moved heaven and earth, but we've only got one fabricator and two tanks to make. This is what happens to the plan."

He tapped the data pad and the boxes on the wall shifted. Lines stretched. One line, darker and thicker than the others, the critical path, changed to run through the Propellant box.

"At least the heat's off the software," someone muttered.

The new schedule added three weeks to the construction schedule. Luckily, Ray didn't have to say anything, because he couldn't think of anything to say. They'd struggled to cut corners, blown through bureaucratic roadblocks, invented new procedures. They'd carried positive attitudes around like armor against the difficulty of their task. Suddenly, he didn't feel very positive.

Schultz stared at the diagram, then used his own data pad to select the Propellant Tank task. It opened up, filling the screen with tables of data and a three-dimensional rendering of the two tanks in the cargo bay of *Defender.*

Defender's laser needed fuel to fire, hypergolic chemicals stored as liquids and mixed to "pump" the weapon. The ABL-1 aircraft carried fuel for fifty shots, an extended battle. *Defender* would carry thirty, enough for three or four engagements.

While the laser and its mirror could be taken out of its 747 carrier aircraft and used almost as it was, the laser's fuel tanks had been built into the aircraft's structure. They were also the wrong size and shape for the bay. New ones had to be made.

Schultz grunted and selected the 3-D diagram. It was replaced by a schematic of the cylindrical tank, not as neat and showing signs of being hurriedly drawn. The date on the drawing showed it was a month old. The multilayered tanks were built up in sections, then the end caps were attached.

"Reduce the number of sections in each tank," remarked the admiral. "That reduces the number of welds to be made."

"We can't make the sections larger," answered Dawson. "They come prefabricated from the subcontractor, and they're limited by the size of the jig."

"Then we reduce the number of shots," Schultz replied. "What if we cut the number of shots in half, six sections per tank instead of three?"

Ray heard an inrush of breath in the room. The laser was *Defender*'s main battery. Halving its firepower was a drastic step.

Schultz said, "Better any laser on time than a laser too late. We can replace the small tanks with larger as soon as they've been built."

McConnell nodded and started working. He ticked off points as he worked. "We'll save weight by carrying less laser fuel, but we'll need more structure surrounding the tanks. It's less weight overall, but it throws off all the center-of-gravity calculations." He paused. "And we only get enough ammunition for two engagements."

While Ray worked on the design, he saw Dawson recalculating the fabrication times. The executive finished first, and Ray watched him send the figures to the main display.

The chart shifted again, shrinking, but not enough. They were still a week late.

Ray spoke up this time. "We need more time. If we can't raise the dam, let's lower the water. Launch another satellite. That gets us a week." That was the decision he couldn't make. Would Admiral Schultz?

"At $300 million a bird, that's a pretty expensive week," Biff Barnes remarked.

Schultz nodded, agreeing with Barnes. "There are political costs as well. The public won't know why. Even the people launching the satellite won't know they're buying time for us."

Ray persisted. "There aren't any more corners to cut."

The admiral sat silently for a minute. Ray prayed for everyone to be silent. Schultz knew the situation as well as anyone in the room. He didn't look pleased, but it wasn't a pleasant situation.

"This is where I start earning my pay, I guess," Schultz announced. "All right. I'll pass this up the line." He looked over the assembled group. "And I'll make it happen. But you should all understand the political capital that will be spent here. We can't do this twice.

"You've got another week. Don't waste it."

INN News
November 11

"The addition of a name, one word, has caused the security dam around *Defender* to burst."

Holly Moore, INN's White House correspondent, reported this piece, rather than Markin, since it covered the political implications more than the military ones. She stood on the wind-whipped U.S. Capitol steps. The image lasted only seconds, though, before being replaced by the cover of the *Defender* design document.

"INN has obtained a copy of this detailed design for an armed spacecraft designed to attack targets in space and on the ground. According to our source, it was widely distributed in classified defense circles.

"Based on the civilian VentureStar spacecraft, soon to be entering commercial service, the design equips it with radar and laser sensors, guided ground-attack weapons, and a laser from the Air Force's Airborne Laser program.

"No one in the Defense Department would comment on the document, and everyone referred us to the Aerospace Defense Organization. We also tried to contact Mr. Ray McConnell, listed on the cover as the designer, but attempts to locate him have failed. There is another list of names on the inside, all described as contributors to the document. The few INN have located have either denied knowledge of *Defender* or refused to comment.

"Sources have linked *Defender* with the mysterious activity at Miramar. Since the initial reports about this Marine air base, security has been tightened to extraordinary lengths, with a recent notice banning all flights within ten miles of the base.

"Opposition to *Defender* has appeared just since reports of its existence were aired earlier today. Some are opposed to the militarization of space. Others don't believe the spaceship can be built in time to do any good, and are asking for an accounting of the cost. Links to websites opposing *Defender*, as well as the original document, are available on our website.

"Tom Rutledge, Democratic Senator from Kentucky, spoke on the Capitol steps moments ago."

The image changed to show a tall, photogenic man with a cloud of salt-and-pepper hair fluttering in the fall wind. "As a member of the Senate Armed Services Committee, I intend to find out why we were not consulted on this wasteful and extremely risky project. The investigation will also deal with the administration's continued inability to cope with this crisis. In less than three weeks, our expensive and valuable GPS satellites will be unable to provide even a basic fix."

Moore reappeared. "Here, with a related piece, is INN's defense correspondent, Mark Markin."

Markin appeared in front of the animated Dragon Gun again. "I interviewed Mr. Michael Baldwin, a well-known expert on the NAVSTAR GPS system. I asked him how long the system would be able to function under continued Chinese attacks."

Baldwin was a slim, long-faced man in his fifties with a short gray haircut. He sat against a backdrop of jumbled electronic equipment and computer screens. He spoke with ease, secure in his knowledge. "The constellation's been severely affected. There are few places on earth now where the military can get the kind of accurate fix it needs for missile guidance or precision navigation. There are a lot of places worldwide where civilian users can't get a basic fix. This has affected not only airline travel, but also more basic functions like rail and truck shipping. We've come to expect that GPS will always be there, like the telephone or electricity."

"How long before it ceases to be any use at all?"

"If the Chinese continue shooting down satellites at the rate of one a week, on November 25 it will be completely unusable."

The reporter asked, "Some people are saying that if we can't destroy the gun with Tomahawk missiles or air strikes, we should use nuclear weapons. What do you think of that?"

Baldwin seemed surprised by the question, but answered it quickly. "Nobody's died yet, but they're hurting the economy, and the military's ability to fight. It's too deep inside Chinese territory for anything but a ballistic missile, but I don't want us to use nuclear weapons. I don't know anyone who does." He grinned. "I'm hoping this *Defender* is real."

Markin asked, "Can we do anything to repair the constellation?"

Baldwin shook his head. "Not until they can protect the satellites somehow."

"So we shouldn't launch any replacement satellites right now?"

The expert shook his head. "That would be lunacy."

Space Force Headquarters, Miramar
November 15

"Be glad you're such a bad typist." The Security director's face was grim, but his tone was triumphant. He stood before McConnell's wall display, which held a diagram. It repeated the same symbol, an icon-sized image of the *Defender* document file. Starting at the left, it was labeled McCONNELL. Line segments connected it to other nodes, each labeled with a name and sometimes a date.

"INN took off the version number, trying to hide the source, but each version of your design had different typographical errors. We were able to determine the version number and its creation date in a half a day."

"Checking the e-mail records you gave us, we found out who received this version of the design. We also could make a good guess as to when INN got their hooks on it. We got a lot of cooperation from some of the addresses, and not much from others, which in itself helped us focus our search."

Ray had listened to the presentation with both anger and fear. INN's scoop had devastated morale. Secrecy had been part of their strength. It allowed them to move quickly, unhindered. Now friend and enemy alike could interfere with a timetable that had no room for delay.

He knew *Defender* was a long shot. The Chinese now knew where they were. Could they take some sort of counteraction? Even well-meaning friends could derail the project.

The Army colonel handed Ray his data pad. "Here's the report. I've found two individuals, one at SPAWAR and the other at NASA. Both received copies of this version, third- or fourth- or fifth-hand, and according to investigators I sent out, both have openly criticized *Defender*. One, at NASA, was quoted saying that, '*Defender* had to be stopped. It could interfere with NASA's plans for developing spacecraft technology.' "

Ray nodded, acknowledging the information, but not responding immediately. The colonel respected his silence, but obviously waited for a reply. McConnell wanted to strike out at these people, but there was little he could do.

Ray stated flatly, "The *Defender* document was never classified, so it's not a crime to release it."

"The ones who gave it to the press certainly weren't our friends," countered the colonel. "And by exposing us, they've hurt our chances of stopping the Chinese. I'd say that's acting against the interests of national security."

"By the time we indicted them, it would be moot. Our best revenge will be to succeed." Part of Ray didn't agree with what he was saying, but he was trying to think with his head, not his emotions.

"I could give it to the press. Fight one leak with another," suggested the colonel.

McConnell shook his head slowly. "Tempting, but that would open the door to more accusations and counteraccusations. I need you for other things, now. All our energy has to go toward finishing *Defender*. We don't have to provide a cover story anymore, but we have to assume they'll try to attack us at this location. Increase our defenses accordingly. If we need to bring in a Patriot battery or a division of paratroopers, that's what we'll do."

"Meanwhile, I'll report to Schultz." Ray knew Schulz wouldn't enjoy his decision, but he knew it was the right one.

The colonel left, and Ray started to get up, to go report to his boss. But Schultz would want to know what they were doing about the exposure, and Ray knew that just increasing security wasn't the full answer.

Opposition to *Defender* was forming fast. Ray had assumed that there would be opposition, but he'd been so behind the idea he couldn't look at it objectively. Web pages already? Congressmen could order the program stopped or delayed for review.

The war in space had turned into an information war. Anyone who'd seen the news knew the media would pick up and report anything that was fed to them. Well, it was time for him to do some of the feeding.

He opened the address book on his data pad. He had contacts all over the defense and space and computer industries. They'd helped him get *Defender* started. Now he needed them again.

He started typing. "*Defender* needs your help . . ."

Six

Assembly

Gongga Shan Launch Site
November 17

Shen had insisted on having the meeting here, in the shadow of the mountain. Ignoring the recall order to Beijing had seemed suicidal, but the general knew that once away from the mountain, any flaw or error here could be blamed on his neglect. So far, the gun had worked perfectly, but that had just made him a more important target.

Friends in Beijing kept him informed. There were those who resented his success, even if it helped China against the U.S. There were those who wanted to weaken him, then take over the gun for their own political empires. Some simply thought he had too much power.

He'd been able to fabricate some sort of excuse for remaining on the mountain, and to his relief Dong Zhi had backed him up. He'd expected the scientist to do so, but the first rule of Chinese politics was that trust was like smoke. When it was there, it blocked your vision. And it would disappear with the first puff of wind.

Instead, Dong and what seemed like half the Politburo now sat in the observation gallery, while an intelligence officer briefed them on the new American warcraft.

The Army colonel had passed out edited copies of the original design, annotated in Chinese with an engineering analysis attached. He'd reviewed the systems—the laser, the projectiles, the radar and laser sensors. The general, Dong, and the other technical people present had been fascinated. It was a dangerous craft. Shen noticed that the politicians had spent more time gazing out the window. Had they already heard it? Or were the exact details unimportant? Maybe they'd already decided.

The colonel finished his briefing, but the Politburo members wanted definite answers. When would it be ready? Would it interfere with the Dragon campaign? How could it be countered?

The colonel refused to make any conclusions. "We're still gathering information, Comrade Secretary. We have no information on how much they've actually accomplished. We're moving agents into place, but it takes time to infiltrate even with normal security, and the safeguards around the Miramar base are extremely tight."

Shen spoke up for him. There was no risk in stating the obvious. "If their design works as shown, it can interfere with our satellite attacks."

"And the chance of that happening?" Pan Yunfeng demanded. The First Secretary had headed the delegation himself.

"Impossible to say, Comrade Secretary. However, this is not something they can build in just a few months. While the VentureStar space vehicle is complete, it had not yet been fully certified for service. It will have to be adapted to the new role, and many of the systems he describes do not exist."

"Is it possible that this is a disinformation campaign?" Pan asked the briefer.

The colonel looked at Shen, who nodded. "Unlikely, sir," the intelligence officer assured them. "The American administration is suffering intense criticism because of this now-exposed secret project. They've gained nothing from the revelation."

"Then what is its purpose?" Pan asked.

Shen replied again, his tone carefully chosen, almost casual. "Oh, they're building it, all right, but there will be very little to defend once it is operational. By that time, the new T'ien Lung II will also be ready. It has stealth features, more energy, armor, and it's semiautonomous. And we have designs for our own armed spacecraft." Shen smiled, imagining Chinese ships orbiting the earth, shattering America's military hegemony.

"We'll use the Dragon's Mother to keep them on the ground. We can destroy anything they launch."

Kunming Air Base, Xichuan Province
November 18

The aging Il-76 transport lumbered off the taxiway and stopped. A cluster of uniformed Chinese and Russian military personnel waited on the tarmac. The instant the rear ramp touched the surface, they ran aboard, and only a few minutes later, the huge GAZ missile launcher rolled out of the aircraft.

The forty-five-foot wheeled eight-by-eight truck inched out of the transport and down the ramp. Four canisters took up two-thirds the length of the vehicle, overhanging the end of the chassis.

The command and radar vehicles were already on the ground and had moved off to a clear area to one side of the hangars. Technicians swarmed over the two vehicles, checking them quickly before letting them proceed. Rail cars and loading equipment stood ready.

The first battery, consisting of the command and radar vehicle and eight launcher vehicles, was already emplaced around the base. It would protect the airfield while the rest of the equipment arrived.

National Military Command Center, The Pentagon
November 19

"At least three batteries of S-400s have arrived so far. One was used to cover the airfield, while one was sent by rail to the Gongga Shan launch site. We believe the other will be used to cover the Xichuan control center."

None of this was good news, but Admiral Overton had more to tell. He displayed a list of Russian military units, along with their strength and their location.

"Additional Russian forces, including aircraft and more SAM units, are heading for the Chinese border. These are not weapons sold to China, but active Russian units stationed in the Far Eastern Theatre. I believe that these units are going to deploy to Chinese bases.

"Although they're deployed defensively, they will free up Chinese units to move south. More disturbing are the close military ties these represent. Russian official statements have always supported the Chinese in the Vietnam crisis, but they've been quiet about their attacks on our GPS satellites. These movements may indicate that they've decided to take sides."

Overton saw their reaction, and mentally throwing the rest of his presentation over his shoulder, just summarized the rest. "A North Korean MiG-29 squadron has moved across the border, while other North Korean units are mobilizing."

He put a new list on the display. "Indian and Indonesian forces are mobilizing, for reasons not clear right now. There are even signs of activity in Iraq."

"We've only seen the early signs of mobilization, but if they continue, other powers like Japan, South Korea, and Malaysia, will have to follow suit."

General Kastner looked thinner after almost two months of crisis. He listened to Overton's brief quietly, then asked, "And the Chinese are still completely ready?"

"All the deployed units are still in place, sir, and they've begun mobilizing other units throughout the country. Half their fleet is at sea or ready for immediate steaming. Stockpiles at staging areas near the Vietnamese border have actually increased, and thanks to the Russians, the Chinese will probably be able to protect them better. They could attack the Vietnamese with less than twenty-four hours' notice."

"They certainly know about the congressional resolution," fumed Kastner. Opposition members in the House had started a resolution cutting funding for troops in Japan and Korea. "With Russia and North Korea holding her coat, the Chinese may now feel free to act."

Kastner looked at the assembled service chiefs. "Are there any other comments?" Only the Marine general spoke. "The Chinese know they have a free hand—against Vietnam, Taiwan, wherever they want."

The Chairman said, "We all know the status of *Defender*, and their request for more time. Do we recommend for or against the replacement satellite launch? General Warner?"

The Air Force Chief of Staff controlled the GPS constellation, although it was used by all the services. "I'd hate to waste the last replacement satellite, sir. We've contracted for new birds, but it will be a long time before they're ready. I say hold it until after *Defender* proves herself."

"If we go to war, we'll need any GPS capability we can get." General Forest, the Army Chief of Staff, wasn't shy. "Even if we can't get full coverage, more partial coverage is better than less partial coverage."

"And when that coverage is lost? We only have the one spare GPS bird," Kastner reminded him. "Once we lose that satellite, we're helpless."

"The Chinese will shoot down one GPS satellite a week whether we launch a new bird or not. This buys us a week. Putting it in my terms, we're fighting a rearguard action, trading casualties for time." The soldier looked grim, but determined.

"And we hope for the cavalry," Kastner concluded. "I'll make the recommendation."

Space Force Headquarters, Miramar
November 21

Biff Barnes resisted the urge to shout, give orders, or any kind of direction. These people were supposed to do their jobs on their own. He'd be too busy to give orders when the time came.

Jim Scarelli, the designated pilot, was off working on the flight-control systems with the techs. The Lockheed Martin test pilot for VentureStar, there was no question of his ability to fly *Defender*. That part was easy.

The rest of them struggled to train on half-built systems in a jury-rigged simulator. Six metal chairs mimicked ejection seats, and plywood and plastic boxes pretended to be control consoles. A plywood arch covered them, because many of the controls were positioned on the overhead. Network and power cables were tightly bundled, but still required attention to avoid a misstep.

Steve Skeldon, the navigator and copilot, sat in the right front seat. A Marine captain, his time flying fighters was less useful than his master's degree in physics. That morning, he had taken over Scarelli's flight duties as well, which made him a very busy man.

Behind the pilot, Sue Tillman, the sensor officer, pretended to scan the earth and space. An impressive array of infrared, visible light, and radar equipment was being installed in *Defender*. Hopefully it would act like the mocked-up control panels. She also took care of the voice and data links that would tie *Defender* in to the ground-based sensors she needed.

The weapons officer on the right was Andre Baker, a captain in the U.S. Army. Although he had no flight experience, he did know lasers, and he was a ballistics expert as well.

Biff sat in the rearmost row. As mission commander, he didn't need to look out the window. The displays on his console gave him the big picture. From the back, he could also watch his crew.

Ray McConnell's chair, for the flight engineer, was on Biff's right, also in the rear. It was empty, as well. Ray was able to train only occasionally, but that was the least of Biff's worries.

Barnes worked the master console at his station. In addition to simulating his own controls, he could inject targets and create artificial casualties for the team to deal with. Right now, he was just trying to get the simulator's newest feature to behave.

"Sue, tell me what your board sees."

"Bingo! I've got an IR target, below us bearing two seven zero elevation four five. Shifting radar to classification mode. I'll use the laser ranger to back up the radar data." She sounded triumphant, and somewhere behind Biff, a few technicians clapped.

"Velocity data is firming up. It should be showing up on your board."

Biff checked his own console, and said "Yes, it is." He'd dialed in a T'ien Lung target for Sue to find, and she had. Considering they'd just installed the infrared detection feature at four that morning, it was a significant achievement.

In spite of the frustration and lost time, Biff smiled, pleased with the results. More than procedural skills, simulators taught the crew to work together through shared experience. These experiences weren't what he'd planned on, but the result was the same.

"It's good to see you smiling, Biff." McConnell's voice would have startled him a few moments earlier, but Barnes felt himself relaxing a little.

McConnell sat down in his designated chair, then clapped his hands. "Attention please! We're short of time, so we can't arrange a ceremony, but I believe these are yours."

Everyone's eyes followed McConnell as he handed a small box over to Barnes. As Biff's hand touched it, a photoflash went off, and he turned in his seat to see a photographer behind him, smiling, his camera still ready.

He opened the small dark box to see a pair of golden oak leaves.

"We thought *Defender*'s mission commander should be at least a major." Admiral Schultz stepped into Barnes's view, reaching out to shake his hand.

Barnes, surprised and pleased, automatically tried to stand, but was blocked by the console.

"At ease, Major," smiled Schultz. "I'm glad to be the first one to say that." As Biff took the admiral's hand, both automatically turned their faces to the cameraman, and the stroke flashed again.

"Thank you, sir."

"Don't thank me, thank Ray. He's the one who insisted you should wear oak leaves. A full year ahead of zone, isn't it?

"And by the way," Schultz said, raising his voice so the flight crew could all hear him clearly, "you're all going to get astronaut flight pay, backdated to the day you reported here for duty."

It was Ray's turn to look surprised. Schultz just smiled. "You had a good idea. I had a good idea."

INN News,
November 23

"Preparations to launch the only available replacement GPS satellite have brought a storm of criticism down on the administration. With only two days until the generally agreed-on deadline date, some observers have interpreted this as a desperate attempt to buy time. Others have suggested that this satellite will be used as part of a U.S. offensive, or that the satellite is being wasted in some American act of defiance."

Senator Rutledge's image, at the podium of the Senate floor, thundered with indignation. "Has our leadership lost all sense of reality? Having lost billions of dollars' worth of hardware, we're about to throw away another few hundred million. This is more than insanity."

Markin's image reappeared. "Congressional support is growing for some sort of accommodation with the Chinese. Few here believe the not-so-secret *Defender* project will ever get off the ground. The latest buzzword around the halls of Congress is 'the new reality.' "

Seven

Deadline

Xichuan Space Center, China
November 23

General Shen watched Markin's report with pleasure. American political will was beginning to weaken. Pan Yufeng, however, did not see it as clearly.

The Party Secretary, along with his aides, had watched the piece, with Chinese subtitles added. He'd only seen the problems.

"Why are they launching another navigation satellite? And how real is *Defender*?" He turned to face Shen, his tone accusing. "Your entire plan was based on the premise that the Americans could do nothing before we gained control of orbital space."

The man's frightened, Shen realized. *He's betting his political life on something he doesn't really understand. He's used to controlling everything, and he can't control this. He's already trying to set me up, digging my grave if this fails.*

"We do control space, Comrade Pan." Shen controlled his voice carefully. He had to be respectful, but the Party Secretary needed a dose of backbone. "Right now, we can kill anything in low or mid-level orbit. Soon, we'll be able to attack even geosynchronous satellites.

"This conflict, any conflict, is about wills. We want to impose our will on the Americans. We've shown them how vulnerable they are in space, and how that vulnerability affects them down here. They are starting to realize that. Their will is starting to break.

"*Defender* is their last hope. We're ready for it. We know enough about the VentureStar design to guess at her performance, and we know they'll be launching from California. Within minutes of her launch, we'll be able to take action."

Space Force Headquarters November 25

Ray McConnell tried to stay focused on the tour as Jenny Oh explained the Battle Center's status. He hadn't seen much of her in the past two months, although they were on the same base, working toward the same goal. He'd wanted to see her, of course, but he didn't need distractions.

Originally, she'd been assigned to set up the communications network that would support the mission. It was an immense job. She had to integrate links between Air Force's Space Command, Navy tracking stations, NASA, and even some civilian facilities. It had to be done quickly and with the real purpose secret.

All that data would be fed to a single point, the Battle Management Center, and her task had such an impact on the Center that she ended up taking over that, too. She'd done both jobs well, almost elegantly.

They'd set up the Battle Center in an empty service school. The classrooms and offices were taken over by the support staff, and the large central bay, which had housed a simulator, now held the command display. The building itself looked weathered, worn, and misused by its new occupants. The few windows had been covered, and other modifications were left raw and unpainted.

She'd met him at the door, standing proudly under a sign that said "Battle Management Center." He'd been glad to see her, of course, and had felt a little of the tension leave. He'd smiled, but it might have been a little larger than he'd intended. She smiled back, but it was a tired smile.

She seemed different, and he realized she looked harder, a little thinner, and wondered if the strain showed on him as well.

Jenny led him down the central hallway, past security, past rooms crammed with electronic equipment or people hunched over workstations. There was more security at the door to the Display Center, and a vestibule that served as a light lock.

They entered the darkened two-story room in one corner. An elevated scaffold had been erected that ran around three sides of the room.

It was about fifteen feet wide, with a waist-high rail on the inside edge. The fourth wall was lined with gray equipment cabinets, and Ray could see more boxy shapes tucked under the scaffolding.

Jenny trotted up the steps to the scaffolding, putting them one story up, then led Ray along the walkway. Desks lined it, facing the center, with an aisle behind them. "This section's communications, that's electronic warfare, that's intelligence." They turned the corner. "This wall is spacecraft systems. We don't get a tenth of the telemetry that NASA gets, but we still monitor critical systems."

They turned the last corner, and she pointed to the last group, on the third side. "Admiral Schultz and his staff will sit here. I've got communications rigged to the White House, the NMCC, and to all the major commands."

He looked around the space. Everything was neatly arranged. The cabinets were fully installed. They'd even taken the time to paint safety warnings near the stairways. "It looks great, Jenny. You've done a wonderful job."

"Don't praise me yet," Jenny replied. "It's looked like this for almost a week. The real test is what's inside."

She walked over to one of the desks, labeled "Staff," and picked up a virtual-reality headset. It was an older model, and still had a cranial framework to hold the eyepieces. Slipping it on easily, she pulled on the gloves and touched a switch on the headset. He heard her say "Begin test three bravo."

The center bay, until then dark and empty, suddenly filled with a bright white sphere, easily ten feet across. It floated in the air halfway between the floor and the ceiling. Ray barely had time to see it before it changed color, becoming a deep blue. Patches of blue lightened to a medium shade, then lightened more, shifting to brown and green. He realized he was watching the world being built, starting with the deepest part of the ocean. Then higher elevations were added, one level at a time.

As Jenny tapped the air with her data gloves, points of light appeared on the surface, and Ray recognized one as Miramar. Lines appeared circling the earth, and he knew they were orbits.

Visually, it was stunning. The implications for command were even more impressive. It was the situational awareness a commander needed to fight a worldwide battle.

"Here's the hard part," Jenny announced. A flashing symbol appeared in southern China, becoming a short red line segment. A transparent red trumpet appeared around the symbol as it quickly climbed toward orbit. "This is a recording of their last intercept," she told him, taking off the helmet and watching the large display. "Here's what we added."

A new point of light flashed, at Miramar. It started to rise, and the display went dark.

The sudden blackness left Ray momentarily blind, and he heard a loud, "Damn! I wanted that to work." He could hear the frustration in her voice.

"The gear was a piece of cake. This display duplicates the one at Space Command, and I could get off-the-shelf components for nine-tenths of what we needed. Hooking it up was straightforward.

"But programming in the new systems has been difficult. We have to be able to track *Defender* in real time. The display was originally designed to show a friendly unit's location based on GPS data. We can't depend on that, so we're using radar and optical sensors all over the world to track your position. That information has to be collected and fused, then sent to the display. That software is all brand-new." She smiled a lopsided smile. "I hear they're having a lot of problems at Space Command as well."

Ray waited for a moment, then asked quietly, "Is there anything we can get that will help you finish on time?"

She shook her head. "I wish I knew what to ask for."

Her tone shook McConnell. He heard someone near the end of her rope. She'd accomplished miracles, but in a week this gear had to be rock-solid. *Defender* needed guidance from the Battle Center. They didn't have the onboard sensors to run the entire engagement from the ship.

He couldn't bring in more people. At this late date, they'd have to be brought up to speed. They wouldn't be ready in time. She certainly didn't need any more gear. If she had the resources, then it was all about leadership.

"You can do this," Ray said carefully. "I can't give you a sunshine speech. Nobody's more committed to *Defender* than you, but I think you're afraid of failing. You care so much about the project that the fear of not making it is tying you up in knots."

She almost shook as she nodded. "I don't like to fail. I never have, more so than most. And this is especially important." Jenny's fatigue was more evident now, as she leaned heavily on the rail.

Gently taking her arm, Ray led her over to a chair and sat her in it. He sat on the edge of the desk. He looked at her steadily.

"You've been a rock for me since the day this began. But also since that day, there hasn't been the time I'd like for us. I've had to say focused, and that's meant putting my feelings for you in deep freeze, until this is over. Your belief has kept me going. I hope my belief in you can do the same."

She smiled and looked up at him. "I want it to."

"Then it will." He stood. Ray tried to sound positive without being too enthusiastic. "We will make it, Jenny, and I'm glad you'll be here in the Center when I'm up."

Ray's phone beeped, and, reluctantly, Ray answered it. It was Admiral Schultz. "They're moving," he said without waiting for Ray to speak.

Ray didn't have to ask who. "Where? What are they doing?"

"Imaging satellites have been watching along the southern border. They're leaving their staging areas. They'll be in position to invade at first light tomorrow."

National Military Command Center
November 26

"There has been no communication from the Chinese government, either to us or to the Vietnamese." Secretary Peck sat next to General Kastner. He'd listened to Admiral Overton's briefing on the movement of Chinese and Vietnamese forces. Now he added a few more details, things the Joint Chiefs weren't normally privy to.

"The Chinese have purchased Russian and North Korean assistance with promises of economic concessions in Vietnam and the Spratlys."

General Forest, the Army Chief of Staff, started to laugh, out of surprise, but stopped himself.

Peck nodded. "I agree. Normally I'd say Moscow and Pyongyang would be fools for agreeing to such an arrangement. Talk about a pig in a poke."

"But the source is reliable," insisted Peck, "and we believe it shows what they all think of our chances. We've been top dog for a long time, gentlemen, but some of the dogs don't think we're that tough anymore."

"It's still a bargain made in hell," Kastner remarked.

Peck nodded. "The President publicly committed us to defend Vietnam from Chinese aggression. Now it's time to put up or shut up."

"The reasons for defending Vietnam haven't gone away," Forest reminded them.

"But the job's gotten a lot harder," said General Warner. Air Force and Navy aircraft would have been the weapons used to stop Chinese forces. Now, their power was reduced, and their vulnerability increased.

"That was the entire purpose of the Chinese plan. They knew we would commit ourselves publicly if our risk was low, and once we committed, they changed the game. It was a setup from the start, and we're trapped."

"It would still be bad if they overran Vietnam," Admiral Kramer observed. "There'd be an economic cost, and domestic and foreign political cost."

"The damage to our reputation abroad could be severe," agreed Peck.

" 'There go the Americans again, not keeping their promises,' " chimed in General Forest. "Let's use a Chinese term. It's about face. They've already gained some by giving us a black eye, and it's paying off. Does anyone want to guess how many new friends they'll have if they actually take over Vietnam?"

General Kastner shook his head. "We can't trade lives for pride."

"I have to disagree, sir," countered Forest. His tone was respectful, but firm as well. "That isn't the trade-off. It's fight here," he paused looking around the room, "and lose some people, or fight later in a lot of different places, and against a stronger enemy. Does anyone think the Chinese will stop here? They've already promised their allies a piece of the Spratlys!"

Peck said, "What if we change the rules? Can we increase their cost?"

"Widen the war," said Kramer. "Threaten them anywhere and everywhere. We can't hit the gun, but there are a lot of targets that are in Tomahawk range, or in range of carrier aircraft. We can sink every naval unit and shoot down every aircraft we can find. And we know about the Spratlys," he said, nodding toward Peck.

"Wide-scale warfare," Kastner wondered out loud, but then his voice changed. "Hit them where they can't hit us back. I agree."

Peck nodded. "It's an option. I'll convey your recommendations to the President."

USS *Ronald Reagan* (CVN-76) in the South China Sea
November 27

On the flight deck, everything was normal, if a maelstrom of noise, metal, and hot exhaust can ever be called normal. Rows of strike aircraft sat armed and ready, while fighters and radar-warning aircraft took off and landed at regular intervals, protecting the task force.

The pilots' orders were clear. Push right up to the Chinese coast. Shoot down any aircraft in Chinese markings you find, sink any ship flying the Chinese flag. But don't cross the coast. Not until we're ready.

Below in plot, they were still trying to get ready, hours after targets had been assigned and authorization received. Squadron commanders waited impatiently while the planners struggled and argued.

The target list was ambitious, with primary, secondary, and tertiary targets assigned to each aircraft. Defense-suppression missions were supposed to arrive moments, just seconds before the strikers made their runs. Enemy defenses were supposed to be located by reconnaissance UAVs that would data-link the position back to command aircraft. Those planes would in turn task in-flight aircraft to attack those targets.

But every step in that process involved a position—a GPS position. The heavily automated precision-targeting systems had to be adapted to other, less precise navigation systems. Those systems had errors, much more error then the planners were used to. In many cases, the errors were too great for the precisely timed tactics of the manuals.

The strikes would launch, late, and the planners could not guarantee that all the strikers would come back.

Space Force Headquarters, Miramar
November 29

Ray heard the klaxon in his office. He ran outside, expecting to see fire engines racing by. His first thought, of the hydrogen and oxygen tanks at the pad, was so frightening that his mind raced, searching for some other emergency. A toxic spill? Did someone fall? Terrible things to hope for, but better than a fire in the fuel area.

He rounded the corner of his office building, which gave him a clear line of sight to the launch compound. It was over a mile away, but seemed normal. Then he heard machine-gun fire. He ran faster.

An open-topped Humvee loaded with armed Marines roared past and he waved frantically, and yelled, still running. He heard someone recognize him. "It's McConnell, hold up," and it skidded to a stop.

They made room for him in front and he jumped in, the driver flooring the accelerator. Someone behind yelled into his ear over the noise of the diesel engine.

"It's a full alert. Radar's detected a slow-moving aircraft headed for the base. He's already inside the prohibited zone, and he won't answer on the radio."

The street ended, and the open area surrounding the launchpad replaced the buildings on either side.

McConnell heard the machine gun again, and located the firer from the sound. It was another Humvee with a pintle-mounted machine gun.

They were stopped, and the gunner was pointing his weapon up. Ray followed the line of tracers, and saw a small speck. It looked like a light plane still a few miles away.

"He can't hit anything at that range," Ray shouted.

"He's trying to warn him off," the driver shouted back. Ray noticed the driver was an officer, a Marine lieutenant. The Marine picked up the vehicle's radio microphone. "This is Hall. I can see him. It's a light plane, a Cessna or something like it. He's at low altitude, and he's headed straight for the pad complex."

"What's he going to do?" asked McConnell.

Lieutenant Hall shrugged. "You tell me. It could be a suicide crash, or loaded with commandos. Or he could drop leaflets that say 'Save the Whales.' "

Hall continued at breakneck speed, arriving at the hangar after the longest sixty seconds of Ray's life. As the vehicle braked, Marines jumped to the ground and ran to take up positions covering the hangar and its precious resident.

Ray could see other squads racing into position, and more weapons opened up on the approaching plane. It was closer, and he could hear the plane's small engine snarl as the pilot opened up the throttle. Its speed increased slightly, and he lowered the nose. Was he going to crash the hangar?

Tracers surrounded the plane. Ray knew intellectually how hard it was to hit even a slow aircraft with a machine gun, but right then he was infuriated with the gunners who couldn't hit something that large, that slow, flying in a straight line.

It was even closer, and he could see it was a high-winged civilian plane, a four-seater. He'd flown them himself. It was nose-on, headed straight for him. The drone of the engine increased quickly, both in pitch and volume.

Although he couldn't see any weapons, he suddenly felt the urge to run for cover, but they hadn't planned for an air raid. The hangar was poor protection. Besides, wasn't that what they were aiming for?

Something fluttered away from the side of the aircraft, and for a moment Ray thought the machine gunners had actually hit. Then he recognized the shape as one of the side doors. A parachute jump? But they were too low, no more than five hundred feet.

They were almost at the hangar, and the Marines nearby had raised their weapons, tracking the plane but not firing without an order.

"Hold fire!" Hall shouted, then repeated the order into the radio. He turned to Ray. "If we hit it now, it could crash into the hangar."

"Assuming that isn't their plan," Ray muttered.

McConnell watched its path, wishing it would vanish. It didn't, but at the last moment it did veer a little to the left, and in a few seconds Ray was sure it was not headed for hangar. He couldn't feel relief.

The plane was headed for the launchpad, about a hundred yards away. He saw a man-sized object leave the plane and drop toward the ground. It had fins on one end and a point on the other. It looked like nothing so much as a giant dart.

Ray stood and watched the object fall, looking even more dartlike as it fell nose-first. Out of the corner of his eye, he saw that the Marines, with better reflexes, were all hugging the ground.

It struck almost exactly in the center of the pad, exploding with a roar. The concussion was enough to stagger him a hundred yards away, and misshapen fragments cartwheeled out from the ugly brown smoke cloud.

Ray was still standing, dazed and unsure of what to do next, when a pair of Marine SuperHornets zoomed overhead in pursuit of the intruder. His eye followed the jets as they quickly caught up with the Cessna, still in sight, but headed away at low altitude.

One of the Hornets broke off to the right, then cut left across prop plane's path. McConnell heard a sound like an angry chain saw, and a stream of tracers leapt from its nose in front of the trespasser. The other jet was circling left, and had lowered its flaps and landing gear in an attempt to stay behind the Cessna.

Lieutenant Hall's radio beeped, and he listened for a minute before turning to Ray. "They've ordered him to land, and he's cooperating." Glancing at the lethal Hornets circling the "slow mover," he said, "I sure would."

Remembering the bomb, Ray ran over to the still-smoking pad. Acrid fumes choked him, but he ignored them, then almost stumbled on the debris littering the once-smooth surface. Slowing down, he picked his way over metal fragments and chunks of concrete.

His heart sank when he saw the crater though the clearing smoke. Easily three meters across, it was at least that deep. Torn steel rods jutted out from the sides at crazy angles.

Admiral Schultz came up though the smoke, standing beside Ray and gazing at the crater. Ray saw Schultz look him up and down, then ask, "You look fine. Is everyone OK?"

Ray stared at him for a minute, then replied, "I don't know."

Schultz shook him by the shoulder, not roughly, but as if to wake him. "Ray, snap out of it. We've got to check for casualties, and see what the damage to the pad is. We can't let this slow us down."

Ray nodded, and started to check the area. He spotted people he knew, and set them to work. He saw Marines working as well, moving from person to person, making sure everyone was all right, helping some who were hurt.

Lieutenant Hall trotted up to Schultz and saluted. "Sir, they've got the intruder lined up for landing."

"Right, let's go, then." He called to McConnell. "Ray! Can you come?" McConnell had overheard the lieutenant and was already heading for the Humvee.

The lieutenant drove almost as fast to the runway as he had to the launchpad. It was located on the part of the base still being used by the Marines, and at speed, it took five minutes to cover.

Ray saw armed patrols all over the base and signs of heavier weapons being deployed. Wheeled vehicles with SAM launchers on top rumbled by, and he saw a column of tracked fighting vehicles being loaded and fueled.

A sentry at the end of the airfield spotted the Humvee's flashing light and waved them onto a taxiway, pointing to the far end. A cluster of vehicles surrounded the Cessna, and the two Hornets whoostled overhead, as if they were daring it to take off.

Ray recognized General Norman, standing to one side, as armed Marines secured the plane. Its two occupants were being half-dragged out of the plane and efficiently searched. A man and a woman, both were in their early twenties, dressed in fashionably mismatched pastel colors, their hair short on top, long on the side. To Ray's eyes, they looked like a couple of college students, straight off the campus.

"Don't put weapons in space!" one of them shouted as he was searched.

"Down with *Defender*!" the girl shouted. "We won't let you turn space into a battlefield."

Ray was in shock. He wanted to grab the two of them, show them the damaged pad, the injured being taken to the hospital. Or show them the Battle Center, and what was at stake.

General Norman's face was made of hard stone, and Schultz looked ready to order two executions on the spot. But they weren't moving or saying a word. Maybe they couldn't. But Ray didn't either. He watched the MPs cuff the two civilians and lead them away.

Later in the day, Ray reported to the admiral. Schultz's office was filled with people. General Norman occupied the only other chair, but a Marine JAG officer, the base's Public Relations officer, and *Defender*'s Security officer took up most of the remaining floor space. They'd all been waiting for Ray.

He didn't bother with introductory remarks. "The engineers say they can fix the pad by tomorrow evening. They'll use the same stuff they use to repair bombed-out runways. It won't be worth much after *Defender* uses it, but it will be fine for the launch. Some of the handling equipment was damaged, but again, it can be repaired quickly." He half smiled. "One of the advantages of jury-rigging all this gear is that it's pretty easy to fix."

Schultz just said, "Thanks, Ray," and turned to the Security officer.

"They're not Chinese agents, of if they are, the Chinese are making some bad personnel choices. Their names are Frank and Wendy Beaumont, and they're siblings, students at UCSD. They're well-known activists at the school, and belong to several political organizations. The plane's their dad's, and both have been taking flying lessons."

"We think they had help with the bomb, but only from other students. It was an improvised shaped charge. The boy, who's a sophomore, described it in detail, and claims he did it all himself, but I doubt it."

Schultz nodded, then looked at the Public Relations officer, a Marine major, who reported, "The press is having a field day with this. Half the headlines read, 'Marines Fire on College Students,' and the other half read 'Marines Fail to Protect Secret Spacecraft.' Either way we can't win. Some of them are even speculating that the *Defender* actually was damaged, and of course we can't show them that it isn't."

Schultz replied, "Let them say it is. If the Chinese think we're hurt, that's fine. Also, show them the people who were hurt in the blast.

"I just got off the phone with the hospital," he continued. "The total is five hurt, one seriously enough to need surgery to remove a bomb fragment. All of them will recover fully."

"I'm glad nobody was killed," General Norman rumbled. "But we can't assume that there won't be another attack. I personally want to apologize for letting that plane get through. It won't happen again. The Commandant has told me I can have anything I need to protect you and this base."

"For as long as you need it, we will stay at full alert. We're keeping fighter patrols and helicopter gunships overhead twenty-four hours a day. There will be no further interruptions."

Space Force Headquarters, Miramar
December 1

Biff Barnes knocked twice on the door to Ray McConnell's BOQ room, then tried the knob. It was unlocked, and as Biff opened it, he heard someone typing. Ray sat hunched over the keyboard, in his pajamas.

"Ray, this is supposed to be a wake-up call. Remember? I told you about something called 'Crew Rest'?"

"I remembered something early this morning that I had to deal with," McConnell answered, his attention still on the screen.

"After dealing with stuff last night until one o'clock." Barnes dropped onto the edge of the bed. "I need you alert and at peak for tomorrow, Ray. When did you wake up this morning?" His question had a slight edge to it.

"Four."

"So you think three hours is enough?"

"Okay, I'll take a nap after lunch."

"That's when we're supposed to review the new sensor handoffs."

"Oh."

"Join us halfway through," Biff told him. "Now I'll see you at crew breakfast in fifteen minutes."

Barnes left and Ray quickly showered and dressed. In spite of his fatigue, it didn't take any effort to hurry, and Ray wondered what percentage of his blood was composed of adrenaline. He'd been running on nerves for way too long.

Feeling like a fool, he put on the blue coveralls Barnes had given him. The left shoulder had a patch that said U.S. SPACE FORCES, and the left breast had one that said DEFENDER, along with his name stenciled below it. Although they were attractive, if flashy, Ray didn't remember approving either design. When asked, Barnes had told him that some things were better left in the hands of fighter pilots.

Barnes had insisted on Ray wearing the coveralls at all times this week. "Of course it makes you stand out. You're flight crew, and that makes you different. Let everyone see it. You not only built *Defender*, you've got the balls to fly in her as well. That's the ultimate vote of confidence, and your people will appreciate it."

The mess hall looked better and better. Geoffrey had changed the décor again, this time from Southwest to Space. Posters of starfields and spaceships filled the walls, and the classical music was appropriately grand.

Ray hurried over to the crew table, and was gratified to see he was not late. Steve Skeldon and Sue Tillman were also just sitting down. Both of them wore military insignia with their coveralls, and made them look natural. Ray thought he probably looked all right, as long as he stood close to one of them. He still felt like a pretender.

Instead of going through the cafeteria line, Ray checked off what he wanted on a menu data pad. The theory was that the crew should be doing useful work instead of standing in line, but it was just another perk, a way of making them feel special. Ray had allowed it reluctantly.

They did work, Barnes drilling them relentlessly on safety procedures, equipment locations, technical characteristics, and each other's duties. His favorite trick was to ask one question, then ask another in the middle of the answer. The victim had to answer both correctly, in order, within seconds.

At first Ray thought Barnes was picking on him, grilling him repeatedly on engine-out procedures. Then after watching him work over the others, McConnell thought Barnes might have been cutting him some slack.

The recital continued throughout breakfast, and Barnes prepared to take the crew to the simulator. Ray found that he wanted to stay with them, but knew that there were too many last-minute problems to fix.

Part of him couldn't wait for tomorrow morning. The rest of him wanted the day to go on forever. He needed the time.

INN News
December 1
2200

Mark Markin stood as close to Miramar's front gate as he could, which meant across Miramar Way, off Highway I-15. At night, there was still a lot of traffic on the arterial, but most of it passed by. The camera followed one heavy truck that did turn in, centering on the armed sentries that surrounded it and checked it carefully before allowing it to move on. It lingered on a dog held by one of the guards.

"Following the attack two days ago, the Marines here have increased security to extraordinary heights. Civilian traffic on and off the base has been severely restricted, and most of the traffic into the base has been official.

"All our attempts to contact the military regarding the damage inflicted by the attack have been fruitless. The Coalition against Military Space, which claims responsibility for the action, says that the launchpad was destroyed and a nearby hangar damaged. Major Dolan, the base Public Relations officer, still denies the existence of *Defender*, and is therefore 'unable to discuss damage to something that doesn't exist.' "

A grainy black-and-white image replaced Markin. It showed a squarish building with rails leaving one side. They led to a rectangular flat area, with a girder structure in the center. The framework was undercut with a sloped trench. It could only be a spacecraft launchpad.

The image was skewed, as if the camera had been tilted well off the vertical. "This photo was taken from an INN plane flying just beyond the prohibited area over the air station. Using a special lens and computer enhancement, we were able to get this image of the 'nonexistent' hangar and launchpad. While there is little that can be seen at this distance, the hangar and pad appear intact. Presumably, *Defender* is undamaged.

"INN news will monitor developments at the base closely and let you know the instant that there are any developments."

Space Force Headquarters, Miramar
December 1
2215

Admiral Schultz turned off the wall display angrily. There was little pleasure in pushing a button. What he wanted to do was push in Markin's face. "War in a fishbowl," he grumbled.

Colonel Evans, *Defender*'s Security officer, could only agree. "Radar's tracked civilian planes flying just outside the prohibited area. There's a good chance at least one of them is an INN plane with a TV camera aboard, waiting for us to launch."

Schultz grinned. "Then let's give them something to look at. I need to talk to General Norman, and Jenny Oh. You might have to wake them, but tell them it's urgent."

Evans asked, "How about McConnell?"

Schultz shook his head. "No, let him sleep. He can't help with this, and he's got a busy day coming." He stifled a yawn. "And once he launches, I'm taking a nap."

Battle Center, Space Force Headquarters
December 2
0200

Schultz had found Jenny Oh at work, testing and refining the tracking software so critical to the mission. She also planned on sleeping after the launch.

Now she sat at the chief controller's desk, considering Schultz's idea. She was tired and worried, but it was an intriguing plan, even if it complicated these last few precious hours.

"We've run similar drills," she replied carefully. She couldn't give Schultz a resounding yes, much as she wanted to. She needed to think it through herself. "And my programmers could continue running their tests separately."

"I don't want to do anything that interferes with readiness for the launch tomorrow," the admiral assured her.

"It would mean transmitting on the launch frequencies."

"We have more than one set, don't we?" he asked.

"Yes, but only a limited number. Once they're used, we have to assume the Chinese or anyone else will be able to monitor them."

"But they're encrypted," Schultz replied.

"I don't assume anything," Jenny answered firmly.

"You're right, of course, but it's worth it." He looked at his watch. "I want it nice and dark, so you'll need to be ready by 0500 hours."

"We'll be ready."

Eight

Arrival

Gongga Shan
December 2

General Shen paced a path in the launch center. The staff, familiar with their duties, gave him a wide berth and paid attention to the upcoming launch. He left them to it. Events were taking their own course. He was no longer in complete control of the situation, and he hated it.

The launch base, always on alert for attack, was on a war footing. Every man of the garrison had been turned out, and patrols went out twice as far as usual. Flanker fighters ran racetrack patterns overhead.

They had cause to be concerned. American strikes up and down the coast had hurt the People's Liberation Army badly. Vital bases were damaged, ships had been sunk, and dozens of aircraft destroyed in the air. The Politburo had forbidden the services to discuss casualty figures, even among themselves.

Still, the American attacks had been carefully chosen to strike weak points. Heavily defended areas had been spared, so far. It was as if the Americans had lost confidence. They no longer believed in their invincibility. He hoped that feeling was right, because it meant they were weakening.

Shen knew it would be difficult for the Americans to strike so far inland, but he had to be prudent. Especially since this was where the real battle lay.

Li Zhang, the Premier, had asked the Politburo if they should seek some compromise with the Americans. Both sides stop shooting, in return for security guarantees. Pan Yunfeng, at Shen's urging, had finally convinced them to continue the launch program without interruption. Shen's reasoning had been irrefutable: Even if *Defender* really existed, there was no way to know when it would be ready to launch. A week? A month?

It was frustrating, but really irrelevant, since *Defender* would be destroyed soon after it took off. Shen was almost eager for the Americans to launch. Its appearance would resolve so much of the uncertainty he had to deal with. Its failure would break their will.

Miramar Marine Corps Air Station
0400

Admiral Schultz watched the pilot preflighting his SuperHornet. It was dark on the flight line, illumination coming from spotlights nearby. The drab gray camouflage scheme didn't reflect the lights, and the plane appeared to be built from angular shadows.

The fighter was unarmed, but carried three of the big 480-gallon drop tanks. The pilot paid a lot of attention to them.

General Norman had joined Schultz on the flight line. "It seems so simple," the general said, looking at the plane's payload.

"It'll work just fine," Schultz reassured him. "We used to have this as a problem with A-6s and F-14s. In fact, once the pilots found out how to do it, we had to explicitly forbid the practice. There are some risks."

"Which Major O'Hara understands," Norman reassured him. "But I'm taking all this on faith. I'm just a dumb grunt."

"And I'm just an old pilot." Schultz grinned at him. "I'm needed elsewhere. Would you care to join me, Carl?"

"I'd love to, Bill," replied the general.

Space Force Headquarters, Miramar
0400

Suiting up for the flight was still a novelty for Ray. He'd practiced the procedure twice before, also a fitting for the suit and other systems. Like the shuttle crew, they would work in a shirtsleeve environment, but for the launch they would wear the full rig.

McConnell moved through the morning in a haze. It didn't feel real. It had happened too fast. He felt adrift. His role in building *Defender* and preparing her for flight was over. He was so used to the pressure of the deadline that he still felt it there. Like taking finals, it took a while to realize they were over.

Add to that the fulfillment of a dream. He would fly in space. He'd flown before, of course, in light planes that he piloted and joyrides in high-performance jets. This would be much different. He'd see and feel things he'd never seen or felt before.

He knew he was afraid. There were risks, of course. Mechanical failure or human error could bring them to grief, but it was the uncertainty of the mission that really frightened him. Did they have the right tools? Ray was so closely tied with *Defender*, he felt part of her, and the thought of her failing almost paralyzed him. He remembered his talk with Jenny, and tried to say to himself the words he'd said to her.

Space Forces Battle Center, Miramar, California 0415

The visit was as important as fueling *Defender* or loading her software. Led by Biff Barnes, *Defender*'s crew filed up onto the scaffolding surrounding the slowly rotating globe of the earth. They were dressed for the mission, wearing their flight suits and, purely for photo purposes, carrying their helmets.

Although nobody announced their arrival, someone, then several people, and finally the entire center clapped and cheered as they made their way to Admiral Schultz's position.

Ray felt embarrassed and proud at the same time. He would depend on these people while he was up. In fact, without them he was helpless. But he and the rest of the crew were the ones taking the risks.

Biff Barnes understood it better. There'd always been a special bond between the people who maintained the planes and those who flew them. *Defender*'s crew was here to acknowledge that bond, and to let the support staff have one more look at the crew before launch. They were the stars of the show, but stars had to let themselves be seen.

Admiral Schultz also wanted to say good-bye and wish them luck as well. After this they would start the final launch preparations, and there'd be no time for ceremony.

Schultz shook everyone's hands, and had a few words for each member of the crew. When Ray took his hand, the normally outgoing admiral was silent for a moment, and finally just said, "Good luck."

Space Forces Launch Center, Miramar, California
0430

The crew left the ready room together and walked outside. Only a few people saw them, but they clapped and waved at the six as they approached *Defender*.

Ray had visited Cape Canaveral several times, and loved the huge Vertical Assembly Building and the massive tracked transporter that carried the assembled shuttle on its six-mile-per-hour crawl to the launchpad. They were tremendous technical achievements, needed because of the shuttle's boosters and fuel tanks. They were also tremendously expensive.

That morning, before dawn, they'd brought *Defender* out of her hangar. Two rails helped them guide her onto the pad, where she was elevated to the vertical for launching. Fueling began as soon as she was locked in place. With an 0300 rollout, she'd be ready for launch at 0600. The sheer simplicity of the preparations amazed him.

She was still an overall white, a broad snowy wedge that reflected the work lights. The swept-back wings on either side only made her look wider and taller. The ship sat on a short framework, the beam used to elevate her now lowered again.

They'd left the American flag, but painted out the Lockheed Martin logo and the VENTURESTAR lettering. Star-and-bar insignia had been added on the wings and the center of the fuselage, top and bottom. Below the insignia, in black capital letters, was her name. To Ray, she was more than beautiful.

The crew access elevator took them two-thirds of the way up, where the square black of the open access hatch led them inside. The moment the last of them was in, technicians closed the hatch and removed the elevator.

Ray became wrapped up in the checklist. The six of them each had their own tasks, and had to work as a team to do it correctly . . .

Runway 15, Miramar Marine Corps Air Station
0530

Major Tim O'Hara smoothly lined up the jet on the runway. Night takeoffs required caution. The lights of the town in the background could confuse a pilot looking for a runway marker or a signal light. He set his brakes and watched the tower. As he waited, he checked his radio again. The transmit switch was off, and would stay off until he was ready to land.

The runway was dry and clear, the weather perfect. He fought the urge to double-check his armament panel. He did double-check that his nav lights were off. He wasn't supposed to attract any attention, and the tower would keep all other traffic clear. He heard them vectoring the standing fighter patrol to the far end of the base.

A green light flashed from the tower, and he pushed the throttle forward to full military. The runway lights slid past him on either side, quickly becoming streaks. With long practice, he pulled back on the stick, feeling the ship almost leap off the runway. He cleaned her up, bringing up the flaps and gear.

Throttling back, he stayed low, and started his first turn quickly. Buildings rushed by frighteningly close below him, but the route had been carefully planned to avoid any obstructions. He had to stay low to avoid the civilian air traffic control radars. You could never tell who had tapped into their signal.

At jet speeds, he crossed the base almost instantly, and spotted the IP ahead. They'd decided to use the motor pool. After his turn there, it would be a straight shot to *Defender*'s launchpad.

He banked precisely over the motor pool's parking lot, then pushed the throttle to full military again. Even at low altitude, he could see the pad ahead of him, and he pointed the nose straight at it.

The jet built up speed again, quickly passing four hundred knots, and passed over a small service building he'd noted on the map. It marked the spot where he had to begin his zoom.

O'Hara pulled the nose up sharply. By the time he'd reached the vertical, he was directly over the launchpad. He hit the afterburner, and an instant later, the DUMP switch on his drop tanks. Fuel sprayed out vents on the back of the tanks and was immediately ignited by the jet's exhaust.

Accelerating, he concentrated on keeping the nose straight up, and hoped someone was getting a picture.

INN News
0532

"FLASH. This is Mark Markin, INN News, outside Miramar. We've just seen a flame rising to the east." Turning to someone off-camera, he asked, "Is it still there? Get it linked!"

Markin's face was replaced by a bright red streak moving against a black background. Jerky camera motion gave the impression of great distance. The end of the streak flickered and wavered. It seemed to be going very fast.

"Less than a minute ago, a red flash appeared in a part of the base used by the *Defender* program. The flash shot up into the sky at terrific speed, and is now fading at high altitude.

"Without any announcement, and presumably to protect the American GPS constellation, *Defender* has launched.

"I say again . . ."

Space Forces Battle Center, Miramar, California
0532

General Norman watched INN's transmission, grinning. "That's what you get for peeping over fences," he joked at Markin's image. The INN reporter was rehashing the recent event yet again.

Schultz was listening on his headset, and watching Jenny move among the launch controllers. Instead of watching their screens, they read from a paper script. Normally used for training, it drilled the controllers in what they were supposed to say at each point as they guided *Defender* during its launch. They'd practiced the procedure dozens of times, but this time their transmissions were being broadcast. Nobody was sure who would be listening in, but if anyone did, they would hear what sounded like the real thing.

Gongga Shan, December 1
0540

From the look on the controller's face, Shen knew it was an urgent call. He took the headset and heard Dong Zhi's voice. "They've launched. It's all over INN."

"What did they show?" he asked, motioning to one of the technicians. Although they had access to the Internet, they were not allowed to link INN except in "special circumstances." Shen thought this would qualify. Along with the launch staff, he watched the launch and heard Markin's commentary.

"Time of launch was 5:30 local, about ten minutes ago," reported Dong. "We've picked up increased radio traffic from Miramar, as well. We're calculating the intercept basket now."

"We're still seventeen minutes from launch here," said Shen, checking the time. He could feel a prebattle excitement build in him. The Americans had moved.

"I recommend holding your launch until we finish the intercept," the scientist replied. "I don't want my staff having to deal with two vehicles at once. Without worldwide tracking, we'll have to move fast once the American appears."

"All right." Shen was reluctant to hold the launch, but agreed with Dong. He knew the staff's capabilities. "I'll wait for word from you."

Dong reassured him, "Preparations for the booster have started and are on schedule. It should launch in ten minutes."

Shen broke the connection and turned to find his launch crew suddenly busy at their posts. He should be worried about the American spacecraft, but felt relieved instead. He really hadn't expected them to launch so soon. It would have a short life.

Space Force Battle Center, Miramar
0552

Wrapped up in the launch sequence, Ray was almost irritated when Schultz's voice came over the comm circuit. "SITREP, people," Schultz announced. Conversation stopped immediately, and the admiral continued, speaking quickly. "We've got a launch."

The crew all looked at their displays, expecting to see a line over Gongga Shan. Ray cursed his luck. Intel had firmly assured him that they would be able to launch before the Chinese sent up another ASAT vehicle—maybe by less than an hour, but they needed that time to get into position.

Then Ray saw it was from Jinan, farther to the north. The thin red line grew slowly, angling east and steadily climbing in a graceful curve. He heard a controller announce, "It's faster than a T'ien Lung."

"A bigger gun?" wondered Ray amazedly.

"No, that's their manned space center," replied Barnes. "It has to be a standard booster. But what's on top?"

"We can't wait to figure that out," Schultz said. "We'll continue with launch preparations while Intelligence tries to sort it out."

It was less than five minutes later when Schultz interrupted their preparations again. With only a few minutes until ignition, Ray knew it would be important news.

"The launch was from their Jinan space complex, and the telemetry is consistent with a Long March 2F booster. That's the vehicle they use for manned launches, but it's moving too fast for a manned spacecraft. We think it has a much smaller payload."

"Aimed at us, no doubt," Barnes remarked. "An orbital SAM."

"Aimed at what they thought was us," Schultz replied. "That fireworks display was more useful than we thought."

"With that much energy, they may still be able to engage us," Ray countered.

"And with what?" asked Barnes.

"Probably another T'ien Lung," guessed Ray. "But it could be modified."

"Nukes?" Barnes didn't look worried, but some of the other crew did.

"Anything's possible."

Schultz asked, "Are we go or no-go? We can hold on the pad."

"With that thing waiting in orbit for us? No way," Ray responded. Suddenly he remembered he was out of line. Barnes should be the one answering. He looked at the major. "I recommend we go, sir."

Biff nodded, then looked at the rest of the crew. All were silent, but they all nodded yes.

"They're still aiming at something that isn't there. Let's go now, before they get a chance to regroup. We're go," Biff answered firmly.

Gongga Shan
0605

General Shen had left the INN webcast on, in the hopes that some additional information might be added, but after running out of ways to repeat themselves, they'd just started speculating. While amusing, it wasn't very useful.

He was in an unusual, in fact unique, situation. The projectile was ready, it had been for almost ten minutes, but they were not firing. Technicians sat idle, the gun crews crouched in their launch bunkers, and they waited. Xichuan was still waiting for *Defender* to appear on their tracking radars, while the interceptor raced to their best guess of its future position.

Shen found himself drawn to the INN show. Much of the material shown was coverage of the war. Most was propaganda, but the coverage was extensive. He learned a few things Beijing would certainly forbid them to discuss . . .

"FLASH. This is Mark Markin, in Miramar, California." Markin's familiar image replaced the physics professor who had been explaining *Defender*'s engines.

"We are receiving many, many reports of a spacecraft launch from inside the Miramar Marine Corps Air Station." Markin looked and acted rattled and confused.

"Our reporters at the scene and numerous civilian sources have reported another launch just a few minutes ago. They described the noise as 'shattering,' much, much louder than the event earlier this morning. What?"

Markin looked off to the side, then answered, "Good, put it up."

"Here is an image of the launch taken by a local resident who grabbed his camera when he heard the noise." The picture showed a blue sky with an angled white pillar, almost a cone, across two-thirds of the frame. A small arrowhead sat on top of the pillar.

Markin's voice said, "We're going to enhance the picture." A box appeared around the arrowhead, and Shen watched as it expanded, then rippled, and finally sharpened. Individual pixels gave it a jagged look, but he could see swept-back wings, and make out clusters of flame at the base.

"Get me Dong!" he shouted to the communications chief, then stared at the image on the screen. "Somebody print that out," he ordered, as the chief handed him a headset.

"Are you watching it, too? I don't know what we saw earlier. This one looks real enough."

Defender
0605

The experience of the launch filled Ray's senses. Every part of him inside and out was affected by the sound, which had faded, and by the acceleration that continued seemingly forever.

One far corner of Ray's mind said something about "time dilation," but the acceleration pushing him down was much more immediate. He found himself struggling to take a deep breath, although he'd been taught to take shallow breaths. The mask gave him all the oxygen he needed. There was nothing for him to do during the ascent, and he forced himself to relax, to accept the weight.

Biff watched the crew and hated the acceleration. The physical sensation was familiar to him, but his mind was filled with the responsibility he held. Mission commander. He tried to take comfort in his training as a combat pilot, but the rules were different. All the rules. Not just movement, but sensors, and weapons as well. He'd drilled himself mercilessly in the simulators, never sure if it was enough. Now he'd find out. At least he didn't have to pull lead.

Ray focused on the board, letting his body do unconsciously what he couldn't tell it to. All the systems were working well, although they'd have to deploy the sensors to really check them out. They'd traded payload for time and overengineered the shock mountings. He had a feeling that would pay off.

Risking a small movement, he touched a switch on his jury-rigged hand controller and checked the tactical display. Two screens simultaneously displayed a side and overhead view of the situation. The Chinese intercept vehicle, marked TL1 on the display, was above them, but eastbound. They had launched to the north, into a polar orbit. Its high velocity would make it difficult, no, almost impossible, to attack *Defender*.

Gongga Shan
0610

General Shen knew that as well. And there were other problems. He pressed his point over the link to Xichuan. "If we try to intercept *Defender* on the next orbit, the T'ien Lung will be out of our view for over an hour. We can't tell what the Americans will do to it during that time.

"Instead, we should use it to kill another GPS satellite. Their orbits are fixed, and it's got plenty of energy for the intercept. I'll attack *Defender* with my weapon instead."

"It's our last shot," Dong countered. "Shouldn't we use it to kill a GPS satellite? Two kills in one day, both while *Defender* is supposed to be protecting them, will be even a bigger embarrassment."

Shen disagreed. "Better to destroy *Defender*. We may have missed with the Long March, but that doesn't change the value of the target."

It was Shen's decision to make, but he wanted Dong to agree. His people would now have to handle the two vehicles, although only for a short time. Although he knew they could, the general asked, "Can you do it?"

"Yes," Dong admitted.

"Then tell them to prepare. We'll be firing in less than five minutes." He raised his voice for the last sentence, and the staff in the center hurried to obey.

"One more thing," General Shen added. "Tell Beijing we need to initiate the special attack." Shen lowered his voice without trying to sound conspiratorial. Security was so tight even his launch staff didn't know about it.

"Good," Dong answered, sounding relieved. "Liang has been after me to use it since the first launch this morning."

Battle Center
0615

Jenny noticed it first. She ran the whole Center, but without communications, there was no Center. Consequently, she dedicated one of her displays to continuously monitoring the data links from dozens of other sites. These included command centers like NORAD and the NMCC, radar-tracking stations, and intelligence aircraft orbiting off the China coast. The Battle Center had no sensors of its own, but took the data from all these sources and created the global situation display.

The audio beep and the flashing red icon had her immediate attention. She called one of the controllers on her headset. "Carol, check on the link to Kwajalein. We've lost the signal."

No sooner had the controller acknowledged her order than another link went red, this time the one to Pearl Harbor. Used to looking for patterns, she instantly compared the two, but could see no similarity. Pearl was a command site.

She started to detail another of her small staff to check out the link to Hawaii when a third one went red, this time in Ascension, and then others, coming so rapidly it was hard to count.

"Admiral, we're losing all our sensors!" Jenny tried to control the panic in her voice. She started to listen to Schultz's reply when Carol cut in with a report on the Kwajalein tracking station.

"I'm in voice comms, Jenny. They say the gear's fine, but they're under electronic attack. Someone's hacking their controller."

"That's impossible," Jenny exclaimed before realizing how silly that sounded. She paused, examining the situation, then suggested, "Their filters must be down. They're supposed to reject anything that's not encrypted."

"They say this stuff is encrypted," Carol explained, "at least well enough to get through the filters."

"We've got another launch," a different controller reported. "This time from Gongga Shan."

Jenny saw the track appear on the globe and checked the sensor log. The detection had been made by an Air Force surveillance aircraft, one of several off the coast. So far they hadn't been . . .

The globe, smoothly rotating in the center of the room, suddenly stopped, then moved jerkily before freezing again. What now?

Even as she switched her headset to the computer staff's channel, Chris Brown, the head of the computer section, reported. "We're being flooded. Someone's sending bogus tracking data over the links."

"The filter's aren't stopping it?" Jenny asked.

"Not all of it."

Jenny walked over to Brown's console and watched him analyze the false information being sent from supposedly secure sites. "Here's the header data on one that got through. It's good."

"They're not all getting through the filters?"

"No, about one in ten makes it." He tapped his console, bringing up another stream of data. "This one has a similar header, but the encryption isn't quite right, and it was rejected."

"But the ones that do get through are enough," he continued. "They force our system to chew on each for a while before rejecting it, and for every real packet, we're getting dozens of these fakes."

"Jenny, I need to know what's happening." Admiral Schultz's voice in her headset was soft, but insistent. She looked across the open space at the admiral, who met her gaze expectantly.

"We're under electronic attack, sir, through our tracking stations. It's sophisticated. They not only deny us sensor information, but they're piggybacking bad data on the links to bog us down."

"How do we block it?"

She sighed. "I'll have to get back to you, sir."

Chris Brown had been listening to her conversation with the admiral, and spoke as soon as she signed off. "It's completely down now. We just lost sensor processing."

Defender
0620

They were still setting up when Jenny called. The pilots, Scarelli and Skeldon, had opened the bay doors, then Andre Baker, the weapons officer, extended the laser turret above the bay. While the specialists readied their gear, Ray watched power levels and the health of the data link.

He'd noticed the problems a few minutes earlier, but had concentrated on the systems at his end. The thought of the Battle Center going down left him feeling very alone.

Her message clarified the situation but didn't help solve it. "Ray, we've lost sensors. We're under attack down here." Her words chilled him, but he forced himself to be silent, to listen. She explained the problem, but its effects were obvious. They were on their own. She could not say when they'd be back on-line.

Suddenly Ray felt vulnerable. Somewhere below, another T'ien Lung was climbing toward them.

Biff Barnes looked at the display screens. They were flat and two-dimensional, nothing like the Battle Center's fancy displays. He selected different modes, looking at projected paths and engagement envelopes.

He ignored the new threat, somewhere below them. They could do nothing about it, so he'd decided to work on the one target they did have.

Ray looked over at Barnes studying the display. "They've missed their chance at us. They'll have to go for a satellite."

"I agree," Biff responded. "Look at this." He sent the plot to Ray's console. It showed the remaining GPS satellite tracks and the area covered by the Chinese tracking radars.

"The easiest one to reach is number eighteen, here." He highlighted one of the satellites. "If they make a course change anytime in the next half hour, they can nail it. They'll be able to watch the intercept, as well."

Barnes waited half a moment while McConnell studied the screen. Ray nodded slowly. "All right," the engineer replied. It was almost a question.

"We're taking it out," Biff stated. "Right now. Before it gets any farther away. Before TL2 shows up to ruin our morning. Pilot, align us on TL1. Crew, engage TL1."

Ray watched the stars and the earth spin slowly as Scarelli oriented the open bay so it faced toward the Chinese spacecraft. The distance was a problem, but at least they didn't have to maneuver to keep the target in *Defender*'s limited sensor arc.

Sue Tillman, the sensor officer, went from busy to extremely busy. She fiddled with the radar settings, then chose one of a number of search patterns for the radar to follow. Everything had to be done manually, and that took time.

The lieutenant finally reported, "I've got a hit with the radar, 151 miles, 330 relative, 80 degrees elevation. Changing to track mode." A few moments later, she said, "Track established."

Checking another display, she reported, "IR confirms."

Ray suppressed the urge to comment on the gear actually working.

By rights, the detection should have been automatically tracked and evaluated. But systems integration takes valuable design time. Instead, it was all done manually, and with each second the target moved farther away.

Captain Baker, the weapons officer, didn't miss a beat. He'd slaved the laser to the data sent by the Tillman's radar. "Ready," he reported, as calmly as if he reporting the weather.

Ray had seen the seven-ton laser turret tested on the ground. The motors made an unholy whine. Now, there was no sound, just a slight vibration felt through the ship's structure, as it tracked the target.

"It's at the edge of our envelope," Ray reminded the major.

"And I figured out what that envelope was. Shoot six shots."

Ray felt more thuds and vibrations as pumps pushed chemicals into a combustion chamber. The intense flash of their ignition "pumped" the chemical laser and a two-megawatt beam angled out and away.

Inside *Defender*, Ray watched five seconds come and go. Sue Tillman, looking disappointed, turned to look over Captain Baker.

The weapons officer watched a spectrograph slaved to the laser mirror.

"Nothing," he reported.

Set for five shots, the laser automatically fired again. McConnell watched a TV camera set to cover the bay. Puffs of vapor left the combustion chamber, and he could see the turret slowly moving, but it was a silent combat.

Both Baker and Tillman spoke this time. The army officer announced triumphantly, "I've got an aluminum line." The laser had caused part of the target to glow. Baker's spectrograph had seen that light, and told him what that part was made of.

Tillman confirmed, "IR's up now. It's a lot hotter than before."

"But it's still there on radar?" Barnes asked.

She nodded. "Trajectory's unchanged."

"Continue firing."

The third shot, five seconds of intense energy, also struck the Chinese vehicle, but with no better result than before. Ray fought the urge to fiddle with the systems display, or remind Barnes that the target was growing more distant with every shot.

They'd spent a lot of time trying to decide how they would know when they'd actually "killed" a target. You couldn't shoot down something in space, and at these distances they couldn't see the effects of their attacks.

During the fourth shot, Biff asked, "Sue, can you measure the temperature rise?"

"No, sir. The equipment's resolution isn't that fine. Physics says it can't radiate heat away as fast as we're adding it, but we're also adding less heat with each shot, because of the increasing distance."

By the time she answered Barnes's question, the fifth shot of the salvo had been fired as well. They'd used up almost half the magazine, but the mission commander didn't wait a moment. "Keep firing. Another five."

Well, we're here to shoot down satellites, Ray thought. He tried to stay focused on his monitors, watching for signs of trouble. It would be hell if a mechanical failure interfered at this point.

Tillman saw it first, on the second shot of the new salvo. "IR's showing a big heat increase!"

"Spectrograph's full of lines!" Baker reported triumphantly. "I've got silicon, nitrogen. . . ."

"Kill the laser!" Biff ordered. "Silicon means the electronics, and nitrogen's either solid propellant or the explosive warhead."

"There's also hydrogen and plutonium," she added, her voice a little unsteady.

Barnes nodded as if he'd expected it. "They were gunning for us."

"Multiple contacts. Radar shows debris as well," Tillman confirmed. *Defender*'s millimeter-wave radar would have no trouble distinguishing individual pieces of wreckage.

"It's a kill," she said with satisfaction. Sue Tillman also handled voice comms with Miramar, and said "They're cheering in the Battle Center!"

Ray noted the time. They'd been up half an hour.

Gongga Shan
0635

"It's gone, sir!" The communications tech handed him the headset. Shen listened to Dong's report quietly. The Americans had destroyed the special T'ien Lung. They'd made the kill at long range, on an opening target. *Defender* was more than capable.

Shen worked to control his surprise and disappointment, making his face a mask. *Defender* had proved itself. Now more than before, it was vital that the second vehicle destroy the American spacecraft. Unfortunately, there was nothing more he could do to ensure its success. Like countless commanders before him, Shen could only wait for the dice to stop rolling.

Battle Center
0635

"It's a brute force attack, Jenny." Chris Brown sat surrounded by display screens. Some showed packets of invading data. Others listed tables of statistical data—numbers of packets sent from each site, numbers rejected by the filter, amount of processor time lost, and many other values.

"They don't have our encryption completely broken, but they've learned enough to get through occasionally. See," he said, pointing to two invading data packets. "The body of the message is the same. And most of the header data is valid. All they have to do is vary the part they don't know.

"And they're getting better at it. Look at this curve." It showed the percentage of successful penetrations since the attack began, and the number steadily increased.

Jenny forced herself to think clearly, to ignore the rest of the center and the craft in space above her. This was a battle of minds.

"The encryption key is time-based," Jenny said. "To mimic it at all, they'd have to be monitoring our communications in real time."

"Then that's what they're doing," replied the computer analyst. "All of the communications are hardened land lines." Jenny had insisted on that, for obvious reasons.

"Except the signal to *Defender*," countered Brown.

"Which we have to leave up," finished Jenny. That link was the reason for the Battle Center's existence. She visualized the flow, out from the Center, picked up by intercept antenna somewhere, then fed back into the system though pirated computers. The Chinese were using their own codes against them.

"Chris, we have to change the encryption schemes."

"That won't help, they'll only . . ."

"Only for the link to *Defender*," she continued. "Right now we all use the same coding scheme. Change the time-based key for *Defender*'s link, and the filters will reject it automatically."

Brown's face lit up. "Yeah, I can even optimize the coding to make it easier for the filters to spot. I can use a modifier . . ."

The analyst trailed off into thought, but quickly resurfaced. "I'll have to upload a patch to *Defender*, but the Chinese haven't interfered with the link. I can have us up in five minutes."

Jenny hurried back to her own console, keying her handset as she went. "Good news, Admiral."

Defender
0645

Brown's patch had an immediate effect. Cut off from the ground, the computer had been displaying the estimated position of the second T'ien Lung. It had been close, but the uncertainty of the estimate had prevented them from taking any action.

Now, within moments, the display flashed with the real position of TL2. A red arc showed its track history, a red dot its present location, and a red cone its possible future position. *Defender*'s orbit lay square in the center of that cone, and another flashing symbol showed the intercept point.

Intercept was only five minutes away. They couldn't hope to set up and kill it before it reached them. Barnes ordered "Countermeasures!" and then told the pilots, "Take this vector. Pull in the turret, close the doors."

Ray saw the stars swing again, then felt pressure against his back as *Defender*'s engines came to life. They quickly increased to full power. The rest of the crew quickly carried out Barnes's orders, bringing the laser turret inside.

The doors might protect the turret against small fragments from the T'ien Lung if it did detonate. Of course, with the doors closed, they were blind as well as defenseless. More than ever, Ray felt grateful for the data link.

Scarelli had oriented the craft so that its top side faced the T'ien Lung. They'd argued about it during one of the many strategy sessions, and decided they'd rather have fragments in the doors and upper fuselage than in the heat shield. They could live without weapons and sensors, but they couldn't reenter without the heat shield.

The acceleration wasn't as bad as takeoff, but it was still intense, and mixed with uncertainly.

His board showed the same tracks as Barnes's, as well as other ship's systems. He watched the radar decoys leave the ship, a cluster of simple radar corners, based on their best guesses about the design of the kill vehicle's sensors.

McConnell also watched as the line of *Defender*'s orbit slowly curved. The engines stopped, and Ray saw that they were just outside the Chinese intercept cone.

The arc carrying the T'ien Lung did not change for two long minutes. It finally started to shift, back toward an intercept on their new course. "Look at that," Barnes said, pointing to the display. "Their reaction times are very slow."

He waited for a moment, then announced, "They're not buying the decoys. All right, pilot, now take this vector. Stand by for a long burn, people."

This time Ray was ready for the acceleration, and better still, welcomed it. The Chinese lag in controlling the T'ien Lung would be their undoing.

Barnes's new course zigged *Defender* away from the T'ien Lung, exactly opposite to the course correction the Chinese vehicle was making. *Defender*'s engines were more powerful than the T'ien Lung's thrusters. The Chinese vehicle had been designed to engage satellites, not maneuverable spacecraft.

"Past closest point of approach!" the copilot reported. Skeldon didn't sound relieved. The Chinese could always command-detonate the warhead if they felt there was a chance of damaging them.

They did, after another thirty extra seconds of distance. There was no sound of explosion, but two sharp bangs, like rifle shots, sounded over their heads, and part of Ray's board went from green to red and yellow. One corner of his eye noted that the symbol for the second T'ien Lung was now gone from the screen.

Ray reported, "We're losing hydrogen pressure. One of the tanks has been holed!"

"Continue the burn," Barnes ordered. "Move as much hydrogen out of the tank as you can before it escapes."

"Doing it," Ray responded. "It'll screw up our center of gravity," he warned.

"Compensating," responded Scarelli. "What about that other strike?" the pilot asked.

"That'll take a little sorting out," Ray replied.

Part of the electrical system flashed red, but what was the problem? Was it a component, or the wiring? They'd installed redundant lines on the critical systems. It was time to see if it was working. He started isolating components. His mind focused on the technical problem, he hardly noticed the acceleration.

There. "Primary actuators for the ailerons are off-line. Backups seem all right." But something else aft still glowed red. He closed a few more systems, but the news wasn't good. "We've lost number three hydrogen pump."

"Which means no number three engine," Scarelli continued.

"We can cope," Barnes reassured him. "We don't have another burn until we reenter."

The burn finished, and Ray was surprised by the sudden weightlessness. His stomach complained a little, but he mastered it.

Barnes asked. "Jim, how long until we're over Xichuan?"

Scarelli checked his plot, then answered, "Twenty-three minutes. That last burn brought our orbit right over them!" He looked at Barnes with a "How'd you do that?" expression.

The major grinned. "I picked the first burn vector directly away from where I wanted us to end up. That way I could make the long burn in the right direction. Set up for ground attack. Here are the targets."

Ray watched as he designated two points on the map display. Scarelli had to make one small burn to refine the course, then he and Skeldon turned *Defender* so her bay faced the globe of earth below.

After that, they waited. Baker and Tillman checked out their equipment, and pilots monitored their course. For the first time since they had taken off, Ray had a moment to realize he was in space.

His stomach was still under control, and they were all strapped in anyway. No floating during General Quarters, he mused. He looked at the monitors, one of which showed the earth "above" them. They were over the North Pole, coming down on the other side of the world from California. It seemed different, somehow. Smaller, and more vulnerable.

"Five minutes," Scarelli warned, and Baker and Tillman both acknowledged. Ray and Barnes both watched silently as the specialists worked.

Tillman reported "Imaging first target," and activated her radar. The millimeter-wave signal easily found the Xichuan space center, a cluster of large buildings. Ray selected the radar display, and studied the buildings. They'd seen it before in satellite photographs, and he quickly picked out the administration buildings, the control center, the powerhouse, and the other structures. The image was clear enough to show the chain-link fence that surrounded the compound.

Baker designated his rods, and Ray saw three small symbols appear over the control center, and two more on the antennas. "Ready for drop," he reported.

"Drop on the mark," Barnes ordered calmly.

"Roger, in ten," the weapons officer replied, and then counted the seconds down. "Dropping now."

Ray saw his board change but felt nothing.

The rods were not as noisy or complex as the laser. Each simply consisted of a long, pointed tungsten cylinder weighing fifty kilograms, with a small motor and finned guidance unit on the back. Springs ejected them in quick sequence from their rack in *Defender*'s bay, and McConnell watched the stream drift clear of the ship.

As fast as the rods had been ejected, their individual motors fired, driving them down toward the earth and reentry. The tungsten projectile would easily withstand the heat, and was aerodynamically shaped. The guidance unit would burn up, but by then they'd be aligned on their target, and with so much speed that nothing would deflect them.

Xichuan was still several hundred miles ahead of them, but of course the rods needed that time to cover the distance to the ground. It also made it difficult for the Chinese to predict where the attack would strike. If they could even see *Defender*. The ship was approaching from the north, where Chinese radar coverage was limited.

"Five minutes to next target," Baker announced.

Gongga Shan
0720

The call came over a standard phone line, not the command net. General Shen Xuesen took the receiver from the communications chief.

"General, this is Wu Lixin." Shen knew the man. He was one of Dong's assistants at the control center. He sounded absolutely shattered.

"Wu, what's happened?"

"They bombed us, sir. Dong is dead, and so are most of the staff. The center's gone, ripped apart."

"Bombs. Was it an air attack?"

"No, no airplane, nothing was seen. No planes, no missiles."

The general felt his heart turn to ice. It had to be *Defender*. So the detonation hadn't hurt them at all. They were still capable.

Shen looked at their predicted orbit. She was moving from north to south, and . . .

"Out! Everybody outside right now! Head for the shelters!" he turned to the comm chief. "Get the gun crews out as well." Theoretically, the gun and the control bunkers were hardened, but Xichuan's control center had been hardened as well.

There was no way to tell when, or even if, an attack would happen, but Shen wasn't risking his people's lives. The instant he saw everyone in the center moving, he headed for the door himself.

He sprinted outside, intending to head for one of the slit trenches that had been dug nearby, but he had made it no more than a dozen steps before the explosions started.

It wasn't from behind him, but from the mountain, to his right. He turned just a little and saw a series of bright yellow explosions ripple over the gun's location. Earth spouted into the air hundreds of feet, and he could feel the concussions from over a kilometer away.

At least three deadly flowers blossomed at the base of the gun, right over the breech. Another four or five landed in a neat line on top of the barrel, and another three clustered closely around the muzzle. In the darkness, the mountain was outlined for several seconds by the flash from the explosions.

One of the first group must have found the liquid-propellant piping, because the entire building suddenly disintegrated in a ball of orange flame. Pieces of debris arced high into the air, and Shen suddenly found himself running again, diving headfirst into the trench as pieces of cement, steel, and rock began raining down on him.

The deadly rain stopped, and Shen untangled himself from the others who had sought shelter with him in the trench. Reluctantly, he knelt, and then stood, a little unsteadily. Knowing and hating what he would see, he nonetheless had to find out what they'd done to his gun.

The breech building was gone, replaced by a crater filled with flaming debris. Most of the installation had been below ground, and the crater had carved a massive gouge out of the mountain's roots.

The slope of the mountain looked almost untouched, but a line of craters neatly followed the path of the gun barrel, and the mouth was hidden in a mound of loose rock.

Five years of work. Ten years of convincing. Twenty years of dreaming, all lost. His friend Dong was dead, with many of China's brightest dead with him. How many bodies would they find just in the ruins below?

Shen realized others were trying to help him out of the trench. Passively, he let them lift him out and steady him on the grass. He turned automatically to head for the center, and saw it was in ruins, flames outlining the ruined walls. He hadn't even heard the explosions.

It was finished. Shen was suddenly very sorry he'd lived.

Defender

With most of their fuel used up, they'd made one small burn to line up for reentry after two more orbits. With nothing to do but wait, Ray felt his sensation of unreality return. His mind and emotions sought to understand this new experience.

They'd fought and won a battle in space. He'd played a role, a major one, in making it happen, but he knew he wasn't the only one. More importantly, others would follow after him. Not all would be Americans, maybe not all of them would be friends, but warfare had changed, as it always does.

Biff Barnes checked the displays over and over again, looking for the smallest fault, but the ship was performing well. Reentry was now only a few minutes away. Scarelli and Skeldon were handling the preparations perfectly.

For some reason Barnes was having problems trying to determine how he would fill out his personal flight log. Would the T'ien Lungs count as "kills"? Three more to become an "orbital ace"? He suspected there would be more missions after this one.

That thought led to another, and he started to make a mental list of improvements *Defender* would need before she flew again.

Battle Center

Jenny Oh fought hard to keep her emotions under control. Her first cheer, when *Defender* had destroyed the first T'ien Lung, had been followed by another when they'd escaped the second kill vehicle. Her heart had leapt to her throat when she saw the symbols for *Defender* and the kill vehicle merge, and then soared when they'd said all were safe.

And that had been followed by the destruction of the Dragon Gun at Gongga Shan. They'd watched it all on *Defender*'s imaging radar, data-linked down to the Center. The sudden transformation of the neat structural shapes to rubble had been unmistakable, and she'd yelled as loud as any of them. It was the success of everything they'd worked so hard for. *Defender* had proven herself.

Jenny had looked over at Admiral Schultz, who sat quietly, his head in his hands. He stayed that way, aware but silent, for some time. After the celebration stopped, he'd left, then come back later, in time to watch the reentry. He slowly walked over to Jenny's station, checking his watch as he approached.

"Check INN," the admiral suggested, smiling. It was just 1600.

Jenny selected to broadcast, and saw Markin's now-familiar face. Behind him was a commercial satellite image of the destroyed gun. Markin was excited, almost frantic.

"Flash! Only a short time ago sources revealed the destruction of the Gongga Shan Dragon Gun by *Defender*, and also the destruction of two orbital kill vehicles. The Chinese attempted to use these to shoot down the American spacecraft and a GPS satellite, but according to my source, both weapons were destroyed after an extended battle."

"Extended battle?" Jenny wondered aloud.

"Well, it was extended in orbital terms." The Admiral's smile widened.

"*You're* his source?" Jenny asked, almost shouting, and then controlling her voice.

"This time, yes. I felt bad about bamboozling him earlier this morning. There's no more need for secrecy, and I figured the best way for the media to get it straight was to get it straight from me."

They watched Markin's piece together for a few more minutes, as he detailed the engagements in space and the damage to the Chinese. Finally, he started to repeat himself, and Jenny checked the status board. *Defender* was now blacked out, and would be until she finished reentry.

The admiral watched her for a moment, then said, "Congratulations, Jenny. You made it happen."

"Congratulations to all of us, Admiral. We all did it."

"We all believed we could make it work, Jenny, and worked our tails off to prove it to the rest of the world. But you and Chris Brown saved the mission. Chris is a civilian, and he'll get a commendation for his civil service file. I'm recommending you for the Navy Cross. Nobody fired a shot in your direction, but you were in the fight as much as anyone. Your quick thinking saved lives, and won a battle."

Jenny felt herself flush, and she automatically came to attention. "Thank you, sir!" Then she wavered. "But what about *Defender* . . ."

Schultz waved a hand, cutting off her protests. "Oh, yes, there'll be medals and parades and all the glory a grateful nation can provide. They've earned all of it."

"Do you think Ray will be able to get a little free time?" she asked quietly.

LARRY BOND is forty-nine and lives with his wife, Jeanne, and daughters, Katie and Julia, in Virginia outside Washington, D.C. After coauthoring *Red Storm Rising* with Tom Clancy, he has written five novels under his own name: *Red Phoenix*, *Vortex*, *Cauldron*, and *The Enemy Within*. The latest is *Day of Wrath*, which was published by Warner Books in June 1998. His writing career started by collaborating with Tom Clancy on *Red Storm Rising*, a runaway *New York Times* best-seller that was one of the best-selling books of the 1980s. It has been used as a text at the Naval War College and similar institutions. Since then, his books have depicted military and political crises, emphasizing accuracy and fast-paced action. *Red Phoenix*, *Vortex*, and *Cauldron* were all *New York Times* best-sellers.

He has also codesigned the *Admiralty Trilogy* series of games, which includes *Harpoon*, *Command at Sea*, and *Fear God & Dreadnought*. The first two have both won industry awards, while the third will be published in late 2000.

Now in its fourth edition, *Harpoon* won the H. G. Wells Award, a trade association honor, in 1981, 1987, and 1997 as the best miniatures game of the year. It is the only game to win the award more than once. The computer version of the game first appeared in 1990, and won the 1990 Wargame of the Year award from *Computer Gaming World*, an industry journal.

CAV

BY JAMES COBB

Excerpts from The New Ways of War: Politico-Military Evolution in the Opening Decades of the Twenty-first Century.
Professor Christine Arkady,
University of Southern California Press, 2035

Much to the consternation of the international community, the African race wars raged on into the new millennium, but not in the format of the old black and white South African conflict. African and *Afrikaner* came to accommodations with comparative rapidity following the end of apartheid in the 1990s. Replacing it was a new, ominous, and growing confrontation between black and brown.

In a great arc across the African *Sahel* from the Atlantic to the Sudan, an almost continuous series of border clashes and minor insurgencies sputtered and flared between the Arabic-Moorish nations of North Africa and the Black African states of the Sub-Sahara. Fueled by racism, newborn nationalistic pride and old tribal enmities, and fanned by self-seeking political leaders and Islamic radicals, the potential for an open conflagration loomed large within the region.

The flash point came in the fall of 2021. The Islamic Republic of Algeria, the new primary troublemaker among the northern tier Arabic states, began beating the drum of *Jihad* against Mali, its immediate neighbor to the south. Taking up the cause of a small Mali-based group of Tuareg separatists with a sudden and suspicious vociferousness, the Algerians launched a major military buildup along the Mali border, all the while calling for a "liberation of our Muslim brothers from the black animists."

This in the face of the fact that the vast majority of Mali's population was also Islamic, albeit of a decidedly more moderate cast than the Revolutionary Council in Algiers.

Mali, in and of itself, was no great prize for any would-be conqueror. Wracked by drought and desertification, it was a strong contender for the title of the poorest nation on Earth. In a strategic military sense, though, it represented a pearl beyond price for any potential empire builder coveting Northwestern Africa. The largest of the West African states, Mali is set in the literal heart of the region. Every other nation around the West African periphery is vulnerable to an invasion staging out of Malian territory.

Reacting to that threat, and to the pleas for assistance from the Malian government, the West African Economic Federation deployed counterforces into Mali in the first major regional security operation ever launched by that fledgling organization. However, although willing, the WAEF combat units were woefully outnumbered and under-equipped to face the armored juggernaut being assembled by the Algerians. Chairman Belewa of the Federation Board of Unity, an intensely realistic statesman, dispatched an urgent request for military assistance to both the United States and France.

France replied with a *Force d'Intervencion* task group built around the First *Regiment Etranger d'Cavalerie*. The United States deployed the Second Army Expeditionary Force with two attached elements: the Thirteenth Aviation Brigade (Support) and the Seventh Cavalry Regiment (Armored Strike).

It was hoped that the presence of the Legionnaires and the Garry-owens on the ground in Mali would serve as a trip-wire deterrent to Algerian military adventurism.

The hope proved to be false.

The Western Sahara
300 Km North-Northwest of Timbuktu
1454 Hours, Zone Time; October 28, 2021

Lieutenant Jeremy Bolde rode in *ABLE*'s open commander's hatch with the balanced ease born of long practice. His wiry, well-muscled form flowed with each jolt and lurch of the big Shinseki armored fighting vehicle in much the same way as a skilled rider moved with the trail pacing of his horse. In that portion of his mind not involved with his focused and deliberate scanning of the surrounding terrain, the words of a song from the old army circled past, his sun-cracked lips pursed in an unheard whistle.

> *"In her hair she wore a yellow ribbon.*
> *And she wore it proudly so that every man could see.*
> *And when we asked her why a yellow ribbon.*
> *She said it's for my lover in the U.S. Cavalry . . ."*

Abruptly, the shrill alarm tone of the threat board squalled in the earphones of his helmet. At the same instant, Bolde felt *ABLE* swerve sharply beneath him as his driver, Specialist Third (Vehicle Operations) Rick Santiago locked the wheel over in an instinctive turn-and-accelerate evasion.

Bolde hit the seat control selector with the palm of his hand, dropping himself down through the commander's cupola and into the cab beside Santiago, the hatch lid thudding closed over his head.

"What do we have?" he demanded.

"Our point drone was just painted by a ground scan radar," Warrant Officer First (Velectronics Operations) Bridget Shelleen reported crisply from behind Bolde's shoulder.

"Any indication of a targeting acquisition?"

"I don't think so." The intense little redhead leaned into the drone operations station on the starboard cab bulkhead, her fingers dancing across the keypads as she pumped a series of commands into the datalinks. "*CHARLIE* was just cresting a dune line when he was blipped. I've reversed him back into the radar shadow. Contact broken. With the luck of the Lord and Lady, they'll think he was a dust transitory."

"How about us, Brid? Are we still clean?"

"No painting indicated. *CHARLIE* is running about ten klicks out ahead of us. We're still below the scan horizon of whatever is out there."

"Right. Recall *CHARLIE*. Low speed. Minimize dust plume. Rick, find us a hide. We're going to ground."

"Doin' it, LT," *ABLE*'s wheelman yelled back over the whir and rumble of the wheels. "We got a *qued* off to the left. I just gotta find us a go-down."

At eighty kilometers an hour, the armored cavalry vehicle roared along parallel to a dry wash. Such *queds* were one of the few, rare terrain variances to be found amid the broad expanses of sand-and-gravel *fesh fesh* plain that predominate in northern Mali.

Driving right-handed, Santiago used his left to manipulate the settings of the ride control panel, backing off the air pressure in *ABLE*'s eight massive Kevlar-belted tires from HARD SURFACE to ALL TERRAIN and dialing a few extra inches of ground clearance into the suspension.

Ahead he saw a point where the *qued* bank had collapsed, giving him a steep but usable access ramp to the ravine floor. "Okay going down. Hey, back in the scout bay! Hang on! Rough ride!"

He braked hard, swung the wheel over, and avalanched his vehicle down the crumbling slope. The suspension sprawled and angled, autoconforming to the terrain and keeping *ABLE*'s twenty-two tons centered over her wheelbase. Tire cleats dug in, then slipped, and the big war machine slither-crashed to the floor of the twenty-meter-wide dry streambed in an explosion of dust and sprayed earth, the pneumatic seats of her crew bouncing hard against their stops. Santiago leaned on his accelerator and *ABLE* lunged forward again, the eight-by-eight drives scrabbling for traction in the sand.

Another avalanche could be seen in the sideview mirrors. *BAKER*, Saber section's second gun drone, waddled down the slope after the command vehicle, its onboard artificial intelligences obediently station-keeping in their tactical default mode.

"How far you want me to work up the wash, LT?"

"Get us clear of our entry point." Bolde computed artillery spread patterns in his mind, judging clearances. When they'd put two bends in the streambed between themselves and the spot where they had disappeared from surface view, he nodded to his driver. "Okay, Rick, shut down and power down!"

ABLE shuddered to a halt, her turbines fading out with a whispering moan. A metallic hiss followed as the cavalry vehicle hunkered closer to the ground, her suspension lowering into a vehicular crouch.

In the forward compartment, an instinctive stream of orders flowed from Bolde.

"Brid, raise the sensor mast and go to full passive scan. I want a threat review! Rick, prep the Cypher for launch. Mary May! Deploy your ground pickets!"

"Yes sir," Spec 5 (Ground Combat) Mary May Jorgenson yelled from the scout team bay back aft. "Ramp going down. Scouts, set overwatch! Go!"

The tail ramp thudded open, and boots rang on aluminum decking.

Even as he issued his commands, Bolde personally involved himself in the security of the laager point. Accessing onboard fire control through the commander's station, he assumed direction of *ABLE*'s primary weapons pack.

In road mode, the boom mount of the weapons pack normally rode angled back over the stern of the cavalry vehicle like the cocked stinger tail of a scorpion. Now it straightened and extended, lifting the twin box launchers of the Common Modular Missile system above the lip of the wash. The telescopic lenses of a target-acquisition sensor cluster peered from between the launchers, as did the stumpy barrel of a 25mm OCSW (Objective Crew Served Weapon). Much like the attack periscope of a submarine, the weapons mount began a slow and deliberate rotation, scanning the horizon.

Scowling, Bolde watched the camera image pan past on his master display. Nothing moved out across the desert except for the perpetual heat shimmer. To the north, toward the rippling dune line, a single thin streak of dust played along the ground. A blue computer graphics arrowhead hovered over it, however, designating a friendly. *CHARLIE* drone returning from his point probe.

As the camera turned to the south, more friendly activity was revealed. A figure clad in desert camouflage snaked over the edge of the *qued*. Carrying his SABR (Selectable Assault Battle Rifle) over his forearms, Specialist Third Nathan Grey Bird snaked across a narrow stretch of gravel in a fluid infantry crawl, vanishing into a low clump of rocks with a deft alacrity that would have brought pride to the heart of his Shoshone-Bannock warrior ancestors.

Specialist Second Johnny Roman had his outpost established on the opposite bank of the *qued* and Specialist Second Lee Trebain could be seen through *ABLE*'s Armorglas windshield, establishing a sentry point farther ahead along the wash floor. Sensor systems were all well and good, but the "mark one eyeball" was still the hardest sensor in the world to fool. Saber section would not trust its security to electronics alone, not while one Lieutenant Jeremy Bolde commanded.

Bolde disarmed the weapons pack and allowed the boom to retract back into travel mode. Arming off his bulky HMD helmet, he replaced it with the dust- and sweat-stained cavalry terai that had been riding atop the dashboard, settling the hat over his short-trimmed, sandy hair at the precisely proper "Jack Duce" angle. The black slouch-brimmed Stetsons had been revived by the new cavalry as their answer to the berets of the Ranger and Special Forces regiments, a distinctive badge of branch individuality. The difference was that the Airborne units looked upon their signature headgear as being, for the most part, ceremonial. The Cav looked upon theirs as essential field equipment.

"Pickets are out, Lieutenant. Ground security set." Mary May Jorgenson came forward from the scout compartment through the narrow passage between the two mid-vehicle powerbays.

Man-tall and broad-shouldered for a woman, Mary May was one of the elite few female personnel to match the rigorous physical parameters required by the Army for a Ground Combat Specialist's rating. Yet for all of her inherent and repeatedly proven toughness, there was still a large degree of the mellow Nebraska farm girl in her blue-eyed and lightly freckled countenance.

Wearing BDU trousers and a flak vest over a khaki tee shirt, she carried an M9 service pistol on her right hip. However the 9mm Beretta automatic was carried in a left-handed holster, butt forward in the old dragoon's draw. She, too, wore a battered terai cocked low over her brows.

"What's up, Lieutenant?" she inquired, leaning back against the rear bulkhead. "Are we in contact?"

"With something," Bolde replied, rotated his seat so it faced the systems operator's station. "How about it, Brid. What do we have out there?"

"A single battlefield-surveillance radar," the systems operator replied, her attention still focused on the telepanels of her console. "With our mast up, I'm receiving an identifiable side lobe from it. Emission ID file indicates a Ukrainian made Teal/Specter system. . . . Multimode . . . About five years old . . . And it matches a unit type known to be in Algerian service."

She sat back in her seat and looked across at Bolde. "We are indeed in contact with the enemy, sir. And given the emission strength and beam angle, the unit must be operating from an elevation."

"Hell!" Bolde permitted himself the single short curse. "They beat us to the pass."

Terrain defines the battlefield. Unfortunately, for all intents and purposes, northern Mali doesn't have any. No rivers, no mountains, no forests, no swamps. Just extensive, arid plains of baked earth and *fesh fesh* intermittently blanketed by the migrating sand dunes of the Sahara.

The one exception was the El Khnachich range. A line of low, rugged hills arcing from east to west, midway between Algerian border and Timbuktu, it was the sole high ground in an ocean of flatness.

The Taoudenni caravan track, the closest thing to a road that existed in this part of the world, ran southward through a pass in the range. For centuries, the Taoudenni track had been a link joining Algeria with the Niger River valley. Thirty-six hours before, when the Algerian army had stormed across the undefended and indefensible Mali border, one entire mechanized division had been vectored down this beaten sand pathway, its mission to seize that route southward into Mali's fertile heartland.

In a countermove, Troop B, First of the Seventh had been ordered north from its patrol base in Timbuktu to meet the thrust, a fanged and venomous mouse charging an elephant. For the first time in modern human history, the hills of El Khnachich were important.

The systems operator called up a tactical map on her main display. The hill range and the pass lay perhaps twenty-five kilometers ahead on the section's line of advance. Blue IDed unit hacks glowed near the bottom of the map, indicating the position of Saber section's dispersed elements. A single hostile target box pulsed in the southern mouth of the pass.

"Darn!" Mary May yanked off her hat and slid down the bulkhead to sit on the pebbled rubber antiskid of the vehicle deck. "I thought the noon sitrep said that the Algies were still watering up at Taoudenni oasis."

"The bulk of the division was," Bolde grunted, his angularly handsome features impassive. "But they were already starting to push their lead elements south. I suspect they rammed some fast movers forward to play King of the Hill. Any sign they've got anything over on our side yet, Brid?"

The SO shook her head, her firefall of hair brushing the back of her neck. "Nothing's indicated. *CHARLIE* didn't spot anything, and I'm not picking up any tactical communications on the standard Algerian bands. If they have any units fanning out on this side of the slope, they're running an extremely tight EMCON, and that's not like them. We'll have to go eyes up to be certain, though."

"Then let's do it. Get off a contact report to Bravo six then put up the Cipher. I want to see what we have crawling around out there."

The Cipher reconnaissance drone was literally a flying saucer. Or perhaps to be even more precise, a flying doughnut, a flattened discoid aeroform four feet in diameter with two contrarotating lift fans in its center. A puff of compressed air launched it out of its docking bay on *ABLE*'s broad back. Bobbling in a hover for a moment over the dry wash, it autostabilized then darted away to the north, skimming an effortless ten feet above the desert's surface.

The drone rotated slowly as it flew. The television camera built into the rim of its sturdy stealth composite fuselage intently scanned the surrounding environment, the imaging being fed back via a jitter frequency datalink to its mother station in *ABLE*'s cab. There, in turn, a slender hand on a computer joystick clicked a series of waypoints onto a computer-graphics map, guiding the little Remotely Piloted Vehicle on its way.

On the main screen, the rusty red wall of the Khnachich range rose above the dune lines.

"I'm not seeing anything moving out there," Mary May commented from her position, seated cross-legged on the deck.

"Nothing as big as an armored column at any rate." Bolde glanced at the ECM threat boards. "And nobody is emitting except for that one radar on the high ground. Brid, take the drone out to the west a ways and then take it up to the ridgeline. We'll move it back east along the crest and have a look down into that pass."

Shelleen nodded her reply, her expression fixed and intent on the drone-control readouts.

Even at the Cipher's best speed, it took over a quarter of an hour to maneuver the drone into its designated observation position. At one point, as the RPV climbed the jagged stone face of the hill range, the video image on the display flickered and the datalink inputs faded as line of sight was broken between the drone and its controller. Instantly, Shelleen's hands flashed across the keypads, rerouting the links through one of the flight of Long-Duration Army Communications drones orbiting over the Mali theater at a hundred thousand feet.

The imaging smoothed out and Bolde rewarded his SO with a slight, appreciative nod of his head.

In due course, the drone's position hack on the tactical display and the image on the television monitor indicated that the drone was approaching the gut of the pass. Shelleen eased the RPV to a hover just below the crest of the last saddleback. "No closer," she advised, "or they'll hear the fans."

"Okay. Blip her up. 'Then we shall see' as the blind man said."

The systems operator tapped a key. Twenty miles away, the drone's motor raced for an instant, popping the little machine an additional hundred feet into the air. For a few seconds before dropping back out of sight below the lateral ridge, the RPV's sensors could look down into the mouth of the pass.

"Oh yeah," Mary May commented. "They beat us here all right."

Bolde reached forward for the monitor playback controls and froze the image.

It was the usual multinational hodgepodge of military equipment that had become commonplace in the post–Cold War Armies of the Third World.

The previously detected Teal/Specter radar track and its generator trailer sat parked in the center of the road. Mounted on the hull of a BMP 3 Armored Personnel Carrier, the radar unit's slablike phased-array antenna swung deliberately in a slice-of-pie scan of the desert below.

Backed deeper into the cut behind it, deftly positioned to blast any radar-hunting fighter-bomber or gunship making a pass on the Teal/Specter unit, was a massive, tracked antiair vehicle, its rectangular turret bristling with multiple autocannon barrels and missile tubes. A Russian 2S6M *Tunguska* or, more than likely, an Indian-produced copy of the same.

Then there were Scylla and Charybdis, a pair of eight-wheeled *Otobreda Centauros* parked out on either flank of the pass entry. The long-tubed 105mm cannon mounted in the turrets of the big Italian-built tank destroyers angled downward, covering the narrow road that switch-backed up from the flats.

In the face of the day's heat, the Algerian crews swarmed around their vehicles, concealing them not only with visual-sight camouflage netting, but also with RAM antiradar tarpaulins and anti-infrared insulation. Stone defensive revetments were being stacked up as well, indicating that this was more than a brief stretch-and-cigarette stop.

"Okay, Brid. Walk us over the pass. Let's see what else they have down there."

"What else" proved to be half a dozen more armored fighting vehicles dispersed along the winding floor of the pass. Tracked and low-riding, with the Slavic design school's distinctive flattened "frying pan" turret shape mounted aft of center, their crews were hard at work digging them in as well.

"Six Bulgarian BRM-30 scout tracks and a pair of *Centauros*," Mary May commented. "That's a full Algerian Recon company. The radar rig and the *Tunguska* would be mission attachments."

"The question being just what that mission is." Bolde slid out of his seat and hunkered down on the deck beside the system operator's chair to get a clearer view of the station displays. "Brid, take us north a little more. I want to get a view of what's happening on the other side of this ridge."

"Not a problem," she replied, setting the new waypoint.

It wasn't. In another minute or two the drone went into hover again, offering its masters a panoramic vista of the plains to the north of the El Khnachich. The caravan road was a pale trace across the desert floor. Clustered about it, perhaps fifteen kilometers beyond the hill range, a number of massive dust plumes rose into the air.

"There's the rest of your division," Shelleen commented, "or a goodly chunk thereof."

"Agreed," Bolde replied slowly, "but not in road column. It looks like they're dispersing."

"They are, LT," Santiago added. The driver had swiveled his seat around, joining the ad hoc command conference. "From the look of that dust kick-up, you got a series of company-sized detachments peeling off the main road and fanning out."

"Yeah." Mary May nodded up from the floor. "If I didn't know better, I'd say those guys were dispersing to go into a night laager."

Bolde glanced down at his head scout. "Why do we know better, Mary May?"

The young woman shrugged. "Because they've no reason to stop and lots to keep going, Lieutenant. You never halt on the near side of a low river ford or a clear mountain pass. It might not be low or clear the next day when you want to move again."

"Yeah. That's how we'd do it. But then the gentleman who's running that outfit may not necessarily play by the same rules that we do." Bolde let his voice trail off as he contemplated possibilities.

"Probably," he said after a half minute's pause, "that Algi division is strung out along a good seventy–eighty kilometers of the Taoudenni road about now. They're stuck with staying on it because their logistics groups are still using trucks instead of high-mobility all-terrain vehicles. They can't move too fast for that same reason. That caravan route is literally just a camel trail.

"Now, a lot of Third World commanders still aren't too comfortable with large-unit operations after nightfall. Let's also say that the Algi general running this outfit is a conservative and cautious kind of guy, again like a lot of Third World commanders.

"He's got night coming on, a replenishment coming up, and he knows that there's likely U.S. and Legion Armored Cav out here hunting for him. The idea of being draped across this range of hills with some of his maneuver elements on one side and some on the other come oh dark hundred might not appeal to him too much."

"It wouldn't to me either," Shelleen noted thoughtfully. "There are things a raider could do with a situation like that."

"Indeed there are, Miss Shelleen," Bolde agreed, lifting an eyebrow. "And I was hoping to try some of them out tonight. Unfortunately, our Algerian friend appears to be playing it safe. He's run a fast recon element out ahead to secure this pass. That will do a couple of things for him. For one, it'll plug up the obvious route another mechanized unit would have to take to get at his main. For another it will give him an observation post on the high ground.

"That battlefield radar will give him early warning of any major force moving in from the south. If one shows up, he can engage at long range with artillery, spotting from the pass mouth. He knows he's got way more tubes and rails on this side of Mali than we do, so he'll have the edge in any potential gun duel.

"So covered, he figures he can safely fort up overnight north of the pass to regroup and resupply. Come first light, when he doesn't have to worry so much about being bushwhacked, he can push his entire division rapidly through the choke point of the pass. Once he's got his maneuver battalions out into open country again, he can trust in his massed firepower to bust him through any light-force screen we can throw in front of him."

Bolde's planning staff exchanged glances, wordlessly discussing their leader's analysis. Bridget Shelleen voiced their findings. "That very well could be what we're seeing here, sir. The question is, what are we going to do about it?"

"What indeed. What indeed." Bolde accessed a secondary screen on the workstation, filling it with a graphics-map tactical display of the immediate region. He added an overlay showing Saber section's position as well as that of the known hostile units. Using the console touch pad, he drew in the potential laager sites of the remainder of the Algerian division. Then he considered once more.

Minutes passed and Mary May Jorgenson stirred restlessly from her seat on the deck plates. "It wouldn't be too much trouble to mess up that recon outfit in the pass. My guys and I could get up on the ridges overlooking their positions and laser designate for our CMMs. We could take 'em out, no problem."

"Yeah, we could do that," Bolde replied slowly. "But how much would that gain us or cost the bad guys? We could kill that recon company, all right. But is that our best potential shot? If we are serious about slowing the Algis down, we'll have to maximize our strike effect. We'll have to nurse as much bang out of our buck as is conceivable, even if it means stretching the sensibility envelope to a degree."

"L'audace, l'audace, toujours, l'audace," Shelleen murmured.

"Precisely. The problem is that we are down here—" Bolde's fingertip touched the blue position hack at the bottom of the map display—"and all the really good stuff is up there." His finger climbed up the map to the Algerian laager zone. "Tonight, the Algis are going to be in static positions, refueling and rearming. Their logistics groups are going to be up forward and intermixed with their maneuver battalions. That's when they will be at their most vulnerable and when we could do the most damage.

"Thing is, the Algis are playing it smart. They've read their copy of *Jane's All the World's Weapons Systems* and they're going to ground far enough back from this hill range so that we can't toss anything over the rocks at them. If we want to hurt them, really hurt them, we'll have to get over on that north side with them, and they can't know we're there until it's too late."

Bolde looked back over his shoulder at his driver. "How about it, Rick? Can you get us over these hills without using the pass?"

The lean and moustached Latino gave a slight shrug. "It's gonna depend on the surfaces and gradients, LT. Miss Shelleen, could you show me the slope profile on that stretch of range ahead of us?"

"Coming up." Pad keys rattled.

A new overlay appeared on the tactical display, a mottled red, yellow, and blue transparency draped across the contour lines of the map. This was a gauging of the slopes and angles of the El Khnachich range as laser and radar surveyed by a Defense Mapping Agency topographical satellite cross-referenced with the cross-country performance capacity of the Shinseki Multi-Mission Combat Vehicle family.

"Yeah, we got somethin' here." Santiago levered himself out of the driver's seat and crowded in with the others around the workstation. "See," he indicated in interlocking sequence of yellow and blue areas on the map. "It looks like I can get us over that next saddleback to the west of the pass. The grades look good anyway."

"How about surfacing?" Bolde inquired.

"I kept an eye on the visuals we were getting from the drone. It looks like we got some shale-and-gravel slopes and some boulder fields, but nothing we can't beat."

"And how about the Algis? Do you think they might suspect somebody could crawl through that hole?"

A faintly condescending smile tugged at the driver's lips. "Treadheads always have a problem believing what a Shinseki can do, LT. The Algerians don't have a vehicle that could get over that saddleback. I'm willing to bet that they'll figure we don't either."

Santiago straightened and took a step back, collapsing into the driver's seat again. "The problem is, sir, while I think I can get us over that sucker, I'm not going to be able to do it fast. Especially if I have to be sneaky while I'm doing it."

"How about if you don't have to be sneaky? We'll be tiptoeing going in, but we'll be pretty much running flat out when we extract. Can you get us back out over this route before the Algis can zero us?"

Santiago held out his hand, palm down, and rocked it in an ominously so-so manner. "The main force isn't what's sweating me, LT. My beast and I can outrun pretty much anything that moves on treads if we get half a chance. What I'm worried about is that recon company up in the pass. They can't cut us off moving laterally along the ridge. Like I said, their vehicles can't hack the climbing. But if they move fast enough, they could either drop down out of the pass and intercept us short of the hills as we fall back, or they could be waiting for us over on the other side. It wouldn't take much. They'd only have to hold us in place for a couple of minutes, just long enough for their pursuit forces to close up and engage and . . . *fiiit!*"

Santiago drew his thumbnail across his throat, matching graphic action to graphic sound.

"A valid point, Rick," Bolde replied, rocking back on his heels. "To secure our line of retreat, we're going to need to give that recon company in the pass something else to think about. Mary May, you were talking about taking those guys out. Do you think you and your team could do the job without the direct support of the vehicles?"

The young woman tilted her head down so that the brim of her hat concealed her eyes and her expression as she thought. When she lifted her head again, she looked composed and confident. Only a faint reddening of her lower lip indicated how she had bitten it. "No problem, Lieutenant. We'll have the terrain and the surprise factor. We can keep 'em busy."

"Okay then. Brid, recall the Cipher." Bolde glanced around the cab of the command vehicle, meeting his troopers' eyes as he spoke. "Here's how we're going to do it. We've got some pretty good cover here, so we'll lie doggo for the rest of the afternoon. We'll keep the pass under observation, run some mission prep and get a little rest. If the Algis do go to ground and if we have the same tactical situation come nightfall, we'll develop an Ops plan. We all good with this? All right, then let us proceed."

The remaining hours of the afternoon passed in a breathless shimmer of heat, the smears of shade produced by the walls of the *qued* a priceless commodity beneath the torchblast of the sun. The expanse of desert around the vehicle hide remained empty, barring the passage of a herd of rare Saharan gazelles. As they materialized out of the mirage fields, their delicacy and grace stood in stark contrast to the harshness of the land.

The only hint of war came when two pairs of frost-colored contrails climbed above the horizons, one pair coming from the north, the other from the south.

They met and tangled lazily in the desert zenith, sparks of sunflame glinting from cockpit canopies and banking wingtips. One by one, over a period of a single minute, the snowy streamers of yarn terminated, turning dark and arcing toward the earth below, or ending abruptly in a smoke blotch against the milky azure sky.

The lone survivor turned away to the south. Bolde and his troopers watched for any sign of a descending parachute but all that was seen was the tumbling flicker of falling metal fragments.

Tired of its day's brutality, the sun drifted below the horizon.

[SABER 6-BRAVO 6***WHAT SUPPORT ELEMENTS WILL BE AVAILABLE WITHIN MY OPSFRAME?]

Jeremy Bolde typed the words onto the flatscreen of the communications workstation, located on the left-side bulkhead behind the driver's seat. Reaching forward, he tapped the transmit key. Instantly, his sentence was encrypted and compressed down into a microburst transmission too brief to be fixed on by a radio direction finder. Tight-beamed up from the dish antenna atop *ABLE*'s cab, the blip transmission was received by a station-keeping relay drone and then fired downward again to the Bravo Troop command vehicle some two hundred miles away to the southeast.

Awaiting the response, Bolde tilted the console seat back, the creak of the chair mount loud against the only other two sounds in the cab, the low purr of the air-conditioning and the quiet snoring of Rick Santiago. *ABLE*'s driver had his own seat tilted back to its farthest stop and his terai tipped down over his eyes, raking in a few precious minutes of sack drill. Even when *ABLE* was in laager, Rick could generally be found lounging behind the cavalry vehicle's wheel, an aspect of the almost symbiotic relationship he had developed with his massive armor-sheathed mount.

Bolde was pleased his driver could get some rest. He wished he could do as well. Maybe later.

Then the answer to his query flashed back on his screen, erasing any thought of sleep.

[BRAVO 6-SABER 6***EFFECTIVELY NONE.]

The datalink transmission continued hastily.

[BRAVO 6-SABER 6***I'M DAMN SORRY, JER, BUT WE ARE AT SATURATION. ALL AVAILABLE IN-THEATER AND LONG-RANGE AIR ASSETS ARE COMMITTED TO SUPPRESSION OPS AGAINST ALGERIAN AIR FORCE. HONCHO 2ND HAS EFFECTIVELY ASSUMED COMMAND OF ALL IN THEATER GROUND FORCES. 1ST LEGION CAV, 2 & 3 OF 7TH, AND WAEF MOBILE FORCE ARE MASSING IN EASTERN SECTOR FOR COUNTERSTRIKE AGAINST ALGERIAN ARMORED CORPS ADVANCING SOUTH ALONG TESSALIT-GAO HIGHWAY. HEAVY INITIAL CONTACT PROJECTED FOR TONIGHT. ALL AIRCAV, ALL L-R ARTILLERY ELEMENTS ARE ENGAGING ENEMY MAINFORCE AT THIS TIME. YOU CAN CHECK THE STRIKEBOARDS BUT I THINK THE CUPBOARD IS BARE UNTIL AT LEAST FIRST LIGHT TOMORROW.

There wasn't anything else to do except to type

[SABER 6-BRAVO 6***ACKNOWLEDGED. ANY FURTHER INSTRUCTIONS.]

[BRAVO 6-SABER 6***JUST SCREEN AND DELAY, JER. 2ND

RANGER, 6TH AIRCAV AND 9TH RIFLE HAVE ALL BEEN COMMITTED AND ARE DEPLOYING BUT WE CAN'T EXPECT TO SEE THEM ON THE GROUND FOR 36–92 HOURS. SCREEN AND DELAY AND BUY US SOME TIME. CARBINE AND PISTOL SECTIONS BRAVO HAVE FOUND ANOTHER TRANSIT POINT OF THE EL KHNACHICH RANGE TO THE EAST OF YOU AND ARE GOING DEEP, HUNTING FOR ALGERIAN LOG UNITS. ALPHA AND CHECKMATE TROOPS 1ST ARE REPOSITIONING TO TIMBUKTU PATROL BASE BUT WILL NOT BE A FACTOR UNTIL 06–07 HUNDRED TIME FRAME TOMORROW. . . .

A secondary screen on the console lit off, indicating that a data dump was under way from the troop command vehicle carrying intelligence updates, refreshed battlemaps, and weather projections, the sole aid their CO could dispatch.

. . . DO THE BEST YOU CAN WITH WHAT YOU HAVE, JER.] [SABER 6-BRAVO 6***IF IT WASN'T A CHALLENGE, SIR, IT WOULDN'T BE THE CAVALRY. SABER-6 DOWN]

Bolde secured the transmitter and retracted the roof antenna. For a long moment, he studied the last glowing lines on the communications screen. After a moment, he chuckled with soft self-derisiveness. What was that line George C. Scott had said in *Patton*? The one just before El Guettar, "All of my life I have dreamed of leading a large number of men in a desperate battle."

Well, while he had no large number of men, the desperation level was certainly adequate. Brid Shelleen, with her somewhat "different" worldview would say that he had created this moment and this situation for himself. He had asked and the universe had given.

For he, Lieutenant Jeremy Randolph Bolde, had dreamed of being a warfighter, not merely a soldier, or a career army officer, but a combatant. For as long as he could recall, Bolde had hungered for what Patton had called the "sting of battle," for the chance to test himself in the ultimate crucible.

Such concepts and attitudes were decisively not "PC" these days, not even within the Officers' Corps, or within his own old Army family. But they had smoldered on deep down in his belly where he lived, and they flared hot and bright now.

Hail, Universe! If this night is your gift to me, I thank you for it.

Bolde called up a large-scale tactical map on the big screen. Tilting the seat back, he studied the display, absorbing each terrain feature and deployment point.

They would be overwhelmingly outnumbered, but that was almost an irrelevancy. Classically, cavalry almost always fights outnumbered. But then again, the cavalry trooper almost always had three good allies ready to ride at his side: speed, shock, and surprise. Utilize them properly, and they could go a long way toward leveling the odds. He must use them in precisely the right way tonight.

Also, while the modern armored cavalry section was, pound for pound and trooper for trooper, the most tactically powerful small military unit in history, he must dole that power out one critically metered spoonful at a time to maximize its effect against the enemy. Definitely a most interesting exercise.

Without Bolde realizing it, his lips pursed and a whispering whistle drifted around the command cab.

"For seven years I courted, Sally,
Away, you rollin' river.
For seven years she would not have me.
Away, I'm bound away, crossed that wide Missouri . . ."

Mary May Jorgenson stood beside *CHARLIE* in the twilight, putting the gun drone through a systems check cycle. As with the section command vehicle, *CHARLIE* was an MM15 Shinseki Multi-Mission Combat Vehicle configured for armored cavalry operations, a sleekly angular boat-shaped hull the size of a large RV, riding on eight man-tall tires. Unlike *ABLE*, it carried a decisively different payload of systems and weapons. *CHARLIE*, and his brother *BAKER*, were the dedicated stone killers of the team.

Configured for robotic operation, *CHARLIE*'s cab windshield and crew gunports had been plated over. Squat sensor turrets were mounted in the driver's and commander's hatches, giving the drone a slightly froglike appearance. A low casemate had been fitted atop the aft third of the hull, the mount for a Lockheed/IMI 35mm booster gun. The slender, jacketed tube of the hypervelocity weapon extended the full length of the drone's spine to a point five feet beyond its nose.

Using the trackball on the remote testing pad, Mary May tested the fifteen-degree traverse and elevation of the booster gun, then cycled the chain drive of the action, carefully keeping the magazines and propellant tanks on safety. Her head tilted in the dimming light, she critically listened to the clatter of the rotary breech mechanism, trusting her own judgment as well as the pad displays.

The blip of another key tested the twelve CMM artillery rounds slumbering in their vertical-launch array in the drone's forward compartment. The touch of a third verified the readiness of the Claymore reactive panels scabbed onto *CHARLIE*'s composite armor skin. Checks done. Boards green. Mary May unjacked the remote pad from the drone's exterior systems access. They were ready to rock.

Boots crunched on the gravel of the *qued* as Nathan Grey Bird trudged up from *BAKER*'s parking point. Her assistant scout leader had been running an identical testing cycle of the second drone. "How's Mr. B looking, Nate?" Mary May inquired.

"Pretty much good," the stocky, bronze-skinned trooper replied. "One of the secondary link aerials was acting sort of shorty, so I replaced it. And that first wheel motor on the right side's leaking oil again. I topped it up and we'll be okay for tonight, but for sure we got a busted seal on that unit."

Mary May nodded. "I'll write it up. The next time we see the shop column, we'll get it pulled."

"Whenever that might be." Grey Bird grinned, white teeth flashing. "We pulling out soon?"

"The LT says as soon as we hit full dark. I'd say that'll be inside the hour." Mary May passed Grey Bird her testing pad. "Secure that for me, will you, Nate. Then go on up to *ABLE* and kill some rations. We'll eat, then switch off on picket with Johnny and Lee so they can get a not-on-the-move meal, too."

"You got it, Five. You comin' along now?"

"In a minute. Save me the pizza MRE if Rick hasn't already snagged it out of the box."

Mary May caught up her carbine from where it leaned against one of *CHARLIE*'s wheels and started back down the wash. Warrant Officer Shelleen had walked down the draw a few minutes before, and the scout wanted to verify that everything was all right with her. Or at least that was the excuse Mary May gave herself.

In actuality, she was motivated by a continuing and nagging curiosity about Saber's systems operator. When Mary May had elected to join the Army, one of her reasons had been to see new things and meet new people. Never in her wildest imaginings however had she ever visualized herself serving beside a genuine, spell-casting, card-carrying witch.

A smile tugged at the corner of her mouth. She never mentioned Warrant Officer Shelleen's religious preferences in any of her letters home. Mary May's family were all hard-shell Lutheran, and she didn't need Uncle Joseph and Aunt Gertrude writing their congressmen.

Mary May lightened her footsteps as she approached the shallow bay in the wall of the wash that she had seen Warrant Officer Shelleen enter, not desiring to disturb, yet aware that she might. In the growing shadows she noted a slender figure kneeling on the sand of the *qued* floor, facing away to the south. A palm-sized splash of diesel oil burned bluely on the ground before her, and the silver-hafted dagger the SO carried lay on the sand at her knees, its blade aimed at the heart of the flame. Bridget Shelleen's arms were uplifted shoulder high, and her head was lowered, a soft whispered pattern of words escaping from her lips.

Mary May hesitated, a ripple of unease touching her, the discomfort sometimes felt by the average person when in the presence of a truly and genuinely devout individual.

Shelleen's whisper faded away and the whicker of the wind in the wash was the only lingering sound. For a long minute, the systems operator continued to kneel, statue-still. Then, gracefully, she leaned forward and scooped up a double handful of sand and poured it over the patch of flame. Lifting the dagger from the ground, she made a decisive gesture with it as if she were slashing through some invisible line or thread that surrounded her. The blade disappeared into her boot sheath and the redhead rose and turned to face Mary May, her movements an effortless catlike flow.

Unnerved at so suddenly finding herself regarded by those large and level green eyes, Mary May asked with a forced lightness, "Casting a spell on the Algis, Miss Shelleen?"

A wisecrack wasn't at all what she had wanted to say but she'd had to do something to recover her equilibrium.

"Oh no," Shelleen replied with a calm seriousness. "The Law of Return would make that a very bad idea."

"The Law of Return?"

"Yes. One of the root laws of all magic," the systems officer replied, picking up her flak vest and pistol belt from where she had set them aside. " 'So as you conjure, so shall you receive back fourfold.' Invoking a negative conjuration, a black magic if you will, against the Algerians could come back and hit us far harder than it would the enemy. I was only addressing the Lord and the Lady, asking them for strength, protection, and wisdom for us all this night."

Mary May tilted her head questioningly. "You mean like you were only praying?"

"Essentially." Shelleen smiled back.

The two women started back up the ravine to the vehicle hide through the deepening shadows. Overhead, the first star seeped through the darkening blue of the sky.

"War," Mary May asked eventually. "Can I ask you something?"

"Why not?"

"Well, the word is that you were once a model in New York or something. How did you ever become . . . a soldier?"

Again, "soldier" wasn't what she'd meant to say, but that's how it had come out. The warrant officer shot her a knowing glance and smiled again.

"Yes, I did have the start of a modeling career once," she replied, slinging her flak vest over her shoulder. "I also had the start of a very unhappy, meaningless, and self-destructive life. So I started to look around for something to hold on to. Eventually, I found the beliefs of my Celtic ancestors, Wicca or Paganism as it is known to some. It was something that worked for me, giving me a degree of peace although not of contentment.

"I continued my studies and, upon my becoming a priestess, I elected to confront my destiny once and for all. I undertook a time of fasting and spiritual seclusion, a spirit quest as it is called by the American Indian. During it, I asked for the Lady to show me the path I should be following during this stage of my life."

"Did she?" Mary May asked, intrigued in spite of herself.

Shelleen nodded. "She did. She came to me as the Lady of the South Wind, armor-clad, the guardian and the woman warrior. I had my answer. So, I went back to New York, fired my agent, tore up my contracts, and joined the Army."

She smiled a sudden impish grin. "And yes, there are any number of people who think that I have gone totally and completely insane."

Mary May chuckled. "A lot of my family think the same thing about me. What do you think now? Was it the right call?"

Bridget Shelleen paused just short of *ABLE*'s tail ramp and swept her arm around the vehicle hide. "Here, I find I am centered," she replied, looking into the scout's face. "Here, for the first time in my life, I can say that I am exactly where I'm supposed to be. If you can do that, I suppose you aren't doing so badly."

Mary May Jorgenson could not disagree.

**The South Face of the El Khnachich Range
Three-quarters of a Mile West of the Taoudenni Caravan Road
2335 Hours, Zone Time; October 28, 2021**

The only illumination within the cab came from the glow of the instrument displays, that odd gray-green unlight that is compatible with night-vision systems. The only light beyond the sloped windshield issued from the cold and distant stars.

At the walking pace of a healthy man, the three vehicles of Saber section ground upward toward the saddleback, the two gun drones trailing *ABLE* nose to tail, like obedient circus elephants. Normal operating doctrine called for an unmanned vehicle always to be out on point, cybernetically scouting and taking the initial risk. However, the rugged irregularity of this night's drive mandated that a human intelligence break the trail.

As *ABLE* hunched and clawed her way upslope, Rick Santiago relished the feel of handling the big war machine. As a kid back in Arizona, there wasn't a tractor pull, off-road race, or monster truck bash within a hundred miles of Wickenburg that he hadn't attended. By the time he'd graduated from high school, he'd built up both a perilously hot Ford F150 pickup and a terror-of-the-desert reputation.

Unfortunately, few job prospectuses listed driving crazy in the dirt as a prime desired attribute.

Then came the day when an enterprising Army recruiter brought a transport variant of the Shinseki Multi-Mission Combat Vehicle to a hill climb outside of Yuma. Rick and a lot of other young people stood by in awe as that magnificent eight-wheeled monster shamed some of the best ATVs and 4X4s in the Southwest, Rick had filled out his enlistment papers that day, sitting in the Shinseki's cab.

"Okay, people," Lieutenant Bolde murmured over the helmet intercom. "We're getting in close. Column stealth up and go to batteries."

Miss Shelleen replied with a soft verbal acknowledgment as she dialed the command into the drone datalinks. Rick answered by clicking a switch sequence. The breathy whine of *ABLE*'s twin turbogenerator sets faded away, leaving only the purr of the multiple drive motors and the crunch of the mountain rubble beneath the mushy all-terrain tires.

The key to the Shinseki's amazing flexibility and performance was its composite electric-drive system. Two lightweight UMTec 1000 ceramic gas turbines spun a pair of electrical generators. The generators pumped power into the banks of rechargeable iron-carbide batteries under *ABLE*'s deck plates, and these batteries, in turn, fed the 150-horsepower radial electric-drive motors built into the hubs of each ground wheel. No gears, no clutch, no driveshaft, just instant power on demand.

There were other advantages as well. Spinning constant speed at their most efficient RPM setting, the turbines drew the maximum power potential from each liter of fuel consumed. And for those times, such as now, when stealth was at a premium, the turbines could be shut down. Operating on battery power alone, the armored cavalry vehicle's thermal and audile signatures were greatly reduced.

Through his night-vision visor, Santiago noted a change in ground texture ahead. A shale patch on the hillside angled down to the left. He eased the all-wheel steering over, hunting uphill for better traction.

But not quite far enough.

Rick felt the hill shift beneath *ABLE*, the deck slewing and tilting as loose shale slid away beneath the left-rear tires. The cavalry vehicle lurched, threatening to twist crosswise and slide in the beginning of its own avalanche. Santiago's foot rocked forward on the accelerator, slamming 1200 horsepower into the ground. *ABLE* responded like a hard-spurred cow pony. Lunging upgrade, she scrabbled to solid ground, tire cleats paddlewheeling in the stone fragments.

Rick Santiago grinned into the night. ¡Hijole! *And they're paying me for this!* "You're gonna want to edge the drones over to the right a few yards, Miss Shelleen," he called back to the systems station. "We got a little patch of soft stuff here."

And then they were at the crest of the saddleback with only the down-slope and a great darkness before them. Bolde cycled through the vision modes of his helmet visor and surveyed that darkness. By standard light, there was only the starblaze of the sky and the black horizon line of the not-sky. By switching to the night brite option, he could use the starlight to make out another great expanse of gravel pan and sand dune stretching out from the northern face of the range.

Here and there, well out into the desert, were also occasional flickers and flares of transitory illumination. Bolde recognized them as light leaks caught by his photomultipliers: dashboard glow, lantern gleam escaping through a gap in a tent door, a sloppily used flashlight. Hints of the presence of a bivouacking army.

It was not until he switched from the gray world of the night brite vision to the glowing green one of the thermographic imager that all was made clear. Glowing cyan geometries like the patterns on a snake's back stretched across the horizon. Other individual dots of light and stumpy luminous caterpillars crept and crawled between them.

This was the infrared portrait of an army at rest. Each geometric was a company-sized laager point, each dot of light the signature of a parked armored fighting vehicle. The steel hulls stood out as they radiated the heat absorbed during the day back into the chilling night. No doubt the Algerians had anti-IR tarps deployed, but insulation could only do so much against the vivid thermal contrasts of the Sahara environment.

The moving green points of light would be liaison and supply vehicles bringing up the food, the fuel, and the thousand and one other things an army on the march required. They were like the red corpuscles of a bloodstream, carrying oxygen to the muscles of a limb, giving it strength. And as with a bloodstream, if that flow was cut off, gangrene and death would rapidly follow.

"Column . . . halt," Bolde said lowly.

ABLE crunched to a stop, *BAKER* and *CHARLIE* following suit in robotic obedience.

"Okay, Mary May. We're at drop point. Your people set to take a walk?"

The scout leader moved forward to crouch beside Bolde's seat, her tall and rangy frame bulked out by full field gear.

Curved ballistic plates of bulletproof ceramic had been slipped into the plate pouches in her BDU shirtsleeves and trouser legs and snugged tight with Velcro strap-tabs. An interceptor flak vest shielded her torso as a combat helmet protected her head. In addition to its integral squad radio and night-vision system, spring-wire leads connected the helmet's HUD (Heads-Up Display) with the SINCGARS Leprechaun B communications and navigation system clipped to Mary May's load-bearing harness and to the BattleMAC tactical computer strapped to her left forearm.

This night she would be carrying thirty-five pounds of body armor and personal electronics alone, without the consideration of weapons, ammunition, incidentals, and the gallon of water in her MOLLE harness reservoir. Such was the reason females were still rare within the Ground Combat Specialists' rating. Even in the twenty-first century, the foot soldier still required a healthy dose of pack mule in their genetic makeup.

"Set, LT," she replied. "Ready to go down the ramp."

"Acknowledged, Five. You've got the drill. Get into position. We'll coordinate the strike and recovery as the situation develops. You've got the satellite beacons with you?"

"Two of them, yes, sir."

"Good enough. Take one of the water cans as well and cache it somewhere, just in case. Bravo six knows you're up here. If something Murphys on us, and we don't make it back for pickup, trigger a beacon and lie low. The regiment will get you out."

Mary May grinned through the black-and-brown camouflage paint that covered her face. "I'm not worried, sir. I always leave the dance with the guy who brought me."

Bolde grinned back. "We'll make that our beautiful thought for the day, Five. Take off."

"Yes sir. See you later guys."

"*Adios*, Five. Watch your ass out there."

"Blessed be, Mary May."

Jorgenson moved aft to the scout bay. A brief rattle of equipment followed a whispered command and the tail ramp whirred down. Boots scuffed on antiskid decking, then crunched on gravel and a cool puff of outside air traveled up the passageway from the rear of the vehicle. The tail ramp closed again and a single whispered word issued from the radio link.

"Clear."

In the starlight beyond the windshield, four patches of shadow trickled up the right-hand slope of the saddleback. The three remaining in *ABLE* cab found themselves acutely aware of their intensified aloneness.

Bolde spoke in the darkness. "You journeyed this night, Brid. What do the spirits of this place have to say about us?"

"The old ones who dwell here wish us neither good nor evil," the Wiccan warrior replied levelly, her face underlit by the glow of her console screens. "They do not know us. They will judge us by our actions and then make their decision."

"Then let the judgment begin. Okay, Rick. Column forward!"

The only sound over the scout team's tactical circuit was the rasp of heavy breathing caught by the helmet lip mikes. It was a half mile climb to the top of the saddleback ridge that overlooked the pass, mostly a thirty-to-forty-degree assault up loose shale and crumbling sandstone. Sometimes the hill was manageable by leaning into the slope, at others a clawing scramble on hands and knees was required.

Boots sank in and slid back ten inches for every twelve gained. Clutching fingers gashed on jagged stone and the dust quenched the flowing blood. Lungs burned and legs ached beyond all conditioning.

Johnny Roman and Nathan Grey Bird bore the primary burden of the Javelin launcher and Johnny considered himself the luckier half of the team. He only bore two reload round canisters and their carbines. Nat had taken the burden of the launcher itself.

The Jav was a good old piece that could still do a thorough job on most anything that might be encountered on the battlefield. But the price paid for that kind of firepower was weight. A Javelin launcher with a missile preloaded in the tube weighed fifty pounds. Johnny wryly acknowledged that you couldn't kill an armored fighting vehicle with something you could carry in your hip pocket.

The other fire team didn't have it all that much better either. He could see Mary May and Lee Trebain laboring farther ahead upslope. They were tricked out for grenadier work with SABRs slung across their backs and half a dozen spare magazines each of 20mm grenade and 5.56mm NATO to feed the over-and-under barrels of the twin gun systems. All that plus another Javelin reload each.

All in all, each member of the scout team was humping the near equivalent of his or her own weight up that night black ridge.

Beside Johnny, Nate Grey Bird's feet slithered out from under him and he went facefirst into the slope with a muffled curse. He started to slide backward and Johnny grabbed out for him, snagging his harness.

"You okay, Nate?"

"Yeah, I'm okay," the fiercely whispered reply came back. "It's just that this goddam piece of sewer pipe won't pack worth shit. It keeps throwing me off!"

"You want me to take it for a while?"

"No, I'm okay. It's only a little way to the crest now. I'm gonna take a breather for a second."

"Good idea."

The two troopers collapsed against the slope, striving to catch their breath long enough to take a swig from their water packs.

"When I get back to Purdue to finish my degree, you know what I'm going to do?" Johnny said after a minute.

"I dunno. What you gonna do, white man?"

"I'm going to write a paper. A combined science and philosophy paper about how environment and situation can affect the theoretically immutable laws of physics."

"I don't get you."

"It's like this. Climbing this damn hill, it feels like we're lugging every damn weapon in the world on our backs. But over on the other side, when the shooting starts, I suspect it's going to feel like we're hardly carrying anything at all."

A dozen yards below the eastern crest of the saddleback, Mary May angled her team into a jagged rock formation that jutted from the scree slope like a miniature castle. "Okay, guys," she said, unslinging the Javelin reload she carried. "Go to ground and set overwatch. I'm going up to take a look around."

"You want me to come too, Five?" Lee Trebain asked from the pocket of shadows he'd claimed.

"Nah, just cover me," she replied, thumbing the takedown stud for her SABR. Disassembling the big weapon into its three primary components, she set aside the grenade launcher and locked the sighting module directly onto the grab rail atop the receiver of the carbine. The repeatedly drilled act took only seconds.

"You sure you don't want me up there?"

"For Pete's sake, Lee, I'm only going to be about forty darned feet up the hill," Mary May snapped back in an aggravated whisper, locking out the carbine's folding stock. "I don't need anyone breathing down my neck. Just watch my back."

Mary May removed an anti-IR cape from a harness pouch. Drawing the foil-lined camouflage cloth around her, she secured it with a silent, "stealth" Velcro neckband and drew the hood over her helmet. Crawling out of the rock outcropping, she snaked her way upslope on knees and elbows. In a few moments she was at the crest.

Still prone, she eased herself ahead the last few feet, then froze in place. The gut of the pass lay below her.

For the next several minutes she lay unmoving, slowly and deliberately scanning the terrain below and across from her. The barren, steep-sided ridges and precipitous ravines reminded her strongly of the Dakota badlands back home. Deliberately she toggled in the night vision visor of her helmet between thermographics and photomultiplier, seeing what each sensor view had to offer.

Her helmet visor had more to offer than just enhanced vision. It also served as a Heads-Up Display for her other systems. A graphics compass rose scrolled across the bottom of her vision field, giving her an instantaneous bearing on anything she observed. Time and radio-frequency hacks glowed in the corners of her eyes and, as she turned her head, threat arrows pulsed redly, aiming down at every known and plotted hostile position in the area, graphics prompts giving her the range to target.

A look back over her shoulder revealed a trio of blue arrows hovering over the rock formation downslope. Her own team, their location microburst transmitted to her Leprechaun B navigation system from the GPS receivers of their own Leprechaun units.

And in the distance, and drawing steadily farther away, another trio of blue arrows, the troop vehicles and their crew en route to this night's destiny. The only other "blues" within a two-hundred-mile radius. Mary May shivered in spite of the growing pocket of body heat trapped beneath the IR cape and returned her attention to the pass below.

One of the Algerian scout tracks was parked within her field of vision, the residual heat signature of its armor beginning to fade with the chill of the desert night. A dazzling point of thermal radiation burned close abreast of it, however, possibly a small fuel pellet stove. Given the steam plume rising above it, someone must be heating water for tea or coffee. Spectral green shadows huddled close about it, Algerian soldiers warming their hands in the stove glow and maybe thinking of the night's watch or about home.

Other luminescent forms hovered away from the stove, one in the track's turret, two more on station above and below the vehicle hide. *Sentries*, she thought, staring out into the dark.

Mary May started to ease back below the ridge crest when suddenly she caught more movement in her visor. She froze in place like a startled lizard.

On the barren ridge across from her, a line of four small cyan dots bobbed slowly along.

Lifting her hand up to her helmet, Mary May flipped up her night-vision visor, blinking for a moment in the onrush of true darkness. Then she lifted and aimed her carbine, not to fire but to utilize the magnification and imaging of its more powerful sighting module. The pressure of her thumb on a handgrip stud zoomed her in on target.

An Algi patrol. Each of those Algerian BRM-30s carried a four-person scout team, just like her own, and one such team was conducting a security sweep along the high ground beyond the pass. And if there was a patrol over on that side, likely there was one somewhere over on this side as well.

The other scouts looked up as Mary May slid back into the shelter of the rock pile. She flicked aside her helmet's lip mike, deactivating her squad radio, then spoke in a whisper. "Here's how we're going to work it, guys. The Algis are deployed below us along about a kilometer of the pass floor. Nate, you and Johnny work your way to the south end of the pass, staying out of sight below the crest of this saddleback. You have the Javelin and you take out the heavies at the pass mouth. Kill the *Tunguska* first! Got that? From down in the bottom of this canyon, the *Centauros* and the BRMs will have trouble elevating their main armament high enough to engage us up here. The quad 30s on that antiair vehicle could saw the top of this ridge right off though. It goes first!"

"He's first blood, Five," Grey Bird's soft reply came back.

"Okay, Lee and I will work our way north. We'll take out the two northernmost BRMs with the grenade launchers, each of us engaging one of the tracks. All initial attacks will be coordinated with Lieutenant Bolde's move on the main body of the Algerian division. We get into position and we wait for the LT to give us the word to open fire. Until we get that word, we are strictly hide and evade. Nobody, and I mean nobody, fires a shot for any reason!

"Once the music starts, the two teams will work in toward each other, picking off the remaining Algi elements as the shots present themselves. These rocks will be our rendezvous point for fallback and extraction. Lock it in."

Fingers touched keypads, calling up and storing GPU fixes in personal navigation systems.

"Set, Five."

"Got it."

"Same."

"Right. Watch your backs. Make your kills. Get back here. That's the show. That and one other thing. We may have some company up here tonight."

Like an infantryman hunkering under cover, *ABLE* retracted its suspension and sank behind the shelter of the low dune, *BAKER* and *CHARLIE* going to ground a quarter of a kilometer off on either flank. Electronic Countermeasures masts unfolded and suspiciously sampled the ether.

The interior of the cab was silent except for the tick and creak of contracting metal and the purr of the systems fans. "Any sign of a ground-scan radar on this side?" Bolde inquired over his shoulder.

"Negative. Just two big air-search systems well off to the east and west," Shelleen replied. "Mobile SAM batteries covering the laager sites. I'm getting tastes of a constant-wave datalink though. They might have a scout drone up."

"We'll watch for it. Rick, you take tactical security while we plot the strike."

"Doin' it, LT," Santiago acknowledged. Accessing the sensors in the commander's cupola via one of the driver's station telescreens, he began a deliberate scan of the surrounding environment.

Bolde assumed control of *ABLE* weapons pack, elevating the boom to its maximum fifty-foot extension for a high-ground overview of their selected objective.

The lead Algerian mechanized battalion had deployed on an open gravel pan, straddling the Taoudenni caravan trail roughly four kilometers beyond Saber section's position. The three maneuver companies were in laager at the points of a two kilometer triangle, the base oriented to the south with the Headquarters Company in the center. Each company position was a weapon-studded island in the desert, creating a mutually supporting archipelago of firepower.

Bolde zoomed in on the nearest laager. The Algerians had learned a few things about desert fighting over the years. They had abandoned the old heavily structured Soviet doctrine in favor of the more flexible and efficient Western-style mixed combat team. One three-tank platoon mated with two four-track infantry platoons. All of the AFVs were parked nose outward in a hundred-meter-wide radial pattern that faced their heaviest protection and armament toward any potential threat.

There would be a sentry posted in every one of those vehicle turrets and a shell or ammunition magazine fed into every gun action. As Bolde looked on, one of the tanks panned its main tube warily across the horizon.

Once upon a time, it had been a Russian-made T-72. However, as Bolde recalled from his technical briefings, little remained that was actually "Russian" barring the bare hull and suspension.

A lightweight Japanese turbocharged diesel had replaced the original power plant, and a Korean-produced copy of a German-designed 120mm smoothbore had been fitted in the turret, replacing the cranky 125mm main gun. A revised velectronics suite had been manufactured in Taiwan, the reactive armor jacketing had come from a factory in Brazil, and the redesign and rebuild had taken place in an Egyptian armaments works.

The end result was an international battlefield "hot rod" considerably more efficient and deadly than the machine that had first rolled out of a Soviet foundry thirty-plus years before. Similar performance upgrades had been applied to the ex-Soviet BMP Infantry Fighting Vehicles of the infantry elements as well.

Again, located in the center of the position, were the unit headquarters tracks and a covering antiaircraft vehicle. Also present were a pair of massive semitankers and a number of smaller deuce-and-a-half utility trucks. The logistics group was up, bearing with it the fuel, food, water, and ammunition that would be needed for the next day's march. Figures worked around the parked vehicles, unrolling fueling hoses and unloading stores, no doubt thankful for the night's cool.

A swift scan of the other company sites indicated that similar replenishment operations were going on there as well. The timing was right, and the Gods of Battle were smiling.

"Brid, we've got sixteen rounds of antivehicle and eight of antipersonnel in the drone silos. You program the AVs. I want one dropped in on each of the fuel tankers and the command vehicles. I'll take the APs."

Overlooking the pass, Nathan Grey Bird and Johnny Roman struggled on against the burden of both the rugged terrain and their augmented munitions load. They were still several hundred meters short of their firing position. Time was growing tight, and the ridgeline looked even more broken ahead of them.

"Hey Nate," Johnny wheezed. "Hold up. I got an idea."

"Such as?"

"Such as, why don't we cache a couple of these spare Jav rounds here so we can move faster. We'll be working back this way again. We can just pick 'em up when we're ready to use 'em."

"Damn, white man! I'm proud of you! You're starting to think like an Indian. Let's do it."

Farther to the north along the saddleback, Lee Trebain peered cautiously through his firing slit between two boulders. The youthful Texan could see his designated target on the floor of the pass below him. His position was good, the BRM-30 had been backed into the slope between a couple of crude stacked-stone fighting positions. Its tail ramp was down, and Trebain could intermittently make out movement both inside the track and in the gun pits.

Moving with silent care, he verified that a clip of smart rounds was in the grenade launcher of his SABR and that the magazine of 5.56 NATO was well seated in the carbine section. Then he slipped a second clip of 20mm antiarmor projectiles out of a harness pouch, setting them where they could be grabbed in an instant. He'd worked out just exactly how he was going to do this thing. All he had to do was to stay ready for the word.

Trebain tried to keep focused, but he couldn't keep from glancing away toward the north. Toward that next blue friendly arrow glowing in his visor display.

She wasn't moving anymore. She must be set, too. And she had to be all right, right? She was on the squad circuit and she could have yelled for help if something had blown. And there hadn't been any gunfire, and, besides, Mary May could take care of herself.

But then, damn it all entirely, wasn't the guy supposed to look after a girl? That's the way it always been where he'd grown up and the instinct was hard to shake, even when the girl was two inches taller than you were and had three grades of seniority. Lee closed his eyes and shook his head, trying to clear it of a confused jumble of emotions and images. He snapped them open them again when the audile prompt of the tactical datalink sounded in his helmet earphones. The glowing line of a communication was scrolling across the bottom of his vision field.

SABER 6 TO ALL SABER ELEMENTSSTAND BY TO ENGAGE***ACKNOWLEDGE READINESS STATE***

Lifting his hand to his helmet, Lee tapped the transmit key at the base of his lip-mike boom, giving his go signal. Flipping his visor up, he settled the SABR against his shoulder and peered through the sighting module. Safeties off. Weapons selector to GRENADE. Mode selector to POINT DETONATION. Finger on trigger.

Lee Trebain's mind was suddenly as cold and clear as a mountain spring.

The same message flashed before the eyes of Nathan Grey Bird and Johnny Roman just as they threw themselves flat on the overlook above the mouth of the pass. Below them, at the foot of a steep scree slope, was a quarter-mile-wide plateau notched into the range side and the fighting positions of the Algerian blocking force. They'd made it, but just barely.

"Johnny, let the LT know we're in position! Then get those reloads ready!"

"Doing it, Nate." Roman blipped the acknowledgment, then popped the end caps off the first of the two spare Javelin canisters.

Grey Bird plugged the connector lead from the missile launcher's firing unit into his helmet's remote jack and a targeting reticle snapped into existence in the center of his field of vision. Choosing the Javelin's "ballistic engagement" option, he eased up onto his knees. The boxlike firing unit with its handgrip nestled against the side of his head, the connected launcher tube swiveled to angle down his back, its muzzle pointing to the sky. Turning his head slightly, he set the death pip of the sight on the top of the turret of the Algerian antiair track.

Nathan felt his lips peel back in a feral grin. Back in Idaho, his sister had never been happy with his decision to go career Army. Intensely into American Indian activism, she had felt he was selling out his heritage by joining the service that had defeated his people. And she had been extremely unhappy when he had chosen the cavalry as his preferred branch.

Nathan had pointed out in reply that their ancestors had been some of the best mounted warriors the world had ever seen. What greater heritage did he have except as a cavalryman?

She had retired grumbling before he'd had the chance to mention that the regimental assignment he'd been given was to the Seventh. *Hoya,* she was going to go through the roof on that one.

Grey Bird eased down the first trigger, giving the missile its initial look at its target.

"All CMMs designated and the scout teams are in position," Bridget said quietly. "No detected changes in tactical environment. Ready to engage on your command, Lieutenant."

Bolde swallowed with deliberation before replying. All of the preparations, all twenty-five years of them, were over.

So you think you're good, Jeremy Bolde, good enough to take your life into your hands this night. But how about these six other lives you'll be carrying? Does your surety stretch that far? It had better, for when this battle is over, whatever remains will be your responsibility.

"Right. Stand by for conversion to direct linkage control. I'll take *BAKER*. You've got *CHARLIE.* Stand by for turbine start. All units!"

"Turbine start armed on drones."

"*ABLE* ready to light off, LT."

Bolde typed the ***ALL SABER ELEMENTS***COMMENCE ENGAGEMENT NOW*** command into the scout team datalink and poised a finger on the transmit key. "Good luck to us all, ladies and gentlemen," addressing those who were present and those who were not. "May we all be discussing this over a cup of coffee come morning. Open fire!"

Flame geysered from the backs of the gun drones. Twelve rounds per vehicle, launching at half-second intervals, a spreading fountain of destruction. The Common Modular Missile rounds, configured for an artillery-fire mission profile, climbed almost vertically until booster burnout. Then guidance fins snapped out of the main stages and dug into the air. Arcing over the Algerian armored formation, the missiles pitched nose down, hunting for targets.

The infrared sensors in the noses of the antivehicle rounds scanned for a specific geometric size and shape on the ground. One that matched that of the prey assigned to them. The antipersonnel rounds steered in via Global Positioning System fix, the proximity fuses in their warheads concentrating on their altitude above ground. As each missile locked in, its main engine ignited, blasting it through the sound barrier and down out of the sky.

The antipersonnels detonated while still a thousand feet in the air. Each "beehive" warhead burst to release a spreading conical swarm of needle-nosed and razor-finned flechette darts, thousands of them, in a supersonic steel rain, a titanic shotgun blast sweeping the open ground clean of life.

The antivehicle rounds arrived a split second later, before the standing dead even had a chance to fall to the earth. Flaming pile-driver strokes that crushed and destroyed.

The targeted fuel tankers popped like bursting balloons, sprayed diesel flaming as the warheads exploded deep in their guts. Likewise the headquarters tracks lurched, belching fire and shredded flesh out through their doors and hatches. The command personnel whose task it was to coordinate a defense, perished before they even knew an attack was under way.

And amid the chaos and confusion, no surviving sentry immediately noted the three small thermal plumes that hazed into existence out in the desert night, the one turning away and the two closing the range.

The charge had been sounded.

From his firing position between the two boulders, Lee Trebain dropped his grenades in around the Algerian scout track, being exceedingly careful *not* to place them too close to the parked vehicle. From personal experience, Trebain knew what the first instinct of a fighting vehicle crewman was when suddenly placed under attack. *Saddle up and get under armor!*

Trebain had no desire to interfere with that instinctive reaction. Not yet.

The turret of the scout track swiveled around and up-angled, ripping off a 30mm reply to his volley of grenades. The autocannon shells tore a gash across the slope twenty meters below his position, kicking up dust and stinging stone fragments. Hot damn! Mary May had called it right! They couldn't fire up out of the gorge!

The turret gun raved off another long futile burst, covering the figures scrambling aboard through the vehicle's lowered tailgate. Through the thermographic sights of the SABR, Trebain saw a luminous green mist belch from the track's exhaust as the engine kicked over, the ramp beginning to close.

Now! Now was the time to take them!

Trebain ejected the empty clip from the grenade launcher and slammed the fresh magazine of antivehicle shells into its place. Holding the death dot of his sights on the turret of the Algerian scout track, he again pulled the trigger.

Like many armored fighting vehicles, the Algerian BRM had reactive armor panels scabbed to its hull and turret. Made up of sheets of low-grade plastic explosive sandwiched between two thin metal plates, reactive armor defeated shaped-charge antitank warheads by exploding upon the impact of the warhead, the counterblast "defocusing" the warhead's detonation, leaving the protected vehicle undamaged.

Unfortunately for the Algerians, each reactive panel only worked once.

Lee Trebain rapid-fired the six rounds in his launcher magazine, the SABR's recoil thumping his shoulder. The first two grenades kicked reactive panel flares off the BRM's turret. The next four drilled cleanly through steel.

The holes punched by the grenades were only the diameter of a pencil. Each puncture, however, spewed a supersonic jet of flaming gas and molten metal into the confined space of the track's interior. One such jet, as hot and destructive as the fire blade of an acetylene torch, slashed across the ammunition tray of the turret gun.

The BRM shuddered to a halt. Its deck hatches blew open and a protracted series of detonations flickered and reverberated within the vehicle, like a string of firecrackers dropped into a trash can. Afterward nothing emerged from the vehicle except for a growing plume of smoke.

Trebain became aware of more explosions around him. Some were nearby and echoing sharply through the canyon. Other heavier blasts rolled in from the northern horizon, a skyline that now glowed an angry flickering orange.

Trebain backed crablike out from between the two boulders and slid a few meters down the reverse slope of the saddleback. Hugging the ground, he flipped his night-vision visor back down. Warily he scanned his environment as he dug a fresh 20mm clip out of a harness pouch.

Running footsteps sounded behind him and he whipped around, freezing his trigger pull as he caught the blue flash in his Heads-Up Display. Mary May dropped beside him a moment later. "How'd you make out?" she demanded.

"Clean house. Track and crew. How 'bout you?"

"Same. That's two down. Let's go see how the other guys are doing."

"Right behind you, Five."

A half klick to the south, Nathan Grey Bird's finger closed around the Javelin launcher's second trigger.

The hollow thump of the launching charge followed, kicking the missile out of the tube. The missile itself did not ignite until it was well clear of the launcher and the operator both. Flaming away in a high-curving trajectory, it dived on its target from above, the one angle of attack unshielded by either reactive armor or heavy steel.

The *Tunguska* exploded spectacularly, bursting 30mm shells intermixing with flaming rocket fuel. “Ayeee!” Grey Bird screamed. “I count coup! Feed me, white man, I’m on a roll!”

“Loading!” Johnny Roman slammed the next missile into the smoking breech of the launcher, then rolled aside. “Round loaded! Clear!”

The launcher barked again and the second round burned across the sky, wobbling slightly as it hunted for the heat signature of its target, stabilizing again as it found what it sought. The more distant of the pair of *Centauro* tank destroyers lifted off the ground on a pad of flame, its turret blowing off and flipping away.

“That’s two! Keep ’em coming!”

Above the crackle of ammunition heat firing in the burning wrecks, screams and shouts echoed up from the pass mouth along with the sound of cranking diesels. The Algerians were reacting to the attack. Wildly and without coordination, but that would come swiftly as the shock effect wore off. Grey Bird and Roman had only seconds of clear time remaining.

The second *Centauro* was the closest of their three targets, immediately below them at the foot of the steep slope that led down into the pass mouth. They’d saved it for last because it would be the easiest snap shot. Nate locked the launcher into direct-fire mode as Johnny slammed the last Javelin into the tube. Springing to his feet and aiming downward, Grey Bird acquired the target in his helmet sight and squeezed the trigger.

At that instant, the *Centauro*’s driver, reacting to the sure and certain knowledge that a moving target is harder to hit, slammed his eight-wheeled mount into gear and floored his accelerator. The tank destroyer lurched forward, not swiftly enough to escape the homing missile fired at it, but enough to divert its impact point. The Javelin clipped the flank of the *Centauro*’s turret and a reactive armor panel detonated, swatting the missile aside. Undamaged, the tank destroyer roared out of its field revetment, its turret gun traversing and elevating.

Roman and Grey Bird could only stare at each other and at the empty launcher.

“Uh-oh.”

“To which I can only add ‘Oh shit’! Let’s get out of here!”

Below, the *Centauro*'s driver rammed the front wheels of his vehicle up the slope, giving his gunner the extra angle he needed to engage the ridgeline. An instant after the two scouts had thrown themselves back down the opposite slope, a 105mm round gouged a notch in the hill crest, the concussion and battering spray of stone fragments sending both men sprawling into the jumble of broken rock that covered this section of the saddleback.

They would become grateful for that momentarily.

Dazed, and with his ears ringing, Grey Bird lifted his head. "Johnny, you okay?" he yelled.

"Yeah. Nate." A familiar but equally groggy voice replied over the squad circuit. "What do we do now?"

"We crawl back and get those other two Javelin rounds, that's what we do. Then we kill that damn tank destroyer before the Five and the LT find out how bad we screwed up."

Grey Bird started to pull himself upright. He spotted Johnny's "friendly" prompt in his helmet visor, pointing down into a boulder field a short distance to his left. However he also spotted an ominous, unmarked green glow downhill at perhaps a hundred meters.

"Algis! Down!"

Assault-rifle fire spattered his rocks a split second after he dived back behind them. With his own carbine still slung over Johnny's shoulder, Grey Bird yanked his Beretta out of his belt holster. A handgun was a poor second in any kind of a serious firefight but at the moment it was far better than nothing.

A short chopping burst of 5.56 NATO sounded from off on his left. "I got four of them spotted, Nate," Roman reported. "They're trying to work a skirmish line up toward us. They must be one of those Algi scout teams the Five warned us about."

Behind their position, another shell ripped into the ridgeline, showering the two pinned troopers with a fresh barrage of stone fragments. Grey Bird burrowed closer to the jagged rock he lay upon.

"You know something, white man?" he said, spitting a mouthful of grit aside.

"What?"

"All of a sudden I'm developing this great feeling of empathy for General Custer."

Jeremy Bolde's hand closed around his console joystick, and suddenly he was looking through *BAKER*'s cybernetic eyes, the imaging from the onboard cameras feeding into the Heads-Up Display of his helmet.

You could maneuver and deploy gun drones via microburst transmissions over a datalink, in effect issuing suggestions to the onboard artificial intelligences. Actual combat, however, required a human telepresence. It was as if he rode the back of the charging steel beast in the ultimate video game gone real.

The system was configured to trackfire mode; the cart-wheel sights of the booster gun hovered in front of his eyes. Wherever he aimed those sights, so would the drone steer itself. Data hacks glowed around the perimeter of his vision: speed, ammunition, vehicle systems status, and ahead glowed a small forest of hostile target arrows stabbing downward accusingly at the enemy. His forefinger tightened on the throttle trigger and a flick of his thumb lifted the safety cover off the firing switch, triggering the hot gun warning tone.

"Right through the middle, Brid," he murmured. "I'll work left to right. You have right to left. Engage."

"Engaging," the quiet one-word reply returned over the interphone.

Bolde laid his sights on the first silhouetted armored fighting vehicle as he might have aimed a target pistol and pressed the thumb button.

Two kilometers away, the first round cycled into *BAKER*'s booster gun. It wasn't a shell in a conventional sense, rather it was a slender "kinetic kill" dart encased in a sabot sheath, a simple finned crowbar of superdense inert uranium encased in a superhard tungsten steel alloy.

The dart itself carried no propulsive powder charge. Instead, injectors spewed a metered dose of a liquid explosive propellant into the breech chamber behind the round. Ignited by an electric arc, the incandescent gas of this initial detonation hurled the dart on its way as with a conventional cannon. However as the projectile accelerated down the barrel, secondary injectors spaced down the length of the smoothbore cannon tube fired in sequence, building the breech pressure and pushing the dart to a velocity far higher than could be obtained from a conventional weapon.

Three rounds were fired in as many seconds, an X of blue-white flame spewing from the cannon's muzzle brake.

Downrange, an Algerian T-72 died. Neither its reactive armor nor the heavier steel beneath were enough to save it. The tungsten-and-uranium darts passed through the tank's hull like heated needles through butter. The passage converted kinetic energy into heat and instead of solid projectiles, jets of metallic plasma exploded into the tank's interior, burning at the temperature of a star's surface.

Bolde swung his sights onto the next target in the laager. Shock and surprise had done their parts. Now they must rely on speed, wreaking as much havoc as they could before the Algerians recovered.

The vehicles around the laager perimeter flared like the candles on a birthday cake as the fire streams of the two gun drones converged. Over the intercom link Jeremy could hear Bridget Shelleen's whispered supplication with each press of her trigger key.

"Lord and Lady . . . Hold your hands above us this night . . . Grant pardon for these lives we must take . . . Grant peace to those we must slay . . ."

"Scout lead! We got trouble here!"

Mary May paused in her jogging run and dropped to a crouch beside a stone slab. Lee Trebain following her lead an instant later. "Go, Nate. What's happening?"

"We're blown," the Indian trooper rasped back over the squad circuit. "We been nailed by an Algi patrol."

"Tac situation? Are either of you hit?"

"We're under good cover, but pinned. Four hostiles on our front. Johnny and me are both okay, but we can't maneuver. We bitched the strike and one of the *Centauros* is still operational. It has the ridgeline covered behind us. We can't fall back."

"Oh, jeez! We're hearing small-arms fire from the south. That must be you guys. Can you hold?"

"For a while, Five."

"Understood," Mary May acknowledged. "We'll be up with you as soon as we can. Hang in."

"We don't have all that much choice," Grey Bird replied with wry grimness.

Trebain had been monitoring the same series of transmissions, and now he scrambled. "The guys are in trouble. Let's go!"

"Like I said, we'll get to them as soon as we can." Mary May started back up to the ridge crest. "We still have four Algi scout tracks down in that canyon we have to take care of."

"Hey, Mary May. Nate and Johnny are in trouble!"

"Darn it, Lee. I know it!" she snapped over her shoulder. "But the lieutenant and Miss Shelleen and everybody will be in trouble if we let those tracks bust out! Now load antiarmor and come on!"

Trebain swore under his breath and followed.

The growl of engines and the squeak and chatter of tracks echoed up from the pass floor. The Algerian BRMs were on the move. Rolling north at a fast walking pace, they had their scout teams deployed as flank guards. Warily, the Algerian mobile troopers advanced, scanning the walls of the pass on either side. There would be no surprising this bunch.

Lying side by side, Mary May and Trebain watched them advance. "How we working this?" Trebain growled.

"You kill that lead track. I'll peel the infantry." Mary May flipped her visor up and settled her eye to the sighting module of her SABR. "One magazine, then pull back fast. On my mark. Three . . . two . . . one . . . shoot!"

The two grenade launchers barked out their vest-pocket artillery barrage. The lead BRM flared and exploded under Trebain's fire stream while Mary May walked a string of laser-ranged airbursts down the left-hand column of dismounted flankers.

The surviving Algerian infantry scattered and went to ground. Their earlier-gen night-vision goggles picked up the muzzle flashes on the ridge crest and assault rifles began to crackle an angry response. The surviving BRMs reversed gear and backed up the roadway like a trio of startled crayfish. In the turret hatches, the track commanders swiveled their deck machine guns in line with the threat and opened fire, hosing streams of greenish tracers into the night.

"Lee, fall back!" Mary May rose to a half crouch, intent on dropping the last shell in her clip in on the second track in line.

"Mary, get down." Trebain lunged to his feet, grabbing for her harness. Then the bullet hail was chopping up the stone around them. Mary May flipped backward off the crest in a credible parachute landing roll. Trebain tried to follow but a 7.65 NATO round took his right leg out from under him. The ballistic plate covering his shin deflected the slug but the limb went numb from ankle to hip.

Lee fell forward in a sprawl. He felt himself start to slide. Good God Almighty, he was falling down the front face of the ridge! He clawed at the crumbling slope, trying for a hold, but he only succeeded in making himself tumble. Caught in the midst of a miniature landslide, Lee lost his grip on his weapon. Stars burst behind his eyes as he found himself battered away from consciousness.

"Brid, cut across the laager and then engage the command company! We'll use the fires for thermal masking."

"I'm with you." The contralto reply remained cool and focused.

"Rick. Drop Jabberwockys and commence disengagement! Head for the extraction route."

"Doin' it, LT!"

ABLE swerved and accelerated, jinking across the pans like a broken-field runner, her belly racks thumping as the first Jabberwocky beacon kicked clear. Inside the cybernetic world of his battle helmet Bolde's eyes flicked over to the time display, counting seconds. The three S's had done as much as could be hoped for and soon the Algerians would be reacting, violently, to this assault.

The danger now lay in the fact that Saber section had revealed itself by radiating. The continuous-wave datalinks that now connected the command vehicle with its fighting drones could be detected and locked in on by radio direction finders. Because of the jitter frequency technology used, it wouldn't be easy, but given enough time, a minute or two, the Algerian Electronic Warfarc battalion would have a fix on them. Once that happened, the word would be flashed to the division's artillery regiment and hellfire and damnation would rain from the sky.

The Jabberwocky decoys, small, high-discharge radio transponders that produced a false signal similar to *ABLE*'s emissions signature, could buy them a little more combat time. So would staying on the move and not presenting a fixed target for the direction finders.

The question was, just how much.

BAKER and *CHARLIE* raced through the perimeter of the shattered Algerian mechanized company. Not a single vehicle remained intact, and flames leaped from the torn hulks. There were still men alive, though, a few stunned survivors, and mostly they fled or cowered in the presence of the angular, multiwheeled demons that had come howling in from the desert. A few, though, still strove to resist.

Bolde caught the backflash of a rocket launch out of the corner of his eye. Some thirty meters to the left, an Algerian infantryman crouched in the shelter of a wrecked BMP, the tube of a light antitank weapon at his shoulder and leveled at *BAKER*. Caught by surprise there was nothing that Bolde could do. However, with light-swift electronic reflexes, the gun drone defended itself.

Thermal sensors recognized the exhaust flare of the rocket and the onboard AIs triggered the Claymore reactive panel in line with the threat. A more sophisticated cousin of conventional reactive armor, the Claymore panel exploded, its front face fragmenting into thousands of small tungsten cubes. Sprayed into the path of the incoming rocket, they chewed the projectile apart in midair. And not the rocket alone, the expanding wave of shrapnel reached out and engulfed the missile man as well.

Moments later the drone tore out through the far side of the laager perimeter and Bolde executed the turn in toward the Algerian Headquarters Company. There was a logic to Bolde's charge directly through the enemy encampment. Any infrared sight aimed at the gun drones from the central enemy position would be blinded by the heat aura thrown off by the blazing hulks of their first kills. Any enemy gunner seeking to engage them would also be presented with the quandary of having his own troops in his line of fire.

The drone's 35s raved on. The last of the communications and command vans died. The mortar carriers and ammo hogs of the Algerian heavy-weapons section exploded, the glare momentarily overloading the videolinks. Wild missiles tore loose from the disintegrating antiair vehicle, jittering madly across the sky. Bolde became aware of a squealing warning tone and a pulsing red flag in his vision field. Barrel overheat! The drones had expended almost half of their two-hundred-round base load, and their titanium-lined gun tubes were going incandescent.

Damnation! Just when they were getting some real work done!

"Brid, deploy smoke! Execute breakaway! Come right to one two zero!"

Multispectral smoke canisters thumped out of secondary projectors, burying the drones in a synthetic fogbank, and the two vehicles turned away from the havoc they had produced, racing back into the undamaged darkness of the night.

Bolde called up a command on *BAKER*'s ordnance menu, releasing a blast of chill carbon dioxide gas down the barrel of the drone's main gun. "Brid, execute a thermal purge. We're going in again."

There was a warning edge to Shelleen's reply. "Lieutenant, may I remind you that we've been radiating continuously for almost five minutes."

"You may, Miss Shelleen, but I want one more Algi company torn up. We'll hit the one to the southeast. Come left to zero eight zero and engage as you bear!"

The drones described a dusty curve across the desert toward their next objective, bucketing over the sand ripples in the plain.

This time it was different. This time the Algerians had been given the opportunity to recover from the initial CMM strike. Tank guns spewed fire and tracer streams snaked along the ground. Bolde weaved and swerved his robotic command, snapping off countershots as his sights aligned. One Algerian vehicle burst into flames. A second, a third . . .

Suddenly the image from *BAKER*'s cameras blurred under a concussive impact. A pattern of red-and-yellow system warning flags blazed in front of Bolde's eyes and he caught the impression of the world rolling over onto its side, then the datalink broke and his HMD fuzzed into static.

"Hell!" Bolde tore up his useless visor. "We just lost *BAKER*!"

"I saw him go out," Brid reported. "Direct hit with a tank round. Dead one. Orders?"

Bolde dialed up the self-destruct code on *BAKER*'s crisis menu and beamed it off, hoping there was a functional receiver to catch it. "Disengage! Show's over! Get *CHARLIE* out of there. Put him under autonomous control and head him for the extraction point, then kill our transmitters. Rick, balls to the wall and clear the area! We've pushed it about as much . . ."

Beyond *ABLE*'s windscreen, the desert exploded.

Mary May skidded down the unstable slope to the sprawled form amid the slide rubble. Lee shouldn't be moved after a fall such as he had sustained, but he was also three-quarters of the way down to the pass floor and lying on an open hillside. Algerians had pulled back around the next bend in the gorge, but they would be probing again soon.

Grabbing on to his harness, she dragged Trebain a few yards cross-slope to a clump of thorny brush. It wasn't much, but it was all the cover immediately available. Dividing her attention between the canyon floor and her wounded trooper, she made a fast assessment of Trebain's condition.

He was unconscious but breathing. The ballistic plate shielding his right shin had shattered from a direct hit, but the bullet itself had been turned. The leg was rapidly darkening with a massive bruise, and Mary May suspected the limb wasn't going to be much good for a while. Trebain's body armor had also shielded him from the worst effects of his fall. Beyond a concussion and a sizable collection of bangs and abrasions he appeared intact. A good thing as there wasn't much she could do at the moment beyond applying a few jets of aerosol disinfectant.

As she completed her inspection, she heard him moan softly.

"Hush, Lee. You're okay," she said quietly.

"Mar . . . Five . . . what happened?"

"You took one on the armor and fell down the wrong side of the hill. How's your leg feel?"

"My leg . . . Christ! I can't even feel if it's still attached!"

"It is," she replied, stretching out beside him. Peering out beyond the brush clump, she established her firing position. "It's just numb from the shock. Enjoy it while it lasts. I'll bet you've got one heck of a bone bruise there."

"I can't even get it to move." Trebain shook his head, becoming more aware of his environment. "Shit! How in the hell are we going to get back up to the extraction point!"

He started to sit up but Mary caught him by the shoulder. "Stay down. We could have Algis moving in on us again. I'm not sure how we're going to get out of here yet, but we are. You're going to be okay, Lee. Nobody's leaving you behind. You got my word on it."

The thermal lobe and glare from the burning Algerian track kept overloading her night brite visor. Mary May flipped it up for a few moments and rested her grainy eyes with a look up at the cool star-speckled blackness of the desert sky. Beside her, she heard a soft, dazed chuckle. "Shit! And all this friggin' time I've been worrying about taking care of you."

Distractedly she reached back and patted Trebain on the shoulder. "We take care of each other, guy."

Flipping her visor down again, she keyed her Leprechaun transceiver onto the voice-channel link with the command vehicle. "I'd better let the lieutenant know we've got problems . . . Scout Lead calling Saber Six. Flash Red. Do you copy?"

She repeated the call three times. There was no answer.

ABLE's hull rang like a beaten oil drum, and shrapnel sparked and howled off of her armor plating. For an instant her crew stared down at the ground through her windshield as the concussion of the multiple shell bursts lifted her tail into the air. Then the cavalry vehicle crashed back onto her eight wheels.

"Incoming!" Santiago bellowed, fighting with the wheel to stave off a rollover.

"Oh really? You think?" Shelleen commented through gritted teeth, clinging to the grab bar above her workstation.

Bolde reached across to the driver's console and slapped the belly rack release, kicking out another set of Jabberwocky decoys. "Brid. Verify that the transmitters are down! Rick. Hard left! Get us out from under the next pattern!"

The driver replied by skidding *ABLE* through a minimum-radius turn that locked the frame levelers to their stops, shooting the cavalry vehicle off at right angles to their prior course. Instants later, chain lightning played across the desert and man-made thunder roared as eight heavy howitzer rounds tore up the ground where they would have been. The Algerian table of organization was artillery heavy, the divisional commander having over eighty tubes and launchers at his disposal. He was employing this awesome sledgehammer now to eliminate the gadfly that had dared to sting his command. The gadfly's only recourse was flight.

"Rick, hard right!"

ABLE swerved again, sprayed gravel roaring in the wheel wells. Flooring his accelerator, Santiago resumed the dash south for the hill range. But again there came the wail and slam of an incoming salvo, the cavalry vehicle barely scurried clear of the shells dropping in its tracks.

A rapid rhythmic thumping came from back aft as the shrapnel-torn rubber sheathing stripped from one of the tires. The wheel held together; its multiple layers of steel and Kevlar cording could withstand more damage then even a conventional metal tank tread, but a limit would be reached . . . soon.

"Dammit! They're tracking us! Brid, are you sure we've got cold boards!"

"Positive," she called back. "We are not emitting, and the threat board is clear. No laser or radar paints or locks!"

"Then there's got to be a drone eyeballing us! Find it! Rick, shuck and jive! Buy us some time!"

Bolde called up the weapons pack on his controller, heating up the pair of CMM surface-to-air rounds that were always carried ready for use in the box launchers. Elevating and indexing the mount, he began searching for the Algerian's airborne spy.

"I verify a drone," Brid yelled. "I'm getting a datalink trace."

"Can you jam it?"

"I'll need a minute to analyze and match the jitter pattern."

"We don't have a minute."

Another salvo dropped in on *ABLE*. Again they didn't hit behind but around the fleeing cavalry vehicle and only the luck of the draw prevented a direct hit. With the range established the Algerian gunners would switch to anti-tank scatter packs for their next volley.

Wildly, Bolde swept the IR sights of the sensor group across the sky. There! Off to the west, the sight crosshairs acquired a smear of ruddy heat against the cold stars. The Algerian recon drone was running roughly three klicks out and paralleling their course, targeting for the enemy Artillery regiment.

A flick of his thumb set the tracking lock and a rock forward on a coolie-hat switch zoomed the camera in. Bolde got a momentary impression of the skeletal frame of a miniature helicopter, internally lit by the glow of its rotary engine.

There was only the momentary impression because he was already squeezing the trigger that sent both of the antiair CMMs on their way. The last imaging sent to the Algerians by their drone was two wobbling fire trails converging on it from out of the night.

Bolde observed the flash of the missile kill. “Brake hard! Now!” he bellowed.

ABLE’s wheels locked up and her tail came around as she broke loose and slithered to a halt, broadside on. And then submunitions shells burst overhead and the desert hissed and sparkled as hundreds of deadly little antiarmor bomblets rained out of the sky just beyond the stalled Shinseki.

“Might as well just let her sit, Rick,” Bolde continued calmly. “If they still have us acquired, we’ll never get out from under the next one.”

The only sound the soft steady-state whine of the turbines. Bolde, Shelleen, and Santiago sat unspeaking in the darkness, thinking their own thoughts and counting the seconds. When fifteen had passed, the next salvo fell . . . half a mile away along the course they had been following. The next dropped at twice that range as the thwarted Algerians stabbed blindly into the dark. Bridget Shelleen chuckled softly at the wonder of being alive.

Bolde released a breath that he had been holding for what seemed to be an amazing length of time. “Rick, get us out of here. Brid, advise Mary May that we’re disengaging and tell her to head for the extraction point. Fun’s over, people, let’s go home.”

At a solid 60 K an hour, *ABLE* and the *CHARLIE* drone roared south toward the looming refuge of the El Khnachich range. Bolde kept *ABLE*’s weapons pack trained aft as they fled, scanning their back trail for signs of enemy pursuit or activity.

Beyond the burning wrecks of the battalion they had decimated, the Algerian division was reacting like a kicked ant’s nest. Thermal blossoms dotted the night as hundreds of vehicle engines kicked over, the neat pattern of laager sits dissolving as unit commanders strove to regroup into combat formation. Flares and flashes of gunfire danced around the perimeter as gunners blazed at ghosts in the darkness or even engaged in “blue on blue” duels with their own side.

Bolde grinned. This kind of battlefield hysteria could do more damage to the enemy in the long run than his own direct assault. The smile rapidly dissipated as Brid spoke up from her station. “We’ve got major problems with the scout team. They’ve got the Algerian recon company immobilized with about half of the elements destroyed, but they’re pinned down as well. They can’t get back to the extraction point.”

“Get me a direct link with Mary May.”

“Not possible. She’s too far down in the pass and we’re radio blocked. All we have is a relay through Nate and Johnny on the squad circuit.”

Bolde twisted around in the command chair. “What in the hell is she doing down in the pass?”

"Lee Trebain apparently took a bad fall down into the cut. Mary May is with him but he's been injured too badly for them to get back up to the ridgeline."

"What about Nate and Johnny? Can they get to them?"

"Again not possible. Nate and Johnny are pinned down by an Algerian patrol at the southern end of the pass about a kilometer away. They haven't taken hits yet, but they can't move. Both fire teams are requesting instructions."

Requesting instructions. The polite military term for begging the CO for a fast miracle. Bolde lifted his wrist to his mouth and wiped away the salty dust caked on his lips. This was his run. He'd set this plan up, and his people had every right in the world to expect that he would get them out the other side of it. Simple statements like, "I misjudged" or "I overlooked something" were not an option. Her face outlined by the screen glow, Brid Shelleen looked at him, calmly, expectantly.

"Brid, tell the scouts to hang on and stand by. We're coming to get them. Then pull *CHARLIE* back in with us. Rick, new game plan. Forget the route over the saddleback. We're going out through the pass."

Through the SABR's infrared sights, Mary May picked out a ghostly pale sphere hovering a few inches off the ground, the face of an Algerian trooper. Gingerly he was crawling forward to peer around the turn of the pass, hugging close to the rubble along the edge of the roadway. The face was there for a moment and then gone as the trooper ducked back.

Flicking the selector setting to AIRBURST Mary May rested the sight crosshairs just above the point where the Algerian had disappeared and squeezed the SABR's trigger.

At the trigger crossed its first detent in its pull, the SABR's ranging laser produced an invisible pulse of coherent light that touched its targeting point and reflected back. The microprocessor in the SABR's stock computed a range from that laser reflection and as the grenade launcher itself fired, an inductance coil wrapped around the launcher's barrel transmitted that range to a microchip buried within the shell as it screamed down the tube.

The shell itself dispassionately counted out the distance in flight and, over the target, it detonated, spraying the environment with a handful of shrapnel.

The Algerian trooper did not return.

"What's happening, Five?" Trebain asked.

"Nothin' much. Just a snooper. How are you doing?"

The breath rasped in the Texan's throat. "You were right about the leg. I liked it a lot better when it was numb. I'm trying to tell myself I'm just imagining it, but I think I got a couple of busted ribs, too."

"That's no fun. That happened to me once when I fell off a hayrack. As long as you're breathing all right you'll be okay. You want a hit of feel good?"

"No. I want to stay clear. Maybe I can do something . . . Mary May, maybe you'd better start thinking about getting out of here. Like you said. I'll be okay."

She rolled onto her side and looked back at Trebain. "What's with you, Lee? Do you honestly think I'm going to run out on one of my guys? Get real!"

"Aw hell, Five. It's just that . . . I don't like the idea of the Algis getting their hands on you is all."

Mary May nestled back behind her weapon stock. "Well, thanks, but I don't like the idea of the Algis getting their hands on any of us. And that's not going to happen. The lieutenant'll get us out of this. One way or another."

Almost as if by one of Brid Shelleen's conjurations, a familiar and most welcome voice sounded in their helmet. "Saber Six to Scout Lead. Do you receive?"

Mary May almost broke the transmit key on her lip mike. "Roger that! We copy, Lieutenant!"

"Okay, Mary May. We've got the Cipher drone up and we're relaying through that," Bolde replied over the circuit. "We also have you and Lee spotted, not to mention our friends the Algerians. We see three BRMs around the bend in the pass about two hundred meters south of your position. Do you verify?"

"I verify, Lieutenant. I can hear their engines idling. We've hurt them pretty bad. I don't think they're exactly sure of what they're up against yet."

"Better and better. We'll be up with you presently, but we're going to need a little bit of assistance. What's your ammunition state in regard to 20mm grenade?"

"Uh, six clips between Lee and me, counting the one in my weapon. Mixed antiarmor and smart round."

"Excellent," Bolde's filtered voice replied with satisfaction. "When I give you the word, I want you to rapid fire it all down the pass in the direction of the Algis. Don't worry about hitting anything in particular. Just make a lot of noise and keep their heads down. Then you and Trebain stand by to mount up fast. Understood?"

"Understood, sir."

"Very well. Then let's proceed. Stand by to commence firing . . . now!"

Mary May's finger closed convulsively on the trigger. As rapidly as she could she hosed the bend in the canyon with high explosives, the sharp popping of the grenade bursts reverberating up and down the pass, the echoes building upon themselves. Ejected shell cases tinkled around her and the frame of the SABR grew warm and then hot as she poured fire through it. Lee, ignoring the pain of his fractured ribs, fumbled clips out of his own harness pouches, feeding her.

She was down to her last three rounds when two massive, dark shapes roared past on the floor of the pass. *ABLE* and *CHARLIE* running side by side and charging headlong for the bend in the canyon. Mary May realized that her barrage had been performing multiple functions. Not only distracting and suppressing any Algerian forward observers but blanketing the sound of Bolde's charge through the pass. In a moment someone was going to be most unpleasantly surprised.

The cavalry vehicles vanished around the curve and the silvery glare of muzzle flashes reflected off the walls of the gorge, strobing with the orange of explosion flame. The hills trembled with the piercing crack of booster-gun fire, the thudding cough of grenade streams and the slam of Claymore panels.

And then silence and darkness and a single satisfied voice over the radio link.

"And some damn fools say cavalry is no good in the mountains."

ABLE reappeared around the bend in the canyon. Rolling to a halt below Mary May and Trebain's position, its tail ramp swung open. Before the vehicle had even come to a halt, however, Mary May had Trebain to his feet. Supporting him they slid-hopped down the slope toward home.

"See, Lee, I told you we'd get out."

The only answer was a tightening of the arm around her shoulders.

Mary May lugged the injured trooper into the scout bay and dumped him into one of the air seats spaced around the bulkheads. As she secured his safety harness, the tail ramp lifted, and *ABLE* rumbled ahead.

"Hey, Lieutenant," she yelled forward. "There's still one tank destroyer left at the mouth of the pass."

"Understood, Five," Bolde called back. "Miss Shelleen is sorting that gentleman out right now."

Wired into *CHARLIE* drone's remote cyber senses through her Helmet-Mounted Display, Brid Shelleen snaked the big robot through narrowing confines of the pass, keeping the throttle trigger pressed to its limits. The enemy knew of their presence and intent. There was no room left for subtlety, no more than there would be in a high-noon shoot out between two old Western gunfighters. Speed and precision would decide this last engagement.

For a split second Brid toggled across to the overhead tactical of the area around the pass mouth. The Algerian *Centauro* was off to the right of the roadway by about fifty meters, covering the exit and waiting.

She built the engagement sequence in her mind. Fire smoke grenades . . . Clear the pass entrance and pivot to the right . . . Switch to thermographics . . . Acquire the target . . . Take the shot . . . *Do it now!*

CHARLIE's grenade throwers hurled a cluster of smoke bombs out into the open ground beyond the pass mouth, the drone plunging into the dense swirling haze produced by the bursting charges. Brid started to brake for the turn when, abruptly, a shadowy outline loomed in her visor.

The problem with any military plan of action rests with the fact that the enemy rarely consults with you concerning his own intents. The Algerian tank destroyer crew had apparently elected at that moment to cut across the entry to the pass. Their intent, no doubt, was to take a snap shot at their oncoming foe. Instead, they had found themselves engulfed in an unexpected smoke screen and had come to a halt directly in the path of the charging US vehicle.

Brid locked up *CHARLIE*'s brakes, but before she could halt the drone it had plowed headlong into the *Centauro,* centerpunching it between its second and third set of drive wheels.

She hit the firing button of the booster gun, but the three-round burst blazed futilely over her opponent's deck. The casemate mount could neither depress nor traverse enough to engage this closer-than-point-blank target. She saw the tube of the *Centauro*'s 105 swing across her video field of vision, then caught the vibration as the gun barrel jammed out of line against *CHARLIE*'s hull. The Algerian gunners were caught in the same conundrum as she, unable to bring an effective weapon to bear.

Unable to reverse away from the deadlock, Brid opted for her only other alternative, she rocked her joystick hard forward and crushed the power trigger to maximum output.

CHARLIE shuddered, its massive tires clawing at the unyielding stone. Red and yellow systems overload warnings flared all around the periphery of Shelleen's Helmet Mounted Display and a grinding vibration blurred the camera imaging. But *CHARLIE* began to gain ground.

As the deck tilted beneath him, the Algerian driver frantically and futilely attempted to break away but the five hundred horsepower of the *Centauro* could not match the twelve hundred of the Shinseki. Remorselessly the gun drone bulldozed the tank destroyer sideways and over, the *Centauro*'s wheels spinning helplessly, until the point of overbalance was reached.

With a final crash the Algerian vehicle went over onto its side. With the deadlock broken, Bridget backed *CHARLIE* off twenty meters and waited. The Algerian crew scrambled out of the hatches of their doomed vehicle, fleeing into the night, and she let them go with a prayer.

I thank you, My Lady, for granting me this option of mercy.

Then she tore open the belly of the tank destroyer with another booster-gun burst.

"The pass mouth is clear, Lieutenant," she said, lifting her voice to the world outside of her helmet display.

Nate Grey Bird fed his last clip of 9mm into the butt of his Beretta. A lot of extremely odd noise had just come from over the ridge crest, and he sincerely hoped it was indicative of a relief-and-rescue operation.

"Nate, what's your sitrep?" Lieutenant Bolde's voice was coming in over the squad channel now.

"Pretty much the same, sir, except the Algerians are getting closer. They're going to be in hand-grenade range pretty quick, and they have four throwing arms to our two."

"That will be an irrelevancy here in a moment, Specialist Grey Bird. Roman, you still with us?"

"Yes sir!" Johnny's enthusiastic response came back. "Right here."

"All right, here's the package. I have fixes on you and Nate as well as on the bad guys. In a second here I'm going to toss some CMMs over the ridgeline and onto the Algi positions. Crawl under your helmets because they are going to be close. After the rounds hit, the two of you fall back to the ridgeline and drop down to where we're waiting. We're parked almost underneath you."

"Uh, begging your pardon, sir." Johnny's voice had lost a great deal of its enthusiasm. "But that descent is almost vertical. How do we get down?"

"The operative word here, Mr. Roman, is 'almost.' As for how you get down, I suggest you step off the edge and let gravity take its course. You can grow some new skin on your next leave. Dedigitate, gentlemen, we do not have a great deal of time here! Rounds on the way!"

Aimed almost vertically, the box launchers belched out their four preprogrammed missiles, the flame spraying over *ABLE*'s armored back.

"Rounds look good," Brid reported from her workstation. "We have hits . . . Johnny and Nate are moving . . ."

"Right. Get *CHARLIE* moving, too, down and out onto the flats. Expedite!" Bolde swiveled the weapons pack around, intent on doing a little housecleaning. The Teal/Specter radar unit still sat at the edge of the plateau. Its crew had bailed out of the unarmed vehicle as the fighting had gotten close, and it was far too valuable an asset to leave intact.

Laying his sights on the generator trailer, Bolde demolished it with burst of 25mm from the OCSW. Elevating fire, he chewed away the antenna array and finally focused on the rear hull doors of the transporter track, caving them in and gutting the systems bay.

"Here they come!" Mary May yelled from the aft compartment. Turning his sights to the rear again, Bolde caught the last of Nate and Johnny's wild slide down the slope face. They still had the Javelin launcher. Good men!

A sharp *tack tack tack* sounded against the windshield and bullet stars danced across the Armorglas. There were still Algerians out there trying to make a fight of it. Bringing the grenade launcher around, Bolde raked the stone outcropping across from their position, covering his last people home.

The ramp dropped and the deck rang as Johnny and Nate threw themselves and their equipment aboard. "In!" Mary May screamed.

Rick Santiago didn't need a "go" order. All hands were thrown back in their seats as *ABLE* lunged forward at maximum acceleration.

Rick fought with the cavalry vehicle's wheel as they tore down the first switchback below the pass. Dios! *This thing is just a goat path! This grade will be hairy enough in daylight and at a sane rate of speed!*

Beside him Lieutenant Bolde chanted a mantra. "Faster . . . Faster . . . Artillery . . . Faster!"

Artillery? Shit! Somebody up there in the pass must still have a working radio. They'd left a whole lot of really pissed off Algerians just on the other side of this hill range, and now they no longer had to worry about the presence of friendly troops!

ABLE tore into the next corner, broadsiding through it like a sports car, her outer set of tires more over the edge than on the road. Rick tore back his night-vision visor and slapped his palm down on the auxiliary panel, kicking on the headlights and running lights full beam. Screw stealth! He had to see!

One . . . two . . . three . . . four . . . five . . . six . . . interminable switchbacks, then a short down grade and then the gravel pans.

"Off the road!" Bolde's yelled command rang in the confines of the cab.

Killing the headlights, Rick swung *ABLE* into the open desert. A dune loomed ahead, and the Shinseki didn't as much drive over it as through it, blasting a bow wave of sand to either side. All eight wheels momentarily left the ground. She hit hard once and then concussion bounced her into the air again as the night cracked open and bloody orange light flooded in. There were no definable single explosions as much as a continuous ear-crushing thunder as the massed time-on-target barrage rained down on the Taoudenni caravan road.

Rick's heart stalled in his chest. But after a moment he realized that they were steadily pulling away from the fire zone. The bombardment wasn't swinging onto them but was only marching down the roadway. The Algerians were firing blind, raking the caravan route, a frustrated tantrum of high explosives hurled after a brazen and escaping enemy.

They were out. They were all out. Backlit by the shell bursts, Rick could even make out the battered silhouette of *CHARLIE* drone lumbering faithfully behind them. Then and there, Santiago made a pledge that the next time he got home, he would remember this night and he would go to church and light some candles. He would also go out and get really, really, drunk, but first, he would light the candles.

Over at the commander's station, Lieutenant Bolde unsnapped the chinstrap of his helmet. Lifting its weight off with a sigh of relief, he ran a hand through his sweat-sodden hair. "Well, that wasn't such a chore now, was it?"

45 Miles Southeast of the El Khnachich Range
0421 Hours, Zone Time; October 29, 2021

"You want me to push her for a while, Rick?"

"Nah, LT. I poured a little coffee down my throat, and I'm good to the replenishment point."

"Just checking."

Steel-splinter stars still gleamed overhead and the cracked cab hatches admitted a stream of pure, chill predawn air that blew away the stenches of powder and sweat and fear. Bolde and Santiago had the driving watch. The others caught what fragmentary rest they could.

Brid Shelleen drowsed intermittently in her workstation seat. Mary May lay on the deck beside her, her head pillowed on her flak vest. Aft, things were silent in the scout bay as well. Even Lee Trebain slept with the aid of a morphine ampoule.

Somewhere over the horizon, an Army heavy-lift quad-rotor was outbound to meet them. Aboard it would be fuel blivets and ammunition reloads and a flying squad from squadron maintenance to help repair their battle damage.

His injured man would be airlifted out to a field hospital for care. And maybe there would be hot A rations and a clean uniform and an extra liter of water for a bath. And maybe a chance to sleep. Maybe really sleep for several hours straight through.

Bolde grinned to himself. Luxury in the eyes of the field soldier. But not yet. Not yet. There were still things to be considered.

What had he done this night? What had he accomplished that had been worth the gamble of the lives of his people?

Destroying the Recon company had poked a sharp stick into the eye of the enemy. Worthwhile. The Algerian army was weak on logistics. There would be no replacements for those destroyed tankers. Another gain. And the attack on that Algerian mechanized battalion would have a cascade effect. Knock out one of a brigade's three maneuver battalions and you cripple that brigade. Cripple one of its three maneuver brigades and you weaken the entire balanced structure of the division. A plus.

More importantly, though, was the time. It would take hours for the Algerians to re-form and resume replenishment. More hours for casualties to be dealt with and replacement supplies to be brought forward. More hours cautiously to probe forward and learn if any new and nastier surprises were set to be sprung.

Half a day bought? Maybe a day? It was enough. What was that rueful joke making the rounds within Third World military circles? *If you are planning a war, best also plan to win it before the Americans can get there.* The Algerian *fait accompli* had been blocked. Their aggression had been stalled. When they finally ventured south of the El Khnachich range, they'd find more than just a scattering of cavalry patrols waiting for them. They'd find an army.

Bolde slouched deeper into his seat. The risk and return had balance. It had been worth it.

Half-asleep at her workstation, Bridget Shelleen lifted her head as she heard a soft trilling whistle grow in the darkness. It had the lilt of the old country to it, and it took her a moment to place the melody over the rumble of the tires. When she did, she smiled.

"Instead of spa, we'll drink down ale.
Pay the reck'ning on the nail.
No man for debt shall go to jail,
For Garryowen and Glory."

GLOSSARY

Common Modular Missile System—The replacement-to-be for the US Army's current TOW and Dragon antitank missile systems. An interchangeable family of warheads, guidance packages, and booster engines, CMM rounds can be assembled in the field to produce a number of differently mission-formatted antiarmor and antipersonnel missiles. Capable of being launched from both Army land and air vehicles.

HMD (Helmet-Mounted Display)—An integral multimode imaging system built into the visor of a combat helmet. It can be used to present readouts of personal or Velectronics systems, as a video display for operating remote-controlled vehicles and equipment via telepresence, or as an access to a virtual-reality environment.

Javelin—A shoulder-fired, infrared-guided, "fire and forget" antitank missile. The replacement for the Dragon ATM, the Javelin is just entering the US inventory at this time, making it a veteran weapons system by 2021.

Laager (modern usage)—A temporary camp for a unit of armored fighting vehicles in the field.

SABR (Selectable Assault Battle Rifle)—The projected next-generation weapons system for the US Army's ground fighter. An assumed given in any twenty-first century conflict situation is that the American foot soldier is going to be massively outnumbered wherever he (or she) is going to be committed to battle. The concept behind the SABR is to give the individual US infantryperson the same enhanced firepower and survival advantages that precision-guided standoff munitions give his (or her) Air Force counterpart.

The SABR is a composite weapon, combining a 5.56mm Heckler & Koch G36 assault carbine with a six-round, clip-fed grenade launcher, the launcher firing a family of 20mm antivehicle and antipersonnel rounds, many of which will be cybernetically fused "smart" munitions.

Also mated to the weapon will be a multimode sighting system incorporating thermographic, night brite, and laser targeting technologies, giving the user the ability effectively to engage the enemy at all ranges and in all combat environments.

OCSW (Objective Crew Served Weapon)—The 25mm big brother to the SABR. Replacing the "Ma Deuce" 50 caliber machine gun and Mark 19 40mm "Chunker," this vehicle- and tripod-mounted high-velocity grenade launcher will also be capable of delivering a wide variety of "smart" and "dumb" munitions.

RPV (Remotely Piloted Vehicle)—A remotely operated, robotic surface or aircraft.

MM-15 Shinseki Multi-Mission Combat Vehicle—An end result of Army Chief of Staff Eric K. Shinseki's "Medium-Weight Force" concept. The replacement for the U.S. Army's current force of heavyweight tracked tanks and Armored Personnel Carriers. The concept behind this family of wheeled Armored Fighting and Support Vehicles is that they are light enough to be airlifted rapidly to any global trouble spot. Yet, at the same time, they mount enough advanced technological firepower to deal with any potential crisis.

Track—Military slang. The term "track" might be used for any caterpillar-treaded armored fighting vehicle other then a true tank or a self-propelled howitzer, e.g., "scout track", "antiair track", "command track," etc.

Velectronics (Vehicle electronics)—A ground-combat vehicle's battlefield sensors and onboard electronic-warfare systems. An increasingly critical factor in future conflict situations.

Author's Note—Following the American Civil War, the Seventh U.S. Cavalry Regiment began using the old Irish ballad *Garryowen* as its distinctive signature march, an acknowledgment to the many Irish immigrants who served with both the regiment and with the frontier army as a whole.

So strongly did the regiment become linked with the song that they became known as the Garryowens, a designation the unit still wears proudly today.

JAMES COBB has lived his entire life within a thirty-mile radius of a major Army post, an Air Force base, and a Navy shipyard. He comments, "Accordingly, it's seemed a natural to become a kind of cut-rate Rudyard Kipling, trying to tell the stories of America's service people." Currently, he's writing the Amanda Garrett technothriller series, with three books, *Choosers of the Slain, Seastrike*, and *Seafighter*, published. He's also doing the Kevin Pulaski suspense thrillers for St. Martin's Press. He lives in the Pacific Northwest and, when he's not writing, he indulges in travel, the classic American hot rod, and collecting historic firearms.

CYBERKNIGHTS

BY HAROLD W. COYLE

One

combat.com

The secluded community just outside of Valparaiso, Chile, slumbered on behind the high walls and steel-reinforced gates that surrounded it. Other than the lazy swaying of branches stirred by a gentle offshore breeze, the only sound or movement disturbing the early-morning darkness was that created by the rhythmic footfalls on the pavement of a pair of security guards patrolling the empty streets of the well-manicured community. The two armed men did not live in any of the homes they were charged with protecting. Even if either one of them had been fortunate enough to possess the small fortune that ownership of property in the tiny village required, neither had the social credentials that would permit him to purchase even the smallest plot of ground within these walls. If they harbored any resentment over this fact, they dared not show it. The pay was too good and the work too easy to jeopardize. Their parents had taught them well. Only fools take risks when times were good and circumstances didn't require it.

Still, the guards were only human. On occasion a comment that betrayed their true feelings would slip out during the casual conversation that they engaged in during the long night. Upon turning a corner, one of the security guards took note of a flickering of light in a second-story window of one of the oversize homes. Slowing his pace, the hired guardian studied the window in an effort to determine if something was out of kilter. Belatedly, his partner took note of his concern. With a chuckle, the second guard dismissed the concerns of the first. "There is nothing going on up there that we need to bother ourselves with."

"And how would you know that?" the first asked as he kept one eye on the window.

"My sister, the one who is a cleaning woman, chatters incessantly about what she sees in each of these houses. That room, for example, is off-limits to her."

Rather than mollify his suspicions, these comments only piqued the first guard's interest. "And why is that? Is it the personal office of the owner?"

Letting out a loud laugh, the second guard shook his head. "Not hardly. It is the bedroom of a teenage boy."

Seeing the joke, the first guard let out a nervous chuckle. "What," he asked, "makes the bedroom of a teenage boy so important?"

"The boy is a computer rat," came the answer. "My sister says he has just about every sort of computer equipment imaginable cluttering the place."

"What does your sister know about computers?" the first asked incredulously.

Offended, his partner glared. "We are poor, not ignorant."

Realizing that he had unintentionally insulted his comrade, the first guard lowered his head. "I am sorry, I didn't mean to . . ."

"But you did," the offended guard snapped. "What goes on in those rooms is not our concern anyway. We are paid to guard against criminals and terrorists, not speculate about what our employers do within the confines of their own homes." With that, he pivoted about and marched off, followed a few seconds later by his partner.

Neither man, of course, realized that the only terrorist within miles was already inside the walls of the quiet little community. In fact, they had been watching him, or more correctly, his shadow as he went about waging an undeclared war against the United States of America.

Alone in his room, Angelo Castalano sat hunched over the keyboard of his computer, staring at the screen. As he did night after night, young Angelo ignored the pile of schoolbooks that lay strewn across the floor of his small room and turned, instead, his full attention to solving a far more interesting problem. It concerned his latest assignment from the commander of the X Legion.

The "foot soldiers" in the X Legion were, for the most part, the sons of well-to-do South American parents, people who could be correctly referred to as the ruling elite. While Angelo's father oversaw the operation of a major shipping business in Valparaiso owned by a Hong Kong firm, his mother struggled incessantly to keep her place in the polite society of Chile that was, for her husband, just as important as his business savvy. Like their North American counterparts, the information age and modern society left them little time to tend to the children that were as much a symbol of a successful union as was a large house in the proper neighborhood. That Angelo's father had little time to enjoy either his son or house was viewed as a problem, nothing more. So, as he did with so many other problems he faced, the Chilean businessmen threw money and state-of-the-art equipment at it.

A computer, in and of itself, is an inert object. Like a projectile, it needs energy to propel it. Young Angelo and the electricity flowing from the overloaded wall socket provided that energy. But engaging in an activity can quickly becomes boring if there is nothing new or thrilling to capture a young, imaginative mind, especially when that activity involves an ultramodern data-crunching machine. Like the projectile, to have meaning the exercise of power must have a purpose, a target. That is where the X Legion came in.

The X Legion, properly pronounced Tenth as in the roman numeral, was a collection of young South and Central American computer geeks who had found each other as they crawled about the World Wide Web in search of fun, adventure, some sort of achievement. In the beginning they played simple games among themselves, games that involved world conquest, or that required each of the participants to amass great wealth by creating virtual stock portfolios. Slowly, and ever so innocently, the members of the X Legion began to break into the computer systems of international companies, not at all unlike those owned or operated by their own fathers. They did this, they told each other, in order to test their growing computer skills and engage in feats that had real and measurable consequences. "We live in a real world," a legionnaire in Argentina stated one night as they were just beginning to embark upon this new adventure. "So let us see what we can do in that world."

At first, the targets selected for their raids were chosen by the legionnaires themselves, without any controlling or centralized authority. This, quite naturally, led to arguments as fellow members of their group ridiculed the accomplishments of another if they thought the object of a fellow legionnaire's attack had been too easy.

"Manipulating the accounts of a Swiss bank must have more meaning," a Bolivian boy claimed, "than stealing from a local candy store." Though intelligent and articulate, no one had a clear idea of how best to gauge the relative value of their targets.

To resolve this chaotic state of affairs, a new member who used the screen name "longbow" volunteered to take on the task of generating both the targets to be attacked by the members of the legion and the relative value of those targets. Points for the successful completion of the mission would be awarded to the participants by longbow based upon the security measures that had to be overcome, the creativity that the hacker used in rummaging around in the targeted computer, and the overall cost that the company owning the hacked site ultimately had to pay to correct the problem the legionnaire created. How longbow managed to determine all of this was of no concern to the young men like Angelo who belonged to the legion. Longbow offered them real challenges and order in the otherwise chaotic and shapeless world in which they lived, but did not yet understand.

When they were sure he was not listening, which was rare, the rank and file of the legion discussed their self-appointed leader. It didn't matter to Angelo and other members of the X Legion that longbow was not from South or Central America. One of the first clues that brought this issue into question was the English and Spanish longbow used. Like all members of the X Legion, longbow switched between the two languages interchangeably. Since so many of the richest and most advanced businesses using the World Wide Web communicated in English, this was all but a necessity. When it came to his use of those languages, it appeared to the well-educated legionnaires that both Spanish and English were second languages to their taskmaster. Everything about longbow's verbiage was too exact, too perfect, much like the grammar a student would use.

That longbow might be using them for reasons that the young Latin American hackers could not imagine never concerned Angelo. Like his cyber compatriots, his world was one of words, symbols, data, and not people, nationals, and causes. Everything that they saw on their computer screen was merely images, two-dimensional representations. In addition to this self-serving disassociated rationale, there was the fear that longbow, who was an incredible treasure trove of tricks and tools useful to the legion of novice hackers, might take offense if they became too inquisitive about longbow's origins. The loss of their cyber master would result in anarchy, something these well-off cyber anarchists loathed.

While the security guards went about their rounds, protecting the young Chilean and his family from the outside world, Angelo was reaching out into that world. As he did each time he received a mission from longbow, Angelo did not concern himself with the "why" governing his specific tasking for the evening. Rather, he simply concentrated on the "how."

Upon returning from school that afternoon, Angelo had found explicit instructions from longbow on how to break into the computer system of the United States Army Matériel Command in Alexandria, Virginia. This particular system, Angelo found out quickly, handled requests for repair parts and equipment from American military units deployed throughout the world.

The "mission" Angelo had been assigned was to generate a false request, or alter an existing one, so that the requesting unit received repair parts or equipment that was of no earthly use to the unit in the field. Knowing full well that the standards used to judge the success of a mission concerned creativity as well as the cost of the damage inflicted, Angelo took his time in selecting both the target of his attack and the nature of the mischief he would inflict upon it. After several hours of scrolling through hundreds of existing requests, he hit upon one that struck his fancy.

It concerned a requisition that had been forwarded from an Army unit stationed in Kosovo to its parent command located in Germany. The requesting unit, an infantry battalion, had suffered a rash of accidents in recent months because of winter weather and lousy driving by Americans born and raised in states where the only snow anyone ever saw was on TV. Though the human toll had been minimal, the extensive damage to the battalion's equipment had depleted both its own reserve of on-hand spare parts as well as the stock carried by the forward-support maintenance unit in-country. While not every item on the extensive list of replacement parts was mission essential, some demanded immediate replacement. This earned those components deemed critical both a high priority and special handling. With the commander's approval, the parts clerk in Kosovo submitted a request, via the Army's own Internet system, to the division's main support battalion back in Germany to obtain these mission-essential items.

As was the habit of this particular parts clerk, he had waited until the end of the normal workday before submitting his required list of repair parts. In this way the clerk avoided having to go through the entire routine of entering the system, pulling up the necessary on-screen documents, and filling out all the unit data more than once a day. Though parts that had been designated mission essential and awarded a high priority were supposed to be acted upon as soon as they landed on the desk of the parts clerk, lax supervision at the forward-support unit where the clerk worked permitted personnel in his section to pretty much do things as they saw fit. So it should not have come as a great surprise that the parts clerk in Kosovo chose to pursue the path of least resistance, executing his assigned duties in a manner that was most expedient, for the clerk.

This little quirk left a window of opportunity for someone like Angelo to spoof the United States Army Matériel Command's computer system. Since the request was initiated in Kosovo and relayed to the forward-support battalion's parent unit after normal working hours in Kosovo, the personnel in Germany charged with reviewing that request were not at their desks. Those personnel had the responsibility of reviewing all requests from subordinate units to ensure that they were both valid and correct. They then had to make the decision as to whether the request from Kosovo would be filled using on-hand stocks in Germany or forwarding back to Army Matériel Command to be acted upon using Army-wide sources.

All of this was important, because it permitted Angelo an opportunity to do several things without anyone within the system knowing that something was amiss. The first thing Angelo did, as soon as he decided to strike here, was to change the letter-numeric part number of one of the items requested to that of another part, an item which Angelo was fairly sure would be of no use to the infantry unit in Kosovo.

The item Angelo hit upon to substitute was the front hand guards for M-16 rifles that had been cracked during one of the vehicular accidents. Switching over to another screen that had a complete listing of part numbers for other weapons in the Army's inventory, Angelo scrolled through the listings until he found something that struck his fancy. How wickedly wonderful it will be, the young Chilean thought as he copied the part number for the gun tube of a 155mm howitzer, for an infantry unit to receive six large-caliber artillery barrels measuring twenty feet in length instead of the rifle hand guards that it needed. Just the expense of handling the heavy gun tubes would be monumental. Only the embarrassment of the unit commander involved, Angelo imagined, would be greater.

Selecting the item to be substituted, then cutting and pasting the part number of the artillery gun tube in its place, was only the beginning. The next item on Angelo's agenda was to move the request along the chain, electronically approving it and forwarding it at each of the checkpoints along the information superhighway the request had to travel. Otherwise, one of the gate-keeping organizations along the way, such as the parent support battalion in Germany, the theater staff agency responsible for logistical support, or the Army Matériel Command in Virginia, would see that the item Angelo was using as a substitute was not authorized by that unit.

To accomplish this feat Angelo had to travel along the same virtual path that such a request normally traveled. At each point where an organization or staff agency reviewed the request, the young Chilean hacker had to place that agency's electronic stamp of approval upon the request and then whisk it away before anyone at the agency took note of the unauthorized action. This put pressure on Angelo, for he had but an hour or so before the parts clerks in Germany and the logistics staffers elsewhere in Germany switched on their computers to see what new requests had come in during the night. Once he had cleared those gates, he would have plenty of time to make his way through the stateside portion of the system since Chile was an hour ahead of the Eastern time zone.

It was in this endeavor that the tools and techniques that longbow had provided the legionnaires came into play. By using an account name that he had been given by longbow, Angelo was permitted to "go root." In the virtual world, being a "root" on a system is akin to being God. Root was created by network administrators to access every program and every file on a host computer, or any servers connected to it, to update or fix glitches in the system. Having root access also allows anyone possessing this divine power the ability to run any program or manipulate any file on the network. Once he had access as a root user on the Army computer system that handled the requisitioning and allocation of spare parts, Angelo was able to approve and move his request through the network without any of the gates along the way having an opportunity to stop it. In this way the request for the 155mm artillery howitzer gun tubes for the infantry battalion in Kosovo was pulled through the system from the highest level of the United States Army's logistical system rather than being pushed out of it from a unit at the lowest level.

To ensure that there was no possibility that the request would be caught during a routine daily review, the Chilean hacker needed to get the request as far along the chain as he could, preferably out of the Army system itself. To accomplish this little trick, he used his position as a root operator within the Army Matériel Command's computer to access the computers at the Army's arsenal at Watervaliet, in New York State. It was there that all large-caliber gun tubes used by the United States Army were produced.

Once in the arsenal's system, Angelo rummaged around until he found six 155mm gun tubes that were already on hand there. Using the actual bin number of the on-hand gun tubes, he generated shipping documents for those items. Copies of those documents were then forwarded to the computers of the Air Force Military Airlift Command. The result of these last two actions would all but ensure that the request would go through. Upon arriving at work the following morning, the Department of the Army civilian employees at Watervaliet would be greeted by Angelo's instructions for the disposition of the gun tubes issued through the Army Matériel Command's computer in Alexandria, Virginia. Odds were the DOA civilian would not question this, since all the proper electronic documentation, including a code designating it as a high-priority item, were valid. At the same time the computers at the headquarters of the Military Airlift Command would spew out the warning order that a priority shipment for an Army unit forward-deployed in Kosovo was due in. As was their charter when dealing with such a request, the Air Force staff would immediately allocate precious cargo space on one of its transports headed for Kosovo, assign the mission a tasking number, generate their own mission tasking orders, and issue them to all commands who would be involved in the movement of the gun tubes. When all was set, the Air Force would relay disposition instructions back to Watervaliet, instructing the DOA civilian employee to deliver the gun tubes to the air base from which the designated transport would depart.

All of this took time, for Angelo needed to make sure that he not only hit every point along the long chain, but that each action he took and document he generated was correct. An error anywhere along the way would result in someone going back, up or down the actual chain, to ask for clarification or a retransmission of a corrected request. The chances of someone catching the hack would, as a result, be all but certain.

It was only when he had dotted his last virtual i and crossed his last digital t that Angelo noted the time being displayed on the upper right-hand corner of his screen. It was nearly 3 A.M. Shaking his head, the Chilean hacker raised his arms and glanced at his wristwatch. Why, he found himself wondering, had all this taken so long? While he appreciated that he had eaten up a great deal of time searching for the perfect target, and then finding an appropriately useless item to send them, Angelo found he could not explain the disparity. He had, after all, been involved in spoofs that were far more complex and involved than the one he had just completed.

Easing back in his seat, Angelo considered this incongruity with the same highly developed analytical tools that all the members of the X Legion possessed. Doing so proved to be no easy task, for his eyes were blurry and his mind, exhausted by hours of tedious labor, was not focusing. While there was always the possibility that the fault lay with the American Army's computers, Angelo quickly dismissed this. They had, as best he knew, some of the fastest and most capable systems in the world. Even when the United States had been in the throes of a major crisis, Angelo had never experienced anything resembling a delay on the networks he so enjoyed hacking. This evening had been a relatively slow evening, with network traffic, if anything, being a bit lighter than the norm. So the young Chilean quickly dismissed this possibility.

This made his computer suspect. Perhaps, Angelo thought, it was time to run a diagnostic check of his system and clean up some old files, repair any fragmented sectors on his hard drive, and generally clean house. So, despite the late hour and his yearning for sleep, he leaned forward, pulled up his utility tools, and accessed the program.

Once the disk-repair routine was running, Angelo had little to do but sit back and watch. The images that flashed across his screen were, to Angelo, a bit silly. It showed a little figure, dressed in white with a red cross on his chest, turning a disk. Every now and then, the figure would stop, bend over, and give the appearance of examining a spot on the disk. After a second, the figure would straighten up and continue his search for another "injured" disk sector. Angelo no more enjoyed watching this mundane sequence than he did sitting before a television screen displaying a test pattern. Yet like the late-night viewer too tired to sleep, the Chilean continued to stare at his screen. Even the fact that the little stick figure before his eyes was going about its mindless chores slowly and with jerky motions couldn't shake Angelo from his inattention.

In was in this semiconscious, almost hypnotic state that something utterly unexpected happened. The entire screen before him simply went blank. There was no flickering or shrinking of the image that is characteristic of a loss of power. Angelo did not hear the snapping that usually accompanies the tripping of the monitor's on-off switch. Nor was there a change in the steady hum of the computer itself that would have occurred if hit by a surge. One second the screen had been up and active. Then the next, it was pitch-black.

After blinking in an effort to clear the glaze from his eyes, Angelo stared dumbstruck at the unnatural blackness before him. Already troubled by the previous problem he had been attempting to resolve, this new development further confused the Chilean hacker. He was just beginning to wonder if the diagnostic tools that he had turned to were the cause of this calamity when, on the left-hand side of his screen, he saw a figure appear. The peculiar figure, attired from head to toe in green medieval armor and mounted on a barded horse, sported a long lance and carried a shield. Mesmerized, Angelo watched as the knight, measuring about two and a half centimeters, rode out into the center of his screen. Once there, the horse turned until the small green knight, lance still held at a forty-five-degree angle, was facing Angelo head-on. The figure paused only long enough to lower his lance and tuck his shield up closer to his body. Then, with a quick swing of his feet, the green knight spurred his mount and charged forward.

Fascinated, Angelo watched. While one part of his mind wondered where this image was coming from, another part of the young man's brain found itself captivated by the details of the computer-generated knight and its lifelike motions. As the virtual knight loomed closer and grew larger, more and more details were revealed. Quickly Angelo came to realize that the knight was not all green. Instead, the armor of the growing image before him began to blossom into a motley pattern of light greens, dark greens, browns, tans, and splotches of black, not at all unlike the camouflage pattern worn by modern combat soldiers. Even the bard protecting the knight's steed was adorned with the same pattern. Only the shield clinched by the charging knight failed to conform to this scheme. Rather, the shield's background was as black as the rest of the screen. Upon that field, at a diagonal, was the symbol of a silver lightning bolt, coursing its way from the upper right-hand corner almost down to the lower left. On one side of the bolt there was a yellow zero, on the other a one, numbers that represented the basic building blocks of all computer languages.

Completely engrossed by the video presentation, it took Angelo's mind far too long to realize that the advancing knight, filling more and more of the screen before him as it charged home, was not meant to be entertaining. Rather the symbol of military virtue, power, and untiring quests was the harbinger of disaster. When this horrible fact finally managed to seep its way into his conscious mind, the young Chilean all but leaped out of his chair, as if struck by a lighting bolt not at all unlike the one adorning the knight's grim, black shield. With a jerk he reached for the master power switch in a determined effort to crash his own system before the unheralded knight struck home and did whatever mischief its creator intended.

Had he been thinking straight, Angelo would have saved himself the trouble, accepted his fate calmly, and enjoyed the show. For the knight he saw was not the initiator of electronic doom, but rather a messenger sent forth from an implanted program within Angelo's machine to announce that a sequence of destruction designed to destroy the Chilean's toy had run its course. The South American hacker had been blindsided by an assault launched across the World Wide Web by another cyber combatant, a young boy not at all unlike himself. Like so many other intruders before, Angelo Castalano had been struck down by America's new front-line guardians, the Cyberknights of West Fort Hood.

Two

Virtual Heroes

The tunnels and chambers that honeycomb the hills of West Fort Hood had been built in another era. They had been part of a national effort to fight a foe that no longer existed, using weapons designed to be delivered by aircraft and missiles that had been relegated to museums. In underground chambers encased by reinforced concrete, nuclear weapons had been stored and assembled before being wheeled out onto the tarmac of the adjoining airfield, where the city-killing devices were hosted in the waiting bomb bays of B-47s. For many years the people of the United States had depended on those bombers to stand guard and protect them from foreign intruders. In time new weapons, weapons that were more precise, more advanced, replaced the free-fall bombs that had once been hidden away under the scrub-covered hills of West Fort Hood.

Strangely, the usefulness of the facilities that had been little more than storerooms during the Cold War long outlasted the weapons system they had been created to house. When the bombers had flown off for the last time, and the bombs themselves moved to other underground bunkers, new occupants moved into the spaces left behind.

This subterranean world had much going for it. For one thing, the earth and rock that concealed the underground work spaces created a constant environment and temperature. Other than providing a steady flow of fresh air, little needed to be invested in the heating or cooling of the facility to a round-the-clock temperature of just under seventy degrees. For those who have not had the opportunity to enjoy the month of August in Texas, this was a very big plus. Nor did people need to concern themselves a great deal with physical upkeep. There were, after all, no lawns, walkways, windows, or exterior walls that needed to be tended to. Even the interior was rather robust and carefree. The baby-shit green glazed tiles that covered the walls, while monotonous and difficult to work with, made painting all but unnecessary. There were, of course, issues and difficulties that were well-nigh impossible to overcome. For one thing, the all-male draftee Air Force of the early 1950s had far different ideas about the minimum requirements when it came to the latrines than did the mixed workforce that followed them in later decades. And when it came to updating the electrical web that supplied power to everything from the overhead lights to high-speed computers, architects and engineers first found themselves having to redefine the meaning of creativity.

The attraction of the underground complex, however, went beyond these concerns over simple creature comfort. The very nature of the facility made access difficult. Since there were so few outlets, movement into and out of the underground complex could be readily controlled. The access tunnels which did connect the outside world to the work spaces within were long, straight, unobstructed, and narrow. This permitted security personnel manning the checkpoints at both ends of these tunnels clean fields of fire. The posts themselves, holdovers from the days when top-secret weapons had been stored there, were in fact bunkers. From behind bulletproof glass and using gun ports designed to sweep the entire length of the tunnel as well as the area immediately outside, the military police on duty could employ their automatic weapons to deny entrance into the complex completely.

This tight control extended to more than the coming and going of those who occupied the complex. Electronic equipment operated within the underground chambers was protected by the same dirt and rock that provided the humans who operated it with a comfortable environment. While not impossible, efforts to eavesdrop electronically from the outside were complicated. Nor could electronic emissions from computers escape, except though the cabling that provided power and communications from the outside world. To prevent this, filters and sophisticated countermeasures at selected points along the wiring leaving the complex denied unauthorized monitoring and filtered out emissions. If the powers that be wanted to, the entire complex could be shut down and isolated in every way imaginable.

Isolation, however, was not part of the charter for those who currently occupied the West Fort Hood complex, known by its occupants as the Keep. Quite to the contrary. From clusters of workstations that numbered anywhere from four to eight, young men and women sat before state-of-the-art computers, following the day-to-day activities of computer operators throughout the entire United States Army. With the twirl of a trackball and the click of a button, the cybersnoops at West Fort Hood could pull up the screen of any Army computer that was plugged into the World Wide Web or one of a dozen closed-loop systems used by units that handled hypersensitive material. Everything the unsuspecting computer operators "out there" did and saw on their machines could be monitored, recorded, and studied from the complex.

While the on-screen antics of some of the Army personnel and the civilians who work alongside of them in cyberspace could be entertaining, the residents of the subterranean labyrinths were not concerned with them. Rather, they searched the Army's network of computers in search of those who did not belong there, young hackers from the outside like Angelo Castalano who used their computers to generate electronic mischief and mayhem on systems the Army depended upon to keep itself going. This, of course, was nothing new and far from being a secret. The hunting down and tracking of unauthorized intrusions into an organization's computer system by the government and civilian businesses was practiced universally.

What made the West Fort Hood cybersleuths different than that of other, more mainstream agencies was what they did once they latched on to someone fiddling about in an Army computer. The computer geeks of the FBI, CIA, NSA, Secret Service, banks, and corporations all relied on laws, both federal and international, or protective countermeasures to deal with violators they came across. While this was usually sufficient to do the job, the use of established courts to punish or end unauthorized intrusions and electronic vandalism took time. In some cases, the lack of laws or a foreign nation's inability to enforce existing laws made retribution impossible. And there were more than a few instances where the nature of the violation demanded an immediate response.

It was to provide the United States Army with the ability to deliver that response that 401st Signal Detachment was created. Sporting a simple black unit crest with nothing but a zero and a one separated by a lightning bolt, personnel assigned to the 401st went about their assigned duties without fanfare. Together this collection of intelligence analysts, computer experts, and hackers stationed at West Fort Hood was rather unspectacular. The didn't sport a beret, worn at a jaunty angle. Nor did they wear a special skills qualifications badge over the upper left pocket of their rumpled BDUs like that given out to paratroopers, expert infantrymen, or combat medics. To those who did not have a security clearance sufficient to read the unit's mission statement, it appeared that the 401st was simply another combat service support unit swelling the ranks of the Army that already had far too much tail and not near enough teeth.

Only a handful of senior officers in the Army knew that this was just not so. The 401st provided neither service nor support. It had teeth, real teeth and a mandate to use them. For the fangs that the 401st sported had not been created to serve as a show of force or deterrent. Unlike their more conventional counterparts, the computer hackers who wore the black "Oh Slash One" crest had but one mode of operation: attack. Collectively known as Cyberknights, their charter was not only to find intruders, but to strike back using every means possible. The motto adopted by this quiet little unit pretty much summed it all up in three words, "Seek, Strike, Destroy."

From their small workstations tucked away in casements where nuclear weapons once sat, the Cyberknights of the 401st went about their task with enthusiasm. For many of the young men and women assigned to the unit, this was the ultimate in jobs, a nonstop video game played against a foe that was always different, and just as articulate as they in the ways of cyberspace. Most of the "foot soldiers" belonging to the 401st were in their early twenties. With few exceptions they had been recruited by the Army on campuses of America's most prestigious universities and colleges. The typical candidates targeted to fill the ranks of the cyberwarfare unit were well-educated students who had more ability than they did drive, ambition, and money. Better than half had been on academic probation when the recruiter from the 401st approached them. Faced with the prospect of being cast out into the real world, where they would not have a degree to help them find a job sufficient to pay off student loans and credit-card debt they had accumulated along the way, the Army's offer was a lifeline.

Without fanfare and often without the knowledge of the administration of the campus on which the recruiting was taking place, the FBI scanned records to detect discrepancies between the potential of students enrolled in computer-engineering courses and their actual performance. When prospective candidates were found, discreet inquiries were made into the habits of the student as well as the reasons for the poor academic showing. When a student matched the profile the 401st had established as being susceptible to what it had to offer, the action was passed off to the administrative branch of the 401st which dispatched one of its recruiters. These officers tracked down the candidate and made offers few in their positions could refuse.

Some in the unit's chain of command disapproved of the procurement practices. Older officers who had been educated at West Point and had proudly served their nation for years without compromising the ethical values which that institution took pains to instill saw the methods used to induce young people at risk to join the 401st as rather predatory, a tad intrusive, and a shade too far over the line that separates that which is legal and that which is not. Few of the former students, however, complained. Plucked out of college just when things in their tender young lives could not have gotten any bleaker, they were offered an academic version of a golden parachute. In exchange for a three-year obligation, debt they had incurred during their ill-fated academic pursuit of excellence would disappear in the twinkling of an eye. While that alone would have been sufficient to bring over a number of prospective recruits, the Army offered more, much more. To start with, there was a tax-free, five-figure cash bonus paid up front. Coupled with this windfall was a college fund that grew with each year of honorable service. And for those who had trepidation about shouldering a rifle or slogging through the mud, a promise that their nights would be spent between two sheets and not standing a watch in a country whose name they could not pronounce was more than enough.

In most cases, however, such inducements were unnecessary once the new members of the 401st entered the Keep. To young men and women who had learned to read while cruising the World Wide Web, the Keep was a virtual wonderland, a field of dreams for cyberpunks and hackers. A flexible budget and a policy that permitted the unit's automation officer to ignore normal Army procurement procedures ensured that the Cyberknights were well equipped with state-of-the-art systems. Once they were on the job, the new Cyberknights employed every cutting-edge technology and program available, not to mention a few that were little more than a glimmer on the horizon in the world outside. This last benefit came via a close relationship the 401st maintained with both the NSA and the CIA. This gave the equipment and technologies procurement section of the 401st access to whatever those agencies had, both in terms of equipment and techniques.

While the Keep was, for the Cyberknights, akin to a dream come true, not everyone found their assignment to the 401st to their liking. As he trudged his way down the long tunnel en route to his office located at the heart of the Keep, Colonel Kevin Shrewsbery tried hard not to think about his command.

An infantry officer with an impeccable record and a shot at the stars of a general, his selection to command the 401st had come as a shock.

The mere fact that neither he nor any of his peers in NATO headquarters in Belgium had heard of the 401st when his orders had come in assigning him to that post should have been a warning. "What the hell are you people doing?" he yelled over the phone to his career-management officer at Army Personnel Command. "Whose brilliant idea was it to assign me to command a signal detachment? What happened to the brigade at Bragg I was promised?"

Equally ignorant of what, exactly, the 401st was, the personnel officer could only fumble about in search for an explanation. "You were asked for by name," he replied to the enraged colonel on the other end of the line. "The request for orders assigning you to the 401st was submitted by the Deputy Chief of Staff for Special Operations himself."

Rather than mollify the irate colonel, this response only served to confuse the issue. In the Army, young up-and-coming officers that bear watching are tagged at an early stage in their careers. The field from which a future Chief of Staff of the Army is chosen is pretty much narrowed down to a select few by the time the rank of major is achieved. Those who have a real shot at that coveted position are usually taken under the wings of a more senior officer, an officer who can guide the Chief of Staff of the Army in waiting along the maze of peacetime career assignments that are mandatory checkpoints. This senior officer, known as a rabbi in the Old Army, ensures that all the right buttons are pushed, and all the right tickets are punched by his charge in order to ensure that his candidate wins the four-star lottery.

Major General William Norton, the current Deputy Chief of Staff for Special Operations, was Shrewsbery's rabbi. So it was not surprising that the designated commander of the 401st took the unprecedented step of calling Norton at his home at the earliest opportunity. With as much respect and deference as circumstances would permit, Shrewsbery pleaded his case. "Sir, I have never questioned your wisdom or judgment. But assignment to a signal unit? What is this all about?"

Since the phone line was a private home phone and not secure, Norton could not tell his protégé a great deal. "Kevin," the general stated in a tone that conveyed a firmness that could not be missed, "the Army is changing. The world of special operations and the manner in which we wage war is changing. In order to advance in the Army today, you must ride the wave of change, or be crushed beneath it." While all of this was sound advice, advice that he had heard time and time again, neither Norton's words or the fact that he, Shrewsbery, would be reporting directly to Norton himself while commanding the 401st did much allay the colonel's concerns. His heart had been set on a parachute infantry brigade. Though considered by many an outdated twentieth-century anachronism, the command of a whole airborne brigade was his dream assignment, a dream that now was beyond his grasp.

That was the first chip on Shrewsbery's square shoulders. As time went on, more would accumulate until it seemed, to Shrewsbery, that he would be unable to walk along the long access tunnels leading into the Keep without bending over.

If there had been a casual observer, one who had the freedom and the security clearance necessary to stand back and look at the 401st from top to bottom and make an objective evaluation of the unit, they would have compared it to a piece of old cloth. In the center, at its core where Shrewsbery sat, the fabric retained its old structure. The pattern of the cloth could be easily recognized and matched to the original bolt from which it was cut. But as you moved away from the center, out toward the edges, the fabric began to unravel, losing its tight weave, some of its strength, and as well as the neatly regimented pattern.

Around the center the observer would see an area populated by the 401st support staff. The recruiters who provided manpower for the unit were assigned here, as were the technocrats who maintained and modified the computers and networks that the Cyberknights used. These staffers liked to think of themselves as the Lords of Gadgets. The Cyberknights called them the stableboys. Also counted as part of the support staff was the intelligence section. While not the equal of the knights in the scheme of things, it was the wizards behind the green door who did much of the seeking.

The intelligence section worked in its own series of tunnels, isolated from the rest of the complex by a series of green doors, a quaint habit the Army's intelligence types had adopted years ago. There they took the first steps in developing a product that could be used by the operations section and, if necessary, the Cyberknights themselves. Rare information concerning computer hacks on military systems was funneled to them from throughout the Army. Once deposited behind the green doors, the intelligence analysts studied each case handed off to them for action. They looked at the incident and compared it to similar events they had come across in the past in an effort to determine if the intruder was a newbie, or someone that the 401st had met before in cyberspace. Next the analysts were expected to make a judgment call, based in part upon the facts they had on hand, and in part on intuition, as to the nature of the hack.

By the time one reached the edges of the material, the original color and pattern could no longer be discerned. All that one could see were individual strands, frayed ends that were barely connected to the cloth. Each strand, upon closer inspection, was different. Each had a distinct character that little resembled the tightly woven and well-regimented strands that made up the center. Yet it was there, among these strands, where the real work of the 401st took place. For these strands were the Cyberknights, the young men and women who sallied out, into cyberspace, day in and day out to engage their nation's foes. And while the terms these Cyberknights used were borrowed from computer games, and the skirmishes they fought with their foes were in a virtual world, the consequences of their actions were very, very real.

While Colonel Kevin Shrewsbery settled in for another long day, Eric Bergeron was in the process of wrapping up his shift. In many ways Eric was the typical Cyberknight. At age twenty-five he had spent five years at Purdue in an unsuccessful pursuit of a degree in computer science. Rail-thin, his issued BDUs hung from him as they would from a hanger, making it all but impossible for him create anything resembling what the Army had in mind when they coined the term "ideal soldier." Being a Cyberknight, young Bergeron did nothing to achieve that standard. His hair was always a bit longer than regulations permitted. The only time there was a shine on his boots was when he splashed through a puddle and the wet footgear caught a glint of sunlight. Only his baby-fine facial hair saved him from having to fight a daily hassle over the issue of shaving.

Making his way along one of the numerous interior corridors of the Keep, Eric didn't acknowledge any of the people he passed. He neither said hello nor bothered to nod to anyone he encountered on his way to the small, Spartan break room. It wasn't that he was rude or that he didn't know the names of those he came across. Rather, his thoughts were someplace else. Like most of the Keep's population, Eric's mind was turning a technical problem over and over again. At the moment he was going over his last engagement. Though he had triumphed, it had taken him far too long to ride down the kid in Valparaiso, Chile. This had brought into question his skills, which he took great pride in, as did most of the Cyberknights. This was a far greater motivational factor than all the inducements that had been showered upon them to secure their enlistments or the official rating they all received periodically.

Recognizing the *Lost in Space* stare, Captain Brittany Kutter waited until Eric was almost right on top of her before she called out to him. "Specialist Bergeron?"

Startled, Eric stopped dead in his tracks and looked around. "Yes?"

When she was sure she had his attention, Kutter stepped up to the befuddled Cyberknight. Flashing the same engaging smile she used when she was about to ask someone a favor that was, in reality, an order,

Kutter motioned with her right hand toward a rather forlorn figure who stood behind her. "I know you've just finished a long shift, Specialist Bergeron, but would it be possible to show a newly assigned member of the unit around the complex while I find out where he will be assigned?"

Eric made no effort to hide his feelings. He hated it when people like the captain before him assigned his tasks in this manner. Why in the hell, he thought, didn't they just behave the way soldiers are supposed to, like the colonel, God bless his little black heart.

Stepping forward, the young man who had been following the female captain reached out, hesitantly, with his right hand. "My name is Hamud Mdilla. I am sorry to be of bother, but . . ."

Realizing what he had done, Eric managed to muster up a smile. "Oh, please. No bother at all."

Taking advantage of the moment, Kutter broadened her smile as she stepped away. "Well, I'll let you two go. When you're finished, come by my office."

Eric waited until he was sure that she was out of earshot before he spoke again. "You'd think," he mumbled, "they'd drop all their phony pretenses once they've reeled in their latest catch and start acting like normal human beings."

This comment offended Hamud. "I am sure that the young captain is more sincere than you give her credit for."

Looking over at the newly recruited Cyberknight, Eric smirked. "Yeah, right." Then, with a nod, the veteran stepped off. "Come on. I'll give you a Q and D."

New to the Army, Hamud hesitated. "Excuse me?"

"Q and D," Eric explained. "Quick and dirty. I'll show you around."

Though the tour was an impromptu one, Eric executed his assignment using the same methodical approach he used when dealing with any issue. As he did so, he engaged the new Cyberknight in conversation. In part, this was to ease the tension that their awkward introduction had created. But Eric also took advantage of this opportunity to probe and take a measure of Hamud's abilities. For even though the foes the Army wanted them to seek out and destroy were the ones lurking about in cyberspace, the Cyberknights engaged in an in-house competition that pitted one against another.

"So," Eric chirped. "Where'd they find you?"

"MIT," Hamud stated glumly. "I was in my third year there."

"MIT! Wow. I am humbled in your presence."

Glancing over at his rumpled guide, Hamud wasn't sure if he was being mocked. "Yes, well, it sounds more impressive than it is."

"The best I could do was a few years at Purdue before I reached the end of the line," Eric countered. "The credit line, that is."

Use of experienced Cyberknights to take newly assigned members of the unit was a practice that Colonel Shrewsbery had introduced. He figured that these soldiers, for all their shortcomings, were no different than any others in the Army. The old hand, he reasoned, would do more than show the 'cruit his way around. He would use the opportunity to lord it over the newbie, to demonstrate his superior knowledge as well as brag about his accomplishments. In this way the new man would have an opportunity to gain insights that a nontechno type could not hope to pass on.

"Not every assault on the Army's network poses the same threat," Eric explained as they wandered about the section of the Keep where the wizards of intelligence sorted through incoming material. "And not everyone who breaches security systems does so for the same reason. Most of the intruders are pretty much like us, young cyberpunks with more time and equipment on their hands than smarts."

Nodding, Hamud listened, though he had never considered himself to be a cyberpunk and very much resented being lumped together with them.

"They utilize their personal high-speed computers and the World Wide Web to wreak havoc on unsuspecting sites for any number of reasons," Bergeron continued. "The sociologists assigned to the unit say most of them are young people harboring feelings of being disenfranchised by whatever society they live in. They use their equipment, given to them by dear old Mom and Dad, to vandalize the very society which their parents so cherish. Of all the intruders that violate Army systems these hackers, known collectively as gremlins, are rated as being the lowest threat to the system as a whole, and generally rate a low priority when it comes to tracking them."

"But they can still cause a great deal of damage, can't they?" Hamud asked.

"Oh, of course," Eric replied as he led Hamud to the next stop. "But nine times out of ten they have neither the expertise, the number-crunching power, or the persistence to crack the really tough security used to protect mission-essential systems."

"The Vikings," Eric stated with a wicked smile as he moved on to the next stop along the tour, "are a different story. They're organized in bands. With their superior organization and, in the main, better equipment they can mount a serious and sustained offensive against the Army's computers. Their ability to network, exchange information, refine techniques, and share insights coupled with an ability to strike along multiple routes using multiple systems simultaneously makes them far more lethal than gremlins. The more vicious bands of Vikings can crash all but the Army's most secure sites." Pausing, Eric turned and looked at Hamud. "But that doesn't keep them from trying."

"Are they all just vandals?" Hamud asked. "Or are some politically motivated?"

"If by political motivation," Eric answered cautiously, "you are referring to terrorist groups, the answer is yes. Though the intel wizards seldom tell us everything, it doesn't take a genius to figure out why the people we are assigned to take down are making the hack."

Pausing, Eric cocked his head as if mulling over a thought. "Of course, there have been instances where a band of relatively harmless Vikings has been hijacked by someone who was, as you say, politically motivated."

Having no qualms about showing his ignorance, Hamud shrugged. "Hijacked?"

"Yes, hijacked," Eric explained as he resumed his tour. "We refer to politically motivated hackers who work for foreign groups or nations as dark knights. Normally, they will operate out of their own facilities, some of which are probably not at all unlike this place. But on occasion a dark knight will search the web for an unattached band of Vikings. By various means of subterfuge or deception, these roaming dark knights, or DKs, work their way into the targeted band. Often, they use bribes such as techniques that he hasn't observed the Viking band he's been tracking use as a means of worming his way into the targeted band's good graces."

When he heard this, Hamud's pace slowed. Turning, Eric saw a pained expression on the new recruit's face. Knowing full well what that meant, the veteran Cyberknight smiled and waved his right hand in the air. "Oh, I wouldn't worry. We've all been duped by some predatory sack of shit. Just make sure you don't get sucked in here."

Forcing a sickly smile, Hamud nodded. "Yes, I can appreciate that."

"Now the DKs," Eric went on as he picked up both his conversation and tour where he had left off, "can be quite vicious. Unlike the gremlins and lesser Viking bands, most DKs and the war bands they belong to have unlimited funds. That means they can not only buy the best that's out there, but even when we fry their little brains, it's only a matter of time before they come back, but only smarter and better prepared for battle."

"So what do you do then?" Hamud asked innocently.

"Then," Eric shouted, thrusting his right arm up, index finger pointed toward the ceiling as if he were signaling a charge, "we have ourselves some real fun."

Three

www.quest

With growing reluctance, Lieutenant Colonel James Mann glanced down at his fuel gauge. In his sixteen years in the United States Air Force, he had never seen that particular indicator dip so low. Drawing in a deep breath, he struggled to control his emotions as he pressed the PUSH TO TALK button. “Quebec Seven Nine, Quebec Seven Nine. This is Tango Eight Four, over.” After releasing the PUSH TO TALK button, Mann stared out of the cockpit of his F-16, vainly searching the night sky as he waited for a response from the KC-10 aerial refuelers using the call signs Quebec Seven Nine.

After what seemed to be an eternity, Mann called out without bothering to use call signs. “Does anyone out there see anything that looks like a tanker?”

At first no one answered as five other pilots craned their necks and searched the black sky that made their isolation seem even more oppressive, more ominous. Finally, Mann’s own wingman came back with the response no one wanted to hear. “Boss, looks like someone missed the mark.”

Rather than respond, Mann flipped through the notes he had taken during their preflight briefing. When he found what he was looking for, he glanced up at his navigational aids. The coordinates, the time, the radio frequency upon which they were to make contact with the tankers all matched. Everything was exactly as it was supposed to be. Everything. Yet, there were no KC-10s out there waiting to greet them with the fuel they would need to complete their nonstop flight to Saudi Arabia.

In the midst of checking and rechecking all his settings on the aircraft's navigational system, another voice came over the air. "Colonel, I'll be sucking fumes in a few. Maybe it's time we start making some noise."

Mann didn't answer. The deployment of his unit was part of a major buildup in southwest Asia in response to threats being directed against the Saudi government. With the exception of conversations between themselves and the aerial tanks, strict radio listening silence was the order of the day. The arrival of the air wing that Mann's flight belonged to was meant to be a surprise to the local despot. "We're going to come swooping down on that little shit," their wing commander told his pilots at their final briefing, "like a flock of eagles on a swarm of field mice." Now, as he peered out into the darkness, Mann accepted the horrible fact that the only thing he and his companions would be swooping down to was the cold, dark Atlantic below. Even if the tankers did show up in the next few minutes, which he doubted, there would be insufficient time to go through the drill and refuel all of the aircraft in the flight. Some, if not all of them, would have to ditch.

Faced with this awful truth, Mann prepared to issue an order that went against his every instinct. "Roger that," he finally responded with a heavy sigh. "Everyone is to switch over to the emergency frequency following this transmission. Though I know some of you will be able to go on for a while, I don't want to make it any harder for search and rescue than it already is. As soon as the first plane goes in, we'll circle around him and maintain as tight an orbit over that spot as we can. Acknowledge, over."

One by one, the other pilots in Mann's flight came back with a low, barely audible "Roger." With that, the Air Force colonel gave the order to flip to the designated emergency frequency and began broadcasting his distress call.

Even before the last aircraft belonging to Lieutenant Colonel James Mann began its final spiral into the dark sea below, frantic efforts to sort out the pending disaster were already under way. When the Kansas National Guard KC-10 tanker failed to rendezvous with Mann's F-16s at the designated time, the commander of that aircraft contacted operations. A commercial pilot by trade, the tanker's commander was less concerned with the operational security than he was with the lives he knew were in the balance.

Back at Dover Air Base, from which the KC-10 had been scrambled for this mission, a staff officer pulled up the tasking orders on his computer screen that had dispatched the KC-10. As the pilot of the tanker continued to orbit at the prescribed altitude, over the exact spot he had been sent to, he waited for the operations officer to confirm that they were in the right spot. Unable to stand the tension, his copilot broke the silence. "That yahoo back in Dover better get a hustle on or there's going to be a lot of unhappy Falcon drivers out here with nowhere to land."

From behind them the navigator glanced down on a sheet of paper he had been making some calculations on. After checking his watch, he cleared his throat. "I'm afraid it's already too late."

Both the pilot and copilot of the KC-10 turned and looked at him. In return, the navigator stared at the pilot. "What now, sir?"

The commander of the tanker had no answer. Without a word he looked away.

When he reached his workstation to begin his shift, Eric Bergeron didn't bother to sit down. Posted in the center of his screen was an international orange sticky note. The reliance of some members of the 401st on such a primitive means of communications caused the young hacker to chuckle. Even in an organization whose whole existence centered on keeping a sophisticated communications network functioning properly, there were many who didn't trust it. Of course, Eric thought to himself as he pulled the note off and read it, after seeing what people like the ones he hunted down could do, he really couldn't blame them.

From his little cubicle next to Bergeron's, Bobby Sung leaned back in his seat until he could see around the divider. "I see you've been zapped by the overlords."

Waving the sticky note about, Eric nodded as he gathered up a notebook he kept next to his computer monitor. "Yes, I have been summoned." In the parlance of the 401st, the overlords were the operations officers, the men and women who assigned the Cyberknights their missions, which the knights themselves referred to as quests. The orange sticky note, reserved for use by the operations section, indicated that this was a priority mission.

"Well then," Sung stated as he made a shooing motion with his hands, "begone with you, oh wretched soul."

Bending over, Eric contorted his expression. Then he did his best to imitate Dr. Frankenstein's deformed assistant as he limped away, grunting as he went, "Yes, master. Coming, master."

In a small briefing room tucked away in one of the numerous casements that sprouted off of the long internal tunnel of the Keep populated by the unit's operations section, Eric met with several members of the staff as well as some outlanders. The conniving officer was no less than the chief of the unit's operations section himself, Major Peter Hines, a name that caused him much grief in an organization with more than its fair share of irreverent cynics. He sat at the head of the long, narrow table in accordance with the military protocol that the regular Army staff stubbornly clung to.

Seated to the major's right, along one length of the table, was the Queen of the Wizards, a title bestowed upon Major Gayle Rhay, chief of the intel section. To her left were the outlanders, outsiders who were not members of the 401st. They wore the typical bureaucratic camouflage that all visitors from Washington, D.C., favored, dark suits and tightly knotted nondescript ties. Farther along that side of the table was an Air Force colonel. That this senior an officer was placed to the left of the pair in civilian attire clued Eric to the fact that the outlanders were pretty well up there on the government's pay scale.

The presence of the outlanders and the officer from a sister service was not at all unusual. Oftentimes the 401st handled a high-priority mission that originated within another service or government agency. What was disconcerting to the young hacker was the presence of the Master of the Keep himself, Colonel Shrewsbery. Seated away from the table against the wall, Shrewsbery was situated in such a manner that only Hines could see him without having to turn his head. Eric had noted that Shrewsbery often did this when one of his subordinates was running a meeting or briefing that he wanted to attend but not, officially, participate in. During the course of the proceedings the chair of the meeting would glance over to wherever Shrewsbery had placed himself, checking for subtle signals from the colonel. There was, Eric concluded long ago, a sort of mental telepathy used by the careerists within the unit that neither he nor any of the other Cyberknights were privy to. Not that he wanted to be part of that strange clique.

Without preamble, Major Hines launched into his presentation. "Our records show, Specialist Bergeron, that you have engaged a DK using the screen name longbow."

Without having to look, Eric knew that the major's use of the term "DK" had caused Shrewsbery to grimace. Despite the fact that the colonel had been with the 401st for the better part of a year, the terms his staff resorted to when dealing with Cyberknights still irked him. To him it was unprofessional to indulge in the video game terminology the Cyberknights favored. Still, like every professional officer who entered the Keep, he adapted.

"Twice," Eric corrected Hines. "Once just last week during our quest against the X Legion down in South America, and a few months ago when he was working with Der Leibstandart in Germany."

"Yes," the major stated, annoyed that he had been interrupted. "I know." Leaning forward, Hines folded his hands on the table in front of him. "Well, he's back."

Now it was Eric's turn to be surprised. "So soon?" Not that this was unexpected. The Cyberknights themselves had reached a consensus after their second run-in with him that longbow was a DK working for a national-level interest. That he was back already, after only a week, confirmed speculation that had been bantered about between the Cyberknights that this particularly bothersome Dark Knight had access to funds and equipment that only a well-financed organization could provide.

Using a pause to break into the conversation, Gayle Rhay provided some additional information. "He's currently using the screen name 'macnife' and, for the first time, making the hacks himself. Yesterday he hit the Air Force."

Looking over at the rep from that service, Eric noted that the Air Force colonel was avoiding eye-to-eye contact with anyone.

Eric was quick to appreciate that the new screen name was a feeble attempt to cyberize the character's name from the song "Mack the Knife." Nor did he entertain any doubt that macnife and longbow were one and the same person. The one thing that he had learned during his tenure with the 401st was that when the military, the CIA, and the NSA were able to put aside their petty turf battles and pool their combined intelligence assets, no one and nothing could get by them. Even the most sophisticated hacker, exercising the greatest of care, left tracks that were both distinct and traceable.

To start with, a hacker tends to use the same system and computer language. Though he may be familiar with many different types, like an auto mechanic he can't be an expert on every system out there. So he specializes. Nor could he change his ways. As with the mechanic, every hacker has a repertoire of tools that he uses when breaking into a system and while rooting about in it. The sequence in which he employs these tools and the manner in which he operates when confronted by security systems may vary some, but not so much that they cannot be used to assist in pegging who's engaged in making the break-in. It was this particular trait that alerted the 401st that longbow was behind the hacks made by the X Legion, for the novice hackers of that Viking band slavishly mimicked everything longbow taught them. "It's like watching half a dozen junior longbows," an intel Wizard told Eric when they were preparing for that counterhack.

Even more insidious, in the eyes of a hacker, was the ability of intelligence agencies such as the NSA to ID an individual by simply studying the speed and manner in which someone typed. It was far more involved than just counting the number of keystrokes someone makes within a given period of time. Certain irregularities, such as the habit of misspelling the same word, or the use of a certain phrase, tagged an individual as surely as his or her own fingerprints. With the enormous number-crunching ability of the NSA, the American intelligence community had the capability to run the record of a hack through their library of past attacks and look for a match. No doubt, Eric thought as he listened to the briefing, longbow and all his past activities had been puked out as soon as they had done this, just as his own would if he were the target of such close scrutiny.

"He managed," Rhay continued, "to change the mission tasking orders for a deploying flight of aircraft."

"The F-16s," Eric chirped with glee as if he had just guessed the right answer to a pop quiz. Then, when he belatedly remembered that all six pilots were still missing and assumed dead, the Cyberknight's expression changed. "He did that?"

From across the table, one of the outlanders joined in. "The administration considers this attack to be nothing less than an act of war." He made this statement using the sanctimonious tone that many from inside the Beltway seemed to favor when dealing with a flyover person. "As such, the President has directed that the National Security Council come up with an immediate and proportional response."

In an effort to regain control of the meeting, Hines cleared his throat as he looked over at Rhay and the two outlanders, using a spiteful glance as he did so to warn them to back off. When he was ready, the ops major took up the briefing. "That's going to be your mission, Specialist."

Given the events that had brought this about, Eric did his best to hide his excitement. Still, he could see something big was in the offing. "Will this be a duel?"

In Cyberknight speak, a duel was a one-on-one confrontation between one of their own and a dark knight.

Shaking his head, Hines continued. "No, not in the traditional sense."

Leaning back in his seat, Eric eyed Hines and the array of faces across the table from him. "You tagged me because I am familiar with longbow, yet you don't want me to go head-to-head with him. Explain, please."

"It is obvious," the older of the two outlanders stated, "that not only is this character very, very good, but he has the backing of a very robust and well-financed support system. This makes him a very dangerous threat, since each run-in serves to enhance both his reputation and his experience level."

The second outlander picked up the thought. "Since we can't seem to terminate this particular hacker by direct means, we have been given the mission of finding another way of putting an end to his career."

Like a wrestling tag team, the older outlander took over. "We hit upon the idea of discrediting this hacker, now operating under the name 'macnife.' "

Looking back and forth between the pair of unnamed outlanders, Eric shrugged. "How do *we* plan to do that?"

Used to working with the Cyberknights and the way they could become quite unruly if allowed to, Major Gayle Rhay cut in. "We are fairly confident that another nation is using macnife, formerly known as longbow, and his nation as a surrogate, a platform from which to strike at the United States."

"Other than raising hell and poking the tiger," Eric asked, "what's their motivation?"

"The second party, the one supplying equipment and funding to macnife's nation for his use, may be doing so in an effort to test our computer security and try new techniques on us," the intelligence officer explained. "By going through a surrogate, the second party nation is able to gain valuable experience without having to expose its own nation's cyberwarfare capability to countermeasures or foreign intelligence agencies."

"Huh," Eric grunted. "Sounds like a Tom Clancy plot."

"Were this not actually taking place," Rhay replied, "it would make a rousing good read. But unlike a technothriller, we can't be sure the good guys are going to win."

Unable to restrain himself, Eric began to grin. "So, you've come to me, the Indiana Jones of cyberwarfare. What, exactly, is it you want me to do this time?"

Without any noticeable objections from Major Hines, the older of the two outlanders gave Eric a quick, thumbnail sketch of what the operation would entail. "You will begin the operation by breaking into the system used by macnife. Once there, you must establish yourself as the root, preferably without anyone noticing."

"Is there any other way?" Eric asked in mock innocence.

In unison, the two outlanders looked at each other, searching each other's expressions in an effort to determine if this was a serious question. Since neither was sure, the older outlander chose to ignore it and continue. "Now comes the hard part. Once in, you're to assume macnife's identity. Using his own system, you're to access several computer systems within the nation that has been supporting macnife's adventures."

"The object here," the second outlander stated in a crisp, monotone voice, "is to create suspicion and distrust."

"I see," Eric replied as he reflected upon the implications. "By making the supplier think that macnife is using their own equipment against them, you're hoping to break this unholy alliance."

"Exactly," the older outlander stated. "Otherwise, the cycle will simply repeat itself, with macnife becoming smarter and the nation supplying the equipment and funding getting away scot-free."

"Do you folks have any specific targets in mind?" Eric asked as his enthusiasm for this operation continued to mount.

"We have been assigned two targets," Major Hines stated as he finally found an opportunity to elbow his way back into the briefing he was chairing. "The first hack is the supporting nation's cyberwarfare center. We want you to get inside the system there and see what you can find."

Excited, Eric blurted out his questions as he thought of them. "Is this a simple snoop and scoot?"

"If possible," Hines stated, annoyed at the interruption, "we want you to plant a Trojan horse, which the NSA rep will provide you with."

To hackers, a Trojan horse is an implanted code or program that runs an operation or performs functions that the host computer user is unaware of or alters an existing program so that the original functions do not behave as they were intended to. If done well, a Trojan is all but impossible to find and can totally corrupt the original program.

"Okay, so far, this sounds like a piece of cake," Eric quipped.

Again, the two outlanders turned to face each other before continuing. "The second hack is a straight-out attack against a chemical plant located within the supporting nation."

Suddenly, Eric's tone changed. "A denial of service attack?" he asked cautiously.

"No," the older outlander stated without betraying any emotion. "The objective of this hack is destruction. Whether this can be best achieved by altering settings or by incapacitating automated safety protocols will be determined once you're into their system. It's the results that matter."

It was more than the words that caused the hairs on Eric's neck to bristle. It was the cold, unemotional manner in which the outlander mouthed them that bothered the Cyberknight. "If it's a chemical plant," the young hacker stated cautiously, "then we're talking serious roadkill. Aren't we?"

Though they never saw it up close and personal, the loss of human life as a result of their hacks, referred to as roadkill, bothered even the most hardened Cyberknight. So long as there was no blood shed as a direct result of their activities, the young hackers belonging to the 401st could engage in a bit of self-deluding disassociation. But once that line was crossed, once they became aware that their activities, if successful, would produce death, many a Cyberknight hesitated. On more than one occasion, a Cyberknight even declined to execute an assigned task.

Realizing what was going on, Colonel Shrewsbery chose this moment to insert himself into the proceedings. "I am well aware of the fact, Specialist Bergeron," he stated in a gruff voice that commanded everyone's attention, "that you do not think of yourself as a soldier, at least not in the conventional sense."

Eric looked across the room and into the dark, unflinching eyes of the colonel. "I do not believe," the Cyberknight whispered, "in the taking of human life."

"Unfortunately," Shrewsbery countered without hesitation, "those who oppose us do not share that sentiment. While it would be wrong to characterize them all as monsters, let there be no doubt in your mind that they are willing to do whatever they need to in order to achieve their national goals." Pausing, Shrewsbery reached down, without breaking eye contact with Eric, and picked a newspaper off the floor. With an underhanded toss, he flung the paper on the table, faceup, in Eric's direction.

Reaching out, the young Cyberknight stopped it just before it slid off the table and into his lap. In bold print the paper announced that any hope of finding the F-16 pilots alive was waning. Below that banner headline was a photo of one of the pilots' wife, looking up into the empty sky, as she clutched a crying child to her side. As Eric read the caption accompanying the photo, Shrewsbery continued. "How many tears do you think the folks behind that hack shed?"

Looking up at the colonel, Eric's resolve hardened, but only for a moment. "I cannot speak for them, sir."

"I'm not asking you to, son," Shrewsbery replied as he moderated his tone. "All I am asking you to do is to do your best to keep that sort of thing from becoming a daily occurrence. While none of us can bring those pilots back, we damned sure can do something to protect those who are still out there, doing their duty, just like you."

Unable to find a suitable reply, Eric again looked at the photo before him. Then he lifted his eyes and looked over at the people gathered about the table. They were all staring at him, waiting for him to say something.

Glancing back at Shrewsbery, Eric found that he was barely able to contain his anger. How he hated it when someone like the colonel rubbed his nose in what he, and the other Cyberknights, really did. Eric knew that the 401st was not a video arcade. He understood, on an intellectual level, that his actions had very real consequences that affected very real people. He just didn't want to be reminded of this day in, day out. Like the bomber crews in World War II, the young Cyberknight managed, for the most part, to insulate himself from what he was doing. That's why he and all the other Cyberknights used the colorful terms they did. Such words hid the meaning of their actions. Nor did the Cyberknights allow themselves to think of their foes as real people. And, like the young men who had flown the planes that had smashed Coventry, flattened Dresden, and eradicated Hiroshima, once they had finished an action, they moved on. No need, he often found himself thinking, to bother himself about what lay behind in his wake. He was, after all, simply following orders. Let the people who generated those orders lose sleep over the price.

But every now and then, reality took a bite out of this cherished isolation. As the saying went in the Keep, even Disneyland has a cloudy day.

"Okay," Eric finally whispered as he took the newspaper before him and flipped it over. Mustering up as much enthusiasm as he could, he turned to face Major Hines. "Let's get it on."

Four

The Pit

The days when a high-school kid, parked in front of his computer in the comforts of his bedroom, could rain down death and distraction upon the world were gone. So was the Lone Ranger approach, especially within the 401st. When executing a major operation, known as a hack attack, the exercise had all the intricacies of a Broadway production. The room in which they made their attack was not as nearly as sophisticated as one would have imagined, though it did have more than its fair share of bells and whistles common to most government operations. Yet even these, like everything found in that room, nicknamed the Pit, had a purpose.

The Pit was isolated for reasons of security. The official name of the Pit, posted on the red door that separated it from the rest of the tunnel complex, was Discrete Strike Operations Center, or DSOC, pronounced "dee sock" by the operations staff. Within the DSOC were two chambers, the Pit itself, where the actual cyberattack would take place, and a second, in which observers, straphangers, and miscellaneous personnel not directly involved in the mechanics of the attack could watch via closed-circuit TV and dummy monitors. The Army staff called this the observation suite. The Cyberknights referred to it as the Spook Booth.

Whenever Eric Bergeron had been in the Pit it had always been dark. The only illumination in the room was that which was thrown off by the computer monitors located there and small reading lights at each workstation. Everything else was so dark that if asked by someone, he would be unable to tell them what color the walls were.

The furniture in the Pit was quite sparse, consisting of two long tables, one set upon a platform behind the other. Along one side of each table were armless chairs. These chairs faced a wall that was actually one huge screen that covered that surface from ceiling to floor. Both tables were fitted out with four computer workstations, though there were power trees bolted at either end of the tables and space to accommodate two more if required. Unlike the normal haunts where the Cyberknights went about their day-to-day activities, there were no dividers between the individual workstations. This was done to permit quick access, both verbal and nonverbal, between the members of the 401st at each of the tables. A person working at one position could easily reach in front of anyone to their left or right to pass on a handwritten note or sketch. Even though everyone in the strike center wore a headset with a tiny boom mike that permitted them to speak to other members of the team, it had been found that there were times when these notes worked best, especially when the personnel in the Pit didn't want those in the Spook Booth to know something.

Located at each of the eight permanent workstations was a computer. Each was set up to perform a discrete function during an attack. The primary assault computer, labeled PAC, was the center-right workstation on the front table. It was from this position that Eric Bergeron would make his way into macnife's computer, then on to those that ran the chemical plant located in the supporting nation. To Eric's immediate right sat the primary foreign language expert, or FLE. While much of the traffic on the World Wide Web was in English, many of the programs and protocols, especially those concerning security and safety, were written in the language of the actual user. Hence there was a need for someone to be there, at Eric's side, to translate in real time. These interpreters, recruited in much the same way as the Cyberknights were, had to be as computer savvy as the knights themselves. This was how Bobby Sung, a second-generation Chinese American, had made his way into the ranks of the Cyberknights. Since this hack attack would be going into the systems of two different nations, there was a second FLE located at a computer at the right end of the table, set up at the overflow slot.

The left-center workstation belonged to the systems expert, or SE. While good, the Cyberknights could not possibly know every nuance and quirk of the computers they were working from or hacking. The SE was one of the many on-site civilian tech reps ordinarily charged with maintaining machines supplied by their companies. During an attack, an SE familiar with the targeted systems was brought in to answer any questions Eric might have during the hack or assist if the Cyberknight came across something that he did not quite understand. Oftentimes these SEs were members of the design team who had actually manufactured the computer being attacked. To the SE's left was a language/programs expert, or LPE. Like the hardware specialist, the LPE was on hand in case Eric needed help with the software he encountered.

Immediately behind the primary assault computer, on the rear table, sat the electronic-warfare station. Manned by a second Cyberknight, the operator of this computer had the task of assisting the hacker whenever he ran into a firewall or other security measure during the break-in. Once the hacker was in, the electronic-warfare knight, EWK for short, monitored the systems admin and security programs of the hacked network. It was his responsibility to protect the hacker from countermeasures initiated by automated security programs or systems administrators.

This feat was accomplished in any number of ways. The preferred countermeasure was simply to lie low, or cease the hack, until any detected security sweep was completed. If it appeared as if someone was starting to become wise to the hack, the EWK attempted to spoof the systems administrator by making him think everything was in order. When this failed and the administrator started to track the unusual activity that the hack was causing, the EWK began to feed his foe data that would create the appearance that the security program was malfunctioning. More often than not, this made the system administrator hesitate as he tried to determine if the suspect activity was nothing more than an anomaly in the system or a glitch with the security program of his computer. When this ploy didn't work, the EWK was forced to employ the least desirable trick in his bag, the dreaded red herring.

Every EWK had a totally fictitious hack sequence loaded on the EW computer and ready to initiate with nothing more than the touch of a special function key. Often they used the screen name and tactics of another hacker that the Cyberknights had come across during their day-to-day efforts to protect the Army's computers. This ruse was designed to be both sloppy and obvious, yet not easily countered. When initiated, more often than not, it gave the primary hacker more than enough time to finish his attack and back out before the system administrator caught on. Occasionally, however, the defensive measures taken against the feint were too quick. When the EWK saw that he was losing the fight to keep their foe at bay, he would call out, "eject," signaling the hacker he had to stop the hack, no matter where he was.

To the right of the EWK was an intel wizard. Major Gayle Rhay herself frequently took this seat. Like the systems or the language/programs experts, the intel officer was there to provide the primary hacker with advice and recommendations should he run across something that was unfamiliar or unexpected. The presence of someone from the intelligence section in the Pit also had the benefit of providing the wizards themselves with valuable firsthand knowledge of the capabilities of their foes.

The station to the left of the EWK was occupied by a recently recruited Cyberknight. Since a highly technical hack attack such as the one Eric was about to undertake was both difficult and involved operations against a sovereign power, only the most senior Cyberknights were permitted to make them. To qualify for what was, among the Cyberknights, these most prestigious assignments, a novice had to observe six actual hacks in the Pit and successfully complete twelve consecutive simulations. On this day, the honor of checking off his first observed Pit hack fell to Hamud Mdilla, the bright young newbie Eric had shown around.

Most people who wander onto the World Wide Web from their home computers give little thought about how their input makes it from the keyboard sitting on their laps to the sites they are seeking. Nor do they much care that so much data about who they are, and where they are, is bounced about the web in a rather haphazard manner, from one web server to another, in search of the most direct route to the site desired. Few appreciate how much personal data is left behind, like footprints, during this process.

Things were not that easy for the 401st. They could not simply dial up a local server, plug into the Web, and charge out into cyberspace in search of hackers messing with the Army's computers. This was especially true when going head-to-head with a foreign power who possessed the same ability to tap into servers around the world in search of a foe. Since this was how the Cyberknights themselves found most of their adversaries, it was safe to assume that their counterparts working for other masters would do likewise.

To counter this threat, every major cyberattack, such as the one which Eric was about to embark upon, followed a pathway along the Web plotted out by a network-routing specialist. To the Cyberknights, they were the pathfinders. Working at the computer located on the far left of the rear table, the pathfinder opened the route the hack attack took through the World Wide Web. This normally involved going through a number of servers located around the world. Unlike the home web surfer, there was nothing random about the pathway that data would travel. Yet it had to appear that way. To accomplish this little trick the pathfinder mimicked the route that a hacker the 401st had dealt with in the past had followed. This not only served to confuse the cyberwarfare specialist who might come back at them later, but it also covered the unit's own tracks as the Cyberknights crawled along the Web en route to their target. Any webmaster monitoring a Web server along the way who caught the Cyberknights hack would think that it was the same hacker who had visited them before.

This intricate course through the Web also served to protect the security of the 401st and the Keep. By knowing, in advance, where the outgoing data packets were going, the EWK would be able to go back, when the hack attack was over, and erase any record of the traffic at selected servers. This would make it impossible for anyone tracing the hack to discover the real point of origin. Since the Keep was, at that moment, a one-of-a-kind facility, protecting it was always a major concern. While the attack Eric and the team assembled in the Pit was important, it was not worth compromising the entire unit, a unit that could very well be needed to parry the opening attack of the next war.

The last member of the assault team, the officer in charge, had a seat at the rear table, but no computer. This paradox was the result of a decision made by Colonel Shrewsbery's predecessor when the operational procedures for the 401st were being drafted. Since the officer in charge had the responsibility for the attack, the first commander of the 401st felt it was important that he or she be unencumbered by a computer. "Who'll be keeping an eye on the overall ebb and flow of the attack, the big picture of what's going on," the unit's first commander pointed out, "if the OIC is fiddling about with a computer mouse." Though none of the Cyberknights since then understood how the OIC of a hack could run things without a computer, the issue was never debated or discussed.

A well-orchestrated hack attack did not simply happen. How various Cyberknights thought of their collective efforts was reflected by the terminology they used. Those who followed professional sports spoke of scoring when they accomplished an assigned task, or fumbling the ball when a hack went astray. Other Cyberknights with an ear for the classics liked to think of themselves as members of a well-tuned orchestra. And, of course, there were those who enjoyed spicing up their mundane lives by taking on superhero personas that would make Walter Mitty blush.

None of these alternate realities, however, could disguise the fact that this was, from beginning to end, a military operation. Once the officer in charge of the hack had assembled his team, all pretenses were dropped. With few exceptions these officers were like Shrewsbery, professional soldiers with a muddy-boots background who had been pulled into the 401st because they had a demonstrated ability to lead troops.

Their task was not at all an easy one. Most hackers, by their nature, were loners. They did not readily surrender their cherished individualism since so much of their self-worth was based upon what they, and they alone, could do. To overcome this common personality quirk, every OIC staged a rehearsal once all the preliminaries had been completed and the various players felt they were ready. While standing before his assembled strike team, the OIC walked through the hack attack step by step, from beginning to end.

Since most of the officers in the 401st who served as OICs for attacks could not hope to match the technical expertise of the people they would be in charge of, these professional soldiers relied upon the published execution matrix. This document, set up like a spreadsheet, listed each and every step that would be made during the attack down the left-hand edge of the page. Across the top of the matrix was the title of each member of the team, listed at the head of a column. By following that column down the page, everyone in the Pit could see what action he or she was expected to take as the attack unfolded.

With this execution matrix in hand, the OIC would point to the member on the team whose responsibility it was to initiate the next action. As he and every other person in the Pit listened, the soldier or technician the OIC was pointing to explained in detail what he would do at that point. When finished the OIC would turn to another team member, sometimes chosen at random, sometimes selected because they were required to support the event in progress, to spell out what was expected of them. Every now and then the OIC threw in a "what if?" scenario before moving on to the next item in the sequence. Though he already had an idea who needed to respond to his hypothetical question, the OIC would not point to that person, waiting, instead, for them to respond to the unexpected situation. Only when he was satisfied that everyone knew his or her role in the pending operation would the OIC report to Colonel Shrewsbery that they were ready to execute.

The timing of these attacks varied. The classic window chosen to hack into a system was during off hours, when the traffic on the targeted system was light and the chances of someone noticing something unusual was minimal. There were times, however, when hackers wanted to get lost in the traffic, or when the traffic on a busy system was actually necessary, especially when the hacker was trying to collect authentic screen names and passwords which he could use later. Because the hack attack Eric was about to embark upon required him to assume the persona of macnife, the attack had to be staged at a time when the real macnife would not be at his computer.

The other factor that played into the equation was the desire to keep the number of casualties at the chemical plant low. When the OIC of the attack, an artillery captain by the name of Reitter, mentioned that during the rehearsal, Eric Bergeron could not help but laugh. Normally such outbursts were ignored. In the eyes of the professional officers assigned to the 401st the Cyberknights were not real soldiers and therefore unfamiliar with the proper military etiquette and protocol normally expected from soldiers belonging to "the real Army." Reitter, however, was the sort that could not let such a breach of decorum go unchallenged. "As best I can see," he snapped back, "there's nothing funny about what we're about to do, soldier."

Eric didn't shy away from the captain's rebuke. "It's not the fact that we're going to be taking human life that I find laughable," Bergeron explained. "What I find amusing is the concept that somehow, by killing only fifty people instead of one hundred and fifty, we're being nice, or compassionate to the poor schmucks we're zapping."

Up to that point, Colonel Shrewsbery had been content to stand against the rear wall of the Pit, saying nothing as he listened while Reitter walked the assembled team through the operation. Eric's comments and explanation, however, were both uncalled for and way out of line. "That'll be enough of that, mister," the infantry colonel bellowed. "We are soldiers, soldiers who have been given a mission. Executing that mission, and that alone, is all we are concerned with. Period."

For several seconds, no one said a thing as Eric and the commander of the 401st locked eyes. Only when he was sure that he had made his point did Shrewsbery look over to where Reitter stood, seething in anger. "Carry on, Captain."

When he was sure that their colonel was not looking, and while Reitter was fiddling with the note cards he had been briefing from, Bobby Sung leaned over till he was but a few inches from Eric's ear. "Ve vere only following orders, herr judge," Bobby whispered, using a mock German accent. Though they often joked about such things, the Cyberknights understood that they were playing the deadliest game there was. Only through the acceptance of the party line, as well as adopting the sort of graveyard humor soldiers have always used to preserve their sanity, did the Cyberknights manage to go on.

The one thing that would not be present in the Pit during the attack was something that no one in the 401st ever gave a second thought to, a gun. Once past the two MPs posted on either side of the Discrete Strike Operation Center's red door, no one was armed. Yet the war that was about to be waged there was just as vicious, and deadly, as any war that had gone before. Only the tools, and the type of warrior who wielded them, had changed.

Five:

Hack Attack

From his post in the Spook Booth, the commander of the 401st watched the bank of monitors as the members of his command prepared for combat. Just as the business community had been dragged kicking and screaming into the information age, so, too, had the Army. Professional soldiers such as Shrewsbery knew, in their hearts, that units like the 401st were necessary. While some saw this change as being inevitable, and others freely embraced it as a brave new world, all who had been raised on the heroic traditions of their fathers grieved in silence as Eric Bergeron and his fellow Cyberknights took their place in the front ranks of America's military machine.

Joining Shrewsbery to monitor the attack were a number of advisors. One of the most important members of this second-tier staff was a lawyer from the Army's Staff Judge Advocate Corps. Of all the people involved, her position in the scheme of things was the least enviable, since everything that was about to happen was illegal. Not only were there no federal laws that sanctioned what the 401st did on a day-to-day basis, the United States supported every effort in every international forum it could to counter cyberterrorism. While they understood the necessity to aggressively seek out and destroy those who sought to attack their country under the cover of cyberspace, it didn't make anyone pledged to uphold the law feel good about what they were seeing.

If all went well, the JAG officer would have nothing to do. Her presence there was in case something went astray and the activities of the 401st or members of that unit had to be defended in a court of law. The JAG officers assigned to the 401st likened their plight to criminal defense attorneys retained by the mob.

Though he was also charged with enforcing the laws of the land, the FBI liaison in the Spook Booth viewed the undertaking with envy. As a member of that organization's computer crimes unit, the FBI Special Agent followed everything that the hack attack team did. His presence there was more than a matter of courtesy. Despite the fact that the Bureau could not use the same aggressive techniques employed by the 401st, watching a hack from inception to completion served to improve his abilities to devise ways of catching domestic cybercriminals his agency would have to combat once his tour with the Army unit was over.

Also joining Shrewsbery in the Spook Booth were the CIA and NSA reps who had generated this mission as well as the Air Force colonel who was, himself, connected to the Air Force's own cyberwarfare center in Idaho. Collectively theirs would prove to be the most difficult burden during the hack attack. While they had been the ones who had come up with the plan, none of them could do a thing once the attack had been initiated. Like the dummy monitors they watched, they would be powerless to influence the action.

This was not true of the final man in the room. As a member of the National Security Council, he had direct access to the national command authority. If all went well, he would have no need to use this access. Like the other people in the Spook Booth who were not assigned to the 401st the NSC rep would merely go back to Washington, D.C., once the hack was over and submit a written report to his superiors on what had happened. If, however, things got out of hand, the NSC rep would be the one who would pick up the phone and talk to the President and his advisors. While the NSC rep was friendly enough, Shrewsbery likened being confined in the small observation room with him to being locked in a cage with a tiger.

"Okay, people," Reitter announced over his boom mike after his assembled team signaled they were ready, "Here we go. Comms, open the channel."

The first step in any hack attack was to connect the Pit to an outside commercial network. This was done to keep dark knights from doing to the 401st what Reitter and his team were about to do to the cyberwarfare center macnife was operating from. The communications section of the 401st, located in another part of the Keep, literally had to plug the cable leading from the Pit into an external access port. These ports were arranged in a row on a panel painted bright red. Each of these connections was covered with a spring-loaded cap that snapped shut when the internal cable was removed. While there were written warnings posted all over the room, across the top of the red access port panel, and over each cover, a further audio warning was initiated as soon as a cap was lifted, announcing that the connection now exposed was a commercial line. When the connection was made a banner announcing that fact flashed across the top of the big screen in the Pit. This cued the pathfinder to initiate the attack.

Entry into the World Wide Web from the Pit was rather unspectacular. The procedure used by the pathfinder was not at all unlike that used by millions of his fellow Americans on a daily basis. The pathfinder dialed up the Internet server he desired and waited for the link to be made. Patiently he watched the display on his monitor. The plotted pathway that would take them from the Keep to macnife's system was displayed using a rather simple wiring diagram. Each server along the chosen pathway was listed in the sequence that it would be tagged. Within the hollow wire box each server was identified using its commercial name, the access code the pathfinder would need to use to connect with it, the type of equipment the server used, the nation it was located in, and the language the local webmaster used when tending to it.

The box representing each of these web servers was initially blue, the same color this particular specialist had chosen for the monitor's desktop. When a server was being contacted the box went from blue to yellow. Once the connection was made, it would turn red on both the pathfinder's monitor and the big screen on the wall. Only in the Spook Booth, where the nontechnicals watched, did the screen displaying the servers the hack was being routed through show up as an actual map. "Nontechnicals" was a catchall term applied to visitors to the Keep like the rep from the National Security Council and people who were not as computer savvy as the Cyberknights or their support team. When the Pit was being set up it had been decided that it would be far easier for these people to understand what was going on if they saw a map rather than the simplistic wiring diagram used by the pathfinder.

When a civilian web surfer goes out into cyberspace, he usually has a destination in mind but little concern over how he gets there. He simply instructs the web navigational program on his computer to take him to a Web address. This program does several things. It translates the user's message into a protocol that will allow the user's machine to interact with all the servers on the Web as well as the system at the destination site. This internet protocol, or IP, creates header information which includes both originating and destination addresses as well as the message or any additional information the sender has included. Once sent, this data is broken down into packets of data which then bounce about the World Wide Web looking for a server that is both available and capable of taking the message along to its destination. When the connection is made between the user who initiated the communications and the site he was looking for, the data packets are reformatted into a computer language that the receiver, or the system can understand. If the data is a simple e-mail message, the traffic is deposited in the memory of the computer to which it was sent or the service provider if a connection to the final destination is not open at that moment. If the sender has a desire to communicate in real time with someone on the other end, or access and manipulate information stored there, the connection between the two systems remains open until one party or the other terminates it.

Since he wanted to hit specific servers in a fixed sequence, the pathfinder had to organize the address portion of the packets so that they followed a specific route. If a selected server had no open ports, progress along the Web stopped until access was gained. Once in a server, the address for that server was stripped away, revealing the pathfinder's instructions to send the routing message along to the next server.

The assembled Pit team sat in silence as they watched the pathfinder's display on the big screen. Bobby Sung, a patient soul, could be as dispassionate as the computer that sat before him. Eric Bergeron, on the other hand, was unable to contain the nervous energy that was gnawing away at him. With nothing better to do with his hands, he tapped the table with a pencil. While there might have been some sort of rhythm in the Cyberknight's head driving this subconscious response, his hand did a poor job of translating it into anything resembling melody. Instead of music, the female interpreter seated next to him heard disjointed thumps that only served to heighten her own jitters. Without a word, she reached over and snatched the pencil out of Eric's hand. Offended by her action, Eric turned and stared at her. The interpreter met his indignant glare with an expression that all but said, "Go ahead, make my day."

In the midst of this nonverbal exchange, the pathfinder broke the silence. "Okay, boys and girls, we're in." After giving the interpreter one more spiteful glance, Eric turned his attention back to the big screen.

By the time he had refocused his attention to the progression of the attack, Bobby Sung was already at work. As the electronic-warfare knight for this operation, it was his task to break through the security systems that protected the host computer macnife worked from. Since the system they were breaking into was based on an American design, and both the network-level firewalls and the application-gateway firewalls had not been modified by macnife's sponsors, this task was relatively easy. For the first time that day, Bobby Sung betrayed the excitement he felt by humming "The Ride of the Walküre" while his fingers flew across the keyboard before him.

In the Spook Booth, the CIA agent chuckled when he heard Wagner's oft-played piece. "Sounds like your people have been spending too much time watching old war movies."

Kevin Shrewsbery looked over at the visitor from Langley. "I'd rather that than have them use the training we give them here to empty my bank accounts."

While the CIA man stared at the Army colonel, the FBI liaison chuckled. "You've got that right."

Back in the Pit, Bobby Sung was finishing his tasks. "Righto, mate," he called out to Eric Bergeron, "we be in business."

Taking a deep breath, Eric studied his screen. "Let's see now," he mumbled. Bobby Sung, using an old technique, had managed to enter an open port in the host computer macnife worked from by sending a message using an address that macnife's system was familiar with. Once past the security gateways, the body of the message was not checked by the security programs, since it followed the address of a trusted user. That body consisted of a sequence of commands, written in the computer language used by the system under attack, that established a new root account.

Neither the nation that had provided the computers nor macnife's native country altered the basic programming language, making it easy for Eric to pull up the directory of the host computer and get to work. The first phase of the attack involved the downloading of a Trojan horse. While there are several variations to this sort of attack, the one Eric introduced to macnife's host computer involved that system's Internet protocol instructions.

Rather than destroy a single computer which could easily be replaced, the NSA had convinced the members of the National Security Council that it could nullify the effectiveness of future attacks by keeping track of where the dark knights from that country were going in cyberspace. Their solution was to modify the header portion of the Internet protocol instructions currently on macnife's host computer so that every time macnife and his compatriots connected with the internet, the NSA would be alerted. The Trojan horse in this case did nothing other than send the NSA an info copy of everything that was sent out onto the Web. With that information in hand, the NSA would be able to warn any site that was the target of an attack as well as gather information on who this particular nation was working with.

Methodically Eric made his way into the operating system of macnife's host computer. With root access, this was rather simple. What was not going to be easy was the substitution of codes. To do that Eric would have to operate on the old code. That could create a momentary interruption in service, much in the same way that a surgeon performing open-heart surgery must stop the heart in order to work on it. Everyone using macnife's host computer that was connected to the Internet would experience a momentary delay of service. If this interruption became pronounced, the system administrator would, quite naturally, assume that there was a problem either with his connections or his system. Either way, he would become active and begin an aggressive effort to resolve the problem while ignoring the phone calls from angry users.

To prevent this Bobby Sung would momentarily block all outgoing traffic. To the average user this interruption would appear to be nothing more than a delay in finding an open circuit at his or her Internet service provider. Even the most astute computer geek would have difficulty detecting the hiccup Bobby Sung's break in service would create.

"Hey, Bobby," Eric called out. "You ready?"

The EWK looked up at the big screen, where he could clearly see that Eric had the existing IP header information highlighted and ready for deletion. "On the count of three," Bobby Sung replied. Then he began his count, "Three, two, one, break."

In the Spook Booth, the NSA agent pointed to the screens displaying what Bobby Sung and Eric were doing. "The interruption in service comes first," he explained to the rep from the National Security Council. "Then the Cyberknight making the hack wipes away the old header information and substitutes the one we came up with, the Trojan horse."

Though he really didn't understand everything that was going on in the Pit, the NSC rep grunted and nodded knowingly.

Back in the Pit, Eric drew his hands away from his keyboard and into the air. "Done!"

Bobby Sung, alerted to this by his compatriot's actions and announcement, removed the block from the targeted system. When the warning banner on his screen was replaced by a "Service resumed" message, the EWK let his hands fall away from the keyboard and to his sides. Dispassionately he watched his monitor, which was now showing him the same thing the systems administrator of the hacked computer was seeing. If anyone had noticed the break in service, they would notify the system administrator, who would, in turn, initiate some sort of action to find out what had happened.

Again the Pit became still as everyone watched for a flurry of activity on the portion or the big screen showing them Bobby Sung's screen display. From his seat the OIC took note of the time. It had been decided that a thirty-minute pause would be sufficient to allay any fears that their insertion of the Trojan horse had gone undetected.

As before, Eric found himself unable to contain his nervous energy. With all his pencils out of reach, Eric began to drum his fingers on the tabletop as he watched the big screen. He was in the middle of rapping out a tune when he felt a sharp slap across the back of his right hand. Stunned, he looked over at the interpreter next to him. Surprised by her action and the scowl she wore, Eric pulled his injured hand up to his chest and began to rub it as he stared at his attacker as if to ask, *"Why did you do that?"*

Having anticipated this, the interpreter shoved a note in front of his face. In angry strokes, the note read, *"Stop with the noise, before I am forced to break your fingers."*

Reaching over and snatching the pencil from her hand, Eric turned as he took up his notepad and jotted out a response. When it was finished, he flashed his response at her. *"Oh yeah!"* it read. *"You and what army?"*

Seeing an opportunity to pass time by engaging in something more exciting than watching the big screen, Eric and the female interpreter exchanged a flurry of notes.

They were still at it when Captain Reitter broke the silence. "It looks as if the Trojan horse is in place and doing its thing. It's time to move on to phase two."

Before breaking off the silent war of words, Eric scribbled out one more message to his neighborly foe. *"We'll continue this later."* After delivering that, he swiveled about in his seat and took up where he had left off. "Okay, Scottie," Eric announced over the intercom, "beam me up."

Without a word the pathfinder prepared to launch back out into cyberspace from the computer they had hacked into and on to the one at the chemical plant chosen for destruction. Using macnife's screen name, he initiated the new hack from macnife's own computer. Unlike before, he made no effort to cover his tracks or weave his way through the Internet along a predetermined route. For this part of the operation to be successful, the pathfinder had to leave a traceable path from macnife's machine to the chemical plant for the cyberwarfare specialists in the other nation to find.

The point of entry at the new site was the computer system at the chemical plant that handled the shipping and tracking of the plant's products. This point, according to the system expert, would be the easiest port through which they could enter and gain access to the rest of the system. While he watched the pathfinder hand off the attack to Bobby Sung so that he could crack the security codes, the system expert unfolded a diagram of the chemical plant's network.

As before, Bobby Sung wormed his way through the security gateways and worked his way through the system until he had reached the network's root directory. From his seat, Eric looked at up the big screen before him. "Gee," he muttered as he took in the screen before him. "I thought you said this plant had been built by a German firm."

"The plant is German," the SE replied. "But the computer network is based upon an American design."

"I sure hope the American firm got some royalties out of this deal," the interpreter remarked.

Bobby Sung snickered. "Not likely."

From his seat, Reitter called out. "Let's settle down and deal with the issue at hand."

Unlike the previous sessions that had passed in near-total silence, a lively exchange began between the system expert, who guided Eric through the computer network that ran the plant, the interpreter, who translated when they came across something in Chinese, and Eric himself, who asked them both questions. To assist in this effort, each of these three had laser pointers with which they could point to the word or section of the plant's computer screen that was now displayed on the big screen.

"Okay," the SE stated triumphantly. "The second file down contains the program that runs the control panel."

"Well," Eric mused as he highlighted the file and clicked his mouse. "Let's see what we shall see."

After taking a moment or two to study the series of computer commands, the language/program expert heaved a great sigh of relief. "They've not changed a thing. All the pre-programmed defaults are still set."

The system expert nodded. "Agreed. We can proceed as planned."

Leaning forward, Eric locked his fingers and flexed them as a concert pianist would before playing. "Thank you, ladies and gentlemen.

Now, for my first number, I shall play, 'Let's fuck with the emergency shutoff.' "

"He's a cocky little bastard," the NSA agent commented to the group assembled in the Spook Booth.

Coming to Eric's defense, Colonel Shrewsbery countered. "He's twenty-five years old, playing the world's most sophisticated computer game." Turning, he looked over at the NSA man. "Like you, we recruit brains, not personality."

Quickly Eric moved from item to item, changing the settings. In some cases he reversed values, so that when the computer screen in the control room showed the operator that a valve was open, it was actually closed and vice versa. Simple mathematical formulas were added to lines that displayed temperatures of the huge vats where chemical reactions and mixing took place. The inserted formulas were written so that the measured temperature at the vat showed up on the control room's computer as being substantially lower than it actually was. Together with the disabling of the automated-shutdown sequence and fire-suppression system, the new settings were designed to initiate an uncontrolled chain reaction. Not only would the personnel in the control room be unaware of what was going on until it was too late, when they did take steps to shut down the plant or activate emergency procedures, the false readings they were seeing and the reversed controls they were manipulating would only serve to increase both the speed of the disaster and its magnitude.

When he was finished, Eric leaned back in his seat, pushed his chair away from his workstation, and looked up at the big screen. Slowly, he checked each line he had altered, character by character. When he had finished, he twisted about in his seat and looked up at Bobby Sung. "What do you think, old boy?"

Sung, who had been watching every move Eric had made, took another long look at the big screen before he nodded in approval. "Bloody good show, old boy. I'd say we have a keeper here."

Though annoyed by their lighthearted manner, Reitter said nothing. The two Cyberknights, like everyone else in the Pit, were under a great deal of pressure.

When the hackers were satisfied, Eric next turned to his left. "Do you see anything that needs a second look?"

Both the systems expert and the language/programs expert took a few extra moments to scan the altered settings and formulas. In turn, each gave Eric a thumbs-up when they were satisfied.

With that, Eric glanced back at the pathfinder. "Okay, Scottie.

Take us home." As was his particular habit, the pathfinder clicked his heels three times, repeating the old cliché, "there's no place like home," each time while he backed out of the chemical plant's main computer and prepared to quit the Internet. Finished, he clapped his hands. "We're out."

Without hesitation, Reitter called out over his boom mike. "Comms, break down the link. I say again, break down the link."

In the Pit, the red banner that warned that they were connected to the World Wide Web suddenly disappeared. Standing up, Reitter looked about the room. "It is now nineteen thirty-five hours. Our initial after-action review will take place commencing twenty hundred in the main conference room." Though this briefing was standard, the assembled team let out a collective groan. Then, without further ado, all of the players began to gather up the material they had brought with them and prepared to leave.

From his seat in the Spook Booth, the representative of the National Security Council blinked before he looked over at Shrewsbery, then at the NSA and CIA reps. "That's it?" he asked incredulously.

As one, everyone connected to the 401st, as well as the special agents from the CIA and NSA, looked about, wondering if they had missed something. Confused, Shrewsbery looked back at the NSC rep. "What were you expecting? Armageddon?"

"Well," the NSC rep asked, still not sure of what had just taken place, "how do you know if you've succeeded?"

Shrewsbery did his best to hide his disgust. It was obvious that this refugee from inside the Beltway had expected to see explosions and death and destruction in real time, just like in the movies. When he had composed himself, Shrewsbery stood up. "Well," he stated as tactfully as he could, "as far as the Trojan horse goes, it will be a few days before the NSA will know just how effective that is."

"What about the chemical plant?"

Shrewsbery shrugged. "My advice is to watch CNN tomorrow morning. If we succeeded, it'll be all over the news."

"And the ploy to foment distrust between the two nations?" the NSC rep continued.

"That, sir," Shrewsbery answered, making no effort to hide his irritation, "we may never know."

Stymied, the civilian advisor stood there, looking about at the men and women gathered about in the Spook Booth. "So, that's it? This is how we will go about fighting our wars in the twenty-first century?"

Bowing his head, Colonel Shrewsbery reflected upon that comment for a moment. He had asked himself the same question time and time again until the truth had finally sunk in. "Yes," he answered, making no effort to hide the regret he felt over this state of affairs. "That's pretty much it." Then, sporting a wicked smile, he looked over at the NSA rep and gave him a wink. "Last person out, please turn off the lights."

Without another word, the infantry colonel pivoted about and made for the exit. In so many ways, his job was finished.

HAROLD W. COYLE graduated from the Virginia Military Institute in 1974 with a B.A. in history and a commission as a second lieutenant in Armor.

His first assignment was in Germany, where he served for five years as a tank platoon leader, a tank company executive officer, a tank battalion assistant operations officer, and as a tank company commander. Following that he attended the Infantry Officers Advanced Course at Fort Benning, Georgia, became a branch chief in the Armor School's Weapons Department at Fort Knox, Kentucky, worked with the National Guard in New England, spent a year in the Republic of Korea as an assistant operations officer, and went to Fort Hood, Texas, for a tour of duty as the G-3 Training officer of the First Cavalry Division and the operations officer of Task Force I-32 Armor, a combined arms maneuver task force.

His last assignment with the Army was at the the Command and General Staff College at Fort Leavenworth, Kansas. In January 1991 he reported to the Third Army, with which he served during Desert Storm. Resigning his commission after returning from the Gulf in the spring of 1991, he continues to serve as a lieutenant colonel in the Army's Individual Ready Reserve. He writes full-time and has produced the following novels: *Team Yankee, Sword Point, Bright Star, Trial by Fire, The Ten Thousand, Code of Honor, Look Away, Until the End, Savage Wilderness,* and *God's Children.*

FLIGHT OF *ENDEAVOUR*

BY R. J. PINEIRO

One

The soft whirl of the Environmental Control and Life Support System broke the silence of space, the dead calm that Russian Mission Specialist Sergei Dudayev had grown to detest since his arrival at the International Space Station three months before. He knew he didn't belong there, in the pressurized cylindrical modules that had been his entire world for what now seemed like an eternity. A place where "up" and "down" had no meaning, no significance. A state-of-the-art rat cage where humans worked, ate, and slept protected from outer space by layers of metal alloys and insulating compounds.

Outer space. Sergei frowned as he gazed out through the Habitation Module's panoramic windowpanes at the light cloud coverage over southern Africa. The Earth looked peaceful, quiet, majestic.

At five-foot-four, the thirty-year-old Russian cosmonaut was a short man, particularly when standing next to his American or European colleagues. With a neatly trimmed beard, hollow cheeks, and charming smile, Sergei gave the impression of someone who found no pleasure in food. In his long, bony face, Sergei's alert, rather feminine eyes had an Italian softness that made people feel at ease with him. Today, he was banking on his natural ability to make everyone inside the International Space Station feel comfortable in his presence.

Closing his eyes, he listened to the sound of his own breathing as he prepared himself mentally for what he had to do. He felt his heartbeat increasing, the adrenaline rush, the perspiration forming on his creased forehead.

He opened his eyes and stared at a perfectly round bead of sweat floating inches from his face. He placed his index finger and thumb around it and toyed with it for a few seconds before squashing it. The silent explosion projected hundreds of tiny liquid particles in an isotropic that slowly trended upward as they got sucked in by the air-revitalization-system extractors overhead.

The time had come. With *Atlantis* heading back down to Earth and the launch of the shuttle *Endeavour* at the cape being delayed by a week, the ISS's regular crew of eight had been temporarily reduced to five, including himself.

The opportunity to take over the U.S. military's GPATS module would never be so easy. The Global Protection Against Terrorist Strikes module was one of several modules that made up the current core of the station. But unlike its sister modules, which served either as living quarters or to run experiments and collect data, GPATS, the highly classified military payload of a shuttle flight a year ago, housed a prototype hydrogen fluoride chemical laser gun powered by an array of solar cells. Initially plagued with bugs, the laser had already proven itself useful six months ago, when a malfunctioning satellite had come dangerously close to colliding with the space station. The laser had managed to transfer enough energy to the satellite to deflect its trajectory, missing the station by a thousand feet. Since then, the Pentagon, in order to protect the station from space junk, had used two shuttle flights to haul a billion dollars' worth of upgrades to increase its power and accuracy, making it capable of disabling enemy satellites as well as incoming nuclear warheads—its design objective during the Strategic Defense Initiative project over a decade ago. But GPATS also housed another weapon, deployed at the request of the United Nations Security Council: thirty BLU-85 warheads, each fitted with individual Earth reentry boosters. The BLU-85 was the largest nonnuclear warhead made by the United States, big brother of the venerable BLU-82 used during the Vietnam era to clear out large areas of forest for helicopter landing pads. The purpose of the BLU-85 aboard the ISS: a tactical, nonnuclear, first-strike antiterrorist-capability weapon that could be delivered with surgical precision anywhere on Earth within minutes. Each warhead provided the equivalent yield of fifteen thousand tons of TNT, or fifteen kilotons—small when compared to the two-hundred-kiloton warheads atop ICBMs, but large enough for its intended application. A single BLU-85 could level a military compound in a hostile nation, vaporize a terrorist training camp, discourage an advancing army, or destroy a cocaine plantation—all with the push of a button, and guided to its target by its own radar in shoot-and-forget mode. In procedures similar to the ones followed for decades by missile-silo crewmen, the weapons were kept in a state of readiness, their launching controlled by two crew members from the United States, the country that footed the entire GPATS bill. GPATS was the United Nations' ultimate hammer against a rebellious nation or terrorist group, capable of delivering a quick and devastating blow without the large overhead of troop deployments or air strikes, or the political and moral problems associated with a nuclear strike.

And now I will use this weapon against the Russian butchers, thought Sergei, who had become aware of this secret payload during the last month of his training.

Sergei Viktor Dudayev was Russian by birth, but his heart belonged to the struggling people of Chechnya, the land where he'd spent most of his youth as the son of a military officer during the final decade of the Soviet Union. Growing up in Grozny, Chechnya's capital, had allowed the young Dudayev to develop strong bonds with the locals, some of whom were killed during the turbulent civil war period following the fall of the Soviet Union. This secret loyalty had remained very much alive inside Sergei Dudayev after he'd left that war-scarred land, abandoning his friends in their fight for independence. The fire continued to burn in his heart even after he had settled in Moscow and tried to start a new life; even as he himself climbed the military ladder of the Russian military, following in his father's footsteps; even as his distinguished career eventually led him to the Russian space program.

Sergei reached into a Velcro-secured side pocket and extracted a small electric stun gun, capable of discharging a single twenty-thousand-volt shock, powerful enough to incapacitate an average man for thirty minutes. His people in Chechnya had managed to smuggle the tiny gun inside a Progress Russian cargo spaceship, which had arrived at the station just last week. Along with the gun came coded instructions from his Chechen contact in Moscow on the critical timing to take control of the station.

"Hey, Serg. You look pretty depressed today." One of the American astronauts floated past him, patted Sergei on the back, and stopped in front of the food galley. The American was the current resident aboard the ISS from the United Nations Security Council. In addition to standard mission-specialist responsibilities, he was also chartered with the protection of the GPATS module. Ever since the UNSC deployed GPATS, a minimum of one crew member aboard the ISS possessed the training and the weapons to defend the military module.

Sergei didn't respond, his eyes shifting from the American's holstered stun gun to the back of his light blue flight overalls, identical to the ones Sergei wore, except that the muscular UNSC soldier filled his, while Sergei's looked a size too big for his lanky frame.

The tall astronaut turned around, his hands fumbling with a brown pack of dehydrated peaches. His round face, pink and white, went well with his short hair. Curious brown eyes blinked at Sergei. "You okay, pal? You look sick. Have you been getting enough sleep?"

His heartbeat rocketing as he tried to hide the stun gun behind his back without looking suspicious. Sergei forced a smile, slightly closing his eyes as he nodded. "Yes, I am fine. Thank you."

The bulky American shrugged, turning his attention back to his dried peaches.

Sergei Viktor Dudayev tightened the grip on the stun gun and gently pushed himself toward the food galley, arming the weapon and pressing its bare-wire ends against the soldier's neck.

A light buzzing sound filled the Habitation Module as the pouch flew off, spilling its contents in a brownish cloud. The American jerked for a moment and went limp, his arms floating in front of his body.

First incapacitate, then kill.

Blocking out all emotions, Sergei choked his victim until breathing ceased. Then he felt for a pulse, finding none. Satisfied, he grabbed the dead man's stun gun before pushing his body aside.

Adrenaline rocketing his heartbeat, Sergei stared toward the other end of the Habitation Module, where sleep compartments occupied both sides of the padded walls and the ceiling. A crewman slept in one of them. Another American, the station commander.

The Russian cosmonaut drifted toward him, coming to a rest in front of the compartment. The commander's arms floated loosely to the sides as his head leaned slightly forward. The Velcro straps securing him against the padded board applied just enough pressure on his body to create the illusion of sleeping in a comfortable bed.

Sergei curled the hairy fingers of his right hand around the plastic case of the UNSC soldier's stun gun, and without further thought, drove the hot end of the weapon into the side of the commander's neck. The astronaut opened his eyes and stared at Sergei in surprise, before his eyes rolled to the back of his head and his arms jerked forward, almost as if trying to reach for his attacker. The motor reflex ended a moment later, and, again, Sergei strangled his incapacitated victim.

The Russian unzipped the front of the American's suit and removed a key attached to a chain around his neck. The American also wore a small badge around his neck. Briefly eyeing the credit-card-size object,

Sergei decided to come back to it later. Right then he needed both ISS master keys.

Sergei Dudayev floated to his first victim and retrieved a second key, before approaching the center of the module and eyeing the closed-circuit TV monitors of the operations workstation. There he verified that the remaining crew members, one British and one Japanese, were still inside the U.S. Laboratory Module, the forty-four-foot-long pressurized cylinder similar in shape and size to the Habitation Module. Satisfied, he inserted both keys on the top of the keyboard of the Multipurpose Application Console, linked to the electronic core of the ISS's network. From here, Sergei had control of all onboard subsystems such as electrical power, thermal control, data management, communications, interface with ground control, and even full space station attitude control and orbit altitude.

Sergei Dudayev bypassed all manual overrides of the air-revitalization system and emergency hatch releases of the U.S. Laboratory Module. A few more strokes of the keys and he heard the alarms going off across the station as the computer system automatically isolated the laboratory from the rest of the station by closing and locking the hatches at both ends of the module.

His eyes drifted back to the flat-panel monitor, which now showed two astronauts frantically waving at the camera and reaching for the radio. Sergei turned the intercom system off. He didn't care to hear their pleas, just as the world had refused to listen to the cry of his people as Russian forces raped his beloved Chechnya.

Visions of his explosive youth, of his slaughtered friends, of his hasty departure filled his mind as Sergei typed again. This time he overrode the air pressurization and revitalization control system of the station and began to bleed the air still trapped inside the Laboratory Module into space. The astronauts continued to wave and scream in front of the camera, but their struggle didn't last long. Soon they began to breathe through their mouths. Their movements grew clumsier, erratic, until they went limp.

The Russian quietly followed the bodies floating in the monitor. His soul could hear their screams now, their shouts and pleas for mercy. All four astronauts had died without really knowing Sergei's motive, without an explanation as to why their lives had to end so abruptly inside this man-made pocket of life traveling at thousands of miles per hour over a fragile Earth.

The two keys giving him access to all modules of the station, including GPATS, Sergei quickly typed the appropriate commands on the MPAC workstation, unlocking the latching mechanism that isolated

GPATS from the rest of the station. Locking the MPAC system by removing both keys, Sergei used a single arm motion to propel his weightless body across the length of the Habitation Module, where a hatch connected that end of the module to Node One, also known as Unity, a pressurized cylinder fifteen feet in diameter and eighteen feet long sporting six hatches that served as docking ports for the other modules. A hatch connected to the U.S. Laboratory Module, another to the GPATS Module, and a third to the airlock, where the crew could suit up prior to EVAs, extravehicular activities, or space walks. The hatch immediately above Sergei led to a Russian-made Soyuz capsule to be used by the crew of the station to return to Earth in an emergency. Sergei planned to use the Soyuz Escape System (SES) to return to Earth after he had completed his mission.

A fifth hatch attached a cupola to Unity. Composed of eight large windows arranged in a circle over the node, the cupola provided the crew of the ISS with a 360-degree field of view in azimuth and complete hemispheric field of view in elevation of Earth. Part of the instrumentation aboard the cupola was the control system for the ISS robot arm, a larger and more versatile version of the venerable robot arm of the space-shuttle program. Unity's sixth hatch was used to dock with visiting shuttles or Russian Progress supply ships. The other end of the U.S. Laboratory Module connected to Node Two, which led to additional modules on that side of the station, including the Columbus research module from Europe, and the Japanese experimental module.

Using the handholds built in along the padded walls lining Unity, Sergei directed himself into the GPATS Module. Placing his feet into the secure straps in front of the latched hatch, he applied nine pounds of pressure on the hatch actuator lock lever, turning it 180 degrees. The hatch opened to the contour of Unity's inner wall. Sergei pulled it toward him about six inches, before pivoting it up and to the right side, exposing the crowded interior of the GPATS module.

Unlike the other modules, illuminated with soft white overheads, the interior of GPATS had a green glow designed to minimize eye fatigue during prolonged combat situations. Viewed from the inside, the module looked like a half cylinder. The side facing Earth was completely taken up by the BLU-85s, each stored in its own individual compartment and stacked ceiling high for the entire length of the module, leaving a three-foot-wide "walkway" between the wall of shelled warheads and the left side of the compartment. The forward section of the side of GPATS opposite the warheads consisted of two large computer consoles, each capable of launching warheads if the order ever came from the United Nations Security Council. The workstation closest to the hatch had a red light above it, meaning it was the system currently designated as active. The other system, set in standby mode, served as backup.

Farther down the left side Sergei saw the single computer system controlling the powerful GPATS laser, gimbal-mounted above the module. Gliding past gleaming instrumentation and displays, the Russian cosmonaut reached the laser system, whose operation he had had to learn before being qualified as mission specialist. ISS regulations dictated that every crew member aboard the ISS knew the operation of the laser in case of an emergency. The operation of the warheads, however, was limited to UNSC personnel, mostly American. In the event that a mission specialist like Sergei figured out how to operate the warhead-launching system, he would be incapable of doing so without the authorization codes, which were kept in a safe next to the workstation. Sergei had picked up bits and pieces of the launching procedure during a recent drill by eavesdropping on an intercom channel. If the order to launch ever came, the authorized crew would use their keys simultaneously to open the safe and extract the sealed envelopes containing the launch codes, which would then be compared with those received from Earth. If the codes matched, the order to launch one or more warheads would be executed. Such precautions were required given the fact that albeit nonnuclear, each warhead was capable of leveling downtown Washington, D.C. However, no authorization from the Pentagon or the United Nations was required to use the laser, particularly if there was a need to deflect or vaporize space junk in a collision course with the station. Its use in an emergency was at the sole discretion of the station commander.

Sitting behind the controls of the GPATS laser, Sergei activated the search-and-tracking radar, which, in conjunction with the tracking systems of three reflectors positioned in geosynchronous orbit 23,000 miles above the Earth, had the capability of detecting and tracking anything in orbit.

Sergei went to work, commanding the laser's search-and-tracking system to scan the space along an east-to-west elliptical orbit of 274 kilometers in perigee and 150 kilometers in apogee with an inclination of 63.4 degrees—the orbit of Russia's latest Cosmos surveillance satellite, currently Russia's eyes over the border between Chechnya and Dagestan to the north. Sergei adjusted the system's sensitivity to filter out objects smaller than ten feet in length. It took an additional minute before the search-and-tracking system came back with an object roughly the size of a school bus.

Sergei Viktor Dudayev smiled.

I see you.

His fingers moved almost automatically, selecting an energy setting, width of beam, and duration of event. Giving the controls one last inspection, he commanded the laser to fire.

The hydrogen-fluoride chemical laser gun, receiving its power from massive solar-rechargeable batteries, created a high-energy beam of light, which streaked across space to one of three reflective mirrors in geosynchronous orbit. The fifty-foot-diameter segmented mirror, actively cooled by a steady flow of liquid hydrogen running below its reflective surface, and whose angle had already been determined by its radio link with GPATS, deflected the beam with only a four percent loss in energy. The beam continued on its new trajectory, which abruptly ended when it came in contact with the laminated twenty-four-karat gold skin of the Cosmos orbital reconnaissance satellite.

Although the beam only remained in contact with the satellite for a few seconds, the laser's energy changed into intense heat, slicing through the skin, evaporating the metal, and instantly frying the sophisticated electronics housed in its core.

Before manning the workstation controlling the warheads, Sergei used the keys to extract the launching codes from the safe next to the system. He activated the system and spent a few minutes typing the thirty-characters-long codes, working through several menus and levels of security. Another set of codes allowed him to move down the encrypted system until he reached the directory where the launching software resided. A few more keystrokes and the twenty-one-inch Sony color monitor displayed a list of warheads, labeled UNSC15KTSN001 through UNSC15KTSN030 in cyan on a black background.

He placed an index finger, trembling from excitement, over a spring-tensioned trackball—a mouse didn't work well in zero gravity—bringing the cursor to the BLU-85 warhead SN#001. Sergei's plan, which he had secretly worked out two weeks prior to his launch with Nikolai Naskalhov, an aide to the president of Chechnya, was simple: gain control of the warheads as a hammer against the Russian troops threatening to invade Chechnya. The destruction of the Russian satellite had been Sergei's message to Moscow that the people of Chechnya now had an ally high above the clouds. As he gained control of GPATS, another message was being delivered to the Kremlin: unless the Russian 157th armored division retreated from the border with Chechnya, he would release a warhead over an undisclosed location. More demands would follow.

The adrenaline rush making it difficult to swallow, Sergei clicked the button beneath the trackball. He wanted to activate the warheads and have them ready for launch at a moment's notice.

The UNSC15KTSN001 warhead turned magenta, and a message appeared:

UNSC15KTSN001 HAS BEEN SELECTED
INSERT VALID UNSC ACCESS CARD TO ACTIVATE
******00:59******

A slot opened beneath the monitor and a red LED began to blink next to it.

Sergei froze.

Insert Valid United Nations Security Council access card?

Why would he need one when he had already logged into the system and entered all the authorization codes successfully?

Confused, Sergei glanced at the screen again. It now read:

UNSC15KTSN001 HAS BEEN SELECTED
INSERT VALID UNSC ACCESS CARD TO ACTIVATE
******00:55*****

And a second later,

UNSC15KTSN001 HAS BEEN SELECTED
INSERT VALID UNSC ACCESS CARD TO ACTIVATE
******00:54******

The Russian's soft eyes widened in fear when he realized the system would not let him start the launch sequence unless he inserted a UNSC access card in the slot within the next fifty-four seconds. The UNSC had added a safety feature that he didn't know existed, and if the system was as secured as he expected it to be, he would probably only get one chance at inserting the card before the computers would lock him out.

But where do I—

You idiot! The station commander! The card! He glanced at the screen once more.

UNSC15KTSN001 HAS BEEN SELECTED
INSERT VALID UNSC ACCESS CARD TO ACTIVATE
******00:47******

Sergei jumped off the chair and propelled himself to the entrance of the GPATS module, floated across Unity, and into the Habitation Module. Shoving aside the American floating next to the galley, he reached the end of the long, cylindrical compartment, halting his momentum by holding on to the edge of the sleeping compartment.

He tugged at the chain around the neck of the dead station commander, but it didn't give. Beads of sweat lifting off his forehead, the Russian raised the chain over his victim's head. Holding the electronic card in his left hand, he kicked his legs against the side of the sleeping compartment, propelling himself back toward Unity. He miscalculated his zero-G flight, crashing his right shoulder against the edge of the passageway. The impact deflected his forward momentum, sending him floating out of control inside Unity.

Wasting precious seconds, ignoring the pain, Sergei clawed at anything within reach to regain control, grabbing on to a built-in handle next to the hatch connecting Unity to the cupola. In the process, he let go of the card, which floated toward his feet.

In one swift motion, Sergei snagged the chain, pulling the card to his chest. Kicking his legs against the cupola's control panel, he shot himself through the D-shaped entry of the GPATS module, reaching the workstation a moment later.

******PROCEDURE VIOLATION******
TIME LIMIT EXCEEDED. SYSTEM RESET IN PROGRESS
******167:59:54******

Procedure violation! He had missed the window by six seconds!

Sergei tried to insert the badge, but the slot was already closed. He tried to type a command to reset the system manually, but the system would not respond. The keyboard was locked. He tried the power switch on the side of the machine, but it did not have any effect. The system was obviously designed to bypass all exterior input after such violation, and it would remain like that for 168 hours—one week—before it would let him try again.

Sergei was familiar with procedure violations, and the only way to reset the system before the stated time was by entering a special access code known only by four people in the world: The U.S. President, the Russian President, the British Prime Minister, and the Secretary General of the United Nations. The procedure was implemented as a safety measure against exactly this type of intrusion. One week was usually enough time to get either a shuttle or a Russian Soyuz packed with armed United Nations forces up here. During his last six months of training at Johnson Space Center, in Houston, Sergei had seen a platoon of UN Security Forces in similar zero-G training exercises. While Sergei trained to use a screwdriver in space, the soldiers practice zero-G warfare tactics.

But fortunately for Sergei, he still had a chance of pulling this off. It just would take a little more time and a hell of a lot more nerve.

Moving up the module to the laser station, Sergei quickly verified his access to the laser. Unlike the warheads, the laser system could never be locked—as long as the user had the right authorization codes. Otherwise, the station ran the risk of getting damaged by space junk. He moved over to the backup warhead-deployment workstation, next to the one he had locked.

Sergei tried his luck at gaining access to the warheads' directory. He got the message:

SYSTEM LOCKED BY OTHER USERS
PLEASE TRY AGAIN IN 167:58:42

Frowning at his own stupidity, but grateful that at least he could defend himself and prevent anyone from getting near the station, Sergei deactivated the system and floated back to the Habitation Module, where he prepared a coded message that he sent to a mobile tracking station in Chechnya ten minutes later, when the International Space Station flew over the Caucasus Mountains.

The reply from his controller was very clear: hold your ground. Regain control of the warheads and advise when Sergei was in a position to launch. He would be provided with a priority list of targets at a later time. Right then control of the ISS played a significant role in the ongoing discussions with Russia, providing Chechnya with bargaining leverage against the Russian armored divisions gathered at its border. He was also told that the hearts of the Chechen people were with him at this time.

Afterward, Sergei dragged the bodies of the four astronauts across Unity and into the hyperbaric airlock, which provided an effective and safe mean for the transfer of crew and equipment between pressurized and unpressurized zones.

He gave the interior of the compartment a visual check to verify that all airlock equipment—including the two AMEX AX-5 EVA hard suits and all power tools—were safely secured, before floating back up into Unity. Closing the hatch, he used the small control panel next to the hatch to depressurize the airlock from the normal atmosphere inside the station of 14.7 pounds per square inch (PSI) to 0.5 PSI. As Sergei remotely opened the airlock's exterior hatch, the pressure differential between the vacuum of space and the low pressure of the airlock sucked the four astronauts out of the airlock and into free space.

Sergei closed the exterior hatch, repressurized the airlock, and headed back to the Habitation Module. Although he felt partially victorious for coming so close to accomplishing his lifelong goal of seeking revenge against the enemies of Chechnya, the cosmonaut couldn't help a wave of guilt. After all, this had been the very first time that he had taken another human life. As much as his mind tried to justify his actions, the plain fact remained unchanged. He had killed four innocent astronauts—people that he knew well after training together for over two years.

Sergei stared at his brown eyes in the small mirror by the module's personal hygiene station. *There is no turning back now.*

Closing his eyes, Sergei saw Nikolai Naskalhov's round face. He remembered Nikolai as he told Sergei of the pain inflicted on the Chechen people by the Russians. The rapes, the killings, the abuses, the humiliation, the agony his people had endured for so long while the Americans stood by, while the rest of the world stood by. But Sergei also remembered the feeling of retribution that radiated from Nikolai's burning stare. The presidential aide had suffered as much as many Chechens but was willing to sacrifice everything to strike back, to stand up for his people.

Filling his lungs with the purified air of the Habitation Module, Sergei Viktor Dudayev watched his reflection in silence.

Two

Wearing one-piece blue coveralls, Mission Commander Diane Williams sat in the rear of one of three firing rooms on the third floor of the Kennedy Space Center's Launch Control Center (LCC), a four-story building located south of the Vehicle Assembly Building, where shuttles were mated to External Tanks and to Solid Rocket Boosters prior to their rollout to Launch Complex 39.

Running a hand though her short, brown hair, the forty-five-year-old astronaut of three previous shuttle flights watched the start of her flight's countdown, initiated with a Call to Stations at T minus twenty-four hours. The retired Marine aviator crossed her arms, which looked as thin as they had been when she was in the military, but without the firmness of daily exercise.

She watched LCC technicians run orbiter checkouts from their workstations by using complex algorithms that monitored and recorded the prelaunch performance of all electrical and mechanical systems and subsystems aboard *Endeavour*. The workstations, linked to the large-scale Honeywell computers one floor below, sent an array of commands to thousands of sensors inside the orbiter. The sensors measured specific parameters and relayed the information back to the workstations for comparison against safety limits stored in the Honeywell's memory banks. The cycle of information and checks would continue nonstop until seconds after liftoff, when control of the mission would be handed off to Mission Control in Houston, Texas.

"What do you think of our new passengers, Diane?" asked Gary McGregor, the thirty-seven-year-old astronaut of one previous shuttle flight scheduled to be Diane's Mission Pilot. McGregor, a former Air Force captain and F-16 pilot, was a short man, almost four inches shorter than Diane's five-ten, with black hair, a carefully clipped mustache, and brown eyes that widened as he grimaced, something McGregor had been doing a lot since the change in mission plans two days before.

Diane glanced at the four "Space Marines," the term adopted by astronauts when referring to the selected team of UN Security Council forces trained to operate in zero gravity.

"Look like your average tough *hombres*," Diane replied with a shrug, her slim brows rising a trifle. "I hope they can handle it up there."

McGregor nodded.

The four soldiers, wearing all-black uniforms, stood roughly thirty feet to Diane's left. Their eyes were trained on a sixty-inch projection screen on the left wall of the firing room, displaying a Titan-IV rocket slowly lifting off Pad 40. The Titan carried a large segmented mirror left over from the Strategic Defense Initiative days. Diane's first priority after reaching orbit would be to chase and rendezvous with the Titan's payload and connect the large mirror to the end of two Remote Manipulator System arms—the fifty-foot-long shuttle robotic arm used to deploy satellites—to protect *Endeavour* from a potential laser discharge by the Russian terrorist aboard the ISS.

Timing was of the essence to complete the mission successfully, before the Russian regained control of the warheads. Diane had to deploy the mirror before the terrorist realized that *Endeavour* had been launched, and he used the laser to destroy the shuttle just as he had the Russian Cosmos satellite. There was a risk of detection, but NASA had minimized it by programming the mission software aboard *Endeavour* to achieve an orbit 180 degrees out of phase with the space station, meaning that the orbiter and the station would be on the same circular orbit, but at opposite ends, with the Earth in between, until *Endeavour* was properly shielded. In addition, to prevent the terrorist from destroying any other satellites, NASA, in conjunction with the Department of Defense, had disabled the mirrors in geosynchronous orbit, and also the Brilliant Eyes search-and-tracking satellites used by the laser's tracking system to zero in on a target. The laser's range of operations had been reduced to detecting and engaging objects within the station's visual horizon.

The UNSC had also considered firing Anti-Satellite (ANSAT) missiles at the ISS to distract the terrorist while *Endeavour* dropped off the Space Marines. That approach, however, carried the risk of a missile slipping through and destroying the station. The ANSAT option then became a last resort if the shuttle mission failed to prevent the terrorist from gaining access to the warheads.

But by the time we get that close, the mirror will protect the shuttle, she thought, as the Titan broke through the sound barrier and continued its ascent undisturbed.

Diane glanced back at McGregor, who for the past day had began to show signs of stress. "You okay?" she asked.

The native of Tulsa, Oklahoma, brushed a finger over his mustache as his eyes stared in the distance. "I'll be fine."

Diane tilted her head toward the UNSC soldiers. "We just have to get those guys close enough to the station. The rest is up to them. Pretty straightforward."

McGregor didn't respond right away. The current mission plan, after attaching the mirror to the robot arms, called for Diane and McGregor to pilot the shuttle to a concentric orbit six miles above the ISS during the night portion of the orbit, when the station's large solar panels were idle and the laser system drew its power from its backup batteries. The terrorist would probably detect the incoming shuttle and most likely blast away with the laser against the shielded orbiter until it ran out of power. Afterward the UNSC soldiers would use a prototype Lockheed boarding vehicle, currently being loaded into *Endeavour*'s payload bay, to reach the hyperbaric airlock of the ISS, neutralize the terrorist, and regain control of the station. It was a simple plan, but the Marine in Diane knew that military missions didn't always go as planned. And McGregor knew it too.

Fortunately for everyone, the Lockheed boarding vehicle, a top-secret Air Force project that was being readied for space at the processing facilities of Cape Canaveral Air Force Station (CCAFS), was scheduled for launch in six weeks aboard *Atlantis*. Now CCAFS personnel were working in conjunction with the Launch Complex 39A team to swap payloads. *Endeavour*'s original payload, two commercial satellites and one Department of Defense (DOD) satellite, had already been loaded back into its payload canister and returned to the Vertical Processing Facility. CCAFS personnel now transferred their secret cargo from the payload canister to *Endeavour*'s payload bay. The operation was scheduled for completion in another two hours.

McGregor shook his head. "I'm Air Force, Diane. I know how these last-minute missions usually go . . ." He lowered his voice a few decibels. "I mean, we had no dry runs here. No simulation time on this type of approach. We're banking *everything* on being able to connect that damned mirror to the RMS arms, and also on being able to control the arms and the shuttle attitude verniers to keep that mirror shielding us. What if something goes wrong? Do you know what that laser can do to the orbiter? And how about that classified Lockheed vehicle we're carrying? Do you know how to use it? And what's that special cargo labeled UNSC CLASSIFIED in the lockers of the crew compartment? Do you know?"

Diane shook her head slightly while giving McGregor a slanted glance, pushing out her lower lip in a resigning pout.

"Neither do I."

"That's not our concern, Gary. We've been given a mission. Those guys have theirs. Period. You served in the military, didn't you? What we're doing's called following orders."

McGregor frowned. "How do you manage to keep it all straight in your head?"

Diane shrugged and looked away. Her mind had already formulated the answer: California. Many years ago. During a training exercise outside the Marines' El Toro Air Station, her F/A-18D Hornet had flamed out, sending her jet into an uncontrollable spin. She had managed to eject in time but injured her back when a gust of wind swung her parachute into the side of a hill.

Diane closed her eyes. She remembered the base's doctor, a petite woman with a heart-shaped face, a pointy nose, and enormous round black eyes wearing a white lab coat and a stethoscope hanging from her neck. She introduced herself as Dr. Lisa Hottle, a physician assigned by the base's commander to look after her. Dr. Hottle explained to Diane the crippling consequences of her spinal-cord injury and the possibility of walking again but only after undergoing extended physical therapy. The Marine aviator immediately withdrew into the tears. Life had dealt her a cruel hand. For the weeks that followed Diane fell into a state of depression. The Marine Corps sent a battalion of psychiatrists to help her cope with the drastic changes in her life, but nothing helped.

Late one evening, Dr. Hottle came into Diane's room to check on her condition. Diane, barely acknowledging the doctor, gazed at the stars through the window next to the dresser. Instead of taking Diane's pulse, Dr. Hottle simply stood at the foot of her bed staring at Diane. *So, you're feeling sorry for yourself?* Dr. Hottle asked. Before Diane could reply, the petite doctor unbuttoned her blouse and reached behind her back, lowering her padded brassiere. The sobering revelation struck Diane with the force of a jet on afterburners as she stared at her breastless chest, a pink scar traversing Dr. Hottle's upper chest from armpit to armpit from a double mastectomy. *You simply go on, my dear Diane. You simply just . . . just fight with all you've got and go on with your life.*

Diane had not only learned to walk again, but within six months of the accident she was back on a Hornet. A year later she had joined NASA and became a shuttle astronaut.

As the Titan rocket shot high above the clouds, Diane Williams let the memories fade. Although she considered this mission the most important of her life, that experience long ago had given her a new perspective in life.

Diane checked her watch. "Looks like the Titan is going to make orbit, and that means we're going up, too. See you in a few."

Diane headed toward the entrance of the firing room, walking by the Space Marines.

"All set, Commander?" asked the senior UNSC officer, a black ex–Army colonel by the name of Frank Ward, his booming voice matching his six-foot-three height and 240 pounds of solid muscle. Ward had been in a bad mood ever since NASA got news of the killings aboard the station. His man aboard the ISS had apparently failed to prevent the terrorist from gaining control of the station. The UNSC had come down hard on Ward, drilling him on every aspect of his operation, questioning his team's capabilities to carry out the assignment for which the UNSC spent over twenty million dollars per year in equipment and training. Now Ward and his team were under extreme pressure to recover the station and save whatever was left of their reputation.

She grinned at the bald colonel with the powerful chest and equally strong arms and legs. A pair of piercing brown eyes stared back at Diane. "We're ready, Colonel."

"Are you certain? This mission is far too important."

"We're *always* ready, Colonel. Are you?"

Ward raised a brow and said, "We'll be there."

"Good. See you at the launchpad."

Three

Fifteen minutes later, Diane peeked inside one of many windowless offices at the KSC's headquarters. A medium-built man in his late forties sitting behind a desk typed on a computer. He wore a pair of dark slacks, a perfectly starched cotton white shirt, and a maroon tie. The keyboard clicking stopped, and he looked up above the edge of the brown monitor, studying Diane for a few seconds through rimless glasses. Narrow streaks of gray on his otherwise brown hair gave him a touch of elegance.

"May I help you?" he asked, returning his eyes to the screen. The clicking resumed.

Diane walked inside the ten-by-twelve office, closing and locking the door behind her. "As a matter of fact I need lots of help."

He looked at her again, smiling. "Exactly what kind of help do you seek?"

Diane reached his desk and sat against the edge, her back now toward him. "Well, you see. I'm about to go on this long and dangerous journey, and I feel I need something else besides my training to help me make it through."

He stood, walked around the desk, and stood in front of her. Standing almost six-foot and weighing 190 pounds, he removed his glasses and, tossing them over the desk, told Diane, "I'm sorry, miss, but I still don't understand exactly what I can do to assist you on this journey."

Diane pulled him toward her before throwing her arms around his neck and kissing him on the lips. A moment later she pulled away, staring into the eyes of Jake Cohen, and saying, "That'll get me from liftoff to Solid Rocket Booster separation. After that I'm afraid I'm gonna run out of motivation."

Jake smiled, taking her in with a greedy stare. He had always loved to play these little games. The businesslike, forty-eight-year-old veteran astronaut and now Capsule Communicator (CapCom) for the past dozen shuttle flights had a private side that never ceased to amaze Diane Williams. Not only was Jake Cohen a refreshing change in Diane's otherwise very organized life, but Jake was also one of the very few men Diane had met who was never threatened by her profession. As a matter of fact, Jake once confessed to her that her brilliant mind and different past had attracted him to her just as much as her stunning looks.

"I heard the Titan launch went clean," Jake said.

Diane nodded while brushing her lipstick off Jake's face. He intercepted her index finger and sucked it gently. She pulled it away. "Pervert."

"Can't seem to control myself around you . . . speaking of which, most everyone's out to lunch, and you did lock the door, didn't you?"

She quickly pushed him away. "You're nuts, Jake."

"Hey," he said, pulling her close. "You only live once."

"Stop it, Jake. Besides, we got a briefing in twenty minutes."

"That's plenty of—"

"No."

"It's gonna be a long and lonely week."

She smiled. "Are you really going to miss me?"

"Yep."

"Liar. But thanks anyway," she said with an odd little glance at Jake, who had always enjoyed spending time by himself. Diane sensed that Jake probably looked forward to just a little space for the next few days. Since their relationship had gone into high gear six months before, neither of them had done much outside of work besides rolling under the sheets at his or her place. As it turned out, both Diane and Jake had not had a sexual partner for some time. So when Jake's hands had ventured inside Diane's cotton skirt after going through a bottle of Chardonnay late one evening at his apartment during their seventh date in three weeks, Diane had not resisted, figuring Jake not only was the most understanding, decent, and honest man she had ever known, but he also had a similar technical background, which gave them a lot more in common.

Jake suddenly turned businesslike. "Are you okay about this flight? You don't have to go if you don't want to. I mean, there is a lot of risk on this one."

Diane put a hand to his face and smiled. "And I love you too, darling."

Jake grimaced. The issue of her going on this mission had come up in every conversation they'd had in the past two days, since NASA settled on a recovery strategy. Jake had volunteered to go in her place, and that comment had resulted in their first fight ending with Jake's quick withdrawal of his suggestion plus a dozen roses. But as charming and intelligent as Jake Cohen was, he was also a hardheaded bastard who would not give up until *Endeavour* left the launchpad. Trouble was, Diane's head was as thick as his.

"Jake, I don't question your professional decisions, so, please, don't question mine. Besides, you'll be with me on the radio every step of the way."

Jake regarded her with a peculiar grin, at once agreeable and frustrated. "You're some strange piece of work, Diane Williams. But at least you're my kind of strange."

"I warned you about getting involved with me. I'm not an airhead in a bikini walking down Cocoa Beach."

Jake laughed, "But you sure look great in one . . . or out of one."

Diane slapped his shoulder.

"Say, speaking of strange, what do you think of your passengers?"

She shrugged. "We both have a mission, but up there I'm *Mission Commander*, meaning it is *my* pond and up to the point that he leaves the orbiter he *will* follow my orders. I think we understand each other. I am annoyed, however, that NASA won't allow me to inspect the gear they're bringing aboard my ship."

"Look, you and I know that this mission is a bit different from what we're used to flying. In the past at least we were told we were carrying classified cargo, and we were even given some level of detail about it, but absolute secrecy on this one is top priority directly from the top. I know it makes you and Gary mad as hell not knowing much about this new boarding vehicle or the stuff that they are hauling inside the crew module, but the reality of things is that you two don't have a need to know. That's Colonel Ward's job. Think of him as a mission specialist. Your job is just to get him and his team close enough to the station and then get the hell out of the range of that laser as fast as possible, and stay out of sight until Ward and his men get the situation under control."

"I'll do my part, Jake. I was in the Marines. I know how to follow orders. When is your plane leaving for Houston?" she asked.

"In three hours. Do you want to grab a bite at the cafeteria?"

Diane Williams nodded and leaned forward, kissing him on the cheek before they walked side by side toward the door.

Four

The waiting never got any easier, decided Diane Williams as the digital display of *Endeavour*'s mission timer showed T minus three minutes. No matter how many times she'd done it before, sitting on top of enough chemicals to create a blast as powerful as the BLU-85 warheads aboard the GPATS module in the ISS made her question whether she had chosen the right career after leaving the Marine Corps.

But the reason why she felt even more concerned at that moment than on any of her previous flights was not the fact that *Endeavour* could become the target in an orbital shooting alley for the terrorist manning the GPATS laser. After all, Diane had been a Marine aviator. She had dodged more than her fair share of antiaircraft fire during the Gulf War. The woman in the astronaut knew there was another reason for her abnormally high heartbeat, for her dried mouth, for her sweaty palms. She had never before felt this nervous about a launch, not even during her first time, shortly after completing her astronaut training.

There was another reason, but it was one the astronaut in her refused to admit, for it made her feel weak in the eyes of her professional mind. For the first time since joining NASA Diane was truly afraid of dying. She had not realized her fear until she'd reached the Operations and Checkout building before dawn that morning to eat the classic steak and eggs breakfast, prior to suiting up and heading for the launchpad. The realization of the danger involved, not only in a routine orbiter flight, but in this particular mission had slowly begun to sink in with every bite she had taken of that medium-well sirloin steak and scrambled eggs. And the reason for the uncharacteristic fear was Jake Cohen. For the first time in her life Diane had fallen in love, and that gave her something that she feared losing.

Jake Cohen filled Diane's life more than anyone or anything else, even flying. She never thought it could happen, but somewhere during the past six months her priorities in life had changed, and the possibility of a life with Jake had superseded all her other ambitions. Perhaps it was the fact that she was forty-five. Or maybe that the pilot in her had seen enough action to last forty-five lifetimes. Or the fact that Jake loved her the way she was. She wasn't sure why it had happened, only that it had. And it had been a revelation she had kept all to herself, refusing to share it even with the man she loved. The fear of lowering her wall of pride and exposing her innermost feelings to Jake Cohen was just as intense as the fear that ran through her body at that moment, while her pale green eyes gazed at a dawning sky through the 1.3-inch-thick windowpane directly in front of her.

Breathing in the oxygen and nitrogen air mixture inside the flight deck while forcing her mind to put her fears aside, Diane checked the timer and gave Gary McGregor a thumbs-up. The Mission Pilot winked and returned the gesture.

The NASA Launch Room controller's voice crackled through the orbiter's speakers.

"T minus two minutes fifty-two seconds. Endeavour: *the liquid oxygen valve on the External Tank has been closed and pressurization has begun."*

The colossal rust-colored External Tank, carrying over 1.3 million pounds of liquid oxygen and 227,641 pounds of liquid hydrogen, and measuring nearly 158 feet in length, began to pressurize the liquid oxygen housed inside its aluminum-monocoque-structured tank to a pressure of twenty-one pounds per square inch—the pressure necessary to force the oxidizer to the three Space Shuttle Main Engines and achieve combustion with the volatile liquid-hydrogen propellant.

"T minus two minutes fifteen seconds: the main engines have been gimbaled to their start position and the pressure on the liquid oxygen tank is at flight pressure. T minus two minutes and counting: the liquid oxygen vent valve has been closed and flight pressurization is under way."

She glanced at CRT#1, one of three CRTs on the control panel between McGregor and her, displaying the status of the main engines. She also glanced at an array of warning lights between CRTs #2 and #3. Nothing seemed abnormal.

"Coming up on the one-minute point on the countdown, everything

is going smoothly. The firing system for the ground suppression water is armed."

Diane battled her rocketing heartbeat. *Just like in the Marines, Diane.* she told herself. *Relax and do what you do best!*

"T minus thirty-seven seconds and counting; switching control of the launch to the computer sequence."

Launch countdown control switched from KSC's Launch Processing System to *Endeavour*'s five General Purpose Computers, four working in parallel, the fifth checking the output from the other four.

"T minus twenty seconds: SRB hydraulic power unit started, the SRB nozzles have been moved to the start position. Coming up on fifteen. Switching to redundant start sequence. T minus twelve . . . eleven . . . ten . . . nine."

Diane closed her eyes and visualized the sound-suppression water system nozzles popping up from the Mobile Launch Platform base, like lawn sprinklers, and beginning to spray water onto the base of the MLP at the rate of 900,000 gallons per minute in anticipation of main engine start.

"Seven . . . six . . . we're going for main engine start!"

The GPCs ordered the opening of the liquid-hydrogen and liquid-oxygen feed valves of the huge External Tank, channeling both propellant and oxidizer to the Space Shuttle Main Engines through seventeen-inch-diameter feed lines, at the rate of 47,365 and 17,592 gallons per minute respectively. The highly cooled chemicals reached each of the SSMEs, where two sets of turbopumps boosted the chemicals to pressures of 6,500 PSI for the propellant and 7,400 PSI for the oxidizer. The chemicals reached the combustion chambers at fulminating speeds before exploding in a hypergolic reaction that created a colossal outburst of highly pressurized steam.

The soul-numbing rumble that followed reverberated through the entire orbiter as each of the three SSMEs, capable of unleashing 375,000 pounds of thrust, kicked into life at 120-millisecond intervals, and automatically throttled up to the ninety percent level.

"We've got main engine start . . . three . . . two!"

The GPCs verified that all three engines had maintained the required thrust level before firing the pyrotechnic device in each of the two Solid Rocket Boosters, and the resulting blast echoed through Diane's soul as the astounding uproar of 7.5 million pounds of thrust thundered against the cushion of water above the Mobile Launch Platform. The acoustic shock wave pounded the ground on this warm and humid dawn as the brightness from *Endeavour*'s engines illuminated the indigo sky, casting a yellowish glow for miles around.

The GPCs verified proper SRB ignition and, a fraction of a second later, initiated the eight explosive hold-down bolts—twenty-eight inches long and 3.5 inches thick—anchoring the shuttle to the Mobile Launch Platform. All three SSMEs throttled up to 104 percent, and the computers started the mission timer. Diane sensed upward motion.

"Liftoff! We have achieved liftoff!"

The 4.5-million-pound shuttle rose vertically in attitude hold until the SRBs' nozzles cleared the tower by forty feet.

"Houston, *Endeavour*. Starting roll maneuver," commented Diane in a monotone and controlled voice, shoving away all of her fears.

Endeavour began a combined roll, pitch, and yaw maneuver to position it head down, with the wings leveled and aligned with the launchpad.

"Roll maneuver completed."

"Endeavour, *Houston. Got a visual from the ground. You're looking good. Mark twenty seconds,"* Jake Cohen said from JSC.

"Roger, Houston," responded Diane.

Diane glanced at CRT#1, where an ascent-trajectory graph showed the desired ascent route and *Endeavour*'s current position as the GPCs issued millions of commands every second to the gimbal-mounted SSMEs and the SRBs to keep the orbiter on track. With this part of the mission totally automated, Diane and McGregor limited themselves to monitoring equipment and instruments as the shuttle rose higher and higher, leaving behind a billowing trail of steam and smoke.

"Houston, *Endeavour*. Mark thirty seconds. Throttling down for Max Q."

"Roger, Endeavour. *Throttling down."*

Endeavour's main engines throttled down to reduce the aerodynamic stress on the 21,000 thermal protection tiles glued to the orbiter's all-aluminum skin as the vehicle approached the speed of sound.

"Passed Max Q. Engines back up to 104 percent," reported Diane, as ice broke off from the External Tank and crashed against the front windowpanes. Diane saw their minute explosions before they disintegrated and washed away in the slipstream. One point three Mach. They had gone supersonic.

"Houston, *Endeavour*. Mark one minute ten seconds," reported McGregor. "Five nautical miles high, three nautical miles downrange, velocity reads at 2,300 feet per second."

Diane's eyes drifted to CRT#1. *Right on track*, she thought. The GPCs and their complex ascent phase algorithms performed beautifully. Right next to CRT#1 were the master alarm warning lights. All looked normal. Below it she saw the mission timer.

"Mark one minute twenty seconds, Houston," Diane read out. "Nine nautical miles high, six nautical miles downrange. Three thousand feet per second. Mark one minute thirty-five seconds."

"Roger, Endeavour. *We copy you at one minute forty-five seconds. You are now negative seats. Repeat. Negative seats."*

"Roger, negative seats," responded Diane as *Endeavour* soared above the maximum altitude for safe use of ejection seats.

Diane checked the chamber pressure of both Solid Rocket Boosters. It had dropped to 55 PSI down from 400 PSI at liftoff. At 50 PSI both SRBs automatically shut off and the GPCs' SRB separation sequence software automatically fired the bolts holding the SRBs to the External Tank.

Diane watched the pyrotechnic display as *Endeavour*, still mated to the ET, rocketed at nearly five thousand feet per second while both SRBs arced down toward the Atlantic almost ten miles below.

"Endeavour, *Houston. Confirm SRB sep."*

"Smooth, Houston. Very smooth," responded Diane. "Mark two minutes twenty-five seconds."

"Roger, Endeavour*."*

Diane and McGregor monitored the readings from the CRTs for the next five minutes as *Endeavour* gathered speed and altitude while depleting the propellant and heavy oxidizer in the External Tank. This made the shuttle progressively lighter without a change in upward thrust, allowing *Endeavour* to accelerate to 24,000 feet per second—the speed necessary to break away from the Earth's gravitational pull and achieve an orbital flight.

"Houston, *Endeavour*. Mark eight minutes twenty seconds, altitude sixty-three nautical miles, 645 nautical miles downrange. Standing by for MECO."

"*Roger*. Endeavour."

Diane watched the GPCs initiating the Main Engine Cut Off sequence. All three SSMEs shut off the moment the feed-line valves connected to the umbilical cords coming out of the External Tank were closed. Eighteen seconds later, the computers jettisoned the ET by firing the explosive bolts anchoring it to the orbiter. Suddenly engulfed by the silence of space, Diane watched the ET separating with a velocity of four feet per second. The tank would continue on a suborbital trajectory, which would take whatever survived the reentry breakup to an impact location in the Indian Ocean.

"Houston, *Endeavour*. We have ET sep," said McGregor.

"Roger, Endeavour. *Eight minutes fifty-eight seconds, confirmed External Tank separation."*

"Roger, Houston. Stand by for first OMS burn," said Diane as she armed both Orbital Maneuvering System engines, vital to perform orbital insertion. With its current altitude of eighty nautical miles and inertial velocity of 24,300 feet per second, *Endeavour* flew a very unstable suborbital trajectory, which would bring the orbiter directly within the range of the ISS's laser. In order to boost the orbiter to a safe orbit fast, one long OMS thrusting burn would be made instead of the usual two. The OMS engines consisted of two pods, one on each side of the upper aft fuselage on either side of *Endeavour*'s vertical stabilizer.

"OMS burn in five . . . four . . . three . . . two . . . one . . . now!"

In each OMS engine, highly pressurized helium forced both hydrazine propellant and liquid oxygen down to the reaction chamber at great speed. The chemicals clashed in a hyperbolic reaction, creating the necessary outburst of thrust. The temporary silence gave way to yet another roaring blast. Diane felt a mild pressure forcing her against her flight seat as the OMS engines, providing a combined thrust of twelve thousand pounds, began to accelerate *Endeavour*.

"Mark fifteen seconds, Houston. All systems nominal. Helium pressure's 3700 PSI on both tanks. Propellant and oxidizer pressure looks good," reported McGregor.

"We copy, Endeavour.*"*

Three minutes and twenty seconds later the OMS engines shut off, and Diane nodded approvingly. Orbital insertion had been as accurate as anyone could have hoped. *Endeavour* flew a stable orbit 180 degrees out of phase with the ISS, and on an intercept course with the Titan payload, which *Endeavour* would reach in another five hours.

"Good job, Endeavour.*"*

"Thanks."

In reality, besides initiating the single OMS burn, her contribution to the mission had been next to none.

But that changes now, she reflected as she unstrapped her safety harness and watched McGregor do the same.

"What do you think so far?" she asked.

"Well," he responded as they floated side by side behind the seats, "I just hope we can attach that mirror to the RMS arms."

"One thing at a time."

She removed her helmet, and her shoulder-length hair floated above her head. She wore a pair of small diamond earrings.

Diane used a single arm motion to push herself gently to the aft flight-deck station to open the payload bay doors and expose the vital heat radiators to space. The radiators, used by *Endeavour*'s environmental-control system, dissipated the heat generated by the orbiter's equipment and also the heat accumulated on *Endeavour*'s skin during the ascent phase.

That accomplished, Diane dived through one of two interdeck hatches on the flight deck's floor down to the crew compartment, where Colonel Frank Ward and his three warriors, dressed in matching all-black uniforms, had already unstrapped themselves from their seats and were going over a diagram of the space station.

Three of the lockers on the forward section of the crew module, opposite the airlock, were already open, exposing a number of black boxes marked with bright yellow codes.

Colonel Ward raised his head and briefly made eye contact with Diane Williams before motioning one of his men to close the lockers.

Since their brief chat at the firing room a couple of days before, the colonel had kept conversation with the former Marine colonel to a minimum, and that suited Diane just fine. The less interaction she had with him or his men, the happier she felt. Jake was right. All she had to do was get Ward and his team close to the ISS, and then move out until it was safe to return. The rest was up to them.

"Everything okay, Commander?" asked Ward.

"No problems, Colonel. You and your men made it fine?"

"Yes. Smooth ascent."

"Good. I know you and your men are taking all the necessary precautions with your special payload, including whatever it is you have stored in those lockers. I'm sure you realize the danger involved if the air inside the crew module is contaminated. You do remember *Apollo* 7, right? The fire inside the capsule that incinerated three astronauts?"

Ward gave her a long stern look before saying, "All of my equipment was approved by NASA, Commander. Why don't you stick to your job and I'll stick to mine?"

"Fair enough," she responded, as Ward lowered his gaze back to the large blueprint floating in between the four Space Marines. Diane checked her watch and looked over to McGregor making his way through a hatch from the flight deck. "Start prebreathing in two hours, Gary."

McGregor also checked his watch before nodding. Prebreathing 100 percent oxygen was required prior to a space walk to remove nitrogen from his bloodstream. Inside the airlock, they breathed a mixture of oxygen and nitrogen at a pressure of 14.7 pounds per square inch, the same as sea level. But once inside a space suit, McGregor would breathe pure oxygen at a reduced pressure of only four PSI—the pressure required by the Extravehicular Mobility Unit suit for ease of limb movement during EVA without excessive physical effort. The rapid drop in pressure around his body would cause bubbles of nitrogen to form and expand in his bloodstream, causing severe nausea, cramps, paralysis, and even death—the same problem faced by scuba divers when surfacing too quickly following a deep underwater session.

Diane headed for the changeout station to the right of the airlock, and, extending the privacy curtain, she changed out of her crash suit and into the blue coveralls standard for shuttle missions.

She floated back up to the flight deck. She wanted to run some tests on the RMS arms. Its proper functionality was paramount to the mission.

Five

The Flight Control Room was located on the third floor of the Mission Control Center at Johnson Space Center in Houston, Texas. Capsule Communicator (CapCom) Jake Cohen sat back on his swivel chair in the rear of the large room, where almost thirty flight controllers for this mission worked behind console computer displays arranged in rows of six or seven across the entire length of the room. A few projection screens on the front wall displayed different mission-related information, including a world chart that plotted *Endeavour*'s location in orbit and actual television pictures of activities inside and outside the shuttle, like the view of Earth on the screen to the right of the world chart, and a view of the payload bay on the screen to the left. Other displays showed critical data such as elapsed time after launch, or the time remaining before the next maneuver, which in *Endeavour*'s case was the time to rendezvous with the Titan target.

Jake removed his glasses, rubbed his eyes, and loosened his tie. So far, so good. Being CapCom was an important but quite stressful responsibility, particularly since he had to pretty much live inside Mission Control for the duration of the flight. But like his predecessors, going all the way back to the Mercury Program of the early sixties, Jake understood the significance of him being here. He was the primary voice that the crew aboard *Endeavour* heard after launch. He was their primary contact while the astronauts traveled in space at over twenty-four times the speed of sound. In his hands, and in the hands of the Flight

Director (called Flight) sitting to Jake's immediate right, rested the responsibility of making sound split-second decisions and passing them on to the crew in space in an emergency. CapComs and Flights have been doing basically the same thing for over forty years: assisting countless crews on countless spacecraft accomplish their missions and return home safely.

Since it opened for business on a 1,620-acre site twenty-five miles southeast of Houston in February of 1964, the responsibilities of the Johnson Space Center have included the design, development, and testing of spacecraft, the selection and training of astronauts, the planning and conducting of manned missions, and many other activities related to help man understand life in outer space. And it all started with the Mercury Program.

The Mercury Program. Jake couldn't help a tiny smile. The term Capsule Communicator was a holdover from those early manned flights, when Mercury was called a capsule rather than a spacecraft. Those had been simpler times, when compared to current events, yet . . . *look at what we have done with our accomplishments.*

Jake felt disappointed that despite all the technical advancements and all the scientific breakthroughs, man was still man. And at that moment one madman was at the controls of the world's most advanced—and most expensive—technological wonder, and the U.S. had sent an equally technological wonder to stop him before he wiped out the downtown area of every major capital in the world—according to a communiqué broadcast just hours ago from Grozny, Chechnya. Unless the United Nations—Russia in particular—agreed to a twenty-point list of demands from the Chechen president, including the acquisition of nuclear missiles to protect itself again future Russian threats, the terrorist would start releasing the GPATS deadly cargo one at a time according to a priority list of targets.

Jake could only pray that Colonel Ward's team was indeed as good as he claimed, and that nothing went wrong with the orbiter. Clearly, there was no other way to regain control of the ISS than by force.

Six

From the aft mission station of the flight deck, Diane Williams guided one of two Remote Manipulator System arms from its stowed position on the main longeron of the starboard payload-bay upper wall to the large segmented mirror hovering thirty feet above the orbiter.

She looked through one of the two rear-facing windows at the fifty-foot-long mechanical arm, which had six joints designed to mimic the human arm. The RMS had shoulder yaw and pitch joints, an elbow pitch joint, and wrist pitch, yaw, and roll joints—all controlled by a joystick-type hand controller.

Slaved to Diane's hand motions, the RMS slowly extended toward one side of the rectangular mirror, nearly as long as *Endeavour* and just as wide as the orbiter's wingspan. Anchored to the end of the robot arm was Gary McGregor in his Extravehicular Mobility Unit (EMU), an untethered pressurized suit that provided McGregor with a one hundred percent oxygen environment pressurized to three pounds per square inch (PSI), the equivalent atmospheric pressure of 14,000 feet in altitude.

They already almost had to scrub the mission because of the difficulties in retrieving the large segmented mirror from a malfunctioning Titan shroud. The procedure, which NASA had scheduled to take only four hours, had actually taken three times as long, requiring two separate space walks because the oxygen supply inside the EMU backpack only lasted eight hours. Using a battery-operated circular saw, McGregor had cut the faulty latching mechanism halfway through his second EVA, allowing the spring-loaded shroud to separate along its longitudinal axes, exposing the mirror, which then had to be unfolded before attempting to secure it to the ends of the two RMS arms.

This flight was the first time that NASA had loaded two RMS arms aboard a shuttle. Normally, only one robot arm was needed to accomplish most operations involving satellite deployment and retrievals, but this situation was quite different. Two arms were required in order to achieve a strong grip on the mirror, particularly during orbit transfer maneuvers, when *Endeavour* would use the Orbital Maneuvering System engines to change orbits and chase the space station. But loading a second RMS arm aboard the shuttle had come at the price of sacrificing the Ku-band antenna, normally used for communication and data transmissions at a much faster rate than the orbiter's S-band antennas. This was a reasonable compromise to increasing the odds of keeping that mirror snuggled tight against the shuttle.

McGregor disengaged himself from the end of the RMS arm and grabbed a handle at the edge of the mirror.

"Tether yourself to the RMS, Gary," she said when noticing that McGregor had not secured his EMU suit to the manipulator arm after disengaging from the RMS. If something went wrong at that moment, McGregor could be sent floating out of control away from the orbiter with nothing to hold him back.

"Okay," he responded as he attached one end of a woven cable to the RMS while clipping the other to a metal ring on the side of his pressure suit. *"All right, now bring the end up . . . nice and gently."*

The arm's standard end was only about three feet from the edge of the mirror. Using the two-position slide switch on top of the rotational hand controller, Diane changed the sensitivity of the arm from coarse to vernier. The RMS motors moved now at a fraction of the speed they did before. Operating in this fine-adjusting mode, Diane positioned the end of the RMS within inches of a special fitting welded onto the aluminum-and-graphite frame supporting the segmented mirror.

"All right. How's that?"

"Almost there. Bring it up just a dash."

Slowly, following McGregor's hand signals, Diane brought the end of the arm in direct contact with the latching pin on the mirror, until the latch snapped in place.

Locking the arm, Diane Williams switched control of the Rotational Hand Controller to the second RMS, set the vernier/coarse switch back to coarse, and mimicked the position of the first RMS. This time she did it without the help of McGregor, who was still strapped to the first RMS and was currently engaged in clamping a high-resolution TV camera to the edge of the mirror to be able to see objects on the other side of the mirror.

One of the complications of having two manipulator arms on board was that Diane could only control one arm at a time. Although the wiring for a second hand controller existed, NASA had never installed it because it had never been needed, until now. But such installation would had taken weeks to complete—time the world did not have.

"All right, Gary. I think you can come in now."

"On my way."

McGregor returned to the payload bay by crawling back along the first RMS. When he reached the airlock he said, *"I'm inside."*

"All right. Good job," Diane responded as she commanded the second RMS to pull the mirror closer to *Endeavour*, leaving just a foot between the orbiter's upper fuselage and the honeycomb frame supporting the mirror.

"How much clearance does that gives us?" said Colonel Frank Ward, who had been standing behind Diane for the past minute. The Lockheed boarding vehicle stored in the payload bay needed at least ten feet of clearance between the edge of the cargo bay wall and the mirror.

Without looking at the large black soldier, Diane said, "Not enough for your boarding vehicle. You tell me when you're ready, and I will lift one side to let you out. Otherwise, I'm keeping that mirror as close as possible to the orbiter."

"That's fine," Ward responded.

Diane felt bad enough that the vertical fin, the OMS pods, and a portion of the nose were not covered by the mirror. She didn't want sections of the wings also exposed by moving the mirror around. The OMS pods and the nose had to be exposed since that was where *Endeavour*'s attitude vernier rockets were located. Those rockets were critical for orbital maneuvering, and their exhaust paths could not be obstructed. But anything else was safely hidden behind the segmented mirror.

NASA had estimated the chances of the laser hitting the unprotected sections of the orbiter at less than three percent. And given the fact that she would just be dropping her load and then quickly getting out of the laser's range, she would be exposed to that three percent for just over twenty minutes. To make matters even safer for the crew of *Endeavour*, the mission plan called for approaching the station during nighttime, when the gigantic solar panels of the station would be essentially off, and the only power available for the laser would have to come from the GPATS module's vast array of storage batteries. According to the laser manufacturer, the batteries would only support somewhere around fifteen laser shots, depending on the energy level used and the duration of each event. After that, the Russian terrorist would be unable to fire the weapon until the station came back around into the daylight portion of the ninety-minute orbit. That gave Diane roughly forty-five minutes to make her approach, take the laser hits, drop the UNSCF soldiers and their gear, and get out of Dodge.

"How much time will we have to clear *Endeavour* once we're in position?" asked Ward.

"About ten minutes."

Ward nodded before turning around and propelling himself down one of the interdeck hatches.

Diane thought of Ward's secret cargo stored in the lockers below, hoping it wasn't anything flammable. An explosion inside the crew module would be bad news for everyone aboard. But she didn't realistically expect NASA to approve the storage of any dangerous substance inside the crew's living quarters.

Diane reached for the intercom. "Colonel?"

"Yes, Commander?"

"Please secure your gear in the crew compartment. We have a twenty-five-minute window to start our approach to the ISS. OMS burn in fifteen minutes."

"No problem."

"Gary? You're through?" Diane asked.

"I'm getting rid of the EMU." McGregor responded from inside the airlock.

"Get up here now."

McGregor floated into the flight deck a few minutes later.

"Diane . . . I think we have a little problem down there," he whispered, pointing to one of the hatches leading to the crew compartment below.

"Yes?"

Swallowing hard, McGregor said, "I got a chance to take a good look at what Ward's been guarding so carefully."

"And?"

"While I was changing inside the airlock, I saw them through the hatch's window."

"What is it, Gary?"

"HEP."

"Wh—what?"

"And from the looks of it, those guys down there were inserting fuses into the plastic. I guess they were waiting until after we reached orbit to arm the explosives to avoid the strong vibrations during ascent."

Putting a hand to her forehead, Diane Williams struggled to calm down. She couldn't believe that someone would be insane enough to bring high-explosive plastic on-board a shuttle. *And armed?*

She rushed past McGregor and dived through one of the interdeck openings.

"Colonel!" she screamed, reaching the crew compartment and startling the four UNSC soldiers, who were setting up the seats in preparation for the orbital maneuvers to chase the station. Each soldier had an oxygen mask over his face. A plastic tube ran from each clear mask to a pint-size tank strapped to the belt of each uniform. The soldiers were prebreathing pure oxygen in preparation for their space walk.

Ward pulled down the mask. "I'm right here, Commander. There's no reason to scream."

"Who gave you permission to bring explosives aboard this orbiter?"

Ward gave her an odd little glance. "I thought we had an understanding here about our respective roles."

"Not when it involves bringing HEP inside my shuttle."

Ward exhaled slowly, obviously not happy that she had found out about the HEP, but still trying to see if he could reason with her. He put his arms in front of him, palms facing Diane while the other soldiers looked on with curiosity. "Look, nothing's going to happen. We are profession—"

"I want to jettison the explosives immediately," she said.

The UNSC colonel simply crossed his arms. "Can't do that, Commander. The HEP's a critical element of our mission. If we can't regain control of the station before the terrorist regains access to the launching software, then my orders are to blow up the module. Besides, HEP doesn't just blow on accident because of vibrations or anything else. It need to be detonated."

"It wasn't a request, Colonel. It was an order."

"Sorry, Commander. That's an unreasonable request. Besides, I only take orders from the Secretary General of the United Nations. This is the way the UNSC has approved to carry out the mission, and the White House has bought into it."

"Do you realize what can happen if any of those charges go off inside the crew module?"

"*Won't* happen." Ward was beginning to show an edge. "The only time we were at risk was during ascent, and during that time I had the detonators removed from the charges. Now I need to get the charges ready for my mission. You've just told me I would only have ten minutes to get ready after reaching the ISS. That's barely enough time to—"

"We're not going anywhere until you lose those," Diane said, pointing a thumb toward the lockers. "And that's final."

"You're compromising my mission, Commander. I have permission from the UNSC to neutralize anyone who jeopardizes my team's ability to achieve our objective." Ward placed a hand on the stun gun strapped to his belt.

Diane tightened her fists and said, "And who's going to fly this shuttle?"

"Your Mission Pilot."

"He's not going to do it."

"Let's ask him."

Diane didn't like the way this was headed. She was losing control. "I'm calling Houston."

"Be my guest. But do it quickly, or we're going to miss our window."

Fuming, Diane headed back up to the flight deck, where a stone-faced McGregor stood by one of the interdeck openings.

"Jesus Christ, Diane. Let's just do it. Let's drop them off by the ISS and get the hell away from there until it's safe to return."

Reaching her seat, Diane put on her headgear and contacted Houston using the S-band frequency.

"Houston, *Endeavour*."

"Endeavour, *Houston. Go ahead,"* came the voice of Jake Cohen.

"Houston, I'm afraid we have a problem. Colonel Ward has stored HEP inside the crew compartment. I want to jettison it. We can't afford to have an explosion in here."

"Ah . . . that's a negative, Endeavour. *The explosives are secured, and are a vital component of this mission. HEP is very safe unless purposefully detonated."*

"Houston, we're talking about high-explosive plastic that could kill us all and destroy the orbiter. This goes totally against NASA policy. Remember *Apollo 7*? We can't allow anything that volatile on board."

"Sorry, Endeavour. *The soldiers must keep the HEP. We don't have a choice on this one. Their orders are to blast the GPATS module if they can't get inside the station. Besides, the* Apollo 7 *incident happened because the capsule had a 100 oxygen environment. You don't."*

"But they already have the fuses in and connected to the detonators. All it takes is one electric charge, and they'll blow!"

"This one comes straight from the top. The HEP stays. And you better get everything secured or you'll miss the window to reach the ISS in time."

Diane inhaled deeply. This was a mistake. A terrible mistake. Closing her eyes, she briefly prayed that nothing went wrong with the approach. Although HEP had a long safety record and was very unlikely to go off accidentally, Diane didn't want to add more risk to their mission. A subsystem could explode if the laser hit the wrong spot on the orbiter. Having explosives on board could create secondary explosions if the initial blast happened to be close to the charges.

"Endeavour, *Houston, Confirm orders."*

Diane shook her head as she said, "I want it on the record that I disagree with the orders, but I will execute them. I will secure all objects in preparation for the OMS burn."

"Roger, Houston out."

Slowly, Diane turned around, only to be welcomed by Colonel Frank Ward wearing a headset. The plastic oxygen mask floated under his square chin. The UNSC colonel had been listening to the conversation. McGregor stood in the back, flanked by two of Ward's men. The short F-16 pilot looked quite helpless next to the large and muscular soldiers in all-black uniforms.

"All set?" Ward asked.

Diane Williams nodded and turned back to her instruments. "We're about to start an orbital-change maneuver. Everyone take your seats."

Ward floated toward the back of the flight deck and disappeared through one of the interdeck hatches. The two soldiers followed him.

McGregor approached Diane as she strapped herself to her seat and put the headgear back on.

"Diane, are you—"

"Is the airlock secured, Gary?"

"Ye—yes. It's secured."

"Good. Strap in. We've got work to do."

Diane refused to let her emotions surface more than they already had. She was a professional. She was *Endeavour*'s commander. She would behave as such for as long as the mission lasted.

Before starting the final approach to the ISS, Diane had to realign the Inertial Measurement Units—three all-attitude, four-gimbal, inertially stabilized platforms that provided critical inertial attitude and velocity data to *Endeavour*'s General Purpose Computers—to maintain an accurate estimate of orbiter position and velocity during the orbital flight.

She did a quick radio check inside the orbiter to make sure all was secured. Satisfied, she reached for an overhead panel and enabled the Star Tracker system. Talk-back lights on the same panel told her both Star Tracker doors just forward and to the left of the front windowpanes had fully opened, exposing the two sophisticated bright object sensors to the cosmos. In addition to the nose attitude-control rockets, the Star Tracker system was another reason why the segmented mirror could not cover the orbiter's nose section.

The Star Tracker system measured the line-of-sight vectors to the two brightest stars within the system's field of view. The data was fed to the GPCs, which calculated the orientation between the selected stars and *Endeavour* to define the orbiter's attitude and relative velocity. A comparison between the calculated attitude and the attitude measured by the Inertial Measuring Unit provided Diane with the correction factor necessary to null the IMU error.

The newly adjusted position and velocity vectors, or "state" vectors, were then compared to the International Space Station's state vectors fed to *Endeavour*'s GPCs via S-band telemetry communications relayed from Houston. Both sets of state vectors, updated once every millisecond as both *Endeavour* and the ISS orbited the Earth, were fed to the Guidance, Navigation, and Control software running in the GPCs, which in turn fired the Orbital Maneuvering System thrusters.

Diane's eyes drifted to the OMS helium pressure and hydrazine propellant indicators as the engines came to life, unleashing twenty-six thousand pounds of thrust for fifteen seconds, directing a tail-first *Endeavour* toward its planned delivery orbit, nicknamed Delta. The mild deceleration force pressed her against the back of her flight seat as the southern portion of South America flashed across the top of the front windowpanes before disappearing behind the edge of the segmented mirror frame. In her mind, however, flashed the armed charges shifting inside their containers.

Focus!

A scan of control panel F7, where three five-inch-by-seven-inch green-on-green CRTs displayed the status of *Endeavour*'s vital systems, showed nominal. The array of talk-back indicator lights between CRT#1 and CRT#2, and directly above CRT#3 also showed no warnings. The OMS helium pressure indicator to the left of CRT#3 marked 3,700 pounds per square inch, matching the digital readouts on CRT#1 directly above.

"ETA to Delta Orbit, fifteen minutes," said McGregor, typing a few commands on the right keypad of the center console beneath control panel F7, while checking the readouts of the rendezvous radar measurement, which provided range and range rate to the station. Unlike the late nineties rendezvous radar systems, which could not be used until the orbiter got within fifteen miles of the target, the new system gave them ranging information from as far away as nine hundred miles.

Diane barely acknowledged it, her eyes switching back and forth between the mission event timer and CRT#1. At Delta Orbit, *Endeavour* would have achieved the necessary translational velocity to maintain an orbit six miles behind the ISS.

The GPCs stopped the OMS engines. "Burn complete," she said as the software programmed the aft and forward Reaction Control System verniers to turn the orbiter without disturbing its translational velocity, positioning the mirror toward the ISS. The moment the inertial system detected that the orbiter achieved the desired attitude, the GPCs fired the RCS thrusters in the opposite direction to counter the rotation.

She briefly glanced at McGregor before using a secured S-band radio frequency and speaking into her voice-activated headset. "Houston, *Endeavour*."

"*Go ahead*, Endeavour." She heard Jake's voice coming through very clear. Audio and video communications, as well as telemetry-data transfer, were established through the S-band frequency. Information from *Endeavour* traveled to one of three Tracking and Data Relay Satellites (TDRS) in geosynchronous orbit, where the signal was amplified and relayed to White Sands Tracking Station in New Mexico, before arriving in Houston. Although the link had been established nearly thirty years before, it still remained the best and most reliable way to establish clean, secured, and uninterrupted communications during a mission.

"Houston, OMS burn complete. ETA to Delta thirteen minutes, twenty seconds, over."

"Endeavour, *you're confirmed.*"

"Will be within firing range in one minute," Diane said while checking the leftover pressure on the OMS helium and propellant tanks, which told her that *Endeavour* now had enough fuel left for two more orbital maneuvers besides the deorbit burn at the end of the mission.

Diane glanced at McGregor, who brushed his mustache with a finger while frowning slightly, obviously feeling as nervous about this whole ordeal as she did.

"We're in range," McGregor said, while releasing his restraining harness and heading to the aft station, where he could make adjustments to the RMS arms if necessary.

Diane turned around and gave McGregor a glance. The Mission Pilot already had planted himself in front of the aft station, his right hand on the RMS hand controller, which was currently set to control the starboard mechanical arm.

As the orbiter quickly reached its orbital position behind the ISS, Diane prayed that the mirror would hold in place and that the soldiers kept the HEP safe.

Seven

His feet secured to Velcro attachments in front of the crew support station of the Habitation Module, Sergei Viktor Dudayev heard the proximity alarms disturb the peaceful whir of the air-revitalization system inside the International Space Station.

He checked the timer on the support station before pulling free of his Velcro anchor and propelling himself across the twenty feet that separated him from the Unity module, which connected to the aft section of the cylindrical module.

His Chechen contacts had been right in assessing the Americans. They were sending a shuttle his way in an attempt to regain control of the station before Sergei could release any of the warheads.

But they do not know what kind of enemy they are facing.

Floating cleanly through the hatch connecting the Hab Module to Unity, Sergei kicked his legs against the padded wall to his right and cut left to snug his short frame through the opening leading to the GPATS module. The screen of the proximity radar, which filled the space three hundred miles around the station with energy, showed an approaching space vehicle. The computers had already identified it as the Space Shuttle *Endeavour*.

Eight

At Houston Space Center, Jake Cohen watched the image displayed on the huge projection screen in the front center of the Flight Control Room on the third floor of the Mission Control Center. The telescopic lens of the camera McGregor had attached to the starboard edge of the segmented mirror captured the image of the ISS in the distance. It looked like a white dot with multiple white lines extending like tentacles. The dot was the core of the station, where all the modules interconnected. The lines were the sections of the scaffoldlike booms supporting the gigantic solar panels. At this moment those panels were not powering the station because the Earth was now positioned between the ISS and the Sun.

Jake clenched his jaw and simply waited for the laser attack that he feared would follow soon.

Nine

"We're here, Colonel. Stay in your seats until we're safe," Diane said over the intercom while still strapped to her seat. Her left hand was glued to the Rotational Hand Controller (RHC), the center stick located in between her legs, which controlled the attitude verniers on the nose and the OMS engine pods. By simply moving the RHC as she would an airplane control stick, vernier rockets in the nose and rear of the orbiter would fire to move *Endeavour* in the desired direction.

A backward glance and she saw McGregor still in front of the aft crew station, right hand on the RMS controller.

"We're gathering our equipment," Ward said over the intercom from below.

"No, no. Stay in your seats. Keep your equipment secured."

"We can't. There isn't enough time."

"But there is no telling how the orbiter is going to take the lase—"

A blinding flash, followed by a powerful jolt. The orbiter suddently went into uncontrollable gyrations.

Dear God!

"Keep that mirror taut against us, Gary!" Diane screamed, realizing a moment later that the laser had either partially struck the nose of the orbiter, or its energy level was far greater than Los Alamos had predicted. *Endeavour*'s nose was not only blackened, but a number of heat-protection tiles were missing while the rest appeared charred. The laser had damaged the nose's rotational verniers. Two of them were firing sporadic bursts of—

A second laser flash engulfed the orbiter, this time without the direct protection of the mirror as *Endeavour* tumbled across space.

An explosion rocked the orbiter, followed by an even larger blast that sent powerful stress waves across the entire fuselage. Warning lights came alive on the control panel as a second explosion rocked the shuttle. The laser must have sliced through the exposed skin of the orbiter, damaging subsystems.

"Smoke! We've got smoke down there!" screamed McGregor from the aft crew station.

Diane turned around and watched black smoke coiling up from the crew module. The smell of cordite assaulted her nostrils.

"The HEP!" she screamed as her fears became reality. "A charge must have gone off!"

"Jesus, what are we going to—"said McGregor.

"Remain at your post!" she commanded, while her right hand applied forward and right pressure to the RHC to get *Endeavour*'s upper side facing the station again. The orbiter, however, would not respond, as the nose verniers continued to fire at random, making it impossible for her to offset their thrusts with the aft verniers.

"Colonel Ward? Colonel Ward? Do you copy?" she said over the intercom.

Nothing.

"Colonel? Colonel?"

No response.

"Let me go down there and check it out," McGregor said.

"Remain at your post!"

The smoke was now beginning to fill the flight deck, but it was not as thick as it first looked. Most of it was already being sucked out by the air-revitalization subsystem, which was still operational after the explosions.

But smoke was the least of Diane's problems. *Endeavour* was still dangerously exposed to the ISS, and she could not bring it back under control.

"Houston, we have a problem."

"We've heard, Endeavour," came Jake's voice. *"You're showing multiple failures of the payload-bay door system, rotational verniers, and—"*

"Houston, I'm having a hard time correcting the orbiter's attitude," Diane said, as she began to move her hand toward an overhead panel, where she planned to switch from General Purpose Computer control, to manual control of the Orbital Maneuvering System engines. But her hand never made it. Instead both arms got thrown forward from the fierce explosion that followed the intense light of a laser beam that caught *Endeavour* broadside.

In a blur, Diane saw a cloud of thermal-protection white tiles bursting off the orbiter's starboard wing. Several crashed against the front and side windowpanes.

"The mirror is loose!" screamed McGregor.

Diane looked up, through the upper windowpanes, and instead of seeing the black supporting frame of the mirror, she saw stars.

"Where is it?" she asked.

"The starboard RMS has broken loose from the payload bay. The mirror's off to the side! I still got ahold of it with the port RMS, but it's no longer shielding us!"

"Jesus Christ," she mumbled as the nose verniers ran out of fuel.

Black-and-white tiles, the Earth, and the stars flashing across her field of view, Diane glanced at the array of warning lights between CRT#1 and #2, and noticed the PAYLOAD CAUTION and the HYDROGEN PRESSURE warning lights on the red. *At least the OMS engines and the aft RCS thrusters are still healthy*, Diane thought as her left hand reached down for the Rotational Hand Controller. Now that she did not have to fight the damaged nose verniers, she had a chance to stabilize the orbiter before using the OMS engines. She could not attempt an orbital burn until the shuttle had achieved the proper attitude; otherwise, the burn would simply send *Endeavour* into even more uncontrollable gyrations.

"Get that mirror under control, Gary!"

"Working on it!"

Her hand applied forward right pressure to the RHC. This time the orbiter responded, but sluggishly because it was operating on only a partial set of rotational vernier engines.

"Houston, Houston, this is *Endeavour*. I'm bringing the orbiter under control. OMS burn in ten seconds. Eight . . . seven . . . five . . . three . . . now." She threw the switch, expecting to feel the slight acceleration from the OMS engines.

Instead, a powerful explosion thrust Diane into her restraining harness. A side view of McGregor's body flying past her and crashing against the front windowpanes brought images of dummies inside automobiles during crash tests. The explosion shook the entire vessel as the CRTs on the center control panel burst in a radial cloud of glass that reached Diane's face before her own hands.

She screamed as razor-sharp glass rushed past her and crashed against the aft crew station of the flight deck.

Bouncing back on her flight seat as the orbiter went into another set of uncontrolled rotations, Diane forced herself to breathe between her teeth to avoid inhaling any glass particles or the floating beads of blood lifting off the multiple cuts on her face and neck. McGregor was out of sight, probably floating somewhere behind her.

Alarms blaring, Diane turned her head, only to see Gary McGregor choking on his own blood from a shard of glass embedded in his throat.

"No, no!" she screamed as their eyes met while she unstrapped her safety harness.

Diane reached him near the center of the flight deck, feeling utterly helpless as McGregor made guttural noises while small clouds of foam and blood left his slashed neck and were inhaled by his opened nostrils. He was drowning in front of her.

Slowly, she reached for the piece of glass and pulled it out, but the stream of spherical blood globules that spewed out of the wound nearly drowned her, forcing her to pull away with her hands on her face.

Holding her breath while waving away the floating blood, Diane refocused on McGregor's eyes, but saw no life in them. She reached with her right hand to close them, but another flash, followed by a horrifying explosion, shoved her against the front windowpanes.

"Oh, God!" she mumbled as her head and right shoulder burned from the impact. Bouncing against the panes, Diane floated right past McGregor and toward the aft crew station, where she hit legs first before bouncing back to the front of the flight deck.

Disoriented from the multiple blows, Diane wildly tried to reach for anything to slow down her momentum and prevent another collision, which came a second later, against the back of her own flight seat.

The disciplined Marine inside her taking command, Diane wrapped both arms around the back of the flight seat and tried to take a peek at the control panel.

Warning lights filled control panel F7, where three rectangular holes showed the place where the CRTs had been a minute before. A look outside the windowpanes revealed nothing but a cloud of broken tiles and other debris she couldn't make out. All she could figure was that the OMS engines had been damaged by the laser and blew up when she had tried to use them.

Finding it hard to breathe, Diane quickly reached for the lightweight headset floating over McGregor's head. She disconnected it from McGregor's portable leg unit, and plugged it in her own unit. Once more she hugged the back of the flight seat.

"Houston, Houston. *Endeavour*, here. Do you copy?"

Nothing.

"Houston, this is *Endeavour*. Do you—"

Another flash, followed by three explosions as the laser cut deeper into the orbiter, destroying its core. The blasts pressed her against the seat with a force so great that for a moment Diane felt she was pulling Gs in an F-18. She felt the sudden urge to vomit, and bending over, she did, coughing a large cloud of blood from a number of burst capillaries in her mouth and throat. Her eyes filled as she turned her face away from the floating blood moving toward the rear of the flight deck, where it mixed with the smoke still rising from the crew compartment below.

Another glance at the control panel told her of the lost cause she faced. All main systems were gone, including the air-revitalization system, which explained why she was having a hard time breathing. Then she saw the front windowpanes, saw the growing cracks streaking across the 1.3-inch-thick panes.

Diane knew what that meant, and without another thought, she kicked her legs against the back of the seat and pushed her bruised body toward the left interdeck hatch, just aft of her flight seat, where she curled her fingers on the side rails and pulled herself into the mid deck compartment. The smoke there was thicker than in the flight deck, but she could still see her way through the—

The sight almost made her vomit, but the Marine in her took over, forcing control as she stared at the mangled and charred body parts floating in—

Hurry.

She had no time to waste. The moment those panes gave, the vacuum pressure would be unbearable as everything loose got sucked through the openings. The sudden loss of pressure would mean instant death.

Her hands reached the airlock hatch actuator lock lever at the rear of the crew compartment, and she turned it 180 degrees to unlatch it, pulling the D-shaped hatch toward her. The massive door pivoted up and to the side, exposing the roomy interior of the airlock. Diane floated inside and closed and locked the hatch behind her just as another explosion shook the vessel, giving Diane the impression that the orbiter would come apart any minute. The blast shoved her against the opposite side of the airlock, where the back of her head struck one of the aluminum alloy handholds on the sides of the locked hatch that led to the payload bay.

In an instant, the madness around her ceased and Diane Williams lost consciousness.

Ten

Sergei Dudayev watched the wingless orbiter tumble away after he blasted it one last time before the battery level dropped below the fifty percent mark. He decided to stop firing to conserve power in case he needed it before the ISS could reach the daylight portion of its orbit and replenish the battery charge.

Sergei adjusted the resolution of the spotting telescope of the GPATS module. At such short distance it gave him a clear view of the broken front windowpanes, which meant that the flight deck and the crew compartment had lost pressurization. He also noticed a missing payload bay door, most of the wings and vertical fin, and nearly half of the thermal protection tiles. The shield, which Sergei assumed was made out of segmented mirrors since it had deflected the initial laser shot, now floated away from the orbiter with one of the RMS arms still attached to it. Farther away, he saw the missing payload door, now a rotating hunk of twisted, blackened aluminum.

Sergei glanced at *Endeavour* one last time and shook his head. *Fools. Maybe now they will concede to my people's demands.*

He shifted his gaze to the locked workstation.

******PROCEDURE VIOLATION******
TIME LIMIT EXCEEDED. SYSTEM RESET IN PROGRESS
******32:28:14******

Soon, he thought. *Soon the warheads will be mine.*

Eleven

"Come in *Endeavour*, over. *Endeavour* come in, over."

In the midst of a chaos inside the Flight Control Room, Jake Cohen waited for an answer, but all he got was the low hissing static noise coming from the overhead speakers.

"Sir," said the Electrical, Environmental, and Consumables Systems Engineer (EECOM) to Jake's far left, a blond-headed man of about thirty with fair skin and a wide nose, wearing black-framed glasses. EECOM was responsible for monitoring *Endeavour*'s fuel cells, avionics, cabin-cooling systems, electrical-distribution systems, and cabin-pressure-control systems. "We're still getting S-band telemetry from the orbiter through the TDRS-White Sands link, and it shows zero pressurization inside the crew compartment and flight deck. I'm afraid that—"

"Yes, I know," Jake said, more to himself than to anyone. "*Endeavour* just got hit multiple times by that damned laser!"

Silence in the control room.

"GUIDO," Jake said a moment later. "Status."

The Guidance Officer, call sign GUIDO, sitting a row in front of Jake, was responsible for monitoring onboard navigation and guidance computer software.

While looking at the telemetry data browsing across his twenty-inch color screen, GUIDO said, "Orbiter tumbling along all three axes while maintaining a concentric orbit with the station roughly six miles away.

Guidance computer software showing a major malfunction. I'm afraid we can't control the orbiter via remote."

Jake glanced to his right at the Propulsion Systems Engineer. "Talk to me, PROP."

The fifty-year-old PROP, a veteran astronaut himself, was responsible for monitoring and evaluating the Reaction Control and the Orbital Maneuvering System engines. He also managed propellants. PROP kept his eyes on the data displayed in his console. "Doesn't look good. Major malfunctions on the OMS engines. Looks like the laser cracked the propellant tanks and they blew the moment Commander Williams fired them."

Damn. I can't believe this has actually happened. And Diane, the crew . . . God Almighty.

And that Russian bastard is still at large.

Closing his eyes, Jake Cohen removed his glasses, rubbed his eyes, and breathed deeply. He looked to his left. The Flight Director had already left the room to brief the NASA Administrator, who in turn would pass the information to the President and his staff.

"Wait . . . wait," said the blond-headed EECOM. "The computers are showing nominal pressure inside the airlock. Oxygen content is at thirty-two percent. Pressure is 14.7 PSI." Slowly, he turned to Jake. "Do you think that—"

Jake snapped forward. "Damned right I do! I say we got us some astronauts marooned inside that airlock! What's the status of the pressure-control system and oxygen supply?"

The EECOM's fingers worked on the keyboard as data flashed off and on the screen. After several seconds, he said, "We're in luck. Pressure system is active and still trying to repressurize the crew compartment. My guess is that we got a serious opening to space inside that compartment and the system can't pressurize it. I'm showing two fuel cells down and one still operational."

Jake nodded. "Redirect the pressure-control system to support only the airlock, nothing else. Disconnect all other systems that might be draining the fuel cell. Let's focus everything we have on keeping the atmosphere inside that airlock within the normal range. That will buy us some time."

"Yes, sir."

Since the pressure-control system didn't have to operate at full power because all it was pressurizing was the volume of air inside the airlock, the single fuel cell could last much longer. This was a significant advantage because the oxygen used by *Endeavour*'s life-support system was the same liquid oxygen used by the fuel cell, along with liquid hydrogen, in an electrochemical reaction to produce electricity. The longer the fuel cell lasted, the longer that airlock would be not only fully pressurized, but also filled with air.

"It's done. At the current load, that fuel cell should last us about twenty-four hours, give or take a few, depending on how many astronauts are alive," commented the EECOM.

Jake stared at the blank screen, where only a few minutes before he had seen the images captured by *Endeavour*'s video cameras. Now he was blind, trying to help a dying orbiter while operating in the dark. *Well, almost in the dark*, he admitted. At least partial telemetry data continued to pour in, giving his support crew the information they might need in order to figure a way out of this mess.

Interlacing the fingers of his hands in front of his face, Jake closed his eyes, praying that at least somebody had made it to the airlock. Based on the conversation aboard *Endeavour* before the attack, Jake felt that Diane and McGregor were the two with the best chance of being inside that airlock because they should have been up in the flight deck controlling the orbiter and the RMS arm at the time of the HEP blast inside the crew compartment below.

I should have listened to you, Diane.

Jake Cohen forced the guilt out of his mind. He needed his logical side operating at full capacity in order to guide his staff through this one. Every piece of telemetry data arriving into the Flight Control Room would have to be scrutinized by itself and in combination with other information to try to piece together a possible salvage operation of an orbiter that already appeared beyond salvage.

Twelve

Diane Williams pulled up so fast after releasing her Hornet's ordnance that she thought the Gs would crush her. Her vision tunneled to the information projected on the F-18's heads-up display. Diane kept the control column pulled back. The Hornet shot up into the overcast sky, its wings biting the air as it rolled above the clouds and the sun filled her cockpit, making her feel so detached from the world below. Flying gave her a sense of omnipotence she could get nowhere else. She belonged to a privileged class, an aviator of the United States Marines, pilot of one of the most coveted and feared war machines in the world: the Hornet. Her Hornet. And Diane pushed it, forced it to the outer limits of its design envelope, rammed it into the tightest turns that its titanium-layered honeycomb structure could take, shoved it across the sky in any imaginable way to accomplish the job. To fulfill her promise to America that she would put every single ounce of her life into doing what she had been trained to do.

But her engines suddenly flamed out. Lights filled her cockpit as her jet tumbled out of control, alarms blaring. But then the noise went away as fast as it had appeared, and Diane suddenly found herself lying in that hospital bed at El Toro Air Station. The room was dark, humid, quiet. The lamp on her nightstand filled the room with yellow light, but it was enough to illuminate the faces of the others present in that room. Diane saw Dr. Lisa Hottle's face giving her a stern, yet compassionate look. Next to the doctor stood Gary McGregor in blue coveralls gazing at the floor, a large piece of glass embedded in his throat. Then Diane turned to the last person in the room, a large black man wearing a dark uniform. It was Colonel Frank Ward, his left hand holding an HEP charge. Then a blinding light filled the room, followed by a loud explosion and alarms, many alarms . . .

Another siren went off, but it didn't belong inside the hospital room. Diane didn't know where it had come from. The siren wasn't part of the nightmare. The siren was here, inside the sealed airlock of the wounded orbiter. It was the alarm that NASA had installed in all shuttles to give crews a five minute warning before the oxygen supply would run out.

Dizzy and in severe pain, Diane kept her eyes closed. The throbbing on the back of her head challenged the piercing pain from her throat, where blood vessels had burst from the G-like pressure induced by the multiple explosions. The coppery taste of blood filled her senses with the same intensity as the general body soreness from bouncing around the flight deck like a rag doll.

Floating upside down, Diane opened her eyes, feeling what had to be the worst headache of her life. The relentless pounding of veins against her temples seemed amplified by the siren telling her she had less than five minutes' worth of air inside that compartment, and from what she remembered she doubted *Endeavour* had any other pressurized compartment that could support life after the laser attack.

And McGregor, the UNSC soldiers . . .

Concentrate.

Turning off the alarm, she glanced through the four-inch-diameter observation window on the hatch leading to the payload bay, and visually checked the main cargo in *Endeavour*'s payload bay: the new and still untested Astronaut Maneuvering Vehicle—a four-person unpressurized prototype module designed by Lockheed to provide teams of UNSC personnel the flexibility of moving in space quickly and efficiently. The first production AMV was not supposed to be ready for another year, but the problems aboard the ISS called for Lockheed to release its only prototype.

"Shit," Diane whispered when spotting the vehicle upside down and jammed against the rear of the bay. Actually, most everything else that she could see through the narrow opening appeared out of place or missing.

Before she could attempt an Extravehicular Activity to check the damage done to the AMV and the other equipment in the payload bay, Diane had to start the hourlong 100 percent pure-oxygen prebreathing.

After a brief check that the integral oxygen tank for prebreathing was not operational, Diane grabbed the emergency portable oxygen unit off a built-in inner wall to her left. She actually needed the portable unit even if she wasn't planning an EVA because the oxygen level inside the airlock was falling below the safety level.

She placed the clear plastic mask over her nose and mouth and turned a red knob on the pint-size canister connected to the mask through a thin plastic tube. Letting the canister float overhead, Diane stripped naked. Next she opened a compartment containing most of the "underwear" garments she would have to put on prior to donning the actual EMU—the space suit designed to provided pressure, thermal and micrometeoroid protection, communications, and full environmental control support for one astronaut. The EMU's thick skin consisted of a number of layers, starting with an inner layer of urethane-coated nylon, followed by a restraining layer of Dacron, a thermal layer of neoprene-coated nylon, five layers of aluminized Mylar laminated with Dacron scrim, and an outermost layer made of Goretex, Kevlar, and Nomex for micrometeoroid protection.

Diane put on the Urine Collection Device—a pouch capable of holding one quart of liquid, derived from a device used by people with malfunctioning kidneys. She followed that with the Liquid Cooling and Ventilation Garment (LCVG) which, similar to long underwear, consisted of a one-piece front-zippered suit made of a stretch-nylon fabric but laced with over three hundred feet of plastic tubing, through which chilled water would flow to control her body temperature.

The undergarments out of the way, and while still breathing directly from the oxygen canister, Diane connected the LCVG's electrical harness to the upper torso section of the multilayered EMU she retrieved from another airlock compartment. She removed the EVA checklist attached to the upper torso's left sleeve and, having done her share of space walks, she gave it a quick scan before flinging it aside.

She attached the electrical harness to the EMU. Because the orbiter's communications system was dead, the electrical harness—designed to provide her with a biomedical and communications link to Mission Control—would not work until she reached the space station.

Next, she grabbed the connecting waist ring of the lower torso section—or suit pants—of the EMU, and, while floating in the middle of the airlock, she guided both legs into it. The lower torso came with boots, and joints in the hip, knee, and ankle to give the astronaut maximum mobility. Briefly removing the oxygen mask while extending both arms straight up, Diane "dived" into the upper torso section floating overhead, reattached the oxygen mask, and connected the tubing from the EMU to the Liquid Cooling and Ventilation Garment before joining and securing the upper and lower torso sections with the waist-entry closures of the connecting rings.

She checked her watch. According to NASA regulations, she had another forty minutes of prebreathing before she could go outside, but because the crippled orbiter could not provide her suit with cooling water, oxygen, and electrical power during the long prebreathing period to conserve the oxygen and battery power inside the EMU's backpack for actual EVA time, Diane decided to risk a prebreathing shortcut to maximize the eight hours' worth of oxygen of the Primary Life Support System (PLSS) backpack unit. Besides, her emergency oxygen canister would be exhausted in another five minutes and the air quality inside the airlock was already below the safe level.

Diane backed herself against one of two PLSS units and secured it in place. She made the appropriate connections for feedwater and oxygen, and secured the display and control module on the front, which showed alpha and numeric readouts of oxygen level, fuel, and power remaining in the PLSS.

She grabbed one of the helmets, a clear polycarbonate pressure bubble with a neck connecting ring, and rubbed an antifog compound on the inside of the helmet. Next she placed a communications cap on her head and connected it to the EMU electrical harness. Grabbing a pair of gloves and putting them on, she fastened the ends to the locking rings at the end of each EMU sleeve.

Taking a final breath of 100 percent oxygen from the portable unit, Diane removed the clear mask and let it float over head. Next, she lowered the helmet and locked it in place. Powering up the PLSS, she breathed again while pressurizing the suit to 16.7 PSI at 100 percent oxygen, two PSI above the airlock pressure, to create a pressure differential. Diane's body responded with a slight discomfort in her ears and sinus cavities. She tried to compensate by yawning and swallowing, but the pressure in her ears remained. Pressing her nose against a small sponge mounted to her right, inside the helmet ring, Diane blew with her mouth closed, forcing air inside her ear cavities and equalizing the pressure.

Her eyes on the display module attached to her chest, she turned off the PLSS and waited one minute to check for suit leaks. The pressure dropped to 16.6 PSI, well within the maximum allowable rate of leakage of the shuttle EMU of 0.2 PSI per minute.

Satisfied, she dropped the pressure to 14.7 PSI and waited ten more minutes while slowly starting the airlock pressure bleed-down. The moment the pressure outside equaled the pressure inside the airlock, Diane checked the chest-mounted timer.

Forty-five minutes of prebreathing. It'll have to do.

She took two additional minutes to bring the EMU pressure down gradually to six PSI instead of the recommended four PSI for maximum EMU flexibility without excessive muscle fatigue. At pressures higher than four PSI, the flight suit became more rigid, but Diane had no choice when presented with the option between risking nitrogen-induced bends and exerting a little more effort to move. In another fifteen minutes she planned to lower it to four psi to extend the life her PLSS.

She lowered a sun visor over the helmet before reaching for the hatch actuator lock lever and turning it 180 degrees. She pulled the D-shaped door toward her a few inches and then rotated it up until it rested with the low-pressure side facing the airlock ceiling.

Thirteen

"What did you say?" asked Jake Cohen, slowly turning toward the blond-headed EECOM, the Electrical, Environmental, and Consumables Systems Engineer.

"S-band telemetry shows zero pressurization inside the airlock, sir."

"Dammit!"

"No, sir. You don't understand. The pressure didn't leak out. It was intentionally bled out by someone inside the airlock. My data is also showing an opened hatch to the payload bay. Someone up there just started an EVA."

"And we can't talk to the astronaut?"

"I'm afraid not, sir. All we can do is read the telemetry data on S-band."

"Damn. I wish that K-band antenna was there," said Cohen. In reality, *Endeavour* had given up the K-band antenna to accommodate a second RMS manipulator arm. The K-band antenna could have allowed an alternate communications channel between the orbiter and Houston Control after the S-band antenna was damaged during the laser shoot-out.

Jake Cohen grabbed the phone to update his superiors. Just thirty minutes ago he had gotten word from Andrews Air Force base that a squadron of F-22s armed with ANSAT—antisatellite—missiles was standing by waiting for the order to shoot down the station before the terrorist regained control of the warheads. Now maybe there was a chance that the station could still be salvaged if the surviving astronauts could reach the ISS in time.

Fourteen

Diane Williams held on to the handrails to push herself through the opening and into the payload bay, where she closed her eyes to avoid getting disoriented from the multiaxial rotation of the orbiter with respect to the Earth. She had not noticed it before because of her enclosure inside the airlock, but now that she was in the bay, her eyes instantly sent an alarm to her brain. *Vertigo. Nausea.*

Fighting what she knew would be deadly spatial disorientation, Diane opened her eyes, but kept them focused inside the payload bay, forcing herself to ignore anything outside her small world. Breathing slow and deep to get her body under control, she decided that her initial observation from inside the airlock had been correct. Everything seemed out of place, with most of the standard equipment missing, including one of the two Manned Maneuvering Units (MMU) or self-propelled backpacks, one payload bay door, both RMS arms, the segmented mirror, video cameras, one Payload Assistance Module, floodlights. All gone.

Diane pushed herself to the rear of the cargo area, where she reached the open-canopy AMV, realizing that it would take a miracle to get any use out of it. The missing MMU had crashed against the delicate control panel of the AMV, smashing the stealth vehicle electronics, which, on closer inspection, she decided were vital for proper operation of the AMV's jet thrusters.

Appalled at her bad luck, Diane exhaled heavily, pounding a gloved hand against the black composite skin of the crippled vehicle, her only way of reaching the station . . . or was it?

Her eyes darted across the payload bay toward the undamaged MMU, the backpack system used by astronauts since the 1980s for untethered EVA. Although NASA prohibited astronauts from using the MMU at distances farther than three hundred feet from the orbiter, Diane knew that as long as there was compressed nitrogen in the MMU tanks, the jets could propel her for miles. The only problem she faced was that she didn't know which way to go. But Diane noticed that the Lockheed AMV carried a small homing unit, which she unstrapped from the side of the vehicle. She also grabbed one of four HandHeld Maneuvering Units from the back of the AMV. The small HHMUs were most likely intended to be used by the UNSC soldiers to maneuver themselves away from the AMV after arriving at the station. Now Diane would use it as a backup in case something went wrong with her MMU.

Armed with the homing device and the HHMU, Diane pushed herself back toward the MMU parked next to the airlock. She stopped in front of the maneuvering unit, attached to the payload bay wall with a framework that had a stirruplike foot restraint. Diane placed both EMU boots inside the stirrups and visually inspected the unit, checking the battery and nitrogen-propellant readings, both of which showed fully charged.

Turning around, Diane backed herself against the MMU, until the PLSS backpack locked in place. She extended both control arms of the MMU and placed her hands on the hand controllers. The right controller would give her acceleration for roll, pitch, and yaw, while the left one gave her the power to produce translational acceleration along three different planes: forward-back, up-down, and left-right.

Diane used her left hand to reach for the main power switch located above her right shoulder, and a second later the MMU locator lights came on. She reached with her right hand for the manual locator light switch over her left shoulder and turned it off. It was bad enough that the Russian aboard the ISS might be able to pick her up on radar. She definitely didn't feel like flashing her location like a beacon in the darkness of space.

Strapping the small HandHeld Maneuvering Unit to one of the MMU arms, and the homing radar to the other, Diane prepared herself to execute a maneuver she had never done before.

She currently moved with the same translational and rotational speed as *Endeavour*. She had to jettison away from the rotating wreckage without changing her rotational velocity with respect to the orbiter so that a section of the orbiter would not come crashing against her.

Since the orbiter seemed to be rotating around an axis close to the center of the payload bay, Diane decided to slowly jet herself toward it, reaching a position nearest to *Endeavour*'s zero-rotation point.

She applied full pressure to the aft-facing jets, which spewed nitrogen in one direction and gently pushed her in the other, along a line near perpendicular to the axis of rotation. Twenty seconds later she had moved close to 150 feet from the orbiter, which continued to rotate just as fast as she did.

The Earth, orbiter, and the cosmos flashing on her viewplate, Diane applied two lateral thrusts to counter her clockwise rotation, making a few fine adjustments until she floated upside down, with a large portion of the South American continent hanging overhead.

At that distance she finally saw the damage done to the orbiter, realizing the power of the GPATS laser. Actually, *Endeavour* didn't look like an orbiter anymore, but more like a black-and-white cylindrical hunk of space junk.

Diane also slowly came to terms with the fact that she was alone, forgotten, probably given up for dead by Mission Control. All she had was the gear she had taken with her. The compressed nitrogen inside her MMU tanks. The eight hours' worth of oxygen and pressurization that the PLSS could provide her EMU suit, plus the thirty-minute emergency oxygen reserve unit below the PLSS's main oxygen tanks. She wished she could use her radio, somehow tell Mission Control—tell Jake—that she had survived. But her only link to ground was through an orbiter that no longer existed. Diane was her own spaceship, her own world. The steady flow of oxygen from the PLSS system—carried through a maze of tubes into the back of her helmet—was her life. She depended on it as much as she depended on the system's heater exchange and sublimator to warm the oxygen before it reached the inside of her helmet to avoid fogging the faceplate. Diane depended on the chilled water running through hundreds of feet of plastic tubing lacing her suit liner to maintain her body temperature. She relied on the multiple layers of insulation of the EMU suit to keep her body from direct exposure to temperatures that would boil her blood in seconds.

Diane Williams drew from a distinguished space career and from her decade of military training to shove those thoughts aside and concentrate on the job. She was Mission Commander. She was in control of her space vehicle, regardless of whether that vehicle measured as large as an orbiter or as minute as her EMU enclosure. Being in charge meant keeping her emotions and fears aside, letting her logical side take over. It meant activating the homing unit and steering her MMU propulsion system toward a space station out of her visual range, but a station she knew floated out there, somewhere in the vast emptiness of space.

Diane Williams glanced at *Endeavour* one last time, thought about McGregor and the UNSCF soldiers for one final moment before using the jets to turn around and align herself with the information shown on the liquid crystal display of the homing device. Diane fired the thrusters until she'd put herself in a collision course with the space station. She hoped her orbital trajectory would get her to the station in less than eight hours.

Fifteen

******PROCEDURE VIOLATION******
TIME LIMIT EXCEEDED. SYSTEM RESET IN PROGRESS
******07:15:14******

Sergei Dudayev stared at the screen while eating from a pouch of dried peaches. The moment was near. During his last orbital pass over the Caucasus Mountains, he had gotten confirmation of the deployment orders. Russia refused to yield to Chechnya's request to take possession of nuclear warheads for self-defense. It had also refused to pull back the tank divisions deployed to the border.

Soon I will show them that we mean our threats.

Sixteen

Seven and a half hours into her journey to reach the station, Diane Williams began to feel the effects of the carbon dioxide her nearly discharged Primary Life Support System backpack could not fully extract from her EMU suit. The centrifugal fan of the PLSS, running at nearly twenty thousand RPM, slowly failed to draw the contaminated oxygen from the normal rate of 0.17 cubic meter per minute down to 0.14 and dropping—according to her chest-mounted display. In addition, the slow warming trend inside the suit also told her that the PLSS feedwater pump and heat exchanger and sublimator, designed to maintain a steady flow of chilled water through the hundreds of feet of plastic tubing lacing the LCVG underwear Diane wore, were also fading.

The situation would only get worse, with the suit slowly turning into a greenhouse as humidity and temperature got out of control, fogging the faceplate and eventually suffocating her.

She had to act, and fast, while she could still see through the pressurized polycarbonate plastic sphere underneath the gold-coated visor protecting her eyes from the blinding ultraviolet rays of a sun that had loomed over the horizon a half hour ago. Diane activated the EMU's purge valve to bleed the carbon dioxide into space before switching to the secondary oxygen pack NASA added to the bottom of the unit to ensure the safety of astronauts in case of main PLSS failure.

Operating in open-loop mode, where the oxygen she breathed did not get circulated back to the PLSS but went through the purge valve,

Diane checked the timer on the chest-mounted display. She had around fifty minutes' worth of oxygen left.

That should be enough.

Squeezing the last of the nitrogen pressure inside the Manned Maneuvering Unit's tanks, Diane used the station's long frame, only five hundred feet away, to block the blinding sun. So far, the station showed no sign of alarm.

Soon that'll change, she decided, aware of the station's proximity sensors. Although they had not been sensitive enough to detect her yet, they were designed to detect any object with a radar cross section larger than a half foot getting within five hundred feet of the station.

Her viewplate beginning to fog and her EMU suit temperature climbing out of the comfort zone, Diane opened the purge valve a bit more, which also meant her oxygen supply would decrease at a faster rate. She didn't have a choice. She had to keep the helmet from fogging at all costs while commanding the MMU to thrust her toward the hyperbaric airlock attached to the Unity Module.

Seventeen

UNSC15KTSN001 HAS BEEN SELECTED
INSERT VALID UNSCF BADGE TO ACTIVATE
******00:59******

Sergei Dudayev was ready when the slot under the keyboard opened. Upon inserting the badge, the screen changed to a blinking:

UNCS15KTSN001 IS READY TO LAUNCH

The Russian cosmonaut smiled. Then the station's proximity alarm went off.

Eighteen

Diane Williams noticed a number of red lights flashing on some modules. The proximity alarm motion sensors had detected her. She needed a decoy.

Unstrapping the HandHeld Maneuvering Unit from the side of the PLSS, Diane disengaged herself from the backpack propulsion system that had carried her all the way there. A hard kick against the MMU to push herself toward the station, and Diane watched the MMU tumble out of control away from her.

Now came the tricky part. All she had to propel herself toward the station was the HHMU, very similar to the ones used for EVAs during the Gemini Program of the 1960s, and seldom used by modern-day space voyagers because of the readily available and highly sophisticated MMUs.

Diane held the three-jet maneuvering gun with both hands. There were two jets located at the ends of the rod and aimed back. A third jet, located at the center of the rod, faced forward. Remembering the technique used by those early space explorers, Diane Williams centered the gun close to her lower chest—the place she estimated to be closest to her center of mass. Visually lining up the rear-facing jets with the airlock hatch roughly three hundred feet away, Diane fired the gun, releasing a symmetrical burst of compressed oxygen from both jets, propelling herself more or less in the desired direction.

Finally learning the limitations of the HHMU—and also the frustration of those Gemini astronauts—Diane found herself making slight correction on the firing angle of the jets while lowering the gun to her waist, below the chest-mounted display to avoid a slight rotational motion induced by firing the thrusters out of line with her true center of mass. Slowly, using a combination of forward thrusts and also firing the reverse thruster to break her momentum, Diane reached the airlock hatch.

Nineteen

The proximity alarms blaring, Sergei Dudayev checked the radar and verified the existence of an object at less than five hundred feet from the station.

Puzzled, he floated back into Unity and up to the cupola. Using a restraint system that enabled him to rotate easily for viewing through any of the windows, the Russian spotted an empty Manned Maneuvering Unit drifting away from the station.

An MMU?

Realizing that the ISS didn't carry any MMUs, Sergei concluded that unless for some very strange law of physics one of *Endeavour*'s MMUs had been dislodged from its flight station and floated in this direction, the presence of the backpack system could only mean one thing.

Twenty

After performing an emergency bleed of the air inside the airlock by using the small control panel built in on the D-shaped EVA hatch door, Diane Williams pressed her left hand against the manual unlocking lever while holding on to the adjacent handle with her right. Three full clockwise turns, and she pulled the hatch door back several inches before a spring-loaded mechanism rotated it upward. Floating inside the airlock, Diane closed the hatch behind her and repressurized the compartment.

Twenty-one

Sergei noticed the red lights blinking on the control panel of the crew support station, which told him that an emergency airlock bleed had been done. The EVA hatch had been opened, then closed, and now the airlock was being repressurized.

Cursing his stupidity for assuming that the crew of *Endeavour* had perished in the attack, Sergei kicked his legs against the side of the cupola and reached Unity, sighing in relief when noticing that the hatch connecting the airlock to the bottom of the node was still closed. Without further thought, he locked it from the inside.

Twenty-two

Diane finished pressurizing the airlock and noticed the green light above the hatch connecting her compartment to Unity turning red. Realizing that the Russian had most likely found her, she decided not to depressurize her EMU suit just yet. Instead, she reached for the communications panel on the side of the airlock wall and set it to the standard EVA mode UHF frequency 121 Mhz. Next, she remotely switched on the station's K-band antenna to close the ISS-Houston link via a TRDS and White Sands Tracking Station.

"Houston, this is *Endeavour*'s Mission Commander Diane Williams, over."

"Wh—what? Come in . . . come in, Commander! Jesus Christ! We thought . . . great to hear from you!" Diane heard an unfamiliar voice coming through.

"I have little time before Dudayev catches on and cuts us off. I've reached the station. I'm trapped inside the airlock and have less than twenty minutes left of oxygen in my PLSS."

"Diane, this is Jake."

Diane smiled thinly. "Jake, the orbiter's gone. McGregor and the UNSCF soldiers didn't make it. The bastard now has me locked out of the station."

"Calm down and listen carefully there might be a way to—"

Diane frowned. "Houston? Houston? Come in, Houston."

Twenty-three

A few keystrokes on the computer keyboard of the Multipurpose Applications Console, and Sergei disconnected the communications link between the airlock and the rest of the station. An American astronaut—Diane Williams—had managed to exchange a few words with Houston Control, and although Sergei had not been pleased with that fact, he had at least gotten a good idea of Diane's desperate oxygen situation. The American was running out of air, and in another twenty minutes she would no longer present any danger to his mission.

He commanded the computer system to purge the airlock.

Twenty-four

"Houston, can you read? Hous—"

The emergency purge alarm went off inside the airlock, conveying the Russian's intentions. Glad that she had maintained EMU pressurization, Diane searched for the maintenance tools stowed inside compartments on all four walls of the airlock, finding what she sought: a heavy-duty, battery-operated drill, to which she attached a four-inch-diameter stainless-steel serrated disk at the end of the drive shaft. She had seen what the tool could do when McGregor had cut open the jammed Titan shroud to release the segmented mirror.

Pressing the tool's on-off switch twice to verify proper operation, Diane unlocked the exterior hatch. Having secured the power tool to a six-foot-long woven line that she clipped to her EMU suit, Diane used the HHMU to move away from the D-shaped opening, past the modules, and toward the long, thin structural framework that ended in one set of solar panels.

Rapidly exhausting the compressed oxygen inside the handheld propulsion unit, Diane grabbed a tubular member of the truss assembly. Painted black, the tube—made of aluminum-clad graphite epoxy—was both lighter and relatively stronger than metal. Diane hugged it with her left arm while strapping the HHMU to the side of the EMU suit.

Crawling inside the tubular framework, Diane reached a black tube running all the way from a set of solar panels, still a hundred feet away, to the center of the station. The contents of the tube—thick electrical cables—fed the massive array of nickel-hydrogen batteries and the power converter that provided the GPATS module weapons system with the necessary energy to generate the destructive chemical reaction. The battery also fed the computer system that controlled the warheads and their launching units.

Pulling on the woven line, Diane clasped the power saw in her gloves and turned it on. The serrated wheel began its silent, high-velocity spin. Diane anchored herself between adjacent beams before pressing the round blade against the side of the tube, immediately slicing through the soft composite material and into the thick wires, which bathed her in a cloud of sizzling debris. On Earth, such action would have resulted in a cloud of sparks, but in the vacuum of space, the intensely hot particles had no oxygen to burn.

Her EMU gloves insulating her from the 208 volts of electricity generated by the solar panels, Diane made several cuts to achieve a clean separation. Satisfied, she crawled back out of the framework and moved toward where the large laser gun stood atop the GPATs module.

Twenty-five

Sergei Dudayev heard another alarm coming from the GPATS module and instinctively pushed himself out of the Hab Module, through Unity, and into GPATS, where one of the computer screens at the front of the module told him of an EPS recharge system failure. The Electrical Power System no longer received a charge from the solar panels, and had automatically switched to the battery packs, which had a charge life of thirty hours—much less if he had to use the laser system.

Cursing, Sergei floated back into Unity and through the connecting hatch to the cupola, where he watched the American astronaut floating by the base of the laser gun.

No! Not the laser!

Returning to the GPATS module, Sergei made up his mind and pressed the launch button for the selected warhead. Its destination: the Russian troops on the border with Chechnya.

Sergei wished he could release the remaining warheads, but he had to take care of the American first. Without the laser the station would be defenseless against another attack.

Floating back into Unity, Sergei used the remote actuators to close the outer hatch before repressurizing the hyperbaric airlock. He opened the inner hatch and floated toward one of two one-piece AMEX AX-5 Advanced Hard Suits, made of aluminum and containing no fabric or soft parts, except for the joints, enhancing mobility and comfort for the wearer. The suit had integrated helmet, gloves, and boots.

Entering the suit from a hatch in the rear, Sergei slipped in both legs first, followed by the upper part of his body. Once inside, he backed himself against a Self-Propelled Life Support System backpack, which perfectly covered the square hatch opening, creating a seal after the magnetic latches all around the joint snapped in place. Pressing two buttons on his chest-mounted display and control panel pressurized the AX-5 to twelve PSI—one of the advantages of the new suit since it eliminated the need to prebreathe pure oxygen prior to an EVA.

The sound of his own breathing ringing in his ears, Sergei depressurized the compartment and opened the hatch. He could waste no time. The American had already disabled the GPATS battery-charging system and was now about to sabotage the laser.

The AX-5 integrated thruster system—a simplified version of the MMU—consisted of sixteen compressed nitrogen jets instead of the MMU's twenty-four. Operating two joystick-type controls on his chest-mounted panel, Sergei fired the aft-facing thrusters to propel himself away from the station and get a bird's eye view of his enemy.

Rotating himself in the direction of Diane, Sergei once more fired the thrusters. This time, however, he did it for nearly ten seconds, giving himself a forward velocity of around five feet per second.

Twenty-six

Diane Williams had just finished cutting the array of cables that controlled the sophisticated servomotors of the gimbal-mounted laser gun when she noticed an external door opening on the side of the GPATS module.

She cringed when a single sleek cylinder, roughly fifteen feet in length by three in diameter, slowly left the station after being pushed away by its spring-loaded release mechanism, designed to get the warhead away from the station before firing its reentry booster.

With less than ten minutes of oxygen left, and with the warhead floating farther away from the station, Diane decided to go after the warhead while it was still floating near the GPATS module.

Switching off the power saw and letting it float at the end of the woven line, Diane reached for the HHMU, but her hands never got there.

Twenty-seven

Sergei rammed the American female astronaut at a relative velocity of nearly five feet per second. The blow, cushioned by the thick aluminum suit and also by the high-pressure environment around Sergei's body, barely bothered him or his heavy high-technology garment, but it sent the American tumbling out of control toward the framework to the right of the U.S. Laboratory Module.

Twenty-eight

The powerful blow took Diane Williams entirely by surprise. Her forehead crashed against the polycarbonate plastic helmet before the Earth and the station flashed around her. In one of the flashes, she caught a glimpse of what had crashed against her. The Russian terrorist had suited up and come after her in one of the rugged AX-5 suits.

She finished that thought when another blow, this one to the back of her head, nearly knocked her out as she smashed into the tubular framework near the . . . *where in the hell am I?* She pulled free of the stiff latticework just to be welcomed by a foot shoved against her chest-mounted display.

"Bastard!" she muttered in between breaths as her legs got caught in the crossbeams and batons of the framework. Blinking rapidly to prevent her tears from separating from her eyes and floating inside her helmet, Diane saw the Russian thrusting himself upward for several feet before an expulsion of compressed nitrogen gas from the upward-facing thrusters drove him back down at great speed. This time both feet stabbed her midriff, hammering her farther into the latticework.

Catching her breath, Diane feared that her suit would rip at any moment. The warning lights on her EMU's chest mounted display told her that Sergei had already damaged something, but with her body lodged in the framework at such unnatural angle she needed time to free herself.

Struggling to remain focused, Diane pulled on the woven line, but before her fingers could grab the power saw, Sergei descended on her once more. Tightening her stomach muscles, Diane took the blow better than her suit, which emitted a high-pitched noise that told her she was losing pressurization.

Sergei floated himself up once more. Diane began to feel dizzy and lightheaded as her suit began to lose life-supporting pressure. Fortunately, her prebreathing had removed all nitrogen from her bloodstream, preventing the bends caused by a sudden drop in external body pressure. Quickly, she turned the emergency oxygen knob fully open to maintain an endurable level of pressure.

With the image of the Russian's boots coming down on her again, Diane Williams switched on the power saw and firmly held it with both hands against the approaching boots. Every ounce of strength left flowed into her arms, locked at the elbow. She could not afford another blow. Her EMU would not take it. She had to stop him.

The Russian landed over her. Diane drove the spinning blade into the base of his left boot, letting the serrated edge sink deep into the aluminum, creating a cloud of sparkling white debris.

Twenty-nine

Sergei noticed that the American held out her arms to prevent him from crashing against the EMU. He sensed the resisting motion and got ready to propel himself back up when he felt something strange. For a moment he wasn't sure what it was. It sounded like a malfunctioning fan, or a grinding noise of some sort.

Suddenly, his suit's pressure began to drop, and a burning pain from his heel reached his brain, telling Sergei that the American had pierced the AX-5. Instantly commanding the thrusters to push him back up, he noticed the white cloud surrounding Diane Williams, and he also noticed the object in her hands.

A power saw!

His suit's pressure dropping rapidly below two PSI, Sergei bent in pain from the millions of nitrogen bubbles expanding in his bloodstream. His joints ached to a climax and the cramps in his stomach and intestines scourged him. He could no longer control his body. He was paralyzed, unable to make the smallest movement, except for his eyes, which he focused on the chest-mounted display that told him that he should already be dead. A moment later he passed away.

Thirty

As the limp body of the Russian floated away from her, Diane Williams used her hands to free her right leg, caught in between two crossbeams. That gave her the leeway to position her body so that it became easy to release her other leg from a pair of tubes running along the length of the latticework.

Feeling dizzy, Diane used the HHMU strapped to the side of her backpack unit to move toward the airlock's open hatch. Finding it harder to breathe, she pushed herself through the opening, forcing her mind to remain focused. Her fingers groped around the control panel on the opposite wall, managing to engage the servomotor to close the hatch before pressurizing the compartment.

She fumbled with the visor assembly latch for a few seconds, finally removing it, letting it float overhead while releasing the helmet joining ring. The locking mechanism snapped, and she pushed the clear hemisphere up.

A breath of air. She exhaled and breathed deeply again, coughing, inhaling once more.

A distant rumble brought her gaze toward the airlock's porthole. The missile's thruster fired to commence Earth reentry. Regretting having disabled the laser, Diane removed her EMU suit, leaving on only the cooling garment as she unlocked and opened the hatch leading to Unity and the cupola beyond it, where she engaged the K-band antenna.

Thirty-one

Jake Cohen sat upright when Diane William's voice crackled through the overhead speakers in the Flight Control Room at Johnson Space Center.

"Houston, come in, over."

"Houston here. What in the world is going on up there?"

"Houston, the station is under control, but we have a serious problem. The terrorist managed to fire one warhead. It just started its deorbit burn."

"Stand by," Jake said over the radio, before calling NORAD to advise them of the situation. He then contacted Andrews Air Force Base to call back the F-22s. The terrorist aboard the International Space Station had been neutralized. The Air Force would try to halt the attack, but Jake was warned that it might be too late already.

The veteran CapCom slowly hung up the phone before reaching for the mike in front of him. He had to warn Diane of the possibility of ANSAT missiles heading her way.

"Houston here."

"I'm still here, Houston, go ahead."

Jake struggled to remain as professional as he could, particularly when all eyes in the Flight Control Room were on him. "Situation report?"

"Just accessed the station through Unity. Currently performing a visual check, looking for the rest of the crew. So far I haven't found anyone else."

"I'm afraid we might have bad news for you. A squadron of F-22s is currently trying to shoot you down with ANSAT missiles. We're trying to call them back, but we might be too late."

"Did you say ANSAT?"

"Affirmative. You're might have to use the laser."

"That's a negative, Houston. I disabled the laser before coming inside the station. It's out of commission until we can get a crew to come up here and repair it. I'm afraid if any of those ANSATs are fired, this place is going be in real trouble."

Jake closed his eyes. "Okay, listen. In that case you need to be ready to get into the Soyuz escape vehicle and leave the station immediately. You've stopped the terrorist from launching any more warheads. We'll deal later with the damage those missiles might do to the station."

"That's a negative, Houston. There has to be another way."

Dammit, Diane! Jake thought, before saying as calmly as he could, "ISS, Houston. There is nothing you can do. Repeat, there is nothing you can do without the laser. If the ANSATs are fired, they will destroy the station."

"Houston, I have an idea."

Thirty-two

Colonel Keith Myers kept the rearward pressure on his sidestick as the F-22 soared above 80,000 feet. Brief side glances out of his canopy, and the forty-eight-year-old colonel verified the tight inverted-V formation of his five-jet squadron.

The F-22 was a beautiful plane, and Myers loved to fly it. The advanced tactical fighter-bomber, brought into full production only last year, was a worthy replacement of the venerable F-15 Eagle, which had carried the Air Force through the latter portion of the twentieth century. Myers had been one of five test pilots of the two prototypes built by McDonnell Douglas, and at the end of the evaluation period he had been assigned to lead the first wing out of Andrews.

A medium-built, muscular man with fair skin and short brown hair, Myers looked and acted the role of the typical Air Force squadron commander. He was cocky and sometimes borderline-arrogant, but he knew how to carry out orders and get his men motivated to follow them as well. On the ground he was a bastard, who pushed everyone to do and act their best, but once airborne, he was the ideal flight leader, wise and courageous, fully capable of making lifesaving, split-second decisions.

Myers definitely knew how to follow orders, even when those orders meant the destruction of one of the world's greatest technological achievements: the International Space Station.

"Leader to Ghosts, Leader to Ghosts," Myers said over the squadron frequency. "Prepare to release."

"Roger," came the response from his other four jets, each carrying a single ANSAT missile attached to the underfuselage pallet.

Myers activated the ordnance-release system. Firing the ANSAT was quite simple because of the nature of the missile, which was already preprogrammed to home in on the station flying 105 miles overhead. There was no radar control from the parent craft or from an overhead satellite to guide it to its target. The ANSATs were shoot-and-forget. According to the briefing, Myers would fire his missile first. Each of his men would follow serially until all five missiles had been fired.

Shoving the sidestick back while pushing full throttle, Myers pointed the nose to the upper layers of the stratosphere before pressing a button on the sidestick.

A silver missile glided upward in a parabolic flight as he rolled the jet and pulled away. The missile continued skyward solely on the momentum it had gained from the F-22, until right before reaching its apex, when the single solid-propellant booster kicked in and projected it up at great speed.

"Leader's out," commented Myers as he watched his wingman get into position for his release.

"Ghost Leader, Ghost Leader, Eagle's Nest, over."

"Nest, Leader, over."

"Abort, Leader. Repeat, abort mission. Authorization code Three-Niner-Alpha-Zulu-Seven-Six-Lima-Charlie."

Myers glanced at the small notepad strapped right below the Heads-Up Display. *Abort Code 39AZ76LC. That's a match.*

"Leader to Ghosts, Leader to Ghosts. Abort, abort. RTB, RTB."

"Roger," responded the other four jets, acknowledging not just the abort, but also the Return-To-Base order.

Colonel Myers watched his wingman rolling his jet out of the climb and returning to formation with the ANSAT still strapped to his F-22's belly.

Myers said, "Nest, Ghost Leader. One demon got away. Repeat. One demon got away. Other four demons secured. RTB."

"Roger, Lead. Will pass it on."

The runaway ANSAT's thruster still burning in the distance, Myers cut back throttles and dropped his F-22's nose. His squadron followed him.

Thirty-three

As she floated inside the Habitation Module, Diane Williams only had two more minutes before the ANSAT missile reached her orbit. She inserted the keys she had removed from the GPATS' launching station into the key slots on the top of the keyboard of the Multipurpose Application Console, connected to the central electronic brain of the station.

The screen came up with a list of menus, each containing its own list of submenus and commands. She chose a menu that controlled the station's rotational verniers. A three-dimensional drawing on the screen showed the ISS's current attitude with respect to Earth, and also indicated that the station was operating under automatic computer control. She switched to manual, transferring control of the verniers to a joystick controller next to the station.

She then programmed the station to split the large screen in two. The bottom section still displayed the station's attitude, but the top section now showed a color radar map of the ISS and its surroundings. The resolution was set to 250 miles out, and it showed no sign of the ANSAT yet.

"Houston, ISS. I'm all set, over."

"All right, ISS," Jake Cohen responded from Mission Control. *"ANSAT is three hundred miles high two hundred ninety miles downrange with a closing velocity of seven hundred miles per hour. It should show on your screen any moment now."*

Diane's eyes never left the display as she said, "I see you." The blue dot entered Diane's range from the east and approached the station at great speed. She estimated another minute to impact.

The fingers of her right hand caressed the plastic surface of the joystick. Her eyes followed the blue dot, blinking its way across the screen.

She waited, knowing she would only have one chance at this. Her military background told her that the radar-controlled ANSAT would home in on the area with the largest mass, namely the core of the station. A direct hit there would certainly destroy the ISS.

The ANSAT got within fifty miles. That was the mark. She moved the joystick to the right, and the station's rotational verniers responded by firing counterclockwise. She watched the screen as the station's 3-D drawing began to rotate. *Twenty seconds to impact.*

The ANSAT was too close to make any large corrections as its electronic brain detected a shift in the relative location of its target's center of mass. The microprocessor stored inside the missile's cone ordered the firing of the small attitude control verniers to make a slight adjustment in the flight path, and in another few seconds the missile struck the south section of the boom, near the only functional set of solar panels, over two hundred feet away from any module. The ensuing explosion severed the solar panels in a brief display of orange flames.

Diane was thrown against the food galley, bounced and landed feet-first against the large panoramic window next to the crew's recreational station. Her shoulders and back burned. Through the largest and thickest piece of tempered glass ever put in orbit Diane Williams saw the damage as the station rotated clockwise, out of control, but at least in one piece. She had spared the core of the station from a direct hit. However, the blast had sent a powerful electromagnetic pulse through the cables connecting the solar panels to the station's batteries, shorting them out.

Alarms blared inside the Habitation Module. Red lights, indicating a major power malfunction, flashed at each entrance to the module. Just as suddenly, sparks and smoke spewed from underneath the floor tiles near the Multipurpose Application Console. The bright overheads suddenly went off, replaced by green emergency lights. The computers, sensing that they had lost power from the main batteries, automatically switched to the emergency shutdown program, which began to power down all systems according to a priority sequence.

Stunned but fully conscious, the forty-five-year-old ex–Marine aviator thrust herself through the smoke and sparks and back to the Multipurpose Applications Console, where she snagged the joystick and tried unsuccessfully to stabilize the station. She tried to switch to automatic control, but the system did not respond.

Another alarm began to blare inside the station. Diane recognized its high pulsating pitch: The station was losing pressurization and oxygen. The air pressurization and revitalization system had shut down. At least the station had survived, but it would take a couple of shuttle flights to get it back in shape to support life.

Time to go.

Finding it harder to breathe, her ears beginning to ring from the air-pressure drop, Diane kicked her legs against the MPAC and floated out of the Habitation Module and into Unity. The Soyuz capsule was coupled to the node through a four-foot-long narrow tunnel.

Feeling dizzy, her vision fogging, Diane reached the connecting D-shaped hatch, opened it, and dived through the tunnel into Russian technology.

Her head feeling about to explode, she floated inside the cramped interior of the Soyuz capsule. Closing the access hatch, locking it in place, Diane strapped herself to the center of three seats arranged side by side.

Her vision tunneling, Diane's fingers groped over the control pane searching for the pressurization lever, finding it, throwing it.

Hissing oxygen filled the capsule. The pounding against her eardrums stopped, and after a few deep breaths, her vision cleared, allowing her to inspect the capsule, which lacked an interior wall. Most of the electronic wiring and hydraulic tubing ran fully exposed along steel walls. A porthole directly above provided her only window to the outside, and at that moment it showed Diane the side of Unity.

Placing her hands on a set of levers on the sides of her seat, Diane pulled them up and twisted them ninety degrees.

The capsule jettisoned away from the station, throwing Diane against her restraining harness. Soon she saw nothing but space through the porthole.

Following a preprogrammed reentry sequence, the capsule fired the attitude-control verniers to position the Soyuz's main thruster in the direction of flight. As she waited for the capsule to reach the point in orbit when the rocket would fire to start the reentry, Diane Williams snagged the radio headset secured with a Velcro strap by her left knee, and put it on. She switched on the communications radio and selected a frequency of 252.0 MHz to make a connection with the TDRS-White Sands-Houston link.

"Houston, SES, over," Diane said from the Soyuz Escape System.

"Diane! What happened. We lost communication!"

"The station lost pressure and oxygen. It lost the south end of the boom and solar panels to the ANSAT. I'm afraid some systems and subsystems may have been damaged. But the station is in one piece and still in orbit."

"Status of GPATS module?"

"Deactivated. I have both control keys—"

Her words were cut short by a powerful jolt as the single thruster fired. "Houston, SES. Just started deorbit burn," Diane reported.

"Roger, SES. We're tracking you. Estimated landing site is southern Ukraine."

"Status of the warhead that got away, Houston?"

"Not good, SES. It struck a Russian tank battalion near the border with Chechnya fifteen minutes ago. First estimates are over two thousand dead and many more wounded."

"Damn."

"It could have been a lot worse, SES. The tanks were spread out over a large area. If it would have hit a heavily populated area casualties would have been much higher." Her eyes watched the star-filled cosmos rush past her porthole as the capsule decelerated from its 24,000-miles-per-hour flight.

The burn ended and was replaced by a strong vibration as the first air molecules began to strike the capsule's underside heat shield, heating it to incandescence.

Soon the vibrations grew, accompanied by a pink glow around the edges of the window. Inside her pocket of life traveling inside a decelerating hell of steel-melting temperatures, Diane Williams sat back and watched the pink glow turn into a bright orange just before the Soyuz craft became engulfed by the flames.

Closing her eyes, the ex-Marine tried to relax. She had made it against staggering odds. The remaining weapons aboard the station would remain safe until NASA could get another crew up there to repair it. But that no longer her concerned her.

The rumble of the capsule rushing through the upper layers of the atmosphere increased to a soul-numbing crescendo. Thin air and insulation compounds collided in a scorching outburst of flames. With the might and beauty of a meteor dropping from the sky, the Soyuz capsule sliced through the air at great speed.

Diane Williams dropped like a rock, the flames slowly fading away as the capsule decelerated to the point when the deorbit program disengaged the heat shield to expose three retrorockets to be used ten feet over ground to cushion the fall. At an altitude of thirty thousand feet, bright red twin parachutes deployed from the top of the capsule, giving Diane the jerk of a lifetime.

The first rays of sunlight shafted through her round windowpane, filling the interior of the Soyuz capsule with wan orange light. Mission Commander Diane Williams watched it in silence.

R. J. Pineiro is the author of several technothrillers, including *Ultimatum, Retribution, Breakthrough, Exposure, Shutdown*, and the millennium thrillers *01-01-00* and *Y2K*. His new thriller, *Conspiracy.com*, will be published in April 2001. He is a seventeen-year veteran of the computer industry and is currently at work on leading-edge microprocessors, the heart of the personal computer. He was born in Havana, Cuba, and grew up in El Salvador before coming to the United States to pursue a higher education. He holds a degree in electrical engineering from Louisiana State University, a second-degree black belt in martial arts, is a licensed private pilot, and a firearms enthusiast. He has traveled extensively through Central America, Europe, and Asia, both for his computer business as well as to research his novels. He lives in Texas with his wife, Lory, and his son, Cameron.

Visit R. J. Pineiro on the World Wide Web at www.rjpineiro.com. R. J. Pineiro also receives e-mails at author@rjpineiro.com.

BREAKING POINT

BY DAVID HAGBERG

Spring
Xiamen, Fujian Province
People's Republic of China

Their black rubber raft threaded silently through the densely packed fishing fleet at anchor for the night, the waves, even in the protected harbor, nearly one meter high. The four men were Taiwanese Secret Intelligence Service Commandos, and their chances for success tonight were less than one in ten. Of course all of Taiwan faced about the same dismal odds when it came to remaining free, squad leader Captain Joseph Jiying thought. But the heavy winds, sometimes gusting as high as thirty-five knots, did not help their chances much. They had been in constant danger of flipping over ever since they had left their twelve-man submarine twenty klicks out into the Taiwan Strait just off the entry between Quemoy Island and the Sehnu Peninsula. Now they faced the danger of discovery by patrol boats that darted around the harbor twenty-four hours per day, or by the underwater sound sensors laid on the floor of the bay, or by the infrared detectors installed on the shore batteries, and by the thousands of pairs of eyes always on the lookout. It was estimated that every fifth person in the PRC was a government informer. It meant that at least one hundred fishing boats at anchor tonight held spies.

Xiamen was a city of a half million people and home to an East Sea Fleet base that along with headquarters at Ningbo seven hundred kilometers to the north, and twelve others, was the dominating presence on the East China Sea and more specifically on the Taiwan Strait. Commanded by Vice Admiral Weng Shi Pei, the base was homeport to thirty-seven ships, among them one fleet submarine, three patrol submarines, including a Kilo-class, two frigates, one destroyer, and a variety of smaller boats, among them fast-attack missile, gun, torpedo, and patrol craft. The bulk of the fleet was berthed in a narrow bay to the southwest of the city, while a small naval air squadron was based at the municipal airport on the northeast side of the sprawling city. The sky was overcast, the night pitch-black, the water foul with stinking garbage, oil slicks, and a brown stain that clung to the carbon composite oars they had used since entering the harbor. It was too dangerous this close in to use the highly muffled outboard motor, but no one minded the extra work. It kept them warm.

They rounded the eastern terminus of the commercial port and entered the brightly lit fleet base harbor, the rubber raft passing well over the submarine nets. Keeping to the deeper shadows alongside the frigates and patrol craft, they made it to Dry Dock A, which an earlier recon mission reported was empty. Its massive steel doors were in the open position, and the box was flooded.

Their bowman, Xu Peng Tei, grabbed the metal ladder at the head of the dry dock, tied them off, and scrambled to the top. He cautiously peered over the steel lip three meters above them, then gave the sign for all clear and disappeared over the edge. At twenty-seven he was the oldest man in the group, and although he was not the squad commander, everyone called him Uncle.

Joseph and his other two commandos stripped the protective sheaths from their silenced 9mm Sterling submachine guns, checked the magazines and safeties, then climbed silently to the top of the dry dock and over the edge.

They dropped immediately into a low crouch, invisible in the darkness because of their night-fighter camos and black balaclavas. Joseph checked his watch. It was three minutes until 0100. They were on schedule.

Xu appeared suddenly out of the darkness and crouched beside them. He had also unsheathed his weapon, and the hot diffuser tube around the barrel ticked softly as it cooled. "It's clear for the moment."

"How many guards, Uncle?" Joseph asked.

"Two, as we expected. One outside, one in the guard post. They're down."

The mid-phase mission clock started at that point. "Ten minutes," Joseph said, and they headed directly across to a low, windowless, concrete building a hundred meters away. Surrounded by a four-meter-tall electrified razor-wire fence, the only way in or out was through a gate operated from the guard shack. The outside patrols were on a fourteen-minute schedule, so ten minutes was cutting it close.

The building was the base brig, and for the moment it contained only one prisoner. The PRC was trying to be very low-key about him, which was the only reason tonight's action had the slightest chance of success.

No one wanted to make waves, Joseph thought. Not the PRC, and especially not the United States. Well, after tonight, waves were exactly what they were going to get. And he expected that when the U.S. was finally pushed to the breaking point they would come through. Either that or there wouldn't be anything left of Taiwan except for smoldering cinders and radioactive waste.

But he was betting his life tonight that the U.S. would save them one more time. If his four years at Harvard had taught him nothing else about Americans, he learned that they loved the underdog, and they loved their heroes coming to the rescue. Superman. It was the one serious indulgence he'd picked up in the States. He had copies of Superman comics numbers five through ten, twelve, fifteen, sixteen, and eighteen, from the thirties, plus a hundred others, all original and all in cherry condition. Truth, justice, and the American way . . . now the Taiwanese way, because he'd rather be dead than under mainland rule.

One guard, a neat bullet hole in the middle of his forehead, lay in the darkness beside the fence, and the other was crumpled in the doorway of the guard post just inside the compound.

The lights were very bright there, but no alarms had been sounded, no troops were coming on the run. But the clock was counting down.

Zhou Yousheng dropped down in front of the fence and quickly clamped four cable shunts across a five-foot section. Next he cut the wire between the shunts with insulated cutters and carefully peeled them back. Although the fence now had a wide hole in it, the electrical current had never been interrupted, so no alarm would show up at Security Headquarters across the base.

Zhou gingerly crawled through the opening and as Chiang Kunren clamped the wires back together and removed the shunts, he darted inside the guard post where he released the electric gate lock.

They slipped inside, dragged the dead guards out of sight, and relocked the gate. Joseph led two of his men up the path to the blockhouse. Zhou remained at the guard post. They all wore comms units with earpieces and mikes. One click meant trouble was coming their way.

Chiang, their explosives expert, molded a small block of slow-fire Semtex into the lock on the steel door. He cracked a thirty-second pencil fuse, jammed it into the plastique, then quickly taped a two-inch-thick pad of nonflammable foam over the explosive to deaden the sound.

He'd barely taken his hands away from the foam when the Semtex went off with a muffled bang.

"One of these days you're going to lose a finger," Joseph observed, and Chiang shot him a quick smile.

"Then I'll have to ask for help every time I need to unzip my fly. Female help."

A long, wide corridor led from the front of the building to the back, five cells on each side. There were no adornments, not even numbers over the cell doors. Only a few dim lightbulbs hung from the low concrete ceiling.

Shi Shizong, who was known in Taiwan and in the west as Peter Shizong, was in the last cell on the left. He rose from his cot when Joseph appeared at the tiny window. He was very slight of build and young-looking, even for a mainlander, to be the PRC's most reviled villain. He preached democracy, and for some reason unknown even to him, his message and his presence touched a deep chord among half of China's vast population. Farmers and doctors, factory workers and engineers, fishermen and even some politicians were buying into his message. In the three years he'd been preaching and somehow managing to stay ahead of the authorities, massive waves of discontent had swept across the country, thousands of innocent demonstrators had been killed, their homes and assets confiscated by the state, martial law had been declared in two dozen cities, and even the West had finally begun to sit up and take notice.

Three days ago Shizong's odyssey had finally ended in a small apartment in Xiamen, with his arrest. The next day he was to be moved to a small, undisclosed city somewhere inland, where he would stand trial for treason. There would be no media, no witnesses, no publicity. He would be found guilty, of course, and would be executed within twenty-four hours of his trial.

His name and philosophy would soon be forgotten. It was something that China needed if its present government were to survive. And it was exactly what Taiwan wanted to prevent, at all costs. Reunification with the PRC was suicide, but reunification with a democratic China was not only desirable, in Joseph's estimation, it was worth giving his life for.

"Here," he called softly, and he waved Shizong away from the door.

Chiang rushed over, molded a small block of Semtex on the lock, cracked a ten-second fuse, shoved it into the plastique and stepped aside. This time he didn't bother with the foam; the building itself would muffle the sounds.

The plastique blew with an impressive bang. Joseph hauled the door open and stepped inside the cell. "We're from Taiwan Intelligence, Mr. Shizong. We're here to rescue you."

Shizong hesitated for just a moment, weighing the possibilities. This could be some sort of PRC trick. "Where are you taking me?"

"Taipei."

Understanding dawned on his face, and he smiled and nodded. "I see," he said, warmly. Joseph was instantly under his spell. Shizong had intelligence and kindness; he and he alone knew the answers for China.

Shizong was dressed in dark trousers, but his open-collared shirt was white. Joseph pulled a black blouse out of his pack and handed it to the man.

"We don't have much time. Put this on over your shirt, please."

Xu was at the front door when they came out of Shizong's cell. He motioned for them to hurry.

Chiang closed the cell door, knocked out the lightbulb above it, and joined them outside as Shizong finished pulling the blouse over his head. The night was still except for the occasional boat whistle outside the harbor somewhere. So far there were no alarms, but the next patrol would be at the gate in under four minutes.

Joseph and Xu hustled Shizong down the walk. Chiang closed the steel door and wedged it shut. The lock was gone, but from a distance in the dark the damage might not be noticeable. At least they hoped it wouldn't be.

Zhou powered the gate open, and as soon as the other four were safely through he hit the button to close and relock it, came out of the guardhouse on the run and just managed to slip through the narrowing opening before the gate clicked home.

The lone sentry came around the corner fifty meters away. Joseph and the others raced across the road and dived for cover in the ditch. The son of a bitch was two minutes early, Joseph thought bitterly.

He laid his submachinegun aside and pulled out a stiletto. If need be he was going to have to take the guard out. But silently. The others understood, and got ready to cover him.

It seemed to take an eternity before the guard reached the gate. He said something that they couldn't quite make out, then peered inside. After several moments he shook his head and continued along the fence past the section that had been cut and reconnected just minutes before.

Joseph released the pent-up breath he'd been holding, sheathed his stiletto, and picked up his gun.

The only thing that they had not been able to find out was how often the gate guard was supposed to check in with base security. Whatever that schedule might be they were racing against it now.

When the sentry finally turned the far corner, they jumped up and raced the rest of the way down to the dry dock, keeping as low as they could. Xu and Chiang went down the ladder first, followed by Shizong and Joseph and finally Zhou.

Fifteen minutes later they crossed over the submarine net, and made their way past the commercial docks and through the fishing fleet. The weather had begun to calm down, but it wasn't until they were well outside the harbor and could start the outboard, that Joseph allowed himself to relax.

"It seems that you've actually done it," Shizong said. He smiled. "Congratulations, gentlemen. But now, as the Americans would say, the fat is in the fire."

Joseph laughed. "Indeed it is," he said. "I didn't know that you lived in the United States."

"It's been a secret. But I spent three years in the Silicon Valley as a spy for Chinese Intelligence."

Joseph decided that nothing would ever surprise him again. "Tell me, do you know anything about Superman comics?"

Two Months Later
The White House

Kirk Cullough McGarvey, Deputy Director of Operations for the Central Intelligence Agency, showed his credentials at the door three stories beneath the ground floor even though the civilian guard recognized him.

"Good morning, Mr. McGarvey, how's it out there?" the Secret Service officer asked.

"Hot and muggy, Brian, same as yesterday, same as tomorrow."

"Worst place in the world to build a capital city."

"Amen," McGarvey agreed. He entered the basement situation room and took his place next to Tom Roswell, director of the National Security Agency. At fifty, McGarvey certainly wasn't the youngest man ever to hold the third-highest job in American intelligence, but he was the most fit and had more field experience than all his predecessors put together.

He'd worked for the Company in one capacity or another for the past twenty-five years: sometimes on the payroll, at other times freelance. But in the parlance of the go-go of days of the sixties and seventies at the height of the Cold War, he'd been a shooter. An assassin. A killer. The ultimate arbiter. Now he was the spy finally come in from the cold.

There wasn't a man or woman on either side of the Atlantic or Pacific who'd ever looked into his startlingly green, sometimes gray, eyes who'd ever come away unchanged. At a little over six feet, with a broad, honest, at times even friendly, face, he still maintained the physique of an athlete because he swam or ran nearly every day, and he worked out at least twice a week with the CIA's fencing team. His enemies feared him, and his friends and allies revered him. An old nemesis had once said that although Mac was an anachronism in this high-tech day and age, he was still a force to be reckoned with. "Never, ever underestimate the man. If you do, he's likely to hand you your balls on a platter."

The long conference table was filled with the President's civilian and military advisors this morning. Among them were all four of the Joint Chiefs, the Secretaries of State and Defense; representatives from all the law-enforcement and intelligence services, including the FBI, Secret Service, and Defense Intelligence Agency, along with the National Reconnaissance Office, which was responsible for all the photographic data received from our KeyHole and Jupiter satellite systems as well as a host of others. His National Security Advisor, Dennis Berndt, and his Chief of Staff, Anthony Lang, were also present. *All the big dogs*, McGarvey thought. But he wasn't surprised.

Roswell had been talking to the FBI's Associate Director, Bob Armstrong. He turned to McGarvey. "You giving the briefing this morning, Mac?"

"Gene will start us off."

Eugene Carpenter was the Secretary of State. Nearing eighty, he was the oldest man in government, but everyone respected his intellectually astute, though usually practical, views. He was sitting slumped in his chair lost in his own thoughts.

"If we don't watch our step, this business over Taiwan is going to jump up and bite us on the ass, because the Chinese sure as hell aren't going to forget the *Nanchong*."

"Just like the *Maine*, is that what you're saying?" McGarvey asked.

"Worked for us," Roswell said.

The *FF502 Nanchong* was a PRC frigate that had been destroyed overnight fifty miles off the southwest coast of Taiwan in international waters. The Chinese claimed that it was attacked by a Taiwanese gunboat or perhaps a submarine, while Taiwan denied any involvement. The PRC's state-controlled media were already clamoring for retribution, and the Chinese military had been brought to the highest state of readiness they'd been in since the Vietnam War.

The President walked in, and everyone stood until he had taken his seat. He looked tired, as if he hadn't been getting enough sleep. It was the same affliction that every president since FDR had suffered; the job was a tough one, and it took its toll. He gave McGarvey a nod.

"People, let's get started, I have some tough calls to make and I'm going to need your help this morning." He turned to the Secretary of State. "Gene?"

Carpenter looked up as if out of a daze, and he sat up with a visible effort. He looked pale and drawn, in even greater need of rest than the President.

"Thank you, Mr. President. Ladies and gentlemen, we're here this morning because of an incident last night in the East China Sea in which a People's Republic Of China warship was blown up and sunk with all hands lost. I'm going to leave the actual briefing to Mr. McGarvey, who warned us two months ago that something like this was bound to happen. But there's something that you all need to know before he gets started. Ever since the most recent round of trouble between mainland China and Taiwan started two months ago, we've been trying to find a way to keep the situation out there stable."

Carpenter passed a hand across his eyes. "It's no secret that we've not done a very good job of it. Eight weeks ago, in response to a PRC naval exercise in the area, we moved our Seventh Fleet out of Yokosuka: the *George Washington* and her battle group north of Taiwan and the *Eisenhower* and her support group to the south. Our committment, of course, was and still is to honor our pledge to keep the East China sea-lanes open.

"China's response in turn was to augment her East Sea Fleet presence in the region with elements of her North and South Sea Fleets, greatly outnumbering us."

Carpenter shuffled some papers in front of him. "Four weeks ago our two Third Fleet carrier battle groups—the *Nimitz* and *John F. Kennedy*—arrived from Honolulu to cover Taiwan's north and east coasts, which prompted China to completely strip her North and South Sea Fleets, concentrating every ship that they could commission in an area barely three hundred miles long and half that wide. In addition, the entire PRC Air Force has been moved east. Along with their army and Missile Service, the entire military might of China was placed this morning on DEFCON One."

"My God, what the hell do they want, war?" Attorney General Dorothy Kress demanded angrily. "Over one man?"

"They've done this before," Admiral Richard Halvorson, the Chairman of the Joint Chiefs, said. "The last time they rattled their sabres was during Taiwan's elections. So long as we stand our ground they back down." He turned to the President. "Hell, Mr. President, Shizong isn't worth that much to them."

"How much is Taiwan worth to us, Admiral?" McGarvey asked across the table. All of them were in for a rude awakening that morning. They would be faced with recommending one of the toughest decisions any president could ever be faced with.

Halvorson shrugged. "That's a civilian policy decision, one thank God that I don't have to make," he said. "Ask me if we can defend Taiwan against a PRC invasion, I'll give you the numbers. And frankly, at this moment they do not look good. We're spread too thinly."

"But that's exactly the decision we're going to have to work out here this morning," McGarvey pressed. He didn't know why he was angry, except that we had worked very hard and long to get ourselves into this position. Getting ourselves back out wasn't going to be easy. Nor would it be safe.

The President motioned for McGarvey to back off for the moment. It was the same game we'd been playing out there ever since Nixon had opened the door and stuck his foot into it, McGarvey wanted to tell them. But they knew it; hell, everybody knew it. China was getting Most Favored Nation trading status because she was a vast market. It had to do with money and almost nothing else. The fact was we couldn't ignore a country whose population was one-fourth that of the entire world's. But we couldn't give in to them either; abandon our friends and allies just as the British had abandoned Hong Kong. When the solution to a little problem was distasteful Americans lately seemed to put it off until the problem got much bigger and the solution became even tougher. Sooner or later, as Roswell suggested, the situation over Taiwan was going to bite us in the ass.

Like now.

"Okay, Gene, everything we've tried so far has failed," the President said. "Tell them the rest."

"I've just returned from a three-day shuttle-diplomacy mission between Beijing and Taipei. I was trying to talk some sense into them; find an opening, even the slightest hint of an opening, so that we could resume a meaningful dialogue." Carpenter pursed his lips. "I was afraid that I was coming back with the worst possible news: that there was going to be no simple way out of the morass except to continue the Mexican standoff between our navy and theirs. I thought that the best we could hope for would be, as Admiral Halvorson suggested, that the Chinese would sooner or later tire of the exercise and go home.

"But then the *Nanchong* incident occurred last night while I was over the Pacific on my way home. Now all bets are off."

"What do they want?" Secretary of Defense Arthur Turnquist asked. His was one cabinet appointment that McGarvey never understood. The man was an asshole; he spent almost as much time saving his own reputation as he did on any real work. But he was well connected on the Hill.

"The mainland Chinese want the immediate return of Peter Shizong, dead or alive. And the Taiwanese want nothing less than their independence unless mainland China is willing to open itself to free elections and a totally free market economy. Neither side is willing to discuss the issue beyond that."

"That's hardly likely anytime soon," the President's advisor on national security affairs, Dennis Berndt, pointed out unnecessarily.

"It comes down to the simple question: Do we abandon Taiwan? Do we turn tail and run? Or do we stay and risk a shooting war?" Carpenter said. "The sinking of the *Nanchong* may well be the catalyst. We have to consider where our breaking point is." He sat back, the effort of bringing the discussion this far completely draining him.

"What's the military situation out there at the moment?" the President asked.

"It's a mess, Mr. President," Admiral Halvorson answered. "We've offered to help with the search-and-rescue mission, but the Chinese have refused, as we expected they would. The actual effect of the sinking was to move the bulk of the PRC's naval assets about twenty-five miles closer to Taiwan."

"What about the Taiwanese military?"

"Fortunately their naval units in the near vicinity have all moved back an appropriate distance, but they, along with their Air and Ground Defense units, are at DEFCON One. In the meantime we're keeping four Orions and five A3 AWACS aircraft in the air around the clock to make sure that this doesn't spin out of control and blindside us. All of our carrier fighter squadrons are at a high state of readiness, as are our Air Force fighter wings in Japan and on Okinawa." The admiral looked around the table at the others to make sure that they all would catch his exact meaning. "If someone starts an all-out shooting war over there, we'll be the first to know about it. The PRC knows that we know, and so does Taiwan."

"If we have the region so well covered, how'd the *Nanchong* get hit without warning?" SecDef Turnquist asked peevishly.

"I can't answer that one, Mr. Turnquist," Admiral Halvorson admitted. "Al Ryland's people are the best, and he told me this morning that he was damned if he knew what happened." Vice Admiral Ryland was the Seventh Fleet CINC. His flag was on the *George Washington.*

"If it happened once, it can happen again."

"No, sir, that's not a possibility you need consider," the admiral said in such a way that it was clear he would not be pushed. "Mr. President, I would sincerely hope that we can come to some sort of an agreement with Tiawan over Shizong. I'm not saying that we turn him over to the Chinese, but Taipei could certainly be made to stop his radio and television broadcasts. Christ, it's driving them nuts." He looked around the table at the others to emphasize his point. "The longer our military forces are in such close proximity to the Chinese the more likely it'll become that there'll be a serious accident. We're going to start killing people over there—our own kids. And on top of that my commanders have their hands tied."

"They are authorized to use whatever force necessary to defend themselves, Admiral," the President said. It was clear that he wasn't going to be pushed either. Unlike his predecessor, he had spent time in the military.

"That's the point. Mr. President. They might need more authority than that, and they might need it so fast that there'd be no time to phone home. Al Ryland would like full discretion—" Ryland was in overall command of the combined fleet.

"No," the President said even before Admiral Halvorson finished the sentence. He sat forward for emphasis in his tall, bulletproof leather chair. "This *will not* spin out of control into an all-out shooting war between China and the United States."

"Then, Mr. President, let's pack our bags and get the hell out of there," McGarvey said from across the table.

The President shot him an angry, irritated look, as if he hadn't expected a comment like that from the CIA, and especially not from McGarvey, for whom he had a great deal of respect. "The CIA does not set policy."

"No, sir, nor will the CIA tell this administration what it *wants* to hear."

"When have you played it any differently?"

McGarvey had to smile, and there were a few chuckles around the table though the mood was anything but light. Friend and enemy alike all agreed that McGarvey never bullshitted the troops. Never.

"Okay, let's hear the CIA's version of the situation, because I sure as hell need the unvarnished truth before I can come to a decision that makes any sense."

McGarvey hesitated for just a moment. He'd been in this kind of a position many times before. It never got any easier. What he wanted to do had one-hundred-to-one odds against it. But the alternatives were either losing Taiwan or going to war with mainland China. In either case tens of thousands, maybe hundreds of thousands of lives would be lost. Needlessly.

"There may be no acceptable solution, Mr. President. At least not in the ordinary sense of the word, because the Chinese themselves engineered this situation."

The Secretary of Defense started to object, but the President held him off with a sharp gesture. "Go on."

"First of all the *Nanchong* was ready for the scrap heap. We believe that she was headed for the cutting yard when she was diverted at the last minute and sent out on this mission. She was a *Riga*-class frigate, built in 1955 in the Soviet Union and transferred to Bulgaria in 1958. Her name at that time was the *Kobchik*, which made her a KGB boat. Navy ships have numbers but no names.

"The *Kobchik* was extensively retrofitted in '80 and '81, and then sold to the PRC in 1987, when she was renamed the *Nanchong*. By that time she was already an outdated piece of junk."

"Like most of the Chinese navy," SecDef Turnquist said. He was going to make a run for the presidency next election, and the rumors were already flying that he was taking Chinese soft money. But McGarvey wasn't going to go there right now.

"The *Nanchong*'s skipper, a man by the name of Shi Kiyang, was convicted of treason eighteen months ago and sentenced to life in prison without parole at East Sea Fleet headquarters in Ningbo. His mother, his wife, and his two children were sent into exile to Yulin, in the far north, and all of his assets, car, bicycles, bank account, Beijing apartment, and furniture were confiscated by the state.

"But he made an amazing comeback. Six weeks ago he was released from prison and sent to Xiamen on the coast. His family was brought back to Beijing, where their old lives were reinstated.

"The *Nanchong* left port three days ago on her one and only mission with a skeleton crew of officers and men who had all been convicted of a variety of crimes from treason to theft of state property."

"Goddammit, we were set up," Admiral Halvorson said angrily. "But why? What did the bastards expect to accomplish?"

"Get our attention."

"Are you telling us that the Chinese sank their own ship?" the President asked.

"Yes, sir."

"They got our attention. What do they want?"

"They want exactly what they told Gene they wanted. Peter Shizong. Dead or alive."

"They're using the *Nanchong* as an excuse to punish Taiwan. I can understand that. But they want us to back off this time, and they're willing to fight."

"That's the conclusion we're drawing, Mr. President," McGarvey said. "They're not merely rattling their sabers this time, they've pulled them. The ball is in our court."

"We have the *Carl Vinson* and her battle group still in Yokosuka. We could park them just offshore from Taipei. Any invasion force would have to get through us first," Admiral Halvorson said. He was mad. "Might make them stop and think before they pulled the trigger."

"They would only be fighting a delaying action," Turnquist objected.

"That's if we stuck to conventional weapons," Halvorson countered. "We have six submarines patrolling the strait, three of them strategic missile boats. Their combined nuclear throw weight is five times that of the entire Chinese missile force."

"Most of the Chinese missiles are ICBMs, are they not?" the President's National Security Advisor, Berndt, asked. He was clearly alarmed. "Capable of reaching the United States a half hour from launch?"

"Our first targets would be their launch sites," Admiral Halvorson shot back.

The President gestured for them to stop talking. "How reliable is your information, Mac?"

"We have a high confidence."

"What do we do about it?"

"Whatever we do, Mr. President, will involve a risk—either of losing Taiwan or of getting into a nuclear exchange with China."

"If it's about getting into a nuclear war, Taiwan's independence isn't worth the price," Berndt said. It was obvious that most of the others around the table agreed with him.

"It's about our word," McGarvey interjected softly.

"That's what was said about Vietnam," Berndt pressed. He was an academic. He'd never been out in the real world.

"Taiwan is an ally."

"So was South Vietnam."

"Maybe we could have won that war," McGarvey said patiently.

After twenty-five years working for the CIA, he didn't think he'd heard a new argument in the past twenty years.

"I'll repeat my question, Mac, what does the CIA suggest we do?"

"Play the PRC at their own game, Mr. President," McGarvey said.

"Okay, how do we do that?"

"You're going to lend me a *Seawolf* attack submarine and I'm going to sink it with all hands lost."

Three Days Later
CVN *George Washington*

Even at a distance from the air the *George Washington* was an impressive sight. At over a thousand feet in length, she displaced more than ninety thousand tons, carried a crew of three thousand men, women, and officers, plus another three thousand in the air wing. The carrier had ninety planes and an arsenal of Phalanx cannons, Sams and Sea Sparrow missiles, and yet her two pressurized water-cooled nuclear reactors, which needed refueling only every thirteen years, could push the largest warship afloat to speeds well in excess of thirty knots. McGarvey peered out the window of the Marine Sea King CH-46G troop-carrying helicopter that brought him and his escort, Navy SEAL Lieutenant Hank Hanrahan, down from Okinawa.

It was early morning, the sun just coming up over the eastern horizon, and the day promised to be glorious. The north coast of Taiwan was a very faint smudge on the horizon to the southeast, and arrayed for as far as the eye could see in all directions were war ships: the *George Washington*'s battle group of Aegis cruisers, guided-missile destroyers, and ASW frigates directly below; Taiwanese gunboats, destroyers, and guided-missile frigates to the east; and the PRC fleet along a three-hundred-mile line to the west. The *George Washington*'s air wing maintained a screen one hundred miles out, which of necessity brought them into very close proximity with the Chinese. And below the surface were six U.S. submarines, four Taiwanese boats and eleven Chinese submarines, three of which were nuclear-powered Han-class boats, old but deadly.

"There're almost enough assets out there to leapfrog from Taiwan to the Chinese mainland without getting your feet wet," Admiral Halvorson had told McGarvey after the President's briefing. What he meant was that once the shooting started it would be impossible to control the battle or stop it until there was a clear victory. In the meantime a lot of good people would be dead for no reason.

"Ever been on a carrier before, Mr. M?" Lieutenant Hanrahan

asked, breaking into McGarvey's thoughts. He was twenty-six, with a freshly scrubbed wide-eyed innocent look of a kid from some small town in the Midwest. But he was a service brat, his dad was a retired navy captain, and he was as calm and as hard as nails as any man in the SEALs. You only had to look into his eyes to see it. He'd been there done that, and when called upon he was ready, willing, and very able to go there again and do it again.

"A couple of times, but you forget how big they are."

"About the size of a small city. Only problem is you can't find a decent saloon anywhere aboard."

McGarvey had to smile. He was being tested. "A decent *legal* saloon, you mean." Hanrahan gave him a sharp look. "I wasn't always a DDO. And grunts tend to hear a hell of a lot more than their superiors. Don't shit an old shitter."

Hanrahan grinned happily. "I read you, Mr. M."

A red shirt guided them to touch down just forward of the island. The Grumman E-2C Hawkeye AWACS aircraft normally parked there was airborne, and for the moment the elevator to the hangar deck was in the up position and clear. Fully one-third of the Seventh and Third Fleet's assets were in the air at any one time, making this one of the busiest pieces of air real estate in the world, even busier than Chicago's O'Hare.

The seas were fairly calm and as soon as the helicopter came to a complete stop, McGarvey and Hanrahan unbuckled and grabbed their bags. There was no sense whatsoever that they were aboard a ship at sea. The deck was as rock solid as a parking lot in a big city, but noisier.

"Thanks for the ride," McGarvey shouted up to the crew forward.

"Yes, sir. Hope you enjoyed the meal service and in-flight movie," the pilot quipped.

"Just great," McGarvey said. A cheese sandwich and a ginger ale while looking out a small window were not usually his first choices for breakfast and entertainment, but he'd had worse.

The red shirt motioned them to the island structure as the chopper was already being prepped to be moved below and refueled for the 350-nautical mile return trip. Just inside the hatch a Marine sergeant in battle fatigues, a Colt Commando slung over his shoulder, saluted.

"Gentlemen, please follow me to flag quarters."

He led them down a maze of passageways, the machinery noises not as bad as McGarvey remembered from the *Independence*, but the corridors just as narrow and covered in stenciled alphanumeric legends. Pipes and cable runs were everywhere, and seemingly around every corner there were firefighting stations built into the Navy gray bulkheads.

The ship was very busy, evident by all the activity they saw through the hatches in the bulkheads, decks, and overheads, and the constant PA announcements.

Men all good and true, busy at the work of war, the line came back to McGarvey from somewhere. Only these days it was men *and women* all busy at the work of war.

Another armed Marine sergeant in battle fatigues was stationed at the admiral's door. He stiffened to attention. Their escort knocked once, then opened the door and stepped aside.

"Gentlemen, the admiral is expecting you."

Flag quarters was actually a well-furnished suite, sitting room, bedroom, and bathroom, that equaled anything that a luxury ocean liner could offer—thick carpeting, rich paneling, nice artwork, expensive furniture, except there were no sliding glass doors or balconies.

"Good morning," Vice Admiral Albert Ryland said. He put down his coffee cup and he and the other two men with him got to their feet.

"Good morning, Admiral," McGarvey said, shaking hands.

Ryland, who was from Birmingham, Alabama, looked and sounded like a tall, lean Southern gentleman from the old school. He was one of the most respected officers in the Navy; it was Halvorson's opinion that he would probably end up Chairman of the Joint Chiefs within five years. "Don't try to hold anything back on him, or he'll cut you off at the knees," Halvorson warned.

"This is the *George*'s captain, Pete Townsend, and my Operations Officer, Tom Byrne."

They shook hands. The captain looked like a banker or the chairman of some board of directors. He wore wire-rimmed glasses, his hair was thin and gray, and his face was round and undistinguished. Byrne, however, was a very large black man who looked like he could play with the Green Bay Packers. His grip was as strong as bar steel.

"Sir, I'm Lieutenant Hank Hanrahan. I have orders to assist Mr. McGarvey."

"You Mike Hanrahan's son?"

"Yes, sir."

"How's your old man doing these days?"

"He misses the Navy, sir."

Ryland chuckled. "This would be just the kind of brouhaha he'd like to be in." He turned back to McGarvey. "Well, the Chinese know that you're here. They're watching every move we make. Satellites and OTH radar."

"Hopefully they don't know who I am," McGarvey said. "And we're going to keep it that way because Hank and I are not going to be aboard very long. Just until nightfall."

"I thought your helicopter was heading back right away," Townsend said.

"We're not leaving that way."

"Unless they're sending another bird for you, I don't have anything to spare."

"We're not flying."

"Are you going to swim?" Townsend demanded angrily.

"As a matter of fact that's exactly what we're going to do, Captain," McGarvey said. "Tonight."

He couldn't blame Ryland or his officers for being in a bad temper. They were in the middle of a likely very hot situation with their hands practically tied behind their backs. This was a fight between China and Taiwan. The U.S. was Taiwan's ally and was supposed to back them up if they were attacked, but the Navy was here only to show the flag. The President's orders remained very specific: Ryland was not to shoot unless the Chinese shot at his people first. In effect if the PRC navy simply wanted to sail right through the middle of the Seventh and Third Fleets, engage every Taiwanese warship they encountered, and then send troops ashore, there was nothing Ryland could do about it.

Ryland shook his head. "Dick Halvorson said that you were inventive."

McGarvey smiled faintly. "I don't think that was exactly the word he used."

"No."

Byrne poured them coffee. "Admiral Halvorson said that we were to give you whatever you wanted." He looked at Hanrahan, who did not avert his gaze. "That's a pretty tall order."

McGarvey took a plain white envelope out of his pocket and handed it to Ryland. He figured that if the flag officers were unhappy before, they would be even less happy after reading the letter.

When Ryland was done he handed it to Townsend, and looked at McGarvey. "Okay, the Chairman of the Joint Chiefs calls to tell me than the CIA's Deputy Director of Operations is flying out, and I'm supposed to give him all the help I can. I'm thinking that perhaps you're bringing a magic bullet to get us out of the mess we're in. And now this."

Townsend had finished the letter, and he handed it to Byrne. He was clearly upset.

"No magic bullets this time, Admiral. But I think we might have a chance of coming out of this situation with our asses more or less intact," McGarvey replied. He had decided long ago never to try to argue with a man who has just been blindsided. If you wanted to get through to him, you waited until he calmed down a little.

"That's a comfort," Ryland said acerbically. "I'm told to defend Taiwan, but I can't fire a shot to do it." He glanced at Byrne, who had also finished the letter. "Now the President tells me that I can't even ask any questions. Christ on the cross, if we lose here, we lose everywhere!"

"If we start a shooting war, it could escalate. Go nuclear."

"McGarvey, there's a real chance that every time we untie one of our carriers from the dock and send her to sea we'll get ourselves into a nuclear war. Are you telling me that Taiwan isn't worth the risk?"

"That's the current feeling in Washington."

Ryland glanced again at his officers. "A dose of refreshing honesty for a change. It's a wonder that you've kept your job for so long. What are we doing here then?" he asked angrily. "Sooner or later there'll be another accident. Then another, and another until all hell breaks loose! That's the way it works, you know."

"The *Nanchong* was no accident, Admiral. The Chinese sank her. That's why the President sent me out here, to work out a solution that'll keep everybody happy—Taipei and Beijing."

"If that's true, it explains a couple of things that we were wondering about," Byrne said. He and Ryland exchanged a look.

"How many men were aboard her?" Ryland asked.

"We're not sure, but probably no more than a dozen. Just enough to take her to sea, but not enough to fight her."

"Gives the PRC a supposedly legitimate reason to be here," Byrne observed.

"And us, too," Ryland agreed. "What do we do about it?"

"We're going to sink one of our own."

Ryland sat forward so fast that he practically levitated from his chair. But he hesitated for just a moment before he spoke. McGarvey could almost hear him counting to ten. "I don't think that you're saying what I just heard. The Chinese may be willing to kill their people, not us."

"Thirty-six hours from now there'll be an underwater explosion a hundred miles from here. Five minutes later one of our submarines, the *Seawolf*, will send up a slot buoy to report that they have engaged an unknown enemy, were damaged, and are in immediate danger of sinking. Before the message is completed the communications buoy will break loose from the submarine, there'll be another intense underwater explosion, and then nothing."

Byrne got a chart of the area, and McGarvey pinpointed the approximate location for them. The *George Washington*'s captain saw the plan immediately.

"That's sandwiched between us and the *Kennedy*. No Chinese assets that we're aware of within a hundred fifty miles." Townsend looked up. "That gives the *Seawolf* a clear path into the open Pacific. Is that what you have in mind?"

McGarvey nodded. "There'll be an extensive search, of course, and some wreckage will be found. Twenty-four hours later we'll announce that the *Swordfish* was lost with all hands, and was probably torpedoed."

"The *Swordfish*? She was pulled from duty six months ago," Byrne said. "She's back at Groton."

"That's right. And when this is over with, she'll be taken in secret and sunk just off our continental shelf."

"If we blame the Chinese, they'll have to figure that we've pulled the same stunt on them that they pulled on the Taiwanese," Byrne said.

"It won't matter," McGarvey told them. "Everybody will back off to let the situation cool down and allow the politicians to hash it out."

"That'll only buy us a few days, maybe a week, and then we'll be right back in the same situation we're in right now," Ryland opined. "What will we have gained?"

"After seven days the PRC Navy will return to their home bases and so will we."

Ryland glanced at the President's letter on the coffee table. "That's the part I'm not supposed to ask any questions about."

"You wouldn't want to know, Admiral. As soon as it gets dark we'll be out of your hair."

Ryland turned to Hanrahan. "You're in on this, Lieutenant?"

Hanrahan stiffened. "Yes, sir."

Ryland waved him off. "Relax, I'm not going to order you to tell me. Except how in the hell do you think you're going to get off this ship without the Chinese knowing something is going on? If you're not flying, you'll have to be transferred to one of our frigates or destroyers, and they'll see that, too."

"Sir, we're exiting the ship from the port hangar deck just forward of the Sea Sparrow launcher."

"What the hell—" Townsend exploded.

"Relax, Pete, I think I know at least part of what they're up to," Ryland said. "The *Seawolf* is coming to pick you up." He shook his head. "That's a dicey maneuver no matter how you slice it." He turned to the captain again. "We'll have to warn sonar."

"That won't be necessary, Admiral. Your people haven't detected her yet, have they?" McGarvey asked.

"No," Townsend said, tight-lipped. "Where is she?"

McGarvey glanced at his watch. It was a few minutes after seven in the morning. "Actually we're passing over her about right now. She's been lying beneath a thermocline nine hundred feet down since yesterday morning."

"We're on a twelve-hour pattern," Townsend said. "We'll be right back here around seven this evening."

"That's about when we go overboard," McGarvey said. "When you're clear, she'll come up to about fifty feet, we'll dive down to her and lock aboard."

"Does Tom Harding know what's going on?" Ryland asked. Harding was the *Seawolf*'s skipper, and a very good if somewhat conservative sub driver.

"No."

"Well, I can think of at least a hundred things that could go wrong. But considering the alternatives we'll do whatever it takes to get you down to her in one piece."

"In secret," McGarvey said. "As few people outside this room as possible are to know that we've gone overboard."

"I'll arrange that," Townsend said, and he shook his head. "I think you're nuts."

McGarvey nodded. "You're probably right, Captain."

1920 Local
SSN 405 *Hekou*

Lying just off the floor of the ocean one thousand feet beneath the surface, the PRC Han-class nuclear submarine *Hekou* was leaking at the seams, the air was going stale, and the radiation levels inside the hull continued to rise, the last fact of which was being withheld from the crew. Her home base was at East Sea Fleet Headquarters in Ningbo, and she had been among the first to sail when the trouble begin. By luck she had been lying on the bottom eight days ago hiding from the American ASW aircraft above while the engineers were frantically correcting a steering problem when sonar picked up the *George Washington* passing almost directly overhead. When the steering problem had been fixed, and the aircraft carrier was well past, the *Hekou*'s skipper sent up a communications buoy to get instructions. He was told to stay where he was, maintain complete silence, and wait for the moment to strike.

The message unfortunately was not clear on when that moment might be. In the meantime Captain Yuan Heishui was having problems keeping his boat alive, and there was the American submarine five hundred meters off its starboard bow, also hovering just off the bottom mush.

Twenty-four hours ago sonar had detected the American *Seawolf*-class submarine approaching their position very deep and very slowly. The approach had been so slow and so stealthy that the Americans had been on top of them before they knew what was happening. Even before Heishui could order his torpedo tubes loaded and prepared to fire, the *Seawolf* went quiet and settled silently in place, apparently completely unaware that they were not alone.

Since that time Captain Heishui had ordered all nonessential machinery and movements aboard his boat to stop.

He picked the growler phone from its bracket, careful not to scrape metal against metal. "Engineering, conn," he said softly.

Their chief engineer, Lieutenant He Daping, answered immediately. "*Shi de*," yes. He sounded harried and in the background the captain could hear the sounds of running water.

"This is the captain. How is it going back there?"

"Without the pumps we're eventually going to take on so much water that we won't have the power to rise to the surface."

"We must not run the pumps. How long do we have?"

"Six hours, Captain, maybe less," Daping answered. Captain Heishui knew the man well and respected him. He came from a very good family, and his service record was totally clean, an accomplishment in itself.

"Seal off the engineering spaces, then introduce some high-pressure air in there. That should slow the leaks."

"I was just about to do that," Daping said. If they could not get out of the fix they were in now and get moving soon, sealing the aft section of the boat would doom the crewmen back there. If the flooding got too bad, there would be no way of opening the hatches.

"I'll do what I can," the captain promised. "But we might have to fight. *Hăo yùngi*," good luck.

"Yes, you too, Captain."

"Conn, sonar."

Heishui glanced up at the mission clock, then switched circuits. "This is the captain. Is Sierra Seven back early?" They had designated the American Aircraft carrier as Sierra Seven and had timed her movements. She was on a zigzag course that brought her back to the same point approximately every twelve hours. It was 1120 GMT, the standard time kept aboard all submarines, which put it at 1920 on the surface. If it was the *George Washington*, he was slightly early.

"She's fifteen thousand yards out, Captain, but it's Sierra Eighteen," Chief Sonarman, Ensign Shi Zenzhong, reported excitedly. "He's moving. He's on the way up, very slowly, on an intercept bearing with Seven." Sierra Eighteen was the American submarine, and the captain could not imagine what he was up to.

"Have they sent up a slot buoy?"

"No, sir. And they're running silent. No one on the surface will hear them." Zenzhong's voice was cracking, and the captain considered pulling him off duty immediately. But the man was the best.

"Have we been detected?"

"I don't think so, sir," the sonarman replied. The captain's calm demeanor was helping him and everyone in the control room.

"Stand by," the captain said. He motioned his XO, Lieutenant Commander Kang Lagao, over. "Get down to sonar and give Ensign Zenzhong some help. Sierra Eighteen is on the way up."

"Maybe they're rendezvousing with the *George Washington*," Lagao suggested. He was the oldest man aboard the submarine, even older at forty-six than the captain. And he was wise even beyond his years. Exactly the steady hand they all need. The American command structure could take a lesson.

"That's what I think, but something is strange about it," Heishui said. "See what's happening and then start a TMA."

Lagao was startled. "You're not going to shoot, are you?" A TMA, or Target Motion Analysis, was a targeting procedure used to guide torpedoes in which the enemy vessel's speed and position were continually tracked and plotted against the relative speed and position of the tracking boat.

"Not yet. But I want to be prepared. There's no telling what they're up to, or when we might have to shoot."

"Very well."

When Lagao was gone, Heishui picked up the growler phone. "Forward torpedo room, this is the captain."

"Yes, sir."

"I want all six tubes loaded, but not flooded, with 65-Es." Heishui glanced over at his weapons control officer and chief of boat, whose jobs he was doing. They were studiously watching their panels. The captain did not want to bring any shame to them, but he wanted to make absolutely sure that no mistakes were made. Their lives depended on it. "I want this done with no noise. Do you understand?"

"Yes, sir."

"I'll send the presets momentarily, but if there is any noise whatsoever, whoever was responsible will be court-martialed and shot as a traitor—if we survive to make it home. Do you understand that as well?"

"Yes, sir. Very well."

"Carry on," Heishui said. He replaced the phone, confused about many things though not about why he was here. Taiwan needed to come home, as Hong Kong had, or else be punished as a naughty child.

1930 local
SSN 21 *Seawolf*

Hearing anything with precision from beneath the sharp thermocline was difficult except for a ship the size of the *George Washington.* Named for her class, the *Seawolf* was the state of the art in nuclear-powered attack submarines. No other navy in the world had a boat that could match her stealth, her nuclear and conventional weapons, her speed, and her electronics. Especially not her BQQ-8 passive sonar suite, which, according to the sonarmen who used it, could hear a gnat's fart at fifty thousand yards. Her mission had been to patrol an area well north of the Seventh and Third Fleets in case the PRC tried an end run on them. The long ELF message they had received forty-eight hours ago irritated the *Seawolf*'s captain because it put his boat at risk without an explanation why. He was ordered to rendezvous with the *George Washington* without allowing the carrier or any other ship to detect her. And less than an hour from now he was to pick up two passengers. The only reason he hadn't "missed" the damn fool message was the last line: *McGarvey Sends.*

"Skipper, we're at seven hundred twenty feet," the Chief of Boat Lieutenant Karl Trela reported.

"Okay, hold us here," Commander Thomas Harding told him. The bottom edge of the thermocline where the water got sharply colder was just twenty feet above the top of their sail. They were at the edge of the safety zone where they were all but invisible to surface sonars. He picked up the phone. "Sonar, conn."

"Sonar, aye."

"Where's the *George*?"

"Four thousand yards and closing, skipper. He's on his predicted course and speed."

"What else is up there, Mel?" Commander Harding asked in a calm voice. The trademark of his boat was a relaxed vigilance. A few of the crewmen called him Captain Serenity, though not to his face.

"There's some action southeast. I think it might be the *Marvin*

Shields. And there're faint noises southwest, maybe thirty thousand yards. My guess would be the *Arleigh Burke*, but I'm not real sure, sir." The *Shields* was a Knox-class frigate, and the *Burke* was a guided-missile destroyer. Both were a part of the *George Washington*'s battle group.

"Any subsurface contacts?"

"Negative, sir."

"Very well. Keep your ears open. I want to know as soon as the *George* has passed us and gets ten thousand yards out. We'll be heading up."

"Aye, aye, skipper."

Commander Harding got his coffee and leaned nonchalantly against the periscope platform rail, a man without a care in the world. Whoever McGarvey was sending down in secret would be bringing the explanation with them. *And it better be damned good*, he thought, *or there will be hell to pay*. But then he'd had dealings with the man before. And McGarvey was, if nothing else, a man of consummate *cojones*. The mission would be, at the very least, an interesting one.

1940 Local
George Washington

Nobody said a thing on the way across the hangar deck. Their Marine escort, Sergeant Carlos Ablanedo, stopped them for a moment behind an A-6E Intruder, its wings in the up position, its nose cover open exposing the electronics inside. There was some activity forward, but it was far enough away, and the cavernous deck was lit only with dim red battle lights so there was no chance that they would be spotted.

Word had been sent down to the various section chiefs to make themselves and their crews scarce from about midships aft between 1930 and 2000 hours. It was done in such a way that no questions were asked. A personal favor for the old man.

The military services were not usually particularly friendly toward the CIA; too many mistakes had been made in the past, not the least of which was the Bay of Pigs fiasco. But McGarvey had to admit that this time they were treating him with kid gloves. They were looking for a solution that would require no shooting, and they were willing to go along with just about anything to get it.

The night was pitch-black, the sky overcast, so that there was no line to mark the horizon. The seas were fairly flat, so the huge wake trailing behind the massive warship was not as confused and dangerous as it could have been. Nonetheless, Hanrahan warned him that once they hit the water they were to swim at right angles from the ship to put as much distance between themselves and the tremendous suction of the gigantic propellers as possible. To help them the captain would order a sharp turn to port at 1950, which would take the stern away from them.

There was no rail on the open elevator bay, and it was a long way down to the water, maybe thirty or forty feet, McGarvey estimated. He and Hanrahan were dressed in black wet suits with hoods, small scuba tanks attached to their chests, buoyancy control vests and swim fins strapped to their backs. Hanrahan also carried a GPS/Inertial Navigator about the size of a paperback book. On the surface it established its location from satellites. Underwater it "remembered" its last satellite fix, and then kept track of every movement: up, down, left, and right, along with the speed to continuously update its position. It was a new toy that the SEALs had been given just two months ago. In trials it had worked like a charm. But this would be its first real-world test. McGarvey carried a bag with his things.

They flipped a pair of lines over the side, attached their hooks to the six-inch lip at the edge of the deck, then threaded the lines through their rappelling carabiners.

"Okay, Sarge, we were never here," Hanrahan said.

"Yes, sir. I'll take care of your ropes, but you guys stay cool."

McGarvey looked over the side at the black water rushing by. "I don't think we're going to have much of a choice in about two minutes."

The sergeant grinned. "At least this ain't the North Atlantic."

"Some guys have all the luck," Hanrahan said.

The carrier began its ponderous turn to port. They could actually feel the list, which McGarvey figured had to be at least five degrees, maybe more. The white wake curled away from them, and Hanrahan gave him the thumbs-up sign.

They went over the side together, rappelling in long but cautious jumps down the ship's flank, until they were just a few feet above water that moved as fast as a mountain stream.

Hanrahan unclipped his line and held it away from his body. McGarvey did the same, and on a signal from the SEAL they pushed off, hitting the water almost as hard as if they had jumped off a garage roof and landed on their backs on a concrete driveway.

McGarvey tumbled end over end and then he was swept deep beneath the surface. It seemed to go on for an eternity, until gradually the turbulence began to subside. When he surfaced, the ship was already ahead of him, and a ten-foot wall of water from the wake was curling around, heading right for him.

He yanked his swim fins free, struggled to put them on, and headed directly away from where he figured he had gone into the water and at right angles to the wake.

After five minutes he stopped and looked over his shoulder, involuntarily catching his breath. The ocean was empty. There was no sign that the *George Washington* had ever been there. No wake, no lights on the horizon, nothing. There were no other ships in sight, nor were there any aircraft lights in the sky. No sounds, no smells. He could not remember ever having such an overwhelming feeling of being alone. Facing a human enemy, one bent on killing you, was one thing. But facing the sea, which was a supremely indifferent enemy, was another matter altogether.

He saw a flash of light out of the corner of his eye to the left. He turned toward it, raised the tiny strobe light attached to his left arm and fired a brief burst in return.

A couple of minutes later Hanrahan materialized out of the darkness. "Are you okay?"

"I'm wet," McGarvey said. "How close are we to the rendezvous point?"

"Just about on top of it."

They donned their masks and mouthpieces, and on Hanrahan's lead they let the excess air out of their BC vests and started down at an angle toward the northeast. Almost immediately the massive hulk of the *Seawolf*'s sail appeared directly beneath them. The submarine had risen so that the top of her sail-mounted sensors were twenty feet beneath the surface.

McGarvey followed Hanrahan down the trailing edge of the sail to the submarine's deck, where the forward escape trunk hatch was open. The trunk was like a flooded coffin: the fleeting thought crossed McGarvey's mind as Hanrahan reached up and pulled the hatch closed. This was definitely not a job for someone with claustrophobia.

2015 Local
SSN 405 *Hekou*

Captain Heishui studied the chart, which showed the present positions of his submarine and the American boat, as well as the track of the *George Washington* and her battle group. He was trying to reconcile what he was seeing with his own two eyes and what his XO was telling him.

"She's on her way back down," Lagao said. "There's no doubt about it. It's my guess that she rendezvoused with the American carrier long enough to exchange messages, perhaps more."

Heishui looked up. "More?"

Lagao was a little uneasy, but he held it well. Heishui was an exacting captain. He did not suffer mistakes very well. "It's possible that the *Seawolf* took on supplies or passengers. He didn't surface, at least Zenzhong doesn't think so. But we may have picked up machinery noises. Possibly the pump for an escape trunk."

"All that information from beneath the thermocline?"

"There have been fluctuations in the temperature and salinity. But it's just a guess, Captain."

Heishui nodded. "I think that you may have something," he conceded. "Let's see what he does now."

"What if he tries to run?"

"Then we will follow in his baffles so that he will not detect us." Heishui studied the chart for a moment, trying to read something from it, some clue. "He can outrun us, of course, but not if he wants to remain stealthy." He looked up again. "That in itself would tell us something."

"We will have to keep a very close ear on him," Lagao warned.

"I want a slot buoy prepared. If he does head away we'll send up the buoy on a one-hour delay to inform Ningbo what we're attempting to do. The delay will give us plenty of time to get clear."

"I'll see to it now," Lagao said.

Heishui called sonar. "What is he doing?"

"Still on his way down, Captain."

"I think he means to get under way as soon as he reaches the thermocline. Keep a close watch."

"Yes, sir."

"Prepare to get under way," he told his Chief of Boat. "We're done waiting."

2020 Local
SSN 21 *Seawolf*

By the time McGarvey and Hanrahan changed clothes and were led down one deck and forward to the officers' wardroom directly beneath the attack center, the *Seawolf* had already started down. The XO, Lieutenant Commander Rod Paradise, who had been waiting for them when they emerged from the escape trunk, shook his head and grinned. "It's getting to be a habit, picking you up," he told McGarvey. "This is one time I think the captain is finally going to be surprised."

On a mission last year the *Seawolf* had rescued him from the Japanese Space Center on the island of Tanegashima. While aboard he'd gotten to know the captain and some of the crew. He had developed a great deal of respect for them. It was one of the reasons he wanted this sub for the mission. Harding was unflappable.

"I'd take five dollars of that," McGarvey said.

Paradise started to say something, but then shook his head. "I don't think I'd care to bet against you after all."

The angle on the bow was sharp. Harding was wasting no time getting back to the protection of the thermocline. But it made walking difficult, especially down ladders.

"Here we are," Paradise said, shoving back the curtain.

Harding was just pouring a cup of coffee. He turned around and smiled pleasantly. "Ah, McGarvey. It's nice to see you again." After the Tanegashima mission they had gotten together with their wives for drinks and dinner in Washington. The women had gotten along very well, and McGarvey and Harding had talked over dinner and then at the bar afterward until midnight. There didn't seem to be a subject that they disagreed on.

"Hello, Tom. Thanks for the lift."

"Getting off the *George* must have been interesting."

"Next time I'll leave it to the kids," McGarvey said. "This is Lieutenant Hank Hanrahan. He's along for the ride."

The captain noticed the SEAL insignia. "I suspect that you're going to have an interesting time of it."

"Yes, sir," Hanrahan agreed happily.

They sat down at the compact table, and Paradise poured them coffee. If anything, it was better than the coffee on the *George*, which was going some because the carrier was the flag vessel for both fleets during this operation.

"Okay, Mac, you're aboard safe and sound, and a lot of people went through a whole lot of trouble to get you here, so what's the program?" Harding asked. He was not a man to beat around the bush; not with his questions, nor with his orders. When you dealt with Harding you were dealing with a straight shooter. It was one of the qualities McGarvey liked about the man.

McGarvey handed him the carte blanche letter from the President. Harding quickly read it and handed it back. He was not overly impressed.

McGarvey handed him another envelope, this one sealed. "Once you've taken a look at that you're committed, Tom."

A flinty look came into the captain's eyes. "I wouldn't have picked you up if I wasn't already committed."

"No one outside of this room can know what the real mission is."

Harding considered it for a moment. He looked at Hanrahan. "Do you know what this contains, Lieutenant?"

"Yes, sir."

Harding opened the envelope, quickly scanned the three pages it contained, then read them again before handing them to his XO. This time he was impressed.

"You'll have to maintain radio silence," McGarvey said. "We're on our own now until we get back to Pearl, no matter what happens."

"All this because the old men in Beijing are frightened," Harding said, amazed. "But this isn't all of it. There's more."

"Frightened men are capable of just about anything."

"The question becomes how far are we willing to go to protect an ally," Harding mused. "We're talking about the potential for a nuclear exchange here. So I suppose just about anything should be considered. Even a stunt as harebrained as this one."

McGarvey didn't have a chance to answer before Harding cut him off.

"I think it's worth a try, Mac," he said. He glanced at Hanrahan. "When I said interesting, that was one hell of an understatement."

Paradise finished reading the mission statement, then reached behind him and took out a chart of northern Taiwan and the waters around it. They moved the coffee cups so that he could spread it out on the table.

"Keelung will be your best bet," Harding said. "It's a big enough city so you might not be noticed. And if we make our approach from the southeast, we'll have deep water to within just a few miles of the coast."

"That's what we thought," McGarvey agreed. "We can get transportation there, and Taipei is only fifteen miles away."

"We can supply you with an inflatable and a muffled outboard, but you'll have to find someplace secure to hide it. I expect that the Taiwanese are a little jumpy about now. They'll have plenty of shore patrols out and about."

"We're going in as just about who we really are," McGarvey explained. "We're American military advisors, so it'll be up to the Taiwanese to keep quiet about us. It's something they'll understand."

"Okay, so that gets you to Taipei, then what?" Paradise asked. "It's a big city, maybe two million people."

"That's why they pay me the big bucks, Rod, to figure out things like that," McGarvey said. There was no reason for him or Harding to know what that part of the plan was. In fact no one knew, not even Hanrahan. Nor would they ever.

"How about a time line, then?" Harding asked.

"If we're not back in twenty-four hours, get the hell out, someplace where you can phone home and let them know that we're overdue. The mission name is MAGIC LANTERN."

"What's the earliest we can expect you?"

"That depends on when you get us to Keelung."

"We could have them ashore by midnight," Paradise said, looking up from the chart. "Even if we take it slow and easy."

"In that case with any luck we'll be back before sunrise," McGarvey said. "But the bad news is you'll have to surface."

"We can mask just about any surface radar, but if a surveillance aircraft or fighter/interceptor gets close enough, the game will be up."

"We'll have to take the chance."

"You're bringing something or someone aboard?"

"Something like that."

Harding looked at the mission outline again. "We have one thing going for us. This side of the island is fairly secure. If the PRC makes a move, they'll come from the west. The bulk of Taiwan's ASW assets are directed that way." He looked up. "Getting in and out will be the least of our problems, I think. Your mission ashore will be the tough nut to crack."

"Like I said, Tom, that's why they pay me the big bucks," McGarvey replied.

2050 Local
SSN 405 *Hekou*

"Conn, sonar."

Heishui grabbed the phone. "This is the captain."

"Sir, Sierra Eighteen is on the move. She just turned southeast, relative bearing two-zero-eight, and she's making turns for ten knots."

Heishui turned to his Officer of the Deck. "Turn right to two-zero-eight, and make your speed ten knots."

"Aye, sir. Make my course two-zero-eight, my speed one-zero knots."

Heishui turned back to the phone. "If he starts to make a clearing turn, or you even *think* that he might be about to do it, let me know immediately."

"Yes, sir."

Heishui replaced the phone. "Prepare to commence all stop and emergency silent operations on my command," he told his COB.

"Yes, sir."

Heishui went to the chart table, where he laid out the American submarine's present position, course, and speed. Projecting her line of advance brought her to the north coast of Taiwan about midnight. *A mystery within a mystery*, he thought glumly.

United Nations Security Council

Chou en Ping, the Chinese ambassador to the United Nations, got slowly to his feet, an all-but-unreadable expression on his flattened oriental face. Until his appointment three years ago he had been head of the Mathematics Department at Beijing University. Very few people in the entire UN were smarter than he was. Sometimes talking to him seemed like an exercise in futility.

"We have come to an impasse," he said in English. He directed his remark to Margaret Woolsey, the U.S. ambassador. "I have been directed by my government to ask that the voice of reason prevail. We call on the provincial government of Taiwan to immediately hand over the criminal Shi Shizong. We are sending a military delegation to Taipei to arrest him within twelve hours."

Margaret Woolsey looked around the chamber at the others, trying to gauge their moods this morning. It was a few minutes after 8:00 A.M., and the session had been going with only a couple of short breaks since nine o'clock the previous evening. They were all tired, their thinking somewhat dulled. It was exactly what Ping wanted. She offered a faint smile. "There will forever be an impasse when it involves the issue of individual freedom," she said. It was the harshest condemnation of mainland China's current actions, and some of the other delegates looked up in interest.

"Do you wish to debate the human rights issue again, Madame Ambassador?" Ping asked, pleasantly. "Shall we begin with Harlem, Detroit, or Watts?"

"Let us start with political asylum."

"That would first presuppose the criminal seeking such protection were to seek it of a legitimate nation. Illinois can no more offer political asylum to a federal fugitive than can Taiwan from China."

Margaret Woolsey felt a cautious thrill of triumph. Ping was apparently as tired as the rest of them. "That's exactly what I'm talking about, Mr. Ambassador."

Ping seemed momentarily confused.

"The issue is Taiwan, not Peter Shizong." She held up a hand before Ping, realizing his stupid blunder, could interrupt. "But I agree that Mr. Shizong's case is a special one of great concern to your government, as well as to mine. It is an issue that should be considered by an impartial panel of judges. I propose that Mr. Shizong be handed over at once to the World Court in The Hague, where he should stand trial to show cause why he should not be returned to the People's Republic of China to face charges of treason."

Ping nodded. "Shall we prepare a list of U.S. criminals who should be handed over to the World Court for the same consideration?"

"If you wish, Mr. Ambassador," Margaret Woolsey said. "Though I would sincerely hope that a connection will be made between them and the current problem between Taiwan and China."

Ping was holding a fountain pen in his hand. He put it in his coat pocket. "Twelve hours, Madame Ambassador. And I do hope that reason will prevail when our delegation arrives in Taipei." His gaze swept around the chamber, then he turned and walked out.

0405 Local
SSN 21 *Seawolf*

McGarvey climbed up into the escape trunk. They were about three miles off Taiwan's coast, just west of Keelung. He was worried that they were running out of time. It would be light on the surface soon. Unless they got off shortly, they would have to withdraw and lie on the bottom until nightfall. As it was they were running way behind schedule. Every hour that the standoff between the PRC and Taiwan, with the U.S. in the middle, continued, the chances that shooting would begin and someone would get hurt increased exponentially.

The problem was the patrol boats. They were unexpectedly swarming all over the place topside. Along with the increased commercial traffic, this part of the ocean was practically as busy as New York's Times Square on New Year's Eve. No one had considered that since the entire west coast of Taiwan was all but cut off from outside traffic, the major ports on the island's east side, among them Keelung, would have to take up the slack. They had been waiting for an opening since before midnight.

The phone outside the trunk buzzed, and Paradise answered it. "This is the XO." He nodded, then looked up and gave them the thumbs-up sign. "I'll tell them." He hung up. "Okay, it's clear for now. The captain says that we'll wait on the bottom here until you get back. Sonar will pick up your outboard, and we'll surface if it looks okay."

There were Chinese spies everywhere. If the *Seawolf* was spotted on the surface, the game would be all but up. "If it's not clear, come to fifty feet and we'll get aboard the same way we did last night," McGarvey said. He did not want to get stuck in the middle of a war zone.

Hanarahan looked startled. "But we were told that he can't swim."

"He'll have to learn," McGarvey shot back.

Paradise picked up on the exchange, but he shook his head. "I don't even want to know what you guys are talking about. We'll be here, okay? Just watch your asses."

"If we're not back by midnight, pull the pin, Rod, and call home."

"I'll tell the captain," Paradise said. He swung the escape-trunk hatch shut. Hanrahan dogged it tight, then hit the flood button, and immediately the cold water began to rise.

"What do you figure our chances are, Mr. M?" Hanrahan asked.

"Name's Mac, and I'd guess about fifty-fifty."

Hanrahan grinned from ear to ear. "Good deal. When we started they were only a hundred to one."

0410 Local
SSN 405 *Hekou*

"Sir, that is definitely their escape trunk," Zenzhong reported excitedly. "The hatch is opening now." The chief sonarman pressed his earphones tighter. "Wait."

"Stand by," Lagao told the captain waiting on the phone.

"They've released something into the water."

"A life raft?" Lagao suggested.

Zenzhong looked up and nodded. "Yes, sir. I can hear the inflation noises now."

"Any idea how many people are leaving the submarine?"

"No, sir. But the hatch remains open, so no one else is leaving the boat."

"Keep a close ear, Ensign," Lagao said. He hung up the phone and walked back to the control room, where he and the captain hunched over the chart table.

The *Hekou* was like a puppy dog lying behind its mother. The *Seawolf* had cleared her baffles three times on the way in, but each time Heishui was just a little faster shutting down because he anticipated the maneuver, whereas the American captain had no reason to believe that his boat was being followed.

"They put someone on the surface with an inflatable, but they left the door open, so it means they're coming back," Lagao said. He had a wild idea what the Americans might be up to, but he didn't dare voice his opinion to the captain. Not yet. It was just too crazy.

Heishui studied the chart. "They went through a great deal of trouble to rendezvous in secret with their carrier and then take someone aboard. That was a very risky maneuver. And now, presumably whoever transferred from the *George Washington* is going ashore. Interesting."

"Yes, sir."

"Navy SEALs?"

"They're trained for such maneuvers," Lagao said. The PRC Navy didn't have a unit quite like the American SEALs. To the average Chinese sailor an American SEAL was ten feet tall, could run the hundred-yard dash in four seconds, and ate raw concrete for breakfast.

"But why go ashore in secret?" Heishui asked. "The U.S. and the criminal government of Taiwan are allies. Why didn't they simply fly in? Unless they didn't want us to know about it."

"That's a reasonable assumption, Captain."

Heishui looked up at his executive officer. "What is it? What are you thinking?"

Lagao was uncomfortable. He had served with many officers in his career but never with one who so hated speculation as Heishui. Yet his captain had asked him a direct question, and one of the primary functions of an executive officer was to make suggestions.

"I was thinking that the reason we're here is to resolve the issue of Shi Shizong. Taipei has gone too far this time. They need to come home."

Heishui looked at his XO thoughtfully. "Go on."

"If Shizong were suddenly to disappear from Taiwan, and show up someplace else, our position would not be quite as tenable." Lagao chose his words with extreme care. He was walking a fine line between reason and treason.

"We have spies at every international airport on the island: He would be spotted if he tried to fly out," Heishui said. "And there are probably others who are very close to him, watching his every move. How else would we know as much about him as we do?" Heishui dismissed the suggestion. "The Taiwanese are not interested in giving him up in any event. They want him as badly as we want him." He shook his head. "And you're forgetting the *Nanchong*."

"What if the Americans mean to kidnap him?" Lagao pressed.

A startled expression crossed Heishui's face. "Take him away aboard the American submarine?"

"However improbable, Captain, it is a possibility that we should consider."

"What would they do with him?"

"It doesn't matter," Lagao said. "The point is he would no longer be on the island. Other than the *Nanchong*, there'd no longer be any current reason for us to be here."

"Unless we could prove that he was aboard the *Seawolf*, and report it to Ningbo," Heishui answered. He picked up the growler phone. "Sonar, this is the captain."

"Sonar, aye."

"What's Sierra Eighteen doing now?"

"He's heading to the bottom, sir."

"What about the inflatable they sent up?"

"It's heading ashore, sir."

"How do you know that?"

"I can hear the small outboard motor."

That's exactly what Heishui thought. "The moment it returns I want to know. It may be hours, even days, but I want to know."

"Yes, sir."

Heishui hung up. "When they come back the *Seawolf* will lift off the bottom. They'll make noise. In the confusion we'll send a man up with night-vision glasses to see with his own eyes who is aboard the inflatable."

0445 Local
Taiwan

"Cut the motor," McGarvey ordered urgently. Hanrahan complied instantly. They were about fifty yards off a commercial wharf. There were no boats tied up, nor were there any lights except for one pinprick of a yellow beam. Hanrahan spotted it.

"A patrol?"

"Looks like it." The flashlight moved slowly to the left, stopping every few feet. At one point the narrow beam of light flashed across the water. It was far too weak to reach out to them, but they ducked nevertheless.

On their chart the dock belonged to a fisheries company. Either the fleet was out tending nets, which McGarvey found hard to believe in the middle of a war situation, or all fishing had been suspended and the boats had been commandeered for patrols. They had expected to find minimal activity there tonight, but this was even better than they'd hoped for.

The city of Keelung, just a few kilometers to the southeast, was mostly in darkness, blacked out because of the threat of invasion. But behind them, for as far as they could see in every direction were the dim red-and-green lights of the commercial fleet and the numerous military patrol boats the *Seawolf*'s sonar had picked out. Coming in had been like playing dodgeball.

After ten minutes the point of light disappeared around the corner of the warehouse and processing center. They waited another full five minutes to make sure that the guard wasn't coming back, then paddled the rest of the way in.

The old wooden docks were up on pilings. They worked their way beneath them, the water black, oily, and fetid with rotting fish and other garbage, then pulled themselves back to the seawall and to the west side, where they found a ladder. The only way anyone would spot the inflatable in what amounted to an open sewer would be to get into the water to make a specific search for it.

They had changed into civilian clothes on the way in: light sweaters, khaki trousers, soft boots, and jackets. After they secured the boat they scrambled up the ladder and stepped ashore with the credentials of U.S. Navy advisors to the Republic of China's Maritime Self-Defense Force.

"Welcome to Taiwan, Lieutenant," McGarvey said, and keeping low they headed across the net yard in the dank humidity of the nearly silent early morning.

0520 Local
SSN 21 *Seawolf*

Harding hadn't slept in more than thirty-six hours. Once they were settled on the bottom, and he had made sure that his boat was secure, he drifted back to his cabin, where he kicked off his shoes and lay down on his bunk. McGarvey was one tough character, and Harding held a grudging admiration for the man that was beginning to grow into a friendship. But in Harding's estimation McGarvey was also one lucky son of a bitch. By all laws of reason he and Hanrahan should have been spotted on their way ashore. Four different patrol boats had come to within spitting distance of their inflatable and yet had passed right by. And they were still going to have to get back tonight after dark if they were successful ashore. There was another worry, too. Paradise had reported the conversation between McGarvey and Hanrahan in the escape trunk. They were apparently bringing someone back with them, and there was only one person on all of Taiwan he could think of who'd be worth the risks they were taking.

The phone over his bunk buzzed. He switched on the light and answered it. "This is the captain."

"Hate to bother you, skipper, but we've got company," Paradise said.

Harding sat up. "What are you talking about?"

"Sonar's picked up some stationary noises. Maybe pumps, nuclear-plant noises. It looks as if we've got a PRC Han-class submarine parked on our back porch."

"I'm on my way."

Taiwan in Country

Hanrahan was in the front seat of the ancient cloth-goods delivery truck speaking Mandarin with the driver. They'd hitched a ride on the main highway into Keelung just as the rain began in earnest. The drab old city was known unofficially as the rainiest seaport in the world, and although it was dawn by the time they reached the train station, visibility was limited to less than one hundred feet in the heavy traffic.

"Syeh syeh ni," Hanrahan told the old man.

"Boo syeh," you're welcome, the driver said, an odd expression on his wizened old face.

Everything that came to Keelung by sea had to leave either by rail or by highway, so the train station was busy twenty-four hours per day. Passengers and small parcels were loaded from the street side through the terminal, while trucks and a special spur line running up from the docks used a commercial loading yard across the tracks.

"Your Mandarin sounded pretty good," McGarvey said as they hurried across the street.

"Thanks, but I only had two years of it at Fort Benning."

"It's gotten us this far."

"Yeah, but I think the old man'll probably never trust an American again. I think I might have told him that I'd love to screw his mother, his sister, and his goat."

McGarvey had to laugh. "Would you?"

Hanrahan shrugged. "Well, maybe not his mother."

The train station was a madhouse, filled mostly with merchants and tradespeople bringing goods and services from Keelung to the rest of the country. Taiwan had only one rail line, which circled almost the entire island along the coast, with only a couple of branch lines. The trains were always overcrowded with people and animals, and loaded beyond belief with everything from candle wax and strawberries to cod-liver oil and machine screws.

Hanrahan headed for the lines at the ticket windows, but McGarvey steered him directly down to trackside, where he produced a pair of first-class tickets to Taipei. The police guards demanded to see their passports before they were allowed to board the train. When they were settled near the rear of the car Hanrahan leaned nearer.

"Good thinking about the tickets, but we're not going to be able to get back this way, not with . . . him."

McGarvey watched the policeman at the gate. He'd not made a move to use the telephone beside him. A couple of Americans boarding a train in Keelung were evidently not unusual enough for him to report to his superior. It was another break for them. But he didn't think that their luck would last forever. It never did.

He turned back to Hanrahan. "We're coming back by car, so keep your eyes peeled on the highway for roadblocks or military patrols. We might have to make a detour."

Hanrahan nodded. "Now that we're here, are you going to let me in on the rest of it, or am I going to have to guess?" He looked out the window at the police. "These people have their backs to the wall. If something starts to go down that they don't understand, they're likely to start shooting first and ask questions later."

"I brought you along to get us on and off the sub, and because you speak Chinese. The rest of it you're going to have to leave up to me."

Hanrahan started to object, but McGarvey held him off.

"We're probably going to run into some major shit in Taipei. And if it does hit the fan, if it looks like some of the good guys might get hurt, you're going to turn around and walk away from it. And that's an order, Lieutenant. At that point it becomes strictly a Company operation, and you're not going to be the one holding the dirty laundry."

The train was completely full now. The conductor came in, shouted something over the din, and moments later they lurched out of the station for the fifteen miles to the capital city.

Hanrahan's jaw tightened. It was clear that he was anything but happy. "Just one thing, Mr. M," he said, his voice low but with a hard edge to it. "I know how to follow orders—"

"Nobody is questioning you. But if something goes down, no matter whose fault it is, who do you suppose they're going to blame? It won't be me. It'll be a grunt lieutenant."

"The SEALs have never left one of their own behind, never," Hanrahan said. "I don't give a shit what's going down, 'cause that's a fact."

East Fleet Headquarters
Ningbo

"Captain Heishui is a reliable officer," Sun Kung Kee, the fleet's political commissar, told the CINC, Vice Admiral Pei. "I know his father. He will do as he is ordered."

"I expect nothing less from all of my officers." Admiral Pei reread the slot buoy message that had been sent last night from the *Hekou.*

"Presumably he followed the American submarine to the coast near Keelung. If he is right, the Americans meant to put someone ashore in secret. Since there have been no incidents reported, we must assume that Captain Heishui is still there and has not been detected."

"Nothing from our satellites?" the admiral asked.

"The weather is too bad for visual images, and nothing has shown up on infrared, Admiral," Commander Sze Lau, his Operations Officer replied.

"What about our spies on the ground in Keelung and Taipei, if that's where the Americans are heading? Have there been any reports?"

"Nothing yet," Commissar Kee told him. "But we must ask ourselves why the Americans chose to put somebody ashore in such a secret manner. The operation was not without its very considerable risks, which means that the Americans must be expecting a very considerable reward."

Admiral Pei put the slot buoy message down and sat back. "Yes?"

"Shi Shizong," the political commissar said, and both officers were startled though it was immediately clear that they understood the logic. "I think they mean to kidnap him."

"Do we know where he is being held?" Commander Lau asked. "We could intercept the Americans and take Shizong ourselves."

"His location is a secret. Apparently they move him every few days. Beijing, however, thinks that the Americans will almost certainly make contact with someone from their illegal consulate, who might know where the criminal is being hidden. If we were to wait there, our agents might be able to follow them to the traitor."

"Beijing was consulted?" Admiral Pei asked, his voice as soft as a summer's breeze but as bitter as a Tibetan winter's gale.

"Naturally I wanted to provide you with all the support you might need without the necessity of asking for it if and when the need should arise," Commissar Kee answered smoothly.

"Go on."

"If Shizong cannot be returned home to stand trial, he must never be allowed to leave Taiwan alive."

"That is a job for your agents on the ground," the admiral said.

"But if they fail, it will be up to Captain Heishui and his submarine."

"It would be a suicide mission."

"An acceptable loss providing Shizong does not escape," Commissar Kee pressed. "Word must somehow be gotten to him."

"It will be difficult without revealing his position, if indeed he is hiding just off the coast from Keelung, but not impossible," Commander Lau said, and Admiral Pei nodded his approval for the mission. The nation was willing to go to war over this issue; what was the possible loss of one submarine and crew by comparison?

Taipei

McGarvey watched from the train window as they entered Taiepi from the northeast. The capital was a city ready for invasion. The government was taking the Chinese threat seriously. Street corner antiaircraft batteries were protected behind sandbag barriers. Rooftops bristled with machine-gun emplacements. He counted six Patriot missile launchers set up in parking lots and empty fields, something the PRC had to be really unhappy about.

"This is going to be on my lead," he told Hanrahan. "You don't do a thing unless I tell you to do it."

"This place is crawling with PRC spies."

"That's right," McGarvey said. "The problem is that you can't tell them from the good guys. And if they get wind that we're here on a mission we're screwed. *Capisce?*"

Hanrahan nodded. Jumping off aircraft carriers, diving down to submarines, and even storming ashore prepared to fight an army of trained commandos was one thing. In-your-face daylight covert operations where you were outnumbered a few billion to one was another ball game.

The press of people on the train platform all the way up to the street-level terminal was constant. They had to bull their way forward in order to get outside to the cab rank, and practically had to knock over three businessmen to get a cab. McGarvey gave Hanrahan an address on Hoping Road a few blocks from the university to give to the cabbie, and they headed away.

The streets were as crazy as the train station. Traffic was all but stalled at many intersections, and their driver had to backtrack and make several detours around the downtown area. Especially around the government buildings. The military presence was everywhere, yet there seemed to be a look of inevitability, of resigned indifference, on the faces of the people here and aboard the train. War was coming, and there wasn't much that anyone could do about it.

"How the hell do they expect to get anything done like this?" Hanrahan asked, watching out the windows. The cab was not air-conditioned, and already the heat and humidity had plastered their clothes to their bodies.

"You oughta see New Delhi at rush hour in midsummer," McGarvey said absently, watching for any signs that an organized resistance movement had been formed.

The Taiwanese were great soapbox orators. They took their politics more seriously than just about any other country on earth. Their representatives regularly got into fistfights on the floor of the legislature. And just like the South Koreans, who were also faced with a constant threat of annihilation, there were staunch Taiwanese supporters for every side of just about every issue that was raised. There was a sizable minority of Taiwanese who wanted a return to the mainland. If they wanted to start something, now would be a perfect time for it. If Taiwan were suddenly to find itself in the middle of a bloody civil war, it would give the PRC one more reason to come in and take over by force: to save human lives.

Taiwan was like a powder keg with a short fuse in the middle of an armory packed with dynamite. Lit matches were being held out from every direction. It was only a matter of time before one of them caught.

The driver left them off in front of the Bank of South Africa building, in an area of offices and apartment high-rises. They had just passed the sandbagged entrance to Taiwan University, where a mob of a thousand or more students wearing headbands and carrying banners was parading up and down in front of a Patriot missile emplacement on the grass. Soldiers had cordoned off the area, keeping the students from spilling out onto the busy street and further disrupting traffic. It was the only evidence of any sort of dissension that McGarvey had seen so far.

The Parisian Lights was a sidewalk café set under a red-and-white-striped awning across Hoping Road from the university demonstration. The place was crowded, but they got a table in the corner. Their waiter spoke French with a Chinese accent. McGarvey ordered coffee and beignets, and when the waiter was gone he used his cell phone to call the American Institute three blocks away on Hsinyi Street.

"Peyton Graves," he told the operator.

"He's not in," she answered.

"Yes, he is," McGarvey insisted. "I'll hold." Graves was the CIA's Chief of Taiwan Station and a very capable old China hand. He was in the hot seat right now, so he wasn't going to be in to most people. It was SOP. McGarvey had met the man only once, and although Graves had struck him as a bit officious and bureaucratic, he was doing a good job for them out here.

"This is Peyton Graves, what can I do for you?"

"Is this a secure line?" McGarvey asked.

"Jesus," Graves said softly. He'd recognized McGarvey's voice. "It can be."

"Switching now," McGarvey said. He pressed star-four-one-one, and his cell phone's encryption circuits kicked in. "How's this?"

"Clear," Graves said. "You're in-country, but nobody said anything to me, Mr. McGarvey."

"I want to keep it that way, Peyton, you probably have a PRC leak in the embassy."

"This place is like a sieve. Where are you?"

McGarvey told him. "We're going to need a windowless van and a driver who knows the city, and someplace to lie low just until tonight."

"I'll have somebody pick you up within ten minutes. It'll be a gray Chevy delivery van, Han Chi Bakeries, Ltd. on the side. Driver's name is Tom Preston. Tall, dark hair, mustache."

"Good enough. No one else is to know that we're here, and I mean no one, not even the ambassador."

"I understand," Graves said. "I'm not even going to ask how you got here without flags going up. The city is crawling with PRC supporters. But if you've come here to do what I think you came here to do, tonight will be cutting it a tad close."

"What are you talking about?"

"Apparently you haven't heard. The PRC are sending a military delegation of some sort over here early this evening to arrest Shizong. Nobody knows how it's going to play, but the word is out that the delegation will at least be allowed to land. From that point it's anybody's guess."

"Does the PRC know where Shizong is being kept?"

"It's possible, but I don't think so. The Taiwanese CIA have been handling it, and they've done a good job so far. But the politicians might take it out of their hands. Taiwan wants to keep him here, but they're afraid that if the PRC pushes it, we'll just sit on our hands and watch."

"They're right," McGarvey said. "Do you know where he's being kept?"

"They switch him around every few days. But for now he's up on Grass Mountain at Joseph Lee's old place." Lee was a Taiwanese multibillionaire whom McGarvey had run up against a couple of years ago in a Japanese operation to put nuclear weapons in low-earth orbit. Lee was dead and the Taiwanese government had confiscated most of his properties, including the Grass Mountain house.

"Who'll be with him tonight?"

"I don't know for sure, but considering what might be going down I'd guess the same team that snatched him from Xiamen."

"I know them. They're all good men."

"Tough bastards," Graves said. "They're not going to take kindly to anyone barging in up there, friend or foe. Especially friend. If the PRC is allowed to arrest him and take him back to the mainland, Taipei will be able to make a very large international stink over it. They'll win *beaucoup* points in the UN. But if you mean to grab him and bury him someplace deep and out of sight, nobody will win. They're not going to want that."

"You're wrong about one thing, Peyton. If we do pull this off, *everybody* will end up on top in the long run."

"Do you want some help then?"

"Just Tom Preston, the van, and someplace to crash until tonight," McGarvey said.

"If anything breaks this afternoon, I'll get it to you," Graves said.

"Thanks. But then forget that we were ever here."

"You'd better take Tom with you. After tonight he'll be useless here."

"Will do," McGarvey said, and he broke the connection.

YAK 38 Forger A
Tail Number 13/13

Captain Xia Langshan was flying right wing escort for the Boeing 727 bringing the arresting officers to Taipei. Lieutenant Qaixo was flying left wing. Their transponders were all squawking 11313, which was the code for a peaceful-mission incursion into Taiwanese airspace. The same code was used when Taiwanese weather-spotting airplanes flew into PRC airspace. They just cleared the beach on their long approach.

"Green One, this is Eagle thirteen/thirteen, feet dry," Langshan radioed his AWACS controller circling at thirty-five thousand feet, thirty klicks to the west.

"Thirteen/thirteen, this is Green One. You are clear to proceed, out."

Langshan switched to the civilian frequency in time to hear the Boeing whose ID was Justice Wind Four receiving its landing instructions from Chiang Kai-shek International Airport at Taoyuan. He could hear the tension in the controller's voice.

"PRC Flight Four, your escort aircraft will not be allowed to land. Acknowledge."

"Taoyuan Airport tower, this is Justice Wind Four on final to one-seven with delta. We acknowledge your last transmission."

"We want your escorts to leave our airspace the moment you land."

"Negative, tower. They have been ordered to remain on station until their fuel has been exhausted, at which time they will be relieved."

"Permission is denied, PRC Flight Four."

"We didn't ask for permission, Taoyuan tower," the pilot, Colonel Hezheng, replied in polite but measured tones. "We will view any hostile response as an act of war, acknowledge."

The radio was silent for several long seconds, and Langshan could almost imagine the scene in the tower as the controllers talked to their superiors by telephone.

"Acknowledge," Colonel Hezheng repeated calmly.

The airport was visible now about twenty kilometers to the west. Langshan's threat-assessment radar was clear, although he was being painted by at least a half-dozen ground-radar sets. None of them, however, were missile-facility radars. Those signatures were different. The Taiwanese military well understood that if they illuminated a target it was tantamount to aiming a loaded gun. It was universally recognized as an act of aggression. In that case Langhsan had permission to shoot, though it was not his primary mission.

"We acknowledge your last transmission," the tower finally responded. "Your escorts will maintain flight level one-zero and remain within ten kilometers of the airport."

"My escorts have been ordered to establish and maintain twenty-five-kilometer patrol zones centered on Taipei."

"Negative, negative, negative!" the tower controller practically screamed.

Colonel Hezheng overrode the transmission, his voice still maddeningly calm. "The provincial government of Taiwan has not adequately informed the people about the real issue of the criminal Shi Shizong. We will drop leaflets guaranteeing the truth of our peaceful mission, and let the people decide for themselves who are the warmongers."

Langshan grinned behind his face mask.

"PRC Four, we will shoot your escort aircraft out of the sky if they stray outside of the airport containment zone."

The 727 was losing altitude for its final approach to landing. Langshan looked over at Qaixo and rocked his wings left-right-left. Qaixo responded.

"If our aircraft are fired upon, they will shoot back, tower. And we will request immediate backup. In force."

The radio was silent again. Civilian traffic to Taiwan had been sharply curtailed since the troubles had escalated in the past ten days. And all traffic for the duration of this mission had been diverted to the airport at Kaoshiung in the far south.

Qaixo peeled off to the north to start the outer leg of his patrol zone. When he got over the city of Taoyuan itself he would begin to drop his leaflets.

Langshan watched for a few moments as the 727 continued gracefully down for landing, then hauled his throttles back and shot northeast directly for the heart of Taipei, maintaining an altitude of ten thousand feet while his mach indicator climbed past .7, the hard bucket seat pressing into his back.

In less than two minutes he was directly over the city, Grass Mountain rising off to his north, Green Lake spread out to his south, and the city of Keelung on the coast lost under a thick blanket of low-lying clouds directly ahead.

His threat-radar screen remained blank, and the moment he crossed the Tamsui River he released the first of his canisters programmed to fall like a bomb to one thousand feet before opening and spreading the leaflets on the wind. At the very least, he thought, the bastards would have a big cleanup job tomorrow. In his underwing pods he carried one million messages on long, thin strips of rice paper, like giant fortune cookie fortunes.

He dropped a second canister near the stadium and a third on the densely populated shantytown in the western suburbs before he continued to Keelung and the coast twenty-five kilometers to the west-northwest. Within a half minute he was enveloped in a dense cloud, rain smashing into the canopy like machine-gun bullets. His forward-looking radar was clear of any air traffic, and his look-down-shoot-down radar showed him exactly what was happening on the ground.

In two minutes he was over the city of Keelung, where he dropped two more of his canisters and then made a long, sweeping turn out over the harbor.

At the last minute, about three miles off the coast, Langshan dialed up a special canister on his port wing rack, checked his position, hit the release button, and then headed back for his second run over Taipei.

1920 Local
SSN 21 *Seawolf*

"Conn, sonar."

"This is the captain speaking. What do you have, Fisher?"

"Skipper, something just hit the water eighteen hundred yards out, bearing one-eight-seven. It's not very big, but from the angle it made I'd say that it was dropped from something moving real fast. Maybe a jet, but definitely not a boat."

"Any idea what it is?"

"I think it's a comms buoy, sir . . . stand by."

Paradise came in from the officer's wardroom with a couple of cups of coffee. He handed one to Harding. It had been a very long day since McGarvey and Hanrahan had locked to the surface. They'd all existed on coffee.

"Okay, skipper, that's definitely a comms buoy. She's started to transmit acoustically."

"Good work," Harding said. He switched to the radio room. "Comms, this is the captain. Somebody just dropped an acoustical communications buoy to our south and it's starting to transmit. It's probably in Chinese and in code, but see what you can do with it."

"Aye, aye, skipper," the radio officer said with even less enthusiasm, for a job he was not equipped to handle, than he felt.

"A message from home for our friend?" Paradise asked.

"So it would seem. Question is, what kind of a message is it?"

"It could be about us," Paradise said. "But you have to wonder what makes them think that they haven't told the entire world where their boat is hiding."

1945 Local
SSN 405 *Hekou*

Z112530ZJUL
TOP SECRET
FR: CINCEASTSEAFLEET
TO: 405 HEKOU
A. ACKNOWLEDGE UR Z145229ZJUL
1. DETERMINE AT ALL COSTS IF SHI SHIZONG IS TRANSPORTED TO SEAWOLF UR REPORT.
2. THIS IS A MOST URGENT OPERATIONS FLASH MESSAGE. COMPLIANCE IS MANDATORY.
3. SHIZONG MUST NOT BE ALLOWED TO LEAVE TAI-

WAN. ALL OTHER CONSIDERATIONS ARE SECONDARY. GOOD LUCK SZE LAU SENDS BT BT BT

Captain Heishui handed the decoded message across the table to Lagao. They were alone in the officers' wardroom. His XO read the message, then read it again before he looked up, a grave expression on his face.

"If they manage to get him aboard the American boat, we will be obligated to attack," he said.

Heishui nodded. "But we would have two advantages," he said. "In the first place, they don't know that we're back here. But even if they do find out, they'll never believe that we would open fire. You have to shoot at an American six times before he will start to respond."

"Yes, Captain. But when he does it's usually fatal."

Chiang Kai-Shek International Airport

Peyton Graves powered down his window and pointed a tiny parabolic receiver at the PRC Air Force 727 as the boarding stairs were brought up and the forward hatch swung open.

A lot of cars and military vehicles surrounded the jet, which was parked in front of the old Pan Am hangar. Everyone seemed restrained. No one wanted this situation to accelerate out of control. There were no media.

Lieutenant Colonel Thomas Daping, chief of the Counterespionage Division for the Taiwan Police, went up the stairs, followed by a lieutenant in uniform whom Graves did not recognize.

They stood at the head of the stairs for a few moments until a full bird colonel in the uniform of a civilian police officer, blue tabs on his shoulder boards, appeared in the doorway. A much taller man in a captain's uniform showed up right behind him.

"Good evening, I am Colonel Lian Shiquan, Beijing Police. I am here with a warrant for the arrest of the criminal Shi Shizong."

Graves turned up the gain on his receiver. Even so it was hard to pick up the Taiwanese officer's reply because his back was turned to the receiver. When it came, however, it was a complete surprise to Graves. The government had caved in even faster and more completely than he thought it would.

"Yes, sir," Colonel Daping replied. "He is being held not too far from here, at a home on Grass Mountain. We have transportation standing by to take you there immediately."

It was too far for Graves to see the expression on the Chinese colonel's face, but he heard the surprise and the smug satisfaction in his voice. "I should think so. There are eight of us, plus myself and my adjutant, Captain Qying. Let's proceed."

Graves tossed the receiver on the passenger seat and headed past the hangars toward the back gate. He used his cell phone to call the safe house where McGarvey was staying.

"Switch," he said as soon as McGarvey answered.

"Right."

Graves hit star-four-one-one. "You've run out of time. I'm just leaving the airport. The Taiwanese are handing him over without an argument. They're taking the PRC delegation up to Grass Mountain right now, so you're going to have to hustle."

"How many of them?"

"Ten PRC and I don't know how many Taiwanese cops. But if you get caught in the middle of them, you'll get yourself shot."

"Thanks for your help, Peyton. We'll take it from here," McGarvey said. "Get back to the embassy and keep your head down, there's no telling what might happen in the next twenty-four hours."

"Good luck."

Taipei

It was after 8:00 P.M., but still light by the time they cleared the city and headed east on the Keelung Highway. Grass Mountain, off to their left, was tinged in brilliant pinks and salmons at the higher levels, but the sky toward the coast was dark and threatening. The highway was choked with traffic of all descriptions, from eighteen-wheelers to hand-drawn carts. There seemed to be tiny scraps of paper blowing everywhere.

"I think we've got a tail," Tom Preston said from the front.

McGarvey crawled forward to the passenger seat, opened the window, and adjusted the door mirror. Preston switched lanes to get around an old canvas-covered flatbed, and a yellow Fiat followed.

"It was outside the apartment this afternoon," McGarvey said. In the middle of an operation he had a photographic memory for people and things. Patterns and anomalies. The ability had saved his life on more than one occasion.

"Sorry, I missed it." Preston had struck McGarvey as easygoing but very capable. He and Hanrahan, who were football fans, had argued heatedly, but good-naturedly, about the Pack versus the Vikes all afternoon. But he was apologetic now.

"I only saw him the one time," McGarvey said, studying the image in the mirror. "Same driver, but he's picked up a passenger." He missed the look Preston gave him.

"They're not our people," Preston said. "I'm sure of at least that much."

"Taiwanese police?"

"No. I know all of their tag series. That's not one of them. Civilians. PRC supporters. Maybe spies. Either they knew about the safe house and were watching it, or someone from inside the consulate tipped them off. Whatever it is, we're going to have to deal with it pretty soon because our turnoff is coming up."

"What do you want to do, Mac?" Hanrahan asked from the back. "We've got the PRC delegation from the airport breathing down our necks, so we don't have a hell of a lot of time."

McGarvey took out his Walther PPK and checked the load. "No matter what happens, we're not going to hurt any Taiwan national if we can help it. That means cops and soldiers as well as civilians." He checked the mirror. The yellow Fiat was still behind them. He holstered his pistol and checked the two spare magazines.

"Here's the turn," Preston said.

"Head up toward the house: I'll tell you where to pull over," McGarvey said. It was an early evening like this when he'd come up here nine months ago. Visiting the spoils of war, he'd told his chief of staff in Washington. In reality he was picking up the pieces of a mission that had nearly cost him his life. After all was said and done he wanted to see the house where Lee had lived in order to get some measure of the man who'd almost brought the world to a nuclear showdown. Not terribly unlike the situation they were in again.

Lee's eighteen-room house was perched on the side of the mountain a couple of hundred feet above its nearest neighbor. A maze of narrow roads led in all directions into narrow valleys and defiles, in which other mansions were built. But Lee's compound was at the head of a very steep switchback that had been cut through the living rock. Except for the helicopter pad, there was only one way in or out. Had the Taiwanese police decided to bring the PRC delegation up by chopper, the mission would have been over before it had begun.

Within a few blocks of the highway the Grass Mountain road rose up sharply from the floor of the valley. The traffic, except for an occasional Mercedes or Jaguar, ended, and a thin fog began to envelop the twisting side streets and houses set back in the trees in an air of gloom and mystery. This was the Orient, and yet a lot of people with money built Western-style homes up here. It was a curious mixture, just like Taipei itself.

"Okay, Lee's driveway is coming up around the next curve," Preston said.

McGarvey had spent only a half hour up there, looking around the house and down across the valley toward the city from the balconies. The view had been nothing short of spectacular. But he tried to recall how steep the slope was just below the house on the side of the compound away from the road. Maybe negotiable, but he wasn't sure. He'd not been on a life-or-death mission that time.

"As soon as we're around the curve and out of sight of the Fiat, you're going to slow down and let me off," McGarvey said. "Then drive past Lee's road, pull into the next driveway, turn around, and wait there."

"What about the guys in the Fiat?" Preston asked.

"I'm going to try an end run. If they miss me, they'll come past you, probably turn around, and wait to see what you're going to do next." McGarvey screwed the silencer on the end of the Walther's barrel.

"You'll need some help. I'm coming with you," Hanrahan said, taking out his Beretta.

"I know one of the guys up at the house. If I show up alone, they might listen before they start shooting."

"Goddammit, Mac, that's not why I signed on—."

"You signed on to take orders, Lieutenant," McGarvey said harshly. "If I can grab Shizong and get him out of there, I'll be moving fast. I'll need someone to watch the back door. I don't want to get caught between the PRC delegation coming up from the airport and the goons in the car behind us. Do you understand?"

Hanrahan wanted to argue, but he held himself in check. "Yes, sir."

McGarvey softened. "If we do this right, nobody will get hurt."

"Here we go, guys," Preston said. They came around the sharp curve, passed Lee's driveway, and Preston jammed on the brakes.

"If the group from the airport makes it up here, give me ten minutes and then get the hell out," McGarvey said. He popped open the door, jumped out on the run, then ducked into the trees and brush beside the road as the van disappeared and the Fiat came charging around the curve.

He got the impression of two men, both of them intent on catching up with the van. He was sure that they had not seen him.

As soon as they were gone he jumped up, hurried across the road, and raced up the driveway, conscious that the mission clock was counting down in earnest now.

The road was steep and switched back several times. In a couple of minutes he reached the top, the road splitting left and right around a fountain in front of the low, rambling, steel-and-glass house. The fountain was operating, and there were lights on inside the house. Anyone watching from the outside would have to assume that nothing suspicious was going on up here. No one was trying to hide anything. Life as normal.

Holding his hands in plain sight out away from his sides, McGarvey headed to the right around the fountain. The hairs at the nape of his neck prickled. He couldn't see anyone at the windows, but he got the distinct impression that he was being watched, and that guns were pointed at him.

A wooden footbridge arched gracefully over a winding pond that contained large golden carp. When McGarvey got to the other side the front door opened and Joseph Jiying stepped out. He wore jeans and an open-collar shirt. He was unarmed.

"Good evening, Mr. McGarvey. I've gotta say that you being up here is one big surprise." Jiying had spent eight months working in Langley on an exchange program. McGarvey had gotten to know him and some of the others; all of them dedicated, and most of them pretty good intelligence officers.

"I've come for Peter Shizong."

Jiying looked beyond McGarvey toward the empty driveway. "Did you come alone, on foot?"

"I have a van waiting on the road below. But we don't have much time. There's a PRC delegation along with a Taiwanese police escort on its way up here from the airport to arrest him."

Jiying's expression didn't change except that his eyes narrowed slightly. "That's news to me."

"They didn't want you to do something stupid, like try to take off or barricade yourselves up here."

"My people would have warned me by now."

"Maybe not if they were ordered by someone high enough to stay out of it." McGarvey could see that Jiying didn't want to believe what he was being told, and yet he could see the truth to it. "If I can get him out of here in time, the PRC won't be able to take him."

"They'd turn Taiwan upside down."

"They probably would. And if you knew where he was, you'd be made to tell them. You know that."

Jiying shook his head, more in anger and frustration than in denial. "There's too much at stake, dammit. We're winning. We're finally starting to make points. We're the good guys here—"

One of his men appeared at his elbow, looked pointedly at McGarvey, then told something to his boss. McGarvey did not understand the Chinese, but he caught the urgency. The expression on Jiying's face changed to one of anger and resignation.

"There was no reason for you to come all this way in secret to lie to me, was there," he said. "There are seven Taipei Special Services Police Humvees on the Keelung Highway." He said something to his man that clearly upset him. He tried to argue, but Jiying barked a command at him, and he left.

"How close?"

"They just turned onto Grass Mountain Road. I hope the van is well hidden."

"It's just past the driveway. Is there another way down from here for me?"

"There's a path on the other side of the house. It's steep, but you should be able to make it."

"There's room in the van for all of us."

Jiying shook his head again. "You'll need time to make it down the hill and then get the hell out. We can delay the bastards all night if need be."

McGarvey understood that it was the only way. "All we need is a couple of hours, Captain. After that give it up. Don't get yourselves killed."

A faint smile curled his lips. "Believe me I'll do my best to make sure I die an old man in my own bed."

The commando returned with a bemused Peter Shizong. Jiying said something to him in rapid-fire Mandarin. Shizong looked at McGarvey, asked Jiying a question, and when he was given the answer he nodded.

"It seems as if I am to go with you, sir," he said.

"I have a warrant for your arrest on a charge of spying on the United States for the People's Republic of China."

"You've come all this way," Shizong said with a hint of amusement. "Will you read me my Miranda rights?"

McGarvey had to smile. "If you wish, and if I can remember them from watching *NYPD Blue*."

"Beijing has sent someone to arrest you," Jiying said seriously. "And my government has agreed to hand you over. Tonight."

Shizong suddenly understood the gravity of the situation. "I see."

"You need to go right now, Peter," Jiying said. He brought his heels together, placed his hands at his sides, and bowed formally.

Shizong did the same. When he rose he said something in Mandarin to Jiying, and then turned to McGarvey. "I have no idea how you mean to get me out of here in one piece, but then some really extraordinary things have happened to me in the last couple of months."

Jiying hustled them to a broad veranda on the west side of the house, where the rock-strewn hill plunged steeply a couple hundred feet to a line of trees.

"The road is just below the trees," Jiying told them.

It was finally starting to get dark. The city of Taipei was coming alive with a million pinpricks of light. What sounded like a fighter jet passed overhead to the south.

One of the commandos called something from inside the house. It sounded urgent.

"We're out of time. Take it easy going down and good luck," Jiying said.

McGarvey started down the hill first, and once they were out from under the veranda it was a little easier to pick out the path. At first he went slowly for Shizong's sake, but within thirty feet he realized that the much younger man was in very good shape and as surefooted as a mountain climber, so he picked up the pace.

They reached the bottom in five minutes and made their way through the dense stand of trees. They came out about twenty yards beyond where the Fiat was parked at the side of the road, facing downhill. McGarvey could not see the van, but he suspected that Preston had pulled into the driveway another thirty or forty yards farther down the hill. The road up to Lee's house was just beyond it.

"Is that our transportation?" Shizong whispered.

"No, they followed us up from Taipei. There's two of them."

"PRC supporters?"

"Yes, but I don't want to kill them unless I have no other choice."

"They wouldn't return the favor, believe me," Shizong said. "What are we going to do?"

"Wait until the delegation from the airport arrives. These guys might follow them up the hill."

"They might not—" Shizong said when they spotted lights coming up the road around the curve. They could hear the Humvees' exhausts hammering off the side of the hill, and after they had all turned up Lee's driveway the night got relatively quiet again. But the Fiat did not move.

"Shit," McGarvey said, half under his breath. He took out his pistol. "Wait here," he told Shizong, and he stepped out on the road. Keeping his eye on the car for any sign of movement, and his pistol hidden behind his leg, he walked down to the Fiat. As he got closer he could see the two men inside, but they were not moving, and it wasn't until he was on top of them that he saw why.

They were both alive and frantic with rage. Hanrahan and Preston had gotten the drop on them and had duct-taped them to their seats. They were covered head to toe except for their noses and eyes.

McGarvey motioned for Shizong to come ahead when Hanrahan stepped out of the darkness below and waved them on. Shizong stopped in his tracks, suddenly not sure what was happening.

"Get the van," McGarvey called down to Hanrahan, keeping his voice as low as possible. He hurried back to where Shizong was about ready to bolt.

"I don't know—"

"It's okay, Mr. Shizong," McGarvey said. The man was only in his twenties, and despite his intelligence, training and charisma he was still just a young man faced with a very uncertain and potentially deadly situation. "There's a submarine waiting for us off Keelung. If we can get you aboard, we'll take you to Honolulu. It's either that or Beijing. But you can't stay here any longer."

The van, its headlights off, nosed out from the driveway.

Shizong looked at the van and then back at McGarvey. "Do you think that I can find some old Superman comics in a shop there?"

McGarvey spread his hands, at a loss. "I imagine you can."

"It's a present for someone," Shizong said, and he motioned toward the van. "I believe that our ride is waiting for us."

Hanrahan was holding the side door open for them. Just as they reached the van they heard gunshots from above, and again Shizong was stopped in his tracks. He turned back, and McGarvey grabbed his arm.

"We have to go now," McGarvey said urgently.

"Those are my friends up there." Shizong tried to pull away.

"And they're also Taiwanese intelligence officers who risked their lives to pull you out of Xiamen. They're buying us some time."

"They might be killed."

"Yes, they might be," McGarvey said harshly. "So might we."

Shizong gave him a look of genuine anguish, and McGarvey wanted to tell him: Welcome to the club. You now have blood on your hands like the rest of us. But he didn't say it because it was too cruel, too without feeling or compassion. It was this business; it made people into its own terrible mold, not the other way around. Shizong still had his idealism. McGarvey hoped that it would last at least a little longer.

They clambered into the van and even before Hanrahan had the door shut, Preston took off down the hill like a rocket, the sounds of gunfire up at Lee's mansion intensifying.

2120 Local
SSN 21 *Seawolf*

Harding was in the control room studying the chart. The water didn't get deep for another five miles offshore, and the Han-class submarine blocked the way. There was no real contest if it came to a battle. But he didn't think that the Chinese skipper wanted to start a shooting war any more than the rest of them did.

He glanced at the boat's master clock. McGarvey had given himself until midnight local before he should be considered overdue. There was no way to tell what was happening ashore. Technically that wasn't his responsibility. His boat and his crew were.

He grabbed the growler phone. "Sonar, this is the captain," he said.

"Sonar, aye."

"What's our friend doing?"

"He's still back there, skipper. Trying to be real quiet. But he's got a noisy motor somewhere. Probably in his air-circulation system."

"Any sign of the outboard?"

"Nothing yet."

"How's traffic topside?"

"That's some good news, Captain. It's thinned out."

"Keep me posted, Fisher," Harding said. He hung up the phone. He had to think it out for only a moment, then he looked up. "Come to battle stations, torpedo," he said calmly.

"Aye, sir, battle stations, torpedo," a startled Chief of Boat responded, and he began issuing orders.

"Load tubes one, two, three, and four, but do not open the outer doors."

"Do we have a target, sir?" the weapons control officer asked.

"Start a TMA on Sierra Twenty-one. I want a continuous solution on the target, and I don't want to lose it no matter what happens."

"Yes, sir," the officer said, impressed. It was the first time he'd ever heard the captain speak that sharply. But God help the poor sorry Chinese son of a bitch if he so much as twitched a whisker.

Keelung

McGarvey watched the road from where he sat in the rear of the van. Traffic had slowed to a crawl outside Keelung because of a military roadblock. Some people tried crossing the fields in the steady rain to reach the railroad tracks, but soon got stuck because of the deep mud. Soldiers went on foot to arrest them.

"There were no roadblocks this morning," Hanrahan said.

It had taken them more than an hour to drive the twelve miles from the Grass Mountain road. Time enough, McGarvey wondered, for the battle at Lee's house to be finished, the house searched, and the PRC spies duct-taped inside of their car to be released and give them the description of the van? If that was the case, they would somehow have to bluff their way through because there was no turning back, the highway was impossibly clogged; and he wasn't going to get into a shooting battle with Taiwanese soldiers doing their legitimate duties.

"What do you want to do?" Preston asked. "In the mood these guys are in it won't take much to set them off."

"We're going to talk our way past them," McGarvey said, an idea turning over in his mind.

"If they're looking for us specifically, it's going to be all over but the shouting once we get up there," Hanrahan pointed out unnecessarily. They all knew it.

McGarvey turned and looked at Shizong who was hunched down in the darkness in the back. Their eyes met, and Shizong nodded and smiled. McGarvey turned back. "I'll do the talking," he told Preston and Hanrahan. "No matter what happens, there'll be no gunplay. Understood?"

They both nodded.

It was another twenty minutes before their turn came. The highway was blocked in both directions, and there was just as big a traffic jam trying to get out of the city as there was trying to get in. Most of it was trucks trying to pick up or deliver goods.

A pair of APCs were parked beside the highway, their fifty-caliber machine guns covering both directions. There were at least five Humvees and a couple of dozen soldiers in battle fatigues, all of them armed with M16s and very serious-looking. There were two lanes of traffic in each direction, each lane with its own cadre of soldiers.

A sergeant and PFC came to the driver's window. McGarvey reached over Preston's shoulder and handed the sergeant his military ID, "I need to talk to your CO."

The sergeant looked at the ID and then looked up at McGarvey. "Get out of the van, all of you," he ordered.

"You're going to be in a world of shit, Sergeant, if you don't get your CO over here on the double. We have something here he's got to see."

"Get out of the vehicle—"

"Call him," McGarvey ordered. "Now!"

The sergeant, a little less certain, checked McGarvey's ID again, which identified him as a captain in the U.S. Navy. He stepped back and said something into his lapel mike. A minute later a young lieutenant wearing camos charged over, said something to the sergeant, and then came over to the van.

"Get out now," he shouted.

"As you wish," McGarvey said. "But there's a friend of yours in back who wants to tell you something." He pulled back and slid open the side door. His eye caught Shizong's. The young man nodded. He knew exactly what he was supposed to do.

McGarvey and Hanrahan climbed out of the van as the lieutenant came around from the driver's side where Preston had dismounted.

There were soldiers all over the place, sensing that something was going on, their weapons at the ready.

"Step away from the vehicle—" the lieutenant said, as Shizong appeared at the open door. Recognition dawned on the lieutenant's face instantly. He was visibly shaken. Shizong had been on Taiwan television for more than six weeks. He'd become a celebrity.

"Lieutenant, come here for a moment, please, I would like to ask you something," Shizong said. Then he switched to Mandarin.

The lieutenant, who had taken out his pistol, lowered it and walked over to the open door. He and Shizong shook hands, and Shizong began to speak, softly, slowly, his voice calm, reasonable, and sympathetic.

Some of the soldiers drifted closer so that they could hear. All of them recognized Shizong. Civilians from the trucks and cars came up, and soon there were at least one hundred people gathered in the chill rain to listen to Shizong, who never once raised his voice. It was, as Hanrahan would later recall, as if he was whispering in your ear; as if he was talking to you personally. It was clear that he affected everybody that way. It was the reason that the old men of Beijing were so frightened of him that they were willing to risk nuclear war to silence him.

At one point the lieutenant looked sheepishly at the pistol still in his hand. He holstered it, then bowed stiffly in front of Shizong. Without looking at McGarvey or the others, he turned and walked away, taking his soldiers with him.

"We may go now," Shizong said. "There will be no further roadblocks."

As McGarvey and the others were climbing back into the van, the APCs were already pulling back, and the soldiers were breaking off from their duties and hustling to the Humvees.

Preston started out, slowly at first but gaining speed as the traffic began to spread out. The rain and overcast deepened the night so that coming into a city that was under military blackout orders was like coming into some medieval settlement before electric lights had been invented.

McGarvey directed Preston past the railroad station to the vicinity of the fisheries warehouse and dock where they had come ashore. They parked the van in a dark narrow side alley and walked back to the still-unattended gate into the net yard.

As before there was no activity there, and this time they didn't even see the guard. Fifteen minutes after leaving the van, they'd made their way down the ladder and scrambled aboard the inflatable, which was tied exactly where they'd left it. They pulled themselves out from under the long dock and began rowing directly out to sea, the rain flattening even the small ripples and hiding everything farther out than twenty yards behind a fine dark veil.

A half mile offshore Hanrahan shipped the oars, lowered the outboard, and started the highly muffled engine; the only question left was how four men were going to get aboard the submerged submarine with only three sets of closed circuit diving equipment.

2305 Local
SSN 21 *Seawolf*

"Conn, sonar, I've got the outboard," Fisher reported excitedly. "Bearing zero-one-zero, range four thousand four hundred yards and closing."

"Okay, prepare to surface," Harding told the diving officer. Paradise looked up from the chart he was studying and came over.

"We're going to make a lot of noise," he said. "The PRC captain will know that something is going on."

"That's right, Rod. But he won't know what," Harding replied. He wasn't in the mood to explain what he was doing, not even to his XO. He had a good idea what McGarvey was facing and what he was trying to accomplish, and he was going to give the man all the help he could.

The diving officer relayed the captain's orders, and the boat was made ready to come to periscope depth for a look-see before they actually surfaced. It was SOP.

"Keep a sharp watch on the target," Harding told sonar.

"Aye, skipper."

"Flood tubes one through four and open the outer doors as soon as we start up."

"Aye, skipper," the weapons-control officer responded.

"Bring the boat to sixty feet."

"Bring the boat to six-zero feet, sir," the diving officer said crisply, and they began noisily venting high-pressure air into the ballast tanks. *Seawolf* started up.

He had everybody's attention now, and they were working as an efficient unit, exactly as they had been trained to do. The real test, however, Harding expected, was yet to come.

"Take Scotty and two other men and stand by the main stores hatch," he told Paradise. "I won't surface until they're on top of us. But as soon as they're aboard we're getting out of here."

"Are you expecting trouble?" Paradise asked. Dick Scott was their sergeant at arms.

"It's possible, Rod," Harding said. "Have Scotty break out the sidearms."

2310 Local
SSN 405 *Hekou*

Heishui was in his cabin looking at a photograph of his wife and daughter, when his XO called him.

"Captain, the American submarine is on the way up!"

"What are the conditions on the surface?" Heishui asked, putting the photograph down. Now was the moment of truth for his boat and crew; and for himself.

"We're picking up the same small outboard engine as before, about four thousand meters out, and traffic is down to almost nothing. We show two targets, both of them outside ten thousand meters and both seaward." Their new Trout Creek sonar suite rivaled that of just about any submarine anywhere. Heishui had a high degree of confidence in it.

"Send up the fire squad. But tell them to make certain they have the right target. If we're lucky, we can end this right now and never have to engage the American submarine."

"Yes, sir," Lagao said.

Heishui took a long last look at the photograph of his family, then buttoned the top button of his uniform and went forward and up one level to the attack center.

"Flood all tubes and open all outer doors," he ordered.

"Aye, sir." The weapons officer repeated the orders.

"Prepare to get under way," the captain told his chief of boat, an icy calm coming over him. It was just as good as a day as any to win or lose, he told himself. Live or die.

2320 Local
On The Surface

"We're on station," Hanrahan said, checking his GPS navigator. The night was completely still except for the hiss of the rain on the water and the soft buzz of the idling outboard.

"They know that we're here," McGarvey said. He did a 360 and so far as he could tell they were completely alone on the ocean. "You'll have to dive down, lock aboard, and bring up some more equipment—"

"But I cannot swim," Shizong interrupted.

"You won't have to do a thing, we'll do it all for you," McGarvey said. "Trust me."

"Periscope," Hanrahan said excitedly.

They all turned in the direction that he was looking in time to see the light at the top of the *Seawolf*'s periscope mast about eight feet out of the water, blinking in Morse code.

Hanrahan held up a hand. "Retreat one hundred yards. We will surface. Repeat. Retreat one hundred yards. We will surface."

Shizong turned to say something, when a narrow pinpoint of red light appeared in the middle of his forehead. It was a weapons guidance laser and it seemed to come from somewhere to the right of the *Seawolf*, very low to the water. McGarvey drove forward, his shoulder catching Shizong in the chest and shoving him back.

"Get down," he shouted.

Preston cried out in pain, blood erupting from a very large hole in his chest. He was flung to the side like a rag doll, out of the raft and into the water.

Hanrahan rolled out right behind him as they continued to take rounds from somewhere in the darkness. He grabbed a handful of Shizong's shirt as he went. McGarvey, holding on to Shizong's arm, followed him, the raft and the water all around them erupting in a hail of bullets fired from at least two silenced machine guns.

"Take Peter and get out of here," he ordered urgently.

Hanrahan grabbed the floundering Shizong. "What about Tom?"

"He's dead. Go!"

Hanrahan wanted to stay, but he started away from the deflated raft with Shizong in tow.

The gunfire stopped. McGarvey found Preston a few yards away, facedown in the water. He turned him over, but the man was dead as expected. Preston had taken a round in the middle of the back, which had mushroomed through his body, tearing a hole six inches wide in his chest. The bastards were using dumdums or explosive bullets.

He cocked an ear to listen. He could hear what sounded like a small outboard motor coming toward him. Off to his left a broad section of water for as far as he could see was boiling, as if someone had put it on the heat. It was the *Seawolf* on the way up.

Hanrahan and Shizong were gone in the darkness, and the motor was very close now. They were PRC, and they had been waiting out here for Shizong. How that could possibly happen didn't matter now. They had probably scoped the raft with night-vision equipment, identified Shizong out of the four men, and had targeted him specifically. They were coming in to make sure he was dead.

McGarvey passed his hand over Preston's chest wound, smeared the blood and gore over his face, and floated loosely on his back, his arms spread, his eyes open and fixed as if he were dead.

The motor was practically on top of him, and he had to let himself sink under the water for a second or two without blinking, without closing his mouth.

A black-rubber inflatable, almost the twin of the one they had brought up from the *Seawolf*, appeared out of the mist and came directly over to where Preston's body had drifted. They slowed and circled, shining a narrow beam of light on his face. They said something that McGarvey couldn't make out, then came over to where he was floating. They shined the light in his face, and he had to fight not to blink or move a muscle.

There were three of them, dressed in black night fighters' uniform, their faces blackened. It came to him all of a sudden that they had gotten there the same way that he and Hanrahan had. They were off a submarine. Possibly a PRC boat that had been lying in wait just off shore for the Chinese attack on Taiwan to begin. The *Seawolf* coming in had missed it.

Something very large and black rose up out of the water to McGarvey's left. One of the Chinese sailors said something urgently, and he gunned the outboard motor. As the inflatable started to pass him, McGarvey reached up, grabbed the gunwale line with his left hand, pulled himself half out of the water, and grabbed a handful of the tunic of the sailor running the outboard motor and yanked him overboard.

The inflatable immediately veered sharply to the left. McGarvey had taken a deep breath at the last moment. He dragged the surprised sailor underwater, the man taking a very large reflexive breath as his head submerged.

The sailor got very still within seconds and as McGarvey surfaced with the body the outboard was circling back.

He took the weapon, which he recognized by feel as a Sterling, from the dead man's hands, reared up out of the water to keep the holes in the silencer casing free, and unloaded the weapon point-blank at the inflatable as it was practically on top of him.

The raft swerved widly to the right, flipping over as it collapsed from the explosive release of air from its chambers. McGarvey dropped the empty weapon and backpedaled, trying to put as much distance between himself and whoever was left alive as possible. But it wasn't necessary. Except for the roiled water behind him, the night was utterly silent.

"Hank," he called.

"Here," Hanrahan replied from somewhere to the left.

"Do you have Peter?"

"Here," Shizong called back, his voice surprisingly steady for a man who could not swim and found himself in the middle of the ocean.

A few seconds later a beam of light from the deck of the *Seawolf* caught McGarvey, and he turned and swam toward it as fast as he could manage. They still weren't out of the woods. Not with a PRC submarine lurking around somewhere nearby.

2329 Local
SSN 405 *Hekou*

"Sierra Eighteen is on the surface," Zenzhong told the captain nervously.

"Open doors one and two," Heishui ordered "Prepare to fire."

"Captain, what about our men on the surface?" Lagao asked at his side.

Heishui turned and gave him a bland look. "It's a moot point, Commander. Either their mission is already a success or they have failed. They can't fight the crew of an entire submarine."

"At least give them five minutes," Lagao pleaded. "Some sign that they are alive and trying to make it back aboard."

The *Hekou* had risen to thirty meters in order to lock them out, and then had settled back to one hundred meters behind and below the American submarine. There was no way that even an experienced diver could make that depth, nor was he going to put his boat and crew at risk by heading back up to rescue them. They knew what they were facing when they had volunteered.

"Three minutes," Heishui said. "It will take us that long to get ready to fire." He turned away.

2332 Local
SSN 21 *Seawolf*

"We have three people aboard, and the hatch is sealed," Paradise called to the captain.

"Get up here on the double, Rod, we have work to do," Harding said. He switched channels. "Sonar, this is the captain. What's the target doing?"

"He's about two thousand yards out, skipper, just lying there. Bearing one-seven-five, and below us at three hundred feet," Fisher reported. "I think he might have opened at least two of his outer doors when we were on the way up."

"If there's any change, let me know on the double," Harding said. He hung up the phone. "Get us out of here," he told the Chief of the Boat.

"Aye, sir."

"Emergency dive to three hundred feet, come right to new course zero-six-zero, and give me turns for forty knots as soon as possible." The submarine had to be at least one hundred feet beneath the surface before she could begin to develop her top speed submerged.

Trela relayed the orders and within seconds the *Seawolf* surged forward, her decks canted sharply downward and to the right.

"Don't lose the solution," Harding warned the weapons-control officer.

"No, sir."

2335 Local
SSN 404 *Hekou*

"He's on the move, Captain," Zenzhong shouted. "Sierra Eighteen is diving, and his aspect is definitely changing left to right."

"He's leaving in a big hurry; do you think that he knows we're back here?" Lagao asked Heishui.

"Perhaps," the captain replied. A million conflicting thoughts were running through his head with the speed of light, his family among them. But his blood was up. Serving on a Han-class submarine for any length of time meant certain death in any event from leukemia or some other form of cancer because the reactors leaked. Only the officers understood that for a fact, but most of the crews knew it, too. Love of country and the special privileges for their families were the incentives to serve. "No word from our crew on the surface?"

"No, sir."

Heishuo gave his XO a look of sympathy, then turned to his fire-control officer. "Do we have a positive solution on the enemy?"

"Yes, sir."

"Fire one, fire two."

2336 Local
SSN 21 *Seawolf*

"Torpedoes in the water!" Fisher called out. "Two of them, bearing one-nine-five, and definitely gaining."

"Turn left, come to flank speed," Harding said calmly.

"Aye, sir, turning left full rudder, ordering flank speed," Lieutenant Trela repeated.

"Time to impact?" Harding asked the sonarman.

"Ninety seconds, skipper."

"Release the noisemakers as soon as we pass three-six-zero degrees," Harding ordered. "Prepare to fire tubes one and two."

"Don't do it, Captain," McGarvey shouted, coming into the control room directly on Paradise's heels.

Harding's head snapped around. McGarvey stood dripping next to the plotting tables, blood covering his face, a wild look in his eyes. "Get out of here, Mac. Now!"

"Listen to me, Tom. We have to make the PRC skipper think that he's destroyed us."

"He very well might do just that."

"Sixty-five seconds to impact," Fisher reported.

"Tubes one and two ready to fire, Captain," the fire-control officer said.

"If it can be done without risking our own destruction, we have to try it," McGarvey argued. "That's the entire point of the mission. Getting Shizong out of here in secret, or making the Chinese believe that he's dead." McGarvey shook his head. "They were waiting for us up there. They knew we were bringing him. And I lost one of my people."

"Captain?" the Chief of Boat prompted.

"Release the noisemakers now," Harding said. "All stop, rudder amidships."

"All stop, rudder amidships, sir," Trela responded crisply after only a moment's hesitation. He hoped the old man knew what he was doing this time.

"Fifty seconds to impact."

Harding looked at McGarvey and Paradise. "I'm sorry that you took a casualty," he said. "Stand by to fire tube one, *only* tube one."

"Stand by one, aye," the weapons-control officer said.

"Sonar, this is the captain. I want you to pull up the BRD program that we were given in Pearl. Feed it to the main sonar dome." BRD was Battle Response Decoy system. The *Seawolf* was supposed to have tested it on the initial part of this cruise, but not under actual battle conditions.

"Aye, skipper, I understand. Forty seconds to impact."

"I'll tell you when to transmit. Just be ready."

"Yes, sir."

Harding motioned for Paradise to man the ballast control panel. "On my mark I want all aft tanks explosively vented." This would fill them with water all at once, making the boat stern-heavy. She would sink to the bottom tail first.

"Thirty seconds to impact," Fisher reported.

"Fire tube one," Harding said.

"Fire one, aye," the weapons-control officer said. "Torpedo one is away."

"Sonar, conn. Stand by, Fisher."

"Aye, sir."

"Send autodestruct," Harding told the weapons-control officer.

The man looked up. "Sir—?"

"Twenty seconds to impact."

"Autodestruct now!" Harding ordered.

The weapons-control officer uncaged the button and pushed it. Their wire-guided HE torpedo, which had not had enough time to began searching for a target, exploded less than eight hundred feet from the *Seawolf*, and directly in the path of the oncoming Chinese torpedoes.

"Brace yourselves," Harding shouted as the first tremendous shock wave hammered the hull.

Both Chinese torpedoes fired almost simultaneously, slamming the *Seawolf*'s hull as if they had been hit by a pair of runaway cement trucks.

"Transmit now," Harding told sonar. An instant later the water all around them reverberated with the transmitted noises of a submarine breaking up; internal explosions, water rushing, bulkheads collapsing, even men screaming, machinery spinning wildly out of control and breaking through decks as the boat was torn apart.

Paradise was waiting at the ballast control panel, and Harding gave him the nod.

"Take us down."

Paradise twisted the controls, air was vented out of the aft tanks, and immediately they began a rapid descent to the bottom. Harding reached up to a handhold on the overhead and braced himself. Everyone else did the same.

2340 Local
SSN 405 *Hekou*

Heishui held the earphones close. He was hearing the noises of a dying submarine. It excited him and saddened him at the same time. More than one hundred officers and men were dead or dying beneath him.

He focused on Zenzhong and the other sonar operators who had done such brilliant jobs. He felt a great deal of respect and affection for them. For all of his crew. They had gone up against one of the best ships in all the U.S. Navy and had been victorious.

"Good job," he said, smiling warmly as he took off the earphones and handed them to one of the sonarmen. "Our mission was a complete success, and now it is time for us to go home."

Zenzhong was busy with his equipment. At least six distinct white horizontal lines were painted on his sonar display scopes. "We have many targets incoming," he said. He marked them on the screen with a grease pencil as quickly as he identified them.

"Then we'll thread the needle," Heishui said. "And you will lead us to safety."

Zenzhong looked up, his eyes wide, but then he started to work out the relative bearings of the incomings.

Heishui went back to the control room. His crew all looked respectfully at him. He smiled and bowed to them all. "Thank you. We have succeeded in fulfilling our orders. We will go home now."

"What is our course and speed, Captain?" his Chief of Boat asked.

Heishui went to the plotting table and took the bearings of the incoming warships as Zenzhong gave them. They were almost boxed in, but not quite. One lane leading out to sea was somehow still open to them.

"Make our course three-five-zero, speed two-five knots," he told the Chief of Boat, who immediately relayed his orders. At that speed they would be very noisy.

Lagao came over and studied the plots. "They have left us a way out," he said.

"Either it's a mistake for it's a political decision on their part," Heishui said, looking up. He felt at peace, but it was clear that his XO was troubled.

"Or it may be a trap."

Heishui nodded. "Prepare a message for Admiral Pei. Tell him that we have succeeded and are en route to Ningbo."

"When shall I send it?"

"Immediately," Heishui said, and he turned back to the chart as his boat accelerated. There was no possibility that they would make it home this time. But their mission was a success. The traitor Shi Shizong was dead, and a war with Taiwan had been avoided. At least for the moment.

Two Weeks Later
United Nations General Assembly

On the way up to New York from Langley, McGarvey had a lot to think about. There was a new, troubling situation heating up in the Balkans, more unrest in Greece, rumors that someone at the highest levels inside the Mexican government was in bed with the leading drug cartels, and Castro's successor was courting Pakistan for nuclear technology.

The funeral for Tom Preston had been a quiet affair at Arlington, with only a handful of friends and relatives. He hadn't been married, and there weren't any children. There'd been some confusion about who he was, but the Taiwanese Coast Guard had finally gotten it figured out, and his body had been flown home.

The Chinese Navy and Air Force had finished their extensive exercise, packed up their toys, and gone home all of a sudden with no explanation about Peter Shizong, or about the apparent destruction of two submarines, an American boat somewhere off Taiwan's north coast and a PRC boat a couple of hours later and fifty miles north. There were no survivors.

The media never got the last story, and at the diplomatic level China and the U.S. politely avoided mentioning the issue at all. It was, as far as both sides were concerned, a completely fair and equitable exchange.

That was a position that the Chinese would regret having taken, McGarvey thought with pleasure as he got off the elevator on the third floor. He crossed the hall and after he showed his credentials was allowed inside the sky boxes, where the translators worked looking down on the General Assembly.

Captain Joseph Jiying, in civilian clothes, jumped up from where he was watching the proceedings, a big grin on his face. "Good to see you, Mr. McGarvey," he said. They shook hands.

"My friends call me Mac, and it's *really* good to see you in one piece."

"It was a little hairy there for a couple of hours, but we finally realized the error of our patriotic zeal, and we gave up. No casualties."

U.S. Ambassador Margaret Woolsey had just come to the podium amid some polite applause.

"You might want to check out Chou en Ping. He's the PRC's ambassador to the UN," Jiying said. He was enjoying himself to the max. "The poor bastard doesn't know what's about to hit him."

"It's not going to be so easy," McGarvey said.

"You're right, of course," Jiying said, suddenly very serious. "Maybe it'll take another hundred years for the mainland to recognize who and what Taiwan has become. Look how long it took before Hong Kong went back." He smiled and nodded as a very large round of applause swept across the General Assembly. "But ain't it great to win once in a while? You know, truth, justice, and the American way?"

Down on the floor Peter Shizong was slowly making his way to the podium, shaking hands as he and his UN-supplied bodyguards were completely mobbed by well-wishers.

McGarvey took a pair of binoculars from Jiying and tried to spot Chou en Ping and the Chinese delegation at their seats, but they had already gotten up and were marching up a side aisle for the exits.

He handed the binoculars back. "Gotta go."

"What's your rush, it's just getting good," Jiying said.

"I'm meeting a friend for drinks. And then our wives are coming up to join us."

"Anyone I should know?"

McGarvey shook his head. "Just an old friend. A submarine driver. Good man to have around in a pinch."

David Hagberg is an ex-Air Force cryptographer who has spoken at CIA functions and traveled extensively in Europe, the Arctic, and the Caribbean. He also writes fiction under the pseudonym Sean Flannery, and has published more than two dozen novels of suspense, including *White House, High Flight, Eagles Fly, Assassin*, and *Joshua's Hammer*. His writing has been nominated for numerous honors, including the American Book Award, three times for the Edgar Allan Poe award, and three times for the American Mystery award. He lives in Florida, and has been continuously published for the past twenty-five years.

INSIDE JOB

BY DEAN ING

One

"The longer I live, the more I realize the less I know for sure." That's what my friend Quentin Kim used to mutter to me and curvy little Dana Martin in our Public Safety classes at San Jose State. Dana would frown because she revered conventional wisdom. I'd always chuckle, because I thought Quent was kidding. But that was years ago, and I was older then.

I mean, I thought I knew it all. "Public Safety" is genteel academic code for cop coursework, and while Quent had already built himself an enviable rep as a licensed P.I. in the Bay Area, he hadn't been a big-city cop. I went on to become one, until I got fed up with the cold war between guys on the take and guys in Internal Affairs, both sides angling for recruits. I tried hard to avoid getting their crap on my size thirteen brogans while I lost track of Dana, saw Quent infrequently, and served the City of Oakland's plainclothes detail in the name of public safety.

So much for stepping carefully in such a barnyard. At least I got out with honor after a few years, and I still had contacts around Oakland on both sides of the law. Make that several sides; and to an investigator that's worth more than diamonds. It would've taken a better man than Harve Rackham to let those contacts go to waste, which is why I became the private kind of investigator, aka gumshoe, peeper, or just plain Rackham, P.I.

Early success can destroy you faster than a palmed ice pick, especially if it comes through luck you thought was skill. A year into my new career, I talked my way into a seam job—a kidnapping within a disintegrating family. The kidnapped boy's father, a Sunnyvale software genius, wanted the kid back badly enough to throw serious money at his problem. After a few days of frustration, I shot my big mouth off about it to my sister's husband, Ernie.

It was a lucky shot, though. Ernie was with NASA at Moffett Field and by sheer coincidence he knew a certain Canadian physicist. I'd picked up a rumor that the physicist had been playing footsie with the boy's vanished mother.

The physicist had a Quebecois accent, Ernie recalled, and had spoken longingly about a teaching career. The man had already given notice at NASA without a forwarding address. He was Catholic. A little digging told me that might place him at the University of Montreal, a Catholic school which gives instruction in French. I caught a Boeing 787 and got there before he did, and guess who was waiting with her five-year-old boy in the Montreal apartment the physicist had leased.

I knew better than to dig very far into the reasons why Mama took Kiddie and left Papa. It was enough that she'd fled the country illegally. The check I cashed was so much more than enough that I bought a decaying farmhouse twenty miles and a hundred years from Oakland.

Spending so much time away, I figured I'd need to fence the five acres of peaches and grapes, but the smithy was what sold me. "The smith, a mighty man was he, with large and sinewy," et cetera. Romantic bullshit, sure, but as I said, I knew it all then. And I wanted to build an off-road racer, one of the diesel-electric hybrids that were just becoming popular. I couldn't imagine a better life than peeping around the Port of Oakland for money, and hiding out on my acreage whenever I had some time off, building my big lightning-on-wheels toy.

And God knows, I had plenty of time off after that! Didn't the word get out that I was hot stuff? Weren't more rich guys clamoring for my expensive services? Wasn't I slated for greatness?

In three words: no, no, and no. I didn't even invest in a slick Web site while I still had the money, with only a line in the yellow pages, so I didn't get many calls. I was grunting beneath my old gasoline-fueled Toyota pickup one April afternoon, chasing an oil leak because I couldn't afford to have someone else do it, when my cell phone warbled.

Quentin Kim; I was grinning in an instant. "I thought I was good, but it's humbling when I can't find something as big as you," he bitched.

I squoze my hundred kilos from under the Toyota. "You mean you're looking for me now? Today?"

"I have driven that country road three times, Harvey. My GP mapper's no help. Where the devil are you?"

Even his cussing was conservative. When Quent used my full given name, he was a quart low on patience. I told him to try the road again and I'd flag him down, and he did, and twenty minutes later I guided his Volvo Electrabout up the lane to my place.

He emerged looking fit, a few grey hairs but the almond eyes still raven-bright, the smile mellow, unchanged. I ignored the limp; maybe his shoes pinched. From force of habit and ethnic Korean good manners, Quent avoided staring around him, but I knew he would miss very little as I invited him through the squinchy old screen door into my authentic 1910 kitchen with its woodstove. He didn't relax until we continued to the basement, the fluorescents obediently flickering on along the stairs.

"You had me worried for a minute," he said, now with a frankly approving glance at my office. As fin de siècle as the house was from the foundation up, I'd fixed it all Frank Gehry and Starship *Enterprise* below. He perched his butt carefully on the stool at my drafting carrel; ran his hand along the flat catatonic stare of my Magnascreen. "But you must be doing all right for yourself. Some of this has got to be expensive stuff, Harve."

"Pure sweat equity, most of it." I shrugged. "I do adhesive bonding, some welding, cabinetry,—oh, I was a whiz in shop, back in high school."

"Don't try to imply that you missed your real calling. I notice you're working under your own license since a year ago. Can people with budgets still afford you?"

"I won't shit you, Quent, but don't spread this around. Way things are right now, anybody can afford me."

It had been over a year since we'd watched World Cup soccer matches together, and while we caught each other up on recent events, I brewed tea for him in my six-cup glass rig with its flash boiler.

He didn't make me ask about the limp. "You know how those old alleyway fire-escape ladders get rickety after sixty years or so," he told me, shifting his leg. "A few months ago I was closing on a bail-jumper who'd been living on a roof in Alameda, and the ladder came loose on us." Shy smile, to forestall sympathy. "He hit the bricks. I bounced off a Dumpster." Shrug.

"Bring him in?"

"The paramedics brought us both in, but I got my fee," he said. "I don't have to tell you how an HMO views our work, and I'm not indigent. Fixing this hip cost me a lot more than I made, and legwork will never be my forte again, I'm afraid."

I folded my arms and attended to the beep of my tea rig. "You're telling me you were bounty hunting," I said. It wasn't exactly an accusation, but most P.I.s won't work for bail bondsmen. It's pretty demanding work, though the money can be good when you negotiate a fifteen percent fee and then bring in some scuffler who's worth fifty large.

While we sipped tea, we swapped sob stories, maintaining a light touch because nobody had forced either of us into the peeper business. You hear a lot about P.I.s being churlish to each other. Mostly a myth, beyond some healthy competition. "I suppose I couldn't resist the challenge," said Quent. "You know me, always trying to expand my education. As a bounty hunter you learn a lot, pretty quickly."

"Like, don't trust old fire escapes," I said.

"Like that," he agreed. "But it also brings you to the attention of a different class of client. It might surprise even you that some Fed agencies will subcontract an investigation, given special circumstances."

It surprised me less when he said that the present circumstances required someone who spoke Hangul, the Korean language, and knew the dockside world around Oakland. Someone the Federal Bureau of Investigation could trust.

"Those guys," I said, "frost my *cojones*. It's been my experience that they'll let metro cops take most of the chances and zero percent of the credit."

"Credit is what you buy groceries with, Harve," he said. "What do we care, so long as the Feds will hire us again?"

"Whoa. What's that word again? *Us*, as in you and me?"

"If you'll take it. I need an extra set of feet—hips, if you insist—and it doesn't hurt that you carry the air of plainclothes cop with you. And with your size, you can handle yourself, which is something I might need."

He mentioned a fee, including a daily rate, and I managed not to whistle. "I need to know more. This gonna be something like a bodyguard detail, Quent? I don't speak Hangul, beyond a few phrases you taught me."

"That's only part of it. Most people we'll interview speak plain American; record checks, for example. The case involves a marine engineer missing from the tramp motorship *Ras Ormara*, which is tied up for round-the-clock refitting at a Richmond wharf. He's Korean. Coast Guard and FBI would both like to find him, without their being identified."

There's an old cop saying about Richmond, California: it's vampire turf. Safe enough in daylight, but watch your neck at night. "I suppose you've already tried Missing Persons."

Quent served me a "give me a break" look. "I don't have to tell you the metro force budget is petty cash, Harve. They're overloaded with domestic cases. The Feds know it, which is where we come in—if you want in."

"Got me over a barrel. You want the truth, I'm practically wearing the goddamn barrel. Any idea how long the case will last?"

Quent knew I was really asking how many days' pay it might involve. "It evaporates the day the *Ras Ormara* leaves port; perhaps a week. That doesn't give us as much time as I'd like, but every case sets its own pace."

That was another old Quentism, and I'd come to learn it was true. This would be a hot pace, so no wonder gimpy Quentin Kim was offering to share the workload. Instead of doping out his selfish motives, I should be thanking him, so I did. I added, "You don't know it, but you're offering me a bundle of chrome-moly racer frame tubing and a few rolls of cyclone fence. An offer I can't refuse, but I'd like to get a dossier on this Korean engineer right away."

"I can do better than that," said Quent, "and it'll come with a free supper tonight, courtesy of the Feds."

"They're buying? Now, *that* is impressive as hell."

"I have not begun to impress," Quent said, again with the shy smile. "Coast Guard Lieutenant Reuben Medler is fairly impressive, but the FBI liaison will strain your belief system."

"Never happen," I said. "They still look like IBM salesmen."

"Not this one. Trust me." Now Quent was grinning.

"You're wrong," I insisted.

"What do you think happened to the third of our classroom musketeers, Harve, and why do you think this case was dropped in my lap? The Feebie is Dana Martin," he said.

I kept my jaw from sagging with some effort. "You were right," I said.

Until the fight started, I assumed Quent had chosen Original Joe's in San Jose because we—Dana included—had downed many an abalone supreme there in earlier times. If some of the clientele were reputedly Connected with a capital *C*, that only kept folks polite. Quent and I met there and copped a booth, though our old habit had been to take seats at the counter where we could watch chefs with wrists of steel handle forty-centimeter skillets over three-alarm gas burners. I was halfway through a bottle of Anchor Steam when a well-built specimen in a crew-neck sweater, trim Dockers, and tasseled loafers ushered his date in. He carried himself as if hiding a small flagpole in the back of his sweater. I looked away, denying my envy. How is it some guys never put on an ounce while guys like me outgrow our belts?

Then I did a double take. The guy had to be Lieutenant Medler because the small, tanned, sharp-eyed confection in mid-heels and severely tailored suit was Dana Martin, no longer an overconfident kid. I think I said "wow" silently as we stood up.

After the introductions Medler let us babble about how long it had been. For me, the measure of elapsed time was that little Miz Martin had developed a sense of reserve. Then while we decided what we wanted to eat, Medler explained why shoreline poachers had taken abalone off the Original Joe menu. Mindful of who was picking up the tab, I ordered the latest fad entrée: Nebraska longhorn T-bone, lean as ostrich and just as spendy. Dana's lip pursed but she kept it buttoned, cordial, impersonal. I decided she'd bought into her career and its image. Damn, but I hated that . . .

Over the salads, Medler gave his story without editorializing, deferential to us, more so to Dana, in a soft baritone all the more masculine for discarding machismo. "The *Ras Ormara* is a C-1 motorship under Liberian registry," he said, "chartered by the Sonmiani Tramp Service of Karachi, Pakistan." He recited carefully, as if speaking for a recorder. Which he was, though I didn't say so. What the hell, people forget things.

"Some of these multinational vessels just beg for close inspection, the current foreign political situation being what it is," Medler went on. He didn't need to mention the nuke found by a French airport security team the previous month, on an Arab prince's Learjet at Charles De Gaulle terminal. "We did a walk-through. The vessel was out of Lima with a cargo of balsa logs and nontoxic plant extract slurry, bound for Richmond. Crew was the usual polyglot bunch, in this case chiefly Pakis and Koreans. They stay aboard in port unless they have the right papers."

At this point Medler abruptly began talking about how abalone poachers work, a second before the waitress arrived to serve our entrées. Quent nodded appreciatively and I toasted Medler's coolth with my beer.

Once we'd attacked our meals he resumed. Maybe the editorial came with the main course. "You know about Asian working-class people and eye contact—with apologies, Mr. Kim. But one young Korean in the crew was boring holes in my corneas. I decided to interview three men, one at a time, on the fo'c'sle deck. At random, naturally."

"Random as loaded dice." I winked.

"With their skipper right there? Affirmative, and I started with the ship's medic. When I escorted this young third engineer, Park Soon, on deck the poor guy was shaking. His English wasn't that fluent, and he didn't say much, even to direct questions, but he did say we had to talk ashore. 'Must talk,' was the phrase. He had his papers to go ashore.

"I gave him a time and place later that day, a coffeehouse in Berkeley every taxi driver knows. I thought he was going to cry with relief, but he went back to the *Ras Ormara*'s bridge with his jaw set like he was marching toward a firing squad. I went belowdecks.

"A lot of tramps look pretty trampy, but it actually just means it's not a regularly scheduled vessel. This one was spitshine spotless, and I found no reason to doubt the manifest or squawk about conditions in the holds.

"Fast forward to roughly sixteen hundred hours. Park shows at the coffeehouse, jumpy as Kermit, but now he's full of dire warnings. He doesn't know exactly what's wrong about the *Ras Ormara*, but he knows he's aboard only for window dressing. The reason he shipped on at Lima was, Park had met the previous third engineer in Lima at a dockside bar, some Chinese who spoke enough English to say he was afraid to go back aboard. Park was on the beach, as they say, and he wangled the job for himself."

Quent stopped shoveling spicy sausage in, and asked, "The Chinese was afraid? Of what?"

"According to Park, the man's exact English words were 'Death ship.' Park thought he had misunderstood at first and put the Chinese engineer's fear down to superstition. But a day or so en route here, he began to get spooked."

"Every culture has its superstitions," Quent said. "And crew members must pass them on. I'm told an old ship can carry enough legends to sink it." When Medler frowned, Quent said, "Remember Joseph Conrad's story, 'The Brute'? The *Apse Family* was a death ship. Well, it was just a story," he said, seeing Dana's look of abused patience.

Medler again: "A classic. Who hasn't read it?" Dana gave a knowing nod. Pissed me off; I hadn't read it. "But I doubt anyone aboard told sea stories to Park. He implied they all seemed to be appreciating some vast, unspoken serious joke. No one would talk to him at all except for his duties. And he didn't have a lot to do because the ship was a dream, he said. She had been converted somewhere to cargo from a small fast transport, so the crew accommodations were nifty. She displaces maybe two thousand tons, twenty-four knots. Fast," he said again. "Originally she must've been someone's decommissioned D.E.—destroyer escort. Not at all like a lot of those rustbuckets in tramp service."

Quent toyed with his food. "It's fairly common, isn't it, for several conversions to be made over the life of a ship?"

"Exigencies of trade." Medler nodded. "Hard to say where it was done, but Pakistan has a shipbreaking industry and rerolling mills in Karachi." He shook his head and grinned. "I think they could cobble you up a new ship from the stuff they salvage. We've refused to allow some old buckets into the bay; they're rusted out so far, you step in the wrong place on deck and your foot will go right through. But not the *Ras Ormara*; I'd serve on her myself, if her bottom's anything like her topside."

"I thought you did an, uh, inspection," said Dana.

"Walk-through. We didn't do it as thoroughly as we might if we'd found anything abovedecks. She's so clean I understand why Park became nervous. Barring the military—one of our cutters, for instance—you just don't find that kind of sterile environment in maritime service. Not even a converted D.E."

"No," Dana insisted, and made a delicate twirl with her fork. "I meant afterward."

Medler blinked. "If you want to talk about it, go ahead. I can't. You know that."

Dana, whom I'd once thought of as a teen mascot, patted his forearm like a den mother. I didn't know which of them I wanted more to kick under the table. "I go way back with these two, Reuben, and they're under contract with confidentiality. But this may not be the place."

I was already under contract? Well, only if I were working under Quent's license, and if he'd told her so. Still, I was getting fed up with how little I knew. "For God's sake," I said, "just the short form, okay?"

"For twenty years we've had ways to search sea floors for aircraft flight recorders," Dana told me. "Don't you think the Coast Guard might have similar gadgets to look at a hull?"

"For what?"

"Whatever," Medler replied, uneasy about it. "I ordered it after the Park interview. When you know how Hughes built the CIA's *Glomar Explorer*, you know a ship can have a lot of purposes that aren't obvious at the waterline. Figure it out for yourself," he urged.

That spook ship Hughes's people built had been designed to be flooded and to float vertically, sticking up from the water like a fisherman's bobbin. Even the tabloids had exploited it. I thought about secret hatches for underwater demolition teams, torpedo tubes— "Got it," I said. "Any and every unfriendly use I can dream up. Can I ask what they found?"

"Not a blessed thing," said Reuben Medler. "If it weren't for D—Agent Martin here, I'd be writing reports on why I insisted."

"He insisted because the Bureau did," Dana put in. "We've had some vague tips about a major event, planned by nice folks with the same traditions as those who, uh, bugged Tel Aviv."

The Tel Aviv Bug had been anthrax. If the woman who'd smuggled it into Israel hadn't somehow flunked basic hygiene and collapsed with a skinful of the damned bacilli, it would've caused more deaths than it did. "So you found nothing, but you want a follow-up with this Park guy. He's probably catting around and will show up with a hangover when the ship's ready to sail," I said. "I thought crew members had to keep in touch with the charter service."

"They do," said Dana. "And with a full complement of two dozen, only a few of the crew went ashore. But Park has vanished. Sonmiani claims they'll have still another third engineer when the slurry tanks are cleaned and the new cargo's pumped aboard."

"And we'd prefer they didn't sail before we have another long talk with Park," Medler said. "I'm told the FBI has equipment like an unobtrusive lie detector."

"Voice-stress analyzer," Dana corrected. "Old hardware, new twists. But chiefly, we're on edge because Park has dropped out of sight."

Quent: "But I thought he told you why."

"He told me why he was worried," Medler agreed. "But he also said the *Ras Ormara* will be bound for Pusan with California-manufactured industrial chemicals, a nice tractable cargo, to his own homeport. He was determined to stay with it, worried or not. Of course it's possible he simply changed his mind."

"But we'd like to know," Dana said. "We want to know sufficiently that—well." She looked past us toward the ceiling as if an idea had just occurred to her. Suuure. "Sometimes things happen. Longshoremen's strike,—" She saw my sudden glance, and she'd always been alert to nuance. "No, we haven't, but little unforeseen problems arise. Sonmiani is already dealing with a couple of them. Assuming they don't have the clout to build a fire under someone at the ambassador level, there could be one or two more if we find a solid reason. Or if you do."

"I take it Harve and I can move overtly on this," Quent said, "so long as we're not connected to government."

Medler looked at Dana, who said, "Exactly. Low-profile, showing your private investigator's I.D. if necessary. You're known well enough that anyone checking on you would be satisfied you're not us. Of course you've got to have a client of record, so we're furnishing one."

I noticed that Quent seemed interested in something across the room, but he refocused on Dana Martin. "As licensed privateers, we aren't required to name a client or divulge any other details of the case. Normally it would be shaving an ethical guideline."

"But you wouldn't be," Dana said. "You'd be giving up a few details of a cover story. Nothing very dramatic, just imply that our missing man is a prodigal son. Park Soon's father in Pusan would be unlikely to know he's put you on retainer."

Quent: "Because he can't afford us?"

Dana, with the shadow of a smile: "Because he's been deceased for years. I'll give you the details on that tomorrow, Quent. Uhm, Quent?"

But my pal, whose attention had been wandering again, was now leaning toward me with an unQuentish grin. "Harve," he said softly, "third counter stool from the front, late twenties, blond curls, Yamaha cycle jacket. Could be packing."

"Several guys in here probably are," I said.

"But I'm not carrying certified copies of their bail bonds, and I do have one for Robert Rooney, bail jumper. That's Bobby."

Dana and Medler both looked toward the counter, at me, and at Quent, but let their expressions complain.

"You wouldn't," I said.

"It's my bleeding job," said Quent. "Wait outside. I'll flush him out gently, and if gentle doesn't work, don't let him reach into that jacket."

I was already standing up. "Back shortly, folks. Don't forget my pie à la mode."

"I don't believe this," I heard Medler say as I moved toward the old-fashioned revolving door.

"Santa Clara County Jail is on Hedding, less than a mile from here. We'll be back before you know it," Quent soothed, still seated, giving me time to evaporate.

I saw the bail-jumper watching me in a window reflection, but I gave him no reason to jump. I would soon learn he was just naturally jumpy, pun intended. Can't say it was really that long a fight, though. I pushed through the door and into the San Jose night, realizing we could jam Rooney in it if he tried to run out. And have him start shooting through heavy glass partitions, maybe; sometimes my first impulses are subject to modest criticism.

Outside near the entrance, melding with evening shadow, I listened to the buzz and snap of Joe's old neon sign. I could still see our quarry, and now Quent was strolling behind diners at the counter, apparently intent on watching the chef toss a blazing skilletful of mushrooms. Quent reached inside his coat; brought out a folded paper, his face innocent of stress. Then he said something to the seated Rooney.

Rooney turned only his head, very slowly, nodded, shrugged, and let his stool swivel to face Quent. He grinned.

It's not easy to get leverage with only your buns against a low seat back, but Rooney managed it, lashing both feet out to Quent's legs, his arms windmilling as he bulled past my pal. I heard a shout, then a clamor of voices as Quent staggered against a woman seated at the nearest table. I stepped farther out of sight as Bobby Rooney hurled himself against the inertia of that big revolving door.

He used both hands, and he was sturdier than he had looked, bursting outside an arm's length from me. Exactly an arm's length, because without moving my feet, just as one Irishman to another I clotheslined him under the chin. He went down absolutely horizontal, his head making a nice bonk on the sidewalk, and if he'd had any brains they would've rattled like castanets. He didn't even pause, bringing up both legs, then doing a gymnast's kick so that he was suddenly on his feet in a squat, one arm flailing at me. The other hand snaked into his jacket pocket before I could close on him.

What came out of his right-hand pocket was very small, but it had twin barrels on one end and as he leaped up, Rooney's arm swung toward me. Meanwhile I'd taken two steps forward, and I snatched at his wrist. I caught only his sleeve, but when I heaved upward on it, his hand and the little derringer pocketgun disappeared into the sleeve. A derringer is double-barreled, the barrel's so short its muzzle blast is considerable, and confined in that sleeve it flash-burnt his hand while muffling the sound. The slug headed skyward. Bobby Rooney headed down San Carlos Avenue, hopping along crabwise because I had held on to that sleeve long enough that when he jerked away, his elbow was caught halfway out.

I'm not much of a distance runner, but for fifty meters I can move out at what I imagined was a brisk pace. Why Bobby didn't just stop and fire point-blank through that sleeve I don't know; I kept waiting for it, and one thing I never learned to do was make myself a small target. Half a block later he was still flailing his arm to dislodge the sleeve, and I was still three long steps behind, and that's when a conservative dress suit passed me. Quentin Kim was wearing it at the time, outpacing me despite that limp. He simply spun Bobby Rooney down, standing on his jacket which pinned him down on his back at the mouth of an alley.

I grabbed a handful of blond curls, knelt on Bobby's right sleeve because his gun hand was still in it, and made the back of his head tap the sidewalk. "Harder every time," I said, blowing like a whale. "How many times—before you relax?" Another tap. "Take your time. I can do this—for hours."

As quickly as Bobby Rooney had decided to fight, he reconsidered, his whole body going limp, eyes closed.

"Get that little shooter—out of his sleeve," I said to Quent, who wasn't even winded but rubbed his upper thigh, muttering to himself.

Quent took the derringer, flicked his key-ring Maglite, then brought that wrinkled paper out of his inside coat pocket and shook it open. "Robert Rooney," he intoned.

Still holding on to Rooney's hair, I gazed up. "What the hell? Is this some kind of new Miranda bullshit, Quent?"

"No, it's not required. It's just something I do that clarifies a relationship."

"Relationship? This isn't a relationship, this is a war."

"Not mutually exclusive. You've never been married, have you," Quent said. He began again: "Robert Rooney, acting as agent for the hereafter-named person putting up bail . . ."

I squatted there until Quent had finished explaining that Rooney was, by God, the property of the bondsman named and could be pursued even into his own toilet without a warrant, and that his physical condition upon delivery to the appropriate county jail depended entirely on his temperament. When Quent was done I said, "He may not even hear you."

"He probably does, but it doesn't matter. I hear me," Quent said mildly. A bounty hunter with liberal scruples was one for the books, but I guess Quent wrote his own book.

"How far is your car?"

"Two blocks. Here," Quent said, and handed me the derringer with one unfired chamber. I knew what he said next was for Rooney's ears more than mine. "You can shoot him, just try not to kill him right away. That's only if he tries to run again."

"If he does," I said, "I'll still have his scalp for an elephant's merkin."

Quent laughed as he hurried away, not even limping. "Now there's an image I won't visit twice," he said.

Twenty minutes later we returned from the county lockup with a receipt, and to this day I don't know what Bobby Rooney's voice sounds like. The reason why those kicks hadn't ruined Quent's legs were that, under his suit pants, my pal wore soccer pro FlexArmor over his knees and shins for bounty hunting. He'd suggested Original Joe's to Dana because, among other good reasons, Rooney's ex-girlfriend claimed he hung out there a lot. Since Rooney was dumb as an ax handle, Quent figured the chances of a connection were good. He could combine business with pleasure, and show a pair of Feds how efficient we were. Matter of fact, I was so efficient I wound up with a derringer in my pocket. Fortunes of war, not that I was going to brag about it to the Feds.

Dana and Reuben Medler were still holding down the booth when we returned, Medler half-resigned, half-amused. Dana was neither. "I hope your victim got away," she said. If she'd been a cat, her fur would've been standing on end.

Quent flashed our receipt for Rooney's delivery and eased into the booth. "A simple commercial transaction, Agent Martin," he said, ignoring her hostility. "My apologies."

She wasn't quite satisfied. "Can I expect this to happen again?"

"Not tonight," Quent said equably.

It must've been that smile of his that disarmed her because Dana subsided over coffee and dessert. When it became clear that Quent would take the San Francisco side—it has a sizable Korean population—while I worked the Oakland side of the bay, Reuben Medler told me where I'd find the *Ras Ormara*, moored on the edge of Richmond near a gaggle of chemical production facilities.

Eventually Dana handed Quent a list of the crew with temporary addresses for the few who went ashore. "Sonmiani's California rep keeps tabs on their crews," she explained. "I got this from Customs."

Medler put in, "Customs has a standard excuse for wanting the documentation; cargo manifest, tonnage certificate, stowage plan, and other records."

"But not you," I said to Dana.

She shook her head. "Even if we did, the Bureau wouldn't step forward to Sonmiani. We leave that to you, although Sonmiani's man in Oakland, ah, Norman Goldman by name, has a clean sheet and appears to be clean. We feel direct contacts of that sort should be made as—what did you call it, Quentin? A simple commercial transaction. Civilians like to talk. If Goldman happened to mention us to the wrong person, the ship's captain for example, someone might abort whatever they're up to. If they see you rooting around, they'll assume it's just part of a routine private investigation."

Maybe I was still pissed that our teen mascot had become our boss. "Implying sloth and incompetence," I murmured.

"You said it, not I," she replied sweetly. "At least Mr. Goldman seems well enough educated that he would never mistake you for an agent."

"You've run a check on him, then," said Quent.

"Of course. Majored in business at Michigan, early promotion, young man on the way up. And I suspect Sonmiani's Islamic crew members will watch their steps around a bright Jewish guy," she added, looking over the check.

Quent drained his teacup. "We'll try to keep it simple; Park Soon could show up tomorrow. Then we'll see whether we need to talk with this Goldman. Is that suitable?"

Quent asked with genuine deference, and Dana paused before she nodded. It struck me then that Quent was making a point of showing obedience to his boss. And his quick glance at me suggested that I might try it sometime.

I knew he was right, but it would have to be some other time. I shook hands again with Reuben Medler, exchanged cards with him, and turned to Dana. "Thanks for the feed. Maybe next time we can avoid a floor show."

She looked at Medler and shook her head, and I left without remarking that she had a lot of seasoning ahead of her.

Two

It was Quent's suggestion that I case the location of the *Ras Ormara* itself, herself, whatever. Meanwhile he made initial inquiries across the bay alone in his natural camouflage, in the area everyone calls Chinatown though it was home to several Asiatic colonies. It was my idea to bring my StudyGirl to record a look at this shipshape ship we'd heard so much about, and Quent suggested I do it without making any personal contacts that required I.D.

StudyGirls were new then, cleverly named so that kids who wanted the spendy toys—meaning all kids—would have leverage with Dad and Mom. Even the early versions were pocket-sized and would take a two-inch *Britannica* floppy, but they would also put TV broadcasts on the rollout screen or play mini-CDs and action games, and make video recordings as well. It was already common practice to paint over the indicator lights so nobody knew when you were videorecording. I'll bet a few kids actually used them for schoolwork, too.

I took the freeway as far as Richmond, got off at Carlson Boulevard, and puzzled my way through the waterfront's industrial montage. Blank-fronted metal buildings with ramped loading docks meant warehousing of imports and exports, and somewhere in there were a few boxcarloads of Peruvian balsa logs. Composite panels of carbon fiber and balsa sandwich were much in demand at that time among builders of off-road racers for their light weight and stiffness. I enjoyed a moment of déjà future vu at the thought that I might be using some of the *Ras Ormara*'s balsa for my project in a few months.

Unless my woolgathering got me squashed like a bug underfoot. I had to dodge thrumming diesel-electric rigs that outclamored the cries of gulls and ignored my pickup as unworthy of notice. Hey, they were making a buck, and this was their turf.

In a few blocks-long stretches, the warehouses gave way to fencing topped with razor wire, enforced isolation for the kind of small-time chemical processing plants that looked like brightly painted guts of the biggest dinosaurs ever. Now and then I could spot the distant San Rafael Bridge through the tanks, reactor vessels, piping, and catwalks that loomed like little skeletal skyscrapers, throwing early shadows across the street. You knew without a glance when you were passing warehouses because of the echoes and the sour, last-week's-fast-food odor that drew those scavenging gulls. The chemical production plants no longer stank so much since the City of Richmond got serious about its air. And beyond all this at an isolated wharf, berthed next to a container ship like a racehorse beside a Clydesdale, the *Ras Ormara* gleamed in morning light. I wondered why a ship like that was called a "she" when it had such racy muscular lines, overlaid by spidery cargo cranes and punctuated by the gleam of glass. I pointedly focused on the nearby container vessel, walking past an untended gate onto the dock, avoiding flatbed trucks that galumphed in and out. I had my StudyGirl in hand for videotaping, neither flourishing nor hiding it. In semishorts, argyle socks, and short sleeves, I hoped I looked like a typical Midwestern tourist agog over, golly gee, these great big boats. If challenged I could always choose whether to brazen it out with my I.D.

I strolled back, paying casual attention to the *Ras Ormara*, listening to the sounds of engine-driven pressure washers and recording the logos on two trucks with hoses that snaked up and back to big tanks mounted behind the truck cabs. I could see men operating the chassis-mounted truck consoles, wearing headsets. Somehow I'd expected more noise and melodrama in cleaning the ship's big cargo tanks.

Words like "big" and "little" are inadequate where a cargo vessel, even one considered small, is concerned. I guess that's what numbers are for. The *Ras Ormara* was almost three hundred feet stem to stern, the length of a football field, and where bare metal showed it appeared to be stainless steel. All that cleaning was concentrated ahead of the ship's glassed bridge, where a half dozen metal domes, each five yards across, stood in ranks well above the deck level. Two rows of three each; and the truck hoses entered the domes through open access ports big enough to drop a truck tire through. Or a man. Welded ladders implied that men might do just that.

I suppose I could have climbed one of the gangways up to the ship's deck. It was tempting, but Quent had told me—couched as a suggestion—not to. It is simply amazing how obedient I can be to a boss who is not overbearing. I moseyed along, hoping I stayed mostly out of sight behind those servicing trucks without seeming to try. From an open window behind the *Ras Ormara's* bridge came faint strains of someone's music, probably from a CD. It sounded like hootchie-kootchie scored for three tambourines and a parrot, and I thought it might be Egyptian or some such.

Meanwhile, a bulky yellow extraterrestrial climbed from one of those domes trailing smaller hoses, and made his way carefully down the service ladder. When he levered back his helmet and left it with its hoses on deck, I could see it was just a guy with hair sweat-plastered to his forehead, wearing a protective suit you couldn't miss on a moonless midnight. My luck was holding; he continued down the gangway to the nearest truck. Meanwhile I ambled back in his direction, stowing away my StudyGirl.

The space-suited guy, his suit smeared with fluid, was talking with the truck's console operator, both standing next to the chassis as they shared a cigarette. Even then smoking was illegal in public, but give a guy a break. . . .

They broke off their conversation as I drew near, and the console man nodded. "Help you?"

I shrugged pleasantly and remembered to talk high in my throat because guys my size are evidently less threatening as tenors. "Just sightseeing. Never see anything like this in Omaha." I grinned.

"Don't see much of this anywhere, thank God," said the sweaty one, and they laughed together. "Thirsty work. Not for the claustrophobe, either."

"Is this how you fill 'er up?" I hoped this was naive enough without being idiotic. I think I flunked because they laughed again. The sweaty one said, "Would I be smoking?" When I looked abashed, he relented. "We're scouring those stainless tanks. Got to be pharmaceutically free of a vegetable slurry before they pump in the next cargo."

"Those domes sitting on deck," I guessed.

"Hell, that's just the hemispherical closures," said the console man.

"The tanks go clear down into the hold," said his sweaty friend.

I blinked. "Twenty feet down?"

"More like forty," he said.

The console man glanced at his wristwatch, gave a meaningful look to his friend; took the cigarette back. "And we got a special eco-directive on flushing these after this phase. We have to double soak and agitate with filterable solvent, right to the brim, fifty-two thousand gallons apiece. Pain in the ass."

"Must take a lot of time," I said, thinking about Dana Martin's ability to make people jump through additional hoops on short notice, without showing her hand.

"Twice what we'd figured," said Consoleman. "I thought the charter-service rep would scream bloody murder, but he didn't even haggle. Offered a bonus for early completion, in fact. Speaking of which," he said, and fixed Sweatman with a wry smile.

"Yeah, yeah," said his colleague, and turned toward the *Ras Ormara*. "For us, time really is money. But that ten-minute break is in the standard contract. Anyhow, without my support hoses it's getting hot as hell in this outfit."

"Hold still, it's gonna dribble," I said. I found an old Kleenex in my pocket, and used it to wipe around the chin plate of Sweatman's suit, then put it back in my pocket.

"Guess I'm lucky to be in the wrought-iron biz," I said. With a smithy for a hobby, I could fake my way through that if necessary.

"My regards to Omaha," said Consoleman. "And by the way, you really shouldn't be here without authorization. Those guys are an antsy lot," he said, jerking his head toward the bridge. It was as nice a "buzz off, pal" request as I'd ever had.

I didn't look up. I'd seen faces staring down in our direction, some with their heads swathed in white. "Okay, thanks. Just seeing this has been an education," I said.

"If the skipper unlimbers his tongue on you, I hope your education isn't in languages," Consoleman joked.

I laughed, waved, and took my time walking back to the gate, stopping on the way to gaze at the much larger container ship as if my attention span played no favorites.

When I got back to my Toyota I rummaged in the glove box and found my stash of quart-sized evidence baggies. Then I carefully sealed that soggy old Kleenex inside one and scribbled the date and the specimen's provenance. I'd seen Sweatman climb out of a cargo tank of the *Ras Ormara* and that fluid had come out with him. Quent might not do handsprings, but the Feebs got off on stuff like that.

I took a brief cell call from Quent shortly before noon, while I was stoking up at one of the better restaurants off Jack London Square. The maître d' had sighed when he saw my tourist getup. Quent sighed, too, when I told him where I was. "Look, the Feds are paying, and I keep receipts," I reminded him.

He said he was striking out in Chinatown, just as he had in hospitals and clinics, but the Oakland side had its own ethnic neighborhoods. "I thought you might want to ride with me this afternoon," he said.

"Where do we meet? I have something off the ship you might want Dana to have analyzed," I said.

"You went aboard? Harve,—oh well. Just eat slowly. It's not that far across the Bay Bridge," he replied.

"Gotcha. And I didn't go aboard, bossman, but I think I have a sample of what was actually in the *Ras Ormara*'s tanks, whatever the records might say. You'll be proud of your humble apprentice, but right now my rack of lamb calls. Don't hurry," I said, and put away my phone.

Quent arrived in time for my coffee and ordered tea. I let him play back my StudyGirl video recording as far as it went, and took the evidence baggie from my shirt pocket as I reported the rest. "We have the name of the pressure-washing firm. No doubt they can tell some curious Fed what cleaning chemicals they use. What's left should be traces of what those tanks really carried," I said.

Quent said Dana's people had already analyzed samples of the stuff provided by Customs. "But they'll be glad to have it confirmed this way. Nice going." He pocketed the baggie and pretended not to notice that I made a proper notation on my lunch receipt. We walked out into what was rapidly becoming a furry overcast, and I took the passenger's seat in his Volvo.

Quent said we'd try an Oakland rooming house run by a Korean family. From the list we had, he knew a pair of the *Ras Ormara*'s crew were staying there. "You, uh, might want to draft your report while I go in," he said as he turned off the Embarcadero. "Shouldn't be long."

"I thought you wanted me with you."

"I did. Then I saw how you're dressed."

"I'm a tourist!"

"You're a joke with pale shins. I can't do a serious interview with a foreign national if you're visible; how can I have his full attention when he's wondering whether Bluto is going to start juggling plates behind me?"

I saw his point and promised to bring a change of clothes next time. Quent found the place, in a row of transient quarters an Oakland beat cop would call flophouses. Without a place to park, he turned the Volvo over to me. "I'll call when I'm done," he said, and disappeared into the three-story stucco place.

I did find a parking spot eventually. My printer was at home, but I stored my morning's case report on StudyBint. Quent called not long afterward and, because he wore a frown only when puzzling things out, I hardly gave him time to take the wheel. "Something already?"

He thought about it a moment before replying. "Not on Park. Not directly, at any rate. But I'm starting to understand why our missing engineer was uneasy." When giving Park's name he had mentioned the ship to the rooming-house proprietor, who said she hadn't heard of Park but named the two crew members who were there. The Korean, Hong Chee, she described as taller than average, late thirties. The second man, one Ali Ghaffar, was older; perhaps Indian. Pretending surprise at this lucky accident, Quent asked to speak with them.

Hong Chee was out, but Quent found his roommate Ghaffar in the room, preternaturally quiet and alert. Ghaffar, a middle-aged Paki, was a studious-looking sort wearing one of those white cloth doodads wound around his head, who had evidently been reading one of two well-thumbed leather-bound books. Quent couldn't read even the titles though he got the impression they might be religious tomes.

Ghaffar spoke fair English. He showed some interest in the fact that an Asian speaking perfect American English was hoping to trace the movements of an engineer off the *Ras Ormara*. Quent explained that Park's family was concerned enough to hire private investigators, blah-blah, merely wanted assurance that Park hadn't met with foul play, et cetera.

Ghaffar said he had only a nodding acquaintance with Park. He couldn't, or more likely wouldn't, say whether Park had made any friends aboard ship, and had no idea whether Park had friends in the Bay Area. Ghaffar and Hong Chee had seen the engineer, he thought, the day before in some Richmond bar, and Park was looking fit, but they hadn't talked. That's when Quent noticed the wastebasket's contents. He began pacing around, stroking his chin, trying to scan everything in the room without being obvious while doing it.

Personal articles were aligned on lamp tables as if neatness counted, beds made, nothing out of place. Quent took his nail clippers out and began idly tossing them in one hand as he dreamed up more questions, and he just happened to drop his clippers into the wastebasket, apologizing as he fished them out with slow gropes of bogus clumsiness.

Quent realized that Ghaffar was waiting with endless calm for this ten-thumbed gumshoe to go away, volunteering little, responding carefully. Quent said he'd like to talk with Hong Chee sometime if possible and passed his cell-phone card to Ghaffar, who accepted it solemnly, and then Quent left and called me to be picked up.

"So I ask you," Quent said rhetorically: "What would a devout Moslem, who adheres to correct practices alone in his room, have been doing in a gin mill, with or without his buddy? Not likely. I don't think he saw Park, I think he wanted me to think Park was healthy. And you haven't asked me about the trash basket."

"Didn't want to interrupt. What'd you see?"

"Candy wrappers and an empty plastic pop bottle. Oh, yes," he added with studied neglect, "and an airline ticket. I didn't have time to read it closely, but I caught an Asian name—not Hong Chee's—Oakland International, and a departure date." He paused before he specified it.

"Christ, that's tomorrow," I said.

"I'm not through. Ghaffar is on the crew list as the ship's machinist. You ever see a machinist's hands?"

"Sure, like a blacksmith's. Like he force-feeds cactus to Rottweilers for kicks."

"Well, at the least they're callused and scarred. Not Ali Ghaffar. He may know how to use a lathe, but I'd bet against it."

"Then who's the real machinist? Ships have to have one."

"Do they? From what Medler and you tell me, and from what I saw on your video, the *Ras Ormara* might go a year without needing that kind of attention."

He checked some notes and drove silently across town like he knew where he was going. Presently he said, as if to himself: "So Hong Chee has dumped what looks like a perfectly good airline ticket for somebody out of Oakland. Wish I'd seen where to. More particularly, I wish I knew how he could afford to junk it. And why he knows to junk it the day before the flight."

"Me, teacher," I said, putting up a hand and waving it. "Call on me."

"Tell the class, Master Rackham," he said, going along with it.

"Somebody else is funding him better than most, and he's changed his departure plans because La Martin and company have put the brakes on whatever he had in mind."

"Take your seat, you've left the heart of my question untouched. Is he worried for the same reasons as Park?"

"Suppose we give him a chance to tell us," I said.

"Maybe we'll do that. But I'm not sure he's making plans for his own departure. Another Asian?"

"At a guess, I'd say the name is unimportant. How many sets of I.D. might he have, Quent?"

After a long pause, he exhaled for what seemed like forever. "Harve, you are definitely paranoid—I'm happy to say. Now you've torn the lid off this little box with a missing engineer in it, and I find a much bigger box inside, so to speak. And there wasn't a second ticket there—so Ghaffar may still intend to go back aboard. Or not. But I'll tell you this: Our machinist is no machinist, and he certainly isn't spending his time ashore as if he had the usual things in mind."

I couldn't fault his reasoning. "So where are we headed?"

"Korean social club. Maybe we'll find Hong Chee there."

"And not Park Soon?" All I got was a shrug and a glance, and I didn't like the glance. Quent found a slot for the Volvo in a neighborhood of shops with signs in English and the odd squiggles that weren't quite Chinese characters; Hangul has a script all its own. "You might try calling Dana while I'm inside," Quent said. "Let her know we've got a gooey Kleenex for her."

So I did, and was told she was in the field, and I tried her cell phone. She sounded like she was in a salt mine and none too pleased about it. She perked up slightly at my offer of the evidence. "I'll pick it up when we're through here," she said, and sneezed. "I thought the incoming cargo might be dirty, but the spectral analyzer says no. A few pallets are too heavy, though. My God, but wood dust is pervasive!"

"You're in a warehouse," I said, glad that she couldn't see me grinning. Climbing around on pallets of logs probably hadn't been high on her list of adventures when she joined up. "I haven't seen the stuff, but if it's that dusty maybe it's not plain logs. Probably rough-sawn, right?"

She said it was. "What would you know about it?"

"I've seen how balsa is used in high-tech panels. The stuff is graded by weight per cubic meter and it varies from featherweight, which is highly prized, to the density of pine. In other words, pallets could vary by a factor of three or so."

"Well, damn it to hell," she said. "Excuse me. Scratch one criterion. What's the significance of its being sawn?"

"Just that it may make it easier for you to see whether some of it's been cut lengthwise with a very fine kerf and glued back."

"What's a kerf?"

"The slot made by a saw. Balsa can be slitted with a very thin saw-blade. It occurs to me that it might be the lighter timbers you should be checking for hollowed interiors. Bags of white powder aren't that heavy, Dana."

I think she cussed again before she sneezed. She said, "Thanks," as if it were squeezed out of her.

"But I don't think you'll find anything," I said.

She demanded, "Why not?" the way a kid says it when told she can't ride behind the nice stranger on his Superninja bike.

"I just feel like whatever's being delivered, if anything, hasn't been. The monkey wrench your people threw into their schedule didn't delay those pallets—*gesundheit*—but they're behaving as if you did delay something. They're waiting, apparently with patience."

She said she'd get back to me and snapped off. To kill time, I played back our conversation on StudyBabe. Dana had a spectral analyzer with her? I had thought they were big lab gadgets. Right, and computers were room-sized—once upon a time.

While I was still muttering "Duhh" and thinking about possible uses of Dana's gadgetry, Quent came down out of a stairwell in a hurry. He motioned for me to drive, pocketing his phone. "You love to drive like there's no tomorrow, and I don't. Please don't bend the Volvo," he begged. "Just get us across the bridge to Jackson and Taylor."

While I drove, he filled me in on his fresh lead. He'd struck out again upstairs, but had just taken a call on his cell phone from Ali Ghaffar. His buddy Hong, said the Paki, had returned. Ghaffar had asked about Park. Oh, said Hong, that was easy; back at the gin mill, Park Soon had said he was considering a move to a nice room in San Francisco for the rest of his time ashore. Corner of Jackson and Taylor.

"Smack-dab middle of Chinatown. Didn't say which corner, I suppose," I said, overtaking a taxi on the right.

"No such luck. But there can't be more than a half dozen places with upscale rooms on or near that corner. We can canvass them all in twenty minutes."

I tossed a look at Quent. "You speak directly to Hong?"

"Watch the road, for Christ's sweet sake," he gritted. "I asked, but Ali said he was gone again. Very handy."

"That's what I was thinking," I said, swerving to miss a pothole on the way to the Bay Bridge on-ramp.

Quent closed his eyes. "Just tell me when we get there."

To calm him down I played my conversation with Dana. It pacified him somewhat, and I turned down the Volvo's wick nearing Chinatown, which was a traffic nightmare long before the twenty-first century.

I chose a pricey parking lot near Broadway, and we jostled our way through the sidewalk chaos together. By agreement, Quent peeled off to take the two west corners of the intersection. Because some of the nicer little Chinatown hotels aren't obvious, I had to ask a restaurant cashier. When she hesitated, I said I had a job offer for an Asian gent and knew only that he'd taken a nice room thereabouts. I said I hadn't understood him very well.

Evidently, Asiatics have their own privately printed local phone books, but she didn't hand it over and I couldn't have read what I saw anyhow. She gave me five addresses, and three of them were on Quent's side. I tipped her, hoping I'd remember to jot it down, and found the first address almost next door.

If there's a small Chinatown hotel on a street floor, it's one I never saw. I climbed three narrow flights before I saw what proved to be a tiny lobby through a bead curtain. A young Asiatic greeted me, very courteously, his speech and dress yuppily American. He heard my brief tale sympathetically. Sorry, he said, but no young person of either gender had registered in several days. Would I mind describing the employment I had to offer?

I said it was a marine engineer's job, and I swear he said, "Aw shit, and me a journalism major," before he wished me good day, no longer interested in my problems.

I crossed the street and began to search for the second address when my phone clucked. "Bingo," Quent said with no preliminaries. "But no joy. Meet me at the car in ten. Until then you don't know me." No way I could mistake the implication.

He didn't sound happy, and when I saw him on the street he had turned away, heading down Jackson. It's a one-way street, and he walked counter to the traffic flow, something you do when you suspect someone may be trying to tail you in a car.

So I did the same on Taylor, which is also one-way, doubling back after a long block to approach Quent's car on Jones—again counter to one-way traffic. If anyone followed me on foot, he was too good for me to make him.

I had paid the lot's fee and was waiting in the Volvo when Quent appeared. "Oakland it is," he said, racking his seat back to disappear below the windowsill. As I sought an on-ramp he said, "A man calling himself Park Soon rented a room for a week, not two hours ago; one flight up, quiet, expensive. Told the concierge he might be staying with a friend for a night or so but please to hold his messages and take names."

"He's not hard up for cash," I said.

"He's also about my height and age," said Quent, who was five-eight, pushing forty.

I'd had Park's description. "The hell he is," I said.

"The man who rented that room with a cash advance is," Quent said. "Unless the lady was pulling my leg. And why would she if she wanted me to think it was Park? Park Soon is five-three. What's wrong with this picture, Harve?"

"I might know if I got a look inside that room."

"That was my thought, but it's a risky tactic in a subculture that's understandably wary, so I didn't even try. The Feds can do it if they want to. They know how to lean on people to, ah, I think the phrase is, 'compel acquiescence.' "

"Our own little Ministry of Fear," I observed.

"Everybody's got 'em, Harve. I even have one," he said with a half smile, and pointed a finger at my breast. "And if I had to choose between Uncle's and the ones run by people who call him the Great Satan, I choose Uncle.

"Meanwhile, we don't know who's pushing our buttons, waiting for us to show up, and watching us flail around all over hell. But I'd bet someone is, and I'd just as soon they didn't pin a tail on us."

I nodded, pointing the Volvo onto the Bay Bridge. "You don't think Park could somehow be in on this," I suggested.

"Not in any way he'd like. I don't think Park is where anyone will find him anytime soon," Quent replied grimly. "Whoever tried to create a fresh trail for him would probably be pretty confident he's not leaving his own trail of crumbs. I really don't like that idea, Harve. Well, maybe I'm wrong. I hope so."

"When are we gonna drop that one on Dana?"

He levered himself and his seat erect; opened his phone. "Right away. She's probably still in the field. I will bet you a day's expenses Mr. Ghaffar knows who took that room for Park; the description fits Hong, of course."

I nodded. "Should we go back and have a talk with him now?"

"Not yet, I want to be very calm for that, and at the moment I am peeved. I am provoked."

"You are royally pissed," I supplied. He nodded. "Me too," I added, as he punched Dana's number.

It was nearing rush hour by that time, but with a few extra twists and turns, I managed to satisfy myself that we weren't tailed while Quent spoke with our pet Feeb. She said she'd meet us in twenty at the boathouse on Lake Merritt, in residential Oakland.

She was as good as her word, looking as frazzled as she'd sounded earlier but even more interesting, which irked me. No Feeb had the right to look that good. She took the perimeter footpath and we caught up to her, two visitors hitting on a cutie. When we found a park bench, she plopped her shoulder bag next to me. "If that specimen's bagged, stuff it in here," she said.

"And if not, where do I stuff it?"

She simply looked toward my partner. "While he figures out the answer to his own question, Quent: We've still drawn blanks at every bus terminal, airport and rail connection between Vallejo and Santa Clara. What's your best guess on Park?"

Quent told her while I put my evidence in her bag. At his bidding I let her review the video I'd made. He described the timing of the connections we'd made and blunted the conclusions he and I had reached together. "Wherever Park is, and for whatever reason, I just have a suspicion he won't surface again in the Bay Area," he said. Then he described the Chinatown lead and told her flatly why he believed it was fugazi, a false trail.

She turned to me. "You're uncharacteristically silent. What do you think?"

"Much the same. And I think Quent ought to borrow your spectral analyzer, if it's small enough to put in a Bianchi rig."

"Mine won't fit in any shoulder holster I've seen," she said, "but some will. The covert units are slower, though. Encryption-linked to a lab in Sunnyvale, which is why they can be so small. I've seen one implanted in a LOC-8. And they are very, very expensive," she added. A LOC-8 was one of the second-generation GPS units with two-way comm and a memory just in case you wondered where you'd been. Combined with a linked-up analyzer it would be worth a new Volvo.

"You want me to ship out on the *Ras Ormara* or something," Quent said to me, amused.

Dana turned to him again. "Better you than King Kong here. You look the part, and you could talk with the crew more easily."

Quent: "You're not serious."

Dana: "Not actually shipping out, but you might try getting aboard while the new cargo is being loaded. A spectral analyzer needs no more than a whiff to do its job, and I'd hate to try to guess all the ways a cargo can be falsified."

Quent was silent for a time. Then, "I'd never get aboard without the rep's authorization, or the captain's. There goes one layer of our deniability but yes, I could try it. Or Harve could, in a pinch."

We kicked the idea around a bit, and then she excused herself and walked off a ways to use her phone while Quent and I watched boats slice the lake's surface under psychedelic bubbles of sail. When she turned back, she was nodding. "You'll need to learn how to use it," she said.

Quent said if it was anything like the one she carried, she could show us using the specimen I'd collected. She simpered for him and said she should've thought of that herself. We found a picnic table and, sandwiched between me and Quent, Dana pulled a grey, keyboard-faced polymer brick from her bag and opened my evidence baggie next to it.

She stuck her forefinger into a depression labeled CRUCIBLE in the brick and pressed the CRU key. When she withdrew her finger its tip was covered by a filmy shroud, which she quickly stuck into my soggy tissue. Then she pushed the fingertip into another depression and pressed SAMPLE, and the brick whirred very faintly for an instant. Dana withdrew her finger, stripped the film off, and let it drop to the tabletop, an insubstantial wisp. Then after a silence, the brick's little screen began to print gibberish at a rate too fast to follow.

"Essentially, a carbon ribbon wipes a bit of the specimen off the film—don't ask me why it's called a crucible—and analyzes it," Dana murmured.

"What if you're testing the air," Quent asked.

"Wave your finger around for a moment. They say the crucible has microscopic pores on its surface," she explained.

"And how many of those little mouse condoms are inside," I asked, unrolling the discarded wisp for a better look.

"Rackham, you are a piece of work," she said under her breath. Then more loudly, "A hundred or so. By that time the battery needs replacing." When the little screen quit printing Martian, it showed a line with several numbered pips of varied height. She showed us how to query each number, which could be shown as chemical symbols or in words.

The biggest pip was for water, the next was for a ketone solvent, then cellulose, then something called Biopol.

I put my finger out and touched the screen. "Bad actor?"

"No. A polymer from genetically altered canola," she said.

"How in the hell would you know that," I demanded.

She let me stew for a moment. Then, "Customs. Biopol was the plant extract on the manifest. Quent would've figured that out and told you anyway," she added grudgingly.

The trace of $C_{10}H_{18}O$, according to the screen, was eucalyptol. Dana pointed out that the heavily aromatic tree hanging over us was a eucalyptus. "So you see it's pretty accurate."

I said no it wasn't, or it would've told us what the little condom was made of. She said yes it was and positively beamed, explaining that the analyzer knew to ignore the crucible's signature. I gave up. The damned thing was pretty smart at that.

"At least we know the cargo was as advertised," Quent said.

Dana nodded. "Including those pallets of wood. We 'scoped enough of it. So now we focus on the next cargo because no one has come ashore with sizable contraband, and the incoming cargo was clean."

"Unless they'd already pumped it out into those trucks I saw," I said.

"They didn't," said Dana. "One of the cleanout crew is one of ours. You don't need to know which one. The *Ras Ormara* crew are watching him carefully enough to make us even more suspicious."

"I wasted my time then," I said.

"You proved the wharf isn't all that secure," Quent mused, and checked his wrist. "If you're going to spring for a couple of those analyzers, ma'am, we should get to it."

She reminded him that it was a loan, and there'd be only one. Thinking ahead as usual, he said as long as we were going to show our hand overtly as a P.I. team, he'd feel better going aboard if I went along. That meant I could contact the Sonmiani rep myself for the authorization and save some time.

"If you drop me off at my Toyota right away," I said, "I might catch this Goldman guy before he leaves his office."

We quick-marched back to the Volvo and Dana agreed to meet Quent back at the Sunnyvale lab in the South Bay.

I knew I was cutting it close for normal working hours but StudyBimbo found the Sonmiani number while Quent drove me to my pickup. I was in luck; better luck than Quent would find. One Mike Kaplan answered for Sonmiani Shipping, and put me through without rigamarole. That's how my brief platonic fling began with my friend, Norman Goldman.

Three

When you first meet someone of your own sex that you like right away, no matter how hetero you are, you tend to go through something resembling courtship. When the other guy is equally outgoing, ordinary things sink into a temporary limbo: time, previous appointments, even mealtimes.

That's how it had been with me and Quent, and it happened again with Norm. The reason he and his staff assistant had still been at the office was that the Goldman suite and Sonmiani's office were over-and-under, in one of the smaller of those old Alameda buildings respiffed in the style they call Elerath Post-Industrial. I guessed that Sonmiani did a healthy business because the whole two-story structure was theirs.

It was a few minutes after five, but Goldman had said he'd leave the front door unlocked. Following the signs, I moved down a hallway formed by partitioning off a strip from the offices, which I could see through the glassed partition. One man was still in there, wearing a headset and facing a big flat screen. He looked up and waved, and I waved back, and he motioned for me to continue.

The place must have once doubled as a warehouse to judge from the vintage—now trendy again and clean as a cat's fang—freight elevator. I obeyed its sign, tugging up on a barrier which met its descending twin at breastbone height. It whirred to life on its own, a bit shaky after all those years of service, and a moment later I saw a pair of soft Bally sandals come into view under nicely creased allosuede slacks. A pale yellow dress shirt with open collar followed, and finally I saw a tanned, well-chiseled face looking at mine. Hands on hips, he grinned. I couldn't blame him; I'd forgotten how I was dressed.

We introduced ourselves before he jerked a thumb toward the glass door of what might have been an office, but turned out to be his digs. "Sorry about the time," I said, as he ushered me into a big airy room with an eclectic furniture mix: futon, modern couch, inflatable chairs, and a wet bar. And some guy-type pictures, one of which had nothing to do with ships. I thought it would stand a closer look if I got the time. "I tend to forget other people keep regular hours," I added.

"Couldn't resist your opening," he said, with a wave of his hand that suggested I could sit anyplace, and I chose the couch. "Anyone looking for the same crew member I'm looking for, is someone I want to meet. Besides, I've never met a real live—ah, is 'pee-eye' an acceptable buzz phrase?" He had heavy expressive brows that showed honest concern at the question, and big dark eyes that danced with lively interest. "And if it's not, would some sour mash repair the damage?" His accent was Northeast, I guessed New York, and in Big Apple tempo.

"Maybe later," I said. "But P.I. is a term always in vogue."

"As long as I'm on Goldman time, I'll have a beer," he said, and bounced up like a man who played a lot of tennis. He uncapped a Pilsener Urquell from a cooler behind the bar, dipped its neck toward me, then took a swig of the brew before sitting down again. "We've about given up on Park, by the way. Do you suppose the dumb slope has gotten himself in some kind of trouble?"

I admitted I didn't know. "That's what the client wants us to find out. At this point, we're hoping his personal effects aboard ship might point us in some direction. With your authorization, of course, Mr. Goldman. That's what we had in mind."

He nodded abstractedly. "Don't know why not. And hey, my father is Mr. Goldman, God forbid you should mix us up." His grin was quick and infectious. "It's Norm; okay?"

I'd intended to keep this on a semiformal level but with Norm it was simply not possible. I insisted on "Harve," and asked him if he ever felt ill at ease dealing with Moslem skippers. He got a kick from that; a ship's captain might be Allah on the high seas, said Norm, but they knew who signed their checks. "No, it's the poor ragheads who aren't all that easy about me." He laughed. "But Sonmiani's directors include some pretty canny guys. As long as I keep cargoes coming and going better than the last rep, what's to kvetch about?

"Actually the skipper probably will anyway. Gent with a beard, named something-Nadwi. A surly lot, Harve, especially when they're behind schedule." He stopped himself suddenly, shot a quick glance at me. "I don't suppose it's my bosses who put you onto our man's trail. Nobody's told me, but they don't always tell the left hand what its thumb is doing. In a way I hope it is them."

"Against my charter to identify a client, but let's just say it's someone worried about a young guy who's a long way from home," I said. A hint that broad was, as Quent had said, bending the rules a bit but that wasn't why I felt a wisp of guilt. I felt it because I knew our real client wasn't a deceased Korean.

Norm was understanding. He said he'd seen Park Soon exactly once, and that, while he was making his own inquiries, a couple of the crew who had their papers had claimed they saw the engineer in a bar. "They may have been mistaken. Or—hell, I don't know. You couldn't pick a more suspicious mix than we have on the *Ras Ormara*. Schmucks will lie just for practice. You can't entirely blame them, you know. Some skippers skim company food allowances intended for the crews, though I don't believe Nadwi does. I won't have it, by God, and our skippers know it. There's a backhander or two that I can't avoid in half the foreign ports. A lot of their manning agencies are corrupt—"

"Backhander?"

"Kickback, bribe. It's just part of doing business in some ports, and the poor ragheads know it, but they never get a dime of the action. Same-old, same-old," he chanted, shook his head, and took another slug of Urquell.

His shirt pocket warbled, and he tapped it without looking. "Goldman," he said, not bothering to keep the conversation private from me. I was struck by the openness of everything, the offices, Norm's apartment, his dealings with people.

"I'm about squared away here, guv," said a voice with a faint Brit flavor. "Thought I'd nip out for a bite."

"Why not? You've been on Kaplan time for," Norm consulted a very nice Omega on his wrist, "a half hour. Oh! Mike, would you mind running up here a minute first? Gentleman in an unusual business here I want you to meet."

The voice agreed, sounding slightly put-upon, and after he rang off I realized it must be the man I'd seen in the office. It was obvious that Norm Goldman had the same view of formalities that I did, but something about his decisive manner said he might crack a whip if need be. I decided he was older than I'd first thought; maybe forty, but a very hip forty.

Then I took a closer look at that framed picture on his wall, a colorful numbered print showing one formula car overtaking another as a third slid helplessly toward a tire barrier. It was the Grand Prix of Israel, Norm said, adding that he was a hopeless fan. I said I shared his failing; worse, that I had half the bits and pieces of an off-road single-seater in my workshop awaiting the chassis I'd build. He crossed his arms and sighed and, beaming at me, said he might have known.

A quick two-beat knock, and Mike Kaplan entered without waiting. He was swarthy and slim, with very close-cropped dark hair and a nose old-time cartoonists used to draw as a sort of Jewish I.D. His forearms said he'd done a lot of hard work in his time. I got up. Norm didn't, waving a hand from one of us to the other as we shook hands. "Mike Kaplan, Harve Rackham. Mike's my second, and when we're both out of the office, our young tomcat Ira Meltzer holds down the fort. Ira's not in his rooms—where the hell is Ira—as if it were any of my effing business," Norm added with a smile.

Mike said how would he know, and Norm shrugged it off. "Let me guess," Mike said to me. "Wrestler on the telly?"

"That's me," I said, and pulled up my pants. "Harve, the Terrible Tourist."

"Come on," Mike said, because Norm was chuckling.

"I didn't know they existed anymore, Mike, but you are looking at a private eye. In disguise, I hope," said his boss, enjoying the moment. When Mike didn't react, he said, "As in, private investigator. You know: Sam Spade."

Mike Kaplan's face lit up then, and his second glance at me was more appraising and held a lot more friendly interest. "Personally, I'd be inclined to tell him whatever he wants to know," he said to Norm. I must have outweighed him by fifty kilos.

"If you knew, you might. But that would more likely be the job of the *Ras Ormara*'s skipper," Norm replied. "You're better at those names than I am."

Mike shook his head in mock censure. "If you worked at it as I do, you'd get along better with them," he said. "Captain Hassan al-Nadwi, you mean." As Norm nodded, Mike Kaplan went on, "And what do we need from that worthy?"

I told him, and admitted we needed to look at the engineer's effects as soon as possible—meaning the next day.

Mike allowed as how al-Nadwi would put up a pro forma bitch, but it shouldn't really be a problem if I didn't mind a lot of silent stares, and people on board who suddenly seemed to know no English at all. He said he'd call the skipper, stroke him a little, lean on him a little. Al-Nadwi knew who held the face cards. Piece of cake, he said.

Norm said he gathered I wasn't working alone, and I told him about Quentin Kim, apologizing for the oversight. "If Park Soon left any notes in Hangul," I said, "it'd be Quent who could read them. He speaks Korean, of course; that's probably why he got the case. I'd be just as useful chasing down other leads."

Norm donated a quizzical look. "I didn't realize there were other leads."

New friend or not, there are times when you see you're about to step over the line. That can reach around and bite you or your friend sometimes in ways you can't predict. I said, "There may not be. If there were, I couldn't discuss them. 'Course, if Quent stumbled on one, it wouldn't surprise me if you got wind of it later." I let my expression say, *the game's a bastard but rules are rules*.

"I respect that. Can't say I understand it, but I respect it," said Norm.

"Good," I said. "So for all I know, Quent may come alone to the ship and send me off in another direction."

Norm's reaction warmed my heart. "But—I was going to go along because you were," he said. "Spring for lunch, pick your brains about racing,—uh-unh; you've got to go along, Harve."

"I'll try, but it's Quent's call. He's my boss," I said.

A sly half smile, and one lifted brow, from Norm. "Well," he said softly, reasonably, "just tell him the real call is Norm Goldman's. And Goldman is an unreasonable asshole."

Mike Kaplan laughed out loud and jerked his head toward Norm while looking at me. "I've been saying that for ages," he said.

After Kaplan promised to set up a visit to the ship for me and Quent, he left us. I told Norm that just about cleared my decks for the day, and said I'd take one of those Czech beers if the offer was still open. We jawed about our tastes in racing—I couldn't see his fascination with dragsters; he thought karts were kid stuff. He showed me around his place while we discussed Norm's good luck in falling heir to a floor of rooms that split so nicely into three apartments. Whatever Sonmiani paid their seamen, Norm and his staff obviously were in no fiscal pain. Finally, we bonded a little closer over the fact that both of us placed high value in working with people we liked.

I promised Norm he'd like Quent because they shared a subdued sense of humor, though he might find my old pal oddly conservative considering the career he chose. That was the chief way, I said, that Quent's ethnicity showed.

Norm said believe it or not, I'd find Kaplan had a touch of the prude. He added that it couldn't be the man's Liverpool upbringing, so maybe it was the Sephardic Jew surfacing in him. It was a comfort, he said, to know he could be gone a week and feel confident that the office was secure in the hands of Mike Kaplan. I'd find Ira Meltzer a frank Manhattan skirt-chaser, he said, which could get a bit wearing but Ira was a real *mensch* for hard work.

I tried to call Quent about the good news, but got his tape. I didn't call Dana Martin because I didn't want to seem secretive, and I sure wasn't going to talk with a Fed in front of Norm.

And when he suggested we go looking for dinner—on him, or rather on Sonmiani, he reminded me—I said it might be better if we called a pizza in because I was tired of people looking at me funny. I was catching on to his dry humor by then, and laughed when he said with a straight face that he couldn't imagine why they might.

"Pizza's a good idea," he said, "but we could order it from anywhere. How about from your workshop?"

He was as serious about it as most race-car freaks, and the idea of a forty-minute drive didn't dismay him. It was long odds against a deliveryman finding my place, I said, but we could pick that pizza up on the way. He'd be driving back alone for the first few miles on dark country roads, I cautioned. He said he had a decent Sony mapper, so he was up for it if I was, but if I had any objection we could do it another time.

Objection? Hell, this would be the first time I could recall that I'd had two guests in one week, and I said as much while we rode the rocking old elevator down.

Eventually, using our phones while he followed me out of town in his enviable, cherried-out classic black Porsche Turbo, I suggested we save time by my cobbling up a couple of reubens on my woodstove. He agreed, and when we hit the country roads I tried Quent again without success.

Now I could call our pet Feeb, who sounded slightly impressed that I was still at work. She liked it even better that Sonmiani's people were receptive to our private search and would help us snoop aboard ship, the next day.

Quent, she said, had taken the Loc-8 with its hidden spectral analyzer after playing with it under lab tutelage. She thought he might be cruising around Richmond trying to find crewman Hong Chee. Reception, especially in some of the popular basement dives, wasn't all that reliable. I told myself Quent could cruise the ethnic bars better as a singleton and besides, I was working in a way, schmoozing with a guy who could hinder or help us. No doubt Quent would call me when he was ready.

Dana wasn't so happy with my suggestion that the Feds canvass airline reservation lists scheduled for the next few days, just to see if they got any hits on the *Ras Ormara*'s crewlist. Did she think it was pointless? Maybe not entirely, she admitted, before she hung up. I still think Dana was simply pissed because she hadn't already gotten around to it.

No need to worry about Norm Goldman's ability to keep my pickup in sight. He stayed glued to my back bumper, perhaps to prove that he had a racer's soul. But Jesus! A Pooch Turbo tailing an old Toyota trash hauler? My sister Shar could've done it. Even so, he must've bottomed his pan following me up the lane to my place. A moment later my phone chirped.

I hoped it was Quent, but, "Harve? Is this a gag? How much farther is it," asked a slightly subdued Norm.

I asked if he could spot the old white clapboard farmhouse past the orchard ahead, and he said yes. "That's it. We're on my acreage now," I said. With hindsight, I think he had started to wonder whether his new friend had something unfriendly in mind for him.

My workshop was still more than half smithy then, a short walk from the house, and we parked beside it. I toggled a key-ring button that unlocked the side door, and its sensor lit the shop up for us as I approached.

Norm stepped inside with the diffidence of an acolyte in a cathedral, ready to be awed by a genuine racing-car shop. It may have been a disappointment. The most significant stuff I had on hand was the specialized running gear, protectively bagged in inert argon gas, but he spent more time studying my half-sized chassis drawings and the swoopy lines I had lofted to show the body shells I hadn't molded yet. When I saw him rubbing his upper arms I realized it was chilly for him. "You might enjoy looking at some recent off-road race videos," I said, "while I get the kitchen stove warmed. Or you could sit on top of the stove," I cracked. "Takes about ten minutes to get that cast-iron woodhog of mine up to correct temperature."

So we closed up the shop and I used my century-old key to get us past the kitchen door. I explained my conceit, keeping the upstairs part of the house turn-of-another-century except for a few sensible improvements: media center, smoke and particulate detectors, a deionizer built into a squat wooden 1920s icebox. I couldn't recall whether I'd left any notes on my desk or screen downstairs, so I didn't mention my setup there.

I showed Norm to the media center in my parlor, swore to him that the couch wouldn't collapse, and left him with a holocube of the recent Sears Point Grand Prix. I'd be lying if I said I was worried about Quent, but while rustling up the corned beef, cheese, and other munchables necessary to a reuben I kept expecting him to call. I thought he might wind up his day by driving out, and we could all schmooze together. I thought wrong.

Just for the hell of it, I opened a bottle of Oregon early muscat for our sandwiches. A bit on the sweet side, but, to make a point, I reminded Norm that Catalonians serve it to special guests and I admired their style.

After supper we skimmed more holocubes and played some old CDs, and I was yarning about the time I had to evade a biker bunch when I heard my phone. It had to be Quent, I thought; and in a way it was. I said, "Sorry, you never know," to Norm, went into the back bedroom, and answered.

It was Dana, terse and angry. "You won't like this any better than I do," she warned me, and asked where I was.

I told her, and added, "I sure don't like it when I don't know what's up, boss lady. Tell me."

She did, and a flush of prickly heat spread from the back of my neck down my arms. I only half heard the essentials, but every word would replay itself in my mind during my drive back to Richmond.

"Give me a half hour," I said. "The Sonmiani rep is here with me. He might be some help tracing some of the crew's movements if there's a connection."

"Say nothing tonight; Sonmiani might be one of those firms that demand advocacy no matter what."

"Firms like yours," I said grimly, and regretted it in the same moment. "Forgive me, I'm—I need to go out and slug a tree. See you in thirty."

Norm must have been sensitive to body language because he stood up as I stumped through the parlor door. I told him I had to drive back into town as soon as I changed clothes. To his question I said it wasn't anything he could help with; just a case that had taken a new turn. He asked whether my Korean boss let me go along on the *Ras Ormara* thing. I replied that there wasn't much doubt I'd make it, and promised to give him an early-morning call. Then I hurried into my bedroom for a quick change, my hands shaking.

As I slapped the closures on my sneakers I heard the Porsche start up, and Norm was long gone when my tires hit country-road macadam.

Not so long gone that I didn't almost catch him nearing Concord. I hung back enough to let him find the freeway before me. After all, there wasn't any need for breaking records now; hard driving was simply the only way I could use up all that adrenaline before I met the Feds off the freeway in East Richmond, near the foothills. I kept thinking that from downtown Richmond to some very steep ravines was only five minutes or so. And wondering whether my buddy Quent had still been alive during the trip.

Linked to Dana by phone, I found the location a block off the main drag, a long neon strip of used-car lots and commercial garages. Evidently Dana's people had shooed the locals away, though a pair of uniformed cops still hung around waiting to control the nonexistent crowd, and I seemed to be it. The guys doing the real work wore identical, reversible dark jackets. I knew that "F B I" would be printed on the inner surfaces of those jacket backs and, when Dana waved me forward, a strobe flash made me blink.

I saw the chalk outline before I spotted the partially blanketed figure on a foldable gurney in the extrawide unmarked van. The chalk lines revealed that Quent had been found with his legs in the street, torso in the gutter, head and one arm up on the curb. The stain at the head oval looked black, but it wouldn't in daylight.

We said nothing until I followed Dana into the van, sitting on jump seats barely out of the way of a forensics woman who was monitoring instruments while she murmured into her headset. The gadget she occasionally used looked like my StudyFrail but probably cost ten times as much. I leaned forward, saw the misshapen contours of a face I had known well. I knew better than to touch him. I think I moaned, "Awww, Quent."

"He was deceased before he struck the curb, if it's any consolation," said Dana. "Long enough before, that he lost very little blood on impact. Presumption is that someone dropped him from a moving vehicle."

I couldn't help wondering what I'd been doing at the time. Nodding toward the forensics tech, I managed to mutter, "Got a time of death?"

Dana said, "Ninety minutes, give or take." I would've been licking my fingers right about then. "We thought it might have been accidental at first."

"For about ten seconds," said the tech dryly. She wasn't missing anything. Her gloved hand lifted Quentin Kim's lifeless wrist. It was abraded and bruised. She pointed delicately with her pinkie at the bluish fingertips. The nails of the smallest two fingers were missing. The cuticles around the other nails were swollen and rimmed with faint bloodstains, and the ends of the nails had been roughened as if chewed by some tiny animal. “He still had a heartbeat when this was done,” she added.

“Pliers,” I said, and she grunted assent. “Somebody wanted something out of him. But how could pulling out fingernails be lethal,” I asked, shuddering by reflex as I tried to imagine the agony of my close friend, a friend who had originally hired me for physical backup. Fat lot of good I had done him. . . .

The tech didn’t answer until she glanced at Dana, who nodded without a word. “Barring a coronary, it couldn’t. But repeated zaps of a hundred thousand volts will give you that coronary. Zappers that powerful are illegal, but I believe Indonesian riot control used them for a while. The fingernails told me to look for something else. Nipples, privates, lips, other sites densely packed with nerve endings.”

“I’ll take your word for it,” I said. She was implying torture by people who were good at it, and I lacked the objectivity to view the evidence.

“But that’s not where I found the trauma,” said the tech. “It showed up as electrical burn marks in a half dozen places where a pair of contact points had been pressed at the base of the skull, under the hair. Not too hard to locate if you know what you’re looking for. The brain stem handles your most basic life support; breathing, that sort of thing. Electrocute it hard, several times, and it’s all over.”

“It’s not over,” I growled.

“It is for him,” the woman said, then looked into my eyes and blinked at whatever she saw. “Got it,” she mumbled, going back to her work.

“Under the circumstances,” Dana said, not unkindly, “you may want to break this one off without prejudice. Even though there may be no connection between this and the particular case you’re working. Quentin had other active cases, and we know he’s not above working two at once, don’t we?”

“I resent that word ‘above.’ We also know how we’d bet, if we were betting,” I said.

“You *are* betting, Rackham. And stakes don’t go much higher than this.”

Neither of us could have dreamed how wrong she was, but I could dream about avenging my pal. I said, “I’m feeling lucky. Where’s that Loc-8 with the analyzer? I’ll learn to use it by tomorrow. Maybe Norm Goldman can divert some people’s attention. He’ll be with me.”

She said she’d be glad to, if she knew where it was. “It might be in Quentin’s Volvo; the Richmond force is on it, too. It could turn up at any time,” she said.

She led me out of the van again and into its nightshadow. "There's not much point in going aboard that ship until we find you an analyzer. Preferably the one Quent had. Don't contact Goldman's people again until we do."

"He might call me. We hit it off pretty well, and he could be an asset," I said.

"He may be, at that," she said as if to herself, then sighed and shifted her mental gears with an almost audible clash. "You may as well go home, there's nothing you can do here. I called you in only because I knew you two were close." A pause. "You'd have told me if Quentin had called you tonight. Wouldn't you?"

"About what?"

"About anything. Answer my question," she demanded.

Before that tart riposte was fully out of her mouth I said, "Of course I'd tell you! What is this, anyway?" When she only shook her head, I went on, "I kept my phone on me at all times because I kept hoping he'd call. I was getting uncomfortable because, normally, he'd have called just for routine's sake. I called *him* a couple of times, that's easy enough for you to check. I'd like to know where you're going with this."

"So you don't feel just a touch of, well, like you'd let him down, left him waiting? A little guilty?"

Her tone was gentle. In another woman I might've called it wheedling. And that told me a lot. "Goddamned right I feel guilty! I did let him down, but not because I put him off when he called. He never called, Martin. Why don't you just say 'dereliction of duty' and be done with it? And be glad you're half my size when you say it."

I turned and stalked off before she could make me any madder, wondering how I was going to get any sleep, wishing Quent had called in so I'd know where he'd gone. Wishing I had that Loc-8 so I'd have a reason to go aboard the *Ras Ormara*. And suddenly I realized how important it was that I find the gadget for its everyday use. Hadn't Dana said she'd be glad to lend me the damn thing if she knew where it was?

I was pretty sure where it would be: in the breakaway panel of the driver's side door in the Volvo. Quent had padded the pocket so he could keep a sidearm or special evidence of a case literally at hand.

But the Volvo was missing. If it were downtown, it should already have been spotted. If it was a Fed priority, the Highway Patrol would have picked it up five minutes after it hit a freeway. Very likely someone had hidden it, maybe after using it to dump poor Quent along Used Car Row. Maybe it was in the bay. Maybe parked in a quiet neighborhood, where it might not be noticed for a day or so. Maybe in a chop shop someplace, already being dismantled for parts for other used cars. . . .

Used Car Row! What better place to dump an upscale used car? I fired up my Toyota and drove slowly past the nearest lot, noting that a steel cable stretched at thigh height from light pole to light pole, with cars parked so that no one could cruise through the lot or hot-wire a heap and cruise out with it. Or dump a stolen car there.

Several long blocks later I lucked out, not in a car lot but at the end of a row of cars outside a body-and-fender shop. I hadn't remembered the license; it was that inside rearview of Quent's that stretched halfway across the windshield just like mine did, one of those aftermarket gimmicks every P.I. needs during a stakeout or traffic surveillance.

Pulling on gloves, I parked the pickup out of sight and flicked my pocket flash against the Volvo's steering column. The keys were in the ignition. Knowing Quent as I did, I avoided touching the door plate. In fact, though the racket should have brought every cop in town, I didn't touch the car until, on my fourth try, the old bent wheel rim I'd scrounged managed to cave in the driver's side window, scattering little cubes of glass everywhere.

By that time the alarm's *threep, threep, whooeeeet, wheeeoot* parodied a mockingbird from hell and for about thirty seconds I expected to see gentlemen of the public safety persuasion descending on the scene. Only after I got the keys out and unlocked the driver's side door did the alarm run out of birdseed and blessed silence overtook the place once more.

Fed forensics are better than most folks think, so while I intended to tell Dana what I'd done, I wanted it to be at a time of my choosing. That's why I didn't climb inside the car. I just opened the driver's door and checked the spring-loaded door panel.

And good old Quent, following his procedures as always, had squirreled away the Feds' tricky little Loc-8 right where it would be handy, and whoever had left the Volvo there hadn't suspected the breakaway panel. I pocketed the gadget, left the keys in the ignition again, and drove like a sober citizen back to the freeway and home. I could hardly wait to check out the Loc-8's memory. Every centimeter of its movements through the whole evening would have been recorded—unless Quent or someone else had erased it.

The normal functions of the Loc-8's little screen hadn't been compromised, so I was able to scroll through its travels beginning with Quent's departure from the Sunnyvale lab early in the evening. I brewed strong java and sipped as I made longhand notes with pen on paper at my kitchen table. Say what you will about old-fashioned methods, nothing helps me assemble thoughts like notes on paper.

Quent had driven back via the Bay Bridge to Richmond at his ordinary sedate pace, and the Volvo had stopped for two minutes or so halfway down a block in the neighborhood where he had spoken earlier in the day with the so-called machinist. If he hadn't found a parking slot, I guessed he had double-parked.

Next he had driven half a mile, and here the Loc-8 had stayed for over an hour. At max magnification it showed he must have used a parking lot because the Volvo had been well off the street. I noted the location so I could interview the parking attendant, if any. From the locale, I figured Quent had been cruising the ethnic bars and game palaces, maybe looking for our missing engineer or, still more likely, the machinist's roomie. Then the car had left its spot, found the freeway, and headed south through Oakland to the Alameda, not in any special hurry.

But when the Volvo's trail traversed a long block for the second time, I checked the intersections. There was no mistake: Quent had circled the Sonmiani offices a couple of times, then parked in an adjacent alleyway, the same one Norm used for his Porsche as access to the garage entrance of the first-floor offices. As well as I could recall, I hadn't been gone from there long when Quent arrived to do his usual careful survey of the whole layout before committing himself. That would fit if he'd intended to meet someone like Mike Kaplan or the other guy I hadn't met—Meltzer. Someone whose phone number he didn't have. Maybe he had been confident I was still there.

But if he had been trying to contact me, why hadn't he just grabbed his phone? Obviously he hadn't thought it was necessary. That meant he wasn't worried about his safety, because Quent had told me up front that he'd rented me, as it were, by the pound of gristle. And, like most P.I.s, Quent worked on the premise that discretion was the better part, et cetera. The P.I. species is often bred from insurance investigators, a few lawyers, ex-military types, and ex-cops. Guess which ones are most willing to throw discretion in the dumper. . . .

Despite the lateness of the hour, my first impulse was to call Norm and ask him a few questions about what, or whom, Quent might have met there. But what would he know? He'd been tailgating me out past Mt. Diablo at that time. Another thing: Nearing my place I had called Quent to no avail. Had he gone inside by then? Or he could have met someone in another car. Illegal entry wasn't Quent's style. I decided that if he had been looking for me, he'd have called before parking there. The car had stayed there for about five minutes and then its location cursor virtually disappeared, but not quite. With its signal greatly diminished, it said the Volvo had been driven into Norm's garage. There it had stayed for about an hour.

Then when the cursor suddenly appeared with a strong satellite signal, the Volvo went squirting through the Alameda as if someone were chasing it. It would've been dark by then as the cursor traced its way up the Nimitz Freeway to the Eastshore route, taking a turnoff near Richmond. I was feeling prickly heat as I keyed the screen back and forth between real time and fast-forward, because in real time Quent never drove with that kind of vigor.

I concluded he hadn't been driving by then. The Volvo had gone some distance up Wildcat Canyon near Richmond's outskirts, now driving more slowly, at times too slowly, then picking up the pace as it turned back toward the commercial district. There was no doubt in my mind where this jaunt would end, and for once I nailed it. The Volvo sizzled past the spot where a chalk outline now climbed a boulevard curb, turned off the main drag, and doubled back and forth on a service road before it stopped. The site was approximately where I had found the Volvo.

The screen said more than two hours passed before the cursor headed toward my place, duly recording the moment when I stole the gadget—recovered it, I mean; Dana had clearly said she wished she could lend it to me. Had she been lying? Probably, but it didn't matter. I had the gimmicked Loc-8 and I had time to fiddle with its hidden functions, having watched while Dana showed another one off while sitting on a park bench between me and Quent.

And I had something else: a cold hard knot of certainty that someone working for my new friend Norm Goldman was no friend of Quent's. Or of mine.

Four

I did sleep, after all. Worry keeps me awake but firm resolve has a way of grinding worry underfoot. I woke up mad as hell before I even remembered why, and then I sat on the edge of my bed and shed the tears I never let anyone see.

Then I dressed for a tour of the *Ras Ormara*. I'm told that the Cheyennes used to gather before a war party and ritually purge their bellies. They believed it sharpened their hunting instincts, and I know for a fact that if you expect a reasonable likelihood of serious injury, your chances of surviving surgery are better on an empty stomach. For breakfast I brewed tea, and nothing else, in memory of my friend.

Around nine, I called Norm Goldman and asked if my visit was on. He said yes, and asked if my Korean boss would be coming, too. I told him I hadn't been able to raise Quent, before I realized the grisly double entendre of my reply. We agreed to meet at the slip at ten-thirty. I went downstairs and made a weapons check. Assuming the guys who took Quent down were connected with the ship—and I did assume it—somehow it just seemed a natural progression for them to make a run on me on what was their turf. Especially if Quent, in his agony, had admitted who was running the two of us.

I ignored my phone's bleat because its readout didn't identify the caller and there was no message, and I figured it might be my Feebie boss with new orders I didn't want to follow.

With my StudyChick in one jacket pocket, the Loc-8 in the other, my Glock auto in its breakaway Bianchi against my left armpit and the ex-Bobby Rooney derringer taped into the hollow of my right armpit, I felt like the six-million-gadget man. My phone chortled at me as I drove into town. Still no ident for the caller, and I didn't reply, but this time there was a message and it was clearly Dana's voice on the messager.

She was careful with her phrasing. "The car's been found, but not our property. Whoever has it is asking for a grand theft indictment. But the real news is, someone with political pull back East has complained at ministerial level about the, and I quote, unconscionable interference with Pacific Rim commerce. We're now obeying a new directive. Absent some solid evidence of illegal activity by the maritime entity—and nothing ironclad is present—we're terminating the operation. Of course last night's felony will be pursued by the metro force.

"I want you to report to me immediately. After what's happened, it makes me nervous not to know whether you're still pursuing the operation. If I knew, it would probably make me even more nervous. Just ask yourself how much your license is worth." No cheery good-byes, no nothing else.

I wanted to answer that last one, though not enough to call her back. While my license was worth a lot to me, it wasn't worth Quentin Kim's life. She might not know it, but I could make a decent living as a temp working under someone else's license. If Dana Martin's people dropped out, whatever the Richmond homicide detail found they'd almost certainly discover that their suspects had sailed on the *Ras Ormara*. Good luck, Sergeant, here's a ticket to Pusan and the damnedest bilingual dictionary you ever saw . . .

I played the recording back again, trying to listen between the lines. If Dana had been thinking how her message would sound when replayed for her local SAC, she'd have said just about what she did say. Did she suspect the Volvo's window had been busted by clumsy ol' Harve, who had the Loc-8 and was now en route to the docks? If so, she evidently wasn't going to share that suspicion with her office.

She had also made it plain that I'd have bupkis for backup, leaving an implication that until I got her message, I was still on the case. Or I could just be reading into it what I wanted to read.

What I wanted to read at the moment were my notes, not an easy task in what had now become city traffic.

With twenty minutes to burn, I pulled over beside a warehouse near the wharf and scrolled over my notes hoping to identify the next cargo. The stuff Sonmiani wanted to load was something called paraglycidyl ether, a resin thinner. Quent had checked a hazmat book on the off chance that it might be really hazardous material.

The classic historic screwup along that line had been the burning shipload of ammonium nitrate in 1947 that was identified only by its actual intended use as fertilizer. However, Quent had found that this cargo wasn't a very mean puppy though it was flammable; certainly not like the old ethyl ether that puts your lights out after a few sniffs.

When I checked the manufacturing location I found that the liquid was synthesized right there, not merely there in Richmond but in one of the fenced-off chemical plants with an address off the boulevard facing me. I drove on and found a maze of chemical processing towers, reactor tanks, pipes, and catwalks a half mile past the *Ras Ormara*. A gate was open to accept a whopping big diesel Freightliner rig that was backing in among the storage tanks, carrying smaller tanks of its own like grain hoppers. For a moment I thought the driver would bend a yellow guide barrier of welded pipe and wipe out the prefab plastic shed that stood within inches of the pipe. Near the shed stood a vertically aligned bank of bright red tanks the size of torpedoes. I recognized the color coding, and I didn't want to be anywhere near if that shed got graunched.

The driver stopped in time, though. He was no expert, concentrating on operating his rearview video instead of using a stooge to damned well direct him, and I thought he looked straight at me when he was only concentrating on an external mirror directly in front of him. He didn't see me any more than he would've seen a gull in the far background.

It was Mike Kaplan.

I couldn't be wrong about that. Same caricature of a beak, same severe brush cut and intense features. And why shouldn't it be him? Okay, using a desk jockey to drive a rig might be unusual, and I had thought Kaplan was slated to take the ship tour with me. But if the Fed-erected barriers to Pacific Rim commerce had come tumbling down during the morning as Dana claimed, an aggressive bunch of local reps might be pitching in to make up for lost time.

I wondered what, if anything, Kaplan might be able to tell me about what had happened in that office building early on the previous night. He had left before Norm and I did, but how did I know when he had come back? The third guy—Seltzer? Meltzer!—was one I hadn't met, but without any positive evidence I had already made a tentative reservation for him on my shit list.

It was only a short drive back to the gate that served the *Ras Or-*

mara. This time the gate was manned, but Norm Goldman, in a ritzy black-leather jacket, leaned with a skinny frizzle-haired guy against the fender of his Turbo Porsche, just outside the fencing. Norm recognized me with a wave and called something to the two guys at the gate as I parked beside the swoopy coupe.

The skinny guy with Norm turned out to be Ira Meltzer, who spoke very softly and had a handshake that was too passive for his work-hardened hands, and wore a denim jacket that exaggerated his shoulders. When Meltzer asked where my partner was, I said he hadn't answered my calls, so I figured he wasn't coming.

Neither of them seemed to find anything odd about that. If Meltzer knew *why* Quent wasn't coming, it was possible that Norm might know. I didn't like that train of thought; if true, it made me the prize patsy of all time. And if they had learned from Quent who it was that had been giving him orders, they would assume I already knew what had happened to him. While I thought about these things, the three of us stood there and smiled at one another.

Then Meltzer said, "By the way, aboard ship it's the captain's little kingdom—except for government agencies. And you're private, am I right?"

I agreed.

"Then if I were you, I wouldn't try to go aboard with a concealed weapon." His smile broadened. "Or any other kind."

He didn't actually say I was carrying, and it took a practiced eye to spot the slight bulge of my Glock, but I didn't need an argument with the honcho on board. "Glad you told me," I said, and popped the little black convincer from its holster. I unlocked the Toyota and shut my main weapon in the glove box. "I carry my GPS mapper; it's a Loc-8. And I've got a StudyGirl for notes. That a problem?"

Meltzer looked at Norm, who made a wry grimace. "Shit, Ira, why would it be? In fact, you might carry one of 'em openly in your hand, Harve. I'll do the same with the other, and I'll give it back once we're aboard. I don't think al-Nadwi will get his shorts in a wad. I'm supposed to carry a little weight around here, even with these ragheads."

Meltzer said he supposed so, and I handed over StudySkirt, carrying the Loc-8 in one hand. We left our vehicles near the gate and walked in side by side toward the *Ras Ormara.*

The commercial cleanup outfit I had previously seen on the wharf was finally leaving, a bright yellow hazmat suit visibly untenanted in a niche near the truck's external console. I recognized two of the three guys in the truck's cab, and Consoleman, now the driver, waved. When Sweatman, the guy who had worn the suit, pretended he didn't notice us I knew which of them the Feds had co-opted on the job. I would've given a lot to talk with him alone right then.

Norm waved back, his good spirits irksome to me though I couldn't very well bitch about it. He kept looking around at the skyline and the wheeling gulls, taking big breaths of mud-flavored waterfront air that I didn't find all that enticing. Wonderful day, he said, and I nodded.

As we walked up the broad metal-surfaced ramp leading to the ship, Norm made a casual half salute toward the men who stood high above on deck to meet us. Other men in work clothes were shouting words I couldn't understand as they routed flexible metal-clad hoses around forward of the bridge. A couple of them wore white head wraps.

The skipper took Norm's hand in his in a handshake that seemed clumsily forced, but he shook mine readily enough, unsmiling, as Norm made formal introductions.

Captain Hassan al-Nadwi had a full beard and an old sailor's rawhide skin, bald forward of his ears, but with chest hairs curling up from the throat of his work shirt. He wore no socks, and the soles of his sandals must have been an inch thick.

He spoke fair English. "You want see engineer quarters? Go. Much much work now," he said, friendly enough though shooing me with gestures. He gave an order to one of the two men, evidently officers, who stood behind him, then turned away to watch his work crew.

"You come, okay. I show where Park, eh, sleep," said the Asian, a hard-looking sort whose age I couldn't guess. He led us quickly through a portal, Norm giving me an "after you" wave, and down a passageway sunlit by sealed portholes. Another doorway took us through a room dominated by a long table surrounded by swiveling chairs that seemed bolted in place. Finally, we negotiated another passage with several closed doors, and as the crewman opened the last door I had a view of the skyline through the room's portholes.

The Asian stood back to let us in, pointing to one of three bunks in the room. "Park, okay," he said, and paused, with a sideways tilt of his head. Somewhere in the ship a low thrumm had started, and I could feel a hum through the soles of my shoes. He seemed to talk a bit faster now as he stepped quickly to a bunk with a half-filled sea bag on it. "Park, okay," he said, then moved to a table secured to the metal. Wall? Bulkhead? Whatever. "Park, okay," he said again. I recalled Quent saying once that all Korean kids took English courses. I figured maybe this guy had cheated on his exams.

I pulled out the table's single drawer, which was so completely empty in a room shared by three guys that it fairly screamed "total cleanout job." "Okay," I said. At my reply the crewman turned on his heel, obviously in a hurry to be off. "Wait," I said. The crewman kept going.

Ira Meltzer said something singsong. The crewman stopped in the doorway, not pleased about it. Meltzer looked at me.

"Ask him if there was any other place Park kept any of his personal effects," I suggested.

"I'll try," he said, and then said something longer. The crewman said something else. Meltzer said, "*Nae*," which was damn near all the Korean I knew, meaning "yes."

The man said something else; glanced at Norm as if fearing eye contact; then, when Meltzer nodded, left hurriedly. "He doesn't know of any. I guess this is all," he said, and nodded at the bunk.

As I unlatched the hasp that closed the sea bag, I could hear quick footfalls of a running man in the corridor. Norm laughed. "Skipper keeps the crew on a tight leash," he commented.

"I don't doubt it," I said. I knew he was explaining the Korean crewman's hellacious hurry to me. And I wasn't sure if that was the best explanation. In fact, I sat down on the bunk so that I wouldn't have my back to my trusty guides while I carefully pulled out the contents of the bag to inspect them, one by one.

A small cheap zippered bag held toilet articles, soap, and a prescription bottle of pills with instructions in Spanish. After that, a pair of worn Avia cross-trainers; socks; a set of tan work clothes, and a stained nylon windbreaker. A heavy hooded rainproof coat; a couple of girlie mags; two pairs of work gloves, one pair well worn. A small, pre-palmtop book full of engineering tables, which I flipped through without finding any handwritten notes.

I saw Meltzer take a peek at his watch, so I decided to use up some more time. "Norm, you have that StudyGirl of mine?"

He handed it over. "You find something?" In answer I shook my head. He squatted for a closer look and, I figured, to see what notes I might make.

I used the audio function, first citing the date and location. As I placed each item back in the big bag I described it, and asked if Norm could translate the label on the pill bottle.

He couldn't, but Meltzer could. While I spelled out "methacarbamol," he said, "Muscle relaxant," practically running his words together.

I announced for the audio that this was my complete audit of Park Soon's effects left aboard ship. I added, in traditional P.I. third-person reportage, "The investigator found nothing more to suggest the subject's itinerary ashore, or whether he intended to return. In the investigator's opinion, the value of the bag's contents would not exceed a hundred dollars." By the time I'd latched the bag and placed it back on the bunk, the combined silences of Norm and Meltzer hung like smoke in the little room. They were being nice, but clearly they wanted me the hell out of there.

And just as badly, I wanted to stick around. I hadn't found anything suspicious to use the analyzer on, and in any case these guys were right at my elbow. Norm stepped into the corridor and waited expectantly.

"Just one more thing," I said, following him into the corridor. "I wonder if the captain would let me see Park's workstation. You never know what he might've left lying around."

Meltzer exhaled heavily as we retraced our steps. Norm shot me a pained smile. "I'll ask. In case you're wondering, they just got their clearance this morning, so they're hoping to get under way today. I'd like to see them do it, Harve."

"Message received," I said. "I guess that's why Mike Kaplan isn't with us."

"He's doing three men's work in the office this morning," said Norm.

And as I tried to read Norm's expression, Meltzer saw my glance and chimed in, "It's always like this at the last minute. He isn't even taking calls."

So he lies and you swear to it, I thought. Aloud I said, "I promise to keep out of the way. I just need to cover all the bases." *And one base is the discovery that my new friend may not be that good a friend.*

We found our way back on deck. A faint, musky odor lay on the breeze, reminding me of rancid soy protein. The rushing thrum in the ship's innards was more pronounced as we neared the bridge. It seemed to be coming from those big cargo tank domes that protruded from the forward deck plates. "Wait here," said Norm.

Meltzer stopped when I did. He pulled out a cigarette and, as he lit it, I could see that his hands trembled. It wasn't fear, I decided; not a chill, either, because of the way he was smiling to himself.

It was suppressed excitement.

And when the phone in my pocket gave a blurt, Ira Meltzer jumped as if I'd goosed him. "It's probably Quent," I said. "Let me take it over here." By now I was virtually certain he knew Quentin Kim would not be making any more phone calls. But maybe he didn't know that I knew.

I walked back far enough for privacy, unfolding my phone, casually holding my StudyWench at my side so that its video recorded Meltzer.

"Rackham," I said. I didn't want to pull the Loc-8 out until I could make it look like a response to this call. I'd lugged the damn thing aboard to no purpose.

"Your location is known," said Dana Martin. Sweatman had evidently done me a favor. "Are we clean?" Meaning, 'is our conversation secure?'

Meltzer was watching my face. "More or less. Our Mr. Park didn't leave anything aboard that might tell us—" I said.

Until her interruption I had never heard her speak with a note of controlled panic. "Get out of there aysap. A.T.F. liaison tells us that ether compound can be converted in the tank to a component of a ternary agent. Do you understand?"

I smiled for Meltzer. "Not exactly. Where are you?"

"Sunnyvale. We have to arrive in force, and that could take an hour. *Listen to me!* Binary nerve gas isn't deadly 'til two components are mixed. A ternary agent takes three. A relatively small proportion of an ether derivative is one. Our other asset just confirmed that the second component is already aboard. No telling how much is there, but to be effective, it's needed in far greater amounts than the ether derivative."

The rushing noise aboard the *Ras Ormara* and the deep vibrations abruptly resolved themselves in my mind into a humongous pump, dumping something into those newly cleaned cargo tanks. A hell of a lot of something. "Does it stink like bad tofu?"

"Wait one."

"Make it quick," I muttered with a smile for Meltzer, seeing Norm as he walked back toward me, a sad little smile on his face.

I was still waiting when Norm showed me a big shrug and headshake. "I'm sorry. Park didn't even have a particular workstation anyway," he said.

On the heels of this came Dana's breathless, "That's what you're smelling, Rackham. Judging from the order form for ether, and assuming they intend to convert it to another compound, we predict an amount of ternary agent that is—my God, it staggers the imagination. Component three is a tiny amount of catalyst, easy to hide. If they have it, you're on a floating doomsday machine."

Norm Goldman now stood beside me. "Copy that," I said, with a comradely pat on Norm's shoulder to show him there were no hard feelings. "Hell of a secretary you are if you don't even know where Quent is. Look, I expect I'll be having lunch with a friend. I'll call in later." With that, I folded my phone away.

Norm took my arm, but very gently. "Part of my job is knowing when not to bug the troops, Harve. Sorry." We moved toward the gangway ramp.

Somewhere in the distance, the double-tone beeps of police vehicles dopplered off to inaudibility. I hoped the audio track of my StudyBroad was picking up the sound of whatever it was that surged into those huge tanks, and then I released the button and pocketed my gadget. If the ether component was still being loaded for transfer, or if its conversion was complicated, there might be some way to slow them down. "About lunch," I began, as Meltzer followed us down to the wharf.

"Hey, listen, I'll have to take a rain check on that," said Norm, as if answering my prayer. "Mike will need help in the office. Before the clearance came through I even had a lunch reservation for a nice place where I run a tab, up in San Rafael. Promise me you'll do lunch there today anyway. My treat. Just give 'em this," he said, fishing a business card from his wallet, scribbling a Mission Avenue address in San Rafael on the back of the card. "Have a few drinks on me. Promise me you'll do that."

"It's a promise," I said, as we walked toward our vehicles. Hey, if he had lied to me I could lie to him. . . .

Because San Rafael lay to the northwest, I gave a cheery wave and drove off as if keeping my promise, tugging on my driving gloves. Then I reached over and retrieved my Glock as I doubled back toward the place where I'd seen Mike Kaplan loading up. Minutes later, while I redlined the Toyota along the boulevard, I managed to call Dana. "I'm circling around to where they're loading ether into a big rig," I said over the caterwaul of my pickup. "Why not call the Richmond force and get them to meet me there until you show up? Someone should've already thought of that."

"They have casualty situations in both high schools at the other end of town, called in almost simultaneously ten minutes ago. Perps are adults with automatic weapons. It's already on the news and traffic is wall-to-wall there. And we're having trouble getting compliance with metro liaison staff."

That was weasel-talk for getting stonewalled by city cops who have had their noses rubbed in their inferiority by Fed elitists too many times and who might not believe how serious the Mayday was. I didn't take time to say, "what goes around comes around." Of course that sort of rivalry was stupid. It was also predictable.

I growled, "I'll give odds those perps are decoys to draw SWAT teams away from here. Bring somebody fast. Strafe the goddamn ship if you have to; I'll try to delay the load of ether. Am I sanctioned to fire first?"

A two-beat pause. "You know I can't authorize that. Let me check with our SAC," she said.

I made a one-word comment, dropped the phone in my pocket, and swung wide to make it through the open gate.

Fifty feet inside was the nose of the Freightliner, and behind it two guys in coveralls and respirator masks stood on its trailer fooling with transfer hoses. A guy in street clothes stood near the gate, jacket over his arm, and it barely registered in my mind that the guy was Ira Meltzer. The yellow-pipe barrier, protection for that long utility shed, ran from beside the rig almost to the gate. I made a decision that I might not have made if I'd had time to think.

My Toyota weighed something over a ton, and was still doing maybe thirty miles an hour. The Freightliner with its load might've weighed over twenty tons, but it wasn't in motion. I figured on moving it a little, probably starting a fire. I popped the lever into neutral as my pickup blew past the openmouthed gate guard, then tried to hit the pavement running. Meanwhile my Toyota screeched headlong down the guide barrier, which kept nudging my vehicle straight ahead. Straight toward the nose of the towering Freightliner.

The scrape of my pickup's steel fender mixed with shouts from the gate man, and I lost my balance and went over in a shoulder roll. Inertia brought me back to my feet and nearly over again, and I heard a series of reports behind me just before my poor old pickup slammed into the left fender of the Freightliner with an earsplitting *wham* that was almost an animal scream.

Guttural little whines told me someone's ricochets were hitting distant metal, and I somehow managed to clear that knee-high barrier of four-inch pipe without slowing. I ducked—actually I tripped and fell—behind the utility shed, and saw the common old lock on its door. I was in full view of the diesel rig and turned toward it, drawing my Glock.

I had expected an instant fireball, but I was wrong. Big rigs have flame-resistant fiberglass fenders these days, and only one fat tire on each side up front. The Toyota's entire front end was crammed up into the splintered shreds of truck fender, and the cab leaned in the direction of my four-wheeled sacrifice. With a deflated front wheel, that Freightliner wasn't going anywhere very fast.

And the reason why nobody was shooting at me from the truck was that the Toyota's impact had shoved the entire rig back, not by much, but enough to crimp the already tight fit of transfer hoses. The guys in respirators were wrestling with a hose and shouting, though I couldn't understand a word. As I stood unprotected in the shadow of the shed Meltzer pounded up, an Ingram burp gun in hand. I guess he didn't expect me to be standing so close in plain sight as he rounded the shed.

Because Meltzer was six feet away when he pivoted toward me, it was an execution of sorts. The truth is, we both hesitated; but my earlier suspicions about his dealings with Quent must have given me an edge. Meltzer took my first round in the chest with a jolt that made dust leap from his shirt, and went down backward after my second round into his throat, and I risked darting farther into the open because I needed his weapon.

A burst of three or four rounds grooved the pavement as I leaped back. I saw a familiar face above a black-leather jacket, almost hidden behind the remains of the Freightliner's fender, holding another of those murderous little Ingrams one-handed. I fired once, but only sent particles of fiberglass flying, and Norm Goldman's face disappeared.

He called, "Majub!"

I heard running footsteps, and whirled to the shed's metal-faced door before they could flank me. With those big red tanks standing nearby I had a good idea what was in the shed, so I put the muzzle of my Glock near the hasp and angled it so it *might* not send a round flying around inside. The footsteps halted with my first round, maybe because the guy thought I could see him. I had to fire twice more before the hasp's loop failed, and took some scratches through my glove from shrapnel, but by the time I knew that, I was inside the shed fumbling with two weapons. A drumming rattle on the shed didn't sound promising.

From behind the Freightliner's bulk, Norm's voice: "You couldn't leave it alone, could you?"

I didn't answer. I was scanning the shed's interior, which was lit by a skylight bubble. About half of the machinery there was familiar stuff to me: big battery-powered industrial grinders and drills, a hefty Airco gas-welding outfit, a long worktable with insulated top, a resistance-welding transformer, and tubes with various kinds of wire protruding, welding and brazing rod. Above the table were ranks of wrenches, fittings, bolts, a paint sprayer—the hardware needed to repair or revise an industrial facility.

And I could hear Norm shouting, and voices answering. Simultaneous with gunshots from outside, several sets of holes appeared in both sides of the shed at roughly waist height.

Norm yelled again, this time in English. "Goddammit, Majub, don't waste it!"

And the response in another slightly familiar voice and genuinely

English English: "Sorry, guv. We do have the long magazines." So Mike Kaplan's name was also Majub. *What's in a name? Protective coloration*, I thought. Noises like the tearing of old canvas came from somewhere near. I squatted and lined up one eye with a bullet hole, but not too near the hole. By moving around, I caught sight of my wrecked Toyota. Norm and a guy in coveralls were ripping the fiberglass away as best they could. It might take them ten minutes to change that tire if I let them.

I darted to the end of the shed nearest the action and put a blind short burst from the Ingram through the wall, with only a fair guess at my targets. Because I stood three feet from the plastic wall, I didn't get perforated when an answering burst tore a hole the size of my fist in the wall.

I had taken out one man and there were several more. They seemed partial to Ingrams, about thirty rounds apiece, meaning I was in deep shit. And when I heard the hiss of gas under pressure, the hair stood up on my nape. Those big red torpedoes just outside were painted to indicate acetylene. I hadn't noticed where the oxygen tanks were, but they had to be near because of the long twinned red and black hoses screwed into the welding torch.

And acetylene, escaping inside that shed from a bullet-nicked hose, could blow that entire structure halfway to Sunnyvale the next time I fired, or when an incoming round struck a spark. I darted toward the hiss, wondering if I could repair the damage with tape, and saw that it was the black oxygen hose, not the red one, which had been cut. A slightly oxy-rich atmosphere wasn't a problem, but if I'd had any idea of using a torch somehow, it was no longer an option.

Outside, angry jabbers and furious pounding suggested that Goldman's crew was jacking up the Freightliner's left front for a tire change. It would be only a matter of minutes before they managed it, and another round through the shed reminded me that Kaplan was deployed to keep me busy. From the shafts of sunlight that suddenly appeared inside when he fired, I could tell he was slowly circling the shed, clockwise.

That long workbench with its insulated top must have weighed five hundred pounds, but only its weight anchored it down. If I could tip it over, it should stop anything short of a rifle bullet if and when Kaplan tried to rush the door, and I could fire back from cover. Maybe.

I took off my jacket to free my shoulders and tried to tip the table quietly, but when I had the damn thing halfway over, another round from Kaplan whapped the tabletop a foot from me and I flinched like a weenie. The muted slam of the tabletop's edge was like a wrecking ball against the concrete floor. My shirt tore away under the arms so badly that only the leather straps of my Bianchi holster kept it from hanging off like a cape.

Then I scurried behind the table and tried to visualize where Kaplan might be. Ten seconds later another round ricocheted off a vise bolted to the tabletop. But I saw the hole where the slug had entered, made a rough judgment of its path, and recalled that Kaplan was still moving clockwise. He had fired from about my seven o'clock position, so I used Meltzer's Ingram and squeezed off three rounds toward seven-thirty. The astonished thunderstorm of his curses that followed was Wagnerian opera to me, but his real reply was a hysterical burst of almost a dozen rounds. A whole shelf of hardware cascaded to the floor behind me, and I crouched on the concrete.

Maybe I hadn't hurt Kaplan badly, but he didn't fire again for a full minute. A handful of taps, dies, and brass fittings rolled underfoot, the kind of fittings that were used for flammable gases because brass won't spark. I stood up and found that I could see through the nearest bullet hole toward the Freightliner. My good buddy Norm was barely visible, wrestling a new tire into position. I thought I could puncture it, too, then recalled that late-model tires would reseal themselves after anything less than an outright collision. Then I noticed that the end of that four-inch railing of brightly painted yellow pipe was within a foot of the truck. The pipe was capped; one of those extra precautions metalworkers take to prevent interior corrosion in a salt-air environment.

And that made me rush to another hole at the end of the shed to see if the other end was capped.

It was.

Which meant, if there weren't any holes in the rail of pipe, I just—might—be able to use it as a very long pressure tank.

I duck-walked back behind the overturned table and routed the hoses with the welding torch along the floor, where they couldn't be struck again. Among all the stuff underfoot were fittings sized to match those that screwed the hoses into the torch, and taps intended to create threads in drilled holes of a dozen sizes. Five minutes before, they'd all been neatly arranged, but now I had to scavenge among the scattered hardware. Not a lot different, I admitted to myself, from the chaos I sometimes faced in my own workshop. My best guess was that I'd never face it again.

Another round from Kaplan struck within inches of the big battery-powered drill I was about to grab, and the new shaft of sunlight sparkled off a set of long drill bits, and I gave unspoken thanks to Mike-Majub while promising myself I would kill him.

I knelt and used a half dozen rounds from the Ingram to blow a ragged hole in the wall at shin height, hearing a couple of ricochets. My Glock wasn't all that big, but its grip gouged me as I wallowed around on my right side, so I laid the weapon on the floor where it would still be handy.

Lying on my side, I could see the near face of the pipe rail in sunlight six inches away, with bright new bullet scars in its yellow paint. Like the big acetylene tanks outside, its steel was too thick to be penetrated by anything less than armor-piercing rounds. That's what carbide-tipped drill bits are for.

One of the scars was deep enough to let me start the drill bit I eyeballed as a match for the correct brass fitting, and while I was chucking the long bit that was the thickness of my pinkie, I heard Mike-Majub yelling about the "bloody helo." A moment later I understood, and for a few seconds I allowed myself to hope I wouldn't have to continue what seemed likely to become my own personal mass murder-and-suicide project. The yelling was all about the rapid *thwock-thwock-thwock-thwock-thwock* of an approaching helicopter.

It quickly became so loud the shed reverberated with the racket from overhead, so loud that dust sifted from the ceiling, so loud I couldn't even hear the song of the drill as it chewed, too slowly, through the side of the pipe rail just inches outside the shed wall. Someone was shouting again, in English I thought, though I couldn't make out more than a few words. A few single rounds were fired from different directions and then the catastrophic whack of rotor blades faded a bit and I could understand, and my heart sank.

". . . Telling you news crews don't carry fucking weapons, look at the fucking logo! Don't waste any more ammunition on it," Norm yelled angrily.

So it was only some TV station's eye in the sky; lots of cameras, but no arms. As a cop I used to wish those guys were forbidden to listen to police frequencies. This time, as the noise of the circling newsgeek continued in the distance, I gave thanks for the diversion and hoped they'd at least get a close-up of me as I rose past them.

The bit suddenly cut through and I hauled it back, burning my wrist with the hot drill bit in my haste to fumble the hardened steel tap into place. Of course I couldn't twist the tap in with my fingers, but in my near panic, that's what I tried.

Another round hit the shed, and this time the steel-faced door opened a few inches. Bad news, because now the shooter could see inside a little. I wriggled to my knees and looked around for the special holder that grips a tap for leverage. No such luck. But another round spanged off the door, and in the increased daylight I spotted that bad seed among good tools, a pair of common pliers. They would have to do.

Because I was on my knees at the end of the overturned table and reaching for the pliers when Mike-Majub rushed the door, I only had time to grovel as he kicked the door open and raked the place with fire. I don't think he even saw me, and he didn't seem to care, emptying his magazine and then, grinning like a madman, grabbing a handgun from his belt as he dropped the useless Ingram.

Meanwhile, I had fumbled at my Bianchi and then realized the Glock lay on the floor, fifteen feet behind me. But I was sweating like a horse, and the irritant in my right armpit was now hanging loose, and the tatters of my shirt didn't impede my grasp of Bobby Rooney's tiny palmful of bad news. Tape and all, it came away in my hand as I rolled onto my back, and the grinning wide-eyed maniac in the doorway spied my movement. We fired together.

Though chips of concrete spattered my face, he missed. I didn't. He folded from the waist and went forward onto his knees, then his face. The top of his head was an arm's length from me and I had made a silent promise to him ten minutes previous and now, with the other barrel, I honored it.

Blinking specks of concrete from my vision, eyes streaming, I grabbed the pliers, stood up, vaulted over the tabletop, and kicked the door shut before scrambling back to the mess I had made. Pliers are an awful tool for inserting a steel tap, but they'll do the job. Chasing a thread—cutting it into the material—requires care and, usually, backing the tap out every turn or so. I wondered who was moaning softly until I realized it was me, and I quit the backing-out routine when I heard the Freightliner's starter growl.

Then Norm Goldman called out: "Let him go, Majub, it won't matter."

The tap rotated freely now. I backed it out quickly. "If he answers, I'll blow his head off," I shouted, and managed to start the little brass fitting by feel, into the threaded hole I had made. When it was finger-tight I forced it another turn with the pliers. Then I pulled the torch to me with its twinned slender snakes of hose, one of them still hissing. To keep Norm talking so I'd know where he was: "Some Jews you turned out to be," I complained. "Who am I really talking to?"

The Freightliner snicked into gear, revved up, and an almighty screech of rending metal followed. The engine idled again while Norm shouted some kind of gabble. Then, while someone strained at the wreckage and I adjusted the pliers at the butt of the torch: "I am called Daud al-Sadiq, my friend, but my true name is revenge."

"Love your camouflage," I called back. Now a louder hiss as the acetylene fitting loosened at the torch while I continued to untwist it. With the sudden unmistakable perfume of acetone came a rush of acetylene, which has no true odor of its own. The fitting came loose in my hands and I shoved the hose through the hole, to fumble blindly for the fitting. "I especially like that 'my friend' bullshit," I called.

"In my twenty years of life in the bowels of Satan I have been a true friend to many," Norm-Daud called back in a tone of reproach, everything in his voice more formal, more rhetorical than usual. Now it became faintly whimsical. "Including Jews. You'd be surprised."

"No I wouldn't," I called, knowing that if a hot round came through now it would turn me into a Roman candle. My own voice boomed and bellowed in the shed. "How else could you learn to pass yourself off as your own enemy?" I tried to mate the fittings without being able to see them. Cross-threaded them; felt sweat running into my eyes; realized some of it was blood; got the damned fittings apart and began anew.

The Freightliner's engine revved again. Norm-Daud called, "Not the real enemy. Western ways are the enemy, but I could be your friend. Heaven awaits those of us who die in the struggle; do you hear me, Majub? What can this man do but send you to your glory an hour sooner?"

I knew he was goading his buddy into trying to jump me or to run. "He's just sitting here with the whites of his eyes showing," I lied, to piss my friend-enemy off. The sigh of escaping acetylene became a thin hiss, then went silent. In its place, a hollow whoosh of gas rushing unimpeded into an empty pipe fifty feet long, starting slowly but inevitably—if the bank of supply tanks was full enough, and if there weren't any serious leaks—to fill that four-inch-diameter pipe that was now a pressure tank.

"We will all find judgment when I reach the *Ras Ormara*," Norm-Daud called happily.

"The Feds know about your ternary agent, pal, and they're on the way. That tub isn't going anyplace," I called.

That set his laughter off. "So you've worked that out? Fine. I agree. And no one else will be going anyplace, downwind, from the Golden Gate to San Jose. What, two million dead? Three? It's a start," he said, trying to sound modest.

Then the Freightliner's engine roared, and the rending of metal intensified. The big rig was shoving debris that had been my Toyota backward. I didn't know how fast my jury-rigged tank was filling, and if I misjudged, it wouldn't matter. I grabbed up my Glock and the burp gun and darted to the door I had kicked shut.

I had jammed it hopelessly.

I began to put rounds through the wall, emptying my Glock in a pattern that covered a fourth of an oval the size of a manhole cover. When I'd used that up I continued with the Ingram until it was empty. The oval wasn't complete. That's when I went slightly berserk.

I kicked, screamed, cursed and pounded, and the oval of insulated wall panel began to disintegrate along the dotted line. With insulation flying around me, the Freightliner grinding its way toward the boulevard in a paroxysm of screaming metal, I saw the oval begin to fail. I could claim it wasn't hysteria that made me intensify my assault, but my very existence had focused down to shredding that panel. When it bent outward, still connected at the bottom like the lid of a huge tin can, I hurled myself into the hole.

For an endless moment I was caught halfway through, my head and shoulders in bright sunlight, an immovable target for anyone within sight. But I was on the opposite side of the shed from the big rig, and when the wall panel failed I found myself on hands and knees, free but without a weapon.

Twenty feet away stood a huge inverted cone on steel supports, and beyond that a forest of braces and piping. As I staggered away behind the pipes one of Norm-Daud's helpers saw me and cut loose in my direction, ricochets flying like hornets. Meanwhile the Freightliner moved inexorably toward the open gate, the Toyota's wreckage shoved aside, the massive trailer trundling its cargo of megadeath along with less than a half mile to go. I hadn't so much as a stone left to hurl at it.

But I didn't need one. Funny thing about a concussion wave: when that fifty-foot pipe detonated alongside the trailer, I didn't actually hear it. Protected by all that thicket of metal, I felt a numbing sensation of pressure, seemingly from all directions. My next sensation was of lying on my side in a fetal curl, a thin whistling in my head. Beyond that I couldn't hear a thing.

I must have been unconscious for less than half a minute because unidentifiable bits of stuff lay here and there around me, some of it smoking. The trailer leaned drunkenly toward the side where my bomb had exploded, every tire on that side shredded, and gouts of liquid poured out of its cargo tanks from half a hundred punctures. Still addled by concussion, I steadied my progress out of the metal forest by leaning on pipes and supports. I figured that if anyone on the truck had survived, I'd hear him. It hadn't yet occurred to me that I was virtually stone deaf for the moment.

Not until I saw the blood-smeared figure shambling like a wino around to my side of the trailer, wearing the remnant of an expensive black-leather jacket. He was weaponless. One shoe was missing. He threw his head back, arms spread, and I saw his throat work as he opened his mouth wide. Then he fell on his knees in a runnel of liquid chemical beside the trailer, and on his face was an unspeakable agony.

A better man than I might have felt a shred of pity. What I felt was elation. As I stalked nearer I could see a headless body slumped at the window of the shrapnel-peppered Freightliner cab. Now, too, I could hear, though faintly as from a great distance, a man screaming. It was the man on his knees before me.

Standing three feet behind him, I shouted, "Hey!" I heard that, but apparently he didn't. I put my foot on his back and he fell forward, then rolled to his knees again. I would have hung one on him just for good measure then, but one look at his face told me that nothing I could do would increase his suffering. Even though his bloody hair and wide-open eyes made him look like a lunatic, a kind of sanity returned in his gaze as he recognized me.

Still on his knees, he started to say something, then tried again, shouting. "What did this?"

I pointed a thumb at my breast. "Gas in a pipe. Boom," I shouted. He looked around and saw the long shallow trench that now ran along the pavement. The entire length of the shed wall nearest the pipe rail had been cut as if by some enormous jagged saw, and of course the pipe itself was nowhere. Or rather, it was everywhere, in little chunks, evidence of a fragmentation grenade fifty feet long.

He looked up at me with the beginnings of understanding. "How?"

I could hear him a little better now. "Acetylene is an explosive all by itself," I shouted. "Can you hear me?" He nodded. "You store it under pressure by dissolving it in acetone. Pump it into a dry tank and it doesn't need any prompting. As soon as it gets up to fifteen or twenty pounds pressure—like I said: boom," I finished, with gestures.

He showed his teeth and closed his eyes; tears began to flow afresh. "Primitive stuff, but you would know that," he accused in a voice hoarse with exhaustion.

I nodded. "The new model of Islamic warrior," I accused back, "so all you know is plastique. Ternary agent. The murder of a million innocents."

"There are no innocents," said the man who had been, however briefly, my friend. Why argue with a man who says such things? I just looked at him. "There are many more like me, more than there are of men like you," he said, the words rekindling something fervid in his eyes. "The new model, you said. Wait for us. We are coming."

My eyes stung from the tons of flammable liquid around us. When I reached out to help him up, he shook his torso, fumbling in his pockets. "Get away," he said. "Run."

Only when I saw that he had pulled a lighter from his pocket did I realize what he meant. I scrambled away. An instant later, the whole area was ablaze, and for all I knew the tanks on the trailer might explode. Daud-al-Sadiq, alias Norm Goldman, knelt deeply and prostrated himself in the inferno as though facing east in prayer as the flames climbed toward his warrior's heaven.

The metro cops got to the scene before anyone else, and after that came the paramedic van. Aside from cuts on my face and arms and the fact that the whistle would remain in my head for hours, I had lucked out. I could even hear ordinary speech, though it sounded thin and lacked resonance.

Captain Hassan al-Nadwi and several of his crew weren't so lucky in my view but, in their own view, I suppose they found the ultimate good luck. Using automatic weapons, they had tried to prevent a boarding party. One competence the Feds do have is marksmanship. No wonder the remaining crew were so hyperactive that morning; they were going to heaven, and they were going *now*.

Dana Martin pointed out to me after I handed over her cracked, useless Loc-8 gadget an hour later, that there had probably never been any intention on the part of the holy warriors to sail beyond the Golden Gate again. Their intent was evidently to start up their enormous doomsday machine and, if possible, set it in motion toward San Francisco's crowded Fisherman's Wharf. The crew would all be dead by the time the *Ras Ormara* grounded; dead, and attended by compliant lovelies in Islamic heaven while men, women, kids, pets, and birds in flight died by the millions around San Francisco Bay.

Dana said, "We came to that conclusion after we found that all the Korean crew members but one had reservations of one kind or another to clear out of the area," she told me. "They knew what was coming. Once we realized how much of the major component they must have to react with all that stuff on the trailer, we knew they were using the ship itself as a tank. An external hull inspection wouldn't pick that up."

"You lost me," I said.

"You know that most ships are double-hulled? Well, the *Ras Or-*

mara is triple-hulled, thanks to a rebuild by the Pakistanis. The main component of the ternary agent was brought in using the volume between the hulls as a huge cargo tank. I think Park Soon must have found the transfer pipes, and they couldn't take a chance on him."

"Three hulls," I muttered. "Talk about your basic inside job. You think the entire crew knew?"

"Hard to say, but they wouldn't have to. It doesn't take but a few crewman to pull away from the slip. The North Koreans helped set the stage, but most of them don't believe Allah is going to snatch them up to the highest heaven," she said wryly.

"I don't get it. Which one of them did," I prompted.

"The one who was an Indonesian Moslem," she said. "He was on the truck crew with the perp who passed himself off as Norman Goldman."

"Then he's a clinker over there." I nodded across the boulevard toward the still smoking ruin. "Really keen of you people, assuring me what a great guy Norm Goldman was. Who did your background checks: Frank and Ernest?"

She didn't want to talk about that. Journalists had a field day later, second-guessing the Feds who failed to penetrate the "legends," the false bona fides, of men who had inserted themselves into mythical backgrounds twenty years before. And in twenty years a smart terrorist can make his legend damned near perfect.

Dana Martin preferred to concentrate on what I had done. I had already set her straight on the carnage at the chemical plant. She had it in her noggin that I had started the fire. The truth was, that's exactly what I would have done first thing off, if I'd had the chance. I didn't say that.

"I still don't see exactly how you detonated your bomb," she said. I responded, a bit tersely, by telling her I didn't have to detonate the damned thing. Acetylene doesn't like to be crowded in a dry tank, and when you try, a little bit of pressure makes it disassociate like TNT.

"I'm no chemist," she said, "but that sounds like you're, ah, prevaricating."

"Ask a welder, if the FBI has any. If he doesn't know, don't let him do any gas welding. End of discussion."

Her big beautiful eyes widened, not even remotely friendly. I knew she thought I'd been carrying some kind of incendiary device, which has been a sore point with Feds for many years, ever since the Waco screw-up. She kept looking hard at me. Well, the hell with her—and that's what I said next.

"You're under contract to us," she reminded me.

"You offered to cut me loose early today," replied. "I accepted, whether you heard me or not. Keep your effing money if you don't believe me. Oh, don't worry about sweeping up," I said into her astonished frown. "I'll testify in all this; I've got nothing to hide."

And while she was still talking, I walked away from there with as much dignity as a man can muster when his clothes are in tatters and his only vehicle lies in smoking shreds.

Actually I did have something to hide: gratitude. I didn't want to try explaining to Dana Martin how I felt about the brilliant, savage, personable, murderous Daud. I wasn't sure I could if I tried.

There was only one reason why he would've made me promise to drive the miles to San Rafael for lunch: to make certain I wouldn't be a victim of that enormous, lethal cloud of nerve gas that would be boiling up from the *Ras Ormara.* And while he could have grabbed my ankles when he set himself alight, he didn't. He told me to run for it.

He would kill millions of people he had never seen, yet he felt something special for a guy who had befriended him for only a few hours. I didn't understand that kind of thinking then, and I still don't.

I do understand this: A man must never trust his buns to anyone, however intelligent and friendly, who believes there's a bright future in suicide. And as long as I live, I will be haunted by what Daud said, moments before he died. There are more of us, he said. Wait for us. We are coming.

Well, I believe they'll come, so I'm waiting. But I'm not waiting in a population center with folded hands. I'm recounting the last words of Daud al-Sadiq to everyone who'll listen. I'm also erecting a cyclone fence around my acreage, and I'm in the process of obtaining a captive breeding permit. That's the prerequisite for a guard animal no dog can ever match.

DEAN ING has been an interceptor crew chief, construction worker on high Sierra dams, solid-rocket designer, builder-driver of sports racers—his prototype Magnum was a *Road & Track* feature—and after a doctorate from the University of Oregon, a professor. For years, as one of the cadre of survival writers, he built and tested backpack hardware on Sierra solos. His technothriller, *The Ransom of Black Stealth One*, was a *New York Times* best-seller, and he has been finalist for both the Nebula and Hugo awards. His more humorous works have been characterized as "fast, furious, and funny." Slower and heavier now with two hip replacements and titanium abutments in his jaw, he pursues his hobbies, which include testing models of his fictional vehicles, fly fishing, ergonomic design, and container gardening. His daughters comprise a minister, a longhorn rancher, an Alaskan tour guide, and an architect. He and his wife, Gina, a fund-raiser for the Eugene Symphony, live in Oregon, where he is currently building a mountainside library/shop.

Harve Rackham and Dana Martin have appeared in two previous novellas, "Pulling Through" from the collection of the same name, and "Vital Signs" which appeared in the science fiction series *Destinies*.

SKYHAWKS FOREVER

BY BARRETT TILLMAN

ACKNOWLEDGMENTS

Wynn Foster, Rick Morgan, George Olmsted, Larry and Janet Pearson, Robert Powell, Dwight Van Horn, Phil Wood, Jack Woodul, Lucy Young, the Skyhawk Association, and Training Squadron Seven.

One

The Boat

"Well, now I almost believe it," exclaimed Michael Ostrewski to his fellow flight instructor from Advanced Training Associates.

"Believe what?" Eric "Psycho" Thaler stood beside him on the flight deck of the former USS *Santa Cruz*.

Ostrewski pointed about him. "That we're really going to carqual on this boat. I mean, as long as she was mothballed in Bremerton, she was just an old Forrestal-class carrier. But now that she's an active ship, here in Long Beach, it looks like we're in business."

Thaler, who with "Ozzie" Ostrewski had gone to war aboard one of *Santa Cruz*'s sisters, envisioned this flight deck in its glory years: when aircraft carriers were named for battles or historic ships rather than mere politicians. He visualized thirty knots of wind over the deck, steam roiling from the catapults, and dozens of sailors milling in organized chaos as twenty-ton aircraft slammed onto the deck at 130 knots. He asked his colleague, "Did you talk to the navy yard guys yet? I mean, about the old girl's condition?"

Ostrewski nodded. "Yeah, just a little. One of the engineers was still aboard after the cruise from Bremerton. He says they worked up to twenty-four knots, but they expect to make thirty by the time we start trapping."

"What about the jobs that weren't finished there?"

"Well, they concentrated on what we'd need to operate six jets. Besides main plant and electrical, we have two good catapults, the arresting gear, and fuel systems. The condensers aren't up to speed, so there'll be limited water, and some of the radars aren't operational. But the mirror system checks out so the LSOs will be happy." He flashed two thumbs up.

Thaler looked around the 328-foot-wide deck where American and Chinese military personnel and civilians were busily engaged. "I guess the chinks will have a smaller crew and air wing, huh?"

Ostrewski nodded. "Smaller air wing fershure, dude. They plan on two Flanker squadrons plus a couple of helo outfits for starters. I don't know how many bodies that means, but a lot less than one of our wings. Probably about two thousand for ship's company, to start."

"Oz, I don't really understand something. This isn't a commissioned naval vessel yet, and far as I know the Chinese haven't paid for it in full. Who's actually responsible for this bird farm? I mean, do they have two captains or what?"

"Yeah, they do. Admiral Rhode at NavAir says the official skipper is Captain Albright, who's about to retire. He has a Chinese opposite number with an exec and department heads on down the line, and most of them have American supervisors. But a lot of the crew is civilian contract labor because there aren't enough white hats available after all that 'right sizing.' "

"They still going to send some talent out from Pensacola?"

Ostrewski nodded. "Yeah, I guess Rocky Rhode and others are nervous about of a bunch of civilians driving a carrier up and down the California coast, and retired guys like us landing on her. We're getting an instructor from the LSO school and a couple of TraCom instructors to monitor our procedures."

"Well, I'm glad to see the Chinese are running their part of it." Thaler waved a hand toward the carrier's island, where a gutted Flanker airframe was secured to the deck by tie-down chains. Even with its outer-wing panels folded, the sixty-eight-foot-long fighter, with its twin tails reaching eighteen feet high, took up a lot of space. The ATA instructors watched "Flight Deck 101" in progress as Chinese sailors rehearsed aircraft handling and servicing in the unaccustomed carrier environment.

"Think they'll get the hang of it?" Thaler asked.

"Yeah. This first class is a mix of navy and air force. The sailors handle the basic chores and the blue-suiters do the aircraft maintenance. They already knew the Flanker systems."

Psycho Thaler was skeptical. "Man, they're sure jumping in with both feet. I'd hate to have to learn everything they need to in a few weeks."

Ostrewski pointed to the sailor doing most of the talking. "See the petty officer who's lecturing? Mr. Wei, our Chinese liaison, told Terry Peters that this bunch started training ashore back in China. They knew all the moves before they got here: the yellow gear, the deck cycle, all that stuff. They even had full-size flight deck and hangar deck mock-ups to practice moving airplanes." He shook his head in appreciation. "Makes sense when you think about it."

Deep in thought, Ostrewski toed a tie-down on the nonskid deck surface. "What is it?" Thaler asked.

"Oh, I don't know." Ozzie looked up again at the bustle around him. "I can't quite get used to the idea of us selling the Commies an operational carrier, then teaching them how to use it." He grinned self-consciously. "Even if our company has the contract."

Thaler nudged his colleague. "Careful—if Terry Peters hears you, it's bad enough. If Jane hears you . . ." He allowed himself a grin. "Besides, like we always said in the navy—it's way above our pay grade. Congress and the administration signed off on it three years ago, so just be thankful that we got the job." Psycho grinned at his former *Langley* shipmate. "Besides, how'd you like to watch some other civilian contractor get a sweetheart deal like this?"

Thaler noticed a stocky Caucasian detach himself from the Chinese. "Hey, there's Igor Gnido. He's the lead pilot with the Sukhoi transition team."

The Russian waved at the Americans, and Thaler greeted him. "Hey, Igor." Ozzie was less effusive; he merely nodded. The Only Polish-American Tomcat Ace respected Gnido's reputation as an aviator but could not bring himself to like the former Soviet combat pilot.

"Good morning to you," Gnido ventured with a smile that Thaler took as genuine. The Flanker pilot waved a hand toward the Chinese sailors. "They getting good start on flight deck pro-cee-dures."

"We were just discussing that," Thaler replied. He watched as a group of "grapes"—sailors in purple jerseys—moved a fuel hose toward the Sukhoi's port wing. "Did the factory specially build this airplane to accept American hose fittings? I mean, like they built the nose gear to fit the catapult shuttle?"

Gnido leaned close, trying to ensure that he understood the question. Thaler made a circle with his left thumb and forefinger and a probe of his first two right fingers. The Russian nodded. "Ah, *da, da*." He nodded decisively. "Nose gear yes. Fuel fittings, not exactly." He shook his head. "All Soviet aircraft were being designed to take your hoses, you know?" He hid any edginess in mentioning a NATO–Warsaw Pact conflict. "Plan was, take European airfields and use equipment already there, you know?"

Ostrewski, whose Polish roots ran deep, absorbed that knowledge and worked his professionalism around the ethical thorns. "Well, I guess that makes sense, if you're going to invade the next country."

Thaler felt moved to intervene. "Does that cause any problems with maintenance, Igor? I mean, having both English and metric systems in the same airplane."

Gnido shrugged eloquently. "Is not being much problem. Just way it is, you know? Like cockpit instruments. In air force Flankers, all is metric. In this airplane for navy, airspeed is knots, altitude meters. Besides, pretty soon America is being all metric, like rest of world. Best for everybody, yes?"

Thaler demurred. "Igor, you'll get an argument about that, I guarandamntee you."

Two

Scooter

Half a dozen staffers of Advanced Training Associates lazed away the shank of the afternoon, sipping slowly and speaking rapidly. The animated atmosphere in ATA's office spaces probably had not been seen since Williams Air Force Base became Williams Gateway Airport south of Mesa, Arizona.

Despite the beer-call military ambience, the atmosphere was post–Cold War business; a corporate foundation overlaid with a lather of friendly rivalry.

One of the partners, Zack Delight, had told an active-duty friend, "Here there be morale." A former Marine aviator, he had retired as a reserve lieutenant colonel, flew for Delta, and now was on his second or third career, depending on how they were reckoned. Pushing sixty, he was stocky, well built, and studiously irreverent. He sat on a barstool, scratching the Vandyke beard he had cultivated to cover a scar obtained in a motorcycle "incident." Now, with the unaccustomed beard, "Pure" Delight said he was still getting accustomed to "that mean-looking bastard glaring at me in the mirror every morning."

Next to Delight was Robert "Robo" Robbins, a retired navy commander and former landing signal officer. Slightly younger, he wore a perpetual smile as if savoring a private joke at the expense of the world around him. Aside from their previous part-time work for ATA, both staffers shared a passion for World War I aviation. They haunted The Aerodrome web site, exchanged arcane information and esoterica, and constantly critiqued each other's alternating chapters in an epic titled *Duel over Douai.*

Delight and Robbins were joined by Ozzie Ostrewski, just back from Long Beach. New to ATA, he was known as an exceptionally fine fighter pilot. Rumor and gossip swirled around Ozzie. Reportedly he had scored multiple kills as a USS *Langley* F-14 pilot during a classified dustup in the Indian Ocean a few years before. He steadfastly declined all efforts to elicit details, both overt and otherwise. Not even his shipmate Psycho Thaler would discuss it; he had been there as well.

"Hey, Oz," said Delight. "Lemme buy you a drink, god damn it." Pure and Robo traded sideways smiles. They knew Ostrewski as a nonimbiber, nonblasphemer, and devout Catholic—a rara avis in military aviation.

"And the horse you rode in on," Ostrewski replied evenly. He was getting good at bowdlerizing. He reached over the bar and pulled a root beer from the ice chest. "Any word yet?"

"Naw," said Robbins. He knew what Ostrewski meant. "The boss is still in the office with the new kid. But I think he's gonna hire her."

"Damn!" Ostrewski slammed his bottle down on the bar harder than intended. It was the direst expletive the normally composed aviator allowed himself. "That's one reason I got out of the navy—the damn double standards and all that bu . . . siness." Delight suddenly realized how upset the instructor really was.

Robbins nudged him. "C'mon, Oz, how bad can it be?"

Ozzie inhaled, held his breath, and exhaled. "Look, it's the accumulation of all this stuff. I don't know about you guys, but I really don't like the idea of teaching Chinese Communists how to land on carriers, let alone go bombing and strafing with them. Add in the trouble we're bound to have with girl aviators, and what was a dream job is going to get screwed up."

"The world's changing, my boy," Robo said solicitously.

"Yeah, I know, I know . . . it's just not *my* world anymore. Not even my same country."

Michael Ostrewski wore his heart on his flight jacket. His friends knew he was intensely proud of his Polish heritage and its Old World values.

"Attention on deck!"

Delight, Robbins, and the others turned in their seats. Striding through the door was Terry "Hook" Peters, six-foot-three-inches of enthusiasm and what the navy called command presence. Peters saw his wife in the room and winked. Jane Peters, five-foot-five-inches of feistiness, blew a kiss at the once-gangly kid who earned an ironic call sign when he forgot to lower his tailhook for his first night carrier landing.

A former Blue Angels commander, he and Jane had invested most of their savings in ATA, and now it had paid off with the Chinese training contract.

With him was a brown-eyed brunette, about five-foot-nine and 135 pounds. She glanced around, noticed Jane Peters, and gave her a shy smile. Jane had liked her immediately and told Terry Peters that Elizabeth Vespa got Jane's vote among the four applicants for the new slot. The fact that Liz and that nice Ozzie Ostrewski were single had not escaped her attention.

"Gang," Terry explained, "I'd like to introduce our new instructor—Liz Vespa, call sign Scooter."

Cheers, applause, and laughter greeted Elizabeth Vespa. A few ATA staffers chuckled at the nickname. Ostrewski muttered to Robbins, "Cute."

"Yeah, she is, kind of," Robbins replied.

"I meant the call sign," Ozzie said in a monotone.

Peters continued the introduction. "Liz comes to us from TraCom. She left active duty as a lieutenant commander, and the navy's loss is our gain. She was an A-4 CarQual instructor before going to T-45s, and that's part of the reason I selected her now that we're progressing with the Chinese students. She's more current on carrier qualifications than any of us, and now, having flown with her, I can say that she's a good stick." He turned to Vespa and grinned. "Liz, welcome aboard!"

Vespa blushed slightly at the attention. Standing with her hands behind her back, she said, "Thanks, Captain Peters." She scanned the room, taking in the faces. "There's no place else I'd rather be than here, flying with you guys." More applause and laughter skittered through the room—except from the crew cut, gray-eyed instructor at the bar who met her gaze without blinking. Even from that distance, Liz Vespa could read the flight jacket patch that said OZZIE.

Three

As Good As It Gets

Peters and Delight watched the two Skyhawks accelerate as Ostrewski led Vespa in a section takeoff. Zack turned toward his partner. "You sure this is a good idea, Terry?"

Peters's gaze never left the TA-4s. "It's Jane's idea. She said that when any of her third-graders didn't get along, she put 'em at the same desk." He shrugged. "Eventually they made up and became friends."

Delight shook his head. "Child psychology applied to fighter pilots." He unzipped a wry grin. "Works for me."

Three miles over Gila Bend, Ozzie keyed his mike. "Ah, Wizard Two, let's go in trail. Over."

Liz smiled in anticipation. That was the agreed-upon signal. "Let's go in trail" actually meant, "The chase is on; see if you can stay with me, cowgirl." But privately she rankled at Ozzie's self-confident call sign: "The Wizard of Oz."

She double-clicked her mike button in acknowledgment.

Two seconds later Ozzie half snapped to inverted and sucked the stick into his stomach. From sixteen thousand feet, Wizard One responded in a mind-numbing split-ess, the Gs building quickly to the grayout stage. His vision grew fuzzy around the edges, narrowing to a thirty-degree cone. In several seconds he would regain full vision and swivel his head to see if he had made any money on Scooter Vespa.

Liz had expected an abrupt move, but the suddenness caught her off guard. She lost a hundred fifty yards before she rolled over and followed Ozzie downward. It was much as she expected: On the ground, Michael Ostrewski was a complete gentleman. Up here, man to man, he was a mongoose. No quarter asked or given.

And damn sure no preferential treatment for girls.

Wizard One pulled through the bottom of the split-ess, and as the nose reached the horizon Ozzie rolled into a ninety-degree bank, still pulling hard. He sensed the Skyhawk approaching the onset of buffet, but a minute adjustment sustained his rate of turn. He felt he was getting maximum performance out of the bird.

From experience and conditioning, Ostrewski was comfortable at four Gs. He looked back over his right shoulder, in the direction of his turn. Vespa's Wizard Two had lost some of its original dead-six aspect, but the contest was far from over.

Ostrewski's testosterone-rich brain was convinced that no woman could stay with him in a sustained high-G contest. He determined to make Sir Isaac Newton his chief ally, wearing down Vespa by the unrelenting pressure of gravity. Besides, it was an accepted fact in squadron ready rooms: Girls can fly, but they can't hack the G.

With her throttle two-blocked, Liz focused her powerful concentration not only on Wizard One, but on its projected path. She knew that Ozzie was unlikely to telegraph his punches, and he could be trusted to do the unexpected, but the laws of physics permitted no amendments; they were enforced equally upon all contenders.

As both jets came around the circle, completing their first 360, Liz perceived that the relative separation had stabilized. Ozzie's initial move had netted him perhaps fifteen degrees. By common consent, the fight would end one of two ways: reaching the artificial "hard deck" of ten thousand feet, or when one of them could track the other in the gunsight for at least three seconds.

Passing through magnetic north, Ostrewski nudged bottom rudder, sliding the TA-4 downward to the right. Liz saw the motion and, momentarily perplexed, jockeyed stick and rudder to follow. She was suspicious; Delight had confided that Ozzie seldom made an error of technique.

As Liz slid down toward Ozzie's six o'clock, he abruptly half rolled to the left, pausing almost inverted. Liz could either try to match the move or risk closing to dangerous range. She followed, smoothly coordinating her controls. The G had abated a little, but the oppressive load still pressed on her body.

Ostrewski smiled to himself as he completed an elegant slow roll, stopped the motion, then stomped left rudder and continued around the circle, sliding outside Vespa's field of view in a lopsided barrel roll.

When he rolled wings level he looked up to his left—about 9:30—and was gratified with a view of Two's belly. He retarded the throttle and hit the button. His speed brakes extended into the slipstream, incurring welcome drag that slowed him further.

With airspeed and G relatively undiminished, Wizard Two edged ahead of One. Liz sensed more than knew what had happened—there was only one way to explain Ozzie's disappearance—and she knew it was seconds before his triumphant "Guns" call ruined her day.

Her mind raced. *He's behind my trailing edge, slowing and expecting me to overshoot. But I've got more energy.*

Liz began a hard left turn, realizing that Ozzie would be cleaning up his speed brakes and adding power before putting his gunsight pipper on her tailpipe. But instead of continuing the turn, she forced the Skyhawk three-quarters of the way around, completing 270 degrees of roll. She stopped the wings nearly vertical to the horizon, then pulled right. She surprised herself with her calmness. *Gosh, I hope we don't collide.*

Ostrewski gaped at the plain view of Wizard Two crossing his nose two hundred feet ahead. With Liz's superior momentum at that point, he realized she would continue the turn into his rear hemisphere before he could regain comparable energy. *Smooth move, Scooter!* He had no chance to make a "Guns" call.

"Hard deck. Knock it off!" Liz Vespa knew the contest was a draw, but her voice carried the ring of triumph.

Ninety minutes later, following the debrief, Ozzie Ostrewski and Scooter Vespa regarded one another across the bar in the Skyhawk Lounge. He clinked his root beer against her Coors Light. "Here's to good times." Clearly the frost had melted.

"Long may they wave." She clinked back.

Ozzie looked at her. "You seem pretty darn pleased with yourself, Miss Vespa."

Feeling flirtatious, she cocked her head. "Why not, Mr. O? I just outflew The Only Polish-American Tomcat Ace."

"Did not."

"Did too."

"Did not!"

"Did too!"

He grinned back at her. "Okay, you made a righteous move after I was kicking your butt. Where'd it come from?"

She set down her beer. "Well, because I made a human being of you, I'll tell you." She pretended to ignore his feigned indignation. "Daddy's best friend flew F-86s in Korea. When I got my wings, he told me about his fights in MiG Alley."

Ozzie nodded vacantly, staring at the mural above the bar. "You know, it's odd. I've seen that move before, too."

"Really? Where?"

His eyes returned to her face. He shrugged.

"Oh." She thought. *They still won't talk about the* Langley *cruise.*

"Well," he said, "it was a great hop, Scooter. You can be my wingman anytime—in Wizard Flight."

She giggled more than she intended. "And like Maverick said to Iceman: 'Bullshit. You can be *my* wingman—in Scooter Flight.' "

Ostrewski gave a noncommittal grunt as he finished his root beer. Two minutes passed before he worked up enough nerve to ask Liz to go dancing.

Four

Gonna Wash That Man . . .

Orbiting at sixteen thousand feet, Liz Vespa relished being alone in a jet. Hawk Twelve was one of four A-4Fs owned or leased by ATA, and the powerful little single-seater was a joy to fly—as Zack said, "Pure delight." Lighter than the two-seat trainers with almost thirty percent more thrust, it was the sports car of Skyhawks.

Nearing the end of the two-week air-to-ground phase, the instructors anticipated live ordnance for qualification. Vespa smiled beneath her molded gray oxygen mask—the feds had gone spastic at the mere suggestion of five-hundred-pound bombs being loaded on civilian aircraft. But ATA's certification with State and DOD, plus some high-level arm twisting on behalf of the Chinese, had resulted in issuance of approval for "owning" and proper storage of destructive devices. Vespa marveled at Terry Peters's patience with fearful, overbearing federal inspectors.

Vespa switched channels on her VHF radio and checked in with the Gila Bend controller. She was advised to watch for two F-16s outbound—Fighting Falcons of the Fifty-sixth Tactical Fighter Wing based at nearby Luke Air Force Base. Moments later she caught them, swift darts rocketing above her to the southwest. For a moment Liz envied the Falcon pilots their high-performance fighters, then mentally berated herself. *I've already got one of the best flying jobs on earth.* She keyed the mike. "Gila, this is Hawk Twelve. I see them. Are we clear?"

"Roger, Hawk. Your range time begins in three minutes."

She acknowledged and switched to ATA's common frequency. "Hawk Lead from Hawk Twelve. Zack, do you read?"

The carrier wave crackled in her earphones as Delight's New Mexico drawl came to her from twenty miles astern. "Twelve from Lead. I gotcha, Scooter. I'm inbound with four good birds. Will proceed as briefed. Out."

Vespa now knew that Pure Delight had launched with three other TA-4Js, all with four Mark 82s beneath the wings. Acting as range safety officer, she would clear the flight into the operating area and coordinate with the ground controller in keeping other aircraft away from the impact zone. She was authorized to cancel operations at any time with a knock-it-off call.

In her fifteen years in the navy, Liz Vespa had seldom seen live ordnance expended. Most of her flying had been in C-9 transports and TraCom T-34s or TA-4s. The closest she had got to tactical operations had been qualification as an A-4 adversary pilot, but even that coveted slot ended when all but two of the squadrons were disestablished.

Quitcherbitchin' she told herself. She leveled the Foxtrot, nosed down slightly, and executed a precise four-point roll. Then for no reason at all she wondered what it would be like to kiss Michael Ostrewski. *Do you, Scooter, take Ozzie . . .*

Liz made a clearing turn to port, expecting to see Hawk Flight inbound. She forced herself to focus on the job at hand, upset that she had allowed her mind to wander in the air. That had seldom happened. It was one of the factors that separated her from so many other aviators, male or female. Her flight evaluations had repeated entries: "excellent situational awareness, full concentration, highly professional." Now she found herself humming the refrain from *South Pacific*, her favorite musical. *Gonna wash that man right out of my hair, and send him on his way . . .*

She told herself she was not in love with Ozzie Ostrewski or anyone else, which was true. She knew that Ozzie had recently met "a nice Catholic girl" at a midnight Mass and presumably he was dating her. Once or twice Liz had thought of asking offhandedly, "Hey, Oz, how's your love life?" She had demurred because she knew that The Only Polish-American Tomcat Ace would certainly interpret it as jealousy. *Men are such swine. Well, at least some men. If only he weren't such a good dancer . . .*

"Hawk Twelve from Hawk Lead. I gotcha, Scooter. I'm about three miles back at your eight. Over."

Damn it! Liz, get your shit together. She was angry at being "caught" by Zack Delight, flying in the backseat of one of the trainers. Vespa felt she should have made the first tally-ho on a four-plane flight instead of being tagged as a single. She knew that, despite his red-meat exterior, Delight was too polite to mention it again, but she also knew she had just dropped a point in the unrelenting tacit competition among aviators.

"Lead from Twelve. Roger, Zack. I'm clearing you onto the range. Check in with Gila Control before your first run."

"Right-o, Scooter."

Resuming her orbit, Liz awaited Delight's initial bombing pass. Each Skyhawk would make four runs: one each from five thousand feet at sixty degrees; seven-thousand at thirty degrees; and two from the low-level pop-up pattern at forty-five degrees. She and Delight would mark the hits on their kneeboards for comparison with the data received from the range personnel before debrief.

Moments later Delight was on the air again. "Gila Control, this is Hawk Lead. Rolling in hot."

Glancing down, Liz saw the jet roll over and slant into its sixty-degree dive toward the northerly target, an ancient truck. She knew that Wang was flying, with Zack observing in the rear seat. The other three Chinese—Deng, Yao, and Hua—were solo.

The lead Skyhawk tracked straight down its chosen path. Liz judged it a decent run, maybe a bit shallow, but the little delta-winged jet smoothly pulled up after making its drop. Wang's lilting accent came to her ears, "Lead is pulling off." Below and behind the TA-4 an orange-white light erupted near the truck, spewing smoke and dust into the air.

Deng was next down the chute with a "Two is in" call. Liz watched with pride as her pupil put his first bomb near the target at five o'clock. If anything, he had released a little high. She imagined him flipping the master arm switch to safe as he recovered and called, "Two off."

"Three going in," came from Yao. Liz rolled port wing low to follow his run. She knew that Ozzie had literally taken the taciturn Chinese under his wing, and evidently the instructor's extra attention had borne fruit. Mr. Yao would never be the best bomber in the class, but he showed steady improvement. For a moment Liz wondered if Ostrewski had invested the effort for Yao, or for himself. She literally shook the thought from her mind, snapping her head left and right. *I've got to get him out of my mind for a while.*

Yao was pressing, no doubt about it. Delight had just called "Three, you're . . ." when Yao dropped. The hit was about thirty feet out at one o'clock. Zack came back on the air. "Too low, Yao. You were probably below twenty-five hundred." There was no reply, so Delight added, "Acknowledge." The hick on the turnip truck was gone from his voice, replaced by the Leader of Men.

"Acknowledge." Liz could tell that Yao resented the rebuke.

As Four rolled in, Delight was climbing back to the perch, leading an aerial daisy chain of pirouetting Skyhawks. Vespa tracked each through the seven-thousand-foot pattern and the first pop-up, observing one hit for each pilot. On his fourth run, however, Hawk Lead pulled out without releasing; Delight had a hung bomb. Clearing the immediate area, he called Vespa. "Liz, I can't get shed of this thing. We're gonna have to divert to Luke. Over."

Vespa realized that Zack Delight had no choice. The FAA had balked at permitting ATA jets to take off with live ordnance; there was no question of allowing anyone to return to a civilian field with a potentially armed bomb aboard, whatever the master switch position. "Roger, Zack. I'll finish the cycle here."

Deng's fourth bomb was the best yet—it obscured the deformed old vehicle. As he called off and clear, Liz directed him to dog in the holding pattern until the others were finished. She wanted to lead a four-ship flight back into the break, "lookin' good for the troops."

Yao called "Three in" and made an aggressive move in his second pop-up. It was immediately apparent at the apex that he was too steep. Liz realized that Mr. Yao was determined to get a center hit, and the onerous Mr. Delight's departure only encouraged the student. She thumbed the mike button. "Three, you're too steep! Pull out!"

The TA-4J continued its plunge toward the chalky circle on the desert floor. Liz felt her cheeks flush. "Hawk Three, this is Hawk Lead. You are ordered to pull out. Now, mister!"

Yao's Skyhawk never wavered in its dive. With her thumb still on the transmit button, Liz watched aghast. *My god, he's going right in . . .*

She was already forming the thought "target fixation" for the postmortem when Yao released. Liz estimated he dropped at less than two thousand feet above the ground, and the lethal blast pattern extended to twenty-two hundred. His nose had barely come level when the Mark 82 detonated.

Five

Thumbs-Down

Hawk Three was obscured in the mushrooming smoke and dust of the explosion. Vespa gave a sigh of relief, surprised to see the Skyhawk recover. She realized he had been caught in the frag pattern. *He must have damage.* She ordered priorities in her mind.

"Knock it off, knock it off. This is Hawk Twelve to all Hawks. Safe all your master arm switches. Acknowledge."

Wang in Hawk Four, the only one still with ordnance, chirped a response at least two octaves high. Liz had Yao's jet padlocked in her vision as she pushed over to join him. Briefly she switched frequencies. "Gila Control from Hawk Twelve. We may have a damaged aircraft. I'm stopping operations."

"Ah, roger, Hawk. We read you. Standing by."

She was back to the common freq. "Hawk Three from Twelve. Yao, do you read me?"

Something rapid and garbled came from the two-seater now less than two thousand yards ahead of Twelve. Liz waited clarification, got none, and called again. "Yao, this is Vespa. I am a mile in trail, overtaking you to port." She could see the stricken jet was streaming something, fuel or hydraulic fluid. Or both. The plane was in level flight, slowly turning northerly, toward Williams.

Yao's gentle turn allowed Vespa to close more easily. She slid up on his left wing and surveyed the damage. Small holes were hemorrhaging vital fluids from the wings and empennage. The Skyhawk's "wet wing" held three thousand pounds of fuel, and most of it was venting through holes in the bottom. It occurred to Liz that this sight had been familiar to aviators of Hook Peters's generation: a battle-damaged A-4 trying to reach home before it bled to death.

She remembered to speak slowly, modulating her voice. "Yao, this is Vespa. Can you transmit? Over."

She saw the student's head turn toward her briefly, a faceless entity beneath the oxygen mask and sun visor. He tapped the side of his helmet, then he nodded vigorously. Placing his left hand on his mask, he shook his head left and right. *He can receive but not transmit.* She rocked her wings. "All right, Yao. Keep this heading." She paused. "Break-break. Four, do you copy?"

"Yes, Miss Vespa. Copy."

"Wang, I want you to safe your bomb and drop it on the nearest bull's-eye. Then join Deng and return to base. Clear each other for hung ordnance before landing. Acknowledge."

Wang replied, then Liz was back to Yao. "Three, this is Vespa again. Let's do a systems check. Show me a thumb's-up, thumb's-down, or thumb's-level for a declining state." She allowed him to absorb the procedure, then began.

"Hydraulics." Thumb down.

"Utility." Thumb level. *Damn, he's losing his controls.*

"Fuel." Thumb level. *He's bleeding fuel and hydraulics.* Vespa was frustrated, uncertain how long Yao could stay in the air.

"Electric." Thumb up.

"Yao, I can clear you for a straight-in approach or you can eject in a safe area." Yao motioned toward the north, nodding for emphasis. "You can maintain control long enough for a landing?"

Yao nodded again, less vigorously.

"All right. I'm calling the tower to declare an emergency."

Assured that the fire trucks were rolling, Liz took stock. Fifteen miles out, it was still possible for Yao to eject into the row crops south of Williams, or she could talk him down.

The steps came to her like multiplication tables. "Yao, get ready. To compensate for hydraulic loss, you'll have to pull the T-handle. First, be sure you're below two hundred knots." Liz glanced at her own airspeed indicator: 210.

She saw him lean down in the cockpit, then straighten. He nodded. "All right, Yao. You're flying by cable now. The stick forces will be very high—especially the ailerons—but you can compensate somewhat with electric trim."

The abused J52 began spitting intermittent smoke. Liz noted that the white mist in the slipstream was nearly gone. *He's about to run out of fuel.* "Yao, listen. You need to switch to the fuselage fuel tank. Do it now."

Yao nodded, then flashed a thumbs-up. Vespa asked, "Fuel flow steady?" Another nod, followed by a thumb level. Liz assumed problems with the fuel pump, but at fifty pounds per minute the fifteen hundred pounds in the fuselage tank would get the wounded Skyhawk home.

Vespa's mind raced, trying to stay ahead of the airborne crisis proceeding at three and a half miles per minute.

He's getting pretty low; he's going to drag it in. "Yao, you're losing altitude. Can you add power and hold what you got?"

Hawk Three seemed to respond, then visibly decelerated. Liz glanced at her altimeter: barely two thousand feet above the ground. *It's gonna be awful close.*

"Yao, listen. I think you're having fuel feed problems. Switch to manual fuel control." A brisk nod acknowledged the order. "Okay, good. Now slowly advance your throttle to eighty-eight percent. Let me know how that works."

Long moments dragged by before Yao gave a thumb's-up.

"All right, Mr. Yao. You're doing fine. Listen, we're going to make a low cautionary approach. I want you to maintain 160 knots indicated, okay?" The two jets jockeyed in relation to one another, speed stabilizing at 165 by Vespa's airspeed indicator.

"Now, one more thing, Yao. I need you to put 110 mils on your gunsight. Understand? At the end of the runway, you will aim for the thousand-foot marker and fly onto the runway. Okay?"

Yao reached up and put the setting on his sight. He looked at Vespa and displayed his left thumb again.

Liz waited a few more moments, trying to gauge Yao's rate of descent against the remaining distance. *Damn it! I need to talk to him.* She waited several seconds more, then regretted the time she spent pondering. "Yao, this is Hawk Lead." She sought to reassert her authority. "You need to decide right away if you can land or if you should eject." She emphasized each syllable for clarity. Yao squirmed on his seat as if trying to make a decision. Following several rapid pulses, he pointed straight ahead.

There's the runway! Vespa could see the perimeter fence and the two-mile-long concrete strip running into the midday mirage. She knew that Yao could stand some good news. "Three, this is Vespa. I have the runway in sight. Come left about fifteen degrees." Slowly, the TA-4 complied, steadying up on the runway heading. Barely two miles now.

Then Yao depressed the landing-gear knob and pulled the emergency gear extension handle. The nosewheel and both mains fell forward, locking under their own weight, incurring horrible drag. Liz Vespa's heart sank. There was no retracting them. "Yao! You're settling too fast! Power, power, power!"

The abused J52-P8 had no more power to give. As the last of the engine oil siphoned overboard, bearings and blades exceeded design limits and the jet began shaking itself apart in its mounts. At best, Liz saw that Hawk Three would impact between the fence and the gravel overrun at the threshold. The extra drag coupled with the straining engine and ponderous controls conspired with gravity to defeat lift. The "zero-zero" specifications of the IG-3 ejection seat flashed on her mental screen: wings level with no rate of descent. *But there's no time!* "Yao, eject, eject, eject!"

The TA-4 shuddered, wavered for a long ephemeral moment, and the airspeed dropped through 110 knots. The canopy shot upward and away from the airframe as Yao began the ejection sequence—two seconds too late. Hawk Three fell to earth and exploded with a low, rolling *carrumph.*

Scooter Vespa landed through the smoke of Yao's pyre.

Six

Post Mortem

Terry Peters was first up the boarding ladder of Hawk Twelve. He ensured the seat was safe, then waved the line crew away.

Liz pulled off her helmet and fumbled for the bag. Peters took the blue-and-white hardhat with the ATA logo and *Scooter* in gold script across the back. "Oh, Terry," she croaked. "It was awful . . ." She choked down a sob and rubbed her watery eyes with a gloved hand. He stretched his right arm between her neck and the headrest and awkwardly hugged her, allowing his forehead to touch hers. "I know, babe. I know."

Slowly she unstrapped and followed him down the yellow ladder. They stood by the nose gear, smelling the smoke and hearing the mindless wailing of the sirens. Peters decided against any preliminary questions. There would be plenty of those, but he felt that Mr. Wei, the program manager, undoubtedly would declare a regrettable loss wholly to pilot error. In this case, the PRC officer would be right.

Liz ran a hand through her raven hair. In that motion she seemed transformed from a shaken young woman into a professional aviator who had just sustained a loss. She looked at her employer with eyes still misted but calm. "We didn't have full comm," she said in an even voice. "He could receive but not transmit, so I gave him the lead. He signaled that he was losing utility and fuel, but he still thought he could make the field. About two miles out I saw he might not make it and I asked if he . . ." She ran out of breath. Inhaling, she continued. "I asked if he didn't want to eject while he had time. But he continued the approach, and . . ." She cleared her throat. ". . . and he dropped the gear too soon. He started a high sink rate, and then he lost power and the bird went in." She dropped her right hand, palm down. "Just like that. He pulled the handle just as he hit."

Peters nodded. "I know, Liz. We heard most of it on squadron common. I don't know what else you could have done . . ." His voice trailed off.

He won't say that I should have ordered Yao to eject sooner. She realized that eventually some of the others might be less reluctant to voice that opinion. With a start, she thought of Delight and Wang, who probably now were landing at Luke. "Does Zack know?"

Peters shook his head. "Negats, unless he monitored our freq, which I doubt. Anyway, I don't want to distract him when he has to land with hung ordnance."

Liz realized that ATA still had a lesser emergency to sweat out before the day could be put behind them. She looked at Peters again. "Ozzie?"

Peters's blue eyes went to the pavement before meeting hers again. "He knows."

Seven

Slaying Dragons

"Ozzie?"

"Yes."

"This is Liz."

Ostrewski's pulse briefly spiked, then returned to his normal fifty-five. But his grip tightened on the phone while he thought of something to say.

"Hi, Liz." He never asked "How are you?" unless he meant it. Whatever his faults, insincerity was not among them.

Her breath was measured, controlled. "Listen, Michael. I really think we should talk. Could I come over?"

"Well, yeah. I mean . . . tonight?"

"Yes, if that's all right."

No point putting it off. "Okay. Ah, sure." He paused, collecting his thoughts. "You're still shook about Yao?"

"He's dead, Ozzie. But you and I haven't said ten words since yesterday morning. The investigation and everything . . ." She swallowed. "I just felt you didn't want to talk to me, you know."

He swallowed hard. "Why, of course I'll talk to you."

"Thanks. I'll be there in twenty minutes."

" 'Bye, Scooter." He hung up. "Damn!"

Fourteen minutes later the doorbell rang at Ostrewski's condo. Before he opened the door, he inhaled, closed his eyes, and did a five count. He did not want to do this—he would rather tangle with two of Colonel Li's MiG-29s again—but he recognized the only way out was straight ahead.

"Hi, Liz. C'mon in." He managed a smile.

"Thanks." She stepped inside and looked around. "Gosh, this is nice. I've never been here before." *Oh, that's original, Liz. Talk about stating the obvious!*

Ozzie showed her to the living room, where he had some ice and soft drinks. "Well, I haven't done much entertaining, you know. At least not before I met Maria."

Liz sat on the sofa, trying to appear nonchalant. "Oh, when do we get to meet her?"

Ostrewski sat in the chair at right angles to the sofa. He poured a Coke for himself and a Tab for Liz. "Oh, I'll prob'ly bring her around one day. We're just now going steady." *Got that out of the way.*

She sipped her drink, trying to decide how she felt about that information. "Mmmm . . . what's she do?"

"She's an MBA; manages the family business—construction. It's a large family, sort of like mine." He waved to a series of color photos on the wall behind the sofa.

Liz turned to study the Ostrewski family portraits surrounding a simple crucifix. A big, happy Polish clan with lots of aunts, uncles, and cousins. The only other photo was a large framed shot of an F-14 squadron. It was labeled "VF-181 Fightin' Felines, USS *Langley,*" and the date. Suddenly Liz felt on safer ground. "Was that your combat cruise?"

"Yeah. The CO was Buzzard McBride. That's me and Fido Colley behind the skipper."

She leaned forward, hands in her lap. "I'd really like to hear about it sometime, Ozzie. As much as you can tell."

He leaned back, a defensive gesture. "I can't say much, Liz. There's a twelve-year hold. I don't even know why. Something to do with intel sources and diplomacy."

"But that's crazy. A lot of people know what happened."

He smiled. "Like the GS-20 said, 'There's no reason for it—it's just our policy.' "

Vespa recognized a no-win setup and changed the subject. She looked him full in the face. "I need to know what you think about Yao."

Well, there it is. "Liz, I think he screwed up—twice. He pressed too low and he stayed with a dying jet too long."

"Some of the Chinese think I'm partly to blame. Damn it, Ozzie, I have to know what *you* think. What you *really* think. He was your student and I lost him . . ." She had sworn she would not cry; she held back the tears. For ten seconds. Then the dam broke.

Michael Ostrewski, who had dueled with the Tiger of the North, shot eight Front-Line aircraft out of the sky, and held the Navy Cross, felt helpless with a weeping female. It was one more Guy Thing.

"Ah, Liz . . ." He moved beside her on the sofa, awkwardly patted her shoulder, then wrapped both arms around her. She leaned into him and let the sobs out.

Nearly three and a half minutes trickled by, two hundred seconds, each with a beginning, middle, and an end. Abruptly she sat up, wiped her eyes with the back of one hand and sniffed a few times. He handed her a Kleenex.

"Thank you. I'm all right now." She blew her nose and Ostrewski had no idea what to say. Instead, he picked up her glass and passed it to her.

She drained the soda, set it down, and looked at him through misted eyes. "I really do need to know, Ozzie. Do you think I could have saved Yao?"

He took her hand. He realized that she needed to know another professional's opinion of her judgment. "Liz, I think if I'd been there I'd probably have told him to pull the handle. But I wasn't there. I didn't know what you knew, and you didn't know what I knew about him."

"What do you mean?"

"Well, I brought him along, that's all. I think I got inside his head. He was insecure about his bombing, and my guess is that he thought by saving the jet he could sort of make up for, you know, screwing up."

Liz dabbed at one eye with the hankie. "Did you like him?"

"What?"

"I mean it. Did you like Yao as a person?"

"Well . . . gee, I don't know. I didn't think of him as an individual human with friends and maybe a family. He was a student who was my responsibility." He shrugged. "It was a professional relationship, that's all." Ozzie looked at her again. "Do you like Deng?"

She smiled. "Yeah, I do. The way he wears his Stetson everywhere. And he has that shy quality about him, you know?" Ozzie nodded. He didn't know.

"But he's a good student, Liz. He follows orders."

"You know they were friends? They'd been squadronmates for about four years."

"He seems to be taking it okay."

She gulped an ice cube. "Better than me, evidently."

"Liz, didn't you ever lose anybody in TraCom?"

"No, not like this. A classmate of mine was killed instructing in T-34s at Whiting, but this was different." Ostrewski shrugged again. "Ozzie, why didn't you talk to me when Yao was killed?"

He exhaled, slowly letting the air out of his lungs. "I didn't know what I felt, Liz. I guess . . . I guess I didn't trust myself to say anything to you before I learned the details because I wondered if you *had* screwed up, and I was even more afraid that *I* had screwed up. Maybe I missed something with Yao. I just don't know." He rubbed her arm. "I'm sorry that I caused you any extra pain. I should have been thinking beyond myself."

"You had your own dragons to slay."

"How's that?"

She smiled. "It's a Chinese saying or something. We all have our emotional dragons to slay." She laughed. "You were one of mine."

Ozzie's eyes widened in apprehension at the implication. *High buffet, airspeed bleeding off. Unload, bury the nose and go to zone five 'burner.* He recovered nicely. "Consider that dragon slain, Scooter."

Ozzie walked Liz to her car and made a point of hugging her again. They kissed good night the way friends do.

Eight

Dead Eyes

There was a little delay in the pace of training after Yao's death. As Peters predicted, Mr. Wei had declared the incident closed long before the FAA, the Air Force, or anyone else had reached the obvious conclusions: Mr. Yao had ignored the minimum recoverable altitude when using live ordnance and had tried to land the aircraft instead of ejecting while he still had control. "Consider it another lesson learned," Wei had said. His next words bespoke his mission-oriented mind-set: "I expect you will proceed with strafing next week."

Sitting with the other IPs in the Skyhawk Room, Robo Robbins absorbed the implication. "Did you ever notice Wei's eyes?" he asked. "He's got dead eyes, like a shark."

"Be that as it may," Peters said, "we're now going to be dead eyes with our guns." There were exaggerated groans at the pun. "To tell you the truth," Peters added, "I'd just as soon wrap up the air-to-ground phase and get on to the tactics syllabus."

Delight rubbed his beard, and asked, "Terry, are we condensing the gunnery syllabus to make up time?"

"Affirm. I talked to Rocky Rhode and held his hand long-distance. He's concerned that the loss would delay carquals and upset Lieu and some others back in D.C. so we're throwing in an extra simulator session with two live-fire hops instead of three."

Peters searched the audience. "Gunner, where are you?"

Warrant Officer Jim Keizer raised a laconic hand at the back of the room. He was a tall, well-built career sailor in his late thirties. Peters continued, "Now that we're done with bombing, your ordies can concentrate on the twenty millimeters. Then you can all go back to Kingsville and rejoin the Navy."

"What? And lose all this per diem? Not likely, sir!" Keizer's retort drew appreciative laughter. Ordnancemen qualified to arm and load bombs and maintain the A-4s' cannon were a premium commodity. Like all seadogs, they knew how to turn their per diem expenses into a profit by careful shopping and gratuitous mooching.

"All right," Peters continued. "We have three days before the first gunnery flights. Jim's crew has done the boresighting, but we need to test the guns on the jets we'll be using in this phase. That's eight launches a day. We have range time tomorrow and the next day to confirm that both guns work in each bird. Everybody gets one hop to fire fifty rounds per gun. Any malfunctions, and I may exert my authority and take the extra flights myself."

Catcalls and two paper cups pelted Hook Peters. Fending off the assault with crossed arms, he intoned, "Hey, it's not my fault. Jane said either she gets a gunnery hop or I sleep on the couch."

Nine

Manly Man Night

"*El Cid*," began Delight, standing at the Skyhawk Bar. "Greatest six-minute sword fight ever filmed—duel to the death for possession of the whole danged city of Calajora. Single-combat warriors like Tom Wolfe wrote about in *The Right Stuff*." He wiggled his eyebrows suggestively. "And Sophia Loren . . ."

"*Fighting Seabees*," countered Robbins. "Burly construction guys who drive bulldozers and earthmovers. They level mountains for airfields while killing Japs and hardly break a sweat."

"Okay, *The Vikings*. You can't get no more manly than they were. Sail the Atlantic in an open longship, then go raping and pillaging—real Manly Man stuff. And remember Ernest Borgnine? Ragnar's feasting hall where they swill mead from horns and throw battle-axes at each other and ravish the serving wenches . . ." Delight grinned hugely. "Come to think of it, kinda reminds me of Animal Night at Miramar . . ."

Robbins nearly choked on his drink, rerunning the long-gone Friday frivolity at Fighter Town USA. He thought fast. "*Taras Bulba*. Those cossacks were really Manly Men—jumped their horses over a huge ravine to prove who was right or wrong." He struck an heroic pose and emulated Yul Brynner. " 'I am Taras Bulba, colonel of the Don Cossacks. Put your faith in your sword, and your sword in the Pole!' " He glanced across the room at Ostrewski. "Oops, sorry, Oz. No offense."

Ozzie, conversing with Vespa and Thaler, flipped him off without looking back.

"*Conan the Barbarian.*" Delight flashed a gotcha smile, confident he could not be topped.

"Beeeeep," went Robbins. "You lose. Conan doesn't count 'cause he isn't real."

Terry Peters entered the lounge with Jane on his arm. He turned to his wife. "Oh, no," he groaned. "They're at it again."

She looked around. "At what again?"

"Richthofen and Brown over there. They play a game called Manly Man Night. One starts by naming a movie and the other has to respond with an equally macho flick until one of them runs out of titles. I think Zack just lost."

Delight saw the Peterses enter the lounge and joined them at a table. "Hi, guys. You're just in time—the party's rolling."

Jane regarded the former Marine, a suspicious pout on her face. "Things never change around here. The monthly Friday night gathering and poor Carol's over there with the rest of the aviation widows." She glanced at the far corner where Carol Delight sat in animated conversation with Kiersten Thaler, Marie Robbins, and some other ATA wives.

Delight waved a placating hand. "Hey, it's an old-married-person trick. You spend the whole evening talking to everybody else so you have something to say to your spouse during the drive home." He looked back and forth between Terry and Jane Peters. Keeping a straight face, he added, "Didn't you know that?"

Jane patted his cheek. "That's all right, dear. I'm sure you have a comfortable couch somewhere." She joined the other ladies, knowing that her husband wanted to speak to their partner.

Peters motioned Delight into a corner. "Zack, I got a call from Congressman Ottmann this afternoon. He wants to meet me for a face-to-face with one of his people day after tomorrow. I should be back Monday night."

Delight nodded. "Sure. You taking the red-eye to Dulles?"

"No, I'm hopping Southwest to Wichita." He looked around to ensure no one overheard. "Look, if anybody asks—and don't volunteer it—I'm looking at a twin Cessna at the factory. Ottmann stressed that we keep this as low-key as possible. I don't know exactly why, but that's how he wants it."

"Okay." Delight thought for a moment. "You figure it has something to do with the Chinese?"

"I don't know what else. Anyway, I'll get back ASAP."

Delight punched Peters's arm. "Okay, pard. You got it." He returned to the bar, where Robbins was still holding forth.

Liz Vespa, intrigued by the arcane male ritual under way, edged closer to Delight and Robbins. Zack offered her the ice bucket. "Hey, Scooter. You need a refill?"

"No, I just wonder how you tell which movie is most manly."

Delight's warning receiver began twitching. He knew that Liz Vespa could kid a kidder. "Well . . . it's, like, a Guy Thing."

"Sort of common consent," added Robbins. His perennial grin seemed to indicate that girls would not understand.

"You want to know what Manly is?" Vespa did not await an answer. "I'll give you Manly. It's PMS . . . actually, it's *flying* with PMS."

Robbins braced himself. *Here it comes. The Girl Speech.*

"Imagine feeling bloated from all the water you're retaining. Then add a migraine headache, plus nausea. Then throw in stomach cramps—the kind that make you just want to curl up and go to sleep." She leveled her gaze at both men. "Now, with all that, imagine making an instrument approach in rough air, at night." Privately, Delight recalled when he *had* felt that way.

Vespa was warming up. "Now, after you've fought off vertigo in an instrument descent, aggravated by your headache and nausea, consider this. You feel that same way during an air-combat hop, pulling four or five Gs and doing that twice a day for a week."

Liz drained the last of her vodka tonic and set the glass on the bar with a decisive clunk. "Gentlemen, I'm here to tell you: only Manly Men can fly with PMS."

The men watched her walk away, too astonished for a reply.

Robbins found his voice first. "Wow! What got into her?"

Delight turned to Thaler, who joined his friends at the bar. "Hey, Psycho. What were you guys talking about with Liz?"

"Well, Ozzie said that he and Maria are getting engaged." Thaler cocked his head in curiosity. "Why do you ask?"

Ten

Almost Human

Mr. Wei Chinglao sat across the desk from Terry Peters and played the game. Producing a pack of cigarettes, he politely asked, "Do you mind if I smoke?" In the months he had been working with ATA, he hardly could have missed the "No smoking" signs, let alone Robbins's hand-lettered "Oxygen in use" beside the WW II LSO paddles on his wall.

Hook Peters had quit smoking three decades before, between Vietnam deployments. He had told his wingman, "If I'm ever about to get captured, you'll have to shoot me. I'd tell the gooks *anything* after two days without a smoke."

Now, Peters regarded Wei's request. *He knows I don't smoke; he knows there's no smoking in the building. If I turn him down, he probably thinks I'll feel I owe him something.* "If you don't mind, Mr. Wei, I'm allergic to tobacco smoke. That's one of the reasons we post the signs in our spaces here."

Wei nodded. "Ah, yes. Please excuse me." He put the Camels back in his shirt pocket. Americans: such a peculiar race. Well, not even a race, he told himself, as mongrelized as they had become. Asia's homogeneous populations had blessedly escaped most of those problems. And such concerns over trivia! The cartoon animal used to advertise Wei's favorite cigarettes had been virtually banned by the U.S. government. All things considered, America was a mishmash of contradictions: constant meddling in the affairs of other nations but unwilling to control its own borders; puritan ethics constantly exposed to public hypocrisy;

a vicious civil war fought to free the slaves, the descendants of whom still suffer in economic servitude; a constitution proclaiming supremacy of the individual but steadily eroded by the power of the state. If not for its technological genius, Wei was convinced that America never could have come to world prominence.

"I am preparing a report for Mr. Lieu at the embassy," the program manager explained. "Now that our pilots are nearing the end of their carrier-landing training, I am required to provide a preliminary assessment of their progress."

Peters turned in his chair toward the "howgozit" chart on the wall. Each PRC flier's name and grades were neatly inked in for each phase of the program. Where a pilot had failed the course was an abrupt, final red X indicating that he had departed. Two, Peters thought ruefully, had departed this life.

"Well, sir, the figures are right there for you. Overall, I think your pilots have done pretty well." He turned back to Wei. "Actually, I was surprised that we didn't lose more pilots or planes before now. The weapons and especially the aerial-tactics refresher programs had the greatest potential for losses, but Yao's incident was the only one directly involved in our training program." He did not need to add that the first loss had involved wake turbulence from a Boeing 757 landing at Williams.

Wei's dark eyes scanned the chart, evidently reading the small, neat letters from fifteen feet. "Mr. Yao brought disaster upon himself, Mr. Peters. My report made that clear." The normal brisk tone of his voice softened perceptibly. "I trust that you know we hold your firm completely innocent in that event."

"Thank you."

"Now, I have been following the field-landing practice as much as possible, and I believe most of our pilots are doing reasonably well. But how many might not achieve your own standards before going to the ship?"

"I was discussing that with Mr. Robbins. We noted four pilots who were inconsistent in the simulated carrier-landing pattern. Two of them have improved this week; the others remain erratic."

"And they are?"

"Mr. Zhang and Mr. Hu."

"I mean, Mr. Peters, who are the four?"

"Oh." Peters was taken aback; he knew that Robbins was inclined to give the first pair "a look at the boat." He referred back to the list. "Mr. Chao and Mr. Wong. But I should note that Mr. Robbins believes they are making satisfactory progress."

Wei scribbled a note, then looked up. "Even if Chao and Wong do not complete the course, we regard this as an acceptable completion rate." He almost smiled. "You have done well."

Peters was surprised; outright praise from Wei Chinglao was unprecedented. "Well, thank you, sir. Of course, we won't know the actual results until after the qualification period aboard the *Santa Cruz*." He opened his mouth, then thought better of it.

"Yes?" Wei prompted.

No point kidding this guy. "To tell you the truth, sir, I'm surprised and impressed with how well your group has done here. They've done quite a lot better than most of us expected."

Wei leaned back—an unaccustomed, almost relaxed, posture. "Mr. Peters, now I will tell you the absolute truth. These pilots are the product of a screening process completely unprecedented in our military history. Not only did we require exceptional pilots by our standards, but exceptional individuals. The language study alone eliminated several of our most experienced aviators."

"Well, yes, sir. We knew that this group . . ."

"Excuse me, Mr. Peters. In all candor, your Navy was told as little as possible about these men. It was considered necessary as a security measure at the time." He looked down, as if composing his thoughts. "When my government accepted your government's ah, *suggestions* as to our internal affairs, there was much resentment. But it was judged worthwhile because of the greater access to American trade and programs such as this."

Peters sat silently, astonished at Wei's candor.

"Now, there is a reason for our pilots' success here," Wei continued. "You know that most of our aviators only fly about one hundred hours a year—roughly half of what most Americans do. But once we selected our people for this program, they were given that extra hundred hours, much of it under Russian instruction. Therefore, some of our people flew far less than one hundred hours. Additionally, the prospective carrier fliers were exempted from most political requirements. Each year the army is mobilized to help bring in the crops when necessary, but none of these men did so." He paused, looking directly into Peters's eyes. "You realize what that meant?"

Peters waved a hand. "Certainly, sir. It meant they were expected to succeed here."

"Precisely. And thanks to your staff, the large majority have done so." Wei stood up, preparing to leave. Peters leapt to his feet as well, ruefully thinking that he had mistaken the man's intentions with the cigarette gambit.

"One final thing, Mr. Peters. You must suspect that I have some aviation background. Therefore, I wish to ask one thing."

"Yes, sir?"

"At a convenient time, may I ask the favor of making a carrier landing in the backseat of your Skyhawk?"

Peters did not even try to conceal his pleasure. He extended a hand, which Wei solemnly grasped. "It's a deal, sir."

Wei bowed slightly and walked out the door as Delight looked in. "Any problems, Hook?"

Peters shook his head. "Just that I'm afraid Wei is starting to act human." He looked at his friend. "And that scares me."

Eleven

Things Unsaid

From seven thousand five hundred feet on a crystalline night, the Phoenix Valley was a splash of multihued color from millions of lights strewn across the black carpet of the Sonoran Desert.

Returning to Williams Gateway after a series of instrument approaches to Sky Harbor, Hawk Six descended through the night sky, running lights strobing from wingtips and fuselage. In the front seat, Liz Vespa concentrated on her approach plate. She knew that she had done well on the instrument-check ride, though not quite as well as she would have liked for this particular check airman. Ozzie Ostrewski rode in the back, keeping notes for the debriefing.

Northwest of the field, Ozzie unexpectedly waggled the stick. "I got it, Liz."

Vespa raised her hands, speaking into the hot mike. "You have it." She wondered if she had missed something, committed a mental error.

"Let's take a look out desert way," Ozzie offered. "I always like to see the desert at night, away from the lights."

"Okay," she replied. *Something's on his mind*, she told herself as the TA-4J banked more to the east. *Ozzie's usually all business once he's strapped into the jet.*

The Skyhawk settled on course 090, south of the Superstition Freeway. Apache Junction and then Gold Canyon slid past the port wingtip before her scan returned to the cockpit, where her practiced gaze registered normal indications in the red night lighting.

Minutes passed without further conversation. Vespa was becoming slightly concerned when Ostrewski was back in her ears. "Maria and I have set a date: two months from now."

Though it was physically impossible, Liz tried to turn her head to look at Ozzie. The fittings on her torso harness prevented her from shifting her shoulders more than a few inches. "Wow. That's great, Ozzie." *He's really going to do it.* "Congratulations." Her voice was flat.

"Thanks. We want to have a church wedding, you know? It'll take a while for my family to make travel arrangements out from Chicago."

Liz's pulse was back under seventy. As seconds passed, she reminded herself to scan the instruments again: fuel flow, engine RPM, tailpipe temperature, the TA-4's own vital signs.

"Michael."

"Yeah?"

"Why did you wait until now to tell me? I mean, why not before we launched? Or after the debrief?"

"Hell, Liz . . . I guess I don't really know. Maybe it just seemed important that we have a little time . . . you know, without anybody else around."

She almost laughed. "Well, this is as private as it gets."

"Ah, I just thought that maybe you'd sort of like some time to, you know, maybe, talk."

She forced her feminine fangs back; she would not coyly ask, *Gosh, Ozzie, talk about what?* "That's sweet of you, Michael."

Liz mentally cataloged everything she did and did not want to say—and everything that she could never again discuss with her friend and rival. In two months there would be no going back.

"I'm going to miss you, Michael."

He knew exactly what she meant. "Thank you, Liz. But Ozzie will still be here. And you'll still be Wizard Two."

"Does Maria understand that?"

He thought for several seconds. "Maybe not quite. But she will. It's part of my job as her husband."

"Roger. Break-break."

Again, Michael Ostrewski perfectly read the intent of Elizabeth Vespa. Ozzie waggled the stick and said to Scooter, "You have it. Come right to two four zero. Descend and maintain four thousand five hundred feet."

Hawk Six banked into a thirty-degree turn in the night sky, leaving something more than jet exhaust in its wake.

Twelve

Who Needs Oxygen?

Four Skyhawks were announced by the Pratt and Whitney whine that once was an ordinary sound at Marine Corps Air Station El Toro, south of Los Angeles. Peters looked up from the flight line, where ATA and the Sukhoi delegations were quartered. "Well, that's the last of them."

The TA-4Js broke up for landing interval, gear and flaps coming visible during the 360-degree overhead break. In a descending spiral, line astern, each pilot allowed sufficient distance behind the plane ahead.

"Lookin' good," Peters commented.

"Damn straight," added Robbins.

Peters shielded his eyes with one hand. "I guess Zack had his division up for practice before they left Williams." He looked back toward the parking lot adjacent to the flight line.

"Expecting somebody, boss?"

"Yeah, Rob. I told Jane about Zack's ETA. She and Carol were going to be here for for his arrival."

Robbins worked his eyebrows. "I thought there was some doubt if Carol would even come."

"There was, up until a couple days ago. I guess it took some begging on a pretty thick rug, but Zack convinced her she'd be better off here with us than waiting back home."

"Roger that." Robbins did not need to elaborate. He had persuaded his own wife to accompany him rather than stay alone in their condo—too many people did not want the program to proceed.

As Hawk Ten taxied into the chocks, Delight waved from the cockpit, his rear seat occupied by one of Chief Dan Wilger's maintenance men. The other three A-4s parked beside Delight's, their noses gently bobbing on the long nose-gear oleos.

The boarding ladder was barely in place before a car horn sounded behind Peters and his entourage. Jane Peters and Carol Delight alit from the rented Ford, waving to the crowd as two security men emerged from the front seat. Delight scrambled down the yellow ladder, tugging off his helmet. He met his wife halfway across the ramp, scooped her up in both arms, and carried her back to their friends. "You fool, put me down!" Carol's demand lacked conviction.

"Hi, sweetheart," Zack cooed. He kissed her warmly, then turned to face Jane Peters. "You too, honey." He leaned forward to touch lips with her.

"Pure, what the hell are you doing?" Hook Peters knew perfectly well what his partner was up to.

"I'm ravishing two gorgeous women at the same time," he declared. "It's a Manly Man kind of thing."

Carol Delight settled more comfortably in her husband's arms, both hands around his neck. "I'm glad you're in a manly mood, dear," she said sweetly. "Jane took me shopping on the way back from John Wayne Airport."

Delight shifted her weight in his arms. "That's as manly an airport as there is. I hope you spent a lot of money."

Carol cocked her head, as if studying him. "Did you get enough oxygen on the way over here?"

"Darlin', I don't need oxygen as long as I've got you."

That saccharine statement prompted a chorus of "Yuuuk" sentiments when Chief Wilger appeared. "Excuse me, folks," he intoned. "You might want to come listen to the portable radio."

"What is it?" Peters asked.

"Well, apparently the Chinese and the Vietnamese are shooting at each other."

At eight that night most of the instructors and their wives gathered in the Peters's suite at the old visiting officers' quarters. Two security guards from the firm contracted by Wei stood outside, guarding the door.

"I want you all to know what's going on in Vietnam and how it affects us," Peters began. He stood by the television set that was turned on but muted. The news graphic headlined, "War in the Tonkin Gulf."

"First, apparently it isn't really a war. It seems to be a limited naval action involving the same area that was disputed several months ago.

China and Vietnam both claim the area where petroleum was found, and Vietnam has been drilling there for a few years. You've heard the same news reports I have, but a couple of my D.C. contacts have more detail."

Peters paced a few steps, staring at the carpet. "Congressman Ottmann is coming out here tomorrow or the next day at the latest. So are a couple of Navy representatives involved with the PRC carrier program. From them, I've learned that Chinese marines occupied two of the three drilling platforms."

Robbins interrupted. "Terry, what's Washington say about the Chinese carrier program? If the chinks are the aggressors, won't that result in some kind of sanctions?"

"I'm just coming to that, Rob. Washington has chosen to treat this as a local feud. Even though Beijing is technically the aggressor, the State Department waffles it enough to say that both sides should stand down." He raised his hands. "That's just diplomatic BS. The president and Congress are in bed with the Chinese too far to back out. The bottom line is markets and money, and in that contest, Hanoi loses every time."

"So you're saying we'll continue with the CarQual schedule?" Ostrewski sat on the floor between Vespa and Thaler.

"Well, as of now I haven't heard anything different. Rob, you were out to the boat yesterday. How'd it look?"

"Fine. Captain Albright was happy with things, and he said he can give us twenty-eight knots. Oh, we heard from Pensacola. Two landing signal officers are inbound tomorrow. They're supposed to clear us instructors for preliminary CarQuals before the Chinese begin trapping."

Peters scanned the crowded room. "Any other questions?"

Liz Vespa voiced the thought in a dozen minds. "Only about a hundred, skipper."

Thirteen

The Truest Test

Peters convened the briefing in Ottmann's suite. Zack Delight, Rob Robbins, Ozzie Ostrewski, Psycho Thaler, Liz Vespa, and Chief Wilger were seated around the dining-room table.

"First," Peters began, "for those who haven't met Congressman Tim Ottmann, I'll introduce him by saying he's on the House Military Affairs Committee. He chairs the Tactical Airpower Subcommittee, which has oversight of the Chinese carrier program. Before that, Skip made a poor but honest living as an Eagle driver." Ottmann shared the group's laughter.

"Before Skip explains the reason for this meeting, one thing has to be clear." As usual when he wanted to make a point, Peters paused. "Everything that's said here stays here. What we're planning is potentially dangerous, and the legal implications are not clear-cut. Zack and I are in, but you have to make your own decisions. So, before we continue, anybody who wants to withdraw, do so now." Peters waited but nobody stirred. Peters then turned to Ottmann, standing at the head of the table.

"Thanks, Terry." Ottmann cleared his throat. "Folks, in no more than seven days Mainland China will invade Taiwan."

Vespa's hand instinctively sought Ostrewski's. Chief Wilger voiced the unspoken sentiment of everyone else. "Holy shit."

"I know your first concern," Ottmann said. "You wonder why the Chinese would pick fights with Vietnam and Taiwan at the same time.

Well, the Vietnam feud is strategic deception—a manufactured crisis to draw our attention away from Taiwan.

"The real reason behind the upcoming invasion is, well, time. The old guard in Beijing—the hard-line Maoists—are dying off. They want China 'reunited' before they go to Marxist valhalla. The new generation is more pragmatic." Ottmann gave an ironic smile. "By 'new generation,' I mean those who don't remember the Long March in 1936.

"Now, they've been very patient. They went along with the so-called internal reforms we wanted because they needed American technology. But there is nothing to prevent the Communist Party from reverting to its old ways once it has what it wants—control of Taiwan. It's a purely cynical view, but remember, these folks insist that Mao Zedung was 'too great a man to be bound by his word.' " Ottmann shrugged. "It's a cultural attitude that we can't change."

Ostrewski leaned forward. "Mr. Ottmann, I don't know much, but I know if China invades Taiwan, there'll be war with the U.S."

"Previously I'd agree with you, but things have changed." Ottmann stopped to organize his thoughts, then continued. "The reason the PRC has initiated its so-called reforms is to increase its influence here. You all know about the scandals that never went anywhere. Well, by making themselves financially necessary to three administrations, the Chinese bought themselves more than political influence. They bought political souls."

Robbins was tempted to mutter, "No such thing" when Liz Vespa spoke up. "My God, how did it ever go this far?"

"Well," Ottmann said, "the Bush administration continued normal relations after Tiananmen Square. Clinton, who hammered Bush for his China policy in the campaign, not only continued that policy, but expanded it." He grinned sardonically. "Hey, Washington runs on hypocrisy like jets run on JP-4.

"Anyway, besides the millions of dollars in campaign money, you had major corporations clamoring to do business with one-third of the human race. After all, most other Western nations already were in bed with Beijing, and our CEOs didn't want to be left out. So they leaned on their politicians, and things just snowballed."

Robbins raised his voice. "Sir, how do we fit into this?"

"Okay. Beijing knows that America can't just lean back while PRC troops walk over Taiwan. There has to be a publicly acceptable reason for us to sit it out and pass some window-dressing sanctions. We'll probably impose embargos again.

"However, the Chinese are hedging their bet. They have a new long-range missile, the DF-41, with technology we either sold them or they stole from us. France and Israel also contributed, by the way. So, in the next few days we expect China to launch a 'test' that'll hit about two hundred miles off the Washington coast. That'll be a warning shot that says, 'America, you don't have any better missile defense than we do.' So ICBMs are a standoff.

"Now, that's where you folks come in. A Malaysian-registered freighter is headed this way with a Chinese crew. Its manifest lists petroleum products. It does not list five backpack nukes."

Ostrewski merely emitted a low whistle.

"No kidding holy shit," Wilger said in a hushed voice.

"We're tracking this ship, the *Penang Princess*, and we expect it to arrive off Long Beach day after tomorrow. The plan calls for her to transfer the nukes to several smaller vessels that will bring them ashore in different places. But one of them will be delivered, minus detonator, to the Chinese consulate in San Francisco. There, the president and secretary of state will be invited to see it, with a promise that four more have been distributed around the country. At that point, China wins. No American politician is going to defend an Asian island at the expense of thousands of American lives—maybe tens of thousands. It's in his interest, and Congress's, to keep the lid on. No overt acts, no hysterical commentary, and damn sure no scandal about giving in to blackmail." Ottmann shook his head admiringly. "You got to admire the plan—it's a beaut. Right out of Sun-Tzu."

"Sun who?" asked Wilger.

"Sun-Tzu, an ancient Chinese military philosopher. He said the truest test of a general is to win without fighting."

"Okay," Robbins interjected. "So what do we do?"

Ottmann looked directly at the LSO. "You sink that ship."

Fourteen

Questions

The responses came with machine-gun rapidity.

"We don't have ordnance!"

"How do we *know* the nukes are aboard?"

"What about the Navy or Coast Guard?"

And, on everyone's mind, "How do we stay out of prison?"

Ottmann raised his hands, asking for silence. "I'll answer as many of your questions as possible, folks. First, we know the backpacks are aboard because one of our sources helped load them. Most of our intel has been back-channel between unofficial contacts on both sides. I can't tell you more for obvious reasons—you were all military professionals. But I'm convinced the intel is real.

"Second, we're not involving the Navy because the people in DC who know about this plan need 'plausible deniability.' That's a buzzword that means you're lying and everybody knows you're lying but nobody will prove it because everybody else lies, too. The *Santa Cruz* is perfect: officially it's not a U.S. or a Chinese ship. It's not yet commissioned in either navy, it has a mixed crew, including civilians, and there's been no transfer ceremony."

Zack Delight spoke up. "Tim knows I'm an all-up round for this plan. But how about explaining the legality?"

"Right. The plan is to launch you during your first qualification period with thousand-pounders that'll be loaded aboard right before the ship leaves the dock. You'll have the location of the *Penang Princess* inside our twelve-mile limit, and a full briefing on her. You'll land back aboard before the *Santa Cruz* returns to U.S. waters, which is a legal technicality, but it preserves the appearance of American neutrality."

"But, Congressman," Vespa interjected, "we'll still have sunk a neutral ship. People will probably be killed. Aren't we—pirates or something?"

Ottmann smiled as he reached inside his sport coat. From the pocket he produced several folded sheets. "These are full pardons, exonerating you for everything since Adam. They're signed by the president but undated. You'll have your copies, notarized by the attorney general, before you take off from here to land aboard the ship. If everything goes well, you won't need them. If things go wrong, you're covered."

Vespa locked eyes with the New Yorker. "So the president . . ."

". . . still denies involvement." Ottmann smiled again.

"Excuse me, sir," Robbins said, "but how do we know these papers are valid? We might be set up, and you wouldn't know it."

"Well, Rob, I could just say, 'Trust me.' But if one of you goes to prison, I'll be there waving bye-bye when you finally walk out the front gate. As deep as I am in this, I'd never see daylight again."

Robbins's blue eyes had a little-boy gleam. "You just told me that you've got the president by the . . ."

"By the plausible deniability." Ottmann grinned.

"A couple of other things," Robbins continued. "If I was smuggling nukes into this country, I wouldn't put 'em all in one basket, and I wouldn't wait until a few days before I might need 'em. Doesn't that seem kind of suspicious?"

"Geez, Robo. You ever consider a career in politics?" Ottmann chuckled at the sentiment. "Your instincts are good, but we know that the Chinese decided not to risk discovery of the backpacks until almost the last minute. And actually they're not putting them all in one basket. As I said, some or all of them will be put in other boats before unloading. That's why we need to sink the ship at a specific time and place."

"We're going to recover them?"

"We're sure not going to leave them on the bottom of the ocean. Tactically, it'd make more sense to sink the ship in deep water beyond our limits. But this way, the U.S. government has full authority over recovery and salvage operations. I believe that a Coast Guard cutter will accidentally be nearby to pick up all survivors—and whatever they get off the ship."

Ozzie gave an appreciative whistle. "Sounds like you have it all doped out, sir."

"Well, it's been a long time planning. But in any operation like this, there's always the Oscar Sierra factor. Just remember that if things do turn to shit, you're covered legally.

"Anything else?" Ottmann asked. Liz Vespa's frown caught Ottmann's attention. "Miss Vespa?"

"Liz," Scooter corrected. "You know, all this seems really well planned, but I don't understand something. Why are the Chinese blackmailing us with ICBMs or backpacks? They must know we can't stop them from taking Taiwan—we don't have the people, the airlift, or the sealift anymore. So if they're willing to accept the political fallout, why not just go?"

"Good strategic question. I wish I could tell you what I know, but I can't right now." He looked around. "Yes, Ozzie."

"With everything involved in a big operation like occupying Taiwan, the folks on that island must know what's coming. I mean, PRC bases for shipping, airfields, and several infantry and armored divisions—all of that's got to draw attention. Why haven't we heard anything from them or the UN?"

"Hell, the UN doesn't matter since China has a veto. As for Taiwan, they've lived in the shadow of the PRC for about fifty years—their military is on constant alert. Also, the Chinese have American politicians in their hip pocket. There hasn't even been any contingency planning for operations involving the PRC for several years now." He snorted his contempt. "Hell, dozens of White House staffers don't even submit to presumably mandatory security checks, so don't expect the military to buck policy. Maybe it would help if some senior uniformed people would stand up and risk their careers, but there aren't any left." He looked around the room full of former military professionals. "There just aren't any left."

Fifteen

Answers

Hijacking a moored aircraft carrier is no small task. It requires planning, cunning, and most of all, nerve.

It also helps to have well-placed contacts.

Representative Tim Ottmann announced a later meeting after the first one broke up. He impressed upon Terry Peters the importance of having everyone involved in the program present to take a tour of the Chinese and Russian facilities at El Toro.

"Have you talked to Captain Albright?" Ottmann asked Peters.

"Yes, he'll be here with his exec. I also told our active-duty instructors to attend. That's Lieutenants Arliss and Horn plus Lieutenant Commander Cartier from the LSO school." Peters inclined his head slightly, regarding the New Yorker with amused suspicion. "You're up to something."

Ottmann made a small come-hither gesture with two fingers. Though they were alone in the room, Peters stepped closer. "I want the Chinese and everyone else to think that we're having a last conference here before qualifications begin day after tomorrow. As far as you and anyone else knows, there'll be a reception until late tonight in my suite. Wei and his students will attend, and I've even invited some of the Russians."

"Okay."

"While the *Santa Cruz*'s captain and exec and the active-duty guys are here, including your LSO, there's not much chance of anyone thinking the ship's going to sail, is there?"

Peters's eyes gleamed in admiration. "You're a sneaky bas . . ."

"Thanks. A helo will pick you up here at 2230. Would it be suspicious if you and Robbins both disappeared at that time?"

"Hell, I don't know, Skip. Are you going to serve booze?"

"All the adult beverages anybody wants to consume. Except your guys, of course. As soon as I get word from you that the ship's under way, I'll tell Zack your overhead time. His flight will land aboard, load ordnance, and get the final brief."

Peters nodded. "Sounds like your plan hasn't changed much."

"Now, there's one more factor in our favor. The harbor pilot is one of our guys, Ben Tolleson. He's a master mariner and probably could run the ship without much help. Except for flight operations, of course. But you'll be in full command once you exit the harbor." Ottmann searched his fellow conspirator's face. "Are you really sure you can drive that boat?"

"Well, it's been quite a few years, Tim. I conned *Independence* before she entered the yard. But yes, I'm sure."

"Okay. Now, while we still have time, I need to let you know about our inside source."

"Why tell me? Do I really need to know?"

Ottmann smiled. "Oh yeah, you really need to know. He's flying in one of the two-seaters tomorrow morning." Ottmann rapped on the wall of the adjoining bedroom. After a few seconds the door opened and Terry Peters gaped at Mr. Wei Chinglao.

Sixteen

Half-Truths and White Lies

Tim Ottmann invited Wei to take the most comfortable chair while the Americans sat on the couch. Wei produced a cigarette holder and inserted a Camel before lighting up. He blew two near-perfect smoke rings before he began to speak.

"Mr. Peters, I have not been completely truthful with you. However, you will understand the need for security."

"Certainly, sir."

The old MiG pilot put down his cigarette. "Mr. Peters, the primary Chinese trait is patience. We take the long view of history, but now, in the twenty-first century by your reckoning, some of us realize that events have accelerated far beyond our accustomed pace. The world economy and global communications have forced a radical change upon us. Unfortunately, most of the venerable leaders in Beijing are unable to grasp that fact. Tiananmen Square was just one example.

"Frankly, various American administrations have made the task of reform-minded Chinese more difficult. Your politicians tried to have things both ways: supposedly opposing the successors of Mao while trying to exploit China's emerging economy. The hypocrisy of Republican and Democrat administrations has left China convinced that America stands only for profit and expediency. That attitude has, ironically, reinforced the old men's determination to seize Taiwan. They believe that after an initial flurry of protests, Sino-American relations will return to the status quo ante."

"Will they, sir?"

Wei looked at Ottmann, who nodded. "Most assuredly. As far as America is concerned, I shall explain the consequences for China. But first, I concede that China has too much influence in your internal affairs to prevent, as you say, business as usual. Too many public figures have accepted illegal contributions; too many are compromised in other fashions." Wei shook his head. "You would not believe how many people or how many ways."

Peters felt a small shiver between his shoulder blades.

"Now," Wei continued, "you ask why my colleagues and I are working with men like Mr. Ottmann. The reason is that we are Chinese patriots. Oh, some of us still believe in Marxism, but that is almost irrelevant. Instead, we look at this Taiwan folly and see unnecessary risks. Therefore, we decided to upset the nuclear blackmail part of the plan. Without the assurance of American capitulation, the operation is too dangerous to proceed. Even if it succeeds, the rest of Asia would unite against us, economically and militarily. We would be forced into the type of military spending that ruined the Soviet Union."

Peters ingested the revelation, emotionally breathless at the implications. "Mr. Wei, why don't the Politburo and the Chairman understand these things?"

Wei dismissed the concept with the wave of a hand. "You know of America's so-called Beltway mentality, Mr. Peters? We have the same thing in Beijing. From there, the world appears logical and orderly, bound to fit the outmoded perceptions of the office holders. Our 'wise old men' still view the world through Marxist prisms, even though many of them are political pragmatists. They know their time is running out, and they are determined to cling to their attitudes until the last moment."

Peters leaned back, rubbing his eyes as if in disbelief of what he had heard. He rolled his shoulders and faced Wei once more. "All right, sir. You convinced me. How do we proceed?"

"Our intention is to have the *Santa Cruz* at sea without anyone knowing of it here until the last possible moment. Surprise will be important in sinking the *Penang Princess*, and we must assume that her captain will have some form of communication with agents here at El Toro or in Long Beach."

"That's right," Ottmann added. "Remember the original plan, Terry? We were going to have your instructors qualify in one day and stay aboard that night. Then the Chinese pilots supposedly would fly out the next day with some of the other instructors to begin the main qualification period."

Peters snapped his fingers. "And we're going to launch the strike the same day as the instructors' CarQuals."

"Exactly, Mr. Peters. However, in our long-range planning we only had a time frame. We knew the best time of year for an invasion of Taiwan, and we knew the decision had been made to insert the nuclear weapons a few days before that date." He raised his hands in a semihelpless gesture. "Therefore, our planning could not be as precise as we hoped."

"All right," Peters replied. "But Mr. Wei, I don't understand something. You got a promise from me to get you a carrier landing. How does that fit into the plan?"

Wei almost smiled. "I made it known to my pilots that I wanted to share their experience. Now, if they see me in one of your aircraft, they are unlikely to be suspicious. But it also suits our larger purpose. First, your government and my faction wish to emphasize the Chinese participation in this operation while minimizing American involvement. My authority is accepted among the Chinese aboard the ship, and will not be questioned.

"Therefore, in keeping with the Chinese emphasis, we will need PRC pilots. I am one; Mr. Hu will be the other."

Peters glanced at Ottmann, then back to Wei. "Why Hu? He's one of those who was almost cut from the program."

"Mr. Peters, Hu is my sister's son. I trust him."

Ottmann could almost hear the wheels clicking in Peters's skull. "Terry, when Mr. Wei says we need Chinese on the mission, it's part of the plausible deniability. No active-duty Americans are involved, and we emphasize that PRC pilots flew the mission."

"I see. We ATA folks are retired while the flight-deck troops are Chinese or inactive American reservists." Peters winked at the congressman. "A half-truth isn't quite the same as a white lie."

Ottmann made a point of shaking hands. "Terry, welcome to the wonderful world of politics."

Seventeen

One of Our Carriers Is Missing

It was just past midnight, but the floodlights on the flight deck, and those along the pier on F Avenue, provided ample illumination for the Jet Ranger that Wei had leased. The pilot, who had flown SH-60s, was more than willing to set down directly on *Santa Cruz*, saving Peters and Robbins a long walk from Navy Landing a mile and a half away. They waved good-bye, then turned and entered the island en route to the bridge.

"Think they'll miss us at Wei's reception?" Robbins asked.

"Not likely, with all the free booze and fresh crab. Did you see how our boy Igor was sucking it up?"

On the O–9 level Peters entered the red-lit bridge. He saw an older man, graying with a two-day crop of stubble, talking to the watch officer. "Mr. Tolleson? I'm Terry Peters."

"That's me," the harbor pilot replied. He regarded Peters openly, assessing the aviator who would take this ship to sea. They shook hands. "Our friend told me to expect you."

"Well, it's early for the usual watch change, but I think we'll do all right."

"I hope so, skipper. I've never hijacked a carrier before!" Tolleson smiled. "By the way, do you know your officers of the deck? Mr. Odegaard and Mr. Mei. Gentlemen, this is Captain Peters. He'll be relieving Captain Albright today."

Peters greeted the American and his Chinese counterpart. "Yes, I've met both these gentlemen." He knew that Odegaard was a retired reserve commander; Mei had been aboard destroyers and frigates; reputedly he was an above-average ship handler.

"All right, gentlemen, let's get started. Captain Albright said to expect four boilers on line and four standing by, provisions for two days, and a full complement sufficient for carrier qualifications tomorrow. We're running under our own power without connections to shore. Also, I'm told we have tugs standing by. Is that correct?"

"All correct, Captain." Odegaard nodded toward Mei. "We've checked with the department heads and we're ready to go."

"Very well." Peters inhaled, held the breath, then let it out. "On the bridge, this is Captain Peters, I have the conn." He turned to Robbins. "Robo, check with the weapons officer—Medesha? I want you to eyeball the Mark 83s before we push off."

"You got it, boss." He disappeared down the ladder.

Peters turned back to his bridge watch. "We'll light off the other boilers as we clear the channel, but right now it's important to get under way without drawing too much attention."

"Aye, aye, sir," Odegaard replied. "The plant is lined up in parallel. We'll use those four boilers to provide steam for the main engines."

"Good. Ah, let's see . . . I know the elevators are raised. Are they locked?"

"Yes, Captain. We can confirm that with the deck division if you prefer."

"Not necessary." Peters strode to the starboard side of the bridge, assessing the topography of his new domain. He turned to the watch standers. "Let's test the rudders. And I'd like to confirm that we have up radar plus navigation and comm."

The helmsman was a retired merchant marine and active yachtsman who relished steering eighty thousand tons of steel. He tested the tiller and reported that he had full control of the two rudders.

Mei came to attention. "Captain, I have personally inspected the navigation equipment. I also consulted the communications watch officer. We are ready."

"Very well, gentlemen." He looked to Tolleson. "Captain, request you make up the tugs, sir."

"Right, Cap'n." While Tolleson communicated with the tugs that would pull the carrier's deadweight outboard against the onshore breeze, Peters saw to the pierside procedure. He waited for word from Robbins before the remaining brow was wheeled back from the starboard quarterdeck. The call quickly came from the weapons division.

"Weps to bridge."

Odegaard responded, leaning into the speaker. "Bridge aye."

"This is Robbins. Tell the captain we're cocked and locked."

Peters grinned beneath the brim of his "A-4s Forever" ballcap. "Cocked and locked" was verbal shorthand for the occasion: Robbins had seen the thousand-pound bombs and confirmed that there were suitable fuzes on hand.

At a nod from Peters, Odegaard broadcast over the 1-MC general-announcing system. "Set the special sea and anchor detail. Single up all lines and make all preparations for getting under way."

Peters waved to his de facto executive officer and the harbor pilot. "Mr. Odegaard, Mr. Tolleson. We'll move to Aux Conn." While they stepped eight feet aft to the auxiliary conning station, sailors on the pier removed the first of two heavy lines securing the carrier to each of eight stanchions along the ship's 1,046-foot length. Meanwhile, Tolleson directed both "made-up" tugs into position at the bow and stern.

Taking nothing for granted, Peters leaned out of Aux Conn, looking fore and aft to confirm that all was ready. He called behind him, "Let go all lines." The order was repeated, echoing metallically through the moist maritime darkness as pierside personnel released the final eight hawsers linking *Santa Cruz* to shore.

Peters turned back inboard to face his bridge crew. "Gentlemen, I see no reason to stand on ceremony. Captain Tolleson, you'll give your orders directly to the helmsman, if you please." He chuckled slightly. "We do things differently in the Skyhawk Navy."

Tolleson scratched his beard, beaming his approval of the nonregulation procedure. "Right you are, Cap'n." He waited until he judged the ship forty to fifty feet from the pier, then said, "Son, give me left standard rudder." As the helm swung through fifteen degrees of arc, Tolleson announced, "Back one-third on number one and two; ahead two-thirds on three and four."

Peters watched the "spinning" maneuver move the bow away from the pier, ponderously swinging to port. The watch officer, peering through the window, called to Tolleson. "We're fair, Pilot."

Tolleson spoke into his walkie-talkie, clearing the tugs of their chore.

As the big ship maneuvered in the turning basin, Tolleson called, "All ahead one-third." *Santa Cruz* grudgingly edged up to five knots as Tolleson smoothly coordinated rudder commands and orders to the tugs. With the bow properly positioned, he turned back to Peters. "She's all yours, skipper."

Peters warmly shook hands with the friend of Wei Chinglao. "Nicely done, sir. You'd better catch your taxi if you don't want to make this cruise."

Tolleson laughed. "I might enjoy it at that." He slapped Peters's arm and disappeared through the hatch, en route to the stern, where he would take a jacob's ladder down to the tug.

Captain Terence Peters, USN (Retired), felt the faint throbbing of the engines through the soles of his brown aviator shoes. Peering ahead into the Pacific darkness, he modulated his voice in what he intended to resemble confident authority. "All ahead two-thirds."

Eighteen

Ready Deck

The A-4s dropped their tailhooks and entered the Delta pattern two thousand feet overhead the ship in a descending left-hand carousel. Thaler, Delight's wingman, crossed his leader's tail from the left to establish right echelon beside Ostrewski with Vespa outboard.

Delight reached the initial point three miles astern of the carrier, approaching parallel to her starboard side. He looked down from eight hundred feet and felt a rumble of excited satisfaction in his belly. After months of planning and training, there was the former USS *Santa Cruz* with a ready deck, steaming upwind and eager to receive him. Zack led his little formation ahead of the ship's white-foamed bow. He checked his airspeed—steady on three hundred knots—and prepared for his break turn.

Ahead of the ship, Delight laid the stick over to port, brought the throttle back to 80 percent, hit the speed brakes, and pulled. His vision went gray at the periphery, but he rolled wings level about a mile and a quarter off the port side, descending through six hundred feet while headed aft.

Delight's left hand automatically found the gear and flap handles, and he felt his A-4F decelerate through 220 under the additional drag. He shot a glance at the angle-of-attack indicator, cross-checking with airspeed.

As the LSO platform seemed to slide past him, Delight turned left, adding power to maintain 130 knots. Turning his head, he saw the mirror's meatball halfway up the deck. He crossed the wide white wake, sucked off a bit of throttle, and stabilized his angle of attack with minute adjustments of the stick.

Meatball, angle of attack, lineup, Delight chanted to himself. He knew that a good start and small corrections were the keys to success. He felt as if the A-4 were balanced on a pencil tip, and forced himself to fly smoothly—too much muscle meant overcontrolling that did bad things to landing grades.

"Pure, this is Rob. Come back." Robbins was avoiding standard LSO phraseology in case somebody was listening.

"Read you, Robo."

"Lookin' good, keep it coming."

Delight liked to fly his approach half a ball high. If he began to settle in close, he could catch it without a fistful of power, and it worked. He added a little power and the meatball stabilized nicely in the center. As his wheels impacted the deck he crammed on full throttle in case of a bolter—and was thrown against his straps as the hook snagged the four wire.

Did it! he exulted. He retarded throttle, tapped his brakes, and raised the hook. Up ahead a yellow-shirted crewman was into his manic arm-waving routine, gesturing Hawk One to the elevator.

Behind Delight, Psycho boltered, shoved up the throttle, and went around. Ozzie snagged the two wire; Liz flew a near-perfect OK-3. Thaler trapped the three wire on his next pass.

The ordies began loading weapons on the hangar deck.

Nineteen

Face of a Stranger

Zack Delight stood at the head of the ready room with the doors closed and guards posted outside. The passageways on either side were blocked with plastic tape, forcing anyone transiting the area to detour around the area.

Delight looked over his bobtailed "squadron" seated in the first row: Ostrewski, Thaler, and Vespa, plus Robbins the LSO. Wei and Hu sat in the second row. On the board behind him was an overhead view of *Penang Princess*, carefully drawn to scale.

Delight mussed his graying hair and grinned to himself. "Never thought I'd be in a ready room again, wearing Nomex and briefing a strike with live ordnance against a real target."

"Neither did we," exclaimed Ozzie. He winked at Liz, who smiled back.

"I never thought I'd brief a strike against a real target at all," she added.

"Okay, folks. Here we go." Delight's face seemingly morphed before his tiny audience, passing in one heartbeat from peace to war. Liz felt a tiny thrill somewhere deep inside her. She realized she was seeing a man she had never met before.

Delight quickly passed through the basics: launch, rendezvous, and the route outbound. Then he addressed communications.

"You have your UHF and VHF frequencies, but we need to run this thing under total EmCom if at all possible. If you do have to transmit, no names or call signs on the radio—no Zack or Pure or Ozzie. We are Papa Flight, for 'Pure.' I'm Dash One, Ozzie's Dash Three and so on. The backseaters are Two Bravo and Four Bravo. The helos are Hotel One and Two.

"If anybody has to abort, keep off the radio. That's only for no-shit emergencies. Just rock your wings and break off. We'd rather not bring live ordnance back aboard, but if you can't find a safe place to jettison your bombs, just be damn sure they're safed. If possible, dog overhead the ship until everybody else is back aboard." He paused. "Any questions?"

Robbins waved a hand. "Zack, let's play Oh shit, like we talked before."

"Right." Peters looked from Robbins back to the front-row aviators. "Over the past couple of days, Terry and Rob and I discussed some of the things that might go wrong. For instance, suppose the guys on that ship know we're coming. Maybe they'll have SAMs or even Triple A. Well, two A-4s will have flare pods and chaff dispensers, and there's no need to conserve them."

Ostrewski piped up. "What if the *Penang* doesn't show up on time? Or we can't find her?"

"Well, in that case our part is over. We return to the boat or land at El Toro. You'll have to recover ashore if you get a hung bomb."

Robbins spoke again. "You want to discuss SAR at this point?"

"Coming to that, Robo." Delight leaned on the rostrum, checking his notes. He picked up the paper and extended it to arm's length, ignoring chuckles from the other pilots. "If anybody has to make a controlled ejection, try to get as close to the carrier as possible. We have two helos aboard, but only one is fully equipped for rescues, so be aware that we need to keep that one nearby as plane guard."

Thaler waved a pen. "Since the *Boorda*'s in the area, what about diverting to land on her?"

Scooter shot a glance at Psycho. "That's right, I forgot. I have a Pensacola classmate aboard, flying Hornets." Vespa's tone told the males that there was probably little love lost between the two women. Ostrewski, who had met slender, blond Lieutenant Commander Jennifer Jensen—"Jen-Jen" the ice princess and admiral's daughter—knew that Vespa resented her rival's influence in getting a coveted fleet assignment.

Delight shook his head at Thaler. "Nope, not unless there's something entirely unexpected. We'd rather you eject and write off a jet rather than show the U.S. Navy what we're doing."

With no further questions, Delight turned back to the board. "Now, here's the crunch. When we positively ID the target, we'll conduct a dual-axis attack with roll in from about twelve thousand feet. Put 112 mils on your sight, and include that in your precombat check. I recommend that you pickle no lower than forty-five hundred feet. Like we practiced at Gila Bend: a five-G pull gets you level by three thousand feet.

"I'll take Psycho in from the bow. That's the best way to attack a ship because it forces you to get steep, and we'll be making sixty-degree dives. By attacking along the fore and aft axis of the target, we have a better chance of getting hits with shorts and overs." He jotted pinpoints along the deck of the *Princess* with his Magic Marker, indicating random hits.

"Ozzie, you and Liz will pull around to the stern. If there's no opposition, wait until you've seen the result of our attack. The fuzes are one-tenth of a second delay, but there'll still be smoke and probably flames. Otherwise, time your roll-in so you're down the chute as we're pulling off." He scrawled two arrows breaking to port from their attack.

"Now, if there's opposition—either SAMs or Triple A—Psycho and I will try to strafe, time permitting. I'll tell you what I'm doing. If we do this right, it'll be the only radio call of the whole mission, because we want to stay zip-lip from startup to attack." He scanned the audience, emphasizing his words with his tone.

"When I roll in, I'll start popping flares whether there's any shooting or not. Ozzie and I in the A-4Fs both have enough flares in our pods to cover this short an attack.

"Mr. Wei, Mr. Hu." The two Chinese sat attentively upright in their seats. "You can help your front-seaters by keeping your heads moving the whole time. Let them know if you see anything unusual. When the attack starts, your video cameras need to stay on the target as long as possible. It may be the best damage assessment we get for a while."

"Except for Eyewitness News," Ozzie ventured.

Wei raised his hand from the second row. "Yes, sir," Zack responded.

"Mr. Delight, perhaps you should describe the return to port."

"I was just coming to that. As soon as we're back aboard, all ATA personnel will jump in both helos and we'll be flown to a vacant lot near Tustin. Two or three cars will be waiting there, and we'll return to El Toro. From that point on, we don't know nothin'." He looked around the room again, noting each flier's face. The Chinese were impassive, whether from temperament or familial trait he could not guess. Robbins was completely relaxed, a professional "waver" waiting to do his job. Ozzie fidgeted slightly; Delight attributed it to excess energy. As for Liz Vespa—well, she was smiling.

Twenty

Been There, Done That

Terry Peters stepped into the ready room, unexpected and unannounced. Liz Vespa saw him first. Partly from impulse, partly from abiding respect, she reverted to naval custom. "Captain on deck! Atten-hut!"

Almost in unison the green-clad aviators shot to their feet. Wei and Hu, untutored in such things, followed the example.

Peters felt a warm rush inside him—something close to love. "Thank you, gent . . . ah, *lady* and gentlemen. Please be seated."

Striding to the front of the room, he collected his thoughts. *A short speech is a good speech*, he told himself. He exhaled, wet his lips, and began speaking. "I just wanted to say how proud I am of you guys—all of you. When we started this project, I had no more of an idea how it would turn out than anyone else. Now that it's about to end, and considering what's at stake, well . . ." He blinked away something and shook his head. ". . . I wouldn't be anywhere else on earth today, or with any other people."

"Neither would we, pard." Delight's eyes were beginning to mist over, too.

"Damn straight," added Robbins.

"Well," Peters concluded, "I'd better get back to the bridge. But first I want to wish good hunting to everyone here." He trooped the line, warmly shaking the hands of his friends and colleagues, squeezing Liz in a bear hug, and solemnly greeting Wei and Hu. Then he stepped back three paces, standing erect. "This isn't regulation the way we were brought up, but this ship is in *our* navy, isn't it?" Peters brought his heels together and whipped his right hand to the brim of his ball cap in a slicing arc that might have left a vacuum in its wake. His aviators returned the gesture for the first time in their lives, as it was contrary to U.S. Navy practice when uncovered. Then he was gone.

Eric Thaler began zipping his torso harness and survival vest while Robbins and Hu helped Wei with the unfamiliar garments. Ostrewski caught Vespa's attention and motioned to the far corner in the back of the compartment.

"How do you feel, Liz?"

She arched her eyebrows. *Now he thinks I'm going to wimp out!* "I'm fine, Ozzie. Just fine. Why?"

He glanced away from her and saw Delight's head turned toward them. Equally quickly, Delight averted his gaze. *Like Ward Bond in* The Searchers *watching John Wayne and his sister-in-law,* Ostrewski thought.

"Well, it's just that this is the only combat mission we'll ever fly together . . ." His reticence finally melted in a rush as he heard himself say, "Ah, hell, Liz." He wrapped his arms around her, awkwardly pulling their bodies together despite the bulky flight gear. Her arms encircled his neck, compressing the collar of his flotation device.

"Michael . . ."

They kissed one another with a tender aggressiveness that trod the neutral zone between the foundation of friendship and the dawning of desire. It lasted an eternal four seconds.

"Now hear this! Pilots, man your planes."

The squawk box on the bulkhead repeated the ritual command, focusing aviators' attention and shattering peaceful thoughts.

Ostrewski pulled back, locking eyes with Vespa. "I love Maria, Liz. I'm going to spend my life with her. But I needed to do that, especially today."

She patted the front of his vest. "So did I, Michael."

He managed a laugh. "Okay—been there, done that."

"Good," she added. "Now, let's sink us a ship."

The pilots emerged from the base of the island and strode onto the flight deck. Wearing helmets with visors lowered, they were unidentifiable to anyone who did not know them well.

As the aircrew approached the yellow boarding ladders on four Skyhawks, each of the fliers paused to look at the thousand-pound bombs beneath each wing. Delight touched a kiss to one of his; Vespa ran a loving hand along the ablative surface of hers. Plane captains and ordnancemen scrambled with last-minute checks as catapult crews stood by.

Lowering himself into the blue-and-white A-4F now called Papa One, Delight glanced up at the bridge. He saw Terry Peters's face in one of the windows and perceived a smart wave. Delight tossed a non-regulation salute to the former deep-draft skipper who had missed his chance to drive a flat-roofed bird farm. Twisting slightly to his right, Zack saw the diamond-design Foxtrot flag snapping from its halyard, indicating flight operations under way. Higher up the mast, appearing in stark contrast to the striped banner he was accustomed to seeing, flew the jolly roger. The leering white skull with crossed leg bones on the black field sent an electric thrill through his body. Below it, expressing no less heartfelt a sentiment, was the light blue ensign of the Tailhook Association.

Zack Delight clasped his hands over his head in a gesture of undiluted rapture. At fifty-nine years of age, he knew that he would never again feel as good as this day and this hour. He felt gleefully giddy as his mind defaulted to the frontier tales of his Southwest youth. *Ya-ta hay!* he exulted. *It is a good day to die!*

Twenty-one

The Oscar Sierra Factor

The beeper sounded on Peters's cell phone, pulling him back from the disappearing A-4s that had been the focus of his existence. He pulled the handset from the Velcro pouch on his belt, hit the button, and said, "Peters."

"Terry, thank God!" Jane was almost breathless.

"Honey, what is it?"

"Terry, I don't know how, but the Chinese here know what you're doing! They've roped off their hangar and they're rounding up people and holding them inside." She paused to inhale. "There's been some shooting, and I saw two bodies on the ground. I think they were security guards."

Peters slid off the captain's chair. "Are you all right?"

"Yes, I'm okay. So's Carol and everyone else I've seen."

"Jane, where are you?" He waited three seconds. "Jane!"

"I'm, ah, I don't think I should say over the phone, darling. We're safe for now, and we're keeping out of sight. But they're guarding the parking lot."

"Have you called the police?"

"No, I called you first."

"Jane, honey, there's nothing I can . . ."

"God damn it, Terry! Listen to me!" The venom in her voice silenced him like a piano smashing a Walkman. "Are you listening?"

"Yes." His voice was muted.

"One of the ordnancemen is with us, Ron. He saw the Chinese loading ammunition in two A-4s, and we heard them taxi out."

"Oh, no . . ."

"There's more."

"They're arming more A-4s?"

"No, honey." She inhaled. "The Russians kept the Flankers fueled, and Ron said they were hanging missiles on the rails."

Peters's eyes widened, saucerlike. "Call me again in ten minutes." He broke the connection, belatedly regretting not asking about Skip Ottmann, about the security men who might be dead—and not telling her that he loved her. But now, sorting priorities, he flipped the switch to the communications division.

"Radio, this is the captain."

"Yes, sir."

"Call Papa Flight and tell them at least two A-4s are launching from El Toro with live ammo. Our people are to assume they're hostile. Get an acknowledgment—to hell with EmCon."

"Yes, sir."

"Wait, there's more. Tell them . . . tell them the Flankers are spooling up, too. And they're armed with missiles."

"Yes, *sir*!"

Peters sat back in his chair, sorting through the phone numbers stored in his Powerbook. He scrolled down the listings until he reached NavAirPac, then punched in the number.

It was forty seconds before he got a tone, and the phone rang four times before the watch stander finally answered. "GoodmorningComNavAirPacPettyOfficerStroudspeakingthisisanonsecurelinemayIhelpyou?" Peters barely understood the rapid-fire babble that seemed mandatory in the modern Navy. He wanted to scream, "Shut up, you bitch!" Instead, he did a fast three count.

"This is Captain Peters, commanding the aircraft carrier *Santa Cruz*, steaming off Long Beach. I am declaring an emergency and I need to speak with Admiral Paulson. *Right now*."

Petty Officer Stroud seemed taken aback; she had never heard of USS *Santa Cruz* and had no idea of the protocol involved in a ship declaring an emergency. "Sir, the admiral's at a conference."

"Then I'll speak to the senior watch officer. Immediately."

"Sir, what shall I say is the nature of the emergency?"

"Listen to me, Petty Officer! You have about twenty minutes before a backpack 'nuke' detonates under your rosy red ass. Now, what part of 'nuke' don't you understand?"

"Lieutenant Commander Paglia. What is your emergency, sir?"

"This is Terry Peters. I'm in command of the *Santa Cruz*, conducting CarQuals off Long Beach. Listen carefully, son."

"Yes, sir?"

"I have four A-4s airborne with live ordnance, operating under orders from the national command authority. Their mission is to sink a Malaysian freighter carrying nuclear weapons into this country." He paused for effect. "Do you understand, Commander?"

Peters could almost hear Anthony Paglia swallow hard. "Yes, sir. Ah, may I request verification . . ."

"Commander, I have no verification. And there's no time for you to call the White House and get it. Is there?"

"Well, I suppose . . ."

"Fine. Here's the situation. My flight is about to be intercepted by two Chinese-flown A-4s trying to prevent us from sinking the *Penang*. Okay? That's not the problem—my guys can take care of themselves. But the Russians who're here to CarQual their Flankers are loading missiles at El Toro this minute."

"Ho-ly . . ."

"Right. So here's what I need you to do, Commander. I assume there's an alert flight on the pad at Miramar." *Please tell me there is!* "I need you to scramble them, get 'em up here at the speed of heat, and contact my mission commander on Baker Channel. He answers to Papa One. Your flight can talk to me on 308.2. Tell your people that under *no* circumstance are they to shoot a Skyhawk. Any Flanker—I repeat, *any* Flanker in the air or on the ground at El Toro is a legitimate target. The ROE is: shoot on sight."

"Sir, are you authorized to establish rules of engagement?"

Peters did not even blink. "Absolutely. Definitely. You can check with CNO. But for now, you have your orders, Commander Paglia. Acknowledge."

"Uh, yessir."

"Fine. Call me back as soon as you know about the Hornets."

"Aye, aye, sir."

Robbins appeared at Peters's side. "How bad, Terry?"

"The Oscar Sierra Factor just kicked into afterburner."

A low whistle escaped the LSO's lips. "What else can we do?"

Peters slumped into his swivel chair. "Wait."

"What do you think about Miramar? Will they scramble or will that O–4 go through channels?"

Peters tipped back his cap, biting his lip. "I don't know, Rob. He seemed like a good kid, but . . ."

"But his career's on the line in a situation that's not covered in the

Watch Officer's Guide." Robbins folded his arms, leaning against the thick glass overlooking the flight deck. "And initiative's been bred out of the system. The 'zero defect' mentality just stifles risk taking, doesn't it?"

Peters closed his eyes. "It doesn't get this way under good leadership."

"Yeah," Robbins replied, "and look who's been 'leading' us recently." He etched quote marks in the air with both hands.

"Bridge, Radio."

Peters leapt to the console. "Captain speaking."

"Captain, we just heard from Papa One."

"Yes?"

"Sir, they can't find the target."

Twenty-two

An All-Up Round

In Papa One, Zack Delight ran his precombat checklist, still savoring the memory of the kick in the small of the back as the catapult threw him off the deck, accelerating the A-4 from zero to 120 knots in three seconds. He confirmed the mil setting on his sight, ensured that his master arm switch was off, and scanned his gauges in one practiced sweep of his eyes. He was, as he liked to say, an all-up round.

Delight raised his right leg and withdrew the chart. After nearly a century of powered flight, the human thigh remained the best map holder yet invented.

The Los Angeles area navigation chart was folded to show *Penang Princess*'s most likely location, given her expected arrival time. Delight had bounded the search sector in red crayon—a twenty-mile-by-ten-mile rectangle beginning five miles offshore. At two thousand feet altitude, he could see fifty-five miles in any direction, haze and smog permitting.

Delight glanced down again, taking in the multitude of ships and vessels approaching or departing the Middle Breakwater. Even allowing for the possibility that her company's green hull and beige deck had been repainted, none of the aged thirty-thousand-ton freighters matched his target's configuration.

With a rising flush of ambivalence, Zachary Delight felt frustrated and proud. *I'm like Wade McClusky at Midway*, he thought. *I've got Heinemann-designed airplanes at my back, looking for a target that's not at the briefed intercept point.* The kinship he felt with the *Enterprise* air group commander nearly sixty years before was diluted by the growing doubt that the mission could be accomplished—and bandits were inbound.

He made a decision and keyed his mike. "Papa Three, look north and west of the track. I'll swing south and west."

"Roger." Ozzie's voice was crisp, professional. He eased into a right bank, leading Liz Vespa parallel to the coast.

The cell phone buzzed and Peters whipped it out of the pouch. "Talk to me!" *Whoever you are!*

"Terry, it's Jane."

"You okay?"

His wife's response was delayed a fraction longer than he had grown to expect in twenty-nine years. He had time to wonder if he had hurt her feelings with his abrupt tone.

"We're still all right. I wanted to tell you that Skip's been on the phone to Washington. He called the Pentagon—he has a cell phone—and now he's talking to somebody at NavAir."

"Rocky Rhode?"

"I don't know, honey. It's . . . awful . . . confusing . . ."

"What about the Flankers?"

"What?"

Peters closed his eyes, forcing composure upon his growing anger and frustration. "Jane . . . honey . . . I asked, what about the Flankers?"

There was no reply. Peters lowered the handset from his ear to look at it, willing the inanimate thing to explain itself. He raised it again and spoke slowly, clearly. "Jane, this is Terry. Do you hear me?"

The line clicked twice and went dead.

Delight and Thaler completed their sweep down the east side of the search area, again coming up empty. Zack's cockpit scan took in his fuel state: twenty-four hundred pounds. *Enough for a little while*, he thought. *Then we'll have to abort.* At his altitude, necessary to ID the target, fuel was going fast.

Decision time, Delight realized. *Either we continue trolling this area or we look elsewhere.* He waggled his wings, signaling Eric Thaler that they were heading east to hunt along the coast. He motioned for Psycho to spread out, expanding the visual limits of their horizon.

"Do you know any satisfying profanity?"

Robbins wondered if Terry Peters would recognize Walter Brennan's line from *Task Force.* The LSO sought any method of easing his friend's gnawing concern about his wife, if only for a few seconds.

"Lots of profanity, Rob. None satisfying." Peters bit his thumbnail and stared northward, as if trying to see inland thirty miles to El Toro from fifteen miles at sea. The uncertainty, the concern, the growing fear all eroded his cultivated composure. Aviator cool was one thing—the modulated voice during an in-flight fire or engine failure. Standing here, feeling 280,000 horsepower throbbing impotently beneath his feet, was an appallingly new experience. He paced a few steps back and forth, hardly noticing that he forced Odegaard and Mei out of the way.

"Why the hell haven't we heard from AirPac or Miramar?"

"I don't know, Terry. Shall I give 'em a call?"

Peters spun on one heel, his face eerily alight. "I should've thought of it before, Rob! The Chinese A-4s!"

Robbins shook his head. "What about 'em?"

"They probably know where the *Penang* is! So would the Flankers. If ATC . . ."

"I'm gone!" Robbins seemed to vaporize as he exited the bridge.

"Captain?" Odegaard stood near the helmsman, wearing a querulous expression.

"I should've thought of it before!" Peters smiled for the first time in an ephemeral eternity. "If air traffic control can break out those A-4s and track them, it'll tell us where the target is!"

The watch officer nodded. "Mr. Robbins is talking to ATC?"

"No, Mr. Odegaard. I suspect he's screaming at them."

Twenty-three

Whiskey Tango Foxtrot

"Peters, what the hell is going on out there?"

Nice to hear from you, too, Rocky. "I don't have much time, Admiral. Tell me what you know and what you can do to help."

A continent away, Rear Admiral Allen Rhode nearly sputtered at the flippancy from a retired captain. Instead, the Vice Chief of Naval Operations gripped the phone harder and fought to control his anger. "Mr. Lieu just called to tell me that *Santa Cruz* has been taken over by a bunch of Chinese dissidents, that they're going to bomb merchant vessels, and you're helping them!"

Peters almost gasped. *So Lieu's behind it! Why didn't Wei tell us?*

Rhode was back inside Peters's ear. "Then Skip Ottmann called. He says you and Wei are going to sink a Malaysian ship with nukes, that he's trapped with your wife at El Toro, that A-4s are taking off, and the goddam Russians are loading goddamn AA-11s on their goddamn Flankers!"

"Okay, Admiral. You got the picture, right? Lieu's the fly in the ointment, and Wei's with us. Now, what're you doing to keep those Flankers off my guys? Hell, they're probably gear up by now."

Rhode's voice came back more modulated. "Yeah. I heard from AirPac that you need a scramble from Miramar."

"Well?" *So Rob called it. Paglia's a wimp.*

"Terry, the Marines don't maintain an alert. At best it'd take them a half hour to upload ordnance. I've given the order, but this'll be over by then."

Peters's heart sank. *Maybe Paglia's not such a wimp*. "What help *can* you get us, then?"

Rhode paused, and Peters uncharitably imagined N-88 calculating the odds of how best to play the hand. "Listen: the *Boorda*'s headed for the SoCal Operating Area. Most of the air wing just flew aboard from Lemoore; they deploy in two days."

Peters's mind raced. The new Nimitz-class CVN with Air Wing 18 would be even closer than MCAS Miramar. "A really tactical guy like Baccardi Riccardi might have a couple of Toms or Hornets on Alert Five."

"Hook, I already made the call. I don't know their deck status, but they'll be talking to you directly. It's best if I stay out of the loop, you know . . ."

Yeah, I know, Rocky. If anything goes wrong . . . "Thanks. I'll try to keep you informed." Peters hung up, then turned to the speaker. "Radio, this is Peters."

"Aye, Captain."

"Rob, tell me something."

Robbins's voice shot back. "Terry, I'm talking to ATC at LAX. They're working the problem, but I think they're more concerned with diverting commercial traffic than finding our bogeys."

"Any joy at all?"

"They had a couple low-level skin paints out around Tustin but nothing definite. The A-4s aren't squawking, of course."

Peters bit his lip. The Chinese interceptors naturally would stay low to evade radar while avoiding transponder identification. "Rob, we need a Hawkeye or another AWACS—something that can break a bogey out of the ground clutter. I need to talk to *Boorda*."

"Rog, boss. I'll keep after the feds."

Peters straightened up, and Odegaard approached him. "Excuse me, Captain. I was just wondering—couldn't our own radar pick up the Chinese?"

"Not over land—too much background clutter. Over water, maybe, depending on their altitude and distance. Otherwise . . ."

"*Santa Cruz, Santa Cruz*. This is USS *Boorda*." The power of the transmission was such that Mei turned down the volume on the bridge console.

Peters answered in person, speaking bridge to bridge. "Lima Delta, this is *Santa Cruz*, Captain Peters speaking." He used the CVN's generic call sign to demonstrate his knowledge and authority. "Good thing we worked with these guys at Fallon," he explained to Odegaard and Mei.

"Ah, yeah, Terry. This is Ben Spurlock. Listen, I'm putting you through to CAG Riccardi in strike ops. Call sign Chainsaw. You copy?"

Peters grinned. Captain Spurlock had been Lieutenant Commander "Spurs" Spurlock in Peters's air wing. "Hey, Ben. Sure thing, put Baccardi through."

". . . ardi here, Terry. You read me?"

"Affirmative, Chainsaw. I guess you know our situation?"

"I understand you have four A-4s on a SinkEx for a Malaysian freighter hauling nukes, that a couple of Chinese A-4s are looking for them, and one or two Flankers are involved. Right?"

"That's right. As yet we haven't found the target, Tony. Now, I'm not worried about the Chinese A-4s 'cause that'll be a straight-out gunfight that my guys will win. But the Flankers . . ."

"Concur. They're the threat. Terry, I'm launching two Hornets right now with a couple Toms several minutes behind them. I'm also trying to get an E-2 up, but that'll take longer. Probably too long."

"That's okay, CAG. Just be sure they know that they shouldn't shoot any A-4s. The odds are seventy-five percent that they're friendly."

"Consider it done. Chainsaw, out."

Peters turned to Odegaard and Mei. "At least there's something going right. Now if . . ."

"Bridge, Radio." It was Robbins's voice.

"Rob, what've you got?"

"LA Center has been in touch with Dougherty Field at Long Beach. Between them they've got a plot on two low-level fast movers headed offshore."

Peters's eyes widened. "Send it!"

Twenty-four

Bogies

"Papa One, this is *Santa Cruz*. Over."

Delight's pulse spiked. *God, I hope they have something for us.* "Papa One here. Go."

"Pure, this is Rob. Listen, *amigo*, LAX and Long Beach both got fixes on two low-level fast movers. They're feet wet at Anaheim Bay."

Delight did the geometry in his head. From El Toro, the Chinese Skyhawks had to overfly the Seal Beach naval weapons station and the wildlife refuge. *They'll get FAA violations fershure*, Delight mused. He pressed the mike button. "Roger, Robo. I'm northbound." He paused for two seconds. "Break-break. Papa Three from Lead. Over."

"I heard it, Lead." Ostrewski's voice came through crisp and clear. "We're inbound."

"Papa Lead, Robo here again. The bogies are climbing, orbiting the area around Island Chaffee. Your signal is Gate."

"Roger." Delight glanced over at Thaler, nodded briskly, and shoved the throttle almost to the stop—"through the gate" as it was known in the propeller era. Almost immediately Thaler called, "Lead, gimme a percent." Delight nudged off a skosh of throttle to allow his wingman to keep up.

In a fast climb, Delight led his section toward one of the four small islands in San Pedro Bay. He marveled that *Penang Princess* could have come so far so soon, apparently to drop anchor virtually within sight of the pier from which *Santa Cruz* had sailed the night before. Subconsciously checking his A-4's vital signs, he began thinking ahead in time and space.

Let's see . . . if they're climbing, it's because they want to intercept us before we roll in. They'll be waiting at twelve thousand feet or higher, probably a little south of the ship. He punched the button again. "Papa Three, Lead."

"Three here."

"I'm going in high, Oz. If you see we're engaged, ingress below the fight. We'll buy you some time."

"Three copies. Out."

On the bridge of his hijacked aircraft carrier, Captain Terry Peters rubbed his chin, staring north into the Los Angeles Basin's perennial smog and haze. Emotionally he was split between his friends, airborne and about to engage in an old-fashioned gunfight and dive-bombing attack, and his wife, who was—what? He began allowing himself to consider the possibility that he might no longer have a wife.

"Captain?" Odegaard was at his side.

Peters was startled by the intrusion. He visibly flinched. "Yes?"

"Well, sir, Mr. Mei and I were looking at the chart. The only way the *Princess* could have got this far north was if she'd been running about three or four hours ahead of schedule. I mean, there wasn't a specific arrival time, but it was a pretty narrow window if they were going to off-load as planned."

Peters felt himself growing short-tempered. "Yeah. So what's your point?"

"Well, sir, presumably the Chinese didn't have time to divert the freighter because they only learned about us this morning. And they couldn't follow their original plan because they know that their leased facility at Long Beach is compromised. But here they are, still one step ahead of us. That means, either they intentionally built this fudge factor into the equation, or . . ."

"Or what?"

"Or they planned to transfer the nukes to other boats all along."

Peters shook his head as if avoiding a nettlesome insect. "What are you saying?"

Mei stepped forward. "Captain, we don't know how long the *Princess* has been offshore. It is possible the backpacks are not aboard her anymore."

Peters slumped in his chair, chewing on his thumbnail, pondering the prospects of his watch officers' assessment. He felt that he should have considered the likelihood himself, and he knew why he had not. *Jane, where are you?*

Finally, he shook his head. "Negative, I don't think so. Otherwise, there'd be no reason to scramble the A-4s and cap the freighter. We'll know more once Zack gets a visual."

Odegaard was dubious enough to press his point. "Skipper, I think we're obliged to notify the Coast Guard or the harbor patrol. At least they could board the *Princess* and . . ."

Peters shot a laser glance at Odegaard. "No, absolutely not! If the nukes are still aboard, the crew is bound to resist, and there'll be casualties. And if there's a patrol craft alongside, more innocent people will get killed. No, Mr. Odegaard. We have to play it out."

Odegaard's eyes widened. "You mean, you'd order the attack even with a Coast Guard vessel right there?"

"I mean that Zack Delight and Ozzie Ostrewski will hit their target unless I call them off. And I won't do that."

"Captain Peters, I wish to object. I still think we have options to . . ."

"Noted. Log it, and I'll sign it. You too, Mr. Mei."

The Chinese officer exchanged glances with his American counterpart. "You mean, Captain, you are accepting full responsibility?"

"It goes with the territory, son."

Peters swung his chair outboard, slightly surprised to find that he cared very little about what happened to *Penang Princess*. Jane's face came to him at the same time as Robbins's voice.

"Terry, I'm still in Radio. I'm hitting Baker Channel."

Psycho Thaler's voice was high-pitched in alarm: "Bogies, one o'clock high!"

Twenty-five

Bandits

Zack Delight had seconds to decide his tactics. Psycho's call told him all he needed to know—the Chinese had altitude on him. He could split the section, relying on his A-4F's superior performance to hold off the hostile Juliets while Thaler bombed, but Delight was the one with flares to deceive heat-seeking SAMs. Or he and Thaler could jettison the two tons of weight penalty they each carried, shoot it out with the bandits, and buy time for Ostrewski and Vespa. Four Mark 83s could sink the ship, but six or eight offered far better prospects. Then there were the Flankers to consider . . .

I'll never get this chance again, he realized. *A pure guts and gunfight; no radar or missiles*. "Two, I'm engaging. ID the target and attack." Delight quickly unlocked the drum on his gunsight, dialed in thirty mils, and locked the lever. At one thousand feet range his sight reticle now subtended thirty feet, slightly more than the wingspan of an A-4. He double-checked his armament switches even as Thaler acknowledged, "Dash Two is in."

Two and a half miles below, riding at anchor off Island Chaffee, was a dark-hulled freighter with light-colored deck and upper surfaces. But Delight's attention was focused on the two Skyhawks slanting toward him from his right front. He resolved to keep his bombs as long as possible, hoping that Psycho could drop, rejoin, and even the odds.

The lead bandit tripped off a short burst of 20mm rounds, accurate in elevation but wide to the right. Delight two-blocked the throttle, resisting the temptation to squeeze off a burst in reply, and wrapped the little Douglas into a shuddering, high-G turn as the aggressor pulled off high and left.

Delight felt an emotional shiver when his opponent zoom-climbed for the perch. It was an unwelcome message: *This guy wants an energy fight; I can't match him with my current airspeed.* He glimpsed the Chinese wingman rolling over and diving after Papa Two. *Well, I can't go vertical with my guy; I'll go down.*

Delight retarded the throttle and rolled over. Through the top of his canopy he caught a view of Thaler's TA-4J diving toward the ship. As Delight pulled his nose through, aligning his illuminated sight with the target, he saw one, then two lights streak upward, corkscrewing awkwardly. "Yeah!" he exulted. *It's gotta be the* Princess *all right!*

The SA-7s shot almost vertically from the stern. One wobbled, perhaps uncertain which heat source to home on, and belatedly tried to correct back toward Papa Two. By then, Thaler was down the chute, tracking for the five seconds he needed. Both bombs came off the hardpoints, stabilized, and accelerated toward the ship.

The second man-portable SAM passed twenty feet beneath Psycho Thaler's aircraft before detonating.

Delight saw the white smoke of detonation, noted Papa Two wobble in its dive and begin a shallow pullout. A human noise chirped in Delight's earphones—something unintelligible. The Chinese A-4—"Gomer Two"—had veered away from the two SAMs, giving Thaler some maneuvering room. However, Gomer One—the intelligent bastard somewhere above and behind Delight—was positioned to kill one or both Americans.

Delight knew he was poorly placed to get hits. His roll-in after avoiding the Chinese leader was too far astern for a high-angle attack, and his sight was calibrated for air-to-air. He quickly reset 112 mils with Stations Two and Four selected. Recognizing he was shallow in his dive, he held half a diameter high, hit the red "pickle," felt the Mark 83s leave the racks, then punched the flare button four times. Beneath Station Five, outboard on his starboard wing, four magnesium flares arced downward, silent sirens competing for the attention of the next SA-7s.

Two blows rocked the A-4, then another. Without needing to look, Delight knew that Gomer One was in range and gunning. The Marine kicked right rudder, slewed to starboard, and pulled the stick into his lap. His left hand shoved up the power and began accelerating through 430 knots.

Now long-forgotten, Thaler's two half-ton bombs smashed into

Penang Princess just aft of amidships. One punched through the deck, exploding two compartments down. The other hit slightly to port, dishing in three-eighths-inch steel plates and destroying a speedboat lashed alongside. The splintered Chris Craft, minus four feet of its bow, flooded and sank as far as its lines permitted.

Delight's bombs struck thirty feet aft of the stern. One was a dud, victim of fuze failure. The other strewed water and steel splinters in a wide radius, adding to the confusion aboard the Malaysian vessel.

Zack pulled off target, coming nose level at three thousand feet, and looked left. Gomer Two was turning in behind Thaler, whose TA-4J was streaming something white—smoke or fuel. Briefly Delight wondered what Mr. Wei must be thinking in the rear cockpit. Then the former Marine was coordinating his controls, feeling some slack in the rudder, cutting the corner on Gomer Two and rotating his sight drum back to thirty. He knew that Gomer One was still back there, but Papa Two needed help.

"Papa One, this is Three. We're rolling in hot."

Thank you, God! Delight forced himself to keep the hostile TA-4 padlocked as Island Freeman careened into view. With Ozzie and Liz now attacking, Gomer One probably would let Delight go, trying to disrupt the greatest threat to the *Princess*.

Probably.

Delight keyed his mike. "Psycho, come right and drag 'im for me."

There was no reply, but Papa Two reversed from left to right, turning northerly toward Island White and the Belmont Pier. Gomer Two fired and missed astern, big 20mm slugs churning the water into tall geysers as the fight descended through one thousand feet. *He underdeflected!* Delight exulted.

The Chinese pilot, either unaware of his peril or boldly ignoring it, followed the turn. Delight, twelve hundred feet back and three hundred feet higher, knew the Gomer would pull deflection on Thaler and Wei after another thirty degrees of turn. But as the hostile Skyhawk crossed his nose and the deflection angle narrowed to nearly zero, Delight nudged back his stick, set the pipper one mil over the canopy, and pressed the trigger.

Beneath his feet, Delight felt the twin Colts pounding out three-quarter-inch-diameter shells at a combined rate of thirty-two per second. He kept the trigger depressed for two seconds, expending one-third of his ammunition.

Gomer Two absorbed fifteen rounds across the top of the fuselage and wings. Delight saw shattered canopy glass glinting briefly in the sun, followed by gouges of aluminum, streams of fuel, and just plain junk whipping in the slipstream. The little jet rolled right, dropped its nose, and went straight in.

Zachary Delight pulled up, savoring the dirty brown-white geyser marking his kill, and screamed an atavistic shout of warrior joy that pealed off Valhalla's golden dome.

At least that was how he felt at that exact moment.

A microsecond later he was back in control of himself. He rolled hard right, turning into Gomer One, who had vanished. Leaving the throttle against the stop, he began climbing back toward the likely roll-in point. Delight could do nothing more for Thaler, but still felt an obligation. "Eric, Zack. You better plant that thing."

"Roger, Zack. Ah . . . I'm losin' fuel, but I think I can make the boat."

"Good luck, pard."

Climbing back to the east, Delight rolled his port wingtip down for a better view. He was just in time to see two more bombs explode amidships of *Penang Princess*.

Three seconds later, missile tracks arced out of the haze, passing well above him on a reciprocal course. Then his friend and coauthor was back on the radio. "Papa Flight, be advised. We have Flankers inbound from the east and Hornets from the west."

Twenty-six

Gomer One

"Four, you bomb the ship. I'll block for you."

With that, Ozzie Ostrewski rolled over and slanted down from thirteen thousand feet. He already had spotted the hostile TA-4 trying to cut off the bomber's roll-in point. Confident that Vespa would hit the target, he intended to tie up the Chinese long enough to afford her a clear shot.

Scooter Vespa flipped MASTER ARM, confirmed her sight setting, and nosed over. She forced herself to concentrate on the fundamentals rather than all that had gone wrong. *We were going to make a coordinated attack on a moving target miles from here, without enemy interceptors.* She came back on the throttle, recalling Zack Delight's combat motto: *No plan survives contact.*

The ship was listing slightly to port, with smoke partly obscuring the stern. From a twelve-thousand foot roll-in, Vespa stabilized her TA-4 at 450 knots. She remembered to tell Hu in the rear seat, "Keep the camera going." She received a grunt of acknowledgment.

Elizabeth Vespa had all the time in the world—ten seconds of time in which to trim out her dive, align the sight with the aim point, and track smoothly to the release point. *This is good,* she told herself. *This is very . . . very . . . good.* She marveled at how . . . ordinary . . . it seemed.

At forty-five hundred feet she thumbed the button.

Ostrewski met Gomer One head on—Ozzie going downhill, Gomer headed up. At six thousand feet they passed, slightly offset, and Ozzie pressed the bomb release. With the fuzing switch on SAFE, both Mark 83s slanted toward the water, ridding Papa Three of unwanted weight and drag.

Ozzie honked back on the stick, using his greater momentum to zoom-climb for the perch. He knew that he had the fight in the bag. His opponent, nose-high with energy bled off from the climb, had nowhere to go. The Chinese pilot's only move was to bury the nose, accelerate away, and try to evade.

That was exactly what Deng Yaobang decided to do.

Gomer One rolled into a diving port reversal, looking for the best cover available. He saw it less than three miles ahead.

Barely a mile away, Zack Delight saw the developing fight. He keyed his mike. "Papa Three or Four, this is Zack. I'll take the Gomer. You guys finish the ship."

Without his bombs, Ostrewski could do no more than shoot holes in *Penang Princess*'s hull. Frustrated at giving up a gun kill—the universal fighter pilot's wet dream—he recognized the wisdom of Delight's call. *At least I might split the defenses for Liz's attack.* He reversed course, expending some of his excess energy in a high-speed descent back toward the target.

Delight came hard aport, cutting the corner on Gomer One, who was leaving a 350-knot wake on the water. The hostile Skyhawk flashed across the bow of the Catalina Island cruise ship, drawing appreciative responses and Kodak Moments from the passengers. Delight was six seconds back.

Deng banked fifteen degrees left to thread his way through the channel between the Downtown Marina to starboard and *Queen Mary* to port. Leaving a rooster tail behind him, he flew under Queensway Bridge, popped up long enough to clear the 710 exit, Anaheim Street and Pacific Coast Highway bridges, then bunted his nose down toward the Los Angeles River.

Delight, with his teeth into his former tormenter, followed Deng beneath the Queensway Bridge without thinking about it. Only when the hostile Skyhawk popped up to clear the next three spans did it really occur to him what he had done. Willow Street, Wardlow, and the 405 all disappeared below their white bellies at six and a half miles per minute.

Delight tried to put the TA-4's tailpipe in his reticle. Down low, with the river channel providing a natural barrier, he thought it might be safe to shoot, but Gomer One's jet wash made steady aiming almost impossible. Even within the confines of the flood-control channel,

Delight knew there would be misses and ricochets. *Besides*, he told himself, *if I do hose the sumbitch, he's likely to crash on the Long Beach Freeway*. Route 710 North lay an eighth of a mile off their port wingtips.

As if reading Delight's mind, Deng abruptly laid a hard right at the 710/91 interchange. Scooting along the Artesia Freeway, he quickly departed North Long Beach, entered Bellflower at fifty feet altitude, and felt safer in a residential area. Delight followed.

Liz Vespa felt the thousand-pounders fall away, counted *One potato*, then began a steady, hard pull. She tensed her abdominal and thigh muscles, straining as six times the force of gravity forced her deep onto the unyielding ejection seat. While her vision narrowed, somehow her hearing improved; she heard Hu's grunts over the hot mike.

With the horizon seemingly descending to meet her jet's nose, Vespa extended her left arm, locking the elbow. The J52 spooled up from 80 to 100 percent. She regained full vision and scanned the panel. *All in the green. Now, where's the ship?*

Vespa kept three G on the aircraft, turning back toward the target so Hu could resume videotaping. Coming parallel to the burning, smoking vessel, the TA-4J was rocked as a white shock wave radiated outward from the hull. One second later the aft sixty feet jackknifed, paused an ephemeral moment, then dropped back in a cascading eruption of smoke, flames, and spray.

Scooter Vespa's eyes widened behind her visor. "Secondary explosions, Hu! Are you getting this?"

"Yes, miss! Hold this angle." She thought she heard him laugh. "This is wonderful!" He depressed the zoom button to get a closer view of the conflagration.

Liz shared the laugh. She felt almost giddy. "We have a saying in this country, Mr. Hu."

"Yes, miss?"

"Film at eleven."

Delight scanned his instruments. RPM, fuel flow, and tailpipe temperature were in the green, but he felt himself losing ground on Gomer One. He reasoned that the battle damage had torn gouges in his jet's aluminum skin, imposing a drag penalty. He was down to nine hundred pounds of fuel, and Gomer seemed headed back to El Toro. *Nothing I can do there*, he thought. Reluctantly, Delight pulled up, briefly wagging his wings in tacit tribute to a bravura low-level performance. As he climbed to a more fuel-efficient altitude, the last he saw of the Juliet was a fast white dart making 400 mph in a 65 zone.

Ozzie called for a joinup; he wanted mutual support in case more bandits arrived. “Papa Four, this is Three. I’ll meet you over Freeman. Angels eight.”

Liz hedged for a moment. “Ah, Four, we’re getting BDA. Please wait one.”

Ostrewski fidgeted on his seat. He understood Vespa’s wish for bomb damage assessment, but the *Princess* was beyond help. For a moment he wondered about the heat-resistant qualities of bootleg backpack nukes.

From long habit, he turned his head through almost two hundred degrees. Looking upward to his left, he froze for two heartbeats. Coming from seaward was the track of an air-to-air missile streaking inland.

Twenty-seven

Light to Moderate

"Missile inbound! Left eleven o'clock!"

"My God! It's . . ."

"Tommy, break! Break left!"

The voices on the VHF circuit overlapped in rising octaves and decibels as twelve miles from the burning, sinking *Penang Princess*, a female section leader screamed at her male wingman. Liz Vespa, hearing the garbled transmissions, fought to make sense of it amid her elation at putting both bombs square amidships.

"Tommy, eject!" The female voice was nearly hysterical now. "My God, oh my God . . ." The hoarse contralto descended into an audible sob before the thumb slid off the mike button.

Five heartbeats later, the voice was back. "This is Bronco Three-Zero-Four broadcasting on guard. Three Oh Six . . . exploded. I'm off Palos Verdes. Send a helo!"

Elizabeth Vespa felt a shiver between her shoulder blades. *My God . . . Jen-Jen!*

Flying alone in Flanker One at sixteen thousand feet, Igor Gnido had an idea that he was too late. That black smoke roiling off Long Beach looked ominous for the prospects of *Penang Princess*, and he could only hope that her cargo had been off-loaded. In truth, there had been little chance of making a timely interception.

Furthermore, the R-73M2s and R-77s had necessarily been in deep storage, and it took time to upload the missiles, especially with the Sukhoi factory crew unaccustomed to handling ordnance. Furthermore, Deng and Li obviously had failed to prevent the carrier-based A-4s from attacking.

Gnido glanced again to the south, where the freighter seemed to be burning itself out. He sucked in more oxygen, mentally tipping his hardhat to Miss Scooter. Not long ago he had plans of bedding her; now he might have to kill her. *Or maybe it will not be necessary, and I will kill her anyway.*

Igor Gnido literally possessed a license to kill. He chuckled at the thought of his diplomatic passport from the Russian government, plus his credentials as a trade representative of the People's Republic of China. The mirth he felt at his present situation—controlling the airspace over Los Angeles, California—was mixed with contempt for politicians and diplomats who made such a condition possible.

The first American fighter had been ridiculously easy to destroy. The R-77—what NATO called the AAM-AE "Amraamski"—had been fired well within range and performed as advertised. The haze made it difficult to discern the fireball fifteen nautical miles away, but the big Sukhoi's sophisticated radar clearly showed the southerly target destroyed. Gnido knew that it had to be a Tomcat or Hornet, and from the its unvarying course he wondered if the pilot had been using his radar-warning receiver. Not that it would have mattered very much; R-77 was a fire-and-forget weapon like the U.S. AMRAAM.

Gnido banked into a tight orbit above Terminal Island, awaiting events. He felt confident that the Americans would not return fire as long as he was over land, where aircraft wreckage or missiles would cause casualties and damage on the ground. However, with his look-down, shoot-down radar, he could easily track anything over water.

To the northwest the radar picture was a cluttered mess. Gnido laughed again at the thought of the panic he must have caused at LAX, where a flock of jetliners was scrambling like a covey of quail. *Ladies and gentlemen, we regret to announce the cancellation of Flight 123 owing to occasional Flankers and light-to-moderate missiles in the area.* It occurred to him that he could hide in the LAX traffic pattern, essentially holding hostage any commercial traffic still there.

A pity I only have three missiles left, he gloomed. There had been no time to load more.

"Papa Three or Four, this is Lead."

Ozzie heard the call and replied first. "Zack, this is Oz. Where are you?"

"Ah, I'm halfway to home plate on the zero three five radial. Getting skosh on fuel. How 'bout you?"

"Dash Four and I have seen missile plumes, Zack, and there's a splash on guard channel. You hear it?"

"Negative. I been kinda busy." There was a pause while Delight sorted priorities. "Four, you copy?"

"Four here. Go!" Vespa sounded calm, even eager.

"You have a visual on Three?"

"Yes, I'm closing on his four o'clock."

Delight mentally computed the relative positions of the three Skyhawks. Ostrewski and Vespa would be below and behind him, still offshore. "Okay. Break-break. *Santa Cruz*, this is Papa One. What dope on Dash Two? Over."

Moments passed before the watch officer replied. "Ah, Papa One, be advised. Papa Two is aboard with a bent bird. Pilot and backseater are both okay. Your signal is Charlie on arrival."

"Roger. See you on deck."

Lieutenant Commander Jennifer Jensen fought to control the palsied trembling of her hands and forearms. For the first time in her naval career she was forced to confront the fact that she was out of her depth, facing a situation that neither seniority nor contacts would alleviate.

That knowledge, combined with the fiery death of her wingman, meant that she was deep-down, bone-chilling *scared*. Just how scared she might have to admit eventually—how else to explain the switchology error in firing a Sidewinder after designating the suspected Flanker for an AMRAAM shot?

Now, with the range closing at six miles per minute, she was barely one minute from the merge with that supremely arrogant Russian. Belatedly, Jensen realized she had not made the obligatory "Fox Two" call, indicating an AIM-9 shot. She knew that she had been too rattled to follow procedure, but with a little luck she might still retrieve the situation. Which would be fortunate indeed, considering that she had not yet received the "Weapons free" call from *Boorda*'s strike operations center.

She inhaled deeply, sucking oxygen into her lungs with the faint molded rubber scent of her mask. She willed herself to project the ice princess tone in her voice as she called Strike Ops. "Chainsaw Strike from Bronco Three-Zero-Four. Request weapons free. Repeat, weapons free."

"Three-Zero-Four, stand by."

God damn it, I can't afford to stand by! "Strike, Bronco. I'm looking at multiple bogies on my nose. My wingman is down, and I'm outnumbered!" Immediately, Jen-Jen Jensen regretted the tremor in her voice—the guys would say she choked—but she realized it could work to her advantage. *Admiral, I was in reasonable fear of my life. My God, they had just killed Tommy Blyden!*

Interminable seconds crawled past. During that infinity of time, Jensen fought a cosmic battle of Ambition against Fear. Ambition whispered in her ear, hinting at glorious rewards that might yet be hers if she succeeded. Fear screamed the banshee wail, the dirge that the only reason that Flanker pilot had not yet destroyed her was his willingness to toy with her until he tired of the game.

"Bronco, Strike. Two Tomcats are launching at this time. You are cleared to fire only in defense of yourself or other aircraft. VID is required. Acknowledge."

Jensen was appalled. *Visual identification? He'll kill me before I ever see him!* Then, like a gambling addict laying her last dollar on the table in hope of beating the house odds, she heard herself say, "Three Zero Four. Acknowledge."

Gnido sought to sort out the confusing radar picture. Amid the multitude of blips on his screen, one American fighter had gone down, another continued toward him, briefly painting him with fire-control radar. At least three more aircraft were below him to the south. He assumed the latter were A-4s but had no way of knowing which were friendly or hostile. One was climbing out to sea, probably returning to the carrier, and that one likely was an American. Gnido placed his cursor on the blip and toyed with the idea of locking it up. *If I had a full loadout . . .*

But he needed to keep his remaining R-73 for the main threat—the fighter pressing inland over the Palos Verdes peninsula. He remained confident that no American officer would allow a BVR engagement over a densely populated area. Therefore, he retained control of the situation, willing and even eager to test his aircraft and close-range weapons against a competent opponent. Whatever the political fallout from the *Penang Princess* debacle, Igor Gnido felt that he stood to gain exceptional benefits both from his Russian employers and his Chinese patrons. "Yes, it was terrible what happened at Long Beach," arms merchants would say, "but did you notice what one Su-30 did to three or four U.S. Navy fighters?"

American businessmen talked of "cutthroat competition." *The comfortable, dilettante bastards.* How could they compare to Igor Gnido, who was turning into a world-class salesman?

Jennifer Jensen was thinking better now. She had broken lock on the presumed Flanker, lest the pilot get nervous and spear her with another long-range Archer. She was willing to go to visual range, which would probably be under three miles in this murk, and if the bogey—no, make that bandit—made a threatening move, she would would use her remaining AIM-9M.

Following the "bandit box" in her heads-up display, Jensen turned slightly to port, keeping the threat on her nose. It was an eerie feeling, knowing that somewhere within the HUD square superimposed on infinity lay the source of the death of Lieutenant Thomas Blyden.

Elizabeth Vespa craned her neck, trying to glimpse the high-performance jets jousting inland. She approved of Ostrewski's decision to remain low on the water, relatively safe from radar detection, but it was about time to head for the boat. The temptation to ask Papa Three his intention was powerful, considering that their survival might be at stake, but Scooter Vespa knew that Ozzie Ostrewski would think less of her for it.

And Scooter was like every other tactical aviator. She would much rather die than look bad.

Gnido had had enough of groping through the murk. Since the carrier aircraft approaching him apparently had not fired, nor even continued targeting him, he realized that his premise was correct. *The Americans will not engage beyond visual range!* But he was under no such stricture. He thumbed his weapon selector to the helmet sight detent, confirmed the symbology, and prepared to fire. As soon as the target emerged from the smog and haze, he would shoot, then decide whether to deal with one of the low-flying targets. A BVR kill, a short-range kill, and then perhaps a low-level over-water kill would look very convincing in the sales brochures.

The Hornet appeared slightly offset to starboard as Gnido's blue eyes focused on the dark shape. *Range four point five kilometers, good enough.* He pressed the trigger.

In Bronco 304, Jensen felt her blood surge as she saw the big Sukhoi. She already had her starboard Sidewinder selected, finger on the trigger, ready to fire. There was the tracking tone chirping in her earphones . . .

And the smoke trail of an AA-11 igniting beneath the Flanker. One four-letter word strobed in her brain as she reacted. Stick hard over, throttles against the stops, and pull.

The Hornet pirouetted about its axis and the nose arced abruptly downward.

Twenty-eight

Two V One V One

Ozzie's experienced eyes picked the Archer out of the sky. He would not have seen it had it performed normally—that is, if it had killed Jennifer Jensen—but its rocket motor described a swirling, corkscrewing path below the haze.

"Papa Four, heads up. Missile shot five o'clock, way high." He thought to add, "No threat. Yet."

Vespa looked over her left shoulder and scanned the upper air. She saw the errant missile a few seconds later. "It's gone ballistic?"

"I think so." Ostrewski estimated the geometry of the situation and decided to face the potential threat. He led Vespa into a forty-degree banked turn, climbing back toward the north-northwest.

Jennifer Jensen rolled wings level at four thousand feet and began her pull. She remembered to call the ship. "Chainsaw! Heshotatmeheshotatme! Iwillreturnfire!"

"Bronco, Chainsaw. Say again? Repeat, say again."

Jensen barely heard the response to her panicked transmission. She fought the oppressive G that she loaded on herself as the Hornet's nose rose through the horizon, her vision tunneling through a gray mist.

As her vision returned to normal, her adrenaline-drenched brain perceived a dark spot almost straight ahead. Her richly oxygenated blood put her in a survival mind-set—eyes dilated, blood pressure, pulse, and respiration elevated. Psych 101, fight or flight. It did not occur to

Jensen that the aerodynamic shape approaching her through the HUD symbology was far lower than the threat aircraft that had just launched against her.

She heard the AIM-9 Mike's seeker head tracking the friction heat generated by the 320-knot airspeed of the target airframe. *They said there might be two Flankers!* With the range down to two and a half miles she pressed the trigger, remembering to call "Fox two!"

From his perch above and behind the plummeting Hornet, Igor Gnido watched in fascination. The sight presented to him was almost enough to erase the anger he felt at the malfunctioning R-73 that had narrowly missed the F/A-18. *The pilot is mad*, Gnido told himself. For the life of him, the Russian could not conceive what the Hornet was shooting at. He eased off some power, brought his nose up, and bided his time.

Ostrewski's combat-experienced mind screamed at him even as his rational side denied what was happening. He heard something garbled on the radio, vaguely imagined it was Vespa, then began dealing with the lethal reality accelerating toward him.

Ozzie shoved up the power and abruptly rolled into a right turn, better to gauge the Sidewinder's aspect and closure rate. Head-on it was nearly impossible to determine the range until too late.

As the smoky trail corrected slightly to rendezvous on him, he told himself to wait. He punched off four or five flares, none of which seemed to deceive the Mike's improved logic board. *Not yet . . . not yet . . . Now!*

It is not enough to change vectors in one dimension to defeat a missile. The trick is to alter both heading and altitude simultaneously, forcing more G onto the mindless killer than its small wings can accept.

Ozzie's stomach was bilious in his mouth, constricting his throat. He did not realize that he stopped breathing.

He snapped the stick back, pitching up abruptly while coordinating aileron and rudder. His high-G barrel roll, executed with less than two seconds leeway, forced the winder to cut the corner at too acute an angle to continue tracking. As its seeker detected that the range was opening, the warhead detonated.

"Knock it off, knock it off! Hornet, knock it off! You just shot at a friendly!" Vespa's voice was a high-pitched mixture of astonishment and outrage. She had no idea who was listening to her frequency, and at that moment she was not inclined to be charitable. She saw Papa Three reappear beyond the smoke of the Sidewinder's explosion, apparently unharmed, but Michael Ostrewski had been forced on the defensive. If the Hornet pressed its advantage . . .

She turned in, savoring the Skyhawk's superb roll rate. *If he turns into Ozzie, I'll shoot.* She remembered Hu in the backseat. "Hu, watch for other planes. We don't know who these people are."

In a Topgun "murder board," the debriefer would have faulted Jensen for turning back to engage. The school solution was to blow through, extend away from the immediate threat, reassess the situation, and set up for another missile shot.

Jennifer Jensen pulled her nose above the horizon, anxious to observe the result of her shot. She needed to know that her opponent had either been destroyed or driven into a vulnerable position for a reattack. As she neared the peak of a chandelle, seeking the target through the top of her canopy, she allowed her airspeed to bleed off more than she intended. By the time she caught sight of the target, which she recognized as an A-4, she was down to 285 knots. She tapped the afterburners, pulling through into a 135-degree slicing turn, ruefully recalling that she had no more Sidewinders. Too close for an AMRAAM, she flicked the selector and her HUD indicator changed from HEAT to GUN.

Something's wrong, she realized. *That's not a Flanker.* She eased off some of the G, retarding throttles slightly to gain more time to evaluate the potential threat.

"Liz, cut him off!" Ostrewski's evasive roll had depleted much of his energy. He stuffed his nose down, pulling back into the threat, but knew he lacked the "smash" to go vertical.

With 375 knots on the dial, Vespa committed to an all-or-nothing gamble. She gauged the distance by the Hornet's size in her thirty-mil reticle, waited three vital seconds, then pulled up. Vespa felt oddly calm, almost as she had during adversary training missions with VC-1 in Hawaii. Tracking the F/A-18 from eight o'clock low, she remembered to fly the pipper through the target, allowing a full ring of deflection.

At nine hundred feet range, she pressed the trigger and held it down.

Gnido shook his head in bemused contempt for the American's folly. How could he allow himself to be sandwiched between two potentially hostile aircraft? And then to compound it by turning back again to repeat the error! The Sukhoi pilot decided to watch the outcome of the Hornet's clumsy attack. Depending on what happened, he would kill the winner, return to El Toro, and try not to smile too broadly when waving his diplomatic passport on his way out of this amazing country.

Jen-Jen Jensen had no idea what was happening. Something like hailstones on a tin roof hammered the airframe behind her. The canopy shattered two feet aft of her headrest. Her initial emotion was confused disbelief; only after the Hornet lurched abruptly and began an uncommanded roll did she realize she had been hit by an unseen assailant. *The other Flanker!* she raged.

Jensen shot a wide-eyed glance at her instrument panel. Master caution, fire warning, and system-failure lights strobed at her in red-and-yellow hues. Wind-fed flames waved angrily orange in her rearview mirrors. For an indecisive moment she wondered whether she should risk taking time to point the nose out to sea, away from the Alamitos Bay Yacht Club. Her father's voice came to her. *Honey, don't ever hesitate in an emergency. The Navy can always buy another airplane.*

The crippled strike fighter dropped into a mind-numbing spiral barely a mile over San Pedro Bay.

"Bronco Three Zero-Four! Mayday, mayday!"

Lieutenant Commander Jennifer Jensen pulled the black-and-yellow-striped handle.

As Vespa passed below and behind the doomed Hornet, Ostrewski had an unforgettable view. In a nose-down spiral the canopy separated, the seat fired with its rocket motor glaring white-hot, and the parachute deployed, pulling the pilot violently erect.

"*Santa Cruz*, this is Papa Three. Be advised, we have an F/A-18 down about one mile off Long Beach Marina. The pilot has a good chute. He'll splash about two miles south of Pier J."

"Roger, Three. We're alerting the . . ."

Vespa's voice chopped off the rest of the message. "Ozzie! Above you! Flanker at six o'clock!"

Taking the warning on faith, Ostrewski responded the only way he could. He turned into the threat.

Igor Gnido saw the nearer Skyhawk reverse its turn, hauling around the corner in a ninety-degree bank. The Russian had not intended to shoot yet, but he relished sparring with what was certainly a more competent opponent than that idiot in the Hornet. He added power, pulled up and executed a high yo-yo, keeping the A-4F on the defensive. The TA-4J was still too far off to pose any danger.

Topping out of his four-thousand-foot pitch-up, Gnido half rolled and brought his nose over the top, toward the southern horizon. He looked rearward between his twin tails, found the Skyhawk where he expected, and retarded his throttles.

Ostrewski had padlocked the big Sukhoi, conserving his available energy for the right moment. *Like a Topgun free-for-all*, he thought: *two versus one versus one*. When he saw Gnido's nose pull through, he pitched up, momentarily spoiling the Flanker's tracking. Both pilots had a chance for a gun snap shot; neither took it.

As they passed one another, offset two hundred yards at twenty-five hundred feet, Ostrewski stomped right rudder, shoved the stick over, and buried his nose. He gained fifteen degrees angle on the Flanker before it rocketed upward again in that awesome climb, this time pulling its vector toward Papa Four. His rapid turn caught Ostrewski by surprise—Papa Three could practically join on his wing, almost too close to shoot.

"All stations, all aircraft over Long Beach Harbor. This is USS *Boorda* on guard. Be advised, two F-14s are inbound. They are armed and cleared to fire at any threat. All aircraft: You will comply with any directions from the mission commander. Out."

Gnido cursed fervently. With most of his weapons gone, he was in no position to tackle two Tomcats. He decided to kill one Skyhawk, disengage, and streak for El Toro at low level.

He felt he was managing the two Skyhawks nicely. Without missiles, they had to gain a close-range tracking solution on him, and as long as he kept both of them off his nose—or well below him—he could not be hurt.

The A-4s could not say the same thing. Gnido had selected his last R-73M2. With the Archer's seeker slaved to his helmet-mounted sight, he could kill up to sixty degrees off his nose; he put the reticle on the two-seater running in from ten o'clock. A sideways glance to his right showed the single-seater to be no threat. It was going to pass close aboard and slightly high, too near for more than a fleeting snap shot.

Gnido pressed the trigger and felt his last Archer come off the rail. He was tracking the TA-4J smoothly, knowing that as long as he kept the Skyhawk in his forward hemisphere it was doomed.

Ostrewski saw the smoke plume as the rocket motor ignited, sending the AA-11 toward Papa Four. His heart was raw in his throat; he knew that Liz possessed neither the time nor the countermeasures to defeat the missile. With thrust vectoring, it was perhaps the most agile air-to-air weapon in the world.

Without room for a decent shot, without time to extend away before turning back in—and without conscious thought—Ozzie made his move.

Vespa saw the smoke trail, knew it for what it was, and rolled nearly inverted. She intended to wait until the last possible instant before pulling into her belly and loading maximum positive G on her aircraft. From 135 degrees of bank, her world was a crazy quilt of three-dimensional geometry with the Russian missile eating up the last quarter mile of airspace.

She shut her eyes, saw her mother's face, and pulled.

Gnido saw the evasive maneuver, admiring the pilot's last-ditch effort while knowing it was futile, and awaited the explosion.

Michael Ostrewski's last view was a windscreen full of Flanker. The two-tone gray paint scheme loomed at him, and his final willful effort was to clamp down on the trigger.

His cannon had hardly begun to fire when the little Douglas speared the big Sukhoi squarely behind the cockpit.

Liz fought the G, realizing that she had bottomed out of her desperate split-ess, knowing that the very realization meant life. *I'm alive. How?* She craned her head, seeking the Flanker that had to be above and behind her, positioned to shoot again.

The first thing she noticed was a corkscrewing smoky spiral as the Archer, devoid of guidance, followed its ballistic path to destruction. Vespa reversed into the threat that now was nonexistent. The visual footprint led to a dissipating fireball suspended in space, shedding fuel, flares, and aircraft parts.

Her pulse spiked at the knowledge that Michael Ostrewski somehow—*somehow*—had gained enough room to pull lead on the Flanker. A warm deluge of adrenaline-rich adoration flooded her veins. *Ozzie, you are one* superb *fighter pilot!* She pressed the mike button. "Three, this is Four. Climbing through four thousand."

She waited several seconds for the reply, believing that the Only Polish-American Tomcat Ace must be savoring his triumph. When no response came, she tried again. And again. Finally, she said, "Hu, look around. Do you see Ozzie?"

The Chinese pilot turned in his seat, swiveling his head across the horizon. "No, miss."

Realization descended on Vespa's brain, draining downward in a chilling cascade that coagulated into a hard, insistent lump in her stomach.

She spoke to the windblown smoke and drifting shards. "Oh, Michael. What did you do?"

Twenty-nine

Last One Back

Peters and Delight were on the bridge, digesting three versions of what had happened to the renegade Sukhoi. Delight, still in his flight suit and torso harness, was coming off an adrenaline high following his kill.

"I still think Ozzie gunned the sumbitch and ejected."

"Zack, radar saw the plots merge. And we have a secondhand report from the Coast Guard reporting a midair collision." Peters slumped against the bulkhead, arms folded. Staring at the deck, he intoned, "They're searching, but . . ."

". . . but Ozzie's probably dead."

Peters nodded.

"TA-4 on downwind, Captain!" Odegaard lowered his binoculars and pointed to port.

With gear and flaps down, Scooter Vespa broke at "the ninety" while Robo Robbins, Psycho Thaler, and Mr. Wei watched from the LSO platform.

Vespa rolled wings level a mile and a quarter from the ramp, making minute adjustments to keep on glide slope. Robbins, with the phone in one hand and the "pickle switch" held aloft in the other, waited for her call.

"Skyhawk ball," she said. "State point six."

Robbins and Thaler silently regarded one another. With six hundred pounds of fuel, she would have only two chances at the deck. "Lookin' good, Liz. Keep it comin'," Robbins called.

Thaler had the binoculars on the TA-4, serving as Robbins's watcher. "Hook!" He turned to look at Robbins. "No hook!"

Robbins made a conscious effort to keep his voice calm. "Liz, drop your hook."

Vespa chided herself for missing the crucial item. *Damn it—I've never done that before!* She reached down for the hook-shaped handle, missed twice, and had to look in the cockpit. When she returned her gaze to the mirror, the ball was a diameter high and she was angry with herself almost to the point of tears.

"Waveoff, Liz. Take it around!"

Vespa knew that she could recover and probably catch a four wire, but obedience to the LSO's command was too deeply ingrained. She shoved up the power and ignored the usual procedure. Instead, she wrapped into a hard left turn, leaving gear and flaps down, rejoining the circuit slightly downwind of the ninety.

Thaler leaned into Robbins's shoulder. "I think she could've made it, Rob."

"I know. But she's gotta be shook about Ozzie, and this way there's less doubt in her mind."

As a landing signal officer, Robbins also was a working psychologist. He knew how frustrated and anxious the pilot must be, especially with a passenger aboard. He keyed the phone. "Don't worry, Scooter. We'll catch you this time."

Vespa scanned the instruments once more, pointedly ignoring the fuel gauge. Over the hot mike, she said, "Mr. Hu, brace yourself for possible ejection. If I miss this pass I'll climb straight ahead and give you as much notice as I can."

"Yes, miss." His tone sounded neutral.

As Vespa rolled out of her oblong-shaped 360-degree turn, the ball was half a diameter low. She called "Skyhawk ball," omitting her fuel state, and added throttle to intersect the glide slope. She barely heard Robbins's "Power" call.

As the ball rose slightly she led it with pitch and power, stabilizing her airspeed at 122 knots to compensate for the light fuel load. *Santa Cruz*'s 328-foot-wide deck was irrelevant to her now. What mattered was the eighty-foot-wide landing area with the lifesaving arresting wires, though Vespa aimed within three feet of centerline.

For the next ten seconds Elizabeth Vespa's attention was riveted on the glowing amber meatball. From the the backseat, Hu appreciated the fact that it remained nailed in the middle of the datum. He heard Robbins's only additional transmission. "Good pass, hold what you got."

Papa Four impacted the deck at eleven feet per second sink rate, the landing gear oleos compressing under pressure as the tailhook snagged the third steel cable. As Vespa added power in event of a bolter, the TA-4J was dragged to a stop.

Mr. Wei Chinglao broke all decorum and hugged Robo Robbins. Psycho Thaler pounded both of them on the back, bouncing on the balls of his feet.

Robbins turned to his writer. "Papa Four, low-state recovery, rails pass. Underfunckinglined OK-3!" As a group, they turned and ran up the the deck to the parking area.

Vespa sat in the front seat, listening to the J52 unspool with its vacuum-cleaner whine. She wanted time to absorb what had happened to Ostrewski, and what she had just done. Hu already had descended the ladder, standing with his camcorder, intending to record his pilot's triumph. He was immediately joined by a crowd of plane handlers, ordies, and the LSO contingent, plus Peters and Delight from the bridge.

Liz dropped her helmet over the side, where the plane captain caught it. She beaned a smile she did not quite feel, blew a kiss at Hu's camera, then pinched her torso harness restraints and eased out of the cockpit. She backed down the ladder but had not reached the bottom before she felt eager hands plucking her up and away. She was afloat on a raucous sea of male faces, borne shoulder high toward the island. For the tiniest instant she thought back to her high-school senior prom and the condescending look of triumph that Christine LaMont had shot her as the tiara was set on the queen's head. *Take that, Christine.*

The men grasping Vespa's legs and thighs allowed her slide off their shoulders. She alit in front of Peters, who grasped her in a crushing hug. When he pulled back he exclaimed, "I am so proud of you."

She blinked back what was rising inside her and managed to keep her voice calm. "Ozzie?"

Peters wanted to avoid her eyes. Instead, he focused on her face and shook his head. "No word, Liz. I think he's gone."

"Scooter."

Liz turned at the sound of her call sign. Delight stood by her left shoulder, and she leaned into him. "Oh, Zack." She wrapped her arms around his neck. He patted her back, exactly the way he had reassured his grandchild after a bicycle spill twenty years ago.

"Did you see it?" He knew what she meant.

"No, hon. I was . . ." He cleared his throat. "I was in the pattern about that time. But . . ."

"But my God, Zack. He died for me!" Her eyes were clear and dry, but she choked on her words. "He died for me . . ."

Delight grasped her by both shoulders. "Listen to me, Liz. Listen to me!" They both were aware of the crowd melting away. The deckhands recognized that this was a moment between friends who had shared something exceptional. "If he was still here, he'd be just as proud of you as . . . we are." Delight allowed her to grasp that sentiment. "Liz, you just sank a ship and got a gun kill on the same mission. Do you realize nobody's done that in about fifty-five years?"

She allowed herself a grim smile. "You got a kill, too."

Delight looked at Peters. "Hook and I both flew a couple hundred missions in Vietnam and never got close to what happened today. But, hell, my mom could have hosed that gomer from six o'clock."

Vespa realized that she had instructed the dead Chinese pilot. "Do we know who was in that airplane?"

"No," Peters replied. "But we'll find out fairly soon."

Delight shook his head, marveling at the pilot he had chased. "I'll bet the ranch that my guy was Deng. I don't think anybody else in the class could've flown that way."

Robbins forced his way through the dispersing crowd. He leaned around Delight and kissed Liz on both cheeks. "Scooter, that was the best pass I've seen in years. You got an underlined OK-3." He grinned hugely. "And after a hell of a mission."

Some of the giddiness was returning even as she wondered, *Have they forgotten that Michael's dead?* But she heard herself responding to the banter. "Even with the low start, Rob?"

He punched her arm. "Hell yes. That was a great recovery, and since *I'm* the only LSO aboard, it's a perfect OK-3."

"Captain from bridge." Odegaard's voice snapped over the 1-MC speaker. Peters looked up at the 0–9 level where a khaki arm waved at him. "Sir, the phones are working at El Toro and your wife's on the horn. She and Mrs. Delight want to know if you will both be home for dinner."

Thirty

Shakeout

"How many federal agencies can there be, anyway?"

Representative Tim Ottmann grinned ruefully at Delight's plaintive query. "Hell, Zack, don't blame me. I voted against every new bureau and agency that ever came up for funding. Even tried to make a couple of 'em go away, but it did no good."

Peters looked around the hotel suite, assessing the collective mood. Besides himself and Jane, the Delights and Ottmann, were Vespa, Robbins, Thaler, Wei and Hu, plus two Washington attorney friends of Ottmann's. One of them, a former A-7 pilot named Brian Chappel, specialized in transportation law, including maritime and aviation. He was cordially detested by the Navy Department and the Department of Transportation.

"In the two days since the excitement, I've heard from the following," Chappel said. "DOT including FAA and the Coast Guard, FBI, ATF, and DEQ. That doesn't count state and local agencies."

Robbins raised his head. "DEQ? What's their take on this?"

"Something about protection of coastal waters. They say that bombing is bad for the fish, and the *Penang*'s oil spill caused some concern."

Peters was anxious to wrap up the meeting. "Okay, Brian. Where is all this likely to lead?"

"My guess is that it'll mostly disappear in a couple of weeks."

"Really?" Jane Peters was reluctantly eager to believe it.

"Yes, Mrs. Peters. Really." Chappel gave her a convincing smile.

"Look, the bottom line is this: Everybody on both sides wants the same thing. To make this go away. State and DOD are red-faced over the way things turned to . . . hash . . . with their Chinese program. The way that heavy ordnance like bombs and missiles were smuggled into this country, or actually purchased here, could force Congress to ask a bunch of embarrassing questions." He looked at his D.C. colleague. "Right, Skip?"

Ottmann gave two thumb's-up. "Guarantee it."

Thaler picked up his glass and slurped the last of his lemonade through the straw. "Mr. Chappel, I understand the PR angle—the government's got to look like it's investigating all this. But you know that the fix is already in with the president and the administration. Those pardons that Skip got for us, in case we need them."

"Yes, that's right."

"So what'll happen in Taiwan?"

"Oh, that plan is canceled. With the assistance of Mr. Ottmann, Mr. Chappel, and some other well-placed individuals, the names and roles of certain prominent PRC officials are being made known on a confidential basis in Washington."

"Which means"—Ottmann grinned—"that the papers and news networks will have all the details in time for today's five o'clock news. With what we can release about bribes, kickbacks, and influence peddling, neither the U.S. nor Chinese governments will risk losing billions of dollars in trade and revenues."

Vespa spoke for the first time. "Mr. Ottmann, what about the backpacks? Are they being recovered?"

"I shall answer that," Wei interjected. The old MiG pilot regarded the American woman frankly. At length he said, "Under utmost secrecy, I confide to you what few people will ever know. There were no nuclear weapons."

Liz involuntarily shuddered; Jane felt the tremors in Vespa's body and put an arm around her shoulders. Liz leaned toward the Chinese. "Michael died for *nothing*?" Her hands clenched into frustrated, vengeful fists.

"Not at all, my dear. Not at all. He played a vital role in carrying out the most important part of our plan. When I said that we knew the weapons were aboard because one of my people helped load them, that was the same information that went to the Premier and the Politburo. Oh yes, packages were placed in the *Penang Princess's* hold, and they would have showed a reading if exposed to a Geiger counter. But they were, ah, your word is—a placebo."

"A fake pill to make the patient feel better." Peters slowly shook his head, marveling at the subtle complexity of Wei's plan.

"Exactly, Mr. Peters. In this case, the patient was the premier and his Stalinist cabal. Now that their 'plot' has been defeated and exposed, China may move on to more productive endeavors."

Liz grappled with the cooling anger she felt. At length she asked, "But what about the people on that ship? Eric and I . . ."

"Miss Vespa, Mr. Thaler, please." Wei managed a note of sympathy in his voice that still seemed out of place for the man. "You knew that people would die when you accepted the mission. The rationale was that a far greater number might be saved. Well, nothing has changed. The eleven men who were killed and the twenty or so injured must be balanced against the losses that would occur in an invasion of Taiwan."

While Vespa allowed herself to accept the fact that she had been skillfully used in a geopolitical chess game, Delight intruded on the hushed silence. "One thing I'd like to ask, Mr. Wei. What caused the secondary explosions after Liz's hits?"

"Explosive charges set near the presumed weapons, Mr. Delight. We wanted to ensure that an independent agency confirmed the presence of nuclear materials. Your emergency disaster crews have reported trace elements in the atmosphere and water—far below any hazardous level, but enough to ensure that protests and diplomatic consequences will result in Beijing." He allowed the ghost of a smile. "Your Navy will 'recover' the weapons."

Thaler swirled the ice in his glass, still shaking his head at the revelations. "How were the charges set?"

"Again, Mr. Thaler, I require utmost discretion. But you have treated me and Mr. Hu with uncommon courtesy, and provided me with the most exhilarating day of my life." He almost smiled again. "When the attack began, one of our operatives set off a timer. Then he escaped over the side."

"And the pleasure craft alongside?" Thaler asked.

"You may consider your effort well spent," Wei responded. "That was a Mexican drug smuggler hired by the PRC agents in Long Beach. He was to disperse the backpacks to other agents throughout the area."

Ottmann noticed Chappel closing his briefcase. "Well, I guess that's about it. Brian, you have anything else for these folks?"

"No, just the usual lawyer-client warning." He smiled at the audience. "The spin doctors will take the lead, but people, please remember this. Don't say a damn thing to anybody without consulting me first."

Peters stood up, resting one hand on Jane's shoulder. "Then I guess we can all go home."

Wei and Hu looked at each other in a way that had nothing to do with family ties. "Not all of us, Mr. Peters," Wei intoned. "Not all of us."

Thirty-one

Scooter Flight

The memorial service at St. Francis Catholic Church was smaller than the wedding would have been. The testimonials had been spoken, the elegy delivered by Terry Peters, the rites performed by Ostrewski's priest.

The mourners rose following the benediction and slowly filed out. The ATA contingent stood by while Maria Vasquez accepted greetings and condolences from friends and relatives.

"By the way," Peters said, "Tim Ottmann is recommending Ozzie for a special orders Medal of Honor. With the political horse trading, he figures it's a cinch for a Navy Cross."

"Oz already had a Navy Cross," Delight replied without irony. "Besides, you know how he felt about this country for the past several years."

Peters chose to ignore the sentiment. "Additionally, everybody else on the mission probably will get a Silver Star."

"I've got a Silver Star," Delight replied—with irony.

Carol Delight leaned over the pew. "I don't understand something. Everybody involved was civilian. How can military medals be awarded?"

"Actually there's precedent—industry tech reps, even war correspondents have received combat decorations. Besides, Tim said something about a videotape of a former secretary of the Navy with a sheep." Delight shrugged, then smiled. "Maybe Skip was exaggerating—I couldn't say."

Maria Vasquez turned from the front row, her obsidian eyes searching the pews. "Mrs. Peters," she whispered. "I don't see Elizabeth. I can't believe she would miss this."

Jane patted the young woman's hand. "Don't worry, dear. She'll be here—I promise." She nodded to her husband, who strode up the aisle in that long, ground-eating gait.

"But the service is over."

"Not exactly, Maria." Jane took her arm. "Let's step outside, shall we?" On their way to the exit, Maria glimpsed Terry Peters speaking into a handheld radio.

Thirty seconds later the screech of low-level jets echoed off the surrounding buildings. "There!" somebody shouted, pointing to the south. Other witnesses followed the gesture and clapped or cheered—or merely shielded their eyes against the glare.

With the effortless grace of jet-propelled flight, the finger-four Skyhawk formation glided eight hundred feet overhead. In unison, they dropped their tailhooks in salute.

"It's illegal as hell," exclaimed Carol Delight. "How'd you swing that?"

Zack whispered in her ear. "Don't ask, don't tell!"

Maria leaned against Jane Peters, one hand to her lips and the other dabbing at her eyes. Jane hugged her close. "That's Liz, Maria. With Eric and Rob and Tim."

From eight hundred feet over downtown Mesa, Arizona, Scooter Vespa added power and abruptly pulled up from the number one position while the others continued straight ahead. The vacant space—the missing man—was obvious to everyone on the ground.

As she laid the stick to starboard, inducing a series of vertical aileron rolls into a cloudless blue sky, Liz Vespa made the call to Hook Peters.

"Wizard Flight, off and out." She paused. "Break-break. Scooter Flight, returning to base."

BARRETT TILLMAN is the author of four novels, including *Hellcats*, which was nominated for the Military Novel of the Year in 1996, twenty nonfiction historical and biographical books, and more than four hundred military and aviation articles in American, European, and Pacific Rim publications. He received his bachelor's degree in journalism from the University of Oregon in 1971, and spent the next decade writing freelance articles. He later worked with the Champlin Museum Press and as the managing editor of *The Hook* magazine. In 1989 he returned to freelance writing, and has been at it ever since. His military nonfiction has been critically lauded, and garnered him several awards, including the U.S. Air Force's Historical Foundation Award, the Nautical & Oceanographic Society's Outstanding Biography Award, and the Arthur Radford Award for Naval History and Literature. He is also an honorary member of the Navy fighter squadrons VF-111 and VA-35. He lives and works in Mesa, Arizona.

THERE IS NO WAR IN MELNICA

BY RALPH PETERS

A workman tossed him a skull.

Green had played football at West Point and should have made an easy catch. But the gesture was unexpected. He got a couple of fingers on the dirty bone, not enough to grip. The skull dropped on a flat rock and rolled into the dirt. Undamaged. Skulls are hard.

The excavating crew laughed and bantered in their own language. Green was supposed to understand, but the dialect was too thick. He smiled, unsure.

"Assholes," Sergeant Crawley said. He canted his head toward the valley. "More company coming, sir."

Green looked down through the trees. Autumn had chewed off most of the leaves on the mountainside, but he still heard the vehicle before he saw it. The putter and choke was a leftover sound of Socialism, from the days when nothing quite worked. Now freedom had come, and some things did not work at all.

A small, light-blue truck with a flat bed bounced up the track that led toward the mass grave. It would have to stop down below, where Green and his NCO had left the embassy's armored Jeep Cherokee. Then the visitors would need five minutes to climb to the massacre site. Unless they were drunk. It was afternoon, and the drinking started early, and the men who drank carried guns. If the visitors were drunk, their climb would take longer.

Green picked up the skull and looked at it. He felt things he could not put into words. Except for the anger and disgust. He could express that. "Fuckers," he said to himself. Then he climbed down into the ravine where the victims had been shot and lightly buried.

His orders were to observe, not to interfere. The embassy had gotten the report the day before. Yet another massacre site, this time in the mountains down south, outside the village of Melnica. The defense attaché, a small, brave man who did not look like a soldier and therefore had not been selected for promotion, had told Green:

"Take Crawley down there for a couple of days and have a look. Get plenty of Kodak moments and GPS the site. Joe Friday them when they give you the song and dance about NATO intervention and American neglect."

Lieutenant Colonel Andretti had been passed over for promotion and was slated to retire, but the Army had asked him to extend his tour as attaché because the system that was forcing him out could find no replacement with his skills. Balkan expertise had long been a career-killer, and now the military was scrambling. Andretti did what was asked of him, with his daughters in high school back in Springfield and their mother remarried. The dark circles under Andretti's eyes reached halfway to his knees. He had been in-country for five years, and none of those years had been good ones.

"And Jeff," the attaché had said as Green was leaving the office, "the cease-fire's holding in that sector. There's no war in Melnica at the moment. Don't you and your cowboy sidekick go starting one, all right?" But Andretti was smiling, kidding. "Take care of yourself."

Green slipped on a clot of leaves, almost dropping the skull again. He resurrected himself and spanked the dirt from his jeans with his free hand. Avoiding the exposed rib cages and hip bones, the femurs and decayed rags of clothing that had emerged from the pit, he made his way toward the foreman of the dig.

The foreman was the only man in uniform, if you called a mismatched collection of military scraps a uniform. He wore an unzipped camouflage-pattern jacket and a gray cap that reminded Green of the German mountain troops he had gotten to know back in his Garmisch days. But the resemblance stopped there. This man was unshaven, despite his captain's insignia, and he carried two automatic pistols on a web belt cinched into his big belly. The calluses on his hands would have stopped a knife. Even his eyes seemed shabby.

The captain saluted Green, despite the American's jeans and Gore-Tex jacket. Green had been open about his rank and purpose. He saluted back, although he would have preferred not to.

He had been trained in Russian, back when the Russians still mattered, and the local language—spoken by all sides in the fighting—was related. He could get through the basics, but could not conduct a geopolitical discussion of any nuance. Two months in-country had not been enough time to gain fluency, but Green understood more than he could form into words of his own.

"Major Green," the captain said in mashed English. "Very bad things *those people* do. You see?" He reached down and picked up a faded rip of fabric. Once, it had been red. "You see?" he repeated, breath steaming in the cold. "Woman's dress. No man's clothes. Dress of woman. Who kills woman, child? Bad, bad."

Green nodded. It was very bad. He offered the captain the skull.

The shorter man seized it and tossed it in his hands. "Maybe woman. Maybe very pretty." He held up the skull. "Not pretty now." Suddenly, his expression blackened. He tossed the skull onto a lattice of bones. "Why America stays away? Those people . . . they kill the little babies. Why America stays away?"

"I'll report what I've seen to the embassy."

"The American Army must come," the captain said in his own language. "With American airplanes. Or there is no justice."

"Listen . . ." Green struggled for words in a language he found as jagged and difficult as the mountains surrounding him, ". . . you need to be careful . . . how you dig up the bodies. You'll destroy . . ." He struggled to remember the word for evidence.

The captain snorted. "Look. You see? Everything is there. How many bodies? I count skulls, I know how many. How many those people have killed of my people. That is all I must know."

Green rearranged what he wanted to say into words he could reach. "All this . . . should be done scientifically."

The shorter man had a lunch of onions on his breath. The workers had sat around the edge of the pit, unbothered, as they ate.

"I fuck science in the ass," the captain said. "Bullets. No science."

Green turned away and took more photographs. The war, in a lull for several months, had left many massacres in its wake. Some sites contained a single family, others an entire village. Some graves held only male bodies, while others had seen equal-opportunity killings. Green had visited two other locations, but the digging had been finished days before he arrived. He had expected freshly uncovered bodies to stink and he had braced himself for it. But the corpses had been in the earth long enough to lose all of their liquid and most of the flesh, and the only smell was of the disturbed earth.

"Call me Frankie," the man from the blue truck said in English. He had introduced himself as Franjo Sostik, late of Milwaukee and now the proprietor of an inn down in the village of Melnica. "No bedbugs or shit like that," he told Green and Crawley.

Frankie had the kind of looks that draw women's eyes, but he was reaching the age when he would no longer be able to convince women he was young. He wore a pullover with the sleeves crushed up above the elbows. His forearms were thick. Black hair grew down onto the back of his hands.

He gestured at the mass grave.

"Can you believe this?" he asked, talking mostly to Green, the officer, but including Crawley with a glance now and then. "Look at this. Like the fucking Middle Ages or something. Is this nuts, or what? I got to ask myself why I came back here."

"Why did you?" Green asked.

Frankie lifted his shoulders and held out his hands, palms up, weighing the air. Black birds settled on the branches above the dead.

"What the fuck you going to do?" Frankie said. "I got relatives, family. They need me. But I don't have to like it. No way, man, am I going to buy into this shit. When the war started, I said, 'To hell with that shit. Frankie-boy's a lover not a fighter.' " He made a spitting gesture, but his lips were dry. "Back in the States? I had me this woman, you know? Drop-dead gorgeous, man. We're talking serious, high-energy pussy. And clean about herself. Not like the barnyard animals around here." He raised a fist, protesting the fate that had brought him back to this place. "Christ, I *love* America. The States are my real home now. But what are you going to do? A man's got to look out for his family."

"You served, though, right?" Sergeant Crawley asked. "In the war?" The NCO's voice remained casual, as if he hardly cared about the answer.

Frankie shook his head in disgust. "Naw. Not really. Not my style, man. I mean, what is this about, huh? Let those people stay on their side, I'll stay on mine. Live and let live, you know? I mean . . . I carried a gun and all that shit. Kind of like National Guard stuff. Weekend warrior. But I was never in any real fighting. Melnica lucked out."

Green looked down at the tangle of bones, at the workmen with their spades.

"Who are they?"

"Local guys. With nothing better to do."

"I mean the bodies."

Frankie shrugged. "Makes you want to puke, don't it? I mean, who needs to kill women and children?" He nodded toward the top of the mountain. The new border lay on the other side of the ridge, in deep forest. "We might be stupid peasants. But those people are goddamned animals. Fucking sickos."

"But the bodies . . . aren't from Melnica?"

Frankie repeated the shrug. It was a gesture that seemed to refresh him, get him going. "Who knows? Maybe some of them. People disappeared. Drive down the road, never come back. Go up in the fields after the cows, never come back. We lost some. I lost family members myself. But I don't want to make this a personal hate thing. The truth is those people could have been marched up here from anyplace in the valley. They're ours, that's all I know. From our valley. Our people didn't do this shit."

The valley. When the Cherokee came down the pass, with SFC Crawley at the wheel, the panorama had been pure tourist brochure: the river reflecting the sun, and the low fields, the slopes open for pasture below an uneven treeline and the leaves falling up above. Tan houses clustered in the villages, while here and there a farmhouse with a tiled roof stood alone. It reminded Green of Italy, where he had taken a girlfriend when he was stationed in Germany.

Then you reached the valley floor and saw the shell holes in the roofs and the burn scars, the windows shot out and the walls pocked by heavy-caliber rounds. Craters pitted the road and half the fields had gone to bracken. Ranks of stumps told where apple and plum orchards had been cut down, for spite, during a slow retreat. Bitterness seemed to have soaked down into the earth, it pierced the air like rot. In the towns, which had changed hands several times, the Catholic and Orthodox churches had been desecrated in turn. There had been few Muslims in the valley and their small mosques were gone without a trace. The Muslims were the Washington Redskins of the Balkan league.

Green already had a catalog of destruction in his head from other observer missions, but the fighting had been particularly cruel here. The combatants had tried to make the towns of their enemies uninhabitable. When they had been in a hurry, they had only destroyed the clinics, schools, and municipal buildings. When time permitted, they wrecked the houses, too, and blew in the water pipes in the towns.

Green had been a mech infantry company commander in Desert Storm, but no one in his entire brigade fired a round in combat. They just steered their Bradleys across the barren landscape, and the troops joked about the most expensive driver's training exercise in the world. The worst thing about Green's experience of war had been the need to wear MOPP gear in the desert heat. But he was a dutiful soldier, ambitious within the bounds of honor, and he had studied war since his plebe year at the Point. He wanted to understand, and he took what books could give. But nothing he had read had spoken of this kind of hatred.

There was an upside, though: the way the people refused to quit. The towns and villages were struggling back to life, with new glass in many of the windows, shops reopening, and posters for the coming election. No one wanted the war to reignite, though everyone said it would.

The Jeep passed a white UN vehicle, its occupants straining not to see anything.

Then, toward the end of the valley, up a mountain road with defensible approaches, the village of Melnica sat untouched, a museum display of a destroyed world. The war had taught the people to pay attention to little details, and they figured out from the license plate and vehicle make that Americans had come to visit. Everyone had been anxious to offer directions to the site of the mass grave, with the men interrupting one another and the children blooming from sullenness to giggles and greed. It had been difficult keeping volunteer guides out of the Jeep.

"Do they listen to you?" Green asked Frankie. The captain down in the ravine had given the innkeeper a vague salute, maybe just a wave, when he showed up.

Frankie spit. "They're dumb shits. Uneducated. Dumb-dick farmers, you know? They don't listen to anybody. But they figure I'm smart because I been to America. I mean, they're *good* people. Just kind of stupid." He gestured toward the riddle of bones. "They don't deserve this shit. Nobody deserves this." He nodded across the mountain again. "Those people . . . they're not Europeans. They're fucking animals."

"You should tell them to be more careful," Green said as a worker swung a pickax in the pit. "They're destroying the forensic evidence."

Frankie looked at him as he might have looked at a child. "They don't want evidence, man. They want revenge."

"Well, if they expect anybody to come to their aid, evidence matters."

Frankie smiled. "Oh, come on. It's like I tell them. When they start all that shit about America riding to the rescue. I tell them, 'Hey, America doesn't even know you exist. We might as well be in goddamned China or on the moon or something. Americans . . . they live good. They don't need our shit. America got no interest in this.' "

Green had not been prepared for the display at his feet, for the rawness of it, and he was trying to keep his temper with the world. How could you prepare yourself for this? It was important not to show any emotion, he knew that. But every word he said felt phony and hollow and useless to him. He believed in justice, and he believed in the goodness of his country, and he only wanted to know who was right and wrong. But he had never been anyplace where right and wrong were so hard to figure out.

He wanted to *do* something. But he did not know what to do.

"Well, if they want anybody to *get* interested," Green said, gone peevish, "it's going to take evidence. Who killed who. When. Whose troops were in control at the time of the massacre. Ages and sex of victims. Proof that they were noncombatants. They need to wait until people get down here from the capital, people who know what they're doing."

Frankie looked at him with an expression close to wonder. "Major . . . Melnica lucked out, you know? Couple mortar rounds. No big deal. But we lost people. In ones and twos, like I told you. Some old farmer. A girl with no sense. Everybody got a missing brother or cousin or something."

"All the more reason they should be careful. So they can identify—"

Frankie closed a hand over Green's forearm. He had a powerful grip. "You don't under*stand*, man. These are mountain people. They don't want . . . like for their daughter or something to become some kind of medical exhibit. The truth is . . . they don't want to know exactly who's in the grave. Not names and shit like that. They've had enough bad news."

Sergeant Crawley, who had spent his career in Special Forces and had over a year in-country, said softly, "Different world, sir."

Green understood that the NCO was telling him to back off and let it go.

A whistling noise came down the mountainside: wind sweeping along like a tide. The pitch rose and then, suddenly, cold air flooded through the trees and poured over the grave site. The captain down in the trench clutched his hat. The earth smell rose, and leaves tore away from their branches. The workmen paused and looked at the sky.

"Hard winter coming," Frankie said. "Like these poor shits don't have it tough enough already. So, hey, tell you what. You're not going back today, right? I mean, you don't want to drive that road in the dark. There's still mines in the ditches. You got to stay at my place. 'Yankee Frankie's.' I even got American music. Liz Phair, man. Hot little bitch like that. And Mariah Carey. All that shit."

Sergeant Crawley, who wore a plaid wool shirt for this peculiar duty, spoke again. With the endless NCO suspicion in his voice: "How much you charge for rooms, Frankie-boy?"

Frankie smiled. "No charge for the room. If it wasn't for America,

I never would've been able to buy the place. You're Frankie's personal guests. You just pay for dinner, cause I got to pay the yokels for the produce and shit, keep the local economy going. But the room's free. I even got running water. But no MasterCard or crap like that. This is hillbilly country, man. Cash only."

Green wanted to be a good officer. He wanted to appear strong, impervious to physical discomforts. But the thought of a warm bed had more appeal than a fall night in the mountains crunched up in the Cherokee, engulfed by the decline of Sergeant Crawley's digestive system. And it was standard practice to stay on the economy when there was no fighting in the area. The small talk with the locals sometimes paid off. Random facts led to revelation.

Green was imagining a warm room and dinner when a worker approached him with a bundle. The man laid the corpse of an infant, reduced to leather, at the American's feet.

"I've been from Bolivia to Bumfuck, Egypt," Sergeant Crawley said, "and nothing's ever simple." He sipped from his can of Coke. *Hergestellt in Deutschland.* The rule was no alcohol during a mission, and Green and Crawley both honored it, though grudgingly. The sign advertising Austrian beer was a wicked tease.

The room held half a dozen tables, a corner bench, and the bar. It was a poor man's copy of a German *Gasthaus*, down to the Balkan kitsch that substituted for Bavarian kitsch on the walls. Business was slow, but the place was warm and surprisingly clean. An old R.E.M. disk whined in the background. America had had its effect on Frankie Sostik, who stood behind the bar, drying glasses and talking to a man with a scar that ran from his ear down across his cheek then back into the collar of his jacket. It was the kind of ragged slash inflicted during a hand-to-hand struggle.

Frankie and his customer were drinking shots. Leaning against the bar, Scarface looked like a made-for-television movie's version of a thug. He showed no interest in the Americans. The only words Green overheard were "girls" and "cigarettes."

"I know it isn't simple," Green said. Crawley was a helpful, closed man, hard to get to know. Shaped by the special ops world, he was a masterful soldier. He made Green, most of whose soldiering had been on training ranges and in schools, feel amateurish. Yet the NCO was never condescending, and he let Green take the lead without resentment. Crawley was a team-player in a world of yes-men who thought they were team players, and Green learned from watching him. In the two months they had been working together, they had spent enough time on the road and in the office late at night to know each other's habits, health, and appetites. They disagreed, almost angrily, on politics and music. But the two men were becoming friends—even though Crawley, with an NCO's reverse snobbery, still refused to call Green by his first name.

"Nothing's simple until the shooting starts," the sergeant said. "Then things have a way of coming clear. Shit, I wish I had a beer." He settled his can on the cardboard coaster.

"Buy you one when we get back. Listen, I know it isn't simple. But you saw the grave. And it's not just one. And there don't seem to be very many of them on the other side of the border."

Crawley made a so-what face. "Most of the fighting was on this side of the border."

"Most of the victims were ethnic—"

"Come on, sir. That's only because these guys didn't have the firepower. If these jokers had had the big muscle on their side, the atrocity ratio would have been reversed. I say to hell with all of them. We don't have a dog in this fight."

Green didn't buy that. "When women and children are butchered, somebody has to be punished. We can't just talk forever. For God's sake, Bob. It has to be clear . . . that atrocities are unacceptable."

The song "It's the End of the World as We Know It," came on the stereo.

"You really want our troops plopped down in the middle of this sewer," Crawley asked, "trying to figure out who's zooming who? These people have to settle their own business. What do you want, major?"

Helpless, Green looked down at the table and pruned his face. "Justice. For a start."

The NCO began to laugh, then stopped himself. "Look, sir. It's ugly. I'm not blind. And I'm not heartless. But I'm not stupid, either," Crawley said. "We can't fix this one, boss. Hell, we can't even tell the players apart."

Scarface dropped a pack of cigarettes on the bar and he and the proprietor lit up. Green sipped his Coke. The German stuff was sweeter than the Coke he was used to. He didn't like it.

"We can't just ignore genocide," Green said. "*I* can't."

But the sergeant was in his stubborn mode. He was a good man, and honest to the nickel, Green knew, but his service and a string of failed marriages had hardened the NCO.

"Why not, major? We always ignored it before and did just fine." His mouth hooked up on one side. "You see genocide, I see the local version of bingo night. Some of these jokers like things this way. I mean, those drive-by diplomats don't understand that there really are evil fuckers in this world. Not everybody wants peace, boss. And people don't execute women and children because they hate the work. Some guys *like* it." Crawley had three years on Green, but he looked a decade older in the lamplight. "Or just look at it this way: we've got our means of conflict resolution, they've got theirs. We sue, they shoot. Every place I've been, people have their own way of settling scores. And, near as I can tell, this crap's been going on forever in Mr. Frankie's neighborhood. We just know about it now. Thank you, Mr. Turner." The sergeant shook his head in naked sorrow. "I've been in seventeen years. And I've seen more damage done by ignorant men with good intentions . . . Christ, I ought to write a book."

Back when the Soviet empire was coming apart, Green had been trained for special duties in the East. One of the bennies had been travel, and one of the trips had taken him to Eastern Europe, just as the locals were slipping their leash. In Poland, he had visited Auschwitz.

There were haunted places on the earth, and the gas chambers of Auschwitz were among them. The ghosts crowded you, and you felt a kind of cold that had nothing to do with thermometers. You felt the weight of death.

Auschwitz had been a benchmark for Green. He was not a particularly sentimental man, and his church attendance was erratic. But he wanted to believe in the goodness of mankind. And he believed that good men had to face down evil.

He believed that someone had to be at fault in the Balkans. Crawley was wrong about that. Genocide was not some kind of local folk tradition that had to be respected by outsiders. When the crime was a massacre of unarmed human beings, someone had to be punished.

Green longed to know who to punish. He knew that Crawley was right about some things, too. It was not simple. So Green went carefully. Waiting for clear evidence, for the muddle to sort itself out, and for more powerful men to decide what must be done.

The sergeant played with his empty soda can. They had eaten spiced sausages, green beans, and peppered rice, with crusty bread and goat cheese on the side. There had even been pudding for dessert. Frankie had pulled out all the stops, to the extent that the war had left him stops to pull. And, to Green's relief, their host had let them enjoy the meal in peace, with no more tales of sexual conquests and the splendors of Milwaukee.

"What the hell," Crawley said abruptly. "Maybe you're right. I *hope* you're right. Because I see us getting into this, God help us, no matter what Sergeant First Class Robert G. Crawley thinks about it. I mean, the president hasn't consulted me personally on this one. And that guy Vollstrom, Mr. Negotiator, he's just set on making his mark on history. We'll be in it, alright. And then I'm going to retire on the spot and set up a concession business selling little touches of home to the GIs. You know, *Hustler, Tattoo World*, action videos." He grimaced. "Maybe get this Frankie-boy to go in with me, take care of the local connections and pay-offs and shit. Start us a real nice whorehouse with the local talent. Because once we're in, we ain't getting out in no hurry. We'll be here till the cows come home. And I figure I might as well make a profit on stupidity of such magnitude."

"You'll never retire."

"Just watch me, major."

"I wish I knew what was right."

Crawley looked at him. "Sometimes, sir, right is just staying alive and keeping your nose clean." He snorted. "Other times, the judge tells you to pay alimony. But it's never like in those books you read."

Green smiled. "And how do you know? If you haven't read the books?"

"Oh, I read them alright. It just wasn't a lasting relationship. Guard the fort, I got to take another piss. Army life's been hell on my kidneys."

When Crawley went past the bar, Scarface held out a glass and gave him a broken-toothed smile.

"Good," Scarface said. "Slivovitz. Very good."

The NCO waved him off. "I gave at the office."

Scarface grumped his mouth for a moment, then knocked back the shot himself. He said something to Frankie in a low voice. Frankie laughed. Then they both stared across the room at Green.

"Hey, major," their host called. "He wants to know what kind of man turns down a free drink."

Green returned the stares.

"There are no free drinks," he said.

Frankie laughed again. Frankie liked to laugh. "I told him Americans get this religious bug up their asses. It makes them crazy."

Yes, Green thought. Except we don't butcher each other over it.

Scarface caught the word "crazy." He tapped a finger against his temple, grinning. His teeth looked like he had been in a thousand fist-fights and lost every one.

"Yeah," Green agreed. "We're crazy, alright."

Scarface muttered again, but he did not lose his smile.

"He says you're crazy for not bombing those people over there. With your *Star Wars* airplanes."

"Tell him we don't want to spoil his fun. He looks like he could handle them all himself."

Scarface liked that. But he was disappointed that Green would not accept a shot of plum brandy in the interests of eternal friendship with America.

"He says, how you going to fight if you don't drink?" Frankie translated.

Green was tired of the game. But he had no excuse for turning his back until Crawley returned. So he said, "Tell him I'm like you. Tell him I'm a lover, not a fighter."

Frankie hooted, then translated. Scarface chuckled. It was the sound of a forty-year-old Ford starting up.

"He says that's worse. Lovers need to drink even more than fighters. Women need to be afraid of you."

A woman appeared in the doorway. Early to mid-twenties, she wore jeans and a purple roll-collar sweater. Dark blond hair fell over her shoulders, and her hair and the sweater glistened from the light rain that had drifted over the village. Even at a distance, Green could see that she wore too much makeup, but so did every woman in the Balkans who didn't walk with a cane. By any standard, the woman was attractive. She did not look like village goods.

She considered Green, then walked hastily to the bar. Scarface grunted at her, but she ignored him and spoke to Frankie. He shrugged his shoulders, his favorite gesture, and the woman nodded and smiled uncertainly.

She turned toward Green. But her steps faltered. It seemed as if she were giving herself orders to keep going. As though she were afraid. A few feet away, she stopped, briefly met his eyes, then looked down.

Up close, she was genuinely lovely. Green hoped she was not a hooker. He did not want any part of that, and he did not want her to be that sort. There was something about her that made you want better things for her. She did not look strong. And war sent people down ugly paths.

"May I . . . speak with you?" she asked. Her voice was low, almost masculine in pitch, but it quaked. "I heard that you have come, and wish to practice my English, please."

Good opening for a hooker, Green thought sadly. But the night wasn't going anywhere. If she wanted to sit, he didn't mind the company.

"Please," he said, rising slightly. "Have a seat."

She brushed by him and he smelled the musk of her, and the wet wool of the sweater. After she sat down, Scarface and Frankie lost interest.

"I am Daniela," she said.

"I'm Jeff."

"Cheff?"

"Right. 'Daniela' sounds Italian."

She smiled. Her teeth were straight and fairly white, a blessing by local standards. Odd, how you noticed different things in different situations, Green thought. In the Balkans, you checked out their teeth.

"I think my parents have taken it from a film. Is it a pretty name, do you think?"

"Yes. Very much so."

Sergeant Crawley came back in, wet. Green realized the NCO had been checking the lock-up on the Cherokee and getting the last of the gear into their room, which was in a double cabin out back. With a good lock on the door. Crawley had little ways of shaming him by taking care of duties they should have shared.

The NCO did a fast intel estimate and headed for the bar instead of the table. Green heard him ask for another Coke.

"I do not ask about my name's attractiveness because I seek flattery," Daniela said. "But for practice."

"Practice is very important."

A thick strand of hair fell forward and she flipped it back over her shoulder. The corner of her mouth began to twitch and she quickly set her fingertips over it. Her fingers were rough and scarred, and cuts striped the back of her hand. The sight startled Green. The hand did not match the rest of her.

When she removed her fingers from her lips, the twitch had stopped.

"So . . . are you a teacher?" Green asked. Trying to figure her out.

She shook her head. "There is no school now. Maybe next year. Do you have a cigarette, please?"

From Belfast to Belgrade, the women of Europe still had not gotten the word. They all smoked.

"I'm sorry. I don't smoke."

She looked down, embarrassed at having asked for something, sensing a greater error she did not understand. "I'm sorry. There is no need."

But Green called to his host, "Frankie? Got a pack of cigarettes?"

"German okay?"

Green looked at the woman. She kept looking down.

"It doesn't matter," she said.

"Whatever," Green said to Frankie. Then he asked the woman, "Would you like something to drink?"

She raised her face. There was a little struggle in her eyes, manners at war with appetite. "I think so," she said. "Perhaps there is coffee?"

Frankie dropped off a rose-colored pack of cigarettes and a box of matches with Cyrillic lettering. Leftovers. And yes, there was coffee.

Green opened the pack and held it out for the woman to help herself to a cigarette. Then he laid the pack down on her side of the table and lit a match for her.

Those scarred hands.

She closed her eyes and sucked the smoke deep. As if it fortified her.

"You wish to know what I do?" she asked.

"If you want to tell me."

"But I cannot. You see, there is nothing to do now. I live with my mother. My father is gone. In the war. We do not know any facts about him. But we have hope." She stilled the twitch at the corner of her mouth again. "I have studied at the university until the war's beginning. I studied English literature. But I do not speak so well now. There is no opportunity here."

"You speak English very well."

"Perhaps you know the books of Mr. George Orwell?"

Green remembered reading *1984* and *Animal Farm* in high school. But he was not certain he was prepared for a literary discussion.

"I think they are very true, the books of Mr. Orwell," she went on. "I cannot agree with the people who say *1984* is wrong because the year has come and is gone. The year is not important. I think it is like walking toward the horizon, you see. This *1984* is always ahead of us, no matter how far we go. I think there are always too many people who would like us to behave in such a way."

Green could only remember Big Brother. And the mask with the rats.

"And I think that *Animal Farm* is very important. There are many such pigs."

Green read regularly, but most of the books he chose were histories or biographies. The last novel he could remember reading was a thriller he had picked up in an airport, a story about Washington intrigue and POW/MIAs seized by the Russians during the Korean War. It had not impressed him.

"But I like Mr. Thomas Hardy as my favorite," the woman said, smoke frosting her thick, damp hair. "He is so romantic and sad. But there is an unfortunate lack of books now."

"Maybe you can go back to the university?"

She looked into the smoke. "I would like that very much. But it is difficult. I think the war will come back. And only the people who make black-market business have money." She lifted her head and managed to meet his gaze for several seconds. Her eyes were green, almost gray in their lightness of color. She touched her fingertips to the side of her mouth and looked down again.

"But I think it is not polite to talk so much about my person. We will talk about you now, Mr. Jeff. Where are you from?" She smiled.

"Wheeling, West Virginia, ma'am."

She nodded. "Wheeling is very beautiful."

That was news to Green. "Ever been to the states, Daniela?"

She shook her head. A decided no. "But I know it is beautiful, and the people are very happy. Except for the Negroes, who are in the cities. Are there Negroes in Wheeling?"

"Some."

"Are you afraid of them?"

"Not particularly."

She considered that. "I think they are violent people. I do not like violent people."

"Not all blacks are violent," Green began. "In America—" He caught himself. It was hardly the time or place for Race Relations 101. "Anyway, Wheeling's not the most beautiful city in the United States. But there's pretty country nearby."

"I think it must be beautiful. I would like to see it very much."

The conversation went dead for a moment. Then Frankie brought the coffee, brewed by invisible hands in a back room. It smelled like instant. But even that was a rare treasure in these parts. In the capital city, though, the war had brought wealth to a new class and you could get espresso, which was the new name for the Turkish coffee that had been brewed in the region for centuries. In the capital city, there were late-night cafes and discos, all smoke and loud Euro-pop, where young men with sleek black hair wore suits with padded shoulders, and the women, faces bitter as coffee grounds, wore short dresses and brutal high heels. Everybody had a deal in the works.

Daniela lit another cigarette before she drank. "Thank you. I think you are a gentleman. Perhaps you are married?"

Green smiled at the transparency of the question. These were direct times.

"No. Not married."

"Then, perhaps, you are divorced?" She pronounced the last word with three syllables.

"Nope. Never married."

"That is very strange, I think. And you are an officer?"

"Yes." I am an officer. And, yes, it's very strange. And I would have married Caroline, and she would have married me, and it was all very beautiful when she flew over to visit and we went to Italy, but it was not beautiful enough. Because she would not give up her career for me, and I would not leave the Army for her. And that was love at the end of the century.

"Why have you never been married?"

She leaned toward him, cigarette between the fingers of her closed fist, head leaned against her wrist. Green wished he could wash the makeup from her face. She was very pretty, maybe beautiful in the way it took a little while to see. It was sad because he sensed she had put on the makeup, which she would have hoarded, especially for him. She made him feel lonelier than he had felt in months.

"Just never found the right woman," he said. "I'm a challenge."

She was not having any of that. "Perhaps this woman will find you," she said firmly. "I think you are a lucky man. You are looking to me like a lucky man."

By local standards, Green figured, he was very lucky, indeed.

"You are living in the capital?" she said. She sipped her coffee with the daintiness of a cat.

"When I'm not on the road."

"You have been there long?"

"Just over two months."

"You will stay for a long time?"

"I'm on a six-month TDY."

She put down the cup, which was chipped around the rim, and looked at him quizzically.

"It means I'm a loaner model. Only temporary. Six months."

She thought about that. "Six months is very long sometimes. I think time is longer in the winter than in the summer. Do you have a girlfriend in the capital?"

Green wanted to be serious, but he could not help smiling.

"No girlfriend."

"You do not think our girls are pretty?" Another cat-sip of coffee.

"Very pretty. But I haven't had much time off."

"I went to university there. If I lived there now, I would show you everything."

He almost said, "Maybe you'll get up there sometime," but stopped himself. He did not want her to read it as an invitation. But he did not want her to leave the table, either.

"It seems like a pleasant city," Green lied. With its obese Habsburg architecture, and its fierce grayness, and the leaden food. The people looked down as they walked, and only the whores and hustlers met your eyes.

"Do you know the cathedral?"

Green nodded. He had gone there, a dutiful tourist. The ornamentation had seemed squalid and fussy at the same time.

"I think it is beautiful," she said.

"Are you religious?"

She laughed for the first time. If sound had color, her laugh would have been amber. "Oh, no," she said. "Only the old people are religious now."

"And the people who made the war?"

Her mouth began to twitch again. It was a slight movement, but he could tell that it shamed her. She did not laugh this time.

"They have no religion. For them it is only words. It is an excuse they make."

"Would you like another coffee?"

She shook her head. "I think it is very expensive. One cup is enough, you see."

"Daniela . . . what's your last name? Your family name?"

"Kortach. And yours?"

"Green. Jeff Green. Pleased to meet you, ma'am."

She smiled and stared off to the side of his face. "*Zelen*. That is 'green' in our language. *Zelen*."

He nodded. Really, he was the one who needed to practice his language skills. But he was tired. And the girl was lovely. And she did not seem to be a hooker. Just another soul washed up and stranded by the war.

You could not let yourself get too close. But it was difficult sometimes.

"I think I must go now," she said. "It has become late. And this is not a good place for a woman. The people in the village . . . they are not open of mind like the city people. They think bad things."

"You should go then."

The words saddened her. He had only meant to be polite, but had said the wrong thing.

She touched her fingers to the side of her mouth. "How long will you stay in Melnica?"

"We go back tomorrow."

She seemed to shrink into her sweater. As if he had slapped her and she was cowering under the threat of the next blow. He made her for a lonely girl desperate for any chance to get out. Suffocating here. With her memories of books and the greater world. Willing to risk her reputation for a slim chance of escape, in a place where reputation still mattered in a way it had not mattered for a century in his own country.

"Perhaps you will come again," she said.

"Perhaps."

"Then you will visit with me. To practice English."

"Yes."

"I hope very much that you will come again."

She stood up. He stood, as well. Old manners. And the miseries of West Point, with its fascist etiquette.

She thrust out her hand to show she was a Western girl. He took it, and let go too soon. Afraid of himself, of doing something foolish. Even if she was a fairy-tale princess, he was in no position to play Prince Charming. A ghost of warmth remained in his grip.

She turned away and he called, "Daniela?"

But he only wanted to give her the rest of the pack of cigarettes to take along.

"I don't smoke," he explained.

Her eyelids fluttered. Too quickly. "I think that is good, not to smoke" she said, turning away again.

She didn't just leave. She fled.

Crawley came over to the table and repossessed his seat. He looked at Green through the veil of smoke the woman had left behind.

"Don't go native on me," the NCO said.

The men at the bar laughed over their own little joke. You could hear the liquor level in their voices. Frankie came over to the table and stood before the two Americans. But he only looked at Green.

"You like her?"

"She's a pretty girl," Green said cautiously.

Frankie grunted. "She's a fucking nutcase. They got her during the war. Gang bang." He punched his fist rhythmically into his palm. "Twelve, fifteen of them." He laughed. "Hell, maybe a hundred. They kept her up in the woods for a couple of days. Now she's the town slut. Would've been better if they'd cut her throat."

Green looked down at the tabletop. The last of the smoke curled and drifted.

"Hey," Frankie said, "you want to fuck her? I'll send her to your room. You can both fuck her. Won't even cost nothing."

"Life sucks, then you die," Crawley said. He sat on his bed checking his 9mm. The oiled-paper blinds were drawn down as far as they would go. A light bulb hung from the ceiling. Commo gear and everything else that could be removed from the Jeep covered the floor between the old iron beds. "Those sausages are doing a number on my stomach. What the hell kind of peppers do they put in them?"

Green was not in a talking mood.

Finally, the NCO laid the pistol on the blanket. "Look, boss man.

I've been around the block. I understand the mope you got on, all right? A good-looking woman all cozy at your table, batting her eyes and getting all soulful with you. Then you find out her life's gone off the rails. Way off. And now you don't want to take her home to meet your parents anymore. But you feel bad about feeling that way, 'cause we're all supposed to be sensitive New-Age guys or something, and, yeah, she got dealt a bad hand." He slapped his palms down on his knees. "Well, let me tell you something. Life ain't fair. If it was, you'd feel as sorry for some pot-bellied creepo as you do for the Sweetheart of the Balkans. But you don't, and I don't. And nobody else will, either."

The sergeant clicked his tongue in a parody of shame. "When they packed my ass off to eastern Zaire—that one really got to me. Not for the right reasons, though. Much as I hate to admit it, those people didn't seem real. Not the way your blondie does. Oh, they smelled real enough. Cholera ain't no air freshener. But even the little kids. In my brain I knew they were human just like me, but it didn't move me the way it should have. Not the way American kids would've done. And you know what really flipped me out? This black captain honchoing our A-team? He had the same goddamned reaction. Couldn't relate to people in funny clothes talking mumbo-jumbo and crapping themselves to death. And that's how we get along. There's plenty of suffering out there. We could just about start a genocide-of-the-month club. So we're kind of programmed to pick and choose. And you've got to do it that way. Sometimes you just have to turn your back. Because there's so much suffering it'll just rip you to shreds if you let it. And if you try to fix everything, you end up fixing nothing. So stay in your lane. And be prepared to keep on marching past other people's misery."

Green snapped the clip back into his own pistol. You didn't make a big thing of it, but you did not go unarmed into Indian country. "Rack time? Listen . . . Bob . . . maybe I'm not the right man for this. I mean, that grave today. The little kid who looked like a piece of beef jerky. Then the girl, on top of everything else. My feelings *do* get in the way. It's sloppy, I know it. Intellectually, I understand. But I can't help it, goddamn it. And I'm not sure I want to help it. Maybe I'm not the right guy for this mission."

"There is no 'right guy,' " Crawley said. "You'll get over it. You get calluses where you need them." He laughed to himself, a rusty-pipes sound. "Want to turn off that light?"

"Door locked?"

"Door's locked, I'm locked and loaded, and the carburetor's under the bed. I would've taken off the tires, major, sir, but it was raining and I'm delicate."

"Screw off, Crawley."

"Sweet dreams, Romeo."

But Green did not have any dreams at all. He lay awake for a time, thinking unhappily about the woman, then disgusted about the way he found himself thinking of her. He decided that Crawley was probably right, that every emotion was driven by biology. But he could not make himself accept the idea. He recognized that there was something cheap and selfish—too easy—about his sense of sorrow, but he still believed it would be worse to feel nothing at all. And he figured Crawley felt more than he was willing to let on. You couldn't go through this and feel nothing. Then Green thought of the woman—Daniela—again. He expected bad dreams. But it had been a long day and when he fell asleep there was nothing on his channel.

The first blast shook the walls and woke him. After a stunned instant, he heard Crawley yell, *"Get down,"* and he rolled off the bed.

He landed on the commo gear and pack frames, all knees and elbows and a thin t-shirt. Then he remembered to reach back under the pillow and grab the pistol. The next explosion hit close, but they got lucky. The concussion shattered the windows without blowing them in, and the blinds channeled the falling glass.

"Fuck me to tears," Crawley said. "Mortars. Fuck me to tears."

"You all right?"

The night was black between the flashes.

Green felt the NCO reaching over him and smelled the man's familiar smell. Then the mattress from his bed fell on him.

Crawley was tucking him in.

"Just stay down," the sergeant said. "I've been through this shit before."

This time, Green heard the whistling before the impact.

Close.

The floor shook and the remaining glass blew out. Stings pierced his socks, down where the mattress did not reach.

"What—"

"They know we're here," Crawley whispered. "This ain't no accidental timing. Let's hope they're just saying hello."

A woman's voice shrieked in the distance. Instantly, Green thought of Daniela. But he made himself focus on business again. He was shaking. But he was ready to go, to move, to act. He just wasn't sure what to do.

"Get your gear on, sir," Crawley told him. "Jeans, boots, jacket. In case we have to run. You hear any more whistling, get back under that mattress."

Green fumbled in the darkness. He had positioned his jeans at the bottom of the bed so he could find them easily. But pulling off the mattress had made a mess of that plan.

Then they heard the shots.

"Oh, shit," Crawley said.

The shouting began.

"You think this is about us?" Green rasped. He had his jeans now, feeling for the leg holes.

"I *know* it's about us. I just don't know what they're out to prove. We need to un-ass this place."

A smaller explosion sounded nearby. Grenade. Then the automatic weapons fire kicked in again. The screaming resumed, and there were male shouts now. Green yanked on his hiking boots. His fingers were unsteady. But they did as they were told.

"Maybe something about that grave," Crawley said. "I don't—"

Something struck the wall inside the room. It was a flat sound, followed by the clang of metal on metal.

"Shit," Crawley yelled. Then he landed on top of Green, covering the major's body with his own, barrel chest grinding Green's head into the floor.

The grenade's blast lifted the sergeant away and stunned Green. He did not even know if he was wounded. He felt as though he had been thumped on every side of his head at once. There was an avalanche in his ears. His body was numb. Then he tasted salt and wet, and sensed the pulsing from his nose.

He could not move, but did not know what that meant. Time warped and would not go forward.

"Bob?"

The sound of his own voice seemed slow to Green. It lingered in the air, surrounded by a bronze roar. In another world, automatic weapons continued to fire. Rounds struck metal. He imagined he was inside a big metal room. There was laughter.

His head hurt. It was so bad his mouth stayed open in a scream without sound. He imagined his skull shrinking, squeezing his brain.

The door swung open. Green wanted to rise, to defend himself. But his body would not move. He could think again. But none of his parts would go. He wondered if that meant he had been paralyzed. The thought stunned him.

Boots. Rampaging through the room. He only realized his eyes were open when a flashlight found them. His neck muscles recoiled.

"On zhiv." The voice seemed pleased and angry at the same time. He heard it over the enormous, constant ringing. *"On zhiv."*

Zhiv. Alive. That was him. A string of obscenities followed.

Suddenly, his arm moved. Without his command. Or maybe he had intended to move it a long time before. Somebody inside him, a ghost from a previous life, reached for the pistol.

A boot came down on his forearm.

Whatever else he had lost, he had not lost his language skills. He understood the words, "American scum."

"Bob?" he called again. It was hard to keep focus. "Sergeant Crawley?"

He had to spit the blood from his mouth. Gagging.

Outside the cabin, a man laughed again. A woman's wail colored the distance.

Rough hands yanked Green to his feet. To his astonishment, he found he could stand. But the darkness would not hold still and he nearly toppled. The sound in his ears rolled and rolled. Instinctively, he raised a hand to wipe the slime from his mouth and chin, but a gunbarrel forced the hand back down.

Someone threw something at him, shouting. He had been unprepared. The object—heavy fabric—hit his chest and fell.

The skull. He remembered the skull.

The voice commanded him to pick up the object and put it on. It was his jacket.

That was when he realized they were not going to kill him right away.

Someone thumped him between the shoulder blades and told him to get outside. Green stumbled toward the different darkness. Dizzy. Nauseated. The air was damp and cold, with the smell of a rifle range. His ears still pushed sounds away, making them small and hard to hear. But he could see clearly.

Where was Crawley?

Dark figures in masks. A fire in a house beyond the inn.

Green bent and hacked up the blood he had swallowed. Then he wiped his face with his hand. No one stopped him this time.

The Jeep rested on flattened tires, shot up. The vehicle's armor was light, intended to stop assassins with pistols and sloppy shooters during a drive-by, and really all it meant was that you could not roll the windows down. Now the Cherokee looked like a butchered animal.

Green was afraid. And ready to puke from his lack of equilibrium. But training counted for something, however useless. He noted the assortment of weapons the men carried. Belgian FNs, Kalashnikov variants, one jagged little HK. He counted seven raiders, then an eighth man came out of the shadows. There was still screaming and clatter up in the street, so there would be more of them. Their uniforms were as confused as their armaments, ranging from full cammo to jeans and leather jackets. The only thing they had in common was the black commando mask each man had pulled down over his head and neck.

Two of the men tied Green's hands behind his back with rubber-coated wire. They were good at their work. Then a tall, thin man with a young voice barked at him in dialect. When Green didn't respond, the man shoved the butt of his rifle into his gut, driving him back against the Jeep.

The rain had blown over and a few tough stars shone between the clouds. But most of the light came from flashlights, a couple of them big and rectangular like the kind a conscientious driver might keep in the trunk of a car back home.

"Get the other one. Let's get going." Green understood that.

There was a brief, low-voiced argument. Then the thin man and another gunman in a ragged *Bundeswehr* parka slung their weapons behind their backs and went into the cabin.

They lugged Crawley's body outside, belly down, and dropped him on the gravel. His back was shredded, the blood dark as wine under the beams of light. His neck was broken and he had bled from the mouth. The sergeant's pants were stained. As if he had been hung.

A stocky man bent over the corpse. Crawley's hair was cut very short and the man lifted the head by an ear. A big hunting knife extended from his right fist. He took a practiced stance and swung the knife down like an executioner's axe. He knew his business, but it still took four hacks to separate Crawley's head from his body.

The butcher laughed and held up the head, giving some sort of cheer Green did not understand. If he could have killed all of them, slaughtered them, Green would have done it. But he just stood against the wrecked Jeep, hands bound, helpless.

The man bent down again and cleaned his knife on Crawley's shoulder, then sheathed it. He took the head in both hands, stretching out his arms, and shook out as much of the blood as he could. Bits of pulp splattered the earth. When the gore tapered to a few drips, another of the men held out a plastic shopping bag and the butcher dropped the head in it.

Routine business.

Green closed his eyes, but it did not help.

A muzzle prodded his bicep.

"Hajdemo!" Let's go.

He did not understand the rules. His captors carried their weapons at the slack, unworried about a counterattack from the villagers. And there had not been much of a fight, really. There was so much Green could not explain. He wondered if Melnica had survived because it had cut some kind of deal not to resist.

They forced him to walk through the spread of Crawley's blood.

In the street in front of the inn, Green saw the woman, Daniela. On her knees. Begging.

The four men encircling her laughed.

"Hajdemo!"

Two of the raiders lifted Daniela to her feet. One of them kicked her.

Green did not even think to protest. He had trouble walking straight. And his hearing still had an underwater feel.

The column turned up the street that led to the mountain. In a little barn, a cow gave an annoyed moo. The houses remained shuttered and blacked out.

Daniela was four places ahead of him in the line. She was not bound, but she did not try to flee. Instead, she pleaded with the men to let her go back to her mother. She sounded like she was ten years old. Except for the occasional joke, the gunmen ignored her.

It was cold. Green had not had the presence of mind to zip the jacket before they bound his hands. And even the thought that he might die soon did not make the cold any less a bother. His feet stung and itched and hurt.

Much of life was adaptation to your environment. Even the shorter, stockier gunmen were accustomed to climbing. Green kept himself in good shape, but his legs soon strained at the steepness and pace. When he slowed even a little, a muzzle jabbed him in the back.

He had seen them cut off Crawley's head. It had been indescribably real, immeasurably repugnant. Yet now, on the mountainside, the death was already hard to believe. He remembered the NCO saying something about the attack being aimed at them. And Green remembered the man covering him with his body. The things men did. The marvel of courage. He doubted his own bravery, that he would have done such a thing. He had-thought of himself as a real hotshot, a first-rate officer. Now he hardly felt like a soldier at all. He felt as though he had been faking it his entire career.

He saw himself as a failure and an ass, and he was afraid. Fighting the tears in his eyes. Glad of the darkness.

They pushed through a grove of evergreens. The wet branches slapped him and soaked through his jeans. But the pine smell was gorgeously alive.

He saw the pulp of Crawley's hacked neck. He saw the head, with the sleepy look of the open eyes.

That was how it looked.

Green fantasized about escaping, trying to imagine how it might be done. But his hands were tied, and the trail was steep, and he did not know the way. They would catch him. In moments. And perhaps kill him for annoying them.

The girl sobbed and kept climbing.

He did not know exactly where the border lay. Somewhere over the crest. But he realized that was where they were going. He was a prisoner of the people from the other side.

Despite the muzzle prodding him, he had to turn from the path and gag up more of the blood he had swallowed. His nosebleed had stopped, though not the dizziness.

Yes. The people from the other side. The butchers. The men who made the mass graves. It was as if they had sensed where his sympathies were headed. And came for him to make him pay.

But what was the angle? What did they hope to achieve? Their leaders were telling every lie imaginable to fend off the NATO airstrikes that had been threatened because of the cease-fire violations. What could they hope to gain by killing Americans? Or kidnapping them?

He knew that not everything had logic here. Or perspective. Perhaps they imagined he was much more important than he was. Or maybe this was just a renegade band with its own lunatic agenda. The attaché had warned him, just after Green signed in at the embassy, that the big warlords could not always control the little warlords, and the little warlords could not always control the militias, and the militias could not control the smugglers, except when they all worked together. And when they were not collaborating with somebody on one of the other sides.

Maybe it was the gravesite. Maybe that was why they had come after him and Crawley. Maybe there was more to it. Maybe he had seen something he did not even realize he had seen. Or maybe they were afraid he might see something and bring down the UN and the NGOs and a major investigation.

What had Crawley said? Something about that. Green could not remember.

He needed to sit down. Just for a minute.

The gunbarrel stabbed his kidneys.

The trees fell away and the trail grew rockier. It made walking difficult. Green stumbled again and again. His legs ached. Then it was so rough for a stretch that he could not think about anything but his footing. He wondered if they would shoot him if he turned his ankle and could not go on. The muzzle kept poking his back.

"Fuck you," he said finally. But he sounded pathetic to himself. The metal bore rammed him again, and he kept marching.

Toward Crawley's head. Floating in the darkness. It was there whether his eyes were open or closed.

He saw the knife descending. Chopping. Hacking. Through flesh so recently alive.

It seemed to Green as though there must be a way to reverse time and undo the damage. How could Crawley be dead? So easily?

That was what the textbooks failed to convey. You read the words. And understood nothing.

Just below the crest, with a high wind blanketing the sound of their voices, the raiders stopped for a powwow.

Witch's sabbath landscape. Rocks pale, the scrub and lichen dark. Blacker clouds in a black sky. And the shrieking wind.

The dark men clustered, masked heads bobbing. Green found himself standing hardly a body length from the woman.

She was looking at him.

This time he was the one who was ashamed, the one who looked away.

He wondered why she didn't run for it. Perhaps she knew they would kill her if she did. She would know the local rules. And dying was the worst thing for most human beings, no matter what the books said.

He hated his helplessness more than he hated his captors now. When he looked up, the woman was still watching him. He could not make out any of the details of her features. Except for her eyes. They gleamed.

The tall, thin gunman broke from the huddle and strode over to Green. Roughly, he undid the cords binding Green's wrists. Then he said something.

Green didn't get it. The dialect.

The man chuckled and tried another word.

He was telling Green to take a piss, if he needed to.

"Stay on the trail," he said. "Landmines."

Green tried to guess how long they had been marching, how far they had come. Still no hint of light in the sky. He felt as tired as at the end of a marathon field exercise, as though he had not slept for days. Only his brain was alive, fueled on fear. Eyes wide, body dead.

No. Not dead. Crawley was dead. That was what dead meant.

The man bound Green's wrists again.

Daniela was squatting with her face in her hands.

"Don't fly away, little bird," the gunman told her.

Then the discussion ended. Three of the men headed back down the trail. Rear guard? Green wondered.

The nine who remained shoved and cursed, far more than necessary, to get their prisoners moving again.

They crossed over a saddle between two outcroppings of rock. The footing was even more treacherous going down the eastern side of the ridge. Green fell once, landing on his backside and bound hands. Rock bit his knuckles.

The man behind him kicked him to his feet. Then they entered the treeline again, going deep into more dark, wet pines, and the trail leveled, traversing the side of the mountain. The party followed it into a draw that was shielded from the wind, a natural refuge. It was so overgrown and deep-set that Green missed the outline of the huts at first. It was a partisan camp. Maybe, Green thought, it had been one for centuries. And a smuggler's lair between wars.

Except for the footfalls and grumbling of the raiders, the world had gone silent.

They gave him another chance to empty himself, an odd courtesy, then tied him, sitting down, to the trunk of a dead tree. The wood was as hard as stone.

"We stay now," a new voice told him, in English.

"What do you want with me?"

"We stay now," the man repeated. "One day." He hitched up his trousers and shadowed off.

The gunmen must have been tired, too. But they were not too tired for the girl. They pulled her toward one of the huts. She fought them now. But only until they beat her to the ground. Then she gave up and let them drag her.

"American," she called. She had forgotten his name. *"Help me."*

Green closed his eyes.

But his hearing had returned unmercifully. The sounds were worse with his eyes shut, and soon he opened them again. The men felt secure enough to light a small stove in the open and they sat around it, sharing a bottle and waiting their turn. The night was so quiet in the glen that Green could hear the bounce of an old-fashioned bed. Sometimes the girl cried out, begging them to stop, not to do any more. Then she would cry for her mother again. One of the men cursed her, and Green heard the sound of fists. The girl screamed, then whimpered, and finally went quiet. The bed started up again.

Green wept. He did not understand this world.

He remembered her scarred hands.

She had told him she was not religious. But when one of the masked men led her out in the morning light, barely able to walk, bleeding and naked from the waist down, she prayed. First she prayed standing. Then, when they nudged her over to the edge of the rocks, she prayed on her knees. Green made himself watch, in penance for his helplessness. He could not see her face now, only the torn purple sweater not quite covering her rump and the bare, dirty soles of her feet. But he heard her, the mumbled familiar rhythms. She was still praying when one of the men put a pistol to the back of her head and fired.

The raiders untied Green's hands and offered him a share of their breakfast. Sliced salami, bread, and gruel. He shook his head.

The man with the tin dish in his hand laughed and told his comrades: "He's angry. He wanted to fuck her, too."

"He can still fuck her," another man answered.

They had not buried her. They only kicked her body off the rocks.

A squat man rose from the cluster around the little stove. He had a businesslike stride. He undid the rest of the cords binding Green. When Green stretched out his legs, it felt so good it made him close his eyes. When he opened them again, he saw the man standing before him, holding out the tin plate. There were stains around the mouth of the man's commando mask.

"Pojesti."

Green shook his head again. It was only a slight movement.

"Pojesti."

"No. Fuck you."

With the speed of a professional fighter, the man dropped the plate and punched Green just below the eye. It knocked his head back against the tree.

He had never been hit so hard. He slumped over. It felt as though his neck had snapped.

The man kicked the plate with its remnants toward him.

"Pojesti."

The instant the man turned, Green launched himself. He hit him behind the knees in a perfect beat-Navy tackle and scrambled on top of him as soon as the man's torso thumped the ground.

Green landed one fist. Then they were all on him. When he woke up, he was tied to the tree again. He had to twist his body as hard as he could not to puke on himself.

His eye was swollen and it left Green with a narrowed view of the world. And his feet itched and burned. It seemed ridiculous to him that, waiting to be executed, he should be so bothered by his feet.

Except for a pair of sentinels, the men drifted into the huts to sleep out the day. Eventually, Green slept, too, head drooped above the lashings that bound him to the tree. He half-woke a few times—once he felt crazed by the unreachable itching and cramping of his feet—but every part of him had worn down and the need to sleep finally slammed him down like a whisky drunk.

He dreamed he was back in Wheeling, buying a new car. Except that the car lot was one he recognized from Copperas Cove, in Texas, and he could not square that because he knew he was in Wheeling. A woman he had dated at Fort Hood appeared, excited him, and vanished. There was a problem with the paperwork at the dealership. He needed to prove something and could not. Buying the car was a major commitment, and he needed to get it done before he thought too much about it. He recognized his weakness, knew he was watching himself in a dream.

He woke to twilight and the smell of grilling meat. The sky was deep and cloudless. The fragrance of mutton, a vivid living smell of death, made his stomach ache.

In the shadow of the trees, the gunmen sat and ate, pulling the meat from the skewers with their fingers and gnawing bread torn ragged from a loaf. They shared an oval brandy bottle. Only five of them left now. The tall, thin boy who had marched him up the mountain was gone, Green could tell that much even though the men still wore their stocking masks.

Three of the remaining men stood up and slung their weapons over their shoulders. Green could not make out what was said, but he sensed it was a parting. And he was right. The brandy went around one more time, then the men marched off in a file. Ten minutes later, Green saw their shrunken figures emerge from the treeline, climbing toward the pass. The man at the rear turned around, as if he sensed that he was being watched. In the dying light, Green saw the white dot of an unmasked face.

The masks had only been for him.

He wondered, for a moment, if he had gotten it all wrong. If these men were not ethnic warriors at all, but only bandits imagining a fat Yankee ransom.

Again, he thought of Crawley's severed head.

Not ransom.

One of the pair who had stayed behind to mind him stood up and swaggered toward Green. He was stocky, with a submachine gun slung across his back. Not one of Green's earlier abusers. He untied Green and pointed toward the little grill and his companion, who sat cradling an airborne-variant AK. Watching.

Green stumbled at first, almost fell. His legs were numb. And he still had difficulty with his balance.

The man who had untied him grabbed Green from behind, taking a fistful of his jacket collar. Abruptly, he steered Green toward the huts. A bolt of panic shot through Green's chest and stomach, piercing right down to his bowels.

Was this it?

No. It couldn't be. They had killed the girl over by the rocks. That was the killing place.

Something else.

What?

Green felt himself shaking. He hated it, did not want to seem a coward, but could not control his body. He felt supernaturally alert, but not in a way that engaged reality. His dream had been more real than this.

He understood it now. Why the people had walked to the ovens at Auschwitz. Because you did not know what else to do, afraid that any action you took would only make things worse. And because you were drugged on hope, even as you faced the executioner.

The gunman shoved him between the huts, prodding him toward a trough that caught the water from a mountain spring. He told Green to wash his face.

The water was beautiful, and delicious.

Afterward, the gunman herded Green to the little stove then pushed down on his shoulder. Green sat. The second raider fingered his rifle, watching everything through the slits in his mask. The stocky one bent down behind Green. A strong-handed man, he jerked Green's left ankle back and tied it to his left wrist, hobbling him but leaving his right hand free.

The stocky man lifted a last skewer of mutton from the grill and pushed the meat off with dirty fingers. The chunks fell on the flattened grass in front of Green.

This time Green ate. The men gave him bread, and offered him their plum brandy. He almost accepted it. But finally shook his head. When the last of the meat was gone, Green licked his fingers. Wanting more.

In the gloaming of the little draw, the stocky man reached toward his comrade, straining to grasp the brandy bottle. And Green saw a flash of pale skin below the mask.

A scar traced down the gunman's neck, from below his ear into his collar.

It was not the smartest thing Green ever did or said. But he was far beyond cool judgment. He spoke to the man on the other side of the stove, the one with the collapsible-stock AK.

"Why'd you kill the girl, Frankie?"

The jerk of the head confirmed it. Even Scarface understood English well enough to understand what had happened.

After a moment, Frankie reached up and peeled off his mask. He ran his hand back over his liberated hair.

"Fucking shit things anyway," Frankie said.

Scarface spoke rapidly. In a tone of alarm. But Frankie made a dismissive gesture.

He looked at Green. "It doesn't matter now. We're going to kill you. You know that."

But Green refused to think about his own death. He kept his eyes on Frankie. "You sonofabitch. Why kill the girl?"

Scarface pulled off his mask and shook his head hard. But he let Frankie do the talking.

"What the fuck do you care? You have plans to marry her or something?" He laughed and said something in dialect to Scarface. Scarface laughed with the old Ford rumble Green remembered.

"Look," Frankie said, "this isn't America. People here have values. You can't just go slutting around in a village like that. That bitch was damaged goods."

"You said she was raped."

Frankie rolled his eyes in the glow of the stove. "And that's supposed to make it all right?" He breathed out heavily, a killer's sigh. "You'll never understand. We have to purify our race. A woman who's been raped . . . by those people . . . she doesn't belong here anymore. Anyway, Daniela was nothing but a slut."

"She was one of *your* people, for God's sake. She was educated. She could have helped you rebuild . . ."

Frankie leaned on his gun. "She was a whore, man. Nobody around here's going to marry a whore. And no whore's going to teach our kids. Shit, she was even ready to go away with you last night. All you would've had to do was ask." His eyes burned. "Do you know it's a scientifically proven fact that every man who screws a woman leaves his trace in her, his mark? Then, when she has a baby, the baby's got traces of all of them, of every one who's been in her. That's why those people rape. To infect our genes."

"That's nuts."

"It's science," Frankie said. "*Sci*ence."

Green closed his eyes. He wished he had not eaten the mutton. "You're sick," he said. "You gang-rape one of your own people . . . put a bullet in her head . . . and that's okay? That's some kind of good deed? To keep the race pure? What fucking race? You're all fucking the same, for Christ's sake."

Frankie's tone turned to disgust. "Don't make some big drama out of it, man. She was a disgrace to our people. *Our* country's going to be built on racial purity. Outsiders don't understand. We can't allow genetic pollution. None of *their* filth. And no Turk filth, either." Frankie glanced at Scarface. "Look at Ivo here. He was her goddamned cousin, man. And he was all for blowing her fucking head off. He under*stands*."

"You're sick," Green repeated.

"Yeah? And you're going to be dead."

In despair, Green spoke aloud to himself. "What . . . in the name of God . . . is this all about?"

Frankie grinned. "Which God? Ours, or theirs?"

"Nothing personal," Frankie told him as they went down the trail in the darkness. Scarface walked point, weapon at the ready. Green followed. Frankie brought up the rear. A three-quarter moon lit the path where it broke out of the trees. The fields shone silver. Frankie spoke in a softened voice, as though listening for danger all the while. "You're a sacrifice for a greater cause. You should be proud."

"Fuck you."

Frankie gave a snorting laugh. "Yeah, well. We owe you. I got to admit. Maybe we'll put up a little monument to you somewhere when all this is over. 'Major Jeff Green, who brought America into the war and rescued our people with his sacrifice.' Kind of nice, when you think about it. I mean, what the fuck, man. *Your* death's going to have meaning. Not like most of the poor suckers who get wasted around here."

"America won't intervene because of one major."

"Oh, yeah?" They passed through another belt of low pines and a branch caught Green across the mouth. "Anyway," Frankie went on, "it's not just you. You're just going to be the straw that broke the camel's back. All the atrocities and that shit. Those people have it coming. And your people know it. They just need a little push."

They marched down the mountainside. Green thought hard. His

mind went too fast or too slow, but never just right. Ideas trotted by, then galloped off before he could harness them. And Sergeant Crawley was always with him. Crawley and the girl.

"All this . . . even the mortars on your own village," Green said. "It was all staged. To look like the other guys killed us, or kidnapped us, or whatever."

"Hey, first prize, Mr. Fucking Wizard."

"And you're taking me across the border . . ." Green had trouble getting the next words out, ". . . so . . . you can kill me on their side. So I'll be found where the guilt will seem indisputable."

"Man, you should be on *Jeopardy!* or something. You know I miss American TV? *Baywatch* and shit. And, by the way, I appreciate your consideration. In not biting it back at the inn. We would have had to lug your dead ass over the mountain, which would have been a significant hassle. And the corpse wouldn't have been nice and fresh for those UN fucks to find."

They passed along the high end of a meadow. The autumn night had a scent of rotting apples. Again, the smell of death made Green feel vividly alive.

"And the head? Sergeant Crawley's—"

"It'll turn up. We'll be sure to let your people know."

Scarface dropped to one knee and readied his rifle. Frankie put a hand on Green's shoulder and shoved him down. His voice was only a whisper now.

"Fuck around, and you die right here."

But there was nothing. Only the mountain ghosts.

They came down into a dead world and there was no more talking. The moon had passed its apogee, and the air was colder in the foothills than it had been on the mountainside. Fields of weeds paled with frost. Green put his pride on hold and asked if he could zip up his jacket. His hands were raw with the cold, but he knew he could do nothing about that. Frankie slapped him hard on the back of the head for opening his mouth, but whispered to Scarface to hold up for a minute. Instead of releasing Green's hands from behind his back, Frankie closed up the jacket himself.

"All comfy?" he asked. "Now shut the fuck up."

They came to the head of a cart track and Scarface consulted Frankie. Then they both nudged Green into the underbrush.

He wondered how deep into the country they planned to take him before they killed him.

"Got to stay off the roads," Frankie said. "Lazy fuckers are all sleeping. They aren't worth shit unless they got artillery behind them. But they drop mines all over the place."

They skirted a farmhouse, and saw the sky through its burned-out windows. It truly was a dead place, with not even a stray dog. The weather had put down the insects. And if there were forest animals, they had learned to lie low. Black, burned-over patches scarred the fields in the moonlight.

They crossed a stream by stepping on rocks. Ivo got a wet foot and started cursing. Frankie told him to shut up in the same tone he had used on Green.

"I guess you're some big deal?" Green said. "Local warlord, the big stud back from America."

"You shut the fuck up, too, smart guy. I told you."

"What have I got to lose?"

Frankie's head shook, silhouetted by the fading moonlight. "Man," he whispered, "you really don't understand shit, do you? I mean, really? You'll be *begging* me. For just one more minute. Just five more seconds of life, man. Everybody does. Except the crazy ones. Like Daniela. The crazy ones know better." He laughed, pleased at his vision. "But you. You remind me of this old guy. This doctor fuck. Thought that made him safe. He stayed behind in a clinic to take care of their wounded. Then he makes this big scene when we start waxing the fucks. All this big-shot, big-shit dignity of human life crap. I took that shitbird outside myself. And when he finally got it through his skull that all that education and what the fuck wasn't going to save him, he starts begging. Like some little kid. 'Please, don't kill me yet. Oh, please, not yet. Just one more minute, just one more minute.' " Frankie gave Green a punch on the shoulder to get him moving again. "I bet that's how you'll be. You still think your fucking passport or the cavalry's going to rescue you. But you're already dead, pal."

Green got the sense that his captors knew the way, but not precisely. Darkness took its toll, and they seemed to wander for a while. He remembered his own confusion at Ranger camp, exhausted in the darkness, trying to follow an azimuth in the mountains of northern Georgia. And he recalled his pride in meaningless achievements. It really was nothing but vanity.

There was no training in the world for this.

The march led past a field of staggered crosses, slapped together from wood scraps. Each cross had two horizontals, the lower one wider.

"We didn't kill enough of them," Frankie said.

They came to a hamlet before dawn. The moon was down and the darkness had the texture of flannel. But you could still see that every structure had been destroyed. On both sides of the lane, broken walls rose and rubble narrowed the passage. The earth crunched underfoot.

Frankie and Scarface had a discussion that turned into a spat. Green got the words "patrols" and "stay." Abruptly, Scarface threw up his hands, giving in. Frankie turned to Green.

"We're going to hang here and check out some property. Find some little fixer-upper. See if we can get a good deal."

They went carefully behind the ruins, nervous of booby traps. They sent Green in front now, telling him where to go.

The only structure that offered a decent hiding place was a barn. It stank, although the village must have been destroyed months, if not years, before. But the sky had begun to gray and it was time to go to ground.

In order to avoid leaving traces outside, they took care of their needs at the back of a stall. Then Scarface tied Green to a post where the barn door opened, making no attempt to hide him from anyone who might come nosing inside. Scarface was in a surprisingly good mood, considering that he had spent all night walking through Indian country and had just lost an argument. He tried his bits of English on his captive.

"Door open," he said. "See American." He cocked his fingers into a play pistol and put the index finger to Green's temple. "Bang, bang."

"What's he's trying to say," Frankie explained, "is that anybody comes around here, they bust in the door and they're going to shoot anything they see alive. So they shoot your ass. And give us time to unload on them. That's how this shit goes down."

"Then what?"

"What?"

"Then what happens? All the killing. Daniela. Me. All the others. What's the point anymore? There's a cease-fire down here. You've got your shitty little country. What more do you want?"

"I want those people dead, man. All of them. They still have our land. It was ours for centuries. I want it back." He made a whistling sound. "And you saw what they did to our people. That grave. Those people are savages. You can't live with them."

It was Green's turn to smile, to share what he had figured out. Maybe Frankie would kill him. But he would not die fooled.

"Yesterday, you mean?"

"Yeah. Like that. Women. Little babies. Those people are fucking animals."

"Except the bodies in that grave weren't your people. Were they, Frankie? That's why you were going at them with pick-axes, wrecking the evidence. You wanted to show us another mass grave, to pile it on. But you didn't want us to look too hard. Because the corpses weren't your people at all. And you knew where the grave was because you did the killing."

Scarface looked at Frankie. Frankie's face had gone mean in the gray light.

"Americans can't understand," he said at last, "what's it's like here. It's kill or be killed. Them or you. There's no choice."

"Women and children? That's real hero's work, Frankie."

"Women have babies. Babies grow up to kill you. Children don't forget."

"So everything's okay. Anything for the cause. Butcher people. Massacre your neighbors." Green glanced back and forth in the murky light that filtered through the walls and the little window. "Destroy villages like this."

Frankie laughed. Green still did not get it.

"*This* village? We didn't do *this*, man. Those people did it for us."

Green looked at him. With a question on his face.

Frankie put on an expression that pitied Green's naivete. "This was a *Muslim* village, man. Nobody gives a shit about those scum. Me, I almost like them, in a way. 'Cause those people spend so much time and energy killing them. A bullet in a Turk's head means one bullet less for mine."

Green leaned back against his post. Scarface said something to Frankie. Frankie nodded. Scarface stood up and drew a dirty rag from his back pocket.

"Too much talk," Frankie explained. "Got to be quiet now."

As Scarface approached him with the gag, Green said, "You're wrong. This wasn't a Muslim village. You can smell the pig shit."

Frankie laughed. Green's was the funniest act of the season.

"I didn't say they were *good* Muslims," Frankie told him.

They did not wait for the twilight this time. The afternoon was falling golden through the window when Scarface kicked Green awake, tore off the gag, and untied his hands. Then Scarface pulled a heel of bread from his jacket pocket and dropped it in Green's lap. Green was so dry he could hardly chew or swallow. But he tried not to waste a crumb. This time, he took a swig of the brandy when it was offered.

"They're lazy fuckers, those people," Frankie explained. "They wrap up their patrols by the middle of the afternoon. Then they get fucking drunk. They have no culture. Just appetites, you know? They're not Europeans. But at least it makes things easier for us."

They let Green go to the back of the stall alone.

"Take a good one," Frankie called. " 'Cause it's going to be your last. We just got time to get to the highway and take care of business before the UN trucks come back." After a moment, he added, "They're stupid, too. I hope those dickheads don't just drive over your body and turn all this into a waste."

Scarface muttered and walked off. He opened the door and brilliant light poured into the barn.

"He's just checking if the coast is clear," Frankie said. "Then it's time for our walk."

The explosion shook the birdshit from the rafters of the barn. Frankie grabbed his rifle and took off, abandoning Green. After a delay of a few seconds, the screams began.

Green had never heard such an intensity of shock and pain in a human voice. Even the girl's cries had not been as piercing.

The window was set high, at the back of the barn. It was small. But Green thought he could fit through it. He was just pulling himself up to the sill, when he heard the voice behind him.

Frankie had come back. *"Get the fuck down. Get out here. Now."*

The sunlight was hard as metal. Scarface lay on a pile of rubble. Thrown there. He had no legs.

He was screaming and rocking, trying to tourniquet himself with a belt. The only words Green could decipher were "Help me, help me."

Scarface looked up from the shreds of meat and bone and rags where his legs had been. Looking at Frankie.

Frankie stood there. Fingering his rifle.

Scarface pleaded. He was nothing but a little pile of bloody meat. Sprawled on blown cinderblocks, broken beams, and masonry. The ultimate bed of nails.

"You." Frankie said, turning to Green. "Get down. Lie down."

Green stared at him.

Quick as a boxer, Frankie slammed him on the shoulder with his weapon, then beat him across the back. The barrel cracked against a rib and the sight tore through Green's jacket.

"Get down, motherfucker. Lie down on your goddamned belly."

Green lay down. A couple of body-lengths away, Scarface shrieked and begged.

"Spread out your arms and legs," Frankie told Green. "*Do* it."

Green did it.

"Now don't move. Or you're history."

Green understood more of what Scarface was saying now. The man was pleading with Frankie to make Green carry him back over the mountain, to help him stop the bleeding, to do something, anything . . .

Frankie picked up a chunk of cinderblock.

Green could just see Scarface's eyes. The terror. The legless man scuttled and twisted, trying to bring his weapon around. But Frankie threw the cinderblock.

It struck Scarface in the chest, stunning him for a moment.

Frankie shoved his AK behind him, grabbing a rock with one hand and another piece of cinderblock with the other. He was quick.

"Ne," Scarface screamed. *"Ne, ne . . ."*

Frankie stood over him and hurled the rock at his comrade's head.

Scarface dropped back onto the rubble. After the pile of rocks and masonry settled again, there were no more sounds.

Frankie switched the piece of cinderblock to his right hand. This time he bent low and brought it down on the side of Scarface's head, with all of his weight behind it. He swung with so much force he fell onto the body.

Green could not quite see the effect of the blow. But he heard the sound of a dropped pumpkin.

Frankie knelt over the man for a moment. Gasping. Then he smashed the chunk of cinderblock down again. Making sure. The shard trailed a spray of blood as it descended. Then more blood splashed upward, catching Frankie's face.

When he stood back up, Frankie had blood on his face and hands, on his jacket and on the legs of his pants. His face had the blankness of an icon in an old church, with a saint's huge eyes.

He let go of the cinderblock and glanced at Green.

"Martyr to the cause," Frankie said.

Green was racing on adrenaline now. It brought his brain back to life. He understood why Frankie had done it. Killed the comrade he could not save and could not leave to be captured. With a shard of cinderblock instead of one clean shot. Because a stray animal can set off a mine, but only human beings fired rifles. At the sound of a shot, the other side would have shaken off their torpor and come at a rush to find out what happened.

Their world had begun to make sense to him. He felt as though he had realized something huge that could not be put into words. Something he needed to tell his own people.

Frankie had gone savage. He beat Green up to his knees with the stump of metal where the rifle's stock collapsed forward. For a bewildered moment, Green imagined Frankie was going to beat him to death, too. But Frankie only wanted to get going. Before a patrol showed up. He made Green bend forward and touch his forehead to the earth, then he hurriedly tied Green's hands behind his back again. Green's wrists were already raw and Frankie pulled the cords so tight it made him wince.

Frankie knew the way now, in the daylight. He steered Green down rows of knee-high stumps that had been orchards and on into the forest. Cursing, yet keeping his voice low. He raged against the Muslims, the "Turks," until the complaints were almost hypnotic.

"Fucking Turks," he said, over and over. "Fucking goddamned animals. Fucking Turks."

Finally, Green said, "How do you know it was the Muslims? How do you know it wasn't the other side? Or even your own people?"

"You shut the fuck up. Just shut up. Only the Turks set booby traps like that. It's the way they think. They don't fight like men. They sneak. Fucking cowards. All they want to do is get Christian women doped up and fuck them. They need to be exterminated. Wiped from the face of the earth. Every one of them."

Madness, Green thought as he listened. And I was wrong. We were all wrong. It's not a little madness, not something you can reason away or treat. Not even with airstrikes. It's a big madness. Devouring. Reason doesn't exist here. It truly is another world.

"That bitch Daniela," Frankie said. "Her goddamned father was half Turk. She was born a worthless slut. You see what happens?"

Madness, Green thought. It struck him with the force of revelation. That one word. *Madness*.

They were crossing a field of stubble when they heard the dogs. Yaps echoing up the valley. They were miles away. But they frightened Frankie.

He still has to get away, Green realized. After he kills me.

"Get going," Frankie said. "Move it."

Green watched for a place where he could make his break. Desperate now. With his hands tied behind his back, he could not outrun his captor. And he certainly could not outrun a bullet. He needed a change in the terrain. A bank he could roll down. Or another village. Some way to put some initial distance between them, or obstacles to make it hard to aim.

The land had flattened. In the forests, the trees were well-spaced, with very little underbrush. The fields had been harvested. Green never found his opportunity.

He sensed death coming. Thinking: This is how an animal must feel. He longed to just run. To take his last chance. But he marched along and went where he was told.

He could not tell if the dogs were gaining on them or not. There was so much distance between them. And, if they closed in, Frankie would certainly kill him first. Even if he didn't, those people would do it and blame it on Frankie.

Green understood them now. He got the logic that was not the logic of his kind. It seemed a terrible waste that the knowledge would die with him. When it could be so useful to those who did not understand. To those who imagined sanity waiting to be awakened like some political Sleeping Beauty.

He did not really believe he would die. Not at every moment. Part of him could not conceive of such a thing. Something would happen. He would be saved. It made no sense for him to die like this.

No, he realized. It made all the sense in the world. In *this* world.

He heard vehicles. The grunt of military diesels. But these, too, were far away.

Frankie marched him faster.

The late afternoon light glazing the land was as beautiful as anything Green had ever witnessed. Indian summer weather back home. The best time of the year. Football games, in high school then at West Point. The scent and feel of the girls as they tested themselves against life. The safe, privileged world from which he came. Where you caught footballs, not bullets, and danger meant getting caught by your father with beer on your breath, then, later, missing your ride and overstaying your weekend pass. Or just an upperclassman in a bad mood.

He recalled the crisp mornings when the hills smoked above Wheeling, then the brilliant days when the wind swept down the Hudson. Young women who never gave a thought to gang rape in their lives, who had left the village a hundred years behind them. Who would never be killed because their father was half-something. His land of wonder.

Vehicles groaned on the other side of the trees. Maybe a pair of football fields away. Abruptly, the motion sounds stopped and the engines went into idle.

Frankie shoved his gunbarrel into Green's back and said, "Get down. Flat."

Green got down. And heard voices. No dogs, except for those in the distance. But voices asked each other questions. He could not make out any words, but the intonation was universal. They were looking for something.

Green wanted to shout. To take his chances with those people. To take any chance left to him at all.

Frankie held the muzzle to his head.

The searchers remounted and drove away. Maybe it had just been a piss stop, after all.

"Get going," Frankie said. "It isn't far now."

They passed through a glade where the earth was suddenly soft underfoot and the colors of summer held out. Dark greens hard as lacquer. And pale woodland ferns.

"Tell me one thing," Green said.

"Shut up. Move."

"Why'd you come back? From the States? For this?"

Frankie did not answer immediately. The ground rose slightly and hardened underfoot. The earth sounded cold under their boots again.

The yapping of the dogs had grown fainter, almost inaudible.

As they detoured around a clearing, Frankie answered him:

"Americans got no pride. No dignity. A man isn't respected."

"Lost your job? Girlfriend dump you?"

"Fuck you. You don't know what it's like. Big-shit officer." They marched a dozen paces. "Here . . . things make sense. People respect you. For the right reasons. Not just because you're some rich Wall Street fuck. Because of your family. Because of who you are. Because of who your old man was."

From a treeline, Green glimpsed a paved two-lane road half a mile away.

That would be it.

Frankie paused for a moment, judging the landscape, the safest approach. Before he got them moving again, he looked at Green. Measuring him.

"You think I'm some kind of nutcase. Right? You probably got your skull crammed full of that equal opportunity shit. All that equality crap just means niggers get to fuck your women and you can't say nothing about it." He pointed to the east with his rifle. "It doesn't make sense to you that those people nailed my grandfather to a tree and skinned him alive and now I want to take a piece of their skins. Does it?"

Green wondered at the man. His teachers had been wrong. They did not even belong to the same species any more. All men were not created equal.

"My uncle . . . my father's older brother . . ." Green said, ". . . was killed by the Japanese. And I drive a Honda back home. We put the past behind us. That's our strength."

Frankie looked at him with raw disdain.

"That's not strength," he said. "That's weakness."

They followed a gulley between two fields. The beeches lining the depression had lost most of their leaves and Green ploughed through drifts of yellow and brown that rasped and splashed around his knees.

Apple cider. Sweaters. Parties. Kids goofy in their Halloween costumes. Vampires and ghosts. Ninjas. They had no idea what was frightening. The really terrifying creatures did not wear costumes or have horns or fangs or claws.

He worried that Frankie was right. That he would beg at the last minute. If he had to die . . . if he was going to die . . . he didn't want the end to shame him.

What was he doing here anyway?

What on earth was he doing here?

He wished he had never become a soldier. Or that he had resigned his commission and married Caroline.

He had been so proud. Of his service, his rank. Of the achievements he had imagined held genuine importance.

This is what it came down to.

The leaves made a heart-wrenching sound as he crushed through them. Brutal with memories.

It was going to break his mother's heart. And his father's. His father had always been so proud of him. It was his mother who worried. About football injuries, or the wrong girl for him. About wars.

Did this even count as a war?

He decided he would fight at the end. No matter what. Even if he could only kick.

Unless he saw a chance to run.

He did not know what he would do.

Behind his back, Frankie was humming. Maybe the beauty of the afternoon had reached him, too.

The road had been built at an elevation above the fields, which lay in a floodplain. Its embankment rose before Green like a wall. The gulley narrowed to a culvert, with a half-blocked drainpipe showing daylight under the roadbed.

"Stop."

Not here. Frankie would want to do it right up on the road. There was still time.

"The UN dicks are always on time, at least," Frankie told him. "French colonel's got himself one of their sluts over in the town. Noon to five, then he's on the road again."

Green waited. He sensed Frankie sniffing, sensing the world, listening.

Silence. No dogs, no motors. Not even a bird. Green shifted his weight and the leaves rustled. He tried one last time to work his hands free. Trying to do it discreetly. But the cords were ungiving.

"Okay," Frankie said. "Get up there. Get going."

The time to run would be just when he reached the flat of the road, while Frankie was still climbing the embankment. That would be his best chance. Run and jump down the other side. Then keep on running like hell. He couldn't see yet, but he hoped the ground might drop even lower on the other side of the road. Maybe there would be some undergrowth. Anything that would give him a scrap of advantage.

He walked across a strip of ploughed-under field. With the air cold and thin in his lungs.

"God, please," he prayed. "Please, help me now."

He started up the embankment, struggling to keep his balance with his hands bound behind him.

As he approached the top, he saw that it was hopeless. There was only another field on the other side, wide open for at least two hundred meters before it ended against the next treeline.

He got ready to run anyway.

But Frankie's hands were not bound. He beat Green to the top and covered him with the rifle, moving just in front of him, stepping backward.

Without prompting, they both stopped in the middle of the road.

"This is it, motherfucker."

Green stared at the man who would kill him.

Frankie wasn't smiling now. "Turn around," he told Green. "You've got one minute. Pray, or do whatever you want. One minute."

The last blue sky.

Green took off. He ran harder than he had ever run on any football field. He ran and waited for the shot.

He heard the crack of a rifle.

But he was still alive, still running.

And the sound had not been right. It had not been close enough.

He ran a little farther. When there was no second shot, he stopped. And turned around.

Frankie lay crumpled in the roadway. With his brains strewn over the asphalt. His eyes were open and stunned.

Green saw them then. Emerging from the far treeline. Someone shouted to him to stay where he was. Men in grayish fatigues. Bearded men. Wearing those little caps that always made him think of the old Howard Johnson's hot-dog rolls. Silly caps. *Those people.*

Green sat down hard in the middle of the road and waited.

The hand-over took place on the border that night, with no time wasted and the usual suspects in attendance: the rag-tag killers who had saved his life, a French colonel, and a Dutch major. The U.S. attaché, Lieutenant Colonel Andretti, was on the receiving end.

Driving back to the embassy, Andretti listened to Green's story. Green did not sugarcoat it.

"I was sure they were going to kill me," Green concluded, rubbing his foot. His feet stank, but Andretti understood. "First that sonofabitch Frankie, then me. And pin it on him. I guess my cynicism's showing."

The attaché snorted and offered him another Diet Coke from the cooler. Real gringo Coke. "You got lucky. One man's misfortune . . . you want another sandwich?" Andretti's rough skin gleamed as a flash of headlights lit the back of the sedan. "Couple of reporters just found the biggest mass grave of the war. Seven, eight-hundred bodies, minimum. UN, Red Cross, NGOs, the press—everybody's all over those people. Even the Russians look like they're ready to back airstrikes against their little bearded brothers." He snorted again. The bad air in the capital city had given Andretti asthma at the back end of his career. "You were their good deed for the day. After a decade of atrocious ones. They had everybody they could muster out looking for you. One-legged distance runners and one-armed paper-hangers. We had to jump up and down to keep them on their side of the border. They figured out what was happening quicker than we did. And they were not going to take that rap, if they could help it. They've got enough on their plate already."

Green considered the universe, then condensed it.

"I keep thinking about Bob Crawley."

The little attaché settled back into his seat. "You'll think about him for the rest of your life, Jeff."

The President's special envoy, a former ambassador playing hooky from Wall Street, had flown into the capital city that morning. His visit had nothing to do with Green, whose disappearance had been a sideshow in the circus of international relations. Nicholas Vollstrom was in the middle of another round of shuttle diplomacy, with airstrikes in the offing if the villains of the moment did not back down and do his bidding.

The diplomats assigned to the region had been trying to communicate the complexity of the situation to the President's envoy for months, but had failed. Now, with Vollstrom anxious to go wheels-up for Brussels, where he had a come-to-Jesus session with the SACEUR the next morning, the ambassador had the attaché usher Major Green into the embassy's secure bubble. In a last attempt to inject some reality into the envoy's view of the world.

Green had not even showered. There had barely been time to wash the last crusts of blood from his face in the men's room and change into the suit he kept in the office for meetings with the local bureaucrats. He had seen Vollstrom getting into a limo once. And he had read plenty about him. In person, the president's man was beefy, running to fat. He wore glasses and spoke in a loud, high-pitched voice.

Green tried to tell his tale soberly and efficiently. But less than a third of the way into the story, Vollstrom cut him off, thumping his fist down on the table.

"I've just spent the afternoon and most of the evening with the president of this republic. With whom I have built a relationship of trust. He briefed me personally on what you were doing down there, major. Clowning around, stirring up trouble. And it backfired on you. Got one of you killed. And now you want to shift the blame." He grimaced in disgust. "You'll be lucky if you aren't court-martialed. Goddamned lucky."

"Sir . . ."

The envoy leaned across the table toward Green. His neck swelled out of his collar and his face turned the color of raw meat.

"Get this straight, son," he said. "There *is* no war in Melnica."

RALPH PETERS is a novelist, essayist, and former soldier. His fiction includes *Traitor, The Devil's Garden, Twilight of Heroes, The War in 2020*, and other novels. He is also the author of the acclaimed book on strategy and conflict, *Fighting for the Future: Will America Triumph?* His commentaries on strategic themes appear regularly in the national and international media. He entered the U.S. Army as a private in 1976 and retired in 1998, shortly after his promotion to lieutenant colonel, so he could write and speak freely. His military service and research travels have taken him to fifty countries, and his duties led him from an infantry battalion to the Executive Office of the President. His novella in this collection, "There Is No War in Melnica," is based on his personal observation of the Balkans from 1972 to the present.